NICHOLAS RAVEN

AND THE

WIZARDS' WEB

VOLUME 3

~ CHAPTERS 86 - 120 ~

THOMAS J. PRESTOPNIK

Visit Thomas J. Prestopnik's website at **www.TomPresto.com**.

Cover Artist: Kelly McGrogan
Cover Layout: Ryan McGrogan
Maps: Thomas J. Prestopnik

Nicholas Raven and the Wizards' Web - Volume 3
ISBN-13: 978-1511432474
ISBN-10: 1511432470

Library of Congress Control Number: 2015905654
CreateSpace Independent Publishing Platform
North Charleston, SC

Printed in the United States of America

For every reader in search
of an exciting adventure.
I hope you find one
inside these pages.

CONTENTS

PART TEN
IN ENEMY TERRITORY

PART ELEVEN
THE LAST STAND

PART TWELVE
THE JOURNEY HOME

MAPS

Map One
The Lands of Laparia

Map Two
The Kingdom of Arrondale

Map Three
The County of Litchfield

Map Four
The Village of Kanesbury

Each map follows twice.
First as a two-page spread, and then on a single page.

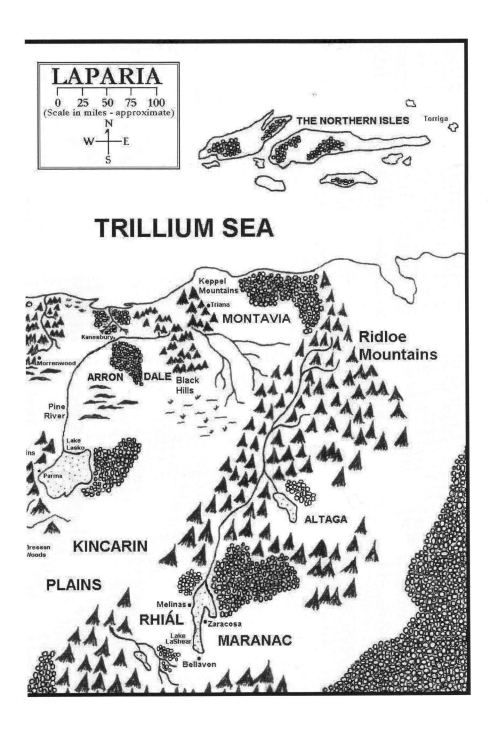

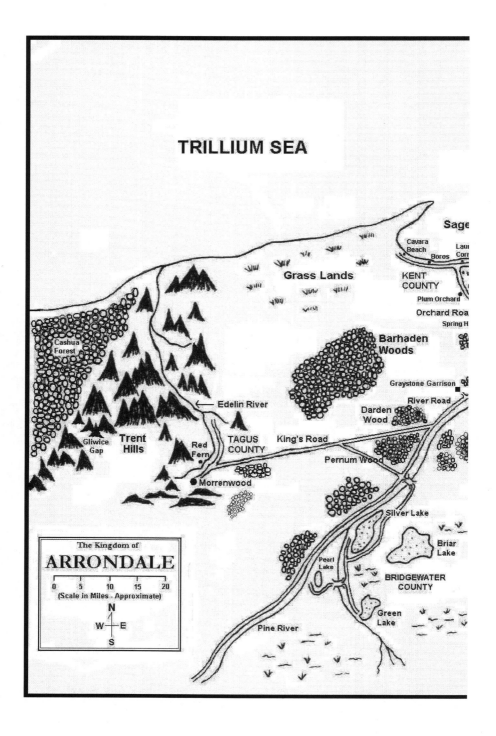

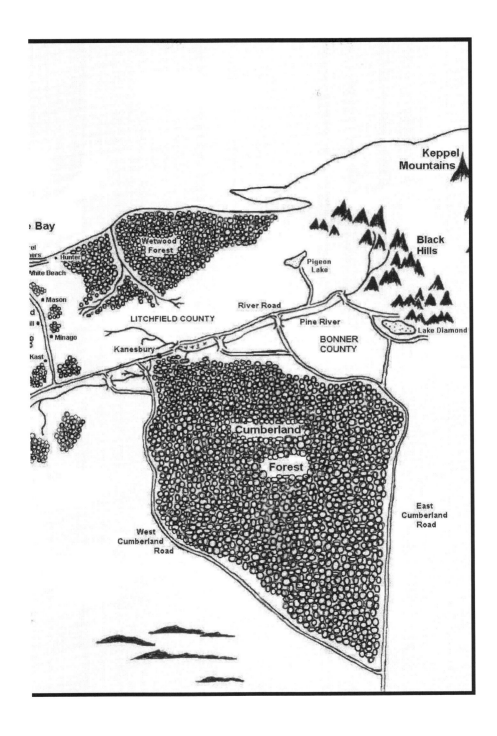

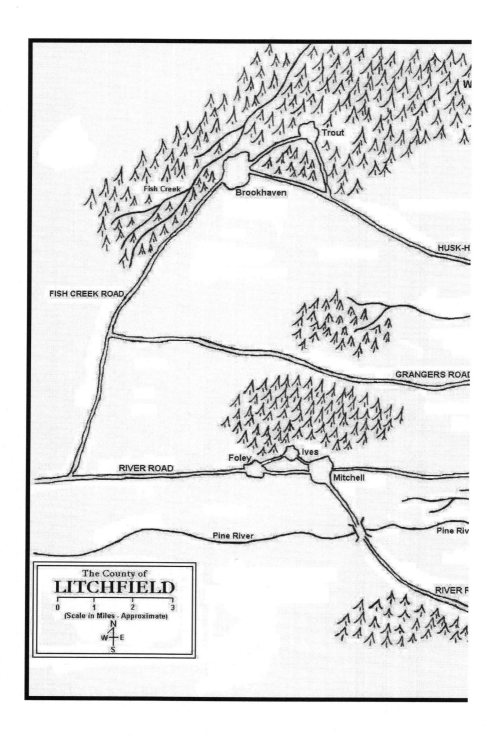

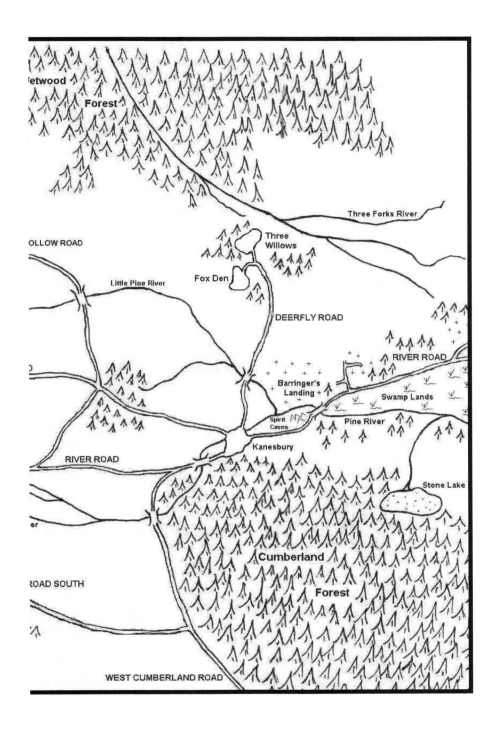

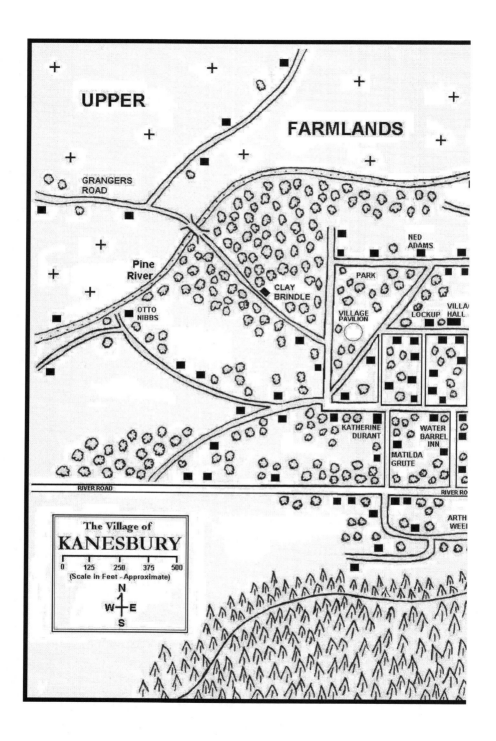

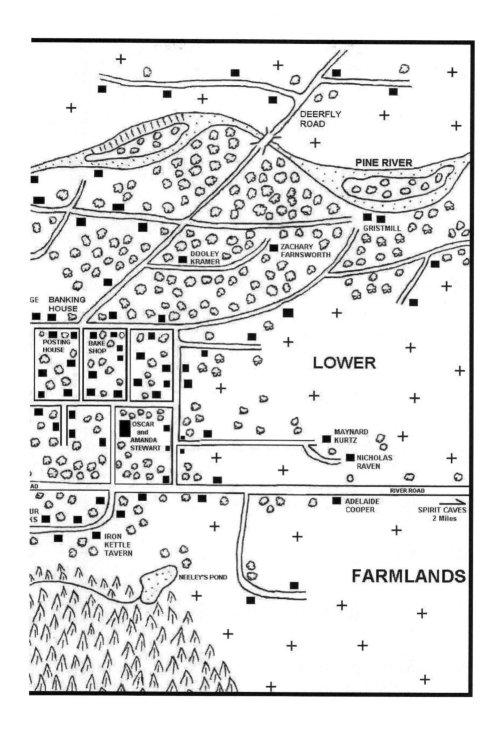

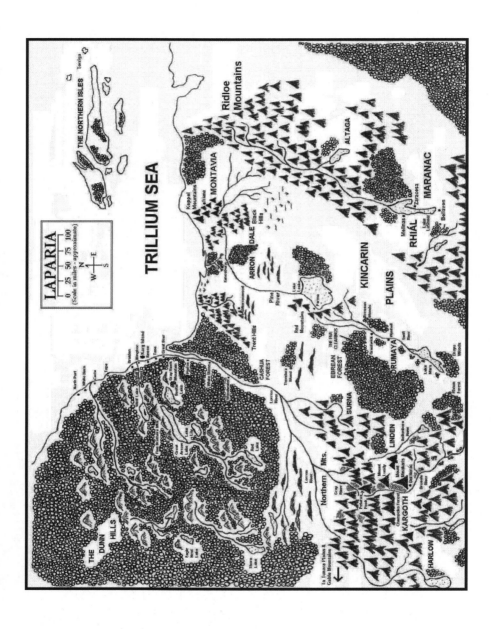

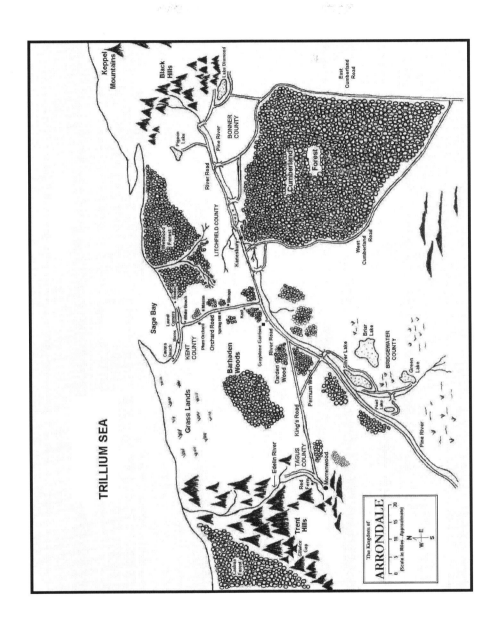

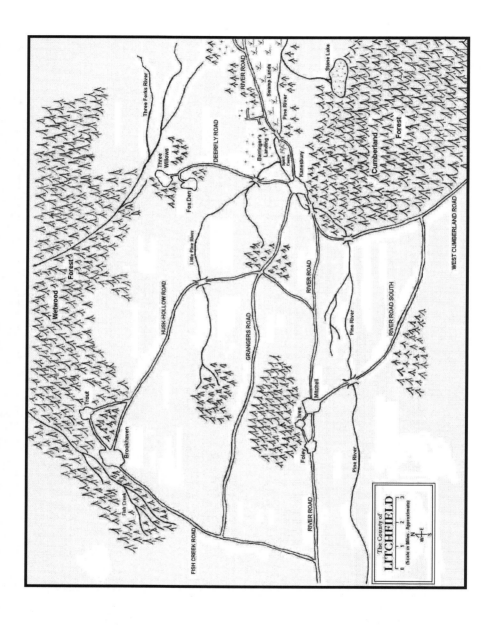

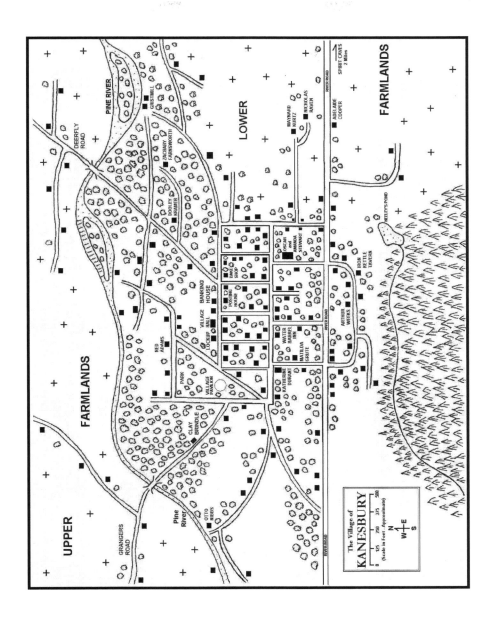

NICHOLAS RAVEN

AND THE

WIZARDS' WEB

VOLUME 3

~ CHAPTERS 86 - 120 ~

PART NINE
THE ROADS SOUTH

CHAPTER 86

The Gray River

Somewhere in the darkness, Ivy's cry for help tormented him, drawing Nicholas ever closer. Her frantic plea pierced his heart like an icy blade. Her frightened voice rose above the slapping sea waves and the crackling flames of the bonfires. He finally spotted her as she was being dragged to the water's edge by two shadowy figures, her arms extended as he raced toward her. His legs felt lead-heavy. He could hardly catch a breath. But her cries grew softer as he neared the stony shore. Nicholas reached out a hand through the spray of seawater, noting the fear on Ivy's face, seeing the movement of her lips, but now unable to hear her words amidst the water and flames. He stretched out his fingers as Ivy did the same, both desperately trying to reach the other, but the dark space separating them could not be breached. With what little strength he had left, Nicholas lunged forward to save her, knowing he couldn't fail. But in the next instant she was gone. His arms wrapped around a black void as he stumbled. He felt himself falling into the sea, slowly drowning yet still alive. His lungs ached, his throat tightened and his heart broke as he tried to swim to the surface. Yet he couldn't reach the cool night air, believing he would suffer this unbearable fate between life and death until the end of his days.

Nicholas opened his eyes. A fleet of milky gray clouds stared back at him in the pale morning light as a cool breeze softly touched his face. He took a deep breath as remnants of sleep swam in his tired head, realizing where he was as the echo of Ivy's voice faded in his mind. For a moment, he was relieved that she was not suffering the torment along the grasslands, but then his heart grew heavy. He was painfully aware that Ivy was no longer at his side as the river, and the sterile landscape just beyond, flowed past in somber silence.

"While you dozed, Nicholas, we entered the Gray River," a voice spoke in the wintry air. "The Lorren is finally behind us. We're making directly for the Northern Mountains whose majestic peaks grace the horizon." Brin Mota's words were filled with reverent awe. He stood near the back of the pine tree-length raft gazing southward, a thin smile upon his whiskered face as the breeze played though a mop of dark hair. He wore a long, brown coat with the collar raised to protect his neck from the biting chill. A sword hung lifelessly at his side. "I've never looked upon the snow-covered tips of one of Laparia's grandest mountain ranges, though I've often imagined what they must look like while studying old maps in the Northern Isles."

"You must miss your home," Nicholas remarked. "Maybe you should go back." He sat against a wooden barrel filled with salted mackerel, his hands tied behind him and another rope binding him to the barrel. A line of other barrels and crates filled with dried food supplies and various brews extended like a small mountain range along the center from one end of the raft to the other, covered with canvas tarps and secured with additional rope.

Brin smirked, turning to his prisoner. "Perhaps one day I will. First I plan to make a name for myself in these mountains, especially in the chambers of Mount Minakaris. Vellan will be pleased that I–"

Nicholas laughed scornfully, anticipating his captor's line of thought. Brin scowled at his prisoner. Two other men, one on either side of the wide raft and separated by the line of barrels and crates, walked silently in unison toward the front of the log vessel. They propelled the raft steadily upstream, each pushing against a long wooden pole behind them whose opposite end was pressed into the river's bottom. Nicholas waited until the two men had passed by before he again spoke.

"Brin, do you really think that Vellan is going to reward you–someone he has never met nor even heard of–just because you claim you're delivering the princess of Morrenwood to him?"

"I'm also delivering King Justin's spy," he replied, squatting down on one knee. "Actually, I think that you might be the better prize for Vellan. He'll be able to extract more information from you than from the girl." Brin raised an eyebrow with ominous intention. "Either by magic or through other means, Vellan will get you to reveal much about King Justin's military designs."

Nicholas shrugged. "You're delusional. But believe what you want. When Vellan discovers that I'm no spy and that Ivy is not Princess Megan, you're the one who'll face the consequences. Don't say I didn't warn you."

Brin grunted and stood up. "I'd never say that because you tediously warn me every single day. Feel free to stop."

Nicholas rested his head against the barrel and kept quiet, not in the mood to verbally spar with Brin as he had done so to varying degrees for the past ten days. As he strolled away, Nicholas' thoughts again turned to Ivy as they did during most of his waking hours. Three times she had been taken from him–first when kidnapped on the streets of Boros, the second time along the shore of the Trillium Sea, and lastly, three days ago. Whenever he replayed those terrible moments in his mind it felt as if his heart were being ripped from his chest until despair or mental exhaustion overwhelmed him. When he recovered, Nicholas couldn't help but repeat the pattern as Ivy was foremost on his mind.

The two steersmen walked to the back of the vessel again and planted the wooden poles into the river to continue the process of propelling the craft upriver. As it floated along vast stretches of browning grassland and scrub brush, Nicholas' thoughts meandered back eleven days ago, the last happy moment he could remember. He had been sitting sleepily against a tree with Ivy in his arms, both admitting how tired they were after enduring the horrific events on the *Bretic* and Karg Island despite a brief recovery in Illingboc. After having drifted off to sleep, they awoke the following day as prisoners on this raft. They soon learned the terrible truth from Brin Mota–that he had drugged them and transported them to the last waiting raft on the Lorren River that was heading to Kargoth. Brin's cousin, Cale, had convinced the Island soldiers on the raft to wait for Brin's arrival and his special cargo for Vellan.

Yet despite their protestations, neither Nicholas nor Ivy could convince their captor that they were not a spy and a princess. Brin's discovery of the royal pendant around Ivy's neck, coupled with Nicholas' involvement with Arteen and his associates, had left him no doubts that he had captured two useful prizes for Vellan. He hoped to advance his career to more dizzying heights than he could ever attain as a mere cog in the military machine of the Northern Isles.

A wintry chill gripped the morning as the sun remained hidden behind a layer of clouds. The distant Northern Mountains stood out like a line of sentries, silent and foreboding. They had been traveling up the Lorren River for ten days, the last few providing a barren and lonely landscape ever since the raft had drifted past the Dunn Hills to the west and the Cashua Forest to the east. How Nicholas missed the green maze of the Cashua despite getting lost inside with Leo. But the passing of recent days had been a blur to him. He tried to guess where Leo and Hobin were right now, hoping that his friends would reach Morrenwood with the key, unaware that Leo had already opened the Spirit Box twelve days ago at dawn.

As the two steersmen passed by on their next circuit, Nicholas recalled how Ivy had been taken from his side three days ago. Twice each day during their travels, Brin would direct the raft to shore and anchor it for a brief meal and a rest. Each evening they would return and make camp for the night. Nicholas was always contemplating a way to escape while he and Ivy were on Brin's floating prison. Whenever they stepped ashore, however, his ideas to secure their freedom would especially take flight despite the watchful eyes of Brin Mota, his cousin and the other four crew members.

Four days ago at twilight they had made camp upon the western bank amid a swirl of bitter snow. Fires were lit and meals were kept brief. All but two watchmen turned in for the night. When darkness encompassed the land, Nicholas freed himself by cutting his bonds with a sharp stone he had pocketed earlier. He stealthily made his way to where Ivy lay. Two crewmen kept watch by a low fire nearby. Everyone else appeared sound asleep. After Nicholas freed her, they made for a patch of scrub brush to the north. But their first taste of liberty was short-lived when Brin discovered their absence and called the alarm. Sleep, as on most nights for Brin of late, was a scarce commodity. Though his eyes had been closed, his ears were sharp and his mind was still spinning plans. Nicholas and Ivy were quickly tracked down and apprehended. Brin guarded them himself until the first light of dawn stretched across the eastern horizon.

"So you'd rather escape into this cold and desolate region," Brin addressed them the following day, "facing hunger and possibly even death, than to remain as my guest upon the river?"

"What do you think?" Nicholas muttered, glaring at him while sitting next to Ivy, their hands tied behind their backs.

"I'll have to double my guard. Clearly you cannot be trusted."

The next day, Nicholas and Ivy's already fractured world tumbled down upon them with the arrival of three men on horseback who slowly made their way downriver along the eastern bank. Brin spotted them at once, and from their attire knew they were fellow Islanders, no doubt on patrol. He ordered the raft to shore to meet with the trio who had stopped upon the grassy bank and dismounted. Brin introduced himself as the assistant captain of the naval ship *Bretic*, neglecting to tell them that it had been destroyed in a massive conflagration.

"You are far from Del Norác," Brin said as the tired men greeted him, eyeing the mountain of supplies secured to the raft. "I didn't think there were Island outposts this far outside the Northern Mountains. You must have offended someone to get such a dreary post," he joked.

"Ours is the farthest post outside of Kargoth," replied the oldest of the trio who was apparently in charge. "But now that winter is here and the rafts from Karg Island have stopped, we'll be moving deeper into the mountains. In the meantime, we would happily take a sack of biscuits and a slab or two of bacon back to our camp if you are so inclined. I'm sure Vellan wouldn't miss such triflings from our Island tribute to him."

A look of disappointment crossed Brin's face, causing the man to fear that his request may have been inappropriate. He quickly smiled, putting the trio at ease.

"I'll see what I can do," he replied, signaling to his cousin who was watching from the raft. "Cale, join us."

As Cale jumped off the raft onto the grassy bank, Nicholas and Ivy glanced at one another with mounting suspicion. Neither was comfortable with the scene playing out before them.

"How many are in your company?" Brin asked after Cale had arrived and was introduced.

"Nearly thirty. Half have already packed up and are making their way to other locations. Though we still patrol the mountains, our work here on the outer edge of these lands is done for the year." The soldier again glanced at the raft, eyeing Nicholas and Ivy who, by their dress, were clearly not from the Northern Isles. "I was surprised to see you poling up the river this morning, believing the last of our vessels had already sailed past."

"This one was delayed," Cale said. "My cousin is conducting a special undertaking for Vellan and–"

Brin raised a hand to silence him, noting a look of surprise upon the faces of the new arrivals. Whether they were impressed at the mention of Vellan's name or merely skeptical of the claim, Brin knew he had gotten their attention.

"My cousin speaks more than he should, but Cale is correct when saying we have a special tribute for Vellan upon our vessel." Brin massaged his chin as if deep in thought, looking at the three men with a gleam in his eyes. "And I would be willing to offer you the food items you requested for your camp, perhaps even above what you ask, but I would need something in return."

"Of course," the lead soldier replied. "Name it."

"Some assistance with an important mission," he said. "Have you more horses available at your camp?"

"A few."

"And you're planning to go deeper into the mountains soon?" Brin asked.

"We are," the man assured him.

"Perhaps even as far as Del Norác?" The three soldiers glanced at one another, suspicious of Brin's intentions, yet ready to hear more. "I'll make it worth your while if some of you leave for there immediately," he promised.

"What would you have us do?" one of the other men asked, eager for a change of scenery. A journey to the capital of Kargoth, even at the onset of winter, offered much appeal after the tedium of monitoring the river over recent weeks.

"I need you to deliver something to Mount Minakaris." The soldiers looked up with both wonder and disbelief, yet Brin already knew that he had secured their cooperation. "Deliver something to Vellan himself–from me."

"What?" the lead soldier whispered.

Brin turned and pointed at the raft, an extended finger aimed directly at Ivy. "*Her.*"

Neither Nicholas nor Ivy heard Brin's softly spoken words as his back was to them during most of the conversation. Both, though, clearly distinguished the last syllable he had uttered when he turned and indicated Ivy with a raised finger. Ivy gazed back uneasily at Brin and the others, certain she was the topic of conversation. Nicholas felt a sickening chill course through him, fearing for her safety. The loathsome expression upon Brin's face and the deadened look in his eyes was proof enough that the situation was about to get worse.

He frantically looked around for a weapon or a way of escape, but since he and Ivy were securely bound with rope, he was simply going through the motions. Ivy noted his pale complexion and sudden look of desperation, imagining the horrific thoughts swirling through his mind.

"Nicholas," she whispered. "What are they talking about?"

"They're talking about *you*, Ivy," he said, glaring back at Brin and Cale who were still engaged in discussions with the Islanders.

"I've been the topic of conversation among many people of late," she replied, trying to keep calm as her heart beat faster. "Any guess as to specifics?"

Nicholas looked at Ivy, wishing he could hold her in his arms as he remembered them dancing together in Illingboc. "I don't–" He took a deep breath to steady himself, imagining the worst. "I don't know what's on Brin's warped mind. But after observing him here and onboard the *Bretic*, I know it can't be anything good."

He gazed into her eyes and took in the long soft strands of her hair as it flowed down a pair of slender shoulders. Ivy's presence calmed him and gave him strength. But when he imagined the extent of Brin's horrid intentions, his heart welled up with pain, fearing for her safety and knowing he couldn't bear to be separated from her again. He couldn't shake the horrible feeling that Brin was going to take Ivy away from him–and soon–though he could not fathom for what purpose.

Ivy noted his ashen complexion, guessing that they were thinking along similar lines. She looked into his eyes, desperately searching for words to calm him while momentarily ignoring the danger she assumed was encroaching upon her.

Nicholas gazed lovingly at her as he struggled at his bonds. But out of the corners of his eyes he noted that Brin and the others on the bank were walking toward the raft. Nicholas' heart pounded. He spoke in rushed and anxious tones. "Ivy, I know we're destined to be together. I can't imagine a better life for me than to walk beside you wherever fate may lead us." Though Ivy looked affectionately at him while he spoke, Nicholas' attention was drawn to the ominous sound of Brin's footfalls as he shuffled through the brittle grass.

"I feel the same way," Ivy replied. "I have for a long time."

"So have I," Nicholas said with a desperate sense of haste as Brin and his men approached. "I love you, Ivy." He gazed upon her as if for the last time. "I always will."

"I love you too, Nicholas," she replied, tearing up. "I can't imagine living–"

"Get the girl!" Brin's order cut through a sharp breeze sweeping across the river. "Hurry up about it. The princess will be leaving us now," he told the men on the raft. Some silently questioned his instructions, wondering why he would send the girl away after going to so much trouble to secure her.

"Take me instead!" Nicholas shouted, tugging at his ropes as he tried to stand up. But one of the men on board went over and pressed a hand upon his shoulder, keeping Nicholas in place while unsheathing a dagger as a warning.

"No need for dramatics," Brin remarked, resting a foot on the edge of the raft as it gently bobbed upon the water.

"Why are you separating us?" Ivy asked, her body trembling.

"He's sending you to Kargoth!" Nicholas shouted.

"Very perceptive," Brin replied. "Now that we're heading deeper into enemy territory, it makes sense to separate you two in case we're attacked. I can get the girl into Vellan's hands much more quickly on horseback. Cale and another of my crew will tag along to let the wizard know that one of King Justin's spies will be forthcoming." He flashed a self-congratulatory grin. "And it won't hurt my cause any to have him eagerly anticipating a visit from me after I've delivered the princess of Arrondale. He'll look forward to my arrival, perhaps offering me a place in his operation as repayment for my initiative."

Nicholas seethed. "You're dreaming, Brin! Vellan will have no use for you. *He* is the center of his world. Why would he want a no-name ship rat from the Isles to assist in his designs on Laparia?"

"I don't have time for this," Brin calmly replied. He snapped his fingers and pointed to one of his men on the raft, indicating for him to escort Ivy off the vessel at once. He again looked at Nicholas, a slight sneer upon his lips. "But perhaps we can talk later, seeing that you won't have your lady friend to converse with anymore. That is, if you'll allow a no-name ship rat to speak with someone as high and mighty as you."

Brin's grating laughter felt like a slap across Nicholas' face until he heard Ivy cry out his name as one of the men forced her to stand up. Her harrowing plea was a knife to his heart, drowned out by his own shouts of defiance as he tried to jump up and save her despite the binds that restrained him. Amid his blinding tears, two pairs of arms pinned Nicholas down as Ivy was dragged away, ripped again from his life as winter's bitter breath swept across the dying landscape.

Nicholas leaned his head back against the fish barrel, mentally exhausted as the flood of emotions from three days ago circulated through his body like a slow-working poison. Each time he remembered how Ivy had been taken from him, he grew angry and sick to his stomach, fearing for her safety. But after hours of fitful worry, his mind and body would collapse into a numb lethargy as he silently gazed at the world passing him by. He was again entering that state, not caring about what might happen to him nor even concerned about getting revenge upon Brin and his men.

At times he would reach a point of giving up, his heart broken and his spirit crushed. He craved sleep if only to forget and to escape his weary bondage, but a deep and continuous slumber eluded him. Nicholas could only close his eyes for an hour or two at most before waking to Ivy's distant pleas that lingered in his mind like a horrible dream. He suffered through the rest of that day and all the next in bitter silence. The raft continued up the Gray River, getting closer to the Northern Mountains whose snowcapped peaks rose like a set of jagged teeth ready to consume them whole. Nicholas, empty and unmoving, stared back at the stone giants with anguished eyes, and for brief and scattered moments, welcomed such a fate.

CHAPTER 87

The Mountain Resistance

Nicholas awoke early the following day, greeted by sunlight shooting through a canopy of bony branches. He was ready to make a joke to Leo about sleeping late when he realized that he wasn't in the Cashua Forest but was instead within a rare thicket of scraggly trees alongside the Gray River where Brin had directed his crew to spend the previous night. A flood of melancholy hit him as he sat up, a cascade of blankets falling from his shoulders. A rope was tied to his ankle and the other end secured to a tree. Lying close by on either side were two of Brin's men, both armed with daggers. Brin and the other crew member sat by a fire engaged in quiet conversation. Brin shot a glance at Nicholas who returned a deadened stare. It had been five days since Ivy had been taken from him. He wondered when his lonely journey would end.

"If you promise to behave, I'll let you help push the raft today," Brin said. "That's a better option than sitting tied up all day."

"Is the work too much for your crew that you want me in the rotation?" Nicholas dryly remarked.

Brin shrugged, not even mildly irked by the comment. "Your choice. Doesn't matter to me either way."

Nicholas sighed, knowing that Brin was calling the shots. He admitted to himself that some exercise would do him good. Putting his pride and anger aside, he nodded. "I'll lend a hand," he replied, grateful for the offer but not willing to show it.

"Good. I'll put you on the first shift," he said as he tossed a stick into the fire. "We'll leave after breakfast. With luck, we'll be nearing the mountains by this time tomorrow. Soon after that, we'll arrive at the headwaters of the Gray River."

"And then what?" Nicholas asked.

"Then we make our way to the Drusala River along a series of diverted streams and dug canals," he explained. "After we entered into an alliance with Kargoth, Vellan instructed the Enâri to bridge the gap between the Gray and Drusala Rivers to provide our rafts swift passage. That saved our men the drudgery of unloading our tribute to him and transporting it several miles over land and rock, avoiding injury, death and much wasted time."

"Lucky for you," Nicholas said. "Not so much for the Enâri."

Brin chuckled. "Vellan can spare them by the thousands. No need to shed any tears."

"Trust me, I'm not. It's *me* that I'm worried about. If Vellan treats his own with such disregard, I can only wonder what he'd do to his enemies."

"You'll find out soon enough. But look on the bright side. Once we reach the Drusala River, we'll be moving downstream. It'll be a much easier and swifter ride for us all."

"Can't wait," Nicholas muttered. "Now when do we eat?"

The first hours on the river that day proved to be as dreary as all the others. East and west, the view was flat and unchanging, a tedious vista of browning grasslands and scrub brush shrouded with overcast skies. By late morning, however, handfuls of pine trees were sprouting up intermittently on both sides of the water, lending color and fragrance to the monotonous landscape and giving the crew hope that a more hospitable environment awaited them. Around noontime, the leaden clouds began to break. The sun appeared from time to time against patches of blue sky, offering more cheer to the men than actual heat or light. Still, all were pleased to see the sun drifting low across the southern horizon between the peaks in the mountain chain. Nicholas gazed at the hazy yellow orb as he repeatedly walked toward it while pushing off the pole in the river, closing his eyes for brief moments and thinking of Ivy as he soaked up the mild warmth upon his face. He wondered whether she had already reached Del Norác, or perhaps by some lucky twist of fate had escaped and fled her captors. The sun moved behind some clouds again, and with it, his hopes for Ivy's safety.

"Break time," said one of Brin's men. He and a second crewman approached Nicholas who was about to walk to the back of the raft to begin another circuit. Dunnic, the second man, held a piece of rope which dangled like a dead snake in his fingers.

"I'm not tired," Nicholas said, enjoying his bit of liberty.

"But I'm bored," the first man replied. "You keep the barrel of salted mackerel company again." Both he and Dunnic laughed.

"Fine," Nicholas said with a disgusted sigh, handing him the pole. He eyed the piece of rope in Dunnic's hand, knowing what was expected of him. "Don't suppose I could trade places with the second poleman for a while?"

Dunnic shook his head. "I'm taking his place. Turn around so I can bind your hands."

With another defeated sigh, Nicholas complied, knowing he couldn't fight off four armed men. On several occasions he had imagined jumping into the water and swimming to shore, though he realized he'd probably freeze to death even after making it back to land. Or if the water didn't kill him, the inevitable knife flung into his back probably would. Yet despite being tied up during most of the trip, he realized that staying with these men would eventually lead him back to Ivy–or so he hoped. Until then, he'd have to keep his desire for revenge or escape in check.

"Not so tight. My fingers turned purple last time," he glumly joked as Dunnic fastened the rope around his wrists. As they walked to the mackerel barrel on the back end, the poleman on the other side of the raft facing the western shore called out to the others.

"We've got company," he said, pointing to a quartet of Islanders who were hiking north along the bank toward them, each dressed in a long brown coat and boots. One of the men was walking briskly in front of the three others who lagged behind.

Brin, on the verge of unsettled sleep, had been resting against a crate of hardtack in the center of the raft. He jumped up, shaking the fog from his head. He curiously studied the four men walking against a backdrop of gray clouds and a clump of stunted pine trees in the near distance, straining his eyes to make out their faces. Something suddenly grabbed his attention.

"Ease the raft toward the bank," he calmly ordered, delighting his men with an unscheduled break. "One of them is injured."

The two polemen, working together, veered the craft toward the western shore. Brin stood proudly on the edge of the vessel as if he were commanding the *Bretic* itself. He clasped his hands behind his back, locking a steady gaze upon the four soldiers as they drew near the sun-speckled bank. Dunnic, standing beside Nicholas, craned his neck to get a better look, wondering if he might know any of the new arrivals from previous assignments. Unable to get a good view over the mountain of supplies, he grabbed Nicholas by the arm and led him around the back of the raft to the other side, pushing him against another barrel of salted fish.

"Stay right here, spy, or you'll regret it later," he muttered, stabbing him in the chest with a finger.

"Duly noted."

Dunnic hurried to Brin's side near the center as the raft approached the grassy bank. "These aren't the ones who took the girl a few days ago, are they?"

"No. Not a familiar face among them," Brin replied, raising a hand to greet the four strangers who had since moved closer to the river and stopped, waiting for the raft to anchor. He turned to Dunnic and softly spoke. "I'll happily give them assistance if they so request, but if they think they're going to board my vessel..." He rolled his eyes. "After all, Dunnic, I have a schedule to keep with Vellan."

Moments later, the steersmen eased the raft alongside the western bank and laid their poles down before dropping two anchors. Four misshapen hunks of iron attached to coils of rope were fastened to each corner of the raft, though only two at a time were used to anchor the vessel depending on which bank of the river it was pulled alongside. The polemen hurried to the two corners facing the open water and shoved the respective anchors off the deck. Each one dropped into the cold water and sank with silent fury, unraveling the rope coils as they disappeared into the gloomy depths.

Brin and Dunnic, in the meantime, stepped off the bobbing vessel and approached the strangers, eyeing the injured man who stood with two of his companions supporting him on either arm. A black and purplish bruise was visible on one side of the man's head with a trickle of dried blood beneath it. The wounded man, slightly stocky with dark, shortly cropped hair, favored his left ankle, raising it up slightly as if it had been sprained or possibly broken.

"Thanks for stopping," said the man standing alone who appeared to be in charge. He was a handful of years older than Brin and introduced himself as Malek. "We didn't expect to see any rafts now that winter has set in. I thought the four of us were going to spend another night with little more to eat than twigs and tree bark," he joked, gently scratching his whiskered face and smiling wearily.

"What happened to your friend?" Brin asked, indicating the wounded man.

"We were attacked at our camp several miles from here before dawn by rebels from Linden. There were so many of them, and all well trained," Malek said, glancing at the ground as if ashamed to speak of the defeat. "Some in our group managed to flee to nearby woods when their numbers overwhelmed us, though many were killed. The four of us headed this way to recover since the rebels were still thick in the south."

"We mean to go back," added one of the two men holding up his injured comrade. "We want to go back, but our friend here makes that impossible. Any chance you could take us upriver and tend to Sala's injury?"

Brin studied their tired faces. "I'll help your friend," he finally said. "Within reason, of course." He pointed to the raft, indicating the two polemen who now stood on the side to watch the proceedings, and Nicholas, still leaning against the fish barrel near the back with his hands tied behind him. "As you can see, we're rather crowded. Besides me and Dunnic, I have two others on my crew and a prisoner from Arrondale. Taking on more passengers is out of the question, especially when I have an important meeting with Vellan to keep."

Malek appeared impressed upon hearing Vellan's name, glancing at his men with what seemed to be deep respect for Brin and his crew. Brin sensed as much and hoped his fellow Islanders would appreciate his unwillingness to take them aboard.

"I guess five people crammed on this supply raft leaves little room for four more," Malek said.

"I'm glad you understand," Brin said. "Still, we'll do what we can for you and your injured friend." He flashed a cordial smile at Malek, happy that he appeared to be so accommodating yet mildly suspicious for the same reason. He knew if their positions were reversed, he would have put up a fierce argument to get his way before giving up so easily. But before Malek could utter another word, Brin posed a question. "Just out of curiosity, on what ship did you and your men cross over from the Isles? My crew and I sailed on the *Bretic*, one of the finest in the fleet before she was destroyed off Karg Island in a wall of flames."

"The *Bretic*? Destroyed?" Malek uttered the words with genuine concern. "What happened?"

"Long story," Brin said. "But needless to say, Captain Okela was devastated, having commanded that ship for almost seven years."

Malek shook his head in dismay. "It will be a great loss to the Island fleet, both Okela and the *Bretic*. But in time, he'll find another ship. I'm sure of it."

Brin nodded. "Still, Okela is always welcomed here if he'd like to take command of my vessel in all its glory," he said. He turned and extended his left arm, pointing at the raft while reaching stealthily inside his coat with his right hand. Suddenly Brin spun around, now armed with a dagger, and confronted Malek, the sharp blade aimed at his enemy's throat. "Who are you?" he demanded. Dunnic and the two polemen on the raft swiftly unleashed their daggers, ready to leap to Brin's defense.

Malek and his men were just as quick arming themselves. He drew a sword hanging from his side and the other three men, each standing in a defensive posture, now held knives similar to their counterparts. Malek flashed a grin in silent recognition to Brin for unveiling their deception so quickly.

"*Hmmm*," he said lightly. "That's four of your knives to our three knives and a sword. I guess we outmatch you, if only slightly."

"*Only* slightly," Brin replied sourly. "Now tell me who you are. You're obviously not from the Isles as you were easily duped by a bit of false information."

Malek appeared unconcerned with the sudden turn of events. "Let me guess—Okela isn't captain of the *Bretic*?"

"Okela doesn't exist," Brin replied. "Captain Kellig, before he turned traitor, commanded the *Bretic*. He has been relieved of duty and his former ship is now a burnt-out hulk sitting off Karg Island."

"Luckily you still have a vessel intact to turn over when I relieve *you* of duty," Malek replied in a jovial tone.

Brin sneered, for a moment letting his seething anger get the best of him. But he decided not to let Malek intimidate him in front of his men. "I'd sooner die than turn over this raft, though I don't think it'll come to that."

"I hope not, but we do mean to take your vessel." Malek indicated the thicket of pine trees farther away. "As a fair warning, we aren't the only ones here. Other eyes are on you, Brin, and they'll kill you if they must to defend ourselves and our land. You are the invaders, and we'll drive you out no matter what it takes."

"Vellan has invited us to these parts!" Dunnic jumped in, his face red with anger.

"Vellan is the prime invader. That wizard settled in these parts fifty years ago and created the realm of Kargoth, attacking our three mountain nations in the process." Malek fumed, his mood darkening. "The government of Surna, my homeland, has been corrupted. Its resources have been pillaged and destroyed by Vellan loyalists, his Enâri creatures, and by Island interlopers like you. The nations of Linden and Harlow have suffered similar fates. But my countrymen and I will defeat you no matter how long it takes."

"And how many lives of *my* countrymen did you take to obtain the Island garb you now wear?" Brin countered, his words dripping with disdain.

Malek sighed with disgust. "None. We raided another supply raft weeks ago that had pulled ashore for repairs. Weapons, coats and uniforms were among the items being transported, so we use them to our advantage to fight the enemy. After questioning and disarming those men, we let them go. I will honestly tell you that that particular crew was eager to flee and start a new life away from the Isles. Apparently not all the Island people support your alliance with Vellan or his relentless quest for power."

"There are always a few weak minds and hearts in any operation," Brin said. "But my crew will not be so easily defeated."

Malek tilted his head slightly as he sized up Brin's resolve to fight to the bitter end. "Are you sure about that?"

He raised his sword high in the air, the blade reflecting scattered sunlight through the breaking clouds. Suddenly an arrow streaked past Brin's left side like a harsh whisper, embedding itself into one of the crates in the center of the raft. Its gray and white feather fletching matched the hue of the clouds overhead. The two polemen, only an arm's length away, turned in unison, both startled when hearing the deadly thud.

Nicholas, witnessing the event on the end of the raft, expected trouble as he frantically tugged to loosen the ropes binding his hands, though no to avail. No matter how the battle played out, he knew he'd be merely an afterthought and wanted to get out of the way as he couldn't defend himself. Escape was out of the question since he would be easily stopped. All he could do to survive an imminent skirmish was to hide on the other side of the raft behind the mountain of supplies and hope for the best. He was prepared to slink away onto the east-facing side of the vessel when Brin responded to Malek's demonstration.

"You have us at a disadvantage," he said after glancing at the arrow protruding from the crate. Brin lowered his dagger and Malek reciprocated, bringing the sword down to his side. "The only sensible thing would be for us to hand over our vessel."

"That would be the wisest course," Malek replied, loosening the grip on his sword, but only slightly, not expecting his opponent to comply. "I promise that no harm will come to any of you. Agreed?"

Brin smiled crookedly and nodded. "Agreed." He glanced at the ground, a thin stream of air passing through his lips as if to punctuate his crushing defeat. "Agreed," he repeated softly as his fingers tightened around his knife handle. "No harm shall come to me or my men. You, sir, however, are a different story."

Suddenly, he swept his dagger through the air directly at Malek, having no intention of losing his vessel or his life. Malek, expecting as much, raised his sword and sharply fended off the blow. At once, Dunnic leaped screaming into the fray, charging at the nearest of Malek's three men and tackling him to the ground. Brin's two polemen jumped off the raft to assist their comrades, but just as one of them stepped foot onto the grassy bank, his body flinched and collapsed to the ground in a dead heap, an arrow with gray and white fletching buried in his chest. Seconds later, three more men armed with swords and bows and dressed like Islanders charged from the nearby pines and raced toward the river to aide Malek and his group.

"You will not take my raft!" Brin shouted, wildly slicing the air with his dagger.

Malek, who could have easily struck Brin down, fended off the strikes one by one, simultaneously watching the others out of the corners of his eyes. As one of his men fought Dunnic in the grass, the other two had barreled toward the second poleman, their daggers raised and their eyes filled with fury. The poleman recoiled in terror and immediately tossed his knife aside and dropped to his knees, raising his hands in surrender. Moments later, Dunnic was also subdued, his face pressed to the ground and one of his arms locked behind his back. Nicholas watched from the raft in silent fascination. When Malek saw that his adversaries were now under control and that more aid was arriving from within the trees, he couldn't help but smile, drawing Brin's ire.

"I swear I'll kill you!" he cried.

"You're taking your time about it," Malek said, turning away another dagger stroke. But Brin, nearly out of breath, countered with even more desperate swings of his weapon as Malek's additional men drew nearer. Growing tired of the match, Malek gripped the hilt of his sword with both hands and swung it with his full force as Brin's knife came down again. He knocked the weapon out of his hand and sent it sailing through the air above the river where it plunged into the water. "Now do you give up?" he asked, breathing heavily yet still in an amiable mood which infuriated Brin. "You must realize that it's all over, my friend."

"I am not your friend!" Brin shouted, clenching his fists and glaring at Malek as if ready to leap at him like a wild dog. "And this is far from over!"

As Brin's face turned a dark shade of red, he screamed in frustration and spun around, sprinting back to the raft. He leaped on board near the center of the vessel where he had been napping earlier and reached underneath the canvas tarp covering the mound of supplies. A moment later, he raised his right arm with a defiant grin, gripping the hilt of a sword he had hidden there earlier while resting.

"Ready for a rematch?" he shouted. He stood upon the edge of the raft as it bobbed upon the water. Beads of sweat dotted his brow. His shoulders rose and fell with each labored breath. "I fear neither you nor your gang of thugs."

"Thugs? That term suits you more than me," Malek replied as he pointed his sword at Nicholas. "It is you, after all, who have a bound prisoner upon your raft."

Brin glared at Nicholas who still stood at the back of the vessel. "That man is a spy for King Justin and deserves the treatment he has received. Vellan, though, will decide his fate when I deliver him to the wizard in person."

Nicholas shook his head, a part of him pitying Brin for not realizing that he was already defeated. "It's over, Brin," he said. "You're not ever going to see Vellan no matter how much you wish it. Hand over your sword to Malek."

"Shut up, you!" he said, waving the weapon at Nicholas. "Or I'll come down there and make you shut up."

"The man is right," Malek said, wanting to redirect Brin's fury at himself. "Lay down your sword so we can discuss reasonable terms. Refuse, and I won't be able to promise a pleasant outcome."

"And why should I trust you? Look at what you did to *him*," he shot back, pointing at one of his crewmen who lay dead upon the brittle grass. "How do I know you won't kill us all once I surrender?"

"You don't," he replied with growing impatience. "But I do. I'm a man of my word. No harm will come to you or your associates if you give up now."

Brin locked gazes with Malek for a moment and then studied the hopeless scene, weighing the option of surrender. The defiant part of him, though, frenetically searched for another way to grasp an improbable victory after such a brutal thrashing.

"Give up, Brin," Nicholas said. "By the look on Malek's face, he's not going to give you much more time to think about it."

"I told you to be quiet!" he shouted. "You're still my prisoner and don't forget that. I'll worry about Malek and–" Brin froze before slowly turning around and glaring at Nicholas from halfway across the raft as a torrent of wild speculation filled his mind. "Now I understand everything. *You* helped to arrange all of this. It's as clear as a full Bear Moon. You're in league with Malek!"

Nicholas' eyes widened in astonishment, believing that Brin had lost his grasp of reality. "I've been your prisoner for the last twelve days. Surely you can see that your claim doesn't make sense."

"Don't patronize me!" Brin raised his sword and stepped closer. "You've been plotting against me since Karg Island. I know it! This has been your plan all along."

As Nicholas stood against the barrel, the ropes biting into his wrists, he noted a desperate, faraway look in Brin's eyes that he had never seen before, fearful that the man was becoming unhinged. Malek wondered the same thing as he stood upon the grassy bank, taking another step closer to the raft.

"Keep your distance!" Brin shouted, spinning around to face him. "I don't know how you and Nicholas kept in contact, but I know you did. Both of you have been waiting to take me down."

"I've never laid eyes on your prisoner until today," Malek calmly told him. "Your mind has taken a flight of fancy."

"You're lying! You and Nicholas are collaborators."

"Malek speaks the truth," Nicholas said, drawing Brin's attention away as Malek took another step nearer to the raft. "How could we possibly know each other?"

"Don't question me as if I'm a child!" he snapped, turning to face the shore. "I said stay back, Malek! Don't come any closer."

"Brin, throw down your sword!" he said, reaching the limit of his patience. "We're ending this now."

"Better do as he says," Nicholas warned.

"Stop talking, both of you!" Brin shouted, his gaze shifting between the two adversaries. With a clenched jaw and groans of frustration, he appeared as if a hunted animal, cornered and ready to spring in one last desperate bid for freedom. "I make the rules around here! I give the orders!"

"Last chance!" Malek cried. "Surrender now, or else."

"Do it, Brin," Nicholas urged. "Save yourself."

Brin, exhausted and enraged, exploded in frustration and ran screaming down the raft toward Nicholas, his sword aimed at him. Nicholas lunged away from the barrel, trying to keep his balance so he could run to the other side of the raft. But as he turned to flee, his foot caught one of the ropes binding a canvas tarp. His body jerked back as Brin's sharp sword zeroed in on him. Nicholas thought only of Ivy in that next instant as Brin was about to kill him.

But in the split second before that fatal blow, Brin's body momentarily froze, arching back at the shoulders and accompanied with a violent intake of breath before he stumbled harmlessly past Nicholas toward the back edge of the raft. Nicholas noted an arrow sticking out of Brin's right shoulder just moments before he heard a terrific splash. Brin tumbled headlong into the water, losing the grip on his sword which sank silently to the river's cloudy bottom.

Nicholas untangled his foot as Brin surfaced and floundered about in the freezing river, coughing and sputtering as he made his way to the raft and grabbed onto the edge. The water about him was tinted scarlet. His hands slipped off the wood as he groaned in pain and reached out again, grabbing the bound logs with his left hand and clutching the iron hunk that served as one of the unused anchors with his right, finally steadying himself.

"Hold on!" Nicholas shouted, standing over his former captor but unable to assist as his hands were tied. He gazed with sickening horror at the arrow protruding from the back of Brin's shoulder. He looked to shore as Malek and his fellow soldiers surrounded the two surviving members of Brin's crew and bound their wrists. One of Malek's men, an archer named Rollin, clutched a long bow at his side. "I need help!" Nicholas shouted.

"Do you think they're going to bother to rush–" Brin took a deep, shaky breath, his head lying upon his right arm as it rested on a coil of rope attached to the anchor. "–rush to my aid?" He raised his tired eyes, offering a grim smile. "I'm as good as dead."

"Climb on the raft," Nicholas said, kneeling down while still struggling at his ropes. "You'll freeze to death in the water."

"Or bleed to death outside of it." He raised his head and gazed at Nicholas with curiosity. "But why should you care?"

"I'm not entirely sure," Nicholas admitted. "But your wound doesn't look fatal. Pull yourself on board and let them help you."

Brin got a more secure grip on the anchor and repositioned himself as spasms of pain coursed through his upper body. His legs, though, were beginning to numb. He imagined that if he let go he would float away down the Gray River until he lost all feeling, allowing death to finally take him. He stared at the coil of rope, gently stroking the fibers with his left hand as Nicholas uttered a few more words of encouragement. But Brin found it difficult to concentrate as his mind began to drift and lightheadedness slowly overtook him. Yet he made a tremendous effort to keep his eyes focused on Nicholas as his fury and disdain began to cool.

"At best, I'll die a–" Brin shuddered as a sharp breeze brushed over the surface of the river. "At best, Nicholas, I'll die a slow and painful death if they can't properly fix my wound." He laughed softly, holding tighter to the anchor with his right arm as he sunk his left hand into the rope and wrapped it once around his wrist. "That is, if they even make an effort to help me."

"They will," Nicholas promised, watching distractedly as Brin worked the rope around his left wrist two more times, wondering if he was going to use it somehow to pull himself onto the raft. Malek and his men, in the meantime, tended to their two prisoners.

"At worst," he continued, his words slowing due to the cold, "I'll survive…and become a prisoner…to them." Brin shifted his eyes to shore. "I could never–"

"Never what?" Nicholas asked, wanting to keep him talking until help arrived. He glanced at the riverbank and shouted. "Would somebody give me a hand?"

Brin bowed his head as he struggled to bring his rope-entangled left hand back to the anchor, hugging the metal chunk with both arms as if never wanting to let go. Suddenly a chill shot through Nicholas when he realized Brin's intention.

"I could never stand being alive…knowing that I failed both Vellan and the Isles," he continued, his face pale and lifeless. "That's a fate worse than death–at least for me." Gathering all his strength, Brin pulled the anchor as close to the edge of the raft as possible with a terrific groan, causing Nicholas to struggle to his feet.

"Brin!"

"Good luck finding…your princess."

With a final effort, Brin pulled the anchor toward him one more time, causing it to topple over the edge and plunge into the water. The rope coil swiftly unraveled. Nicholas barely had time to call for help when the rope around Brin's left wrist tightened like a noose and yanked him under the surface, the anchor dragging him down into the river's darkened waters. Nicholas stared dumbfounded into the murky liquid. A second later, the rope stopped uncoiling as the anchor reached the river bottom. Nicholas felt a thousand miles away and a thousand days out of time's reckoning. He didn't even hear Malek walk up behind him and call out his name. He took no notice until Malek grabbed his hands from behind and cut the binding ropes with a dagger.

He spun around and caught Malek's steely gaze. "Brin went under. He needs our help." His voice sounded far away.

Malek gently rested a hand on Nicholas' shoulder. "Brin is beyond our help now, and you're not to blame. He chose his fate." Malek bent down, grabbed the rope and cut it loose with his knife, dropping the free end into the water like a dead snake. "The river will bury him," he remarked. "Now come ashore with us, Nicholas. We have things to discuss before we move this raft farther upriver."

"All right..." he said, hearing Malek's words but not really comprehending them.

Nicholas still pictured Brin's pale face the moment it was pulled underneath the surface, questioning why he felt a void inside for such a terrible person. The image both sobered and bewildered him as he followed Malek off the raft and onto the grassy bank. He noticed the body of the other dead man whose face had since been covered with his own coat. He wondered if Malek would have his men bury him or consign his remains to the river. He sighed wearily as the voices of the others slowly came into focus. He realized how tired he was and how much his shoulders ached from having had his hands tied behind him so many times over the past several days.

Nicholas recalled walking through Kanesbury shortly before the Harvest Festival, certain then that he had found his path in life and a door to endless adventure when he decided to join the King's Guard. But when he looked around at the strange faces inhabiting this desolate land with the smell of fresh blood and death swirling in his nostrils, he realized that this wasn't the adventure he had had in mind. But imagined or not, it was an adventure he was now a part of, and for the moment, one in which he could find no way out.

CHAPTER 88

A Deed Well Done

Within the hour, Nicholas was again aboard the raft traveling slowly up the Gray River, only this time not as a prisoner but as one of the crew. After Malek and his soldiers had commandeered the vessel, Nicholas was politely informed that he must accompany them until he was thoroughly questioned about his involvement with the Islanders and about Brin's charge that he was a spy for King Justin.

"As to me being a spy, Brin had quite an imagination," he had earlier told Malek while on shore. They spoke in private as Malek's men buried the dead steersman. The sun had since disappeared behind a new bank of thickening clouds moving in fast from the west.

"Imagined or not, when we reach camp, some of my friends and I would like to have a long conversation with you about your recent whereabouts," Malek said. "I usually trust my first impressions and believe you are no threat to our cause. But one can never be too careful in these turbulent times."

Nicholas sighed with frustration. Though he guessed that this man from Surna was only seven or eight years his senior, he detected a confidence in Malek that seemed beyond his years, no doubt developed and honed during his time spent fighting in the wild against Vellan. But not wanting to appear ungrateful after being rescued, Nicholas calmly uttered a simple sentence.

"So, am I your prisoner now?"

"Indeed not. Your hands are no longer bound and no sword is pointed at your chest. Trust me, I understand the reason behind your question. Yet I would be derelict in my duty if I just let you roam free without learning your story." Malek, his hands shoved in his coat pockets, leaned back and stretched his back to fight off the day's weariness. His cool green eyes, framed by a head of light brown hair, focused on Nicholas' dubious expression. He knew he had not completely gained the young man's trust.

"Why do you even need to know my story?" Nicholas asked. "You have the raft and supplies now. What more do you want?"

"Information, and the certainty that I'd be doing the right thing by releasing you. But I won't force you to come with us," he said. "If you wish it, I'll question you here. But that would delay us and keep the raft possibly exposed to enemy eyes. There is a tributary several miles ahead on the east called Kaddis Creek. I had hoped to pole up that watercourse and into the trees to get out of harm's way. Though the last Island vessels have passed by for the winter, there are still enemy stragglers on foot roaming the mountain valleys."

Nicholas glumly nodded, recalling the men who had taken Ivy. Yet if he was to find her again, he suspected he would have a better chance with some help rather than going it alone. He wondered if he would ever have rescued Ivy from Karg Island without the assistance of Arch Boland, his sister Hannah and so many others. If he was once willing to rely on Brin Mota to lead him to Kargoth, surely he could trust Malek to do the same. But as he shook his hand, agreeing to leave on the raft at once, Nicholas knew it would be a difficult task to convince him to arrange an expedition to Vellan's stronghold. For Ivy's sake, he couldn't fail.

Light snow fell on the Gray River as twilight encroached. The raft made steady progress with eight men rotating among the two positions of steersmen. Nicholas was currently on duty, wearing a hood and a pair of gloves. He walked the circuit on the east side of the raft, thinking about Ivy as he did during most of his waking hours. The other men were scattered about the vessel, some napping, others engaged in quiet conversation and one guarding the two prisoners from Brin's crew. Sala, walking the west circuit, called out to Nicholas in the deepening gloom as he operated the pole with his beefy arms.

"The turn into Kaddis Creek is just beyond that trio of pine trees up ahead," said the man who had convincingly faked his injuries to catch Brin off guard. He wore no hood as if unbothered by the cold. "Know how to turn one of these things?"

Nicholas smirked in the shadows. "I've had nothing better to do for twelve days than observe Brin's men poling upriver and veering to and from shore. I could handle this with my eyes closed, Sala. But I'll let you call out the commands just to be safe."

"Eyes *open* would be preferable," Malek joked as he walked up to him. "Kaddis Creek, though wide, is not as deep as the Gray River. We don't want to get stuck on a sandbar. Sala will capably guide you."

As they passed the trio of pines, Sala quietly called out instructions to Nicholas to maneuver their poles and slowly turn the raft to the left where the two watercourses converged. With little difficulty, the pair steered the vessel directly into the center of Kaddis Creek and moved eastward along the waterway. When Nicholas looked around, he was thankful to see the beginnings of a thin forest sprouting up on both sides of the creek and noticed thickening foliage farther south in the shadows of the looming mountains. Here the air smelled sweet and fresh which invigorated his spirit. For a moment he was confident that he would find Ivy, yet managed to keep his emotions in check as he helped guide the raft nearly two more miles up the Kaddis. He and Sala brought it to a rest on the southern bank in a secluded spot beneath some overhanging branches.

"Now what?" Nicholas asked as darkness took hold.

"Now we eat," Malek replied. "A brief meal and a warm fire will do us all good before our next task."

"No rest for the weary tonight?" Sala asked with exaggerated dismay as some of the other men gathered around.

"Though you all deserve a good night's sleep," Malek said, "we must work a few more hours to bring some of these supplies to camp."

"How far is that?" Nicholas inquired, happy with the change of scenery.

"Less than three miles into those woods. We'll take only what we can carry on our backs in one trip. After all, we need to bring something back for our comrades to prove we haven't been idle while we were away tracking this raft."

Nicholas raised an eyebrow, intrigued by the revelation. "So you had planned this caper all along? You didn't come upon Brin by chance?"

Malek shook his head as he stepped ashore, the scent of cold soil and pine dancing thick in the air. The snow had since let up, though the threat of more hung palpably in the low lying clouds.

"Our group paddled over to the western shore and observed Brin's craft for over two days after one of our scouts first reported back to camp upon sighting it. Up until then, we believed that the last of the Island vessels had passed by for the winter. We saw an opportunity to nab this solitary raft. That it was manned by such a small crew only played to our advantage."

"Luckily for me that you took the chance," Nicholas said appreciatively. "Brin had commandeered this craft near the mouth of the Lorren for his own purposes, expecting to strike a deal with Vellan and reap the rewards. Otherwise the raft would have made its way upriver in the company of several others."

"Brin's greed was our gain," Sala remarked.

"Tomorrow we'll return with flat sleds and bring about half the supplies to camp," Malek continued, pointing out three members of his crew. "You men will stay here overnight to guard the raft."

"Why only half?" Nicholas asked. "What of the rest?"

"The remaining goods will stay onboard and continue up Kaddis Creek for several more miles to another landing point closer to other camps to repeat the process."

"I'd like to learn more about your operation," Nicholas later said to Malek as they looked over which supplies to carry back to camp. A few torches had been lit which erratically reflected upon the water's dark, oily surface.

"Perhaps you will during our question and answer period," he replied, handing Nicholas a sack filled with hardened biscuits from a crate he pried open with a metal bar. "Though I suspect I will be doing most of the questioning." He handed him a second sack. "Take another. They're light. The men will enjoy them dipped in hot tea."

Nicholas slung the sacks over his shoulder, happy to be of use again in a cause greater than himself. Though he and Leo were instrumental in reforging the key to the Spirit Box, he still wondered if their efforts had borne any fruit. But this simple act of providing some hungry soldiers a bit of food seemed almost as great an act of heroism as his grueling trek through the Dunn Hills. He took modest pride in the small deed, eager to learn more about the people who had banded together throughout the Northern Mountains to fight Vellan's iron rule, and hopefully one day, defeat him.

After trudging through darkness for what seemed like hours, they finally reached camp deep inside the woods. About twenty men greeted the new arrivals, some stepping outside their crude tents while others had been tending to a few bonfires. A half dozen other men were still concealed in the shadows, keeping silent watch around the perimeter. A modest one-story cabin had been built in the center of camp which served as a meeting and dining place for the group. Another small storage building had been constructed off to the right where the men deposited all the goods they had carried with them. Soon after, Nicholas found himself sitting at a table inside the cabin with Malek and Sala. Also joining them was Tradell, another member of the camp who coordinated its day-to-day operations. The oldest of the trio with a military background, Tradell exhibited a cautious gaze above a thin, brown mustache and a deadpan expression. Nicholas listened to the questions they politely posed to him while all enjoyed hot tea and some of the biscuits Nicholas had carried in.

The cabin, though consisting of one large room, was divided into four semi-open areas—one for eating, one for meal preparation, another for sitting and holding meetings and the last one as wood storage and sleeping quarters for whichever group was assigned to cabin duty. In the center of the structure stood a large square fireplace constructed of rounded stones with an opening on each of the four corners, above which rose a single, shared chimney. Here the crackling fire was kept burning all day and night in cold weather. A few men milling about in the other cabin sections kept their voices low so as not to disturb Malek as he questioned Nicholas.

"I avoided asking specifics about your life earlier," Malek said as he began his friendly interrogation. "I thought it best to let you get to know us better before we spoke in earnest." He sat back in a wooden chair, warming his hands against a mug of steaming tea. Nicholas was seated opposite him with Sala and Tradell positioned on either side of the main table. Other empty chairs were scattered about and a smaller, second table against one wall held a plate of biscuits and a wedge of cheese. "So, where should we start? Do you care to tell us how you got tangled up with a man like Brin? Or is there somewhere else you'd like to begin your tale? We have all the time in the world."

"I may need it," Nicholas said, enjoying the comforts of the cabin as compared to his last several days as a prisoner on the raft.

As he sipped tea and glanced at his eager audience, he felt no fear or distrust as he might have if he had met these men during his trek to Wolf Lake. But since all Nicholas wanted was to find Ivy as quickly as possible, he decided that being honest would offer him the surest path to that goal. Besides, now that the business with the key was out of his hands, and King Justin and Prince Gregory had by now led their armies to Rhiál and Montavia, he knew there was nothing he could say to endanger his friends and their missions. All he wanted was Ivy.

"I'll start by telling you where I come from and about the journey I've been on for the last three months or so," he said with little hesitation, noting the surprised yet appreciative expressions upon his companions. "My home is in the village of Kanesbury in Arrondale. And yes, Brin was somewhat correct when he said I was a spy for King Justin," he added matter-of-factly, taking another sip of his drink. Malek and the others leaned forward in anticipation of a stirring account. "However, Brin was merely speculating at the time and knew nothing about my true relationship with the King."

"So you really know King Justin? And you're willing to tell us about it?" Malek asked, not fully believing him yet.

"Yes," he replied. "But whether you take me at my word is another story. I just hope that when we're through, you might trust me enough to lead me to Kargoth and help rescue someone I love. That's all that matters to me now."

"Then begin, my friend," Sala encouraged him.

Nicholas recounted the highlights of his life since fleeing Kanesbury. He spared no details about Dooley Kramer and Arthur Weeks framing him for the gristmill robbery, his chance meeting with Princess Megan, or the failed attempt to rescue Ivy along the Trillium Sea. He painted an honest and heartfelt narrative to earn the trust and respect of his newfound friends. He also told them about Carmella and Jagga, the medallion and his meeting with King Justin.

Sala nearly interrupted when Nicholas mentioned the Spirit Box and how Tolapari believed the medallion could be remade into a key to open it and destroy the Enâri race. But Malek and Tradell cast sharp glances his way, cooling Sala's desire to comment on the matter. When Nicholas mentioned that he and Leo had volunteered to search for the wizard Frist in the Dunn Hills, Malek was pleased with the information, confirming the first impressions he had developed about the young man. And with a trace of melancholy, Nicholas recounted how he had learned the truth from the wizard about his father's death during an Enâri raid.

"If what Frist told you is true, Nicholas, then perhaps you were destined to have a greater role in the troubled events of our times," Malek quietly remarked as the crackling flames cast a warm, flickering glow upon their faces. "After what the Enâri did to your father and to your village, it's fitting that you should be the one to hasten their downfall." He leaned back, considering his next question. "Were you and Leo successful in your quest?" he asked, casting a knowing glance at Sala.

"We were," Nicholas replied. "Frist remade the key, though I'm sad to say that it cost him his life in the end." He lifted the round, silver amulet from underneath his shirt and held it up for all to see.

"What's that?" Sala asked, impressed by the craftsmanship as he leaned forward for a closer look.

"Frist made this for me before he completed his work on the key," Nicholas said, "with what little life and magic was left inside him. He hoped that it would lead me to those I wished to find and preserve life wherever death and destruction lurked."

"Perhaps it helped save your life on the raft," Tradell said, "if you can imagine Frist's hand guiding an archer's well-aimed arrow."

"I can. In fact, it happened twice. I was saved by another arrow a couple days after donning this amulet," he said, recalling his first meeting with Hannah along the banks of the Wolf River. "Now if only this amulet would lead me to Ivy."

"It may. In any case, treasure the gift. Maybe Frist somehow walks with you while it is in your possession," Malek said as Nicholas slipped the amulet back beneath his shirt. "Or maybe you're just an extremely lucky individual. Now tell me, were you successful in returning the key to Morrenwood and opening the Spirit Box?"

"I wish I had an answer," he said, shifting in his seat. "That's where my story and Leo's diverge, and my encounter with Brin Mota begins."

After pausing to refresh themselves with some food from the other table and more hot tea, Nicholas continued with the next chapter of his adventure. All listened without interruption as he told them of his meeting with Arch Boland and Arteen, his first encounter with Brin Mota and the ensuing conflagration on the *Bretic*, and Ivy's rescue on Karg Island and the death of Tarosius Lok. Nicholas fondly recalled dancing with Ivy a few days later in Illingboc, thinking then that his life had finally taken a turn for the good.

"Little did I know that Brin was yet lurking out there, still convinced that Ivy was a princess and that I was a spy." He glumly related how he and Ivy had been drugged and then awakened as prisoners on Brin's raft before she was taken from his side and sent on ahead to Vellan. Nicholas leaned back in his chair and sighed, appearing tired and grim as if the stress of the last several days had suddenly caught up with him. "Now, Malek, you know everything about me since I left home. Judge me as you see fit, and if you deem me not an enemy, then I'd ask you to release me so I can go to Kargoth. But if you deem me a friend, perhaps you might provide me with supplies and the company of a few men to guide and assist me. In any case, it's in your hands."

He gazed at the trio of men, looking for any subtle clues as to their decision. When he saw Malek and Tradell glance at each other in a jovial manner before exchanging a few whispers, he couldn't tell if they had taken his plea seriously and was visibly disappointed. Sala, too, seemed light of mood, confusing Nicholas even further.

"Nicholas is wondering if we deem him a friend or not," Malek said, addressing Sala and Tradell as he stood and walked around the room. He wore a boyish grin as if privy to some secret.

His camp mates were also in good spirits, anticipating what Malek was about to say. "Do either of you care to comment?"

"Oh, friend indeed," Tradell replied, receiving a slight nod of mystified thanks from Nicholas. "Though I suspect he is at a loss as to why."

"My thinking, too," added Sala with a good-natured smirk.

"Agreed." Malek took his seat and looked at Nicholas. "It's unanimous. The three of us find you a worthy addition to our camp, as I'm sure the others will once they hear your story. And if anyone has earned some help to get to Kargoth, it is certainly you," he said, eliciting a cautious yet hopeful smile from Nicholas. "But first there's something I need to tell you now, something I apparently have the honor of telling you by the good fortune of our meeting." Malek still exhibited a cheerfulness that Nicholas could not fathom.

"Tell me what?" he asked, his mood lightening and his smile growing though he didn't know why. "It's apparent that you've just learned a bit of good news, yet I cannot explain when you received it as you've been sitting here with me all this time."

"Half true," Malek said. "I received this good news about eight days ago, though only moments ago did my friends and I learn of its origins, all thanks to you."

"To me?" Nicholas crossed his arms and tilted his head in a slightly bewildered manner. "I don't understand."

"Tell him already!" Sala excitedly said. "If anyone deserves to know, he does."

"Tell me what?" Nicholas asked.

Malek leaned forward, his elbows resting on the table and his hands clasped together as he offered Nicholas a congratulatory smile. "Sala wants me to tell you that your plan succeeded. The long trip through the Dunn Hills with Leo and Hobin was worth the sacrifice."

"But I already told you that the key was remade," Nicholas said, not grasping the intent of Malek's statement. "Frist successfully forged the medallion back into his original creation with the magic still intact."

"Which Leo apparently brought back to Morrenwood for its intended purpose."

"Well, I hope he and Hobin make it back to the capital and…" Nicholas paused as Malek and the others stared at him with amused wonder as if he didn't comprehend the punchline of a joke. Suddenly he felt a chill run up his back. "Am I hearing you correctly? Our plan–*succeeded*? Do you mean to say that Leo–"

"–used the key to open the Spirit Box?" Malek sat back and nodded, a satisfied grin upon his face. "Indeed he did, or at least somebody did. Of that we are now certain."

Nicholas was struck silent. "How do you know this?" he finally asked, his voice nearly a whisper, his eyes wide in disbelief.

"As I alluded to earlier, I received some good news eight days ago," he said. "A scout from another camp miles to our south sought us out with information he'd received two days before. Word is traveling like wildfire from Kargoth and the other nations in the Northern Mountains that the Enâri race is no more."

"The Enâri have been literally wiped off the face of Laparia!" Sala excitedly interjected. "Their dusty remains were scattered to the wind near the break of dawn fourteen days ago, so we were told. All of them were destroyed according to the many stories circulating. Whether referring to the thousands upon thousands of Enâri residing in Del Norâc itself or those scattered among the villages up and down the Drusala River, it appears that every last one of them suffered the same fate. All of them–gone!" He clapped his hands with a stinging crack. "Even the Enâri forces that occupied parts of Surna, Linden and Harlow were annihilated as well as those patrolling throughout the mountain valleys. And I say good riddance! Let them go back to the dirt and rock from which they came through Vellan's twisted craft. I'll sleep much easier now."

"The only sad thing," Tradell added, "is that Vellan didn't suffer the same fate. Still, we should be pleased with the luck we've been given."

"Nicholas' trek to Wolf Lake was more than just luck," Malek said, "and the men, women and children of our three mountain nations owe him and his companions a debt of gratitude. The elimination of the Enâri race puts us years ahead in our fight against Kargoth. It's a major turning point."

As Nicholas listened to the heady words swirling around him, he still couldn't fully believe what he was hearing and held up a hand to pose a question. Malek observed the bewilderment on his face and beckoned him to fire away.

"This happened fourteen days ago?" he asked, performing a mental calculation. "That would have made it, uh…" He grinned sheepishly. "I seemed to have lost track of days while on the river."

"Who wouldn't have?" Malek said with understanding. "But I can help you out. The Enâri met their demise at dawn on the second day of New Winter. Today is the sixteenth day of the month. When did you and Leo depart from Morrenwood?"

"That I remember clearly," he said, recalling the cold night when Nedry escorted them through a minor back gate of the Blue Citadel to their horses and supplies as the Edelin River flowed nearby along a fragrant stretch of pine. How long ago it seemed, as if part of another life. "We left before midnight on the thirteenth day of Mid Autumn. It took us about three weeks to find the wizard Frist, which included getting lost in the woods before we had hired our guide. That would have brought us to, let's see, the eleventh day of Old Autumn, if I'm figuring correctly. I parted with Leo and Hobin–and the key–two days later, though it seems like a year ago," he wearily admitted. "So if the Enâri were destroyed on the second day of New Winter, then Leo and Hobin had about two weeks to get the key back to Morrenwood." Nicholas yawned, recalling the tiresome parts of his journey. "Only now am I beginning to feel the weight of my travels. I could sleep for a week if you'd allow it."

"At the very least you've earned one good night's sleep tonight," Malek said. "Though when word spreads through camp of your accomplishment, I can't promise you much rest after that. The men will be eager to hear of your adventure. It has been such a long struggle for all of us, and to finally hear some good news will be intoxicating. Many have not seen their families in months since we have taken up the fight against Vellan. The sun lilies were just blooming in Mid Summer the last time that I saw my wife and twin daughters." He smiled wistfully, recalling the two weeks he had spent with them after returning home to Surna for that all-too-brief visit.

"How old are your girls?" Nicholas asked, seeing the longing for his family clearly upon Malek's face.

"Teal and Rosa were born on the first day of New Summer four years ago," he said. "I had hoped to see them again before winter set in, but all of us here were fully occupied in the fight. I fear I shall not see my family until spring arrives, if even then."

"Perhaps we will order you home," Tradell remarked lightly, "whether our fight with Vellan is finished or not. But fear not, Malek. The political winds are shifting. Spring may bring us more gains if we can just hold on a little bit longer."

"I know," he quietly responded.

Nicholas noted a peculiar tone in Tradell's voice as if he knew more than he was letting on. "You say the political winds are shifting? What do you mean by that?"

Tradell glanced at Malek as he silently inquired if they should impart more information to their guest. Malek considered the situation for a moment while taking a slow sip of his drink.

"We have many other things to discuss with you, Nicholas, assuming that you'll stay and join our fight," Malek said. "We know you're anxious to get to Del Norác, hoping you'll find Ivy, but–"

"She's there!" he vigorously chimed in, dismissing the imagined implication that she might not be or that his search for Ivy would have no chance of succeeding from the outset. "She has to be," he added in a softer tone that bordered on hopelessness. But when seeing nothing but compassion in all the eyes upon him, Nicholas sighed with regret. "I'm sorry, Malek. I didn't mean to raise my voice. I guess I'm more tired than I realize."

"Think nothing of it. All of us in camp have gotten on each other's nerves over the months, usually out of sheer boredom. But what I wanted to say was that journeying alone to Kargoth might not be the wisest course right now as winter can be especially brutal in these mountains. You might not survive the trip. However," he quickly added, seeing that Nicholas was about to voice another reservation, "we do have a shared destination in mind and would be more than willing to help you when the time is right."

"And when would that be?" Nicholas asked, feeling all hope draining out of him.

"In all honesty, at the first sign of spring." Malek observed a shadow of defeat upon Nicholas' face, yet he fully empathized with him since he had felt the same longing and melancholy during the long separation from his own family. "Though we and others plan to move our camps deeper into the mountain valleys and closer to Kargoth as long as the heavy snows hold off, it will not be long before winter will rule with an iron fist. Cold and hunger would take you before you completed a third of your journey."

"But I have to try!" Nicholas said, though realizing the logic of Malek's words. He knew in his mind that Ivy's voice and smile and touch would be lost to him in the cold void of winter for weeks to come. Yet his heart needed more convincing.

"It is well over a hundred miles to Vellan's stronghold in Mount Minakaris," Tradell explained, "and that is traveling along the straight path of a hawk. You would have snow-choked mountains and woods and valleys to traverse for many more miles than that. So to be blunt, if you truly love this woman, you shouldn't throw your life away before you actually find her."

Nicholas said nothing, knowing he had lost the argument. The others sensed his quiet resignation and knew that the next few days would be especially tough on him. Sala piped up, hoping to put a pleasant face on the situation.

"Look on the bright side, Nicholas. We're already more than halfway through New Winter. Maybe the next two months will fly by too, or if we're fortunate, we'll be blessed with an early spring." Nicholas merely raised his eyes and scowled, though for a moment his spirits were temporarily lifted by Sala's determined enthusiasm. "It could happen."

"We should be so lucky," Malek replied. "Still, Nicholas, there is some good news I'd like to share before we let you have a proper meal and some sleep. There is something you should know now that your story is told. It's about the war between Rhiál and Maranac which you referenced earlier."

"You have news about King Justin's army?" he asked, perking up.

"Very good news," Malek said. "Less than two weeks ago we received word that the war between the two lakeside kingdoms had ended. The forces of Drogin were defeated thirty days ago. Drogin perished while trying to flee Zaracosa. Sadly, King Basil of Rhiál has succumbed to ill health as victory was upon them."

Nicholas' heart raced. "And King Justin? What of him?"

"He returned home in fine form after the successful campaign, as did King Cedric of Drumaya who had joined him in battle with our brethren from the Ebrean Forest. But we can discuss that later," he said. "Tradell and I first need to check on our two prisoners. It's now time for them to answer a few questions."

"Please answer one more of mine first," Nicholas pleaded as Princess Megan's wellbeing weighed heavily on his mind. "Did you receive any news about Prince Gregory? He was to lead another army to Montavia to wrest that kingdom from Caldurian's grip."

Malek shook his head. "We have no word yet, though are awaiting information on that and other matters." He stood and stretched, glad to be back at his temporary home. "I don't know which has tired me more, my time in the wild or all this seemingly endless talk. Yet alas, both are necessary in these troubled days." He turned to Tradell, about to say something before pausing, having suddenly changed his mind. "I think the prisoners can wait a little while longer, don't you? Let's join Nicholas for a hot meal in the adjoining area and enjoy a conversation about unimportant matters for a change, if only to clear my mind."

"A great idea," Tradell replied. "Besides, I don't think I can face those Islanders on an empty stomach."

"Me either," he agreed, sniffing the air and smiling. "I smell venison stew, though it is not the feast you deserve, Nicholas, after all you've done for our three nations."

"It'll seem like a feast to me," he said, "of which I'll be honored to partake."

"The honor is all ours," Malek said, extending a hand and shaking his with gratitude. "Yours was a deed well done, my friend. A deed well done."

CHAPTER 89

The Waiting Game

Nicholas awoke several hours before dawn to the smell of burning wood. He was lying on a straw-filled mattress in the cabin and noted the reflection of yellow and orange light upon a stack of split wood against the wall. The pungent scent reminded him of the Dunn Hills. He slowly sat up. The fireplace opening facing his section flickered with a low, steady flame. A wide bed of glowing embers beneath the crackling logs appeared as an ever-changing swirl of red, orange and black speckles, as if a thousand shifting eyes were silently watching him with curiosity and suspicion.

"Did I wake you?" a voice whispered in the gloom. Nicholas recognized Sala's figure stooping over the fireplace and noted the cheerful edge to his voice despite the early hour. "I was putting more wood on the fire. I'm a light sleeper."

"You didn't wake me," Nicholas softly replied, wrapping his blankets around him as a current of cold air drifted past.

"I'd stepped outside. It's really coming down out there."

Nicholas scrunched up his face as remnants of sleep enticingly tugged at him. "What is?"

Sala chuckled. "Snow, of course. Lots of it." He added a few more sticks to the fire and fully revived it. "Good thing we rescued you when we did. I can only imagine how bad the weather is along the river right now."

"Please imagine it quietly," another voice gruffly mumbled in the darkness. "We're trying to sleep, Sala."

"Sorry," he whispered, turning to Nicholas. "I'm going to get some leftover stew. Want some?"

Nicholas grinned in the darkness. "No thanks. I'm going back to bed," he said, falling onto his mattress and burrowing into the blankets as Sala trudged away.

As Nicholas slowly drifted off, he imagined the snow piling up higher outside until the cabin was buried beneath a towering white mountain set among trees of green. Despite the occasional gust of wind whistling through cracks in the cabin walls and the gentle creaking of the towering pines, a part of him still regretted not going after Ivy. He wondered where she and her Island captors might be, whether still on their way to Del Norác, perhaps lost, or maybe even now in the presence of Vellan himself.

When he finally dozed off, he dreamed of a tall, snowcapped mountain looming ominously before him. He walked slowly in its shadow, desperately trying to reach the towering mass yet unable to make any progress despite his many steps. And though he had never been in this part of Laparia before nor had looked upon an image of that particular peak, in his dream Nicholas knew that he was gazing up at Mount Minakaris, where at the southern base near the waters of the Drusala River, Vellan had built his stronghold.

The snow was nearly boot-high early the following morning. It had stopped falling and was feathery in texture, so making walking paths through it proved easy. The pine boughs overhead had captured a good share of the snow, its crisp, white highlights running along the dark branches and dispelling the gloom left over from autumn's last days. But Malek was happy to see the frosty white blanket upon the ground for another reason.

"Now we'll have an easier time maneuvering the flat sleds," he told Nicholas outdoors while inhaling the fresh air as the camp was waking up. "After breakfast, ten of us will hike to the raft with five sleds. We'll need two men on each sled to bring them back loaded up. I'll send another ten for the second trip after we return."

"Sign me up for the first crew," Nicholas said, eager to move after spending so much idle time on the river. "My muscles need a challenge. They're screaming out to be put to good use."

"Oh, they'll be screaming all right after you complete your first run," he replied with a chuckle. "Screaming in pain."

Nicholas shrugged with indifference. "They were screaming in pain when I climbed Gray Hawk Mountain. This should be a breeze compared to that."

"We'll see," he replied, happy to see that Nicholas' demeanor had lightened since last night. Though Ivy would most certainly be on his mind more often than not, Malek knew that the young man would only drown in discouragement if he didn't focus on other aspects of life during his and Ivy's long separation over winter.

Nicholas seemed none the worse for wear when he returned to camp from the raft with the first group shortly after noontime. Two individuals, one pulling and one pushing, were assigned to each toboggan-like sled filled with a small portion of the crates and barrels of foodstuff and other items retrieved from the raft, including a few casks of ale and wine. Nicholas felt invigorated after the workout and looked forward to sampling some of the provisions for lunch after they unloaded the haul and piled it in the storehouse. Later though, while roaming the campgrounds with Sala, he privately admitted that he was feeling a few distinctly different aches and pains after the sled run as compared to his climb up Gray Hawk.

"A good night's sleep should work them out of my system," he said matter-of-factly over the crackling wood of a nearby bonfire. "Tapping one of those casks of ale might help, too."

"Malek, I'm sure, will parcel out that treat judiciously," Sala replied. "Just be ready for tomorrow's run. After a few more trips, we should have the raft half unloaded. Some of us will take the rest up Kaddis Creek to unload at another camp."

Soon they passed two men splitting wood in a small clearing. The sharp crack of maple and pine logs being ripped apart echoed in the brisk air. As Sala continued with Nicholas' tour, voices of other men joking and laughing around a roaring fire caught their attention. As Sala went over to talk to them, for a wistful moment Nicholas was reminded of the many occasions he enjoyed frequenting the Water Barrel Inn. Whether throwing dice while savoring a mug of ale or conversing with friends by the fire, he only remembered good times visiting the establishment, that is, until the first night of the

Harvest Festival. Everything had changed that day as accusations of robbery were flung about in front of his friends and neighbors.

Nicholas missed his old life, uncertain if he could ever get it back. Despite all he had done to fight against the Vellans, Caldurians and Loks of the world, he wasn't sure if those deeds would absolve him of fleeing Kanesbury after Constable Brindle had taken him into custody. For all the weeks and miles he had traveled, he wondered if anything in his personal life had really changed.

"They want to talk to you," Sala said, having spoken to the men. He gently tapped Nicholas on the shoulder. "Did you hear me?"

"*Hmmm?*" Nicholas looked up, his thoughts scattering.

"Ivy on your mind?" he asked. "You were standing there still as a tree. I didn't know if you were sleeping or taking root."

Nicholas grinned. "There are other things I think about, but I won't bore you with the details."

"Good, we don't have time," Sala replied, leading Nicholas to the others gathered around the fire. "These fine gentlemen want to hear all about your story."

"My story?"

"We heard you had quite an adventure of late," someone in the group remarked.

Nicholas looked at the five men of varying ages huddled in the glow of the firelight, all unshaven and with a veneer of fatigue from their months in the wild. Yet all had a gleam of hope in their eyes and were genuinely pleased to meet Nicholas. One older man with long locks of gray hair peeking out beneath his tattered hood was stirring a large kettle suspended over the fire on a tripod of sturdy branches, its bubbling contents steaming in the cold air.

"Seems Sala and I are just in time for lunch," Nicholas said, eliciting a round of laughter.

"Not quite," the older man replied, signaling him to look at the boiling concoction.

Nicholas obliged, leaning in to better observe the brownish liquid, not quite sure what kind of stew the man was preparing. But when he placed his nose above the kettle and inhaled, he grimaced and lurched backward to the amusement of the others.

"What in Laparia is that?" he cried, cringing at the odor.

"That's Fedwin's famous brew," Sala told him. "But it's not for drinking."

"Unless you want to double over and writhe in pain, or so I'd imagine," Fedwin replied as he continued stirring the kettle with a large wooden paddle. "We use it to coat the bottoms of the sleds to make them move easily over the snow. A formula I perfected after many failed attempts."

"Fedwin was an apothecary in the village of Ipa in the north region of Surna," one of the men explained. "He has a wizard's touch with roots, herbs and the like."

"But I'm not a wizard," Fedwin replied. "What I've got here is some bark from several biliac trees, a handful of gingish root and a few other secret ingredients. After it cools and I strain it, the others will brush it onto the bottom of the sleds and let it dry. They'll glide over snow as if you were moving across ice."

"My sled could have used another coat," Nicholas joked as he rubbed his sore shoulder, already feeling part of the group.

"All of them will get a new coat overnight," Fedwin assured him. "But enough about sled maintenance. We want to hear some exciting stories from our guest."

"Tell us about your journey through the Dunn Hills," said the youngest in the group who appeared a few years older than Nicholas. "We heard rumors that you were searching for a real wizard. No offense, Fedwin."

"And there was also talk of a magic medallion, and a key to something or other," remarked a second man who sat comfortably upon a tree stump. He stood and insisted that Nicholas have his seat. "We're eager to learn how you defeated the Enâri."

Nicholas glanced wide-eyed at Sala. "Word gets around."

"It's difficult to keep a secret among a bunch with too much time on their hands," he joked. "But go on, Nicholas. Have a seat and start talking. We're starved for entertainment."

"Very well," he said, uncomfortable with all the attention yet pleased to be accepted so quickly. After a round of introductions by Sala, Nicholas described his flight from Kanesbury and setting out on an adventure he had never expected. "One moment I'm hiding in Amanda Stewart's ice cellar fast asleep, only to be awakened and discover that I'm wanted for murder. But that turned out to be the least of my problems," he told his captive audience as the forked flames licked the cold air like snake tongues.

As he watched the mesmerized faces in the fire's glow, a sense of joy welled inside him that he had not experienced since dancing with Ivy. For a moment he felt as if he were back home on a brisk autumn night among friends, whiling away the hours with food, drink and stories without a care in the world. Nicholas savored each moment as the words poured out of him and the fire danced wildly, blissfully unaware of the passing time and the uncertainties of life that only moments ago had haunted him.

Over the next two days, Nicholas and the others repeated their trek to the raft and hauled more goods to camp, following the snowy paths through the maze of leafless trees and towering fragrant pines. When the vessel had been half emptied, Malek appointed Sala and four others to guide the raft several more miles up Kaddis Creek the following day. There the remaining goods would be retrieved by a second camp. Nicholas volunteered for the mission at once, so Malek relented and added him to the crew.

Early the next morning as a light snow fell, Nicholas readied his gear for the journey. He was anxious to get out, fearing the onset of boredom if he remained at camp. But just as he and the others were about to leave, an individual wandered into camp from the north. He trudged wearily through the trees and snow, his tall, large frame bundled in a weather-stained coat. A hood was pulled down over his forehead and a wool scarf wrapped tightly around his neck and face. As Nicholas looked upon the stranger with suspicion, Malek hollered out in joy.

"Maximilian! I'd recognize you behind that ratty scarf even in the dead of night," he said as the man approached.

"My dear Idelia knitted this ratty scarf," he replied, his voice deep and pleasantly gruff. Slowly he unwound the woolen article from around his face and removed the hood, revealing a short brown beard, a mop of curly hair and a mischievous smile. "But I won't tell her what you said the next time I get home."

Malek introduced the visitor to Nicholas. "Max has been gone for almost six weeks, serving as our eyes and ears abroad. He's one of our finest scouts."

"Pleased to meet you," Nicholas said, extending his hand to Max who held it in a vice-like grip for several seconds.

"Likewise," he replied, gazing curiously at him and the other five men who were preparing to leave. "What's going on?"

"We have good news," Sala told him.

Max appeared only mildly impressed. "As do I. But I'd wager mine's better than yours."

"You can tell me after I bid these men a safe journey," Malek said, suddenly signaling to Nicholas. "I've reconsidered and think you should remain here. I want you to hear what Max has to say. There are other things I need to discuss with you, too."

"Are you sure?" Nicholas asked, disappointed that Malek had altered his plan seemingly on a whim.

"You'll be glad you stayed behind. I'll send someone else in your place."

Nicholas relented, offering a perfunctory nod. "If you think it's best."

Malek returned a knowing smile and motioned to Tradell who stood nearby. "How about sending one of the two prisoners as a replacement for Nicholas? Maybe it would be good to separate them for a while and have one do some work other than piling firewood or hauling water from the stream."

"My thought exactly," he said. "But not that vile character, Dunnic. He's been corrupted by the Northern Isles beyond any point of reason. I don't think there's a chance he'll ever see things our way. But Brezzan, the other one, might cooperate. His heart doesn't seem to be in the fight anymore. A few days among some decent company and he might not *want* to leave us."

"We'll turn him into a proper citizen yet," Malek replied. "Let him go on the raft if he chooses, under strict supervision, of course."

After Tradell left to recruit the prisoner, Malek said goodbye to Sala and the others. He then escorted Nicholas and Max to the cabin. A meal was prepared for Max, and soon the three were sitting down in the eating area when Tradell entered the cabin.

"The six are on their way to the raft," he said, pouring himself a mug of hot tea from a kettle hanging over the fire and joining the others. "Brezzan was more than happy to go along for the ride. He admitted that Dunnic was getting on his nerves, endlessly prattling on about loyalty to Vellan and the like."

Nicholas chuckled as he sipped from his mug. "Apparently Dunnic is just another version of Brin–and I thought Brin was one of a kind."

Max wore a tattered vest over several thin shirts and smelled of wood smoke. "Who's this Brin fellow?" he asked. He dipped a piece of bread in venison stew and shoveled it into his mouth. A shower of crumbs fell over his beard and into the bowl. "And prisoners?" he added in a darkly comedic tone. "Are we running our own Deshla here?"

Nicholas furrowed his brow, glancing across the table at Malek and Tradell. "Deshla? What's that?"

"Vellan's infamous prison in Del Norác," Max casually replied. He raised a spoonful of stew to his lips. "He had it built at the base of Mount Minakaris not far from his stronghold."

"We'll talk about that shortly," Malek said, casting a sharp glance Max's way. "It's one reason I invited you to this meeting, Nicholas. But first let's hear what Max found out on the road."

"All right," he replied, his curiosity rising. "So I gather the boy here doesn't know about our plan to–"

"He knows very little," Tradell coolly jumped in, catching Max's eye and silently warning him to stick to the matter at hand. "What did you learn up north?"

"Oh, sorry," he said as he downed another spoonful of stew, realizing that there were still some secrets at the table. Max reached for a loaf of bread and tore off another piece. "I had some interesting news during my travels," he continued. "I ran across troops from Arrondale along King's Road on their way back to Morrenwood. They had just returned from fighting in Montavia."

Nicholas' eyes lit up. "Was Prince Gregory there?"

Max leaned back, both surprised and intrigued that Nicholas knew something of the events so far north. "So you're familiar with the state of affairs in Montavia, Nicholas, and act as if you know the King's son. Do you have Prince Gregory's ear?"

"I was privy to some of the plans King Justin and his son had made to oppose Caldurian in Montavia."

Max raised his eyes. "I'm impressed. Still, I hope you don't know what information I'm about to reveal or else my time scouting will have been in vain."

"I assure you that I don't, Max. I'm as anxious as the others are to hear what you have to say."

"Good!" he replied with an enthusiastic slap of his hand upon the table which rattled the bread plate and bowl. "I like an attentive audience, but I won't keep you guessing any longer. Word from up and down the military lines was that the occupation of Montavia is over. Caldurian and the Islanders were handed a swift defeat after the arrival of Prince Gregory's troops."

"Wonderful news!" Tradell chimed in. "I only hope that that wizard was one of the casualties of war. I've heard many unsavory rumors about that foul apprentice to Vellan."

"Sorry to say, but he isn't dead, though more about him later. Anyway, Caldurian's downfall isn't the best part of my story," he continued while sopping up the last drops of stew in his bowl.

"Oh? Then what is?" Malek asked.

Max glanced up. "Those Enâri troops that the wizard used as his personal army? All destroyed, to the very last one."

"All killed? Or was it something else?" Malek inquired, appearing more inquisitive than surprised.

"Killed, yes. But from what I was told, they were obliterated in mere moments," he explained. "All of them–and all at once. They just disintegrated into the sand and soil they were made from. A most peculiar sight according to the soldiers I spoke with."

"I can imagine," he replied, glancing at Nicholas. "So Frist's lethal spirit sought out the Enâri wherever they were gathered, and not just in Kargoth. A potent strain of magic in that particular spell."

"The spirit had twenty years to incubate," Nicholas replied. "Who could say what strength it possessed when finally released? Frist wasn't even sure."

"I wish I had been there when the key was turned," Malek said, picturing the momentous and turbulent moment in his mind.

Max cleared his throat with mild irritation as Nicholas and Malek, engaged in a private conversation, had seemingly forgotten he was sitting there. The two men turned simultaneously to Max with apologetic smiles.

"Sorry, Max. As you might guess, there are a few important matters you need to know," Malek said.

"So it seems," he said, pushing his bowl aside. "Tell me, who's this Frist you speak of? And what of this talk of lethal spirits? I'm guessing that my news of the Enâri defeat isn't the wild revelation that I thought it would be."

"Not totally." Malek asked Nicholas to briefly tell his story to bring Max up to date. He did so as Max listened with fascination, absorbing every captivating detail.

"I'd like to hear more about your journey from Kanesbury to here when we can spare the time, Nicholas. You've apparently seen more adventure in your several weeks abroad than I have over the last year," Max replied with a hint of feigned envy.

"Some of that adventure I wish had never happened," he said with thoughts of Ivy on his mind. But not wanting to sidetrack the meeting with his problems, he pressed Max with a question. "Did you speak with Prince Gregory? I'm eager to hear of his march to war."

"Yes, but only for a short time. The prince was nearly a mile away at the head of the line when I finally approached him for an audience. But by the looks of me after so much time in the wild, I didn't think he'd grant me one," he added with a cheery laugh. "But I jest. I've met the prince several times before on my travels and have developed a bond of trust with him. He's aware of our efforts here in the Northern Mountains against Vellan's forces and was kind enough to indulge my inquiries. I even caught a glimpse of Caldurian who was being taken to Morrenwood as a prisoner."

Tradell gasped. "Caldurian?"

Max nodded. "According to the wizard Tolapari who had accompanied the prince to war, Caldurian was rendered powerless, at least temporarily so, yet was still under heavy guard near the front line. I didn't get all the particulars as to why, and unfortunately, I wasn't allowed to talk to the wizard or even get near him."

"Still, you must have learned much," Nicholas said. "When were the Enâri destroyed? And did Prince Gregory mention anything of Leo's return to Morrenwood?"

"*No* is the answer to your second question," he said. He reached into an inside vest pocket and removed a thin, narrow rectangular piece of maple wood. It was the length of his hand and

74

four fingers wide, having been striped of its bark and smoothed with a sharpening stone. There were several tiny notches and other marks that had been pressed into the wood with a knife, some impressions larger than others and in varying directions. "Though Prince Gregory and his army had waited as long as he could for Leo's return, they finally departed Morrenwood on, let me see here–" Max quickly consulted the markings on the piece of maple, counting some of the notches with his finger. "–on the twenty-fourth day of Old Autumn. The Enâri creatures were destroyed shortly after the prince attacked Caldurian's forces at dawn six days later–*hmmm*, the second day of New Winter according to my notches. So Leo obviously returned to Morrenwood shortly after the prince and his army had departed."

"Luckily for all of us," Tradell remarked before telling Max how the Enâri army had also met its demise in and around Kargoth. "It will help us greatly not having to deal with that mindless horde."

"One of them wasn't so mindless," Nicholas said, reminding him of Jagga's attempt to save himself by stealing the key and having it melted down. "His bit of thievery may hasten an end to this war."

"But you told us he killed someone to get the key," Tradell said. "Still, I see your point. Vellan's numbers have diminished and cannot be supplemented any time soon now that winter has set in. We must launch our campaign at the first sign of spring before more Islanders start poling up the Lorren River again."

"Do you intend to attack Vellan's stronghold in Del Norác?" Nicholas asked.

"Close," Malek said over the rising steam from his mug. "We'll attack his prisons."

"Oh," Nicholas said. "You mean Deshla."

Nicholas was told about the large prison that the Enâri had constructed in the base of Mount Minakaris. Deshla was situated about a mile west around the mountain from Vellan's stronghold. Malek estimated from stories floating about the region that at least a thousand men from Surna, Linden and Harlow, or perhaps even more, had been locked up in Deshla over the past few years as Vellan grew more bold in his reach. And while men from the Northern Isles ran the prison itself, a large contingent of Enâri troops had been stationed less than a quarter mile away in a garrison alongside the Drusala River.

"That hive of Enâri creatures always gave us pause to launch a raid," Malek admitted, "though I and the leaders from other camps continued planning for a strike. This coming spring was our target date. And now that the nearby garrison is empty, or at worst, lightly occupied by Island soldiers, its threat has been greatly diminished."

"An opportune moment," Nicholas said.

"Exactly, and one which I intend to take." Malek stood and walked to the fireplace, grabbing a few pieces of wood to stoke the fading flames. "Though Vellan may reinforce the number of guards at the prison now that his Enâri protectors are gone, he might also do the opposite." He noted the confusion on Nicholas' face. "Vellan has other places throughout Kargoth he probably needs secured–key villages, food stores, armories and the like–but now that his creatures have been eliminated, many of those places stand unprotected. He'll have to spread out his remaining forces to keep them out of rebel hands. So if ever there was a time to storm Deshla…"

"I see your point," Nicholas said, anticipating a journey to Del Norác to find Ivy. And though he guessed that she would be taken directly to Vellan, assuming that Cale and the others could actually find him, he suddenly latched onto the horrible notion that Ivy might be languishing inside a prison cell in Deshla. His heart raced at the dark thought as the others talked among themselves. "Couldn't you plan this raid during winter?" he asked as Malek returned to the table and sat down opposite Nicholas, locking gazes with him.

"I know what you're thinking," he said sympathetically, "but Ivy could be anywhere in Kargoth. There are other prisons besides Deshla, including those in Vellan's bastion at the foot of Mount Minakaris. I can't risk sending my men on a grueling and likely futile march through treacherous mountain paths in winter on a slim hope, Nicholas." Malek's tone was firm yet gentle. He knew that the man across the table would never stop thinking of a way to rescue the woman he loved, nor did he expect him to.

"I know," Nicholas replied in a voice barely above a whisper, lowering his eyes and staring at the tabletop. "Still, I had to ask."

"But it's not just Malek's decision that's stopping you from getting your way," Tradell added. "The raid on Deshla will be a combined operation composed of men from dozens of camps in the region north of Del Norác. But before we launch, the camps must combine. In the coming weeks we'll make our way southward along with other camps and integrate our troops and resources. The spoils from Brin's raft will go a long way in that goal."

"So you'll have plenty to do, Nicholas, to keep both mind and body occupied while waiting for your chance to hunt down Ivy's captors," Malek said. "Come springtime, you'll have the resources of an army at your side."

"I guess I can't ask for anything more," he said, forcing a grateful smile despite his heavy heart. "How far south will we move this winter?"

"We have a designated meeting area in the north end of the Champeko Forest just past Mount Lundy. That's more than half the distance to Mount Minakaris from here. All of our forces to the north will make for that spot over winter," Malek said. "Once there, we'll begin our final trek to Deshla when the weather turns warmer. Expect three long marches–and lots of sled pulling–throughout the rest of winter to get to Champeko. Needless to say, you will not be bored."

Nicholas chuckled. "I had no worries about that. But if I do get bored, I can always talk to Max," he added, glancing at his new acquaintance. "You said you wanted to hear more about my journey from home, and I have no shortage of stories to tell."

"And I'll take you up on your offer," Max replied, "but that'll have to wait until I return from my next journey."

"*Next* journey?" Malek inquired. "Where are you off to now?"

"Well, with all this interesting talk about Deshla prison and the Enâri creatures–or what's left of them–I never got to finish my story," he said, noisily sliding his chair back so he could fold his arms and stretch his legs. "I have to do a bit of scouting up near Thendara Wood, or perhaps more accurately, a bit of waiting. I won't be gone too long, but I'm not yet leaving for a few days."

"Who are you waiting for?" Tradell asked.

"I'm waiting for information from Morrenwood," he replied. "After I spoke with Prince Gregory, he took me aside for a private conversation. Apparently there's going to be another war council in the Blue Citadel." The others were surprised yet appeared pleased with the announcement, anticipating a future attack on Del Norác by the King's forces. "While the prince was in Montavia, he received a correspondence from his father containing details about the council. King Justin plans to host this meeting on, now wait a moment..." Max again consulted his notched board to the amused delight of the others. "On the twenty-sixth day of New Winter."

"That's six days from today," Malek said. "Had I known earlier, I might have gone myself. Despite the greater distance, the journey from here to Morrenwood in wintertime is far easier than the treacherous maze to Kargoth through the unforgiving mountains."

"Yet a dreary journey as Nicholas can attest to. Nothing for miles around in places," Max said. "But you needn't fret over not attending the second council. From what Prince Gregory told me, it will be a simpler affair and sparsely attended. It seems that everyone invited already agrees that Vellan must be confronted once and for all, and after the victories in Rhiál and Montavia, the will to act is there. This meeting will emphasize planning rather than debating."

Malek grinned. "I had heard details of that last boisterous affair, but the handful of dissenters eventually came to their senses."

"My friends and I arrived at the Citadel just after the first council had concluded," Nicholas said, recalling the hubbub in the corridors. "From what I saw and heard, I'm certain that King Justin would have led an assault on both Drogin and Caldurian without any allies if it had come to that. He knew he had no choice as Vellan undoubtedly eyed Arrondale as his top prize–and still does."

"I look forward to bringing the fight to his doorstep," Max said, "starting with our raid on Deshla. But we should coordinate our plans with King Justin. Prince Gregory promised to send an informant to meet me on the western edge of Thendara Wood as soon as this war council is concluded. He expects it to be a short affair."

"When will you get back?" Malek inquired. "No doubt we'll already have moved south by then to our next location."

"I'll find you," he said without concern. "I'm familiar with the paths you plan to follow. Give me a few days to rest and resupply, then I shall leave. Expect me back by–wait, I can do this one in my head." Max craned his neck back, the gears in his mind turning. "I'll probably return in one and a half weeks time, more or less, if I leave here three days from today. That should give me a nice respite as even I need a holiday off the road from time to time." He shot a mirthful glance at Nicholas. "But only a short holiday, mind you. I get easily bored sitting around plotting and planning. I leave those duties to Malek and Tradell who have a bit more patience than I do."

"Would you like company on the road?" Nicholas asked. The urge to travel again stirred within him after having endured days of tedium while on Brin's raft and foregoing the trip up Kaddis Creek with Sala and the others.

"Your offer's much appreciated," Max said, "but I like to work alone, thank you. No offense intended."

"None taken," he replied.

"Anyway, you've had plenty of adventure lately. A little staying in place for a while might be a good thing," he advised. "And to be truthful, I've found that I do my job much better and faster when I do it my way. More times than not, offers to help lessen my workload–no matter how well-intentioned–just end up making more work for me, if you understand."

"I do," Nicholas said, thinking how much Max's personality reminded him of Hobin. Both men were set in their ways in the best sense and nobody would ever change that. He then thought of Emma, Hobin's one true love from the past. Maybe there *was* somebody who could shake him from his fixed ways, he quickly reconsidered, though that was yet to be seen.

"Besides, I won't be alone. I'll have Graylocks for company," Max continued, describing a horse that Prince Gregory had given him after their last meeting. "I left him with one of the sentries to drink at the stream." He looked askance at Malek. "You didn't find a barrel of carrots on that raft, did you? Or apples perhaps? Oh, Graylocks would surely be in your debt if you did."

CHAPTER 90

A Vast and Mighty Herd

On a gray, bitter morning three days later, Max quietly left camp. He headed northeast to Thendara Wood while most of the men were still asleep. Nicholas had hoped to talk with him at breakfast, but Malek said that leaving unannounced was simply Max's way.

"I stopped expecting a proper farewell from Maximilian years ago after he left on a month-long campaign several summers back," he said. "But when you least expect it, he'll reappear through the trees or along a riverbank with a treasure trove of information–and usually a compelling story or two. He's very good at what he does, so I leave him alone and let him do it. Our cause is in his debt."

Max's departure was forgotten in the commotion the next day. A dozen men with empty sleds arrived from another camp two day's march to the south, having received word from one of Malek's scouts of the haul of goods from the raft. The new arrivals were happy to see the additional provisions as their own supplies were dwindling and not likely to be replenished much, if at all, during the winter months.

"We'll load you up and you can depart tomorrow," Malek said. "But you'll have company. Our camp is ready to move on its first leg south to the Champeko Forest."

"As are we," said one of the men. "When we arrive at our camp, we'll rest a day before heading to the first gathering place near Petaras Peak. No doubt, others are already congregating there."

"How far is that?" Nicholas asked, eager to leave.

"Several days of marching," Malek informed him. "Possibly longer depending on the depth of snow and the weather, but nowhere near as far as Max had to travel."

"Still, he had a horse," Nicholas quipped as they made for the cabin to provide the men a hot meal after their journey.

All that day they loaded up the sleds with provisions from the raft and items from camp that would be needed. The tents would be disassembled the next morning and packed away last of all. Malek hoped for an early start, though a trace of melancholy gripped him as he stood near a towering pine and looked upon the snow-covered cabin. Smoke spiraled from its chimney as a hint of purple twilight splashed through the trees and blanketed the frozen ground.

"We'll never look upon this place again," he said to Nicholas. "Come springtime, we will either defeat Vellan and return home to our respective countries or die in the attempt. This place, which has been a second home, will only know the slow decay of time."

"Perhaps some lost travelers will find it one day," Nicholas suggested, noting the sadness in Malek's eyes.

"Anything is possible," he said, shaking off his glum thoughts. "Still, once I get home and see my wife and daughters again, this camp will be the last thing on my mind."

"I hope that day comes soon," Nicholas replied. "For us all."

After they loaded the sleds and secured the goods with tarps and ropes, everyone gathered around the cabin for a final celebration. Amid laughter, storytelling and the aroma of roasted venison, a deep and contemplative darkness gradually encroached. Warm, yellow light poured from the cabin windows and the open doorway, serving as a gentle beacon beneath the cloudy, moonless night. Nicholas sat on a low pile of wood near the front of the building, conversing with one of the visiting campers. As he stood to get a second helping of ale, he heard a familiar voice through the trees.

"What's the occasion?" Sala called out as he and four others approached the cabin. "And why weren't we invited?"

"Look who's back!" Nicholas said, greeting his friend with a handshake.

"We planned to save you some cold leftovers," Tradell joked as he emerged through the crowd. He noted that only five of the six men had returned from Kaddis Creek. With a furrowed brow, he took Sala, Nicholas and the others aside, inquiring as to the whereabouts of Brezzan, their prisoner.

"Not to worry," Sala replied. "He proved to be a fine worker and asked to join the other camp. They were happy to have him."

"Why?" Tradell asked.

"He wants to start a new life away from the Islands–a free life–just like Nicholas' friend, Arteen. Brezzan thought it best to disassociate himself with Dunnic in order to do that," he explained. "I couldn't have agreed more."

"Nor could I," Nicholas said, having heard and witnessed much about life on the Northern Isles that stifled a man's spirit and freedom. "Brezzan will be better off living anywhere else in Laparia compared to that place."

"And we'll have one less prisoner to worry about," Malek said as he walked up and joined the group, having overheard the last few remarks. "I think he made the right choice, too. Now I suppose, Sala, that you and your men are hungry."

"Famished."

"Then just one more piece of business before you eat. You can fill me in on the other details later," he said. "Shall I assume that our neighboring camp has the remainder of the goods and that the raft has been put out of commission?"

"Yes to both. We cut the ropes binding the raft and let the pieces flow back down Kaddis Creek," Sala said with a frown. "Too bad though. It was a nice craft."

"But it's much safer for us to travel unexposed, even in the dead of winter," Tradell said. "No sense in taking a chance, however slim, that the raft would fall back into the hands of some Islanders. It has served its purpose."

"True," Sala remarked, before breaking out in a grin. "Now more importantly, what's for dinner? Not to boast, but we have far better cooks here than they do upstream. And frankly, I am due a good meal." He raised his head, sniffing the aroma dancing upon the winter air and frowned. "Venison? *Again?*"

They departed the next day after sunrise. Through breaks in the clouds, intermittent stabs of sunshine shot through snow-covered tree branches like swords of golden light. Sala took it as a sign of good fortune and smiled at the brilliant display so rare this time of year. But his smile faded when he looked back at the cabin, now dark and still, its windows shuttered and the chimney uncharacteristically cold and smokeless.

"First the raft and now the cabin," he muttered while stepping into the loop of rope attached to his sled and lying on the snow like a sleeping snake. Affixed to the center portion of the rope was a bundle of padding which he lifted to his chest, preparing to trudge forward. "Things are changing fast, Nicholas."

"Don't fret. In about two days you'll have a new place to call home." He stood in back of Sala's sled, ready to push from behind. "At least until we leave there and head for Petaras Peak. But you'll be okay. We all will."

"I hope so." But before Sala could put his next thought into words, Malek's voice crackled in the cold, bright morning.

"Onward, men!" he shouted with steady confidence. "And watch your footing. I want you all to arrive in one piece."

"So do I," Sala lightly remarked as he pulled the rope taut.

In unison, nearly thirty flat sleds scattered across the snowy terrain set forth like a herd of lumbering bison, moving south through the trees until they funneled into a handful of well established paths. Sharply defined sun rays cut through the clouds in the southeast and down through the treetops, causing the men to squint or shade their eyes when they passed into the light. As Malek marched forward, he noticed that Dunnic was pulling a sled farther ahead in the adjacent line to his right with another man helping to push from behind. Rollin, the archer who had helped capture Brin's raft, walked alongside the sled to keep a constant eye on the Island prisoner.

"At least we're getting more work out of Dunnic today than simply having him pile firewood," Malek commented to Tradell who was pushing his sled in back.

"Seeing that he hasn't paid even a measly copper half piece for his room and board, it's the least he can do," he said with a smirk.

Malek glanced back as he marched through the snow, able to see Tradell bundled in his hooded coat from his shoulders up. "I had my doubts when Rollin told me that Dunnic volunteered to pull a sled rather than walk with his wrists bound." He adjusted the padded rope across the front of his chest, breathing steadily. "Still, I'll keep a close eye on him."

"As you should," Tradell said. "Now less talking so you can conserve energy. I'll take the reins after our first stop."

Malek chuckled. "I'm ten years younger than you, Tradell. You should be the one worrying about running out of fire. But I'll shut my mouth for a while as I know how you like to think."

"It's a challenge to plan for the uncertain days ahead with a full camp to supervise at the same time. My duties will multiply as the various units in this region converge and grow into a little army."

"All of us will have more work," Malek said, "but I have total confidence in my men, including you. I wouldn't have chosen you to help me administer this camp otherwise."

"Thank you, sir," he replied. "I appreciate your trust."

"Same here," Malek said, trudging steadily through the snow. "But as I've asked you before," he said, glancing back, "please don't address me as *sir*. You're not part of the Linden military anymore."

Tradell shrugged. "Hard to break old habits." As they moved silently ahead, he wondered what was left of his nation's once modest, yet proud army from which he had fled after Vellan's proxies in Linden had infiltrated and corrupted the institution. He sighed and put it out of his mind, concentrating on the myriad tasks before him.

The sleds arrived at camp late the following day. There the residents were loading their possessions onto additional sleds to join in the trek to Petaras Peak in two more days. The weary travelers spent the remainder of that day and all the next resting from their grueling journey as more clouds moved in and the dreariness of winter returned. The camp, in a deep wooded area two miles east of the Gray River, wasn't much different from Malek's camp except that it had two central cabins among the field of tents necessitated by its larger population.

But the following day in the gloomy hours after dawn, those permanent structures were also abandoned, left cold and lifeless as the growing herd of sleds, now numbering near fifty, departed southward. Because there were more men than needed to drive all the sleds, about two dozen individuals were free to walk along with the moving mass, trading places with the sled runners after each shift to afford everyone a proper and much appreciated period of rest.

The next morning, on the first day of Mid Winter, Nicholas found himself paired with Malek as they maneuvered across a long, narrow clearing. As Nicholas pulled the sled, he was happy to see the open sky in the west in contrast to the wall of trees stooping over on his left like a line of spying giants. Off to his right loomed a distant mountain surrounded by a scattering of trees, its peak shrouded by a thick canopy of iron gray clouds.

"By tomorrow, the eastern trees should start thinning out for several miles," Malek said. "We should be able to see Petaras Peak far in the south if it's not too cloudy."

"We're that close?" Nicholas inquired with surprise.

"Not quite," he said as he pushed the vehicle forward, each determined footstep crunching down upon the smooth layer of snow left behind by the passing sled. "We're still six or seven days away, I'd guess, depending on the weather." The steady, almost hypnotic sound of sleds gliding across the wintry landscape cast a languorous calm over the brown, green and gray-hued lines of travelers slicing through the white blanket of snow. "Fedwin's latest batch of goo seems to be working wonders. The sleds have never moved so well."

"Good thing he joined your group," Nicholas said as he took a few deep breaths and readjusted the padded rope. "How long has he been here?"

"Over a year," he replied. "He had been with another camp but likes to move around to study the flora in different regions of the mountains. He got that opportunity with us. It's the apothecary in him, I guess. Fedwin has helped several men through many illnesses with his various brews–and he makes the sleds run efficiently, too."

"How long have you been fighting in the wild?" Nicholas asked, delighted to engage in conversation to help pass the time.

"Just over two years, which are two too many as far as my wife and daughters are concerned," he replied with a heavy heart. "I've managed to get home on a few occasions to see them, but not often enough."

"That's a hardship on all of you," Nicholas said, his thoughts turning to Ivy, Maynard and so many others he cared about and had left behind. Yet unlike his own, he reasoned that vastly different emotions must be tugging at Malek since he had left home voluntarily and for a worthy cause instead of fleeing in the dark of night to save himself. Nicholas suddenly wished he had kept his questions private.

"You and I are a lot alike," Malek remarked.

Nicholas was caught off guard. "How so?" he asked, curious to hear the answer as he was genuinely surprised by the comparison.

"We both left our homes and loved ones for a greater cause. Granted, we departed under different circumstances, but both of us made sacrifices for something we believe in."

"But my mission for King Justin came about by chance. I didn't leave my village with the intention of hiking through the Dunn Hills to search for a wizard."

"And protecting a princess," he added. "Don't forget that."

"I suppose. But even for all we've accomplished, you left on your own accord with the specific purpose to do what you're doing."

"Pushing a sled full of blankets, stale biscuits and dried beef through the snow?" he joked.

"You know what I mean."

"It doesn't matter," he insisted, momentarily locking gazes with Nicholas as he glanced back. "You also did what you did in the end when you could have walked away and played it safe. That took courage and selflessness, and that's what counts. All those other nagging details are irrelevant. In fact, I think you've accomplished more in the three or so months you've been on the road than I have over the last two years. The Enâri are no more thanks to you. Think of it. What greater achievement could you want?"

Nicholas again looked back briefly. "Finding Ivy."

Malek nodded understandingly. "Just don't sell your other accomplishments short. Supposedly far greater men than you would never have volunteered for what you and Leo did. Families across Laparia owe you their thanks."

As Nicholas let those words sink in, he allowed himself a moment to savor his victories and take pride in his deeds. Yet as Ivy's wellbeing still lingered in the back of his mind, he wouldn't let himself wallow in such a state for too long. He knew he had to keep things in perspective. Until she was safe, none of his other successes, no matter how significant, really mattered that much to him.

"Tell me about *your* triumphs, Malek," he said, happy to shift the focus back to his friend. "Surely after two years you and your men have much to be proud of."

Malek furrowed his brow, thinking deeply as the cold air pressed against his face and the sweet scent of pine lingered lightly in the air. A murder of crows squawked above the treetops to the east. "I'm proud that we stepped up to take the fight to Vellan, but to tell you the truth, our successes have been few and scattered. At times I've wondered if the sacrifice was worth the trouble and considered packing up and leaving Surna with my family altogether. Yet those moments were few, I'll admit."

"Still, you had to have done some good. Your numbers aren't insignificant."

He nodded. "We raided a few Island rafts from time to time when an opportunity presented itself as with Brin's, so I suppose that must have put a minor dent in Vellan's plans. And while teaming up with other camps, my men and I were involved in several skirmishes with both Enâri and Island soldiers, driving them away from a few farmsteads and villages here and there. But those actions were against small roving bands that we had the numbers to overwhelm. Most of the places where the Enâri have congregated in Kargoth and the surrounding nations, well–let's just say that their numbers are insurmountable. Correction–*were* insurmountable. We never had the forces to directly take on such overwhelming opposition. Vellan created a vast army over the years and he easily replaced any of his creatures that had been killed or died naturally, if the word *natural* was ever applicable to that strange species."

"Now you have a chance to really take it to Vellan," Nicholas said encouragingly. "The odds have moved closer to your favor."

"Thanks to you, though Vellan yet has the advantage. Still, we plan to hit him hard at Deshla once our camps in this region combine forces. That will be a victory worth savoring in light of all the awful tales I've heard about that place. After that–who knows?

We may just march up to Vellan's front door and give a little knock."

"It'll be something to tell your wife and children about," Nicholas said, stopping for a moment to drink from a water skin draped over his shoulder. "I'm parched."

Malek quenched his thirst from his own water skin as he watched the other sleds move across the landscape at varying speeds. He felt a mighty force gathering and hoped that they would make a real difference for once in the long and weary fight against the enemy.

"You honestly thought of leaving your homeland for good?" Nicholas asked as he placed the water skin back over his shoulder and picked up the rope, trudging forward.

"It had crossed my mind," Malek admitted, straining to push the sled during those first few steps until they were gliding steadily across the snow again. "I did, however, move my family from our village in southern Surna to a less populated area in the north where the Enâri rarely made an appearance. My wife, children and I made the trip with several close friends before I enlisted with the mountain resistance. They live a simpler life, but hopefully we'll all be able to move back home now that the Enâri have been annihilated. I don't think even Vellan can quickly replace their vast numbers. In the meantime, we have our best chance ever to finish the job and regain our homes."

"And I'm happy to help," Nicholas said. "I learned there was a heated discussion during the war council involving a representative for the citizens of Surna, Linden and Harlow. Apparently others had fled to the Ebrean Forest to start new lives because of the corruption that had befallen your governments. Do you know of them?"

"Only a little as many had left several years before our resistance was formed," Malek replied. "But they didn't leave simply to start new lives and forever turn their backs on their homelands. They planned to grow their numbers and train for an eventual confrontation with Vellan. Recent reports we received about Rhiál's victory over Drogin had mentioned the army from the Five Clearings. They had marched with King Cedric from Drumaya and were instrumental in bringing about Drogin's defeat. I'm proud of my self-exiled brothers," he said. "And if we're fortunate, they'll come back and aid us now that war is to be unleashed at winter's end."

"If only they were with us now," Nicholas said. "Imagine the look on Vellan's face were we all to stand outside his stronghold."

"That would be a sight, but everyone must contribute to this fight as they see fit. It will take the actions and resources of many people spread across distant lands before this mess is settled," he admitted. "And if that means some people hide and fight among the mountains while others nurture their strength inside a forest–or even if a very few trek through wild hills to find a wizard to remake a magic key–then so be it. We must accept help as it is freely given and do our best with what we've got," Malek said, his words unadorned with emotion. "That said, however, a stable of horses right now would be a welcome addition!" he added with a cheerful laugh.

The sun was imprisoned two days later behind thick clouds that dropped a steady snowfall between the mountain valleys. Soon the winds picked up and visibility along the trail had been all but eliminated. The men took refuge in a stretch of woods to the east and made a temporary home until the weather lifted. Tents were raised and fires built amid a whirlwind of snow. For the rest of that day and all of the next, the caravan was stopped dead in its tracks.

The southward journey resumed late on the fifth day of Mid Winter. The first miles were slow and laborious as the wind-whipped snow had created banks and drifts that needed to be maneuvered through and around before the sleds could travel again at a steady clip. The travelers formed a marching line three men wide and trudged through the snow, clearing a path for almost two miles until they reached a point where the snow was low enough to move easily through. After a brief rest, everyone turned around and hiked back to the encampment, further packing down the snow. Only then did the sleds finally leave their woodland hideaway and pass along the newly created path in single file. When the last sled made it through, deep twilight had settled upon the land. The camp once again stopped for the night along the banks of a partially frozen creek.

"And you wanted to go to Del Norác on your own," Sala remarked to Nicholas as they sat by a fire enjoying a meal of tea, biscuits and bacon. "We weren't exaggerating when we said that the mountain weather shows mercy to no one."

"Now I understand," he said as he dipped a biscuit into his tea before taking a bite. "But I still don't have to like it."

They continued on the next day, tired and glum, but made much progress despite the lingering snow flurries and a thin but persistent breeze. All were bundled up with hoods and scarves, wishing to be back at camp and feeling as if the coming spring was simply a delusion in their frozen minds. This monotonous routine continued for three more days. Early the following morning, five days after abandoning their shelter in the woods, the weather gradually cleared. The peaks of distant mountains were again visible, standing majestically against intermittent patches of blue sky and vibrant streaks of sunlight. Though the air still contained a biting chill, the men's spirits lifted considerably, especially upon seeing the tip of Petaras Peak to the southeast.

"We veered too far to the west," Malek informed Tradell as they paused to gauge their path ahead. "But not terribly so. We should reach the meeting grounds sometime before sunset. Everyone can then rest for a week or so before we begin the next leg of our trip. There'll be much planning to do in the meantime and consulting with the other leaders already encamped there."

"Finally something constructive for me to do," he remarked. "This endless sled pushing will be the death of me."

"They get lighter with each meal we consume," Malek said.

Tradell grunted. "Not if you're hauling crates of daggers and bundles of spare Island uniforms." They soon rejoined the caravan, cheered greatly by the relatively bright morning and the sight of Petaras Peak looming ever closer.

The morning hours passed swiftly. When noontime rolled around, a tattered fleet of clouds passed low overhead and cast flickering shadows upon the snow. After lunch, Nicholas was again teamed up with Malek, this time pushing the sled from behind.

"Seems lighter today. Did we luck out and get a haul of feather pillows and biscuits?" he joked.

"Maybe you're just getting used to all the exercise," Malek replied. "You could probably pull the sled yourself."

"Don't let him put any such idea in your head!" a voice humorously called out to Nicholas from behind. Soon Rollin was briskly walking alongside the sled and smiling.

"Who's watching the prisoner?" Malek asked.

"Sala has taken over for the time being," he replied, pointing to a group of sleds weaving among some scattered pine trees to his right. "Sala was bored, and as I was tired of looking at Dunnic, or more precisely, *listening* to Dunnic, I happily traded the rest of my shift with him. Dunnic does go on a bit about the defeat that awaits us if we attempt to confront Vellan. Tedious drivel. I'll be glad when we arrive and can store him away somewhere more secure."

"We should have left him on the raft without a pole and let the currents take him back to the Trillium Sea," Nicholas suggested.

"Too late for that," Malek said. "Still, an inspired solution."

"Is there anything I can get for you men before I continue my rounds?" Rollin playfully asked, his boots leaving a line of regularly spaced tracks parallel to the sled trail. "Hot tea perhaps? Or maybe a plate of roasted pheasant?"

"Definitely the pheasant," Nicholas said. "And a mug of ale each from whatever cask is available. We're not choosy today."

"I had to stay sharp whenever Sala was around any of the wine or ale as he was eager to try a sample if he could get away with it," Rollin replied with a laugh that seemed to warm the winter air. He then veered off to the right to speak with other sled teams. "Still, he somehow manages to pilfer from the biscuit sacks when nobody's looking!" he added with a wave as he and his words drifted off.

Nicholas shook his head and sighed. "With all this talk of food, I'm hungry all over again," he told Malek as they continued forward. "And we just ate lunch!"

The afternoon hours melted away as the ashen clouds thinned, allowing more light to slip through the snow-coated trees and play in spots upon the crystalline ground. After a short break, the herd of sleds again plowed toward the southeast like tired oxen as Petaras Peak grew steadily closer. Now, less than an hour before twilight, its snowcapped summit was bathed warmly in a pink and tangerine glow as the setting sun peeked through a large break in the clouds. Though near exhaustion, the men eagerly anticipated arriving at their temporary home with childlike excitement. The chance to sleep late the following morning meant more to them right now than sitting down to a sumptuous feast or drinking the most potent ale the Northern Mountains had to offer.

"It could have been worse, but we're only two days behind schedule," Malek said as he walked up to Nicholas from behind, enjoying a break from sled duty. "Otherwise we'd be sitting in front of a fire right now and sampling that Island brew. Still, about an hour from now we may be doing just that."

"Only after we unload the sleds, raise the tents and gather the firewood—all in darkness, mind you," joked a man who pulled the sled as Nicholas pushed from behind.

Malek laughed. "By the sound of it, Averill thinks I'm some horrific taskmaster, Nicholas. What are your thoughts?"

"No comment. I'm staying out of family arguments."

"You're a part of this family now, like it or not," Malek said with a brotherly fondness. "And though we have many jobs before us after we arrive, I plan to let everyone enjoy some well-earned leisure in the days ahead. But right now at least, take time to soak in the beauty of the region. After being outcasts on the desolate northern perimeter for so long, it's a joy to be standing among the trees and mountains despite the task in Kargoth awaiting us."

After Malek waved goodbye and meandered off, Nicholas glanced up and soaked in the wintry panorama as he continued pushing the sled. He exhaled deeply, his breathing keeping tempo with his footsteps as his breath rose in the cold air. To his left stood a dark green swath of trees extending south toward the northern slope of Petaras Peak less than two miles away. Another stretch of woods graced the southwest horizon. Several clumps of pine and other deciduous trees dotted the snowy tract of land in between. A handful of mountain peaks in the area, some craggy and others graced with elegant lines, reached up to the dimming skies as silent monuments to the ages. He wondered what Hobin would think of this chain of mountains, each one vastly taller and more formidable in appearance than any in the Dunn Hills. And though Nicholas thought that both regions possessed stunning beauty and awe inspiring vistas, he felt that the Dunn Hills offered a homespun charm he would prefer if forced to choose. For a moment he missed tramping about their winding, frothy streams, smelling the bittersweet aromas of soil and moss, and hiking along the leafy hillsides dyed in brilliant autumn shades of amber, crimson and orange. Nicholas, knowing that Hobin would want to map every peak here, chuckled to himself, catching Averill's attention.

"What's so funny?" he asked, tossing a backward glance.

"Just thinking about a wonderful guide who took me and a friend through the Dunn Hills," he said wistfully. "He'd love it here as he was fond of mapping–"

Suddenly a voice cried out across the snowy expanse, sending a chilling mix of shock and terror through the hearts of everyone. Nicholas and Averill stopped the sled at once as did the others spread out across the field. All eyes shifted to one particular sled near the head of the pack on the right where the shouts originated.

"That sounded like Sala!" Nicholas said, hurrying across the snow for several steps before stopping to get a better view as a wave of fear overwhelmed him.

When Averill joined him, Nicholas pointed to a slight dip in the terrain in the near distance. It appeared that a man was lying on the ground and another was running toward the trees in the southwest. Sala's voice, now clearly recognizable, still rose in the frosty air in frantic bursts, crying for help as a flock of men trudged through the snow toward him. Nicholas watched as Malek sprinted across the white frozen surface several yards ahead toward the apparently injured man. Nicholas and Averill swiftly followed.

"He's getting away!" Sala shouted amid a rising chorus of voices speculating about what had happened and who was running.

"Hurry!" Nicholas shouted to Averill when he finally spotted Sala's figure in the growing gloom and ran toward him. Sala wildly signaled with his hands near the fallen man as others swarmed to that location. Looking beyond Sala's frenzied gestures, Nicholas saw another man stumble in the deep snow. He slowly got up and changed direction, making for a different section of the tree line where the snow was less deep and his path more maneuverable.

"What do you think happened?" Averill asked.

"Don't know," Nicholas said as he pushed his way through a handful of men hastily advancing from other directions.

"A sledding accident?"

"Maybe. But then why would someone be running *away* from our group? Do you think that–?"

But Nicholas' words were drowned out. Thunderous footfalls rapidly closed in from behind and swiftly passed by him and Averill in a gray blur and a swirling gust of fine snow that momentarily blinded them. Shouts of surprise welled up, and when Nicholas' vision cleared, he saw a large man upon a gray horse expertly weaving a path among the scattered lines of men while heading toward the fleeing stranger. As the horseman shot past Sala's sled which stood close to the fallen man, he grabbed a filled cloth sack sitting atop one of the crates with one hand while controlling the reins in the other. He pressed forward as the galloping horse raised clouds of fine snow and zeroed in on the escaping individual. But just as the runner briefly turned around to get a better glance at his pursuer, the horseman swung back the sack in his left arm like a pendulum and propelled it forward with all his might, hitting the man squarely in the jaw and knocking him off his feet as the horse flew past like a blazing arrow.

Though dazed and disoriented, the man struggled to sit up. He glanced over his shoulder, noting that the horse and its rider had sped well beyond him and were only beginning to slow down and turn around. With a grueling effort, he scrambled to his feet and looked frantically about for the next best path of escape before the horseman returned. But something else caught his attention. Another man in near hysterics was running toward him.

"Dunnic!" Sala's voice was filled with anger as he barreled toward the escaped prisoner with both fists clenched. A chorus of voices called out to Sala to come back, shocked that he had bolted at the enemy so fast and unarmed.

Dunnic, seeing no way of escape, pulled a bloody, knife-like object from his belt and raised it in the air, running headlong at Sala. "I'll kill you too!" he screamed, charging through the snow as Sala moved ever closer, apparently not aware or not caring that Dunnic was armed.

As the other sledders hastened to Sala's defense from the north, the horseman snapped his reins in a desperate race to reach Dunnic before he collided with Sala in an almost certain bloody encounter. As Dunnic pressed forward, a vicious smile spread across his face. He knew he would reach Sala before any of the others could save their friend. He gripped the blood-stained weapon and prepared to spring, not caring about what would happen to him once he killed his foe. At that same moment, with almost slow-motion awareness, Sala realized the danger he had rushed into when observing the murderous intent in Dunnic's eyes. The sound of thunderous horses echoed in his mind like death itself. Sala slowed down as he blindly reached for a sword that wasn't at his side. Dunnic, nearly on top of him, was ready to lunge forward, his blade in motion, his teeth bared, savoring his final victory he knew was but a moment away. Sala, trying to turn away, slipped on the snow and toppled backward, expecting pain and death.

But in that same instant, Dunnic felt as if he had crashed headfirst into a stone wall. He fell flat on his back, seeing Sala's face disappear from view and replaced by a backdrop of deepening blue skies, ashen clouds and then a blinding white light in his mind. He sensed a cold, burning sensation deep inside as he tried to take a breath, but his lungs felt as feeble and useless as clumps of wet parchment. He saw an arrow sticking out of his chest. His vision began to blur. Soon he felt only cold numbness as a collage of distant voices collided in his mind in the swiftly fading light. Then he felt nothing at all, neither heat nor cold nor the snowy ground beneath him. Slowly his eyelids closed for the last time until he lay as still and unmoving as the mountains.

Sala sat up as Nicholas and many of the others gathered around in stunned silence, grateful that their friend was unharmed while trying to make sense of what had occurred. Sala shook the snow from his hair and looked about in dazed wonder.

"What happened?" he said, breathing heavily, his face flushed. "How did–?" When Sala saw Dunnic sprawled dead on his back a few feet away, he went instantly pale, pointing incredulously at the corpse. "Who did that?"

The others turned their heads and gazed upon his rescuer. Sala looked up. Through the open spaces between the men he saw Malek standing near a body lying in the snow beside a sled. He held a bow in his outstretched arm, his eyes yet fixed upon the invisible path of his flying arrow. He slowly lowered the weapon and set it aside before attending to his fallen comrade. Tradell and several others joined him.

Just then, the man on the gray horse sauntered up to the crowd from the opposite direction, the cloth sack still in his hands.

He let it drop near Sala's legs. "Here are your biscuits," Max dryly remarked before dismounting his steed.

"Welcome back," Nicholas said, shaking his hand as Averill and another man helped Sala up. "You're timing was impeccable."

"What's going on?" he asked with concern while fingering his beard and indicating Dunnic's body with a tilt of his head. "Is that one of the men from the raft?"

"Yes," Nicholas said, bringing Max up to date on the events he had missed since departing fifteen days ago. "It would have been better for us if he had joined Brin at the bottom of the Gray River."

"But such wasn't our fate." Slowly, Malek made his way to the front, pale and shaken. He gripped Sala on the shoulder, thankful that he was unharmed. "Dunnic was simply another Brin through and through, warped in his mind and blindly devoted to Vellan." His words were tinged with bitterness as the news he carried was both grave and heartbreaking. "Our good friend, Rollin, has fallen at the hands of that–" He couldn't complete his thought as he gazed upon Dunnic's body as three men examined the corpse.

"How'd he get his hands on a knife?" Sala asked.

"It wasn't a knife," answered one of the men near Dunnic's body. He bent down and picked up the weapon in question and presented it to the onlookers. "It's a piece of wood, most likely a bit he snapped off a chunk of the firewood he helped carry."

"He must have pocketed it on the sly and sharpened it with a stone," Sala concluded with disgust. "We should have kept that miserable thing tied up at all times."

"But we didn't," Malek said. "I'll assume the blame for that."

"What'll we do with him?" asked the man holding the bloody weapon.

Malek thought for a moment. "Bury him under a snow mound where he lies. Let nature take care of his body as she sees fit when warmer weather arrives."

"And Rollin?" Sala asked.

"We'll empty the sled he was pushing except for a layer of crates," he instructed. "We'll set his body upon those, covered and with much honor, and transport it to the encampment. There we'll dig a spot for his final resting place and send word to his family when time and weather allow. But it will be a bitter spring." Malek walked back to Rollin's body, now covered with a blanket as Tradell stood over him and softly uttered words for the dead as several men listened with heads bowed.

A short time later as several men split into two groups to tend to the bodies, Malek took Max aside to talk about his meeting along Thendara Wood with Prince Gregory's scout. He signaled for Nicholas, Tradell and a few others to join them near a cluster of pine trees as the dimming light cast a bluish hue across the snow. Max reached inside his coat and pulled out a parchment envelope sealed with a blot of blue wax pressed with the prince's royal imprint.

"You'll want to see this," Max said, handing the unopened envelope to Malek.

Nicholas, noting that Max's name had been elegantly printed on the front, looked at him curiously. "You are a patient man, not having bothered to read it yet."

Max quietly laughed. "Patience has nothing to do with it, Nicholas. Though I recognize my name on the front, I've never really taken to the written word. Just a handful of necessary ones, mind you, to get me by on the road. Perhaps some day."

"You have the honors," Malek said despondently, handing the envelope to Nicholas. "My thoughts are still elsewhere. Give us the highlights if you would, then later we can pore over the details when more time is available."

"All right," he said, pleased to accommodate his request as the others looked on. After sliding a finger under the flap and breaking the seal, Nicholas carefully unfolded the piece of parchment. Prince Gregory's handwriting in dark brown ink filled the entire page. He skimmed the small and neatly penned words as the last thin rays of sunlight dipped behind the line of peaks in the southwest.

"What's it say?" Max asked, his wide brown eyes darting back and forth between Nicholas' face and the letter.

"Well, after a few details about the winter war council–which was a brief and cordial affair this time–Prince Gregory writes that King Justin's army and his allies from Montavia will march south at the first sign of warm weather. They will make for the city of Grantwick in Drumaya," he continued, his eyes fixed to the letter, "and there join forces with King Cedric's army and any soldiers that Prince Victor and Princess Melinda can spare from Rhiál and Maranac." Nicholas looked up. "It seems that they want to contribute to the fight, even if modestly so, in repayment to the Kings for deposing Drogin and ridding their lands of Vellan's influence."

"All contributions are welcomed," Malek said gratefully.

"What else does he write?" Tradell asked.

"Soldiers from the Five Clearings in the Ebrean Forest will also march, most anxious to continue their fight against Vellan."

"And finish it this time," Sala said with growing hope. "It's a good omen to have our countrymen join us. May they all soon be living again in their respective homelands."

"That's the crux of the message," Nicholas went on, quickly reading toward the end of the letter. "The several armies will leave Grantwick and continue southwest along the Swift River and Lake Mara. After passing beyond the southern border of Drumaya, they'll turn northwest into Kargoth and march along the path of the Drusala River." He paused as he reread some of the words before looking up apprehensively. "They'll head directly to Vellan's stronghold in Del Norác to *conduct their business* as he says. Prince Gregory and his father look forward to meeting with one of our scouts, or *two*, near the southern tip of Lake Mara at the first sign of spring to coordinate our efforts." Nicholas looked up as he folded the letter and handed it back to Malek. "*Respectfully yours, Prince Gregory of Arrondale.*"

Malek took the letter and offered a slight smile. "Apparently they are readying for this springtime conflict with gusto—and so shall we. Max, I assume you will be volunteering to travel to Lake Mara sometime before spring to get the particulars."

"As if you needed to ask."

"I think the letter mentioned *scouts*," Nicholas chimed in. "More than one."

"Oh, did it really," Malek casually replied.

Nicholas shrugged as he ground the tip of his boot into the snow. "Well, I suppose one could interpret it that way. Besides, it might be wise to send a pair of scouts to retrieve such important information just in case one was injured along the way."

Max furrowed his brow as he caressed his beard, feigning deep thought. "You do have a point there, Nicholas, though I was considering breaking my rule this once and taking someone along with me—just in case, as you say. Know any volunteers?"

Nicholas smiled. "As if you needed to ask."

"I guess it's settled," Malek said with growing weariness, handing the letter to Tradell for safekeeping, his demeanor solemn once again. "Now we should press on for camp while we still have the twilight to guide us. I'll pull the sled carrying Rollin. Tradell, will you accompany me on his final journey?"

"It will be my honor," he replied.

"Thank you. Now let's close out this dreadful night," he said with a heavy heart, wishing that springtime were upon them. But he humbly accepted the long and perilous winter still ahead.

CHAPTER 91

Something in the Air

King Justin opened his upper study window in the middle of a quiet morning, inhaling the late-winter air. He gazed north upon the rich green swath of pine trees along the Edelin River that was still ice-encrusted in spots as it flowed behind the Blue Citadel. Below to his right were the fruit orchards, the apple and pear trees in neat rows waiting to burst forth with blossoms and leaves once winter's frosty breath receded. It had been a long, grueling winter. The King felt a cool breeze brush across his face. Gray and white clouds scraped across the tips of the Trent Hills farther north. Fifteen days remained until the beginning of spring and a brand new year.

He had stood alone at this open window many times during the last month in the midst of war preparations. The second council had proceeded swiftly and without altercation when it was convened five weeks ago. Now, and over the last ten days, volunteer troops were arriving from across Arrondale, ready to march south at a moment's notice. Most of the men were encamped in a large field a mile east of the Citadel with smaller camps scattered about where room allowed. Even King Rowan and Prince William had returned from Montavia with their small army, ready to play a part in what everyone thought would be the last major battle of the time. Scouts had fanned out southward to get the lay of the land after winter's handiwork. They were expected back soon to report on current travel conditions along the main roads as far south as the Red Mountains. King Justin wanted to move as soon as the roads were passable.

Moments later a pair of blue jays alighted on a branch of an apple tree below, their excited calls bouncing sharply off the northern face of the building. The King remembered what a voluminous word fest the first war council had turned into as he tried to corral the various factions into pursuing one common goal. A pleased smile formed beneath his ice blue eyes as he savored the coalition army's victory over Drogin. But the satisfaction was brief as the indelible memories of the dead overshadowed that victory like a pall. A high price, though sadly necessary, had been paid. He vowed never to forget those who had sacrificed the best years of their lives to secure the liberty of so many others on either side of Lake LaShear.

He sighed, mentally preparing for the next march south, yet grateful that the Enâri would no longer be an obstacle. Thanks to Nicholas and Leo, the confrontation with Vellan would be a much more even match, though he still gave Vellan an edge. He recalled the morning in this room when he, Nedry and Tolapari had discussed details of Nicholas and Leo's mission. Both young men admirably proved themselves at a task that he, on very rare occasions, had privately thought was a hopeless cause. Now with the elimination of the Enâri, the pieces on the game table were repositioned more in his favor, but King Justin knew he would have to strike fast and strike hard to gain the upper hand.

He breathed deeply again, happy that another matter was not as troubling. He now had no qualms about his granddaughter falling in love with a man like Leo Marsh and perhaps someday marrying him. Such a proposition may have been unthinkable before since Leo was not of royal lineage or wealthy social standing as were previous suitors who had tried to catch Megan's eye in the past. Yet Leo's deeds and manner spoke volumes about his character, surpassing that of others who had called upon his granddaughter. But since Megan possessed a stubborn streak much like his, the King knew in the end that she would have things her way in life, particularly in affairs of the heart. And that suited him just fine.

He next thought about Nicholas' search for Ivy, wondering what had become of him after he undertook that desperate journey. But King Justin told himself not to give up hope despite Nicholas' seemingly impossible odds. He thankfully had been proven wrong in his occasional nagging doubts in the matter of reforging the key, so why not again this time? He deeply wished it so.

As the minutes drifted by, the King stepped back from the window, not wanting to attend an upcoming meeting with some of his ministers regarding rather mundane affairs. But since it couldn't be put off any longer–as Nedry had reminded him three times since yesterday–he began to close the window, preparing to face his tedious duty. Suddenly a gust of air squeezed through the opening and rustled a pair of long, thick drapes and a cluttered pile of parchment accumulating on a nearby table.

As he breathed in the blast of fresh air, faded recollections stirred in his mind like long forgotten items discovered tucked away in a musty storage trunk. Memories green, tender and full of warm light were awakened. He detected a subtle hint of fresh soil, sweet cedar and distant rain that revived delightful images from his youth and lightened the burdens of his heart. He sensed spring itself in the air, an eager spring trying to break through despite the last stubborn layer of winter still adhering to the hard ground, frosted rooftops and winding stone walls. And though the next breeze that slipped into the room again felt bitter and cold, King Justin took this brief episode as a sign that maybe, just maybe, an early spring was near.

He closed and latched the window with trembling hands and rushed out of the chamber. He needed to find Nedry to cancel the meeting with his ministers and arrange another one with King Rowan, Prince Gregory and a few others to discuss their journey south. With his heart racing, King Justin passed through the Citadel corridors like the wind itself, ready to cut loose his army as soon as possible to catch Vellan and his Island collaborators unprepared. Timing now was everything. It would either be his greatest ally or his worst enemy, all depending upon how he played his next move.

That same morning, Leo and Princess Megan were lost in quiet conversation, wandering hand in hand along snowy walkways through one of the Citadel's courtyard gardens. Megan wore a sky-blue cloak, the hem trailing across the frozen ground, her dark brown hair flowing beneath the hood lying lightly upon her head. Leo was bundled in the long wool coat he had worn while hiking through the Dunn Hills. He also sported a pullover cap knitted by one of the seamstresses to keep him warm during his three days recuperating in bed after opening the Spirit Box. The young couple, alone in the courtyard, wandered past a snow-filled water fountain that had been drained last fall and now looked like some mythical creature that had curled up and fallen asleep for weeks among the melancholy surroundings. When they reached a stone bench along a row of hedges, Leo brushed off the snow upon it and they sat down. Megan took his hand in hers and looked at him with a quiet, hopeless sigh.

"So tell me again why you think you must go south with my grandfather's army. Haven't you done enough already for the cause?" she asked. "Father and Grandfather have both suggested as much. You needn't prove yourself any further."

Leo smiled and softly caressed her cheek. "You never seem to tire of this conversation," he replied sweetly, "though I suppose I can't blame you. But my answer hasn't changed, Meg. I want to help in the war effort because I think I can make a genuine contribution. I know I'm not a warrior, but I can serve as a scout or in some similar capacity for your grandfather. I did find my way to Wolf Lake."

"With Hobin's help," she added with a cheerless laugh.

"He'll be with me again. Hobin wants to get out and about, too. Besides, he promised to keep an eye on me at your insistence," he reminded her.

"*Still...*" Megan's shoulders slumped, her breath rising above the hedges. "Leo, I'd think that destroying the Enâri race and nearly dying in the process should spare you from additional military duties. It would if I were in charge."

"Some day if you're queen of Arrondale, you can decree it so," he joked, wrapping an arm around her and kissing her cheek.

"I'm being serious," she replied, playfully pushing him away.

"I just think you're going to miss me."

"That too."

Leo took her hand. "There is another reason I need to go, though I haven't mentioned it," he admitted, his tone now somber, his mood contemplative. "With a simple turn of a key, I destroyed the Enâri race, Meg. And though I don't regret it because of the death and misery they've wrought, I still need to see the aftermath for myself. I want to travel to where the bulk of the Enâri once existed, though I don't think there'll be much left of them to actually see. But you understand, don't you?"

"I'm trying to."

"Meg, I know Vellen created and bred the Enâri to do the awful things that they did—and they had to be stopped—but it's not a deed I can just shake off after the fact. I thought I would be able to, but..." Leo looked into her eyes, seeking comfort. "I have dreams about it, tiring and uneasy images that fill my sleeping hours. I dream about the spirit that nearly suffocated me in the upper chamber, but in those dreams the windows never shatter outward and—" He took a deep breath and looked at the ground, wondering if it was a mistake to mention this to Megan and worry her even more. "But thankfully, I always wake up just before..."

Megan gently squeezed his hand and smiled lovingly at him. "I'm sorry, Leo. I never thought about your ordeal in those terms. I wish you had told me earlier."

He shrugged. "I didn't want to make a fuss. But it's nothing. People elsewhere are facing worse things right now than wrestling with some silly dreams."

"It's not nothing. And if you really think you need to march south to—to Kargoth," she said, her voice quavering, "then I suppose I'll understand. I'll have to."

Leo lifted her hand and kissed it. "I appreciate that, Meg, especially since I'm abandoning you again."

"Well, I didn't want to make a fuss either," she said with light humor. "Still, we've had a wonderful winter together during your recovery, so I suppose you've earned some time out of the Citadel." Megan shook her head with disappointment. "Yet I do regret keeping you from visiting your family in Minago."

"They're doing fine according to the post I received last week," he reminded her, "though I kept some of the unpleasant details out of my letter that your grandfather's scout delivered during his errands in the east. I'll save the more dreadful particulars when I speak to my parents face to face."

"Perhaps that's best," she agreed.

"And don't ever think that I regretted even a minute of this long, lovely winter spent here with you," he added, kissing her softly on the lips. "These have been the best weeks of my life."

Megan blushed in the cool winter air. "Mine too."

"Which brings me to another subject I've wanted to address for a while. I, uh..." Leo reached into his coat pocket, nervously searching for something. "When we visited my parents after our little adventure along the grasslands, I gave them the money from the apple sales I made up north. My father immediately paid me my share as he always does."

"That seems ages ago," she replied. "But why are you telling me this?"

"Because I didn't spend all the money," he continued, eliciting a curious look from Megan. "I kept a silver and a copper half piece safely tucked away in my pocket."

"What exactly do you plan to do with all those riches?" she inquired with a grin.

"It's what I've already done with them that I want to show you," he said, removing a small item from his pocket. Leo placed a silver chain in the palm of her hand. Attached to it were two interlocking metal rings, finely crafted from the two coins, one of copper and one of silver. "One of the smithies in the Citadel made it for me. Now I'm giving it to you, Megan. I hope it'll remind you of me–and of us–while I'm gone."

"Leo, it's beautiful!" she said, on the verge of tears. She held it up to catch the dull winter light. "I'll wear it always."

"I hoped you might like it, especially since Ivy still has your royal silver medallion. I know it's not the same thing…"

"…but it's wonderful just the same," she replied, kissing him. "I suppose the two rings represent the rising Fox and Bear full moons, just like the image engraved on my medallion. That celestial event augurs good fortune, Leo."

He nodded, an awkward smile upon his face. "Well, it *could* represent that, Meg. But that lunar phenomenon occurs about every eight months. I was thinking this little trinket might have an even more special meaning."

"I can't wait to hear," she replied excitedly. "But first fasten it around my neck, please. I'm so eager to show it off."

"Show it off? Uh, perhaps you should wear it underneath your blouse," he suggested as she handed him the necklace. "Just as you did with your medallion."

"I suppose I could do that," she halfheartedly agreed, "though I'm still eager for others to see it."

"Yes, well about that," he said as he slipped the chain around Megan's neck, her back to him as he carefully locked the clasp. "I gave this to you for another reason."

"*Oh?*" she asked, fingering the pair of rings with a smile as she turned to face Leo.

He smiled back as the glow of winter softly touched her cheeks. "I don't know if I'm doing this properly, you being a princess and all, but I…" Leo swallowed hard, his heart beating rapidly. "I want to marry you, Megan, and this charm is a small token of my love for you. The two rings represent us, together forever. And should you accept it–"

"I do!" she said, the two simple words reaching Leo's ears as pleasingly as the sweet scent of pine and apple blossom wafting upon a spring breeze. "And I will." Leo's eyebrows rose questioningly. "Marry you, of course!"

He burst out in a wide grin. "You will?"

Megan nodded, unable to stop smiling. "Yes, and without a second thought."

Leo hugged Megan and held her tightly, never having felt so alive and wishing the two of them could start their lives together right now. When he leaned back, a shade of anxious worry spread across his face. "But *I* just had a second thought. Do I need to ask your father's permission first?" He swallowed hard again. "Or your grandfather's?"

Megan's jaw dropped. She raised her hands to her face in sudden alarm. Leo paled instantly and shuddered, believing he had committed the worst royal offense imaginable. But an instant later, she broke out in a smile and brushed her fingers alongside his cheeks. "I'm only teasing," she said. "We'll ask them together, Leo. That would be best, I think."

"Still, do you think I did the right thing? Maybe I should have waited until after I returned from down south before springing this upon you. But honestly, a part of me didn't want to wait."

"I'm glad you didn't, Leo," she replied, her moment of elation tempered with the knowledge that he would soon be leaving her. "I do love you, and though my wait for you will be miserably difficult when you march off with my grandfather's army, this moment, and your lovely gift, will make it much more bearable."

Megan kissed him and held up the silver and copper rings, gazing at them with delight before looking at Leo with uncertainty.

"What are you thinking?" he asked.

"I'm wondering if…" She attempted a smile. "Will we have a summer wedding? Or perhaps in the autumn?" Her melancholy words seemed merely a simple inquiry on the timing of the event. Yet beneath the surface, though she tried to ignore it, Megan couldn't help but wonder if the wedding would ever take place at all.

Leo sensed her unspoken apprehension and took her hands in his. "It will be a lovely wedding, whatever the season," he assured her. "I promise."

They smiled at one another and kissed again in the courtyard garden. A late-winter breeze rustled through the hedgerow and across the snowy paths, a vague hint of springtime buried somewhere within the mischievous and fitful currents.

CHAPTER 92

Through the Gates of the Citadel

The following morning, Nedry strolled past an open window on the third level of the Blue Citadel, a stream of cool air replacing the stale ambiance within. Slightly hunched over, his gray hair disheveled, he mirrored the melancholy vista of winter's last days lingering upon the gently rolling hills of the southern countryside. He glanced out the window as he walked by and then suddenly stopped, taking a step back and pressing his face to the breezy opening. Sauntering up the road outside the main gates of the courtyard were two of King Justin's scouts upon horses outfitted with gear from the royal stables. They had departed ten days ago to gauge the conditions of the southern roads and terrain should the King decide to unleash his army in the days, rather than weeks, ahead.

Nedry felt a burst of energy and bounded down the corridor to find King Justin. He was just as eager as the King to launch the army, hoping and praying each day for Vellan's defeat. As King Justin's primary advisor, this was the last item on his agenda that he felt he must see through to the end. After that, he looked forward to a quiet retirement. Nedry could no longer handle sleepless nights and chronic indigestion due to a constant string of hastily eaten lunches and dinners–or from too many missed meals altogether. He advised himself that it was time to take life at a slower pace while galloping down a stairway and then racing through a corridor to find the monarch.

To King Justin's delight, the two scouts provided him the detailed report he had hoped for through fretful days and sleepless nights. Prince Gregory and King Rowan, who were also present, offered their agreement as the King appeared to favor the army's swift departure. Prince William and Nedry listened attentively in chairs off to the side.

"The snow is thin beyond the hills south of Morrenwood, but the fields and main roads are still hard from winter," one of the scouts said in the King's private study overlooking the encampment a mile away in the eastern field. "The way will be easily passable until the first spring rains arrive in the weeks ahead."

"I'm not worried about mud right now," King Justin said. "Only the high snows."

"Much of it has blown across the plains," the other scout remarked. "As far down as the northern arm of the Red Mountains, snow has been light since late winter. Word there is that the first months of winter were harsh, but an early spring seems likely."

King Rowan cast a sharp eye upon his fellow monarch as they sat near a fire. "Perhaps fate or other unseen forces are preparing the way, Justin, urging you swiftly ahead to this final confrontation with Vellan." He sat back in his chair and folded his arms, a black, gray and white checkered tunic visible beneath a heavy woolen shirt. "I would back your decision to leave early even if Caldurian and his followers hadn't invaded my kingdom," he added, his voice steady and assured as he looked into the fire. "Vellan has been a menace for decades. He must pay for his ill deeds! He must pay for his crimes and those committed at his behest, especially those against–"

King Rowan abruptly stopped speaking, gripping the arm of his chair like a vice. As he glanced up at the others, he caught their compassionate gazes, including that of his grandson. All stared back with respectful silence, guessing that Brendan was foremost on the King's mind. He smiled awkwardly and sighed.

"It's apparent that my support for a quick resolution isn't totally for altruistic reasons," he continued sheepishly. "I suppose a thirst for revenge, however much I deny it, has tainted my words."

"Who can blame you?" King Justin replied. "But such feelings do not invalidate your position."

"Indeed they do not," Prince Gregory chimed in. "And it's time we face Vellan toe to toe. This is probably the best opportunity for victory." He was more than prepared to engage in battle at a moment's notice should his father will it. "A few more weeks of rest and preparation may seem a wiser move in any other campaign, Father, but the men in camp are as ready as you are to go. Most have anticipated such a course all winter."

"So you're saying they've been thinking like me?" he replied with a hearty chuckle. "I don't know if that should comfort me or send shivers up my spine."

"Definitely the former," King Rowan said. "Your wisdom is evident in their training."

"My captains train my men," he remarked.

"And your captains train them after having first absorbed much from you, Justin. I've noticed a vast and positive difference in my army after many of my soldiers took instruction in Morrenwood." King Rowan indicated William with a slight turn of his head. "And *that* young man privately told me that he refocused his view of some personal matters after talking with you near Lake LaShear. People take your wise words to heart, my friend, and they have seen wonderful results."

King Justin nodded with thanks before addressing his scouts again. "So, gentlemen, have you anything to add?"

"Only to reiterate that if your army moves south in the days ahead, though while still facing a cold and dreary journey, it shouldn't encounter the snowy obstructions we were treated to earlier in the season," the first scout replied.

"In our humble opinion," added the second scout.

"As long as it's a reasoned opinion," the King said.

"It is."

"Well then," he uttered with an air of finality. "After having a few of my doubts allayed, I've finally reached the decision I had hoped for all along. We will march south, and very soon, if there are no objections. If so, speak them now."

Everyone glanced at one another in that charged yet somber atmosphere, offering their quiet approval as the King scanned each face for any objections. Nedry cleared his throat and spoke up.

"It seems, King Justin, that unanimity has been expressed by our silence." He folded his arms and stroked his thin, whiskered face. "At least that is how I read the situation."

"As I have wisely followed your advice through the years, my dear Nedry, I shall not stop now," he replied. "So the only question that remains is—when do we leave?"

Two days later, the armies of Arrondale and Montavia gathered on the frozen grounds and roads around the Blue Citadel. Beneath a pale mid-morning sun behind a thin blanket of clouds, the soldiers assembled after having dismantled their tents and packed their gear. A cool breeze swept through the leafless trees in the main courtyard and across the low hills lying south of Morrenwood like a sloth of snow-covered bears in hibernation. The soldiers, dressed in various forms of protective gear, carried sharpened swords, expertly strung bows or other such weapons, all bearing insignias of their respective kingdoms. And though Arrondale's troops outnumbered their Montavian counterparts, the courage and determination of all the warriors was indistinguishable.

Nervous energy spread through the ranks as the soldiers anticipated the call to move out. At the head of the line far outside the courtyard gates and beyond the last homes on the edges of Morrenwood, Kings Justin and Rowan were engaged in last minute discussions with some of their captains. They stood on a dirt road caked with trampled snow. Their horses grunted restlessly nearby as a chilly breeze sliced through the air. Prince Gregory and Prince William were in the vicinity with Nedry. Though the King's trusted advisor would not be going on the journey, he wanted to see the troops off.

"I shall lose much sleep worrying night and day until you all return," he remarked to the two princes while standing among brittle grass alongside the road. Dozens of conversations buzzed around them as other soldiers milled about. "But what else is new?" he said with a chuckle. "Retirement can't come soon enough."

"You can discuss your concerns with Miss Alb over tea," Prince Gregory said playfully. "I've bumped into her from time to time this winter. She often inquired how you were doing. Apparently she hasn't seen much of you these past few weeks."

Prince William grinned teasingly. "Miss Alb, the head seamstress?"

"We just had lunch last week, if it's any of your business," he replied with mock indignation. "With all the war preparations, I was lucky enough even to arrange that. But I suppose my schedule will be less cluttered now that you're all finally on your way."

"My best to her whenever you see her again," Prince Gregory replied. He craned his neck to see if his father and King Rowan had concluded their discussion farther down the road. "I wish they'd hurry things up."

"When either of us becomes king, let's promise fewer words and more action," William said.

"If only," he replied. "I believe that we'd– *Now* what's going on?" he asked, glancing toward his father a second time. He noticed with apprehension that Caldurian, under heavy guard, had entered the discussion after some of the initial participants had drifted away. "What could that be about?"

"Shall I nose my way over there and find out?" Nedry offered.

Prince Gregory sighed. "Better not. Father will tell me in his own time, though I cringe just imagining what that troublesome wizard could want."

"All I want is a few moments alone with my former student to discuss old times," Caldurian calmly explained to King Justin. King Rowan silently looked on. "What's so complicated about that? Word has come to my ear that Carmella will be accompanying your army on the road to Kargoth."

"She is merely *traveling in the same direction* as she put it," the King impatiently replied. "She wants to find her cousin who had fled that way after the assault on the Citadel. I relented since she was instrumental in helping us rid Laparia of the Enâri creatures. I owe her that much. But I certainly owe you no favors, Caldurian." King Justin frowned at the wizard as he wrapped his cloak tightly about his shoulders. "So why do you continue to badger me these last few days? What are you up to? I trust you as much as I trust Vellan–and I'm certain you can guess how much that is."

Caldurian stared at the ground for a moment, looking tired and dispirited. "If you want the truth, Carmella and I didn't part on friendly terms when we last saw each other twenty years ago."

"You had cast a sleeping spell upon her in her own home," the King replied. "And you turned Madeline against her, too. What makes you think that Carmella would want to see you? She made no mention of it over winter while you were a prisoner in the Citadel."

"And a far-too-well treated prisoner at that," Tolapari piped up as he strolled over to the group, his dark blue robes fluttering in the breeze like the black wavy locks of his unkempt hair. "I also talked to Carmella a few times when she was here visiting Princess Megan. And your name, Caldurian, rarely came up during our chats."

"Then you clearly need to find more interesting topics to discuss," he shot back with a subtle glare. "By the way, Tolapari, this is a private conversation as far as that is possible around here," he added, glancing at the ring of guards keeping a cautious eye upon him. "Don't you have spells to practice now that your powers have returned after that brazen demonstration of the âvin éska?"

"Don't believe everything you hear, Caldurian. Or imagine." Tolapari looked briefly askance at King Justin before taking a step closer to his fellow wizard, a contemptuous scowl upon his face. "The state of my powers is known only to me–but a clever attempt to extract information nonetheless."

"You would have been disappointed if I hadn't tried," he remarked with a glint in his eyes before turning to King Justin. "But back to my argument, sir. I know in my heart that if you asked Carmella, she would be more than willing to meet with me. There is much I could teach her despite my current incapacity."

"That worries me, too," the King replied. "Now enough has been said on this subject to the point of boredom, Caldurian." He signaled to the guards. "Take our guest back to his horse. The army has dallied here long enough."

"But I beseech you, King Justin. I *have* changed," the wizard replied with heartfelt sincerity. For a moment neither King Justin, Tolapari nor King Rowan could tell if he was earnest or perhaps veiled with some mild magic produced through sheer force of will. "You may not believe me, but I am a humbled man since my powers were taken away. Humbled and repentant."

King Justin locked gazes with him. "No, I don't believe you, Caldurian. You were neither humble nor repentant after your defeat in Kanesbury twenty years ago, only coming back more devious and vindictive. And if you had even a portion of your powers right now, I can't imagine you not inflicting some harm upon me." He sighed with disgust. "I'll never forget your part in helping to implement Vellan's plan to have me replaced with that hideous impostor, the same evil being who killed King Rowan's grandson. No, Caldurian, you are not to be trusted! Everything you do or say will be suspect to me and to a good many others for as long as you breathe."

Caldurian appeared genuinely hurt by the King's words. "Then maybe you should put me out of my misery now and be done with it," he muttered.

The King studied the wizard's defiant expression. "Judgment will come your way, Caldurian, when our score is settled with Vellan. In the meantime, I fear I cannot leave you here in Morrenwood and out of my sight should your powers return–if they have not already returned to an extent."

"Have they?" Tolapari asked, eyeing his counterpart. But Caldurian kept silent.

"So for the last time, this discussion is over," the King said, signaling to his guards. "Please return to your horse, Caldurian, unless you'd rather walk to Kargoth like most of my men."

The wizard flipped the hood of his cloak over his head and grumbled. "Fine. I'll do as you say," he said, abruptly turning to follow the guard in front of him while the others fell in to keep watch on either side and from behind. "And all I wanted was a bit of conversation with an old acquaintance," he muttered under his breath as he walked away. "You would think that I had asked for the keys to the Blue Citadel itself!"

"Though I wouldn't be surprised if he had already tried to lift them," Tolapari commented when Caldurian was out of earshot.

King Justin chuckled, looking up at King Rowan and the wizard. "Gentlemen, to our horses, please. It is twelve days to spring, and at the rate we're going, spring might arrive before we finally take to the road."

"Those were some fine words you threw at the wizard," King Rowan remarked as they moved through the soldiers to where their steeds patiently awaited. "Pointed and well delivered. I fear I would have erupted like a volcano if I had addressed the scoundrel."

"As I said, he will be judged in a more formal setting. There you can pummel him with your words, measured or otherwise. William might wish to speak then, too, on behalf of his brother."

"Perhaps," King Rowan said with difficulty, turning aside to mount his steed.

King Justin then stopped for a word with Tolapari who was adjusting the saddle straps on his horse a few steps away. He kept his voice to a whisper. "Are your powers any stronger today?"

The wizard smiled as he stroked the nose of his horse. "I am nearly back to normal, Justin. As per the design of the spell, the one who cast it should recover first and much more quickly than the intended victim. It has been seventy-one days since I performed the âvin éska and things are progressing much as I had anticipated."

King Justin massaged his chin. "Eight weeks as of tomorrow. And how do you size up Caldurian?"

Tolapari looked around to make sure no one was in listening range before leaning in closer to speak. "He has showed no signs to me or any of his guards that he yet possesses his former powers, though I suspect that at least a small portion of his magical abilities must be regenerating. Still, he wouldn't tell us if they were, but I don't believe he is at a point where he can endanger anyone yet. It should be several more weeks, perhaps even a few months, before Caldurian is his old self again."

"That's a bit of good news," the King replied, "though I hope long before then we'll have settled the Vellan issue so we can proceed to settle the *Caldurian* issue, whatever form it takes."

"Simply survey a handful of people throughout Laparia and you'll receive a long list of some rather creative solutions."

"I'll keep that in mind. Now it's time to move."

The King mounted his horse and signaled to one of his captains to sound the call to move out. Moments later, a series of clear and rousing horn blasts echoed off the high walls of the Blue Citadel and swept across the low, snowy hillsides to the south. Upon hearing the stirring yet simple notes, hundreds of horses and thousands of men prepared to move forward, all to be accompanied by a seemingly endless supply line of carts and carriages that would stretch for miles if in single file. King Justin looked behind him at the sea of soldiers. As he gazed northward over the rooftops of the homes and farmsteads of Morrenwood all the way back to the Blue Citadel, he felt the collective pulse of both armies beating steadily in the invigorating air. He glanced at King Rowan to his left and Tolapari to his right before surveying the long road ahead.

"Now is the time to act, for good or for ill. And this is where it starts," he said, his eyes fixed to the south. "Let us begin."

King Justin drew his sword and raised it high in the air so that it reflected the dim light of the late-winter sky. He pointed it sharply forward and the massive army slowly began to move along the hard dirt road. Various images of Kargoth swirled inside the mind of every soldier with a foot either upon the ground or lodged in a cold stirrup. All expected a long and weary journey.

A chill coursed through Megan's body when she heard the call to move out floating high upon the breeze. She and Leo stood facing one another by a row of hedges near the main entrance of the Citadel, talking softly and holding each other's hands. The sounds of busy soldiers and jittery horses ramping up activity escalated all around them as they prepared to vacate the courtyard. Megan gazed into Leo's eyes, realizing that it was finally time for him to leave.

"When you returned from the Dunn Hills, I thought we would have all the time in the world together, Leo. I thought winter would never end." Megan's eyelids briefly closed and she bowed her head, the cold burrowing into her bones despite the heavy cloak wrapped about her shoulders.

"I'll be back before you know it, Meg. I promise."

She looked up as a few tears streamed down her face. "I was very worried when you and Nicholas headed west, but now…" She took a deep breath to steady herself. "Now I'm frightened, Leo, and I'm not ashamed to say it."

"Frightened?" He smiled, hoping to ease her fears. "I have an army to back me up this time, Meg. And Hobin, too." He pointed to his former guide who was talking with Carmella near her horse and wagon under a nearby tree.

"It's not the same," Megan said, dabbing at her eyes. "But I've recited my concerns enough times to bore you to death, Leo. I'm sorry. You deserve a proper goodbye and not another lecture."

116

"I love your lectures," he said with a smile as he hugged her. "And I can't wait to get back to hear another one."

"Then you had better leave now so I can write it down," she replied, putting on a brave face though her heart was breaking.

"We still have a few minutes. It'll be a while before the front lines move far enough forward so we can file out of the courtyard." Leo placed his hands upon her cold cheeks to warm them and playfully kissed her nose. "I'll miss our quiet lunches together in that tiny room with a view of the river. Those were special times, Meg."

"I can't understand it, Leo, but hardly anyone ever uses that room," she said, holding back another stream of tears. "And it does have such a lovely view."

Leo hugged her while she sobbed on his shoulder. Carmella and Hobin strolled over through the bustling crowd. Carmella, in her colorful cloak and beige gloves, noticed Princess Megan's distraught condition. She gently pulled Hobin back with a tug on his coat sleeve. They kept a respectful distance until Megan finally looked up with a budding smile upon her face.

"I'm quite all right now," she said with a sniffle, beckoning for Carmella and Hobin to come closer. "I think I'm finally cried out–until later tonight, no doubt, when I'll be thinking about how much I miss all of you."

"And we'll miss you," Carmella said with motherly affection. "I enjoyed our little talks over tea during these past few weeks. But Kargoth isn't at the end of the world, so expect a detailed accounting soon when I get back. When we *all* get back."

"But soon isn't soon enough," she said, giving Carmella a hug. "I don't suppose it'd do any good to ask you again to abandon your search for Madeline. I don't feel comfortable that you're going to Kargoth even in the company of two armies."

"But I'm not going with them," Carmella replied. "I just happen to be traveling in the same direction. My agenda is separate. And if I should ever lay these gloved hands upon that devious cousin of mine…"

"Don't do anything rash," Leo said. "She's had far more training than you. Perhaps you can reason with her to reverse that pumpkin spell."

"*Humph!* Liney cannot be reasoned with." Carmella shook her head in disgust. "I stood behind the Citadel and saw the damage she had caused. Liney is not one to engage in rational talk. She must be defeated. And if that means tracking her and her scheming associate all the way to Del Norác, then so be it. This sorry chapter in our lives must come to an end, and only one of us can be the victor."

"Then do what you must do," Megan said with a supportive smile, though unable to completely hide the gloom upon her heart. She glanced at Hobin, his tall frame, weathered coat and aqua-colored eyes exuding an air of quiet confidence that gave her comfort and peace of mind. "Please keep a sharp eye on Leo and Carmella for me, if I may ask such a favor."

"You may, Princess Megan, and I will," he replied. "After all the courtesy shown to me by your grandfather and so many others during my stay in the Citadel, it's the least I can do."

"King Justin was impressed with the maps you created for his library," Leo said.

"Those were only preliminary works, drawn after a few short hikes through the Trent Hills. I'll create better maps after this to-do in the south is resolved. Still, I shall bring my drawing supplies with me and make sketches in the Northern Mountains. I hear they're magnificent. Perhaps I can return there in peaceful times."

"Oh, I do hope for that–the peaceful times," Megan said. At that moment there was some greater movement within the courtyard as an initial line of wagons and one company of soldiers slowly headed toward the main gates. Megan looked somberly at Leo.

"Well, I think we should go now," he softly said to her before glancing uneasily at Carmella and Hobin who understood that he wanted one last moment alone with Megan.

"Goodbye, Megan," Carmella said with a brief yet hopeful smile before turning and walking off to her wagon.

"Thank you again, Princess Megan," Hobin added with a slight bow of his head. He donned his hood and followed Carmella to where his and Leo's horses were tied up near her wagon.

Leo looked into Megan's eyes, noting the fear and sadness swirling within their depths and wishing he could ease her pain. But he knew all too well that every step toward Kargoth he was about to take was the very cause of that pain.

"You're not to blame for my distress," Megan told him as if she could read his mind. She kissed him tenderly on the cheek. "I will be strong like a princess is supposed to be and stop acting like a fussy child. I know you'll return to me. After all, I won't let you back out of your promise to marry me that easily."

"Not to worry," Leo said. "That's one promise I *promise* to keep." He took her in his arms and kissed her long and lovingly near the hedges as several eyes throughout the courtyard watched with elated discretion.

A short time later, a crowd of locals gathered near the front gate to see off the last of the army. Megan stood with them, though feeling alone as she watched Leo, Carmella and Hobin slowly disappear down the road and out of her life. She observed with sadness and longing, her right hand tightly clenched yet lovingly held to her chest. Secure within her fingers was the pair of interlocking silver and copper rings hanging from the delicate chain around her neck that Leo had given her in the snowy courtyard garden.

CHAPTER 93

The Road to Drumaya

The long road to Drumaya brought back painful memories for Prince William. He felt his brother's presence in the cool air as the armies of Arrondale and Montavia trekked southward. On the third morning of their journey, he rode alongside his grandfather, King Rowan. With them was Captain Grayling of Morrenwood who had helped rescue the King and William's mother from their Enâri captors over two months ago. The sun reflected off the dark waters of the Pine River whose course they now followed, and upon the thin crust of snow coating the fields on either side with diamond-like brilliance.

"I'm glad Brendan and I spent those days together on the road," William said, his eyes fixed upon the soldiers and supply lines moving in front. "I enjoyed talking and joking about whatever came to mind–even though I'm the better joke teller," he boasted as the sun highlighted his thick blond hair. A hooded, brown cloak hung from his shoulders.

King Rowan smiled. "I'm also glad you shared that special time even though you tricked King Justin to get permission."

"Yes, there was that," he admitted with amusement.

"The open road allows for such camaraderie among friends," Captain Grayling said. "And though I've heard you speak of some competitiveness between you and your brother while growing up, I'll wager that you both enjoyed a solid friendship even if it was an unspoken one at times. But that is natural among young brothers as I can attest to with my own."

William sighed wistfully. "Brendan was not only my brother, Captain Grayling, but my future king whom I would have happily served. Not that I was in any hurry for you to vacate your position, Grandfather," he added with a playful glance at the King. "But you both must understand what I mean. Brendan was older and smarter than I and more suited to such a station many years down the road."

"And now you see that once-imagined future for yourself–ruler of Montavia, only without a brother to lean on," his grandfather replied. "And because we ride to war, the possibility of such an outcome probably worries you even more." The young prince simply shrugged in reply. "Well rest assured, William, that I will make every effort to avoid the swipe of a sharp sword or a well-aimed arrow."

"Avoid even the stray ones, too," he said.

"I'll try my best," the King replied with an affectionate smile as he gazed southward across the sea of soldiers.

The snowy tips of the Red Mountains and the vast waters of Lake Lasko were still about two days away. King Rowan knew that bitter memories would be dredged up for his grandson the farther south they traveled. Yet being here with him, he hoped that sharing in William's grief would help ease it, though the anguish and heartache would always be a part of his grandson's life until the end of his days.

"I wish I had been a better fighter when Brendan and I–"

King Rowan stopped him in mid sentence. "And I wish I had been there to save you both. But life unfolded as it did. So do not linger in that dark corner of your mind, at least not as we prepare for our next task." He glanced at William with a reassuring smile. "Fortify yourself with more wholesome memories for strength and protection in the fight ahead. The bleak ones will still be there when our job is done. I know of what I speak."

"Understood," he replied as memories of his deceased father surfaced in his mind, guessing that his grandfather was sharing similar thoughts. As he lightly clutched Lester's reins, William suddenly thought about Brendan's horse and fondly wondered how

Chestnut was faring under Eucádus' care. He couldn't wait to see them both.

Late the following morning, clouds moved in from the west, creating an ominous, charcoal gray sketch against the horizon. As the wind picked up strength, King Justin scowled beneath his hood, imagining his troops doing the same. The air had turned damp and cold in the last few hours. The miles of hard road were peppered with ruts and dried weeds. The soldiers on foot kept to the uneven terrain on either side of the road, allowing the supply wagons the easier course. Moments later though, all were reduced to a near standstill as large, wet snowflakes fell in a wind-whipped slant, reducing the army to a crawl.

"Maybe those scouts want to revise their weather reports," one soldier muttered to another as he held the tip of his hood to keep the wind from filling it like a ship's sail. He adjusted the heavy pack on his back with a few jerking motions of his shoulders while he trudged blindly forward, thinking about the warmth of his tent when he had been encamped in the field near the Blue Citadel.

"Maybe Vellan will have a kettle of hot soup waiting for you," his friend remarked with a snicker.

"And maybe I'll throw you in the Drusala River when we get there," he replied. "Then you can willingly serve Vellan his meals and scrub his floors."

"At least I'd be warm," he said as the snowflakes pummeled his cheeks. "I don't think we'll be building a fire any time soon."

"I suppose not," the other miserably replied, bowing his chin to his chest.

But the line moved sluggishly and silently onward. More and more gray clouds sailed overhead as if winter were only beginning and not near its end.

Spirits lifted when the snow suddenly stopped two hours later and the sun peeked out through breaks in the thinning clouds. Cheering broke out among the troops as the day brightened and warmed. Hoods were removed and coats unbuttoned as boots and wagon wheels plowed onward through a coating of slush that now carpeted the countryside. King Justin, riding alongside Tolapari, noted his cheerful expression.

"Why so happy?" he asked with exaggerated gruffness. "Our cloaks are wet and heavy and my horse seems determined to pick out the most uncomfortable path on this dreadful thoroughfare."

"Despite the inclement weather, I'm enjoying a moment of contentment that it is all finally underway. We are at last heading to Kargoth to lance a boil that's been festering on Laparia for fifty years." The wizard shook the melting snowflakes from his unruly hair. "I choose to see that as a success and want to enjoy it before the ordeal begins." He glanced at the King. "And don't worry about the weather. You made the right decision to leave Morrenwood early. It is still nine days to spring. Winter is simply having a last laugh on its way out, so cheer up, Justin."

"A cup of hot tea would go a long way toward that end," he replied as the sun neared the noon position and burned away more of the tattered clouds. "I think I shall have one when we stop for lunch. I'll allow for fires and an extended meal today to give everyone a chance to dry off. We can't have the men so miserable at the front end of this journey that they'll lose heart by the end."

"That's the spirit," Tolapari replied, his eyes forward. "And Megan, I'm sure, is fine under Nedry's supervision. So you needn't overly worry about her either."

"You've sensed that, too?" A slight grunt accompanied the King's smile. "Very well then. *Overly* is out. I'll keep my worrying between *regularly* and *often*, if you don't mind. But this grandfather does have eyes. I see the love blossoming between Megan and Leo. Still, I couldn't ask the young man not to accompany us, even for Megan's sake." King Justin breathed in the late-winter air and sighed. "She will be devastated should anything happen to him."

"We'll keep an extra careful watch over Leo as danger nears, though he needn't dash out onto the battlefield to prove himself," Tolapari said. "Leo is a capable scout as he demonstrated in the Dunn Hills. Anyway, the services of many scouts will be needed the closer we get to Del Norác. Leo, with Hobin at his side, could be sent out on one of the less precarious missions," he suggested. "A quiet word by me to a few of your captains will do the trick."

"But I don't want it to be obvious to Leo that he's being protected." King Justin shook his head. "You had better say nothing. I'll let this play out as it will and make my decisions accordingly. I don't want to sully a future relationship with the possible husband of my granddaughter. Oh, I would never hear the end of it!" he said, tiredly massaging his forehead.

"I think Leo would quietly accept your decision. He respects you too much."

"I was referring to Megan."

"*Ahhh...*" the wizard replied. "Then perhaps your decision is the right one after all." He glanced at the King. "But do you actually know something regarding their future?"

"No, no," he said. "Just speculating. But as I've never seen Megan so enthralled with one of her previous suitors before..." The King softly chuckled. "It's funny to think that she found Leo because I had sent her away to Boros for safekeeping."

"Funny indeed. But if you hadn't, then Princess Megan and her newfound friends would never have met Carmella and brought her and the medallion to the Citadel. Think where we'd be right now if that little episode had never played out."

King Justin nodded, never having thought about it that way. "I guess my apprehensions about Megan's safety paid off in the end if you look at the grand tapestry of life. That puts a new slant on things, doesn't it, Tolapari?" he asked with a relaxed smile.

"Certainly on your disposition," he replied.

"Very good then. I'm glad we had this conversation." He sat up straighter in his saddle, his shoulders back, savoring the mix of cool air and warm sunshine brushing gently upon his face. "Now that I'm feeling better, perhaps we'll even take time for a second cup of tea at lunch. What do you say?"

By early afternoon the next day, the road brought them into the shadow of the Red Mountains looming to their right with silent majesty. It was one of the smaller mountain chains in Laparia and cradled the western shores of Lake Lasko. Its darkened peaks rose proudly in the sunshine that highlighted patches of white snow upon each of its summits. The woods, fields, rivulets and dozens of villages in the surrounding region were on the verge of waking from winter's slumber. As dusk deepened a few hours later, the front lines reached the lapping waves on the northern shores of Lake Lasko, a welcomed sight to eyes grown weary of barren surroundings and ears yearning to hear more than thin breezes sweeping across brittle grasses.

The army encamped in a large field close to the shoreline. The troops scouted for driftwood, built bonfires and cast their lines for delicious lake trout for a late dinner. As Kings Justin and Rowan made their separate rounds of the settlement, both detected a holiday atmosphere among the soldiers. Arriving here marked a natural end to the first leg of their journey, putting most in a celebratory mood. King Justin was pleased with the state of morale after five days on the road, reassured that he had made the correct decision to leave before spring had arrived. The sounds of laughter among the crackling flames up and down the shoreline bolstered his spirit, giving him an insight into his soldiers' current state of mind. He realized he still had their full support and let them enjoy their time on the water's edge. Later, though, when he saw William sitting alone on a rock picking at a plate of roasted fish outside a circle of firelight, the King saw that one individual was not sharing the others' enthusiasm. And he already knew why without having to ask.

They were nearing the village of Parma where Brendan and William had met the wizard Arileez disguised in human form and using the name Sorli. The King correctly guessed that foul memories of that night were occupying William's thoughts as he brooded over his meal. King Justin recalled their conversation about that incident while sitting in King Basil's garden overlooking Lake LaShear. He debated whether to join William and talk to him about it again, but decided to leave the boy alone with his thoughts so he could perhaps draw strength from his meditation. Instead, he sought out a group of soldiers gathered around the next fire, simply acknowledging William with a pat on his shoulder as he walked past the boy who sat cloaked in a mass of inky shadows.

They traveled along the western shore of Lake Lasko the next day, passing through Parma as evening approached. But William, still in a melancholy state, never caught sight of the Silver Trout, the inn where he and Brendan had dined with Sorli. Most of the army units traversed nearby fields and minor roads to the west while the supply lines kept to the main thoroughfare, passing by the inn and groups of curious spectators. King Rowan thought it just as well that his grandson had avoided seeing the establishment. He mentioned it to King Justin as they guided their horses along a dusky road beneath the budding stars. The Fox and Bear moons were at varying positions beneath the eastern horizon, each still a few hours from rising.

"William has kept to himself all day, Justin, acting gloomy and distant. But I thought it best to leave him alone with his mood."

"I did the same when I saw him eating by himself last night," King Justin replied. "His troubled demeanor at being back in this region is only natural, I suppose."

"I agree. He has taken his brother's death hard, and despite the passing of winter, the events are still fresh in his mind," King Rowan said. "I see traces of his mother's temperament in him. Vilna was devastated by the news of Brendan's death. I don't know if she'll ever smile again or fully enjoy life at Red Lodge."

The King gazed into the growing shadows, looking forward to stopping for the night. He was dead tired and wondered if William would enjoy a good night's rest as well. That same worry lingered in his mind later as he lay upon the ground bundled in a blanket until a deep and fitful sleep overwhelmed him. But when King Rowan happened upon his grandson the following morning having breakfast with Leo, Carmella and Hobin, he happily noted that the young man was laughing with his friends and in fine spirits, having apparently worked through any grief that had recently tormented him. The King was delighted that William seemed his old self again and left him with a reassuring smile to enjoy his meal with the others.

"Your grandfather seems in a good mood this morning," Carmella noted a few moments later. She and the others sat around a crackling fire near her enclosed wagon amid a sea of encampments spread across a large field. Patches of snow were visible upon the withered remains of grass, weeds and scrub brush left over from autumn. Wisps of fog lingered near the ground and wrapped around a scattering of tree trunks as gray and blue tendrils of wood smoke rose high into the air to greet the new morning upon a freshening breeze.

"He's happy with the progress we've made, as is King Justin," William said while adding a few twigs to the snapping flames. "Grandfather has kept me apprised on some of the discussions he's had with King Justin and Prince Gregory. If we can reach Grantwick without any major weather delays, they all feel we should have little to worry about during our march beyond there."

"Until we reach Kargoth," Leo remarked. "Who knows what the weather will be as we head into the mountains along the river?"

He sat bundled in his wool coat, the hood of which was flopped over his head already topped with a knitted cap. He cradled a mug of steaming tea in his hands to fend of the morning chill that burrowed determinedly into his body. Ever since he had been overwhelmed by the spirit in the Citadel's upper room, Leo felt sensitive to cooler temperatures, something that had never bothered him before. The lingering chills he experienced from time to time reminded him of the cold, lifelessness exuded from the invisible specter that nearly suffocated him upon opening the Spirit Box. He longed for the soothing warmth of spring to truly take hold.

"I can't wait to reach those mountains," Hobin said, standing to stretch his legs. His hair, damp with the morning air, settled on the frayed collar of his brown coat. "Having traveled in the open like a herd of cattle for most of this trip is not what I'm used to. I prefer wending my way through trees and hills, though I'll admit that the Red Mountains here seem nice enough." He suddenly lowered his voice. "I've heard that the wizard Caldurian was from this region."

"Born and raised here," Carmella said. "When he trained me for a short time at my home near Morrenwood, he mentioned a few stories about growing up close to the western slopes of the Red Mountains about a day's ride north of here." She sipped her tea while gazing into the fire. "King Justin told me in private that the wizard has been asking to meet with me."

"Why?" Leo asked with a wary inflection in his voice.

"To perhaps apologize for the way he treated me twenty years ago?" she suggested. "The King said that Caldurian simply wanted to talk to his former student and perhaps advance my learning."

"You don't plan to speak with that menace, do you?" Hobin asked, leaning against the side of the wagon.

Carmella shrugged. "I'm considering it, though only if King Justin is comfortable with the arrangement. Currently he is not." She thought back to the first few days when she had met the wizard. She had learned much about the magic arts in that short time and savored the sense of accomplishment she had achieved upon mastering a few simple spells. "I would be lying if I said I wasn't excited by the possibility of sharpening my skills under Caldurian's instruction."

But just as Leo, William and Hobin were about to protest, Carmella raised a hand to stop them. "But knowing what a scoundrel he's turned into, I could never be his student again simply to better myself. It would be unseemly."

Leo sighed with relief. "I'm glad to hear you say that."

She looked over the tips of the snapping flames and caught his gaze. "However, I might consider using him to prepare myself against my cousin. You all know, as does King Justin, that I mean to find her somewhere in Kargoth. And if Caldurian wants to make his time and skills available to me, who am I to argue?"

Leo shook his head with worry. "You know that Caldurian probably has an agenda of his own by wanting to meet with you."

"Oh, I realize that. He's *Caldurian*, after all," she replied with a chuckle. "But if he can help me, I'm going to consider it. And I don't want the three of you to breathe a word about this to anyone," she added, shaking a finger. "Trust me, I will be wary of Caldurian's words and actions should we meet. But this discussion may be for nothing since he is presumably still without his powers."

"I still wouldn't trust him," William replied. "Caldurian is as dangerous whether armed with magic spells or his own arrogance."

"And he has plenty of the latter from what I've heard," Hobin muttered. "But I'm not too concerned with that wizard's plight right now. I'm facing a far worse one."

"Oh?" Leo asked with unease. "What exactly?"

Hobin was riddled with grave concern. "Boredom! I'm eager to engage in a bit of scouting right about now. Waiting here day after day for King Justin to give the word is nearly killing me."

William laughed. "You'll soon have plenty of opportunities. After we pass beyond the southern borders of Drumaya, teams of scouts will be dispatched often to assess the way ahead."

"No doubt Vellan will have his scouts doing the same," Carmella said, sipping her tea. "After all, there's no way to hide this army from his eyes. He'll be aware of our approach to his borders soon, if not already."

"And he'll be prepared for us," Leo warned. "Vellan has many scores to settle, even without his Enâri creatures to back him up. So for all our worries about Caldurian," he added, giving the fire a quick stir and creating a sudden burst of sparks, "that wizard is merely a gadfly compared to what's waiting for us in Del Norác."

They broke camp in early morning and continued south along Lake Lasko. By early afternoon, after traveling miles upon rutty roads and across hilly terrain, the choppy lake waters faded from view as the army veered southwest, funneling into a valley between the second and third southernmost peaks in the Red Mountains. The tired troops camped for the night by one of the tributaries to the Swift River, then traveled for two more days through fertile farmland and along rushing rivers as the Red Mountains retreated behind them.

By early afternoon on that second day, the northern tree line of the Ebrean Forest, alive in rich hues of emerald green, slowly came into view as the army trekked down the western banks of the Swift River. They had at last entered the kingdom of Drumaya. Hours later, the armies of King Justin and King Rowan approached the city of Grantwick as the sun dipped in the southwest against a gauzy swath of orange and purple clouds. The blazing sphere appeared to fall into the green embrace of the Ebrean during its slow and steady descent. As the forces approached the city from the north, spread out across the field that lay between Grantwick and the Ebrean Forest was another city of sorts. Thousands of soldiers from the Five Clearings moved among a mass of gray and white tents and blazing bonfires. William was enthralled by the sight.

Shortly after their arrival, Kings Justin and Rowan, along with Prince Gregory, Prince William, Tolapari, Captain Grayling and a handful of other soldiers, passed through the western gate in the barricade that surrounded the center of Grantwick before the gates closed for the night. Leo, Carmella and Hobin also accompanied the group as everyone made their way on horseback to King's Quarters. A long line of budding oak trees stood guard near the main entrance. A while later, King Cedric greeted his guests inside, an infectious smile upon his oval shaped face. With him was Minister Nuraboc who ushered everyone into a reception area to enjoy some food and drink.

"Though I was delighted to visit you both at the Citadel this past winter," King Cedric remarked to his royal counterparts, "I am even more pleased to welcome you to Drumaya on the verge of a new spring and a new year four days hence. Winter has faded fast. A buried spring has been resurrected throughout the countryside. It will be a glorious season, I expect."

"If Vellan is defeated, indeed it will," King Justin replied, flashing a hard smile beneath his ice blue eyes. "But there is much work to be done."

"My army is ready and waiting," King Cedric assured him.

"As is mine," a familiar voice chimed in near the doorway. A tall man, freshly shaven, with light brown hair and leaf green eyes, walked confidently into the room and greeted the arrivals. "Sorry we're late," he said, "but some meetings never seem to end." Behind him was another man, slightly taller, his long, black hair tied up in back with a blood red piece of cloth.

"Eucádus!" William exclaimed, greeting his friend with a hug before looking up with an expectant smile. "Tell me, how is Chestnut doing these days?"

"I'm glad to see your priorities are in order, Will," he replied with a grin. "Your brother's horse is fine. And I'm not doing so badly either since our adventure in Rhiál."

"Glad to hear it," he said before greeting Ranen.

"Pleased to see you again, too, Eucádus," King Justin added with a handshake. "Sorry you couldn't attend our winter get-together at the Citadel, but I'm delighted to see that the army of the Five Clearings is camped outside with King Cedric's forces."

"We wouldn't have missed this for anything," Ranen jumped in with a fiery glint in his eyes. "Vellan is long overdue for a visit from us, and a rather raucous visit at that."

"Well said," the King replied, greeting the leader of the Oak Clearing before turning to King Cedric. "Now before we proceed, and with your indulgence, I would like to make a few introductions."

"By all means," said King Cedric. "Though many of our paths have crossed, all here are not yet acquainted with one another."

King Justin quickly introduced King Rowan, Leo, Carmella, Hobin, Captain Grayling and a few of the other men to Eucádus and Ranen. King Rowan was happy to meet Eucádus and thanked him for the kindness he had bestowed upon his grandson.

"William speaks highly of you and values your friendship," he said. "I'm honored that you've watched over him through many hardships."

"The honor is mine, King Rowan. Prince William has proved to be both a good friend and a fighter," Eucádus replied. "He has contributed much to our cause. And if he has not told you in detail of his exploits, then I'll be sure to do so one of these days."

"I look forward to it."

William, blushing slightly, looked at King Cedric. "I would be more than pleased, sir, if you would start this meeting at once so we can discuss more important matters."

"Understood. But first I think Eucádus and Ranen might like to know a little bit more about one of the guests here, specifically, Leo Marsh."

Leo shot a surprised glance at King Cedric, wondering why he had mentioned his name. Though he had met the King a few times when he visited the Citadel during winter, Leo had not developed a close relationship to him and had no idea why he had singled him out.

"Me, sir?" Leo asked respectfully.

King Cedric turned to Eucádus. "This is the young man I was telling you about a few days ago when you arrived. He is one of the two who volunteered for the mission to the Dunn Hills."

Eucádus appeared astounded by the news, stepping forward to shake Leo's hand with overwhelming gratitude. "So you are the one who helped rid our lands of the Enâri menace. King Cedric told me all about your journey through the Dunn Hills with another named Nicholas Raven and of your search for the wizard Frist. As I recall, he mentioned things about magic spells, a reforged key and a spirit imprisoned in an iron box for twenty years. They were heady words when I first heard them, the stuff of legends. But King Cedric insisted it was all true after hearing the tale himself from King Justin."

"He didn't mislead you," Leo replied, uncomfortable with the sudden attention. "Nicholas and I had set out from Morrenwood over four months ago to seek out Frist, not knowing if he was still alive." He told Eucádus and Ranen some of the details of his journey to their amazed delight. "But I will not take all the credit. Carmella brought us the medallion. Were it not for her befriending an Enâri creature, your three nations would still be under their grip." Leo indicated Hobin who stood quietly behind him. "And you must also thank Hobin for guiding Nicholas and me through the Dunn Hills, otherwise we would never have found our way to Wolf Lake."

"The citizens of Harlow, Linden and Surna are indebted to a great many people for ridding our lands of the Enâri, and on their behalf, I thank you," Eucádus said gratefully. "When word from our scouts first reached us in the Clearings that Vellan's creatures throughout the Northern Mountains had suddenly collapsed into piles of sand and garments, no one could believe it. But some of the scouts had seen the transformation with their own eyes and swore to the fact. And when people finally did believe that the stories were true, no one could explain why."

"We were astonished," Ranen added, "but no one could explain such a wondrous miracle until a few days ago. That's when King Cedric told us about Frist and the spirit he had created. Word of that peculiar tale had never reached our lands over the years."

King Justin looked up. "Vellan knew all about the Spirit Box, the contents of which were a constant threat to his prized creation. Caldurian, his loyal apprentice, got word to him twenty years ago after his defeat and humiliation in the village of Kanesbury. But fate was apparently on our side from the moment that Jagga had stolen the key until Leo turned it and opened the Spirit Box."

Eucádus was wide-eyed. "You *opened* the box, Leo? That detail I did not know."

"It's a detail I don't particularly like to think about," he said with a sad look in his eyes. Eucádus immediately picked up on it and avoided further mention of the topic.

"Still, I would like to thank you all again. Your deeds have begun healing our mountain nations and will be remembered with honor," he promised. "One day I hope to meet Nicholas Raven. Is he with you now?"

"No," Leo replied with a trace of hopelessness in his voice. "After completing our mission, Nicholas entrusted me with the key and went his separate way on another mission of sorts, a personal one. But we can discuss that later if you wish, though I have no knowledge of his whereabouts at the moment."

"I'll take you up on that offer," he said.

King Justin, sensing that Leo wished to change the subject, intervened. "There'll be time enough later for these harrowing stories and heroic accounts. But now I think we should press on with the meeting and discuss the next leg of our journey."

"Which fortunately, like the winter war council, will be refreshingly brief as most of the details have already been discussed in Morrenwood," King Cedric said. "Today's meeting is simply to gather together all the principals in this grand effort and make sure we're thinking with one mind before we continue on to Wynhall. There we will have more friends waiting to join us on our way to Kargoth."

"And there are even others besides them eager to join the fray," Prince Gregory informed the gathering, "though they will not be accompanying us on this march."

"Why not?" Ranen asked.

"Because they are already in Kargoth, or near enough."

Eucádus appeared stunned by the news. "Who are these warriors you speak of? A secret force you've already slipped into that vile land?"

"Not quite," he replied. "I refer to your own countrymen from the three mountain nations. They have banded together in the wild to fight against Vellan as best they could. Like those in the Five Clearings, they have given up relying upon the corrupt and weak governments of Harlow, Linden and Surna and have taken matters into their own hands."

"We know of a scattered resistance in the mountains, though we were doubtful of its effectiveness. Are they now prepared to fight?" Ranen excitedly asked.

"They have already done so," the prince continued, "though on a much smaller scale than what we have seen in Rhiál and Montavia. Mainly small raids against the Island invaders. But I have kept in contact with one of the groups and learned of a spring offensive they are planning. Various camps throughout the mountains were going to combine their men and resources throughout winter and converge at a secret location near Del Norác. They propose to raid Vellan's most notorious prison come springtime."

"Deshla," Eucádus said in a whisper. "I have heard stories of it, and none too pleasant. It is a facility under the command of the Islanders as far as I knew."

"Maybe your countrymen will have more than a good chance to free those held inside now that the Enâri have been crushed," King Justin said encouragingly.

"For that reason and another," Prince Gregory said. "The mountain resistance plans to coordinate their raid on Deshla with our actions against Vellan to optimize their success. I will meet with my contact, a scout named Maximilian, near the southern shore of Lake Mara so we can hash out the details."

"You're sure he will be there?" Ranen asked.

"Max is punctual if anything," the prince said. "We made arrangements for this meeting over winter. He will be there, no doubt impatiently waiting for us."

"I look forward to seeing him," Eucádus said.

"As do we all," King Cedric added, noting a hint of impatience on Minister Nuraboc's face. "But we can save some of this talk for later. If you would all join me at the table in the next room, we can begin our meeting."

"If you would please follow me," Minister Nuraboc said as she escorted the delegation to the meeting room with her usual no-nonsense efficiency.

"Judith will quickly tick off the items on the agenda, and with luck, you'll be enjoying a proper dinner before the hour is out," King Cedric announced while everyone filed out of the reception room.

"That's my kind of meeting," Hobin whispered to Leo. "Short and to the point."

Leo chuckled to himself, as eager as Hobin to be on his way to Kargoth. He wanted to end this chapter of his life so he could begin another with Megan. A short time later at the meeting, his thoughts again drifted to his true love. He imagined Megan thinking about him at that very same moment while wandering the corridors of the Citadel or walking along the melting snow banks on the Edelin River. With a sigh, Leo wondered when he would hold her hand again without the threat of war hanging over them like a fleet of storm clouds ever looming on the horizon.

CHAPTER 94

Spring's Healing Touch

The next day, Kings Justin and Rowan let the troops enjoy a one-day respite from their long and tiring journey. But when the second morning dawned upon the field, the armies of Arrondale and Montavia were ready to move, this time accompanied by King Cedric's forces and those from the Five Clearings. After tents and supplies were packed away, the orderly units of soldiers and well laden supply lines proceeded on their southerly march beneath blue skies. The gentle warmth of uninterrupted sunshine competed with a cool, steady breeze barreling down from the north along the path of the Swift River.

They made for the village of Wynhall about a day's march from Grantwick in good weather. Since the traveling conditions were exceptional, the army arrived that same day as purple twilight settled over the smoky rooftops and fallow fields of the community. Fiery stars peeked down from a crystalline sky, reflecting in the river's mirror-like surface that had calmed with the sudden deadening of the afternoon breezes.

Greeting the trio of warrior kings was Captain Silas from the army of Rhiál. He stood with a few of his men at the foot of a stone bridge spanning the Swift River. Prince Gregory, Eucádus and a few other captains were also present. Sprawled out upon a large field on the opposite side of the river below the eaves of the Bressan Woods was an encampment of nearly one thousand men, all citizens of Rhiál and Maranac.

King Cedric and the others dismounted and greeted Captain Silas like an old friend. The soldier's hazel eyes and shortly cropped hair were accentuated with a beaming smile of gratitude for the sacrifices these men had made to save Rhiál from Vellan's grasp. But King Cedric and his companions were just as grateful by the presence of Silas and his army, surprised to see so many men here after their conflict against Drogin.

"King Victor of Rhiál and Queen Melinda of Maranac send their greetings," Captain Silas said with a modest bow of his head. He wore a brown, weather-stained coat that matched his pants. Visible beneath the unbuttoned coat and over his gray woolen shirt was a dark blue vest with tiny nautical insignia stitched along the seams that brought to mind the vast beauty and windswept waters of Lake LaShear. "And though both King and Queen wish they could have sent more recruits, this is all they could spare. Some of our troops are still recovering from wartime injuries while many others are engaged in rebuilding the two kingdoms after Drogin's destruction."

"Your contribution is beyond what we had anticipated," King Justin replied, "and it gives me hope that we may nearly match the numbers that Vellan might throw at us now that his Enâri creatures are out of the count."

"But it will still be a formidable force," Prince Gregory said. "Though Vellan's troops have been reduced, he may substitute that lack of manpower with a more ruthless vengeance."

"I'll confidently put our forces up against anything Vellan has to offer," King Cedric remarked with a gritty smile. "We've already stopped his puppet, Drogin, and his Enâri thugs, so we can do the same to him."

"We'd received word of the Enâri demise some weeks ago," Silas said. "It was astounding news. I would like to know more."

"As would I," Eucádus said. "And to that end I promise to round up Leo Marsh later on, an individual instrumental in that affair. He can provide us additional details at his leisure. In the meantime, how is King Victor's health these days after his imprisonment? And when was he installed as Rhiál's monarch?"

"Both he and Queen Melinda were coronated in brief, simple ceremonies in their respective capitals a few weeks after the war. But with much urging from the public, they promised to hold a more formal ceremony in conjunction with their wedding later in the summer after the wounds of war have begun to heal."

"A wedding?" King Justin said. "I had thought such would be in the offing when I saw them holding hands on the balcony in Zaracosa. It will be a wholesome tonic for the kindred kingdoms."

"Soon again to be united," Silas remarked, explaining how King Victor and Queen Melinda had recently asked their respective populations about merging Rhiál and Maranac into a nation called New Maranac. "Public votes were arranged and the citizens on both sides of the lake resoundingly approved to bury the political mistakes of the past and unite again as one. New Maranac will officially come into existence on the first day of autumn several weeks after Victor and Melinda are married. The new capital city of Bellavon has been refurbished for their arrival."

"I'm glad at least one corner of Laparia seems to be healing," Prince Gregory said. "But what of the new King's wellbeing?"

"King Victor's health is progressing nicely. His knee injury is nearly mended so that he hardly needs his cane." Silas softly laughed. "He conveniently forgets it most times despite promptings from the Queen when she visits from across the lake. But King Victor would not yet be able to bear a long ride across the Kincarin Plains or endure the rigors of a battle in Kargoth despite his protests to the contrary. He desired to lead our men here, but after much convincing–though I do not think he was *fully* convinced–he relented to the sage advice of the royal physician and his bride-to-be."

"Rhiál needs the presence of a strong king during turbulent times," King Rowan interjected. "I know that from my trials in Montavia. And after King Basil's death on one side of Lake LaShear and King Hamil's assassination on the other, Victor and Melinda's proper places right now are in their respective capitals."

"I agree," the captain replied. "So as his representative, I will go into harm's way on this side of Laparia in repayment to all of you for restoring liberty in the future kingdom of New Maranac. It is a debt my soldiers and I are most honored to repay."

A veil of mist lay upon the river the next morning. Captain Silas' men crossed the bridge and joined the other armies on the west side of the water, all joyfully welcomed as brothers-in-arms. A shroud of hazy, white clouds lingered over the greening landscape as the sun rose above the horizon on winter's final day. But by noontime, the clouds had thickened and a steady drizzle of rain fell, dampening the army's spirit as it trudged along the river's reedy banks, yet the temperature moderated the farther south they moved.

They passed through several small villages, cheered on by locals who offered food and drink to lucky soldiers positioned on the edges of the lines. Most of the time, however, the troops saw only muddy farms awaiting spring planting or miles of scrubland dotted with an occasional outcropping of rock or rolling hills.

"I look forward to gazing upon the waters of Lake Mara," King Rowan remarked to Kings Justin and Cedric who rode on either side of him during this latest leg of the journey. The three Kings were warmly cloaked, their white breaths faintly rising as raindrops dripped off the edges of their hoods. "I've never traveled so far south in Laparia on this side of the Kincarin Plains."

"The blue water of Lake Mara is a sight to behold, especially in dazzling sunshine," King Cedric replied. "We'll reach the north tip by nightfall. Tomorrow you'll see her under a splendid sunrise."

"A spring sunrise," King Justin reminded them. "Tomorrow marks the first day of New Spring and the new year."

"But we were so enjoying this one," King Cedric joked.

King Rowan sighed as a thin smile faded from his lips. "May the year seven hundred and forty-three be a healing year for all of us–and a far sight better than seven forty-two," he said as his horse trotted contentedly along under a gentle rain. "Though that shouldn't be too difficult a goal to achieve."

"Many won't be sorry to see this year fade into history," King Justin said, his eyes fixed on the road ahead. "Though we've had our successes, it has been a grievous one for sure."

"We'll bid it farewell at the break of dawn tomorrow," King Cedric added with hope in his voice despite the lingering rain and the memories of a bloody year past. "May the new year bestow upon us thrice the blessings as compared to the sorrows visited upon Laparia over the last four seasons."

"I'll happily drink to that," King Justin said, "even if it be only with hot tea–assuming we can get a fire going when dusk nears and Lake Mara beckons to us."

King Rowan simply nodded, overwhelmed into silence by the many fond memories of Prince Brendan weaving lightly through his mind like a capricious spring breeze through an open window.

They neared the north tip of Lake Mara as evening shadows stretched eastward under a cloudy, moonless sky. The rain had ceased two hours ago, and the pleasant aromas of clean lake water, fresh ground foliage and rich soil mingled in the air. Campfires appeared up and down the lakeshore and on either side of the main road as the men pitched tents and enjoyed a warm meal. Thickets of budding deciduous trees and towering pines dotted the landscape and the water's edge. The glow of firelight flickered upon the water as sweet smelling smoke rose above the encampments and lingered over the troops like a hazy roof.

As the hours passed, the fires faded to glowing embers and soldiers took their rest except for those on guard duty. Sometime after midnight, the waning crescent Fox Moon rose in the east behind thinning clouds and cast its subtle light across the tops of the ghostly billows. Three hours later, the Bear Moon, a much thinner waning crescent, ascended in the east as the men slept and dreamed. In time, a light breeze stirred in the west. The clouds broke up and scattered, allowing the dual moons to gently illuminate the encampment below as they continued creeping westward.

Dawn broke a few hours later as a milky gray line stretched across the eastern horizon. The sky, now clear of clouds, shimmered in rich shades of ebony and deep blue as a multitude of stars blinked open like watchful eyes for the remaining moments of darkness.

Slowly, the first warm rays of the rising sun leaped above the horizon directly in the east. The sharp curve of the brilliant yellow sun gradually ascended above the cool waters of Lake Mara, marking the first day of a brand new spring with little fanfare, scattering a healing warmth and radiant light upon the plains, rivers and mountaintops. The year seven hundred and forty-three had arrived.

William enjoyed breakfast along the shoreline with Eucádus, Ramsey and other soldiers that morning, reminiscing about the war in Rhiál. Sunlight sparkled upon the waters of Lake Mara and sliced through nearby tree branches, their supple edges glowing with an emerald luminescence. The cool, crisp air of the first spring morning revived everyone's hope and strength.

"I'd like to visit the Star Clearing one more time," William said as he munched on a honey biscuit and sipped from a mug of steaming tea. He sat on a rock embedded in the dirt as a fire crackled and sparked amid swirls of gray and blue smoke. "But regardless of the war's outcome, I don't suppose you'll be going back there."

"If things go ill, we definitely won't return," Ramsey said, "mainly because we'll probably all be dead." He rubbed his whiskers and grinned upon hearing William's laughter at his dark joke.

"On the other hand," Eucádus jumped in, "should we defeat Vellan–and I intend for us to do so–we'll most likely make a short visit to the Clearings to retrieve our possessions before moving back to Harlow, Linden and Surna. Despite becoming a dear second home, most of us miss our real homes even though the Five Clearings were the only dwellings some of our children had ever lived in. But I don't expect anyone will want to continue living in the Ebrean Forest if our nations are eventually freed."

"You're probably right," William said, eyeing the ground as he took another sip of tea. "Still, it'd be nice to see the Star Clearing one last time–and areas thereabouts."

Eucádus shot a knowing glance at Ramsey before speaking to William with gentle understanding. "We would be honored to take you back to the cabin where your brother is buried, Will. Ramsey had mentioned that very thing to me only yesterday. We also discussed the subject with your grandfather when he inquired about doing so."

"Really?" William looked up hopefully.

Ramsey nodded. "After this war is over and we're still breathing, we can return to Brendan's resting spot and retrieve his body. King Rowan wants to transport him back to Montavia with honor for a proper burial at home."

William smiled with relief. "That would soothe my troubled heart very much. Ever since traveling in these lands again, that awful day in the cabin is all I seem to think about. Taking Brendan's body home will help ease the grief of many people, especially my mother. She was devastated by my brother's death."

"Vilna seems very strong in spirit from what your grandfather had told me," Eucádus replied. "Despite a heartache that will never subside, she will endure and thrive just as you have, which is an admirable trait and a lasting tribute to your brother."

"She'll be glad to have him back home," he said, gazing at the tendrils of steam rising from his cup. "And so will I."

The journey commenced after breakfast. Lake Mara remained a constant companion on the troops' left, sometimes disappearing in part behind thickets of trees or dense brush, while other times gazing upon the soldiers like a vast blue eye, windswept at times though always lapping upon shores of stone, sand or spongy grass depending on the terrain. By midmorning the sun climbed above the water, but the air remained cool and comfortable with the scent of a new spring day rolling lightly upon the air.

"What would you do with moonflowers, Carmella, if you found any?" Leo posed this question as his horse sauntered alongside her enclosed wagon to his right as they moved southward amid a sea of supply carts. Hobin rode farther up the line with King Justin and Tolapari to discuss his plans for mapping portions of Arrondale.

"The leaves of the moonflower can be used in many potions," she said, "though they are hard to come by in parts north. They are plentiful in the southern regions of the Northern Mountains."

"Near the southern border of Kargoth?" Leo asked with much concern.

Carmella nodded. "I asked Prince Gregory to mention it to King Justin before I approach him. I want to slip away for a few hours some evening and search among the foothills for specimens. It will be well worth the effort."

"If he grants permission, Hobin and I will accompany you. Even though we'd still be far from Del Norác, I don't want you wandering alone in Kargoth, especially at night."

"That's the best time to pick moonflowers as they are at their most potent," she explained. "Besides, the Enâri are no longer a threat. I'll be perfectly fine."

"Vellan has other allies roaming about his lands, some even miles away from the capital city," he warned. "I'm going with you. Megan would scold me for sure if I didn't."

"We'll save this debate for another time," Carmella said with good humor as her wagon rattled along the well-worn dirt road. "But in the meantime, I– Oh, look," she said, pointing up ahead to a horse slowly making its way toward them among the lines of wagons. Atop it sat Prince William who waved at Carmella and Leo as he drew nearer. "We have a visitor this morning."

"A bored visitor," William said as he expertly turned his horse around and was soon accompanying Carmella to his left. "I just came back from riding with Eucádus and the others about a quarter mile up the line. He was going to send a messenger, but I volunteered to dispel the monotony."

"It's not much more exciting down here," Leo said. "What did Eucádus want?"

"He was hoping you might join them, Leo, and recount your mission to the Dunn Hills. They all have many questions. Besides, we've talked to death about our adventures in Rhiál and are in desperate need of a new topic of conversation. If you're willing to indulge us, it would be greatly appreciated."

Carmella smiled broadly. "I think Leo would be more than happy to follow you back, Prince William. Though he probably won't admit it, I suspect he's getting rather bored by me prattling on about moonflowers and magic."

"I've been quite fascinated," Leo replied. "But if Eucádus has requested my presence, who am I to refuse?"

"Then you had better go," she said pleasantly. "It will give me time to think."

"About what?" William asked.

"About, well–moonflowers, of course," she replied.

Moments later, Leo and William disappeared on their steeds among the other wagons, leaving Carmella alone with thoughts about the path she would take in the days ahead–a solitary path, if she could pull it off. She lightly held the reins, plotting out a string of steps that she hoped would lead her straight to Madeline.

Leo followed William out of the swarm of wagons rumbling along the main road. They guided their horses to a wide, grassy strip between the road and Lake Mara. They could move faster now and soon passed the front of the supply line. There was an empty space in the road at that point until they reached the tail end of a company of marching soldiers just ahead.

"Eucádus and the others are farther up the road," William said, pointing south.

His gaze shifted left about a quarter mile ahead toward the lakeshore where he spotted a thin trail of bluish smoke snaking into the air from a single campfire. He didn't give it a second thought though because Prince Gregory, also on horseback, suddenly stepped out of the unit of marching soldiers just ahead of them. William and Leo sauntered up to him and were greeted with a smile.

"What mischief are you men up to today?" the prince asked, reining his horse to a halt.

"Will and his friends apparently need to be entertained," Leo joked, briefly explaining where they were going.

"Inspecting the troops?" William inquired of his fellow prince.

"Not quite. I see someone camping by the shore," he replied, pointing to the rising smoke William had noticed moments ago. "I'm guessing that Maximilian has showed up, early as usual. He had promised to meet me near the southern portion of Lake Mara so we could coordinate our strategies. His resistance fighters in the Northern Mountains are preparing to strike Deshla prison. They want to launch their attack as we strike Vellan's stronghold at Del Norác."

"I hope Maximilian's fellow soldiers possess a better sense of direction. He is quite far from the southern end of the lake."

Prince Gregory chuckled. "No doubt Max had reached the appointed spot days ago and got bored waiting there. He must have hiked up along the lake knowing he would eventually run into us. Max gets restless when he's not busy. I'll introduce him to both of you after we discuss our itineraries."

"I look forward to it," Leo said. "But please excuse us now as I have to discuss my adventures in the Dunn Hills–*again*–with some who haven't yet heard the entire story."

"Enjoy the attention while you can because one day people might stop asking," Prince Gregory advised. "You performed a task you should be proud of, Leo. Certainly many others are proud of you, so enjoy hearing about it."

"Since you put it that way, maybe I can embellish the details a bit for their enjoyment. But just a bit."

He indicated for William to lead on. They continued along the roadside as Prince Gregory made his way to the campfire on the edge of Lake Mara and soon disappeared from view.

Minutes later, William and Leo waded into another company of soldiers. Many in this unit were also on horseback. Soon they found Eucádus engaged in lively conversation with Captain Silas and Ranen. Also riding with them were Captains Tiber and Grayling as well as Ramsey and a few other soldiers. All were in high spirits.

"Ah, just the man we're looking for!" Eucádus said when he saw Leo approach, greeting him with a sense of familiarity as if he had known him for years. Leo was put immediately at ease. "Thank you for stopping by on such short notice."

"And for elevating the quality of our conversation!" Ramsey quipped.

Eucádus turned more serious as he beckoned Leo to his side. "If it's not too much to ask, you must recount the adventures of you, Nicholas Raven and your guide to reforge the key to the Spirit Box. Since you rid our homelands of the Enâri pestilence, it is a story I must tell my wife and children." He offered a heartfelt smile. "We are in your debt, Leo Marsh."

"You are overly kind." Leo noted the glances tossed his way by the others. Even William's interest seemed piqued though the young prince already knew much of the story. "Now where should I begin? When I first met Nicholas and Princess Megan who involved me in all this intrigue?" He smiled, recalling his introduction to Megan moments after he had landed headfirst in a large mud puddle. "Or should I start when Nicholas, Megan and I met Carmella on the road with her Enâri companion, Jagga, the one who had given her the magic medallion?"

Eucádus leaned back in his saddle, relaxed and enjoying the outdoors. "It's a long journey to the southern border of Kargoth, Leo, and then a substantial trek from there to Del Norác. You might as well give us the extended version."

"Very well," he replied. "Just don't complain if you start to get bored. You had your chance for a more concise account."

Leo began his tale when Nicholas and Megan arrived on his father's apple wagon one glorious autumn evening. Fifteen minutes later, with all ears and eyes of his audience still attentive, his narrative had reached the seaside village of Boros. But just as Leo had his listeners on the edges of their saddles awaiting more details, a frantic call sliced through the air from outside the line.

"Prince William! Leo!"

Leo stopped speaking as he and the others glanced left. All were surprised to see Prince Gregory guiding his horse to the center of their gathering with a look of stunned disbelief. Leo and William eyed one another, fearing that Maximilian had revealed some terrible news to the prince.

"Trouble, Prince Gregory?" Eucádus inquired, his senses on alert. "The enemy?"

"No, not the enemy."

"Did Maximilian bring ill tidings?" William asked. "By your startled expression, I'm guessing your meeting didn't go as planned."

"It did not. And about Max, well he…" Prince Gregory was momentarily distracted, observing the boy's face as the sun reflected off the youngster's blond hair and light brown eyes. "No, it didn't go as planned, Will." He then addressed Captains Silas, Tiber and Grayling. "I need you three to halt this line at once. We must make an unscheduled stop. Fan out with those you need and spread the word."

"At once," Silas replied, nodding to his fellow captains. Soon the three departed with several aides, riding up and down the lines to bring the army to a standstill.

"Ranen and Ramsey, can you find our trio of Kings and send them this way at once?" he continued. "My father was near the head of the line with Tolapari and Hobin the last I heard. Kings Cedric and Rowan were making their rounds along the western flank."

"They're as good as here," Ranen assured him as he and Ramsey hurried off.

"What is going on?" asked Eucádus.

"I'll tell you shortly," Prince Gregory replied. "But follow me first. William and Leo as well."

Moments later, Prince Gregory waited on the grassy strip of land with his three companions as word spread through the army about the unscheduled stop. In time, the marching troops, trotting horses and rumbling wagons grinded to a long and slow halt as a gentle spring breeze swept across the lake. Minutes later, Kings Cedric and Rowan rode up on the grass and greeted the others with bewildered expressions. But before Prince Gregory could explain anything, King Justin approached from the distance and joined the gathering, a stern, questioning eye aimed squarely at his son.

"You will appreciate my reason, Father, if you and the others follow me to the lakeside." The prince indicated the spiraling trail of wood smoke drifting into the air near the camp now a short distance to the north. The army had since passed by that spot when Gregory first approached Eucádus and the others.

"Lead on," King Justin calmly replied, though with a gruff edge to his voice. "Ranen told me that Maximilian had arrived. He had better have some especially compelling news to justify bringing this army to a standstill."

"Rumors of Maximilian's appearance are just that–rumors," the prince said. "But follow me and all will be explained."

King Justin threw skeptical glances at the other two Kings, wondering if they shared his nagging doubts. Prince Gregory guided his horse north along the grass for a short distance before veering right toward the lone campsite on Lake Mara. The soldiers on the roadside watched in respectful silence. A few whispered among themselves about why the army would suddenly stop near a single campfire and a thicket of pines trees overhanging the water and the grassy shoreline.

As the seven riders neared the site, the aroma of cooking fish filled the air. A gutted trout fixed to a wooden spit was roasting over a low fire. Through a haze of bluish smoke and a shimmering veil of heat rising above the circular fire pit, the seven men observed another man standing by the water's edge with his back to them, unmoving while gazing contemplatively across the lake. The stranger wore a long brown coat, weather stained and frayed along the bottom hem, with the hood thrown over his head and his arms hanging at his side. At first glance, Leo thought there was something oddly familiar about the person. Suddenly it struck him just as it did the others as they all dismounted. Leo and the man by the lake were wearing the exact same coats, only Leo's garment was much cleaner and in better condition. He immediately thought of Nicholas, knowing that the seamstresses in the Blue Citadel had sewn identical coats for their journey to the Dunn Hills. Leo was about to call out his name when Prince Gregory stepped forward and spoke to the man by the water.

"I've returned with my friends," he said in a calm voice, causing the stranger to slightly flinch as if he had been lost in a daydream. "We'd like to talk with you."

Slowly the man turned around, his face partially obscured by his hood and the wavering shadows created as the sun flickered through the branches of sweet pine. He stood there for a moment and faced the new arrivals before raising his hands and gently pulling back the hood of his coat. A wave of stunned silence swept across the seven men as they gazed upon the face of a young man only a couple of years older than William. His sea blue eyes framed by locks of blond hair looked back with calm curiosity.

William's heart leaped in his chest. He took a deep breath, unable to believe what he saw. He tried to speak for several flustered moments, only able to move his lips at first, until he finally found the wits and ability to whisper one word.

"*Brendan?*"

King Rowan's hands shook when he saw his oldest grandson standing only a few feet away from him, the grandson whom he thought had been killed in the woods of the Ebrean Forest miles to the west. He couldn't find any words to say and simply walked toward the young man as did William, both with tears in their eyes, until they stood face to face with their long lost loved one.

"I can't believe my eyes," King Rowan said as a smile slowly replaced his mystified expression. He gently laid a hand upon Brendan's shoulder to make sure he was a living being and not an apparition or a figment of his imagination. "But here you are."

"How is this possible?" William asked, looking up at his brother, his eyes wide with wonder and delight. He was about to speak further, but nearly bursting with joy he instead lunged forward to Brendan's surprise and hugged his brother with all his might as more tears welled up in his eyes. He still couldn't fully believe that his brother was here even though his arms were tightly wrapped around his shoulders.

"Will, let Brendan catch his breath," King Rowan said with gentle laughter after a moment had passed.

William finally stepped back, smiling as he repeatedly wiped the tears from his cheeks. He gazed at Brendan until he trusted his instincts that it really was his brother standing there. Through his dizzying shock, he at last managed to ask the question on his lips.

"Brendan, how did you get here?" he said breathlessly. "How are you—*alive*?"

Brendan stared at William and his grandfather as a warm wind blew. A kind yet bemused look was upon his face as he tried to guess their thoughts. "*William*?" he finally replied, his eyebrows rising as his brother nodded, eagerly awaiting Brendan's next words. "Do we know each other?"

END OF PART NINE

PART TEN
IN ENEMY TERRITORY

CHAPTER 95

Numerous Narratives

Nicholas and Max sauntered along the southwestern edge of the Ebrean Forest on horseback, each with coats buttoned high and hoods draped over their heads. It was a gray and misty morning three days before the new year. The sweet scent of pine lingered in the air with the aroma of rich soil lying beneath the grassy expanse to their right. The recently melted snow had renewed the landscape, giving promise of an early spring that would also arrive in three days. They had left the encampment in the northern reaches of the Champeko Forest four days ago on their journey to Lake Mara.

Earlier in Mid Winter, Malek had led Nicholas and the other rebels to their temporary camp near Petaras Peak. Ten days later, they continued south through the mountains over several wintry weeks until reaching the northern border of the Champeko Forest. There the resistance fighters from dozens of camps had gathered, finalizing plans beneath snow-laden trees for their springtime raid on Deshla prison. As winter released her grip, Max and Nicholas bid their friends goodbye. They set out eastward to meet with Prince Gregory and coordinate the coalition army's attack against Vellan with their own raid on Deshla.

For two days, Max had guided Nicholas east through a stretch of smaller mountains beyond Mount Lundy and Mount Minakaris until they reached the Bellunboro River on Linden's western border. They spent the night along the water miles from the nearest village or farm. With the Enâri threat eliminated and no sign of Vellan's collaborators from the Northern Isles, both enjoyed a restful night's sleep.

"I'm guessing that whatever presence the Islanders had here in Linden or in the other mountain nations has been greatly reduced after the Enâri met their demise," Max had told Nicholas as they ate a brief meal that night. "Most, if not all of the Islanders were probably ordered back to Del Norác to bolster Vellan's depleted army."

"Those who haven't already deserted," Nicholas replied with a chuckle. "The Islanders have to suspect that King Justin will be coming for them after the victories in Rhiál and Montavia. I'll bet many of them wish they had never crossed the Trillium Sea."

"Maybe so," Max said as he stoked the campfire. "But they're here regardless–and soon war will be here, too. And such is the state of affairs," he said with a sigh. "Now we just have to weather it."

Nicholas nodded, having acknowledged such obvious wisdom many times since leaving Kanesbury. He wistfully wondered when, or if, he'd ever return.

They followed the Ebrean Forest on Linden's eastern border for two full days and part of a third, reaching the southernmost point of the trees at midday and entering the realm of Drumaya. From there they veered slightly southeast away from the woods and into the gently rolling hills and farmland of the kingdom's southern region, making for the south shores of Lake Mara. They spent that night, the last day of winter, among a thicket of budding maple trees along a rushing stream. Nicholas was happy to be out and about the open countryside again, having felt confined living among the mountains during winter, all the while tormented by thoughts of Ivy's plight. But now that spring had arrived and the raid on Deshla was in the offing, he hoped to get his life moving again, and that meant resuming his search for Ivy. Deshla would be the first placed he looked.

"How horrible a place is that prison?" he asked Max early the following morning. They guided their horses through a small valley thick with new foliage amid cool breezes and abundant sunshine, an idyllic first day of spring.

Max guessed that Nicholas had imagined Ivy languishing in that dreadful spot. "I've heard awful stories about what the prisoners of Deshla endure–lack of food, brutality, isolation." He noted Nicholas looking askance at him, his complexion pale, his features hardened. "Yet I've never spoken to anyone who escaped or was released from the place. And nobody I know has talked to a former prisoner either, so I can't say anything based on fact, only rumor."

Nicholas sighed, steeped in misery. "That's not a good sign, Max. If nobody has spoken to a former prisoner, maybe nobody ever gets out of Deshla alive."

"No, I'd guess not." He glanced at Nicholas who now looked straight ahead, his hood draped over his shoulders as a thin breeze tousled his hair. "Still, we can't know for sure if Ivy is there or with Vellan or–"

"–or lost altogether?" Nicholas eyed Max, his expression indecipherable.

Max offered a reassuring smile. "Let's meet with Prince Gregory first. We'll sort out the rest later."

Nicholas nodded and turned his melancholy gaze back upon the green vista ahead, yearning to see the welcoming blue waters of Lake Mara looming upon the horizon.

Later that morning as the sun climbed higher in the east, the weary travelers arrived at the lake's stony shore. Gentle waves lapped upon a blanket of colorful, smooth stones littering the water's edge that was partially shaded by several large pines and other deciduous trees still in their budding stages. Seeing no signs of a recently passing army over this open, roadless region, Max suggested that they set up camp near a clump of trees for the remainder of the day and enjoy some well deserved rest.

"Tomorrow we'll head north along the lake." Max removed his gear and supplies from Graylocks. "We're sure to encounter King Justin's troops one of these days. I don't want to waste my valuable time waiting here until they show up."

"I won't mind sitting by a fire and doing nothing for a while," Nicholas replied as he similarly unburdened his horse, a light brown steed with a narrow white stripe running down its nose. He led the animal to the water where it joined its companion for a drink.

"Then find some dry wood and start one while I check our provisions," Max said. "We should have enough food left until the army arrives, though a bit of roasted fish will be a nice change. I'll toss a line in the lake and see how the new year rewards us."

"Kindly, I hope." Nicholas set out to scour the area for firewood. "I'm tired of dry venison and even drier biscuits."

He fondly recalled all the delicious foods he and Ivy had enjoyed at the party in Illingboc. One full season ago life had been good, offering music, dancing and precious time with the woman he loved. Now, three months later, with the sun shining down from cobalt blue skies and the air warm and light, Nicholas' heart felt empty and cold. He wondered if his journey had been in vain. But less than an hour later as he sat against a tree near a crackling fire and stared across the lake, he silently vowed to trudge on and continue searching for Ivy, whatever her fate. With a heavy exhalation, his eyes closed as soothing sleep gently took hold of him.

They slept under a cold, starry sky that night. Nicholas and Max took turns tending to the campfire as they lay bundled up in their coats and blankets. They rose early the next morning as the sun peeked over the misty lake like a curious eye, scattering its golden light through gauzy vapors floating upon the tranquil waters. After breakfast, they ambled north along the lake for a couple of hours as the day slowly warmed. The sharp cries of distant blue jays competed with chattering clouds of blackbirds perched in nearby trees.

The terrain slowly rose by midmorning. Nicholas and Max now traveled upon a tree-lined ridge overlooking the lake as gentle waves lapped against the shoreline below. Both men savored the stunning view over the next couple of miles, but it was short-lived. In time the elevation gradually descended until they were again at water level. Billowy clouds passed overhead from the west, shielding the sun from time to time. But the sky remained blue and crisp as far as the eye could see.

"It's time we ate lunch," Max suggested a few hours later. They stopped along a narrow, stony stretch of shoreline bordered by wild grass and weeds to the west, dotted here and there with clumps of trees. "Build a fire while I hook a few more lake trout. The ones I prepared yesterday were particularly delicious, if I do say so myself."

"They were." Nicholas stretched when his feet hit the ground. He felt in a fairer mood today, having enjoyed the leisurely ride north. The open solitude served as a balm for his weary limbs and bruised spirits. He began to appreciate Max's desire to take on missions by himself, learning to value time alone and clearing one's head of distractions.

They lingered after lunch, allowing the fire to burn down to a pile of embers that glowed like watchful eyes. Nicholas settled in for another nap against a large oak. Max tended to the horses, cleaning their hooves and brushing them down. The chirping of distant birds and the lapping waves cast a hypnotic serenity across the landscape. But only minutes later Max looked up, thinking he had heard a distant rumble of thunder. He scanned the northern horizon and soon three men on horses drew near. Seeing Nicholas still asleep in the cool shade of the oak, Max let him enjoy his rest and greeted the visitors. He immediately recognized one of the faces and smiled.

"Punctual as usual," Prince Gregory said as he dismounted. He extended a hand to Max. "It's good to see you again, my friend."

"And you, Prince Gregory, though I anticipated waiting a few more days. I've timed my arrival perfectly." Max eyed the other two men on horseback and scratched his head. "So is this the army that your father sent to confront Vellan?"

The prince laughed. "The rest are about a mile back just beyond that low ridge," he replied, pointing north across the lush landscape. "You'll see them shortly. I, however, spotted the trail of smoke from your fire and decided to investigate for myself, assuming that this time it was really you camped out along the lakeside."

Max furrowed his brow. "*This time*? Have you met others along this desolate stretch?"

The prince nodded, a vague smile upon his lips. "It's a long story which I'll fill you in on later, but first we need to–" He suddenly cut his words short when he saw a man emerge from the shadow of the nearby oak, stretching and running a hand through his mop of brown hair. "You brought company along, Max. It's so unlike you to–" Prince Gregory again stopped himself as Nicholas drew nearer. His eyes widened in disbelief when he recognized the young man's face, though he continued to look on in bewilderment. Nicholas hurried over to greet him.

"Prince Gregory!" he piped up with a smile as he shook the man's hand. "Happy to see you again. It's been far too long."

"Nicholas Raven?" he replied, his tone a mix of astonishment and disbelief. "What in all of Laparia are you doing here?"

"That, too, is a long story," Max said, "though Nicholas will be happy to recount the details at your convenience."

"I can't wait to hear them." The prince looked upon Nicholas as if he had seen a ghost, almost at a loss for words. "This marks two days in a row that I've been astounded by a surprise visitor on the shores of Lake Mara."

"What are you talking about?" Nicholas inquired.

Prince Gregory shook his head, trying to make sense of all that had happened in so short a time. "I'll explain later, but first tell me this. Did you find Ivy? Leo Marsh told us of your quest after he returned to the Citadel with the key." Nicholas' smile quickly vanished and Prince Gregory needed no further explanation.

"I'm still searching," he said, "yet haven't given up hope."

"Nor should you," the prince replied with heartfelt sincerity. "And when you feel up to it, I'll be eager to hear all that has transpired, as will Leo."

Nicholas was taken aback. "Leo is here?"

Prince Gregory nodded. "He refused to remain at the Citadel. Your guide, Hobin, accompanied him as well. And Carmella, too."

A smile returned to Nicholas' face. He couldn't wait to see his dear friends and asked where they could be located. Just then, the front lines of the army advanced over the low ridge. Prince Gregory dispatched the two soldiers on horseback to find King Justin and inform him that Maximilian had arrived with a surprise visitor. They rode out as the lines of soldiers and supply wagons slowly came to a stop a quarter mile up the lake.

"My father will allow the army an extended rest for the remainder of the day now that you're here," Prince Gregory told Max. "All of us could use a break after the many miles we've endured over the past thirteen days. In the meantime, we'll coordinate our respective timetables for the attacks on Del Norác and

Deshla. If you'll follow me, we'll find the King and his counterparts. My father will be eager to see you both."

"If you don't mind," Nicholas said, "I'd like to pay a surprise visit to Leo and Hobin first. I'll be the last person they ever expected to see here."

"You'll probably find both of them with Carmella somewhere on the east flank along the last third of the line. Just look for her rickety wagon and colorful cloak."

"I remember both with clarity," he said. "And I promise to pay my respects to King Justin shortly thereafter."

"Take all the time you need. After having had that key remade and returned to the Citadel, my father will allow you all the leeway in the world."

After gathering their things, Nicholas and Max climbed on their horses and accompanied the prince toward the now motionless army. Nicholas took leave of his companions when Max and the prince veered to the west side of the massive military line to locate King Justin. He eagerly continued along the lakeside for several minutes, passing companies of soldiers who had already spread out in an orderly fashion over the open field to set up their encampments. Tents were quickly raised and firewood gathered among a scattering of tree thickets for the extended stay until tomorrow morning.

Soon Nicholas neared the supply lines on his left, keeping his eyes peeled for any sign of Carmella's boarded-up wagon. All the horse-drawn carts filled with food and other supplies were being spaced out forward and to the west to create enough room where the drivers and their staffs could set up individual camps next to each vehicle. Nicholas weaved his way in and out of the grunting horses and bustling workers who were tending to their temporary quarters while simultaneously planning for the distribution of food rations for the evening meal. Some of the soldiers were sent out with nets and lines to fish on the lake while others hunted in a stretch of nearby woods and fields for small game to supplement and extend the supplies of preserved meats and other provisions.

Finally, through a small crowd of shifting people carrying armfuls of firewood and baskets of food, Nicholas spotted a woman sitting on a small crate in the near distance with a cloak of bright colors draped over her shoulders, her back partially turned to him.

He had found Carmella, noting her light blond hair slightly unkempt as usual, and a pair of beige gloves extending up to the middle of her forearms. Her horse and wagon stood under the thin shadow of a bony maple tree. Carmella was talking to a man building a fire in a small circle of rocks. Nicholas smiled as he observed Hobin, happily busy in his element as he struck a pair of fire stones over dry tinder to start a blaze. Sitting on another crate to Carmella's left was Leo. He wore an unbuttoned wool coat and a knitted cap despite the mild weather. Nicholas dismounted and observed the trio from a few yards away as they talked among themselves, unaware of his presence. He was delighted to see his friends again as the torment and loneliness of the past several weeks slipped off his shoulders like a burdensome traveling pack.

"What I'd give for some fresh game right now," Hobin said as the first flaming tongues reached up from the fire pit. He added bits of kindling to fuel the blaze, blowing a gentle stream of air at the base. "I'll head out into the field shortly and see what these lands can provide. A bit of turkey or rabbit would go down nicely. Or maybe I should try my hand at the lake?"

"Can't you sit still even for a moment?" Carmella asked with a cheery laugh.

Hobin glanced at Leo who appeared distracted by a pleasant daydream. "Are you imagining the enticing aroma of roasted turkey?"

"No," he replied. "I was recalling a wonderful meal I had at the Plum Orchard Inn. Roasted pork and vegetables, freshly baked biscuits and a bowl of–"

"–apple-cinnamon relish. Here we are on the verge of battle, and all you and Hobin can think about is food?" a voice interrupted from behind. In unison, Leo and Carmella turned around in their seats and Hobin looked up from the fire, all wide-eyed with mouths agape as Nicholas stood before them wearing a crooked grin.

"*Nicholas*?" Leo jumped up and did a double take upon seeing his friend, unable to fathom how he could really be here as he walked over and gave him a hug. "I can't believe it's you!" he excitedly said, rapidly firing a series of questions about how he had arrived and where he had been. But before Nicholas could answer, Leo looked around, noticing that he was alone. His enthusiasm waned, replaced by an air of cautious optimism. "And Ivy?" he softly added. "Did you find her?"

"Yes and no," he replied with little emotion, dampening the celebratory mood. "I'll explain soon, but first I want to hear from all of you. I've missed you terribly."

"As have we," Carmella said, standing up and wrapping her arms around Nicholas as if he were her son. "I was heartbroken when I learned that Leo had returned to the Citadel without you, but your being here is the best news we've had in quite some time."

"My sentiments exactly!" Hobin added with a hug of his own, delighted to see his hiking companions together again. "I honestly didn't think I'd ever see you again, Nicholas, as you had your heart set on going to the Northern Isles."

"I had my heart set on finding Ivy," he replied. "Fortunately though, I didn't have to go there."

"Oh? Tell us what happened," Carmella said. "You've been on our minds every day since you left the Citadel."

"I can say the same about all of you," he replied, gazing fondly upon his friends.

The four were soon sitting in front of the fire discussing their adventures, seemingly in a world of their own as the army units went about their business. Nicholas recounted his time in Illingboc, his adventures aboard the *Bretic* and his rescue of Ivy on Karg Island. All listened with amazement as his story continued up the Lorren and Gray Rivers, and then with dismay as he explained how he and Ivy were forcibly separated.

"Though my search has been a leap of faith, she is most likely in Del Norác," Nicholas said. "And my only companion most of the way has been blind hope, at least until I met Malek and his friends. Despite the impending raid on Deshla, my prospects of finding Ivy don't look encouraging."

"You found *us*," Carmella said with a buoyant smile. "Take heart in that for now."

"I will," he said, bowing his head with a hint of despondency. Suddenly his mood changed and he looked up at the others with a smile. "But you're not the only ones I found. I had nearly forgotten."

"What are you talking about?" Leo asked.

"You won't believe who Ivy and I visited on our way back to Morrenwood before Brin took us captive. You especially, Hobin."

Hobin furrowed his brow. "I don't know anybody in those parts."

"Oh, I think you might." Nicholas described the time he and Ivy spent in Illingboc, including the party they had attended. "While leaving the festivities, we met a young lady named Miriam who wore a stone pendant tinted a light shade of blue. It gave off silver flashes when the light hit it." He caught Hobin's steely gaze now filled with a swirl of heartfelt memories. "The stone was identical to the one you carry, Hobin. Miriam said that her Aunt Emma had given it to her."

Hobin sat speechless, his mind drifting back years ago to the shores of Lake Lily where he and Emma had found the pair of stones and fell in love. "What'd she say of her aunt?" he asked after clearing his throat.

Nicholas recounted the visit to Emma's farmhouse. "Her name is Emma Covey, but she lives alone as her husband had drowned years ago when they lived near the sea. She never remarried. Emma was moved when she saw the stone again." He explained that Emma had left a note for Hobin with a neighbor twenty years ago before her family moved away from Lake Lily. "Over the next two years, she and her family had moved to other temporary homes until they eventually left the Dunn Hills and settled down along the Crescent."

"I never received her note when I returned to the lake that following summer," Hobin sadly replied. "Maybe whoever held it had moved on as well, or lost it or forgot about it. I asked for information about Emma and her family and even searched for her in some nearby villages, but no luck. Too much time and distance had intervened. And now..." Hobin sighed, looking at the ground.

"And now she still loves you," Nicholas said. Hobin slowly raised his head upon hearing those words, filled with mixed emotions. "She told Ivy and me that she had never stopped loving you and would like to see you again. I promised to get word to you, assuming I'd see you either in Morrenwood or back home in Woodwater." He chuckled to break the tension, putting Hobin at ease. "As you can see, that didn't work out very well."

A thin smile crossed Hobin's face. "No, I guess not." He stood up, folding his arms tightly about his chest as he haltingly paced about. "Emma actually said that she wanted to see me again?"

"Several times. All you have to do is ride north. I can draw a map to her house."

Hobin caressed his chin. "Well isn't that something, and after all these years."

He continued to pace, silently debating with himself as if the others weren't present. Nicholas, Leo and Carmella glanced at one another and smiled, delighted for their friend. Curiosity got the best of Carmella and she asked Hobin pointblank.

"So, what are you going to do about it?"

Hobin turned and glanced at his friends, startled back into the moment. "I'm going to think about it," he said, sitting back down. "And I'm going to think about it *alone*." He shot a glance at Nicholas. "Still, you might want to start drawing that map."

"Happy to."

"A good first step, Hobin," Carmella said encouragingly, patting his arm. "And if you'd like to talk more about it later..."

"That's the last thing I want to do," he grumbled, though his mood was still upbeat. "Now can we please change the subject?"

"I think we'd better," Leo chimed in with amusement. "Let's not push the man."

"Thank you," he replied as he added fuel to the fire. "Now, Nicholas, tell us about Ivy. That's a bit more important than a twenty-year-old romance, don't you think?"

Nicholas nodded, happy to change the subject for Hobin's sake. "I'll travel through Linden with Max and head back to the Champeko Forest," he explained. "From there we'll position ourselves closer to Del Norác and await King Justin's signal before we launch our attack. But if Ivy isn't a prisoner in Deshla, I'll have to look elsewhere. Malek said he'd allow some in his army to help with my search, but the closer we get, the less I sense that Ivy's welfare is anyone else's top priority. There's so much other work to do." He gazed at the snapping flames, taking solace in their mesmerizing dance as the merriment of moments ago dissipated and his mood dampened. "As the prospect for war grows, the plight of a young woman easily gets lost in the commotion."

"Sorry to hear that," Hobin said. He caught a telling glance from Leo and immediately guessed what he had in mind. Hobin nodded in silent reply as Nicholas still stared at the fire. "Sometimes it feels like you're alone even with an entire army behind you."

Nicholas looked up. "Malek's army can't match this one in size, but I understand your meaning."

"Which is why you won't be alone no matter what happens," Leo said, noting the bewildered expression upon Nicholas' face.

"*Hmmm?*"

Leo rolled his eyes good-naturedly, realizing that his friend hadn't yet grasped his point. "Hobin and I are going with you, Nicholas. It's time the three of us got back together on the road."

Nicholas shrugged with bemusement. "And when did you both decide this?"

"Probably a moment after you stepped into our circle," Carmella remarked with a delighted laugh. "And if I were you, I wouldn't argue the point."

"I'm more than grateful for the offer," Nicholas said, "but aren't you two obligated to King Justin's army?"

"Luckily, I know the man very well," Leo said. "I'm certain he'll grant Hobin and me his leave."

Hobin chuckled. "Returning the key to the Blue Citadel and opening the Spirit Box has given Leo some sway around here, though he's never used it."

Nicholas turned to Leo in surprise. "*You* opened the Spirit Box?"

He nodded. "I had hoped to hand the key over to King Justin and be done with it, but things didn't work out that way."

Nicholas told them how he had learned about the destruction of the Enâri race after journeying to Malek's camp. "I figured that you and Hobin were safely back in Morrenwood by then, but assumed King Justin would have the honor of opening the box."

Leo grunted in amusement. "*Safely back? Honor?* There's a lot you need to learn about life in the Citadel after we returned."

"I think I'm about to find out."

Leo, with comments from Carmella and Hobin, explained how the key had come back to Morrenwood and told of the invasion of the Citadel and the nearly successful attempt to replace the King. Nicholas listened in shocked disbelief about Leo's fight with Mune in the upper chamber, Carmella's fiery encounter with her cousin and Jagga's demise upon the opening of the Spirit Box.

"Opening that box wasn't the tame affair I had expected it to be," Nicholas said.

"Considering that I literally had to get Mune off my back before I could turn the key, I'd say no."

"And you still feel the effects?" Nicholas asked, indicating the knit hat and wool coat Leo was wearing in the near balmy weather.

"Some days are better than others. But a few chills are a small price to pay compared to what others endured," he said. "It was a bloody day, Nicholas. Several of King Justin's finest men lost their lives in the attack, including one who accompanied me to the stairwell of that upper chamber. Mune had killed him," he said with bitterness. "Stabbed him to death just to get his hands on that key."

"I'm glad you got the best of him. He and Madeline were the ones who kidnapped Ivy. I can only imagine what other havoc they've spread across Laparia."

"When I last saw them outside the Citadel, they had decided to travel to Kargoth to visit Vellan himself," Carmella said. "Liney, rather, proposed that foolhardy notion. Mune reluctantly went along. I guess his heart wasn't in it from what I overheard."

"Whether they reached Kargoth or not, I hope they both come to a sorry end," Nicholas said. "They're as great a menace as Vellan or Caldurian."

"Which just goes to show that you don't have to be a towering figure to cause lots of damage in this world," Hobin said with dark humor. "Apparently any old fool can demonstrate that same talent and ruin a perfectly good day."

"And today is a fine day indeed," Carmella said, "now that Nicholas is here."

"And yesterday was an astounding one," Leo added, "now that Prince Brendan has returned."

"Returned?" Nicholas curiously asked. "Where did he go?"

CHAPTER 96

A Wizard's Web

Nicholas and Leo walked among the lines of mud-splattered wagons, rows of gray and white tents, and companies of soldiers building fires, preparing meals or engaged in mock swordplay. In time they spotted King Justin emerging from his tent on the lakeshore near a trio of pines. A campfire smoked and sputtered nearby. Exiting the tent with him were Prince Gregory, Max and the wizard Tolapari, followed by Kings Cedric and Rowan along with Eucádus and Captain Silas. All had been discussing the upcoming battles at Del Norác and Deshla prison. When King Justin saw Nicholas approach, he smiled with gratitude, greeting the young man with a brisk handshake and an affectionate slap on the shoulder.

"I don't know why I've been blessed with two glorious spring days in a row," the King said, "but fortune has smiled upon me by your appearance. Upon all of us."

"Two glorious days? You must be referring to Prince Brendan as well," Nicholas replied. "Leo told me some of his amazing story on the way over here, though the importance and manner of his return far outshines mine."

"The presence of you both has been like a salve upon an open wound. You've lifted our spirits," the King said. "I am so glad to see you again, Nicholas."

"Thank you, sir," he replied. "And pardon me for not accompanying Prince Gregory to your tent, but when I learned that Leo, Hobin and Carmella were here…"

"Think nothing of it," King Justin said. "Max and I have settled our business. As the two armies move into place, all that's left now is for ours to signal theirs as to when the action begins."

"And a high and fiery signal it will be," said Max.

King Justin introduced Nicholas to those whom he hadn't met, all who expressed thanks for his contribution to the fight against Vellan. Eucádus was especially delighted to meet the other half of the team that helped free his homeland from the Enâri menace.

"Leo provided an account of your adventures," he said. "I hope that before you return with Max, you might also give me your impressions of the journey to Wolf Lake. It's an important piece of history that my fellow citizens of Harlow and the other mountain nations will want to know."

"Happy to," Nicholas replied, "though with King Justin's permission, Max and I won't be returning alone."

"What's all this about?" Max said with mock concern. "I broke my rule once about letting someone tag along with me. I'm setting a bad precedent."

"If you already broke your rule, then two additional people won't make much difference," Nicholas said. "Besides, extra hands mean extra help preparing meals and gathering firewood." He introduced Leo, informing Max that both Leo and Hobin had volunteered to accompany them back and help search for Ivy. "And being a stubborn lot, they wouldn't take no for an answer."

"Then I won't argue the point," Max replied.

"Nor will I," King Justin said, granting his leave to Leo and Hobin. "Anyway, Max already informed me that he had anticipated two extra guests on the return journey and asked for my permission."

Max, feigning disappointment, quietly remarked to the King. "With all due respect, sir, that bit of information was supposed to stay between us."

Nicholas smiled. "Max, I think you enjoyed my company traveling here. Maybe it'll become a habit from now on."

He grunted. "Hardly. When this mission is over, I'll have grown tired of the jabbering and the slower pace and will gladly send you all on your way. So don't get used to this arrangement."

Nicholas turned to Leo. "Sounds like Hobin," he playfully remarked. "Think they could be related?"

"Two of them? Don't know if I could tolerate that," Leo said with exaggerated concern. "Double the moodiness and evasiveness whenever we have a conversation–that is, if they agree to talk at all."

"And twice the rush to get moving early each morning!"

King Justin cleared his throat. "Are you two quite through?"

"I believe they were just getting started," King Rowan said, amused by Nicholas and Leo's banter. He was more appreciative of the lighter moments in life now after all the difficulties he had recently endured. "These two remind me of another pair of close friends who had spent too many weeks apart and are trying to make up for lost time. William and Brendan have been inseparable over the last day since my grandson's memories have returned."

"Will follows his older brother around like a shadow," King Cedric remarked. "He is happy to see him and is quite protective."

"That's only natural after what they've been through," King Rowan replied. "It will help them both heal."

"Do you have time to tell me about your grandson's story?" Nicholas asked. "Leo only touched upon the highlights."

"Prince Brendan can tell you himself," Eucádus said, pointing north up the lakeshore. "Here he comes now with Will at his side."

Everyone looked on as the two brothers walked along the edge of the lake while dodging the lapping waves upon the stony shore. They were engaged in an animated discussion, laughing from time to time as one or the other's hands would flail in the air depending upon who was emphasizing which particular point, and both oblivious to the many eyes watching them.

Caldurian was also observing at that moment. He sat alone by a fire farther south down the shoreline and away from the lake. He had just finished pitching a small tent where he spent his nights. Four teams of two guards had each made their own camps short distances away. They surrounded the wizard at four points in a large square and kept a collective, watchful eye on his seemingly pedestrian activities. Occasionally one of the soldiers in a fit of boredom would wander over and speak with him, but usually both Caldurian and his guards would keep to themselves. Today, however, when the wizard saw Brendan and William in the distance, he decided to make his move. He had heard stories about Brendan's miraculous return and thought about nothing else, including how it might benefit him. The wizard strolled over to one of the guards who was eating lunch.

"May I have a word?" Caldurian politely asked, noting a flash of skepticism upon the man's face. The wizard's gray robes, faded and weather-beaten, were topped by a black cloak equally distressed by the elements. "I need to speak with King Justin."

The soldier, holding a wooden bowl of stew in one hand and a spoon in the other, appeared quite skeptical. "Again? The King of Arrondale grows weary of your requests to meet with Carmella."

"No! It is not about that, I assure you. I must speak to him about another matter, a very important matter."

The soldier sighed as he finished off a spoonful of stew. His first instinct was to reject Caldurian's request, but he and his fellow soldiers were instructed by King Justin to show a modicum of respect and civility to their charge. He looked up at the expectant wizard.

"Since I said *no* the last two times you asked me, I will relent this once if you would give me a few minutes to finish my meal. Then I will ask my captain for permission to escort you to King Justin's tent–again–so you can present your inquiry."

"That is more than fair," Caldurian replied.

"But do not betray my kindness by badgering the King with your usual request," the soldier warned, "or I will conveniently lose my hearing the next time you badger *me*."

"Oh, do not worry," Caldurian assured the man. "What I have to say to King Justin, he will very much want to hear."

Nicholas smiled upon greeting Brendan and William, recalling their first meeting in the Citadel. Then, the two brothers had appeared young, energetic and innocent despite their daring escape from home. But now nearly five months later, he noted a striking change. Beyond their cheerful smiles and mops of blond hair, deep in their eyes were traces of pain and weariness not typical for two so young. As Nicholas listened to a brief recounting of their journey, he sadly learned the source of the brothers' hidden sorrow yet admired their triumph to exist beyond it now that springtime had reunited them.

"But you must tell me what happened yesterday. How did you arrive at the shoreline?" Nicholas requested of Brendan. The group had comfortably settled around a small fire near King Justin's tent, some sitting on rocks or pieces of split wood while others leaned against trees or stood in the background. "More importantly, how did you defeat death itself?"

"That was the question on all our minds yesterday," King Rowan said. "But considering the circumstances, it was a delightful sense of uncertainty to possess."

"It was hours before I finally convinced myself that I wasn't dreaming," William added.

"And you still aren't," Brendan said. "Shall I pinch you again to make sure?"

"Not necessary," he replied, rubbing his upper right arm.

"So what happened?" Nicholas eagerly asked.

Brendan took a deep breath and spoke of his last frantic moments of life in the cabin one hundred and sixteen days ago. "After Arileez' hand had transformed into a sharp talon, he stabbed me once and I fell. I heard my brother scream as the light faded. After that, I remember nothing," he said, "until eleven days ago. That's when I woke up in the Ebrean Forest wrapped in a blanket, struggling to free myself while lying amidst a circle of split firewood. I assumed I had been buried beneath a stack of it, though I don't remember knocking the wood over."

"Ramsey and his men had piled a mound of firewood around Brendan's body," William explained. "It had been well constructed, so I'm sure neither wind nor animal could have dismantled it as my brother described."

"Regardless, that is how I found myself," he continued. "Lost, tired and without any memories. I was confused, yet grateful for the abandoned cabin nearby where I took refuge for three days. As my strength returned, I sought a way out of the forest. I walked, having no sense of direction at times since the trees were numerous and the sun stayed hidden behind a veil of thick clouds for hours at a stretch. Eventually I emerged near the southeastern edge of the woods before my food ran out. I hiked east across the countryside of Drumaya, encountering no individual or any villages along the way. In time I reached the northern shores of Lake Mara and made camp.

With time to think but still no memory, I hiked north along the shoreline, not knowing why I chose that direction."

"Something deep in your mind must have pulled you that way," King Justin said, "silently telling you that that was the way back to your family, to your home."

"I journeyed for a short time, stopping now and then to rest or eat until I at last met someone on the long and lonely road in my new life. It was yesterday at midmorning when Prince Gregory visited my campsite, cheerfully though mistakenly greeting me by the name Max until he drew close enough to see my face."

"That's when my cheer turned into shock," Prince Gregory said. "To have seen Brendan standing in front of me after I heard of his tragic demise, why I–" He rubbed his unshaven face, shaking his head. "Even now I haven't the words to describe my astonishment and then soaring elation upon that strange encounter."

"It took time for Brendan to fully trust us," King Rowan told Nicholas. "He looked upon us all as strangers at first. His memories slowly returned later that afternoon as his brother talked incessantly to him like an excited magpie."

"But it worked," William replied. "I made him remember."

"Yes, your persistence broke through and my memories flooded back," Brendan said. "And so that, Nicholas, brings you up to date to this very moment."

"Except for one question," he replied. "How did all of these strange events happen to begin with? How did you cheat death?"

"To be precise, those are *two* questions," a voice uttered from behind them. "But I may be able to provide some answers if King Justin will allow me to speak."

"Caldurian, what are you doing here?" Tolapari snapped at his fellow wizard, his words threaded with contempt. "Haven't you annoyed King Justin enough already?"

At the mention of Caldurian's name, Nicholas shot a fiery glance at the wizard and locked gazes with him as he passed by. Each silently studied the other, their faces grim and hardened. Though never having laid eyes upon him before, Nicholas fumed inside, knowing so much about the wizard and his terrible deeds. Caldurian, at the same time, returned a perplexed yet cautious gaze, drawn to the young man's stare as he wondered who he was, yet feeling that he might already know him.

Nicholas took a deep breath when the wizard finally turned his head away with a struggle, breaking eye contact. At last he had met the man who had brought so much chaos, death and destruction to his village twenty years ago. He recalled Frist's astonishing words about his father's demise. And though a particular, faceless Enâr had struck the fatal blow, Nicholas still blamed Caldurian and Vellan for the actual deed. He glanced at Leo, no words being necessary to convey his troubled state of mind.

"Steady now," Leo whispered, grabbing Nicholas' coat sleeve in case he harbored thoughts of lunging at Caldurian. "The wizard is harmless now from what I've heard."

"What?" he quietly replied, shaking his head in confusion. "What is he doing here? And why didn't you mention it earlier?"

"The reason is obvious, though I planned to tell you at some point–preferably when Caldurian wasn't in your line of vision." Leo shifted Nicholas' attention to King Justin. "Let's hear him out first," he said, slowly releasing the grip on his sleeve.

The King walked to Caldurian like a weary teacher prepared to discipline a frequently disruptive student. "*No!*" he said before the wizard could speak, flashing an annoyed glance at the guard who had accompanied him here.

"But, King Justin, I'm not here to talk about visiting *her!*" he insisted. "Trust me, you will want to hear me out. I have news regarding King Rowan's grandson, the one who has returned from the grave. And related information about *your* wounds."

"What are you talking about?"

Caldurian looked at all the disapproving stares and whispered to the King. "Perhaps we should have this discussion in private."

"Anything you have to say to me, you can say to everyone. Besides, Prince Brendan and King Rowan deserve to know what's on your mind as does anyone else who has suffered because of your actions. So get on with it or return to your tent."

"Very well. I'll tell you and your friends what I know, or at least what I theorize," he said, adjusting his cloak. "While I was your prisoner over the winter, I told you how I had freed Arileez from his confinement in the Northern Isles. The Umarikaya had been isolated on the island of Torriga since childhood by a powerful magic spell."

"Yes," the King replied. "We discussed many things, like the spy you cleverly planted in the rafters during the war council. I also remember you saying that Vellan's plans had become misguided."

"Yes, yes! But both those points are–beside the point," he sheepishly replied to the quiet surprise of the others.

"Anyway, after Vellan learned of Arileez' existence," the King continued, "you said that Vellan created a potion to counter the spell that bound him to the island. He sent you to deliver the tonic, if I remember correctly."

"You do, and I did. And after Arileez consumed the potion, he was able to leave Torriga after years of captivity, grateful to serve Vellan in exchange for his freedom."

King Cedric scoffed. "Grateful? I can only imagine the lies and wild tales that Vellan ensnared Arileez with to get him to agree to replace King Justin. Or did Vellan place an enchantment on the pitiful being as well to gain his service? Perhaps he tricked Arileez into drinking from the Drusala River."

Caldurian looked askance at the King of Drumaya. "It didn't take much convincing for Arileez to throw in his lot with Vellan. After all, Arileez, like Vellan, had been shunned and cruelly treated by his people."

"Vellan was not treated unfairly by his fellow wizards!" Tolapari jumped in. "He simply couldn't control his ambitions and desire for power. He created one excuse after another to justify the chaos he had spread across Laparia for the last fifty years."

"Regardless, the Umarikaya was more than happy to assist him. Let's not quibble about details," Caldurian replied. "That is not my point."

"Then make your point," King Justin said. "What has any of this got to do with Prince Brendan's or my injuries?"

"The potion that Vellan had created to free Arileez contained, how shall I say, a little more kick to it than the unsuspecting Arileez was led to believe," he said. "Vellan had added a second, secret spell to that potent blend about which only he and I knew."

"To do what?" Tolapari asked. He and King Justin looked on with simmering disdain, both expecting some treachery in the offing.

"Once Arileez drank that potion, his fate was sealed. The slow and stealthy magic had already gone to work to–" Caldurian seemed ashamed for what he was about to say, causing him to look briefly at the ground. "That second spell slowly reversed Arileez' magical powers, including his ability to transform into other shapes. In time, and without his knowledge, he would have been rendered a mere mortal."

"Vellan betrayed one of his own?" Eucádus remarked with a trace of disgust. "Though I don't know why that should surprise me."

"I'm not surprised," Tolapari replied, combing a hand through his tangled locks. "Evil has a tendency to collapse upon itself, to feed on itself. It is not unexpected that Vellan, and those like him, eventually turn against their own to survive and prosper." He glanced sharply at Caldurian. "For that is what Vellan intended from the start, am I right? I can already see into his twisted motives from what little information you've provided."

Caldurian nodded. "Vellan did just that. Once he learned about Arileez' transformational abilities which outrivaled anything that he or any other wizard could do, he knew he must get rid of him. He saw Arileez as a threat, wanting to prevent a future rival from vying for dominance while using him at the same time."

King Justin sputtered in outrage. "Diabolical! And if Arileez had succeeded in taking my place–running the affairs of Arrondale as Vellan saw fit–I'm guessing that he would have eventually lost his transformational powers and have been stuck in my form for the rest of his life, serving as Vellan's puppet."

"That was the plan. That was how Vellan had timed his spell to work," Caldurian said, flashing a heartless smile. "Once Arileez' powers were gone, Vellan assumed he would have accepted his life as king. And if he somehow learned of Vellan's grand plan and exposed it to the masses, he risked that people would think him crazed and perhaps demand that Prince Gregory rule in his stead."

"Sorry to disappoint," King Justin replied, "but my reign is secure. Your fate and Vellan's, however, remain to be determined. The two of you might have been further ahead in your deranged goals if you had left Arileez alone."

"It was our deception of Arileez that saved *his* life!" he countered, pointing at Brendan. "That is what I came here to tell you. Because Arileez had consumed that potion which slowly depleted his powers, I am guessing that Vellan's spell was also introduced into Brendan's body–and your own, King Justin–when you were both wounded. Arileez struck each of you with an extension of his body, his own skin and bone, rather than a sword or dagger of inanimate construction. Vellan's spell must have reversed your injuries just as it was doing to Arileez' own capabilities." Caldurian's theory captured everyone's attention. "You told me in the Citadel that the cut to your upper arm had swiftly healed despite the depth of the wound. Prince Brendan's fatal blow took far longer to undo considering the magnitude of the injury, but as he is now sitting here among us, can you doubt my explanation? What greater proof do you need?"

King Justin remained silent, digesting Caldurian's words. But as wild as they sounded, the wizard's reasoning contained a nugget of logic that was difficult to refute.

King Rowan grudgingly spoke up. "I will accept your explanation. But do not be so pleased with yourself, Caldurian. You have the audacity to say that your deception of Arileez saved my grandson's life. But it was your meddling in the affairs of Laparia that killed him in the first place!" The King's chest heaved with each deep and angry breath as he recalled the emotional devastation his daughter-in-law, Vilna, was continuing to endure since learning of her son's death. "Only by sheer luck did Brendan survive the attack of that crazed wizard. So don't take credit for something good that happened simply due to the fact that you provided Arileez a drink!"

"I don't mean to take credit for it," Caldurian replied, "but only hope you appreciate the fact that I took the time to tell you what I know. Perhaps that will begin to atone for what happened to your grandson, if only slightly."

King Rowan scowled, prepared to utter the inflammatory words on his mind before he abruptly turned around. He stood protectively behind his grandsons, thinking it better not to escalate the growing tension.

"Apparently *only* slightly," Tolapari dryly remarked, glancing sharply at his fellow wizard.

"I agree," King Justin added in a calmer tone. "You have a long way to go to atone for your misdeeds, Caldurian, though I doubt that that is even possible. But for the sake of sparing this one restful day for the soldiers, I will offer a simple *thank you* for the information before sending you back to your camp. Unless, of course, you have other particulars you'd like to impart."

"Let's not get carried away," he replied. "My amends for one misdeed per day are plenty, don't you think?"

King Justin said nothing, signaling for the soldier to escort Caldurian back to his tent. Nicholas, though, having silently sat through the wizard's performance, could not let him leave without at least one comment, however unwise he knew it might be.

"Amending *one* misdeed each day?" he said standing up, coldly eyeing the wizard. "Then by my calculations it should take you about twenty years to atone for all the damage you've done. Sound about right?"

Caldurian stared back with a bewildered air, not sure what to make of the individual who held him in such contempt. Nicholas, churning inside with anger, stood a few feet from Caldurian, his eyes never releasing their hold upon him as wisps of smoke from the fire rose ghostlike in the space between them.

"You have me at a disadvantage," Caldurian said with forced friendliness. "I don't know your name, yet you obviously know me. And by your tone, you apparently have a gripe or two against me."

"Keep counting," Nicholas said.

Leo noticed his friend's wavering poise and stood next to him, preparing to intercede should Nicholas attempt something rash. King Justin also noted the young man's anxious state and intervened.

"What Nicholas refers to, Caldurian, is your infamous dealings with the citizens of Kanesbury twenty years ago. That is his home village, and so his reaction upon meeting you for the first time should be understandable."

"And were I as callous as you, and you were not so well guarded," Nicholas added, "you might be lying in a pool of blood right now. After all, the Enâri horde you released upon Kanesbury was responsible for the death of my father, Jack Raven, as I recently learned from the wizard Frist."

"Raven, you say?" The mention of Nicholas' surname sent a nauseating chill through the wizard. "*You* met with Frist?" He looked at Nicholas with a befuddled sense of wonderment, his mouth agape. "Does that mean you were the one–"

"–who brought Frist the medallion to be remade into the key to the Spirit Box?" Tolapari smiled with subdued satisfaction upon seeing Caldurian's look of distress. "Yes, by their brave deeds, both Nicholas Raven and Leo Marsh here have set Vellan's plans back quite a few steps. Despite your machinations, the free peoples of this corner of the world will never give in. They'll overcome whatever you and Vellan throw their way."

Caldurian ignored Tolapari's remark, instead fixing his thoughts upon Nicholas. He wondered how this lowly farm worker and gristmill accountant had caused him so much grief. Through his spies, the wizard had learned about Nicholas' life in Kanesbury, particularly his close relationship with Maynard Kurtz, which forced him to hire others to get rid of Nicholas before he could exact his revenge upon Otto Nibbs. But Caldurian had never laid eyes on Nicholas before as most of his groundwork had been done by intermediaries. He had considered Nicholas merely an afterthought, a faceless nuisance that had to be gotten rid of to achieve a greater aim. Now Caldurian stood before that very man who, once a simple pawn in a larger game, had ended up besting the wizard regarding the fate of the Enâri.

Caldurian suddenly wondered if Nicholas had also discovered who arranged for his life to be turned upside down. But who would have told him the truth behind the strange goings-on in Kanesbury? Certainly not Mune or Madeline, nor even the slightly incompetent Zachary Farnsworth and Dooley Kramer. But the wizard wanted to be sure, fearing that his revenge against Otto might unravel if Nicholas traced his troubles back to him. Right now, that satisfying bit of vengeance was all Caldurian had to sustain him. He wouldn't give it up for anything.

"I won't say I'm proud of my past," Caldurian remarked, hoping to draw out more information, "but if that one incident from twenty years ago is your only grievance against me, then maybe I can make it up to you. You need only say how."

"That one incident is a mighty big grievance and can never be made up for," Nicholas replied, his temper having cooled while observing what a wretched being Caldurian really was. "And as much as I'd like to take a swing at you, or avenge my father's death at the point of a knife, I'll let King Justin and others work out the details of your final judgment. I'm sure there are many recent crimes you've committed that should take precedence over my complaint."

"Wise words from someone so young," he said, convinced that Nicholas didn't suspect he was behind his personal troubles at home. "I'm fortunate you have bestowed such compassion upon me."

"Fortunate that we didn't let him have at you," Max softly muttered while standing next to Prince Gregory. Most heard his words with quiet amusement, including Nicholas and Leo who appreciated Maximilian's Hobin-like demeanor.

"And on that note, Caldurian, I think it's time you were escorted back to your tent," King Justin said, signaling to the guard. "And the sooner the better, if you please. I have more important things to do right now, and the first is to enjoy a leisurely lunch. I don't know about the rest of you, but this endless talk has given me a most monstrous appetite."

The army resumed its march early the next morning. By mid afternoon, they reached the southern tip of Lake Mara that bordered on the lush eaves of the Braya Woods. Emotions were mixed as soldiers marched or rode past the last rippling images of the lake, some feeling as if they were saying farewell to a trusted friend while others looked forward to a change of scenery. Soon the various companies marched through fresh, thick grass while framed against a line of trees, appearing as long strands of brown and gray ribbons stretched across a sea of soft green. Near twilight they halted, now a few miles away from the southern edge of the forest. Here they made camp, gazing west across a twenty-five mile gap between the Braya Woods and the Rhoon Forest, the army's next destination. Beyond the Rhoon lay the Northern Mountains and the realm of Kargoth.

A cool, clear night gave way to a sunny but chilly morning as the army began the next leg of its campaign. Nicholas and Leo had said their goodbyes to Carmella who stayed near the back of the supply line. They now rode alongside Prince Gregory and King Justin at the head of the army, preparing to part ways shortly and veer northwest into Linden with Max and Hobin. The two guides, having become fast friends, rode close behind with Kings Rowan and Cedric and Tolapari. Each regaled the trio with competing tales from the Northern Mountains and the Dunn Hills, urging them to choose a favorite. Nicholas and Leo, hearing their friendly argument, couldn't help but laugh to themselves.

"We'll have that to look forward to," Nicholas said. "The miles along the Bellunboro River will be entertaining, if anything."

"Enjoy it while you can," King Justin said, "for at the end of both our paths lay Del Norác. I envision little laughter there."

"As do I," said Prince Gregory, his grim expression making Nicholas suspect that he had more on his mind than the impending conflict. "Remember, if negotiations with Vellan fail–which I suspect they will, if they happen at all–then a volley of flaming arrows will fly at dawn sixteen days from today to signal the start of our war."

"And our raid on Deshla," Nicholas said gravely. "Sixteen days. I'll remember."

"That's on the twentieth day of New Spring, giving you enough time to reach Max's people in the mountains," he continued, "and giving us several days' leeway to reach Del Norác. Max has already notched that date for when he makes his report."

"We'll be traveling in parallel directions around one long loop," said Leo, anticipating the miles ahead. "I look forward to seeing you again when our respective roads meet, but I fear there'll be the sound of clashing swords in the air when we do."

King Justin gazed contemplatively across the grassy vista and gently rolling hills. "I never had any illusions that our march upon Vellan's stronghold would produce a result other than warfare. But that is our fate, as unpleasant a fact as it is."

"Speaking of unpleasant facts," Prince Gregory remarked, tossing an uneasy glance at Nicholas, "there is something I need to tell you before we part ways. I was going to mention it the day you arrived, but seeing how your introduction to Caldurian played out, I thought it best to hold off. After all, there is nothing now that can be done regarding some unfortunate happenings in Kanesbury that began late last autumn."

Nicholas expected the worst. "Unfortunate happenings? I'm afraid to ask, but tell me what you know."

"This is according to Len Harold. I talked with him while leading my troops through Kanesbury. He told me that Caldurian had attacked your village with a company of Island soldiers. They controlled Kanesbury for nine days in the month of Old Autumn."

Nicholas shook his head in disbelief. "Caldurian was in my village–*again*? Why?"

Prince Gregory told of the disruptive events as Len had described them, including the hording of people's food, Caldurian's dramatic reappearance and Otto's public sentencing. The look of dismay upon Nicholas' face was heartbreaking when he learned of the hardship and humiliation his fellow villagers had endured at the hands of the wizard. Nicholas was especially shocked when informed that Otto Nibbs was currently in prison awaiting trial and that Maynard Kurtz' whereabouts was unknown.

"Maynard had left your village to meet with my father at the Citadel and inform him of Caldurian's reappearance."

"I was off to war in Rhiál by then," King Justin said. "I was later informed that Mr. Kurtz never arrived at the Citadel nor has been seen since. I sent scouts out to help search for him when I learned of the news, but to no avail."

"I can't believe this," Nicholas muttered.

"Len informed me that a man named Zachary Farnsworth was serving as acting mayor," the prince said. "But where things stand in your village since we left Morrenwood, I cannot say."

Nicholas' thoughts spun like a wintry gale, unable to make sense why Caldurian would assault his village after all these years. He wondered about Katherine Durant and others close to him back home, imagining how they had fared during that horrible week as prisoners in their own village. He just couldn't understand why.

"All are safe and Caldurian is our prisoner," Prince Gregory said, "so you needn't worry about that aspect of the situation."

"Why bother when there are so many other disturbing aspects to worry about?" Nicholas replied with bitter sarcasm. A new thought suddenly struck him. "I already figured out that Dooley Kramer and Arthur Weeks had framed me for the gristmill robbery, though I could never come up with a good reason as to why. But since they also had possession of the key until Jagga got his hands on it, then they must have had some dealings with Caldurian, too. Doesn't that make sense?"

"Dooley and Arthur?" Leo asked skeptically. "From what you told me about those two, I find it difficult to believe that they would know how to cultivate a relationship with the likes of Caldurian, much less find him in the first place."

"But they might have worked for someone who could," King Justin suggested.

"Who?" Nicholas wondered aloud. "It may sound farfetched, but I'm beginning to wonder if Caldurian was behind the incidents that happened to me during the Harvest Festival. But why would he care one whit about me or want to ruin my life?" He chuckled, his words suddenly sounding ridiculous to his ear.

"I suppose it's possible," Leo said, offering support.

"Thanks, but I'm grasping at phantoms. Just because Dooley may have had dealings with Caldurian while trying to frame me at the same time could merely be a coincidence. I had no knowledge of the key's whereabouts nor can think of anything I did or knew or possessed that would have made me a threat to the wizard." Nicholas shrugged. "Maybe I'll never know the reasons behind what happened to me unless I ask Dooley himself. That seems to be my only recourse if I ever make it back to Kanesbury."

"You could ask Caldurian," Leo suggested. "He's only a mile or so behind us."

King Justin shook his head. "Definitely not. Though I know that Leo jests, I would not recommend it. I see only trouble coming from such a confrontation."

Nicholas put the King at ease. "So do I. Though the wizard would deny his connection if there was one, I don't want to cause any unrest now that you're close to confronting Vellan," he said. "Nor do I want to jeopardize my own life when I'm so close to finding Ivy. Until she's safe, I can live with the web of mystery and deceit I'm entangled in. I have no choice."

"A sensible course," the King replied, "though I suspected that you and Leo had a firm footing in the arena of commonsense since I first met you. You've grown wise during your time on the road, Nicholas Raven."

"Thanks," he replied with a faint smile. "But the road has made me weary, stretching on far longer than I ever anticipated. I'll be happy when it comes to an end."

Several miles and a few hours later, the rich green expanse of the Rhoon Forest appeared on the western horizon as the army's front lines advanced up a gently sloping ridge. The southernmost peaks of the Northern Mountains lay sleepily in the background behind a tranquil, blue haze. Here is where Nicholas, Leo, Hobin and Max bid their friends goodbye, wishing them a safe journey until they would meet again in Del Norác. The quartet, on horseback and loaded up with fresh supplies, veered northwest, planning to skirt around the Rhoon's northern tip and enter the mountain nation of Linden.

King Justin and the others watched as they slowly trotted off under the warming sunlight of late morning, silently wishing them a safe journey. A short time later, Nicholas and his companions had diminished into mere specks against the horizon before disappearing altogether. The vast army now trudged southwest, making for the southern edge of the Rhoon Forest, and beyond that, the realm of Kargoth.

"I wonder how long until we see them again," William said to his brother a short time later. "For I do expect to see them again."

"Oh?" his brother asked.

William nodded. "You returned, after all, unscathed. I'm guessing Nicholas and the others will have an easier time of things compared to what you went through."

"Let's hope they do," King Justin said. "And let's hope they have that same assured attitude of yours, William. Such an advantage will serve them well."

"Vellan's arrogance and overconfidence may be our greatest advantage," Tolapari said, his eyes fixed ahead on the gently rolling landscape. "He already lost two battles by stretching his armies thin, and his Enâri forces were destroyed in the blink of an eye. Vellan's house is crumbling and we must provide that last push to topple it."

"Let's push hard and fast," King Rowan replied. "And though you earlier said that evil tends to collapse upon itself, we can't manipulate the turmoil inside Vellan's stronghold or depend on him to make any more mistakes. We must give our all, perhaps our very lives, to end this scourge. If not for us, then for the generations ahead."

"Well said," King Cedric remarked, giving him a reassuring nod. "Eh, Justin?"

"*Hmmm?*" King Justin snapped to attention, having been mulling over King Rowan's statement. "Yes, yes. I heard and agree. *We can't manipulate the turmoil*, etc..." He glanced at his fellow Kings as a swirl of muddled thoughts crystallized in his head. "Well spoken, Rowan," he replied with a perfunctory nod. "Well spoken indeed."

They camped at twilight after reaching the drooping and somnolent eaves of the Rhoon Forest and traveling southwest alongside them for a couple of miles. Wisps of purple and orange clouds lingered above the horizon, reflecting the last rays of the setting sun upon their gauzy edges. Small bonfires popped up one by one in the numerous camps scattered along the tree line and about the adjacent field. And though the army was still many miles away from Kargoth, the spirits of most were contemplative and subdued tonight, knowing that they were so close to Vellan's backdoor.

Caldurian sat alone by a snapping fire later that evening beneath a star-strewn sky. His tent was situated on an edge of the field away from most of the others, though four pairs of guards still kept watch at a respectful distance on four corners of a surrounding invisible square. The wizard gazed into the hypnotic dance of flames as black shadows wavered upon a handful of nearby saplings. He looked up warily when hearing whispers from somewhere in the darkness. A silhouette among the gloom walked toward him. He sat up on his pine log seat, recognizing King Justin's familiar outline.

"To what do I owe this nighttime visit?" he pleasantly asked. "It's rare that you come to see me."

"Evening up our score," he said. "But I won't take much of your time, Caldurian. I know how you like to use your free moments to think."

"I've had much free time lately, King Justin. A visit is appreciated, though I don't think you're here on a social call." The wizard indicated a small pile of split wood next to the fire. "Pull up a chair."

"No, thank you. I'll make this brief. I wish to retire early."

"I rarely sleep of late," he replied. "I can only manage a few hours at a stretch. I guess the effects of the âvin éska might have something to do with it."

"Perhaps you have a case of melancholy brought on by Vellan's recent failures," the King remarked dryly. "More specifically, *your* contributions to those failures."

"Many have contributed," he replied with a hint of annoyance. "But your point is well taken. Now how may I help you?"

"I just spoke with Carmella. She is camped out near those trees," the King replied, pointing into the shadowy darkness beyond the tent.

"And how is my former student doing these days?"

"Just fine." King Justin folded his arms, caressing his chin with one hand as he cautiously eyed the wizard. "I told her that I no longer would object if she wished to accept your invitation to meet with her." Caldurian flashed a surprised glance at the King. "She said she would like that. Tomorrow, if it suits you."

"Very much so!" Caldurian replied, his tone sincerely grateful.

"But you will still be under guard, mind you, though I have informed my men not to interfere with your visits."

Caldurian held his breath. "*Visits*? Are we allowed more than one meeting?"

"I suppose so. At least until we are deep into Kargoth," the King said. "We'll play it by ear after that. Still, one wrong move to betray my trust…"

"Fear not, sir." He stood up, bowing his head slightly. "I wish to thank you, King Justin, for this most unexpected change in attitude. But I'm curious if you're allowing this visit because of the information I provided about Vellan's second spell."

The King smiled slyly. "And I'm curious if you gave me that information just to get a visit."

The two men stared at one another for a long, silent moment as the flames snapped and a cool, thin breeze rustled through the grass.

"Well, I guess we both choose to remain curious," Caldurian replied pleasantly, retaking his seat.

"I suppose so," King Justin said amiably. "And now I must bid you goodnight. Enjoy your fire."

"Enjoy your sleep."

With that, King Justin disappeared into the darkness, leaving Caldurian alone as he had found him. The wizard, soaking in the warmth of the flames, smiled to himself, concluding that King Justin consented to his meeting with Carmella out of a grudging sense of obligation as he had hoped. He saw it as a sign of weakness on the King's part, wondering if Tolapari had raised any objections.

But it was done, and that was all that mattered. Caldurian reached into one of his deep cloak pockets. He removed the small, amber-colored vial containing the remaining potion that Vellan had created to doom Arileez to a mortal life. He gazed into the liquid now wildly illuminated by the firelight. Caldurian saw himself standing on Vellan's mountainside balcony that overlooked Del Norác, soaking in the view of his new domain.

"In time," he whispered to himself. *"All in good time."*

CHAPTER 97

Where There's Smoke

Caldurian tossed a chunk of wood onto the fire the following evening. It erupted in a swirl of sparks that cut through the night like a cloud of fireflies, illuminating the curious skepticism on Carmella's face as she sat by the blaze. The wizard sat down beside her, flashing a friendly smile at his former student. The army was encamped along the eaves of the Rhoon Forest. Caldurian, with King Justin's consent, had asked his guards to escort him to Carmella's camp.

After engaging in small talk, the wizard and former student stared at one another until their uneasiness subsided. Caldurian, wrapped in a black cloak, blended in with the night. Carmella seemed to mirror the firelight in her brightly hued cloak and beige gloves. Eight members of the King's Guard, in four sets of two, observed them from a respectful distance and just out of earshot from their usual square-corner positions.

"Let me begin by apologizing for my behavior two decades ago, Carmella. Your cousin and I took advantage of your hospitality. We used your home to escape from our foiled kidnapping plot and concealed five hundred Enâri in the nearby woods without your knowledge."

Caldurian's seemingly sincere words mixed with the eddying smoke trails rising above the crackling flames. Carmella grimaced slightly, not wholly convinced of their authenticity, though she had no intention of shooing the wizard away.

"No apology for casting a sleeping spell upon me?" she asked.

"Yes, that too," he replied. "Not my finest moment, but I was in desperate straits."

"Yes, you and Liney had certainly made a mess of things back then," Carmella remarked with a pensive sigh as she looked into the fire. "*Now*, too," she added, throwing a sharp glance his way. "So that naturally leads me to this question–why should I believe anything you say tonight? What are you really after, Caldurian?"

The wizard seemed taken aback, appearing hurt by such blunt words. Slowly, his lips morphed into a thin smile.

"You see right through me, Carmella, even after twenty years, though part of my apology was sincere. That bit about the sleeping spell, I mean. How long were you out?"

"Almost three days. It was more than enough time for you to flee Red Fern before I contacted the authorities. But King Justin and his men eventually caught up with you in Kanesbury which turned out to be the slow start of Vellan's undoing."

"Yes, that blasted business with the key! Had I never ended up in that trifling village, then Frist wouldn't have sown the seeds of the Enâri's destruction."

"You did that, Caldurian, by your misguided actions. Don't blame Frist for cleverly finding a way to take down Vellan's army years later. And who would have ever guessed that I would be a part of it?" Carmella again gazed into the fire. She recounted how she had met Jagga and told of his final moments as he disintegrated before her eyes while fighting Madeline. "I'll never forget that haunting image. And though a part of me grieves for that one particular creature, I do not regret the demise of the rest of them."

"I can't even imagine Vellan's state. I don't think he could recreate the Enâri race again. Not at his age. It would take too much out of him. Their deaths, I'm sure, weakened him." Caldurian sounded almost hopeful when he spoke those words. "No, he cannot be a happy man of late."

"Nor is my cousin," Carmella remarked. "When Jagga melted into a mound of sand upon her, Liney went into hysterics. I think at that moment she feared for Vellan's wellbeing more than anything else, and for any possible future she may have had at his side." She looked askance at Caldurian. "Perhaps as Vellan's next apprentice?"

Caldurian flinched. "Is that why your cousin fled to Kargoth?" he bitterly inquired. "To be at *his* side and to ease *his* sorrows?" The wizard scratched distractedly at his beard. "Traitors! They abandoned me while I was a prisoner in Montavia, only to crawl back to Vellan, no doubt begging for his forgiveness though they hardly know him. Mune has never even met the wizard, though I can picture him groveling before Vellan. He's only in this for profit and cares nothing about reordering the state of affairs in Laparia. But I thought that Madeline had a bit more character to her, a bit more integrity." He angrily tossed a few twigs into the fire, quietly fuming. "And a bit more loyalty to me."

Carmella noted the hurt in his eyes, tempted to feel sorry for him. "Maybe now you're seeing my cousin as I see her. Liney is in it for herself. She always thought too highly of herself, even while growing up. Her drive and ambition have loosened her grasp on what's important in life. It's distorted her senses," she said. "But you and Vellan are just the same. You elevate yourselves above everyone else, all the while rationalizing the horrific deeds you do. You're no better than common criminals."

"Whom you have chosen to associate with," Caldurian dryly replied. "The only question is–why?"

"You requested this meeting with me, Caldurian, so I'll ask you the same question," she said, tightening the cloak about her shoulders. "Why?"

The wizard sat silently, carefully weighing his next words. Slowly his facial muscles relaxed as he glanced at Carmella, having decided that the truth might suit him best. "Let's not engage in a dance of words. We both know what the other wants."

"And that would be?"

"To get to Del Norác, of course, preferably unencumbered by this monstrous army. You want to find your cousin and I wish to consult with Vellan," he said. "No surprise to either of us."

"Agreed," she replied. "So is that the only reason you ever wanted to meet with me? To help you escape?"

"Of course not. While I was a prisoner in the Blue Citadel over winter, I requested several meetings with you, but King Justin would have none of it. I wanted to get information about Madeline and learn of your story since our last meeting. Hearing that you had kept up your pursuit of magic in your own fashion over the years, I was curious as to what influence I might have had in that decision."

"And perhaps recruit me as your apprentice?"

Caldurian softly chuckled. "My powers are a bit off as of late thanks to Tolapari's meddling, so I don't know how good a teacher I would be."

"So I've heard."

The wizard furtively looked around at his distant guards who nearly blended in with the shadows. At the moment, the soldiers appeared more bored than attentive with their assignment. Caldurian lowered his voice to a faint whisper.

"Still–and I've revealed this to nobody until now–I have regained some of my powers, but only a little," he admitted. "Only enough to perform a handful of minor spells, though even those can be tiring as I recover. But I go about my business as if I still suffer from the full extent of the âvin éska, though I suspect that Tolapari suspects I might be putting on a show. Yet we play our little game."

Carmella's suspicion was evident. "Why are you telling me this, Caldurian? I might go back and inform King Justin about your confession. He might double or triple the guard around you, or worse. Perhaps Tolapari might slap another spell upon you before your strength fully returns."

"You could do that, and I suppose I wouldn't blame you. But I was hoping to build a bond of trust between us." He turned to her, appearing at her mercy. "We need each other right now, Carmella– you, to get me out of this place, and me, to lead you to Del Norác, into Vellan's very stronghold where we both assume that Madeline and Mune are currently his guests." The wizard furrowed his brow. "Or perhaps prisoners. One can't be too sure. But I'd rather pay him a visit on my own terms, as I'm sure you would, rather than being dragged there." He pointed to Carmella's gloves. "You don't want to live with pumpkin-colored hands all your life, do you?"

"I've grown attached to them. The color complements my wardrobe," she replied with a smirk before her expression grew serious. "Liney's amusing little spell isn't the only reason I've been seeking her out for the last twenty years. I have others, too, though I wouldn't expect you to understand them."

"Try me."

Carmella, a bit uncomfortable, decided to open up to cultivate a bond of trust. By doing so, she hoped the wizard might teach her some spells before she encountered her cousin the next time. A bit of candor was a small price to pay for some lessons in magic.

"I'll tell you why I've been searching for Liney, but you may change your mind about forming an alliance with me," she replied. "In addition to getting my misguided cousin to lift her spell, I was hoping to draw her away from you and Vellan. She's my blood relative. She was like a sister to me in our younger days. And though the odds are against me, I must try. Liney was a headstrong woman as she grew older, yet we remained good friends despite our disagreements. But seeing what she had become after throwing in her lot with you and Vellan, why, it nearly broke my heart."

"Madeline never talked about her family," Caldurian said, "except for you on occasion. How did her parents react to her sudden departure?"

"They were devastated," she replied, as if the answer should have been obvious. "Liney was their only child who had left them without as much as a goodbye. Later, when they heard rumors about what kind of life she was leading and the trouble she had caused, they felt as if their daughter had died. My aunt and uncle spent years grieving for her even though she was still alive. That's why I promised them that I would find her, and if possible, bring her back home." Carmella recalled the wonderful times she had shared with her cousin during childhood, picturing the younger Madeline as an entirely separate being from her current self. "But sadly, my aunt and uncle, along with my parents, have since passed away before I could fulfill my pledge. Still, I will keep trying, though this will probably be my last chance with war about to break out and all of us in the middle of it." Carmella sighed. "And all of this mess can be traced back to you, Caldurian, when you seduced my cousin when she was a nursemaid in the Blue Citadel."

"I suppose it can," he admitted, "though I never considered matters from your point of view. All I ever saw in Madeline was a vast potential to master the magic arts. All I wanted was to teach her what I knew, just as Vellan had done for me. I never bothered to learn much about her personal life, though she rarely talked about it anyway. I simply acted and she followed."

"Maybe you *should* have bothered, but I suppose that's not a priority when one doesn't have a sense of honor or a conscience."

"My, but we are being honest this evening, aren't we."

"I am." Carmella's words dropped like a heavy stone. "And regardless of any agreement we make to help each other, I am in no way excusing you for your past transgressions. I'll help you escape if you help me find Liney. But I do not now nor ever shall consider you a friend. Your charms will not work on me, wizard."

"Fair enough," he said.

"And," she quickly added before he could utter another word, "I insist that you teach me a few magic spells as part of our bargain. Enough to give me a fighting chance against my cousin should our next encounter prove less than civil."

"I suppose I can instruct you in a few basic spells despite my incapacity. In fact, I could show you a simple one right now that you might find intriguing," he said with a glint in his eyes. "It may come in useful down the road."

"In what way?"

"Ah, one step at a time." Caldurian stood in front of the fire and warmed his hands over the flames. "Now pay attention please."

Carmella watched intently as the wizard moved his hands over the flicking flames. Bluish-gray streams of smoke escaped between his fingers like twisting snakes. After several moments of intense silence, he cupped his hands together, palms down, and allowed smoke to collect beneath his fingers. He uttered a string of short phrases, his soft, whispery words nearly inaudible and in a language Carmella didn't recognize.

"What are you–?"

"*Shhh*," he replied, not looking at her nor missing a beat while uttering the mysterious incantation as his eyelids slowly dropped.

The wizard grew silent. His facial muscles tightened under a wave of exertion that suddenly took hold of him. Caldurian cupped his hands closer together, squeezing them several times as if forming a snowball as he stepped away from the fire. He spoke more words in the same strange language and slowly opened his eyes. In a single swift motion, he separated his hands and displayed the palms upward. A perfectly formed sphere of smoke, seemingly of solid construction, drifted upward and floated across the tips of the flames toward Carmella.

"Amazing!" she whispered as the smoke ball hovered before her. Carmella gazed upon it with awe and delight. She passed a finger through the sphere which felt like warm fog against her skin. She glanced at Caldurian with a pleased smile and then touched the smoke creation again, only to have it disintegrate before her eyes.

Caldurian feigned an expression of dismay. "All that work now up in smoke," he remarked, breaking out in a tiny grin.

"Sorry," Carmella said. "I didn't mean to ruin it."

"Don't worry. It wouldn't have lasted much longer anyway, though I could have added a few additional incantations to give it more durability," he explained. "I just wanted to give you a brief demonstration on manipulating smoke."

"It was wonderful! Did you teach that trick to my cousin?"

"She learned it in no time, and I'm sure you can, too. But Madeline can also manipulate water vapor and fire. She was particularly adept at the latter."

"Perhaps I can equal her proficiency with the proper training, but let's hold off on the fire and continue with manipulating smoke," Carmella replied. "My fingers are already orange. I don't want to singe them black as well."

"As you wish," he said. "If only I had my crushed herbs and powdered pigments. We could create some spectacular displays."

"I have a variety of items in my wagon. Shall I get a few?"

"Next time. This demonstration has tired me somewhat as I am still not operating at full strength." Caldurian stretched his arms and breathed in the night air. "But I shall get a good night's rest so that when we meet again, I will be refreshed and ready to teach you two or three lessons at a time. Tomorrow night?"

"I look forward to it," Carmella said. "And I'll visit you next time. This way your guards won't have to leave their quarters and I'll be allowed more time for training. I need all the lessons I can get before we reach Kargoth. I don't expect King Justin will let us meet so freely once we're in Vellan's territory."

The wizard shook his head, his eyes reflecting the reddish-orange flames. "No, he will not. So don't be late for class. We have lots of material to cover," he said. "And plans to make."

The army traveled along the Rhoon Forest the next day under a thin veil of clouds. The smell of distant rain lingered in the air. King Justin rode among the troops later that morning with Tolapari at his side. Brendan and William rode farther ahead with a company of soldiers from Montavia, both talking up a storm with their fellow countrymen to while away the dreary hours. The King was happy to see the siblings together again, hoping that a similar joy would soon spread throughout Laparia after Vellan was defeated and families were reunited.

"Justin, please do not take this comment with any disrespect," Tolapari said, "but did you not have any qualms about allowing them to meet?" The wizard kept his voice low so that the troops riding in the vicinity would not hear.

King Justin smiled as he fixed his eyes on the gray-soaked terrain many miles in the west—a wide, river valley bursting with muted shades of green and a cluster of mountain peaks nestled sleepily beyond it. Looming closer in the northwest on the far edge of the Rhoon were a handful of slate-gray mountains standing taller than their distant counterparts and ominously guiding the army closer to Kargoth.

"Of course I had qualms, my friend. And doubts, second thoughts and misgivings, too," he replied. "But since Caldurian freely provided us with information about Brendan's astonishing return from the dead, I decided that a little reward was in order. King Rowan, after all, was greatly relieved upon hearing the wizard's theory. He later told me in private that his mind was eased upon learning what had really happened. Until Caldurian offered the information, the King confessed that a small part of him kept wondering if *this* Prince Brendan was really his grandson. He thought it might be some elaborate plot of Vellan's to retake Montavia. Now he is sure that the real Brendan is back." King Justin indicated the sibling princes who were happily talking with the troops. "Allowing Caldurian to meet with Carmella is a small price to pay for Rowan's peace of mind."

Tolapari silently grumbled. "Since you put it that way, I suppose so."

"And Carmella wanted to learn more about the life her cousin had led for the past twenty years in Caldurian's company. After bringing us the medallion, she has earned an opportunity to speak with the wizard," the King said. "I'm taking a chance that Caldurian will be true to his word in this one instance."

"I still don't trust the man. I suspect he has some of his powers back though he will not admit it." Tolapari emitted a sigh of concern. "No, I do not trust him in the least."

"Overall, neither do I."

"Still, I will trust to your judgment as your decisions have never disappointed me in the past."

"Never?"

Tolapari smirked. "A few have come close, but I've learned to live with them."

"Good. Then live with this one as well," he replied. "Anyway, Caldurian is under the eyes of eight watchful guards. It's not as if he can wander off without being noticed, so what's the worse that can happen if he and Carmella have a few chats?"

"Do you really want an answer?"

King Justin smiled, hearing William and Brendan's laughter in the air. "Not really. We can debate this another time. But for today, let's enjoy the glorious scent of spring wafting around us. While we still can," he ominously added. "The aroma of war, I fear, will be thick in the air before long."

The clouds increased overnight, hanging low and dark in the sky the next morning. The army awoke to an oppressive dampness in the air and a pervasive sense of gloom throughout the ranks. They had encamped along the southwestern edge of the Rhoon Forest and were anxious to move on and get an open view of the mountains to their north. But before the first breakfast fires were lit, the sky suddenly let loose with a pounding rain that lasted until late afternoon. Rumbles of thunder reverberated down the nearby river valley as a wild lightning storm exploded miles away above the mountains. Reluctantly, King Justin ordered the army to stay put that day. Visibility was reduced to almost nothing and the path ahead would surely be a muddy mess. The only concern anybody had was to stay dry inside their tents and wagons as rain fell relentlessly from the charcoal clouds.

Caldurian invited Carmella to his tent later that morning where they discussed the magic arts. The wizard was immensely pleased that she easily grasped the finer points in his lessons.

"I had no doubt that Liney was my superior in the magic arts," Carmella admitted as the rain bombarded the wizard's tent, "but I'm not the slouch she thought I was. With a little more training, I could have held my own against her in a few tests of skill."

"Now you are getting that training, and I have full confidence that you just might surprise Madeline should the two of you meet again."

Caldurian smiled kindly upon his student amid the steady beat of raindrops. He sensed an intense eagerness in Carmella to learn the magic arts similar to that of her cousin, yet that interest seemed leavened with an appreciation for the subject that Madeline never fully possessed. The wizard was delighted to impart his knowledge and felt joyous that Carmella seemed genuinely grateful for the opportunity. He wondered where he might have ended up in life had she been at his side these past twenty years instead of her cousin, imagining a world far different from the one he now inhabited.

By nightfall the rain had ceased. A refreshing breeze swept down the river valley and slowly dried the ground. Soon a string of fires were ignited throughout the waterlogged camps, including outside of Caldurian's tent where he and Carmella had just finished a meal of soup and bread. After setting aside his bowl, the wizard looked upon Carmella with a professorial air.

"Now that the rain has stopped, it is time for our next lesson—and a most colorful one at that." He indicated Carmella's wagon with a slight turn of his head. "I'll need to borrow a few items from your inventory. Are you ready?"

Within the hour, Carmella had proudly created several of her own gray smoke spheres, each one holding its shape longer than the previous. When she released the last one from her hands, she was nearly flawless in her ability to direct its motion, circling it around the flames toward Caldurian. There it remained stationary in front of him until he forcefully slapped it away into a puff of smoke.

"It had a sturdier composition than the previous ones," he said. "It looked solid, indicating much progress on your part." The wizard glanced delightedly at Carmella. "Congratulations. Lesson passed. Now on to the next step."

"Which is?"

"First we need more items from your cart to add some color."

"To the spheres?"

Caldurian smiled. "Spheres? That's child's play at this point. Tonight I will create something more elaborate. By tomorrow night, you'll be just as proficient in the task. Who knows, but soon you may be looking for your own apprentice."

The following night, just as Caldurian had predicted, Carmella wildly advanced in her lessons. She beamed with pride in the glow of firelight while gazing upon her latest creations that danced lithely and silently above the snapping flames with multihued vibrancy. One after another, they fluttered lightly on warm currents as she directed their moves with a keen mental discipline she had developed with the wizard's assistance.

Earlier that day, when the army had finally passed beyond the Rhoon Forest, a handful of towering mountains were fully exposed on their right flank in the north. By noontime, the skies had cleared and the sunlight chased away a chill that had swept down the Drusala River valley. By nightfall, as the crescent Bear and Fox moons both waxed in the west, the army made camp on a wide field upon a low rise a couple miles north of the Drusala River. In the waning twilight, all gazed uneasily from afar upon the shadowy waters as the Drusala flowed southeast like a dark and graceful ribbon through the narrow realm of Kargoth. Many silently wondered how many people had fallen victim to its terrible enchantment, by force or by accident.

When darkness enveloped the weary encampment, the waters of the Drusala and the destination ahead were temporarily put out of mind as everyone enjoyed a warm meal, the dry terrain and an early night's rest. Carmella and Caldurian, however, stayed near their fire far into the night, having quiet discussions and practicing advanced smoke manipulation as if the rest of the army was nowhere in sight.

A soldier approached King Justin early the next day as he was breakfasting with Kings Cedric and Rowan. A fiery sunrise bloomed above the distant green splash of the Rhoon. King Justin recognized the soldier from one of the rotating teams who kept watch over Caldurian. He excused himself to talk privately with the young man amid a sea of campfires, tents and bleary-eyed troops.

"What's on your mind, Nemus?" the King inquired. They walked to a spot where several horses were drinking from a stream and lazily munching on tufts of fresh grass.

"Good morning, King Justin," he replied. "Forgive me for interrupting your meal, but I have some news that I thought you should hear at once."

"Would it have anything to do with our special guest?"

"Most definitely." Nemus, a tall, gangly figure with hair down to his shoulders, sported a worried expression as he stood with his hands locked behind him. "I think we have a problem, King Justin. As requested, we've given Caldurian a wide and respectful berth while keeping a discreet watch. But, sir," he excitedly added, leaning in close and lowering his voice to a frantic whisper, "I think he may be up to something. Last night we saw butterflies, at least what looked liked butterflies, fluttering madly above his campfire while he was entertaining Carmella. Butterflies, I tell you, surviving directly above the heat of a fire! Something is not right here."

King Justin gravely shook his head. "No, that does not sound right or natural, and you were wise to report it." Slowly the King offered a knowing smile and looked less worried, putting Nemus at ease. "Unless, of course, it means that Caldurian has started to regain his powers and was showing off to Carmella with a bit of trickery."

"Should I report this to Tolapari?" he breathlessly asked.

"No!" King Justin insisted. "I will handle this matter while you and the others continue your watch. This may be a good thing."

Nemus furrowed his brow. "How so?"

"If Caldurian's magic is returning, we need to find out how much and how fast. He'll never divulge the information voluntarily," the King said. "But if we leave him alone, he'll feel more and more comfortable and let down his guard, allowing us to observe at what rate he is progressing. That is the best way to gage his true powers."

"A clever idea," Nemus agreed.

"And as I speak with Carmella from time to time, she will happily provide me with insight about Caldurian's intentions."

"Of course. That only makes sense," he replied sheepishly. Nemus perked up when noticing Carmella approaching the King in the near distance. "Why, here she comes now, seemingly eager to speak with you."

"What? *Really?*" The King spun around and saw Carmella making a beeline toward him. "Perfect timing," he muttered.

"I would be more than interested in hearing what she has to say about the butterflies," Nemus said, looking hopefully at the King as Carmella approached.

"Let me handle this," the King replied. "Wait here." He went to greet Carmella, quickly taking her aside to another unoccupied space near a thicket of saplings along the stream. "Good morning, dear woman."

"And good morning to you, King Justin," she said with a cheery smile. "I hoped I might find a moment to speak with you, and well, here you are."

"Yes, yes," he said, lowering his voice and indicating for her to do the same. "Always delighted to talk with you, but let's keep our business to ourselves, being on the border of Kargoth and all. Now what can I do for you?"

"I want to confirm the permission you earlier granted me about heading out to search for moonflowers," she said. "The sky will again be clear tonight and both crescent moons are waxing, so there'll be sufficient light to guide me the short distance I have to go. Night is the best time to search for moonflowers as their petals are most potent then."

King Justin smiled wearily. "Yes, my son informed me of those particulars when he relayed your request several days ago."

"Prince Gregory said you had approved my request–"

"–on the condition that my scouts verify the safety of the areas you wish to explore." The King noted a dismal frown upon her face as if she were expecting an answer of *no*. "But I recently talked to the last group of scouts who returned at dawn and they reported no sign of the enemy over the next several miles into Kargoth. In fact, there are no signs of life at all. The few tiny villages located in this region had been abandoned long ago. It appears that most of the structures had been taken over by the Enâri, and well, you know what happened to them."

Carmella cheered up. "So I'm free to go?"

"Yes, but still be mindful of your location and don't stay out too late."

"Only a few hours," she promised. "I don't expect to travel but a mile or two to locate the moonflowers. There are many wood thickets along the river valley that I spotted from here. The flowers should be plentiful along their edges."

"Then best of luck on your search," the King replied. "If you want, I'd be happy to send a few of my men as escorts."

"Dear me, no. I won't inconvenience them," she remarked with a bit of nervous laughter.

"Very well. I'll inform the sentries on the perimeter that you have my permission to wander tonight so they won't hold you up." He eyed Carmella with a mix of affection and concern. "Have a safe and fruitful journey tonight–*wherever* it takes you."

Carmella locked gazes with the King, smiling pleasantly. "Indeed I will."

Moments later, she departed the way she had come. King Justin turned around, longing to finish his breakfast without further interruption. But when he saw Nemus still standing patiently in the distance, he hurried over to him, eager to shoo him away.

"I waited here as you requested, sir," he said, bubbling with curiosity about the King's conversation with Carmella.

"Yes, so you did," he replied with an impatient sigh.

"Is there anything I should know?" he jumped in before King Justin had a chance to dismiss him.

The King thought for a moment and then looked Nemus directly in the eyes, lowering his voice to a whisper. "When I spoke with Carmella, she verified everything you told me about Caldurian's powers returning. She, too, was concerned."

"Even about the butterflies?"

King Justin raised his eyebrows with a grave and deliberate slowness. "*Especially* the butterflies! So my best advice, Nemus, is to continue your excellent watch and to keep your distance. Let's have this play out for a while longer and see what happens."

Nemus nodded. "I understand. Like you said, let Caldurian show us who he really is and then clamp him in chains."

"Yes, something like that," he said, giving him a fatherly pat on the shoulder. "Now return to your camp, Nemus, and remember– business as usual tonight."

"Understood," he replied before heading back.

When he was finally alone among the horses, King Justin shook his head as a swirl of conflicting thoughts battled one another in his weary mind. He hated deceiving people, but some matters couldn't be divulged just yet, even to his closest friends and advisors. After giving himself a moment, he soon rejoined King Cedric and King Rowan around a small fire where they had remained enjoying their breakfast.

"Justin, your tea is probably as cold as stream water," King Cedric remarked while munching on a biscuit. "Sit down and relax. You'll have all day to address the minor concerns thrown your way."

"Oh, I don't mind," he replied. "There were a few lingering matters I was happy to get out of the way before we start moving."

"Anything we can do?" King Rowan asked.

"No. Just minor concerns as Cedric rightly guessed," King Justin replied with a gracious smile. "Just minor concerns."

The Fox and Bear moons shone brilliantly later that evening as they dipped in the west. Carmella took a short break from one of her lessons and sat by the wizard's campfire. She gazed up at the lunar pair, pleased with the amount of light they offered, thinking it sufficient to help guide her way into the valley.

Suddenly a burst of sparks erupted from the fire, startling her. At that same moment, the wizard emerged from his tent carrying a small torch, hunched over and appearing tired like a bear lumbering outside its cave after a long hibernation. The tent flap had been tossed over the roof edge, leaving a yawning opening in the darkened structure.

"I can't find that blasted vial of ground gerka root!" Caldurian spouted in frustration. "And I couldn't find it earlier in your wagon."

"It was next to the rasaweed. I know we had plenty of it left."

"But I can't find it!" he snapped. "We must have used it up."

"Well, you're in a mood tonight," Carmella replied. "But to make you happy, I'll check my supplies. Maybe we can substitute if we need to."

"Substitute? I think not! Maybe we should call it a night." The wizard stretched his arms with the torch still in hand. "These lessons have been taxing. Perhaps you could use a break, too."

"Surely we have time for one more lesson!" Carmella pleaded. "I don't want to stop now that I'm making progress." She grabbed the torch from the wizard and climbed up the three steps set near the back of her wagon. "I'll find that gerka root. Let me take another look." She pushed the door open and stepped inside.

Caldurian shook his head and sighed. He followed her into the wagon and partially closed the door behind him. "All right, but only one more lesson," he uttered in strict tones as his words seeped out through the narrow opening and drifted across the tall grass. The Fox and Bear moons inched westward in their silent journey.

A few minutes later, Carmella's disappointed words seeped out the back of her wagon. "*Hmmm*, so I guess we did use it all up." Slowly the door opened and she stepped out with the glowing torch in hand.

"That's what I told you from the start!" The wizard's voice angrily boomed within the shadows behind her. "So with that, I'll be off to bed."

"Fine!" Carmella replied, climbing down the steps with the torch held aloft. The wizard emerged through the doorway a moment later, following closely behind. "But I wouldn't be surprised if you hid the rest of that gerka root on purpose," she added with a backward glance as she walked toward the campfire. She disgustedly tossed the torch into the flames which sent up a shower of dancing sparks. The wizard in the meantime, slipped quietly into his tent, slowly shaking his head as Carmella shuffled back to her wagon. Suddenly she stopped and spun around, going to Caldurian's tent. She poked her head through the opening. "Just so you know, I expect an extra lesson tomorrow!" she demanded before dropping the tent flap and sealing the wizard inside.

Carmella trudged to her wagon, muttering as she lifted the set of steps and slid them inside the back before pulling the door closed. She walked to the front, gently patting her horses before climbing up onto the seat and grabbing hold of the reins. With a gentle command, the wagon rattled across the grassy terrain until it rolled outside the border of Caldurian's invisible square prison. Carmella offered a gentle wave and a friendly smile to one of the guards as she departed.

"See you tomorrow night if he's in a better mood," she said as she passed by, noting an amused grin upon the soldier's face.

But instead of retiring for the night, Carmella continued driving along the southern edge of the encampment. As she slowly rattled past a series of bonfires, the steady glow of reddish-orange flames projected thin, wavering shadows upon an array of tents whose walls undulated in a gentle breeze. She noted the distant line of the Drusala River to her left as it flowed with a mirror-like stillness. The dual moons cast their subtle light upon the enchanted waters, unfazed by the strength of Vellan's spell.

In time, the last camps receded against a velvety black backdrop. Carmella glanced over her shoulder for a final look. She didn't encounter any of the perimeter guards though guessed that they had most likely seen her as they blended in with the night. Being true to his word, King Justin must have informed his sentries of her late-night excursion and told them not to bother her. She sighed, wondering if she would ever see the kindly King again.

Carmella veered southwest, heading for a stretch of trees about a mile away from King Justin's army. The land had gradually sloped downhill in spots and she took her time navigating the bumpy and hard terrain. About ten minutes later, the ground leveled off and she headed directly west again. A scattering of trees grew to her left that soon thickened into a dense wood. A half mile farther south, and now out of her view, lay the Drusala River.

She pulled gently on the reins moments later and brought her team to a stop, releasing a stream of air through her tightly pressed lips. She leaned back in her seat for a moment and looked up at the dual moons plowing through a field of stars.

"Well, here goes nothing," she whispered to the darkness as a sliver of doubt overshadowed her finely crafted plan. "Or maybe not," she added with a shrug before climbing off the cart. The silvery light of the two crescent moons splashed upon the colorfully embroidered stars, comets and other fantastical shapes on her cloak.

She walked to the back of the wagon whose faded sides were painted as wildly as her flowing cloak. With a rapidly beating heart, Carmella pushed open the back door, reached inside and removed the steps. She set them on the ground and then stepped back into the moonlight, gazing apprehensively into the black void of the wagon's interior.

"You can step outside," she softly said. "We're far away from the encampment."

For a moment there was utter silence except for the rustling wind through the trees. Carmella noted a wavering shadow moving inside the wagon, the vague object nearly indistinguishable from its murky surroundings. Finally, a tall figure emerged through the doorway and into the moonlight.

"Well done," said Caldurian while standing on the top step, a satisfied smile upon his face. "It seems, Carmella, there's a bright future for you in the world of smoke manipulation, and perhaps in theatrics as well. Congratulations on this impressive first showing."

CHAPTER 98

Varied Paths

Carmella guided her horses through the moonlight of southern Kargoth with Caldurian by her side, both pleased with their clever deception. Earlier at the army encampment, they had combined their limited powers to create a smoke replica of the wizard inside her wagon, and then together, manipulated it to walk back to Caldurian's tent. Now, both traveled through the night, finally in control of their fates when it mattered most.

They took a break past midnight near a stream flowing down from the mountains to their north, believing they were safe from the King's patrolling scouts. Following the wizard's advice, Carmella had veered gradually toward the mountains and away from easier paths along the river valley. Caldurian believed that King Justin would dispatch search parties up the Drusala River and into the woods along its banks when his absence was discovered the next morning.

"After one whiff of the stale smoke and sooty remains inside my tent, it won't take long for Tolapari to figure out how I made my escape," he said with a mirthful chuckle. "But we have enough time to put plenty of distance between us and them. Still, it might be wise for you to unhitch this wagon in the stretch of woods up ahead. We can make better time riding the horses to Del Norác."

"I won't leave my wagon behind," Carmella insisted. "This vehicle has been my home away from Red Fern for many years. I couldn't bear the thought of abandoning it."

"But if we—"

"But nothing," she replied. "If it takes a bit longer to reach Vellan, then so be it. I will not inconvenience myself for his sake or for yours. That was not part of our deal."

Caldurian sighed. "Very well. As far as getting to Del Norác, I will leave our fate in your hands. But once there, please let me direct the way. I've been to Vellan's abode in Mount Minakaris many times and have sway with his people. You are a stranger and would be arrested on the spot."

Carmella shrugged. "What's wrong with that? I want to find my cousin. Being arrested would be a logical step toward that goal."

"Unless you're killed in the process," the wizard gruffly replied. "Or worse yet, taken to Deshla prison. Madeline, I'm certain, is in Vellan's stronghold if she's still alive. And though Deshla and Vellan's quarters are both built into the mountain, they are still a distance apart. Deshla is farther west around the base of Minakaris, and from the stories I've heard, you most definitely do not want to end up there."

"You've never paid it a visit?" Carmella asked with an uneasy heart, knowing that Nicholas and Leo were taking part in a raid upon the compound. When she thought of Ivy possibly languishing in Deshla, she couldn't help but fear the worst.

"Vellan never gave me a tour, and truthfully, I wasn't eager to see his operation," he admitted. "While I have the stomach to endure much that is unpleasant, even this wizard has his limits. So do not be flippant about wanting to be apprehended by Vellan's soldiers. They might toss you in Deshla for sport before questioning you—or into the Drusala River—which would end your quest in a flash."

"Point well taken. Anything else?"

"Yes. Since you refuse to relinquish your wagon, I suggest you veer left about a half mile after we pass the woods coming up on our right. As I recall, the land is more easily passable just south of here with a few villages and fertile farmland scattered about." The wizard looked askance at Carmella. "Yet I can't say when the fields have last been tilled or planted. The Enâri and Islanders had swept into most regions of Kargoth that were once productive. Many residents fled who were not loyal to Vellan or under his enchantment. But now that the Enâri no longer exist, many farms have probably been abandoned. The same goes for the iron, coal and silver mines Vellan operated in the surrounding mountains."

"Vellan had a hand in several lucrative undertakings."

"Magic *and* a fattened treasury allowed him local control and influence abroad. But those ventures must be at a standstill since the Spirit Box was opened. All the people of Harlow, Linden, Surna and Kargoth combined, even if under Vellan's will, couldn't match the population of workers provided by the Enâri horde. Vellan's success was due to their vast numbers and unthinking devotion."

"But now that they've been removed, he doesn't have a leg to stand on," Carmella remarked. She gently snapped the reins, passing several tall trees to their right.

"I wouldn't paint an image of Vellan as that crippled, but I see your point. Still, King Justin and his allies had better watch themselves. A cornered animal at wit's end is both dangerous and unpredictable. Best to keep that in mind."

"I suppose Vellan may yet have a few surprises up his sleeves."

"As should we all," Caldurian replied, his face bathed in moonlight and shadows as he felt for the small glass vial deep inside his cloak pocket. "As should we all."

Carmella and the wizard rode throughout the night, agreeing it would be safest to sleep during the day until they had a better feel for the lay of the land. An hour before sunrise, Caldurian eyed a small farmhouse standing sleepily against the ashen gray horizon. They headed for the structure along a rutted, grassy path. A storage barn and a small shed, visible to the right, slouched among the gloomy surroundings. Another farmhouse stood at the far end of an adjacent fallow field, each building once part of a thriving community that had gone to seed.

"Hardly a top rate establishment, but it will do," Caldurian tiredly remarked, gazing at the one-story clay brick building with a thatched roof. Last autumn's dried weeds encroached upon the front door and shuttered windows.

"I can barely keep my eyes open," Carmella said with a deep yawn as she brought the wagon to a halt.

"Me either, though I don't especially mind," the wizard replied. "Sleep has not been a loyal companion ever since I fell victim to the âvin éska. But I suspect the abundant fresh air and my first taste of freedom in quite some time have finally tired me out."

Carmella unhitched the horses and let them drink from a stream running through the property. Caldurian wandered to the front door and cautiously placed an ear to the wood and listened, but heard nothing. He leaned against the door and gave it a firm push with his shoulder. It opened, allowing a gush of stale air to flow out into the cool, predawn air. He then grabbed a stick lying on the ground, and after whispering a few words, its tip began to glow until it burst into a small, steady flame.

"I'm happy to say that smoke isn't the only thing I can manipulate again," he commented in the shadows as Carmella approached from behind. "Who knows, but by the time I reach Kargoth, I may be my old self again."

"That would be a shame," Carmella replied as she stepped into the circle of light. "I believe your temporary inability to dabble in magic is what spurred your desire to meet with me and take me on as an apprentice. Had Tolapari never used the âvin éska against you, can you honestly say that you would have had any interest in our alliance?" Caldurian returned a wounded gaze. "I'm only speaking what's in my heart."

"Perhaps so, but your comment is still a weighty nugget to digest," he replied with a faraway look, causing Carmella some concern. "But do not misinterpret me. I am neither offended nor upset. I'm merely considering the possibility that your words just might be true." He stroked his beard, his thoughts running wild. "If things had turned out otherwise and I wasn't forced to sit for weeks in the Citadel pondering my fate and past deeds, perhaps I might still be the same old Caldurian." A vague smile appeared on his lips. "Then again, maybe I still am. These few days together have been lovely, but is it possible that most people remain who they really are deep down inside regardless of temporary shifts in circumstances?"

"Perhaps–or perhaps not," Carmella replied, rubbing her arms as dampness and fatigue took its toll. "Time will tell. But it's far too late–or early, I can't tell which–to have a philosophical discussion."

"You're right," he said, indicating for her to follow him inside. "Sleep is our first concern. We'll evade no one if we succumb to a deep slumber while traversing the roads of Kargoth, such as they are."

He stepped inside the farmhouse with Carmella close behind. The light from the torch seemed to be eaten up by the darkness. Slowly their eyes adjusted to the gloom and both looked around in the small kitchen of sorts. A chairless table kept company with a tiny fireplace, its yawning hearth holding a pile of charred logs upon a bed of cold ashes. As they wandered a few steps during their cursory examination, the tip of Carmella's boot hit a heavy object lying on the ground, briefly startling her.

"Nothing to be frightened of," Caldurian said, holding the torch aloft. "No one else is around."

"I'm on edge from a lack of sleep," she replied as the wizard bent down to examine her discovery. "What is it? A dead animal?"

"No," he replied. He stood and held up the object for her to see. "It's only a boot."

"A boot?"

He nodded with a grim façade and slowly tipped the boot upside down. A stream of sand spilled out like a narrow waterfall, momentarily baffling Carmella.

"There's a second boot beside it that's also filled with sand," he said. "And a pile of ragged garments."

Carmella gazed at the shadowy floor before glancing up wide-eyed at the wizard, suddenly understanding. "Enâri remains," she whispered. "One of them must have died here."

"Perhaps several." Caldurian walked to the fireplace and noticed another dark mound on the floor. Upon closer inspection, he discovered a second set of sand-filled boots and a pile of tattered garments. He grabbed a charred stick from the fireplace and ignited it with his torch, providing more light in the room. He handed it to Carmella so they could better search the property inside and out.

In all, they located the sandy remains of twenty-six Enâri creatures within the three buildings on the farmstead. An additional seven were found at various spots outdoors. Carmella felt queasy upon the first few discoveries and decided to sleep through the approaching morning in her wagon. She wished Caldurian a good rest in the farmhouse.

"I'll have fitful bouts of sleep if I stay in there," she said near the front door. "Still, I think Jagga's last moments will haunt my dreams tonight regardless of where I sleep."

"Experiencing pangs of guilt for taking that medallion to King Justin?" the wizard inquired. "It's not easy having the fates of tens of thousands of beings on your conscience, even ones as unnatural as the Enâri."

"I suppose it isn't," she said before trudging off to her wagon. She slowly turned around, her expression steady and confident. "But I don't think I could have lived with myself either if I *hadn't* brought the medallion to the Citadel. The fates of many innocents would have weighed more heavily on my mind if I did nothing." She shrugged, offering a grim smile. "In the end, Caldurian, I suppose I shall get the sleep I deserve according to my actions. As you probably will, too," she said, making for her wagon. "Goodnight. And pleasant dreams."

After waking several hours later and eating a brief meal, they took to the road at noontime. They traveled near woodland stretches whenever possible, feeling a sense of security beneath the eaves of tall trees coming back to life. But the region seemed otherwise desolate. On rare occasions they spotted smoke rising from a distant chimney of an isolated household and avoided those areas altogether. They traveled northwest, following the course of the Drusala River several miles to their left. Depending on the elevation and openness of the terrain, they could view the dark, watery strip flowing through Kargoth like a deadly snake. But they preferred to keep closer to the mountains that gazed down upon them on their right.

They stopped for supper near a craggy rock formation upon a field littered with saplings and wild grass. As Carmella heated water for tea over a small fire, Caldurian glanced at her long, beige gloves and smiled in amusement.

"If I had my full powers, I could remove that silly pumpkin spell," he said, his legs dangling from the large flat rock he sat upon. "No need to go chasing Madeline all around Laparia."

"I told you that that wasn't the only reason I've been pursuing her," Carmella replied. "I want to draw her back to being the person she once was, however slim the chances. And one indication that I'll have succeeded in that task is to get Liney to willingly lift her spell. In the meantime, I'll endure the pumpkin hue."

"Suit yourself, though the color does complement your cloak. And your wagon," he added, glancing where the horses contentedly munched upon some grass. Suddenly he turned his head, listening for a subtle sound that had caught his attention. But other than the snapping flames or the cry of a distant bird, all was quiet.

"What is it?" Carmella asked.

"I thought I heard something," he replied, his dark, brooding eyes scanning the terrain. Soon he relaxed and seemed at ease again. "Probably my imagination."

"At least we know the Enâri aren't stalking us," she joked.

"I can't imagine Vellan rebuilding that army after such a debilitating defeat. His only allies left are from the Isles and those citizens in the Northern Mountains he either duped or forced to drink from the Drusala." Caldurian glanced about the area a second time. "I'm guessing that most of them have regrouped around Del Norác to await King Justin's army. That is why our way through this section of Kargoth has been undisturbed. But as we near Vellan's stronghold, our movements must be more discreet. I can't assume anyone I meet on the road will show me the same loyalty that *this* loyal apprentice shows to Vellan," he warned, pointing to himself.

Carmella looked up as the water began to steam. "*Loyal* apprentice? So your desire to meet with Vellan is simply to do his will and nothing more?"

"You ask that as if you doubt my intentions."

"A little. You've suggested that you could do a far better job in his place," she said. "Though for the life of me I can't figure out what Vellan's job in life is."

"Yet you think that I believe I would be much more suited to the task." Caldurian grinned. "Well, that's one vote of confidence for me. But what do *you* think?"

Carmella gazed at the wizard through the veil of rising steam. "To be honest, I don't think you would have been much different from Vellan despite the fact that you haven't reached his level of ability in the magic arts nor possess your own Enâri army."

"True. I'd never be able to create such a race of beings."

"You would have recruited an army of your own. And even if your desire to defeat or enslave the kingdoms of Laparia might be a bit less ambitious than Vellan's, you'd still be just as ruthless and determined ruling over whatever smaller slice of the region you carved out for yourself. Perhaps even more so."

"Interesting," he said, dropping to his feet and leaning against the rock. "I suppose that extra ruthlessness you assume I'd possess would be to make up for the fact that I'm not one of the true wizards from the Gable Mountains. Just a pale imitation at best?"

"Those are your words, Caldurian. But that's not what intrigues me most."

"Oh?" He folded his arms. "Go on. I want to hear more."

Carmella stepped back from the steaming kettle and walked over to him, feeling more his equal than his student. "Since spending time with you lately–and most of it not unpleasant, mind you–I've often wondered if you would have turned out differently had you apprenticed with another wizard instead of Vellan."

"Another teacher? I couldn't imagine that," he replied. "I met Vellan twenty-seven years ago when he was traveling through the Red Mountains near my village. I was nineteen, working on farms, chopping wood and harvesting ice depending on the season. But less than a year later he took me on as an apprentice after I helped him secure supplies and served as a messenger and gatherer of information while he spent time in the region. I gained his trust so much so that seven years after I met him, he had sent me off to Morrenwood to negotiate an alliance with King Justin."

"And how did that work out?"

Caldurian grimaced. "That's irrelevant. But as to your original remark–*no*. I couldn't imagine having another teacher."

"Perhaps you're imagining the wrong type of teacher. Perhaps the wizard Frist?" Carmella suggested. "Where would you be now had your path and Frist's crossed years ago and he had taken you on as an apprentice? Your fate would have been far different." She looked up with grave concern. "The lives of many people would have been spared much death and hardship because Vellan wouldn't have had you doing his dirty work."

"He would have found somebody else to train and perform those same tasks," Caldurian said. "I am not the only one who has fallen under his sway."

"But your loyalty to him is unequaled–though Liney comes close." Carmella hoisted herself upon the rock to sit, her feet dangling over the edge. "From my last impression when I talked to her, I'd say that you two are of the same mind. Liney oozed a chilly devotion to Vellan despite having rarely met with the wizard as you told me."

"Anyone who meets Vellan is quite taken by his intellect and strength of personality, and is happy to do his will," he replied. "Your cousin included. But if I had met Frist instead of Vellan, I suppose things might have turned out differently."

"Well, now you've met me again," Carmella said. "Maybe my good nature will rub off and turn you from your current path in life."

Caldurian sighed. "My path is my path," he said resignedly, staring straight ahead to avoid her probing gaze. "I've spent too much time in Vellan's service to change on a whim now. His ideas have shaped my ideas."

"But you've helped to train me, Caldurian, and I'm the enemy from your point of view," she said, briefly catching his eye. "So you must have changed a little bit to want to associate with me."

He looked kindly upon her and smiled. "We both know we're with each other now because we are *using* each other–willingly, of course–and nothing more. I needed you to help me escape and you need my expertise to find Madeline. I haven't really changed except for suffering the effects of the âvin éska–and those, thankfully, are subsiding."

Carmella eased herself off the rock and stood toe to toe with Caldurian, looking up with skepticism. "If you haven't really changed, how do I know that you'll keep your word and not turn me over to Vellan? Since I gave the medallion to King Justin, I think Vellan would be delighted to kill me or have me as his prisoner."

"You have nothing to fear, Carmella. I promise to keep my word and help you find your cousin and avoid Vellan if I can. And though I probably won't change much beyond that, consider this pledge my one attempt in life to perform a noble, selfless deed. I wouldn't be here without your assistance, so I am in your debt and will repay you in full."

"The old Caldurian would not have done this."

"*Hmmm*, then perhaps I've changed a little. But I assure you, the change does not run deep."

"I'll take whatever I can get," she replied. "And to show my appreciation, I promise not to turn you over to King Justin's troops or his allies should the opportunity ever present itself."

"I assumed we had a tacit understanding regarding that," he replied with mock surprise. "Still, it's good to hear you say it."

"Just be careful you don't get yourself in a fix if you go wandering," she warned. "I won't turn you in, but don't expect me to jump to your rescue if it'll stop me from reaching Del Norác. I'm still loyal to Arrondale and won't betray my homeland to save your neck for anything–well, at least not a second time. Are we clear on that?"

"As clear as a starry sky. And I think that–"

Caldurian suddenly looked up and scanned the rock formation and the surrounding area. A sense of uneasiness overwhelmed him. Carmella took immediate notice.

"Again?" she asked warily.

Caldurian returned an uncertain gaze. "I feel as if eyes are upon us," he whispered.

"Maybe the King's scouts have taken up positions nearby." She looked around with equal alarm but spotted no threat. "We should move on anyway and find a place to make camp for the night. We can see if this feeling persists while we're traveling."

The wizard agreed and they swiftly took to the road. The rock formation, now tinted in soft shades of red and gold from the setting sun, slowly receded in the distance. The stern and regal mountains looming to their right looked on, urging them forward in silent haste while standing guard amid seas of green foliage and narrow, winding valleys.

The air held a biting chill the following day. Though the sun shown brightly among a collage of swiftly moving clouds, the day felt more like late autumn than early spring.

"The weather has a mind of its own in the mountains," the wizard said. "As we slowly rise in elevation, I wouldn't be surprised to run into a blast of snow."

Carmella fixed her eyes on the hard, grassy terrain. "We don't need surprises on this trip. The solitude is nerve-racking enough."

Shortly afterward they were greeted not with a surprise but with a stark reminder of recent events. Just ahead on an area flecked with small trees and scrub brush, lay a dark, bumpy line that first appeared to be a narrow stretch of soil that had been dug up and left to the elements. But as Carmella's wagon rolled past the curious sight, she and the wizard recognized the composition of the slightly wavering trail alongside them. They stopped and climbed down to take a closer look.

"How many?" Carmella asked, gazing upon a pair of boots and a pile of ragged clothes. One of the boots, standing upright and once filled with the sandy remains of an Enâri creature, was now packed to the ankle with globs of wet mud resulting from the melted snow and early spring rains that had swept through the valley.

"Fifty pairs or so," Caldurian replied as he surveyed the path of mud-caked boots, tattered clothing, leather belts and sheathed daggers. "Perhaps they were marching to Del Norác, though most likely to one of Vellan's nearby garrisons which are probably now abandoned." The wizard cast a grim eye upon Carmella. "None of them ever knew that death was heading their way."

Carmella sighed, recalling Jagga's last moments. "I can assure you that it was a complete surprise to all."

"There'll be ghoulish exhibits like this throughout Kargoth." Caldurian walked among the solemn display of footwear and weaponry, gently moving a boot here and there with the tip of his own. Any sandy remains of the Enâri, other than what was left behind inside some of the boots, had long ago been washed away and reabsorbed into the soil.

"We should go," Carmella said uncomfortably. "I don't want to linger here."

"You of all people wouldn't," he said, turning around amidst the morbid remnants. But when noting the distress on her face, he apologized. "I didn't mean for that to sound crass. I was just–"

She raised a hand to gently silence him. "No offense taken."

The wizard walked toward her. "You're right. We should leave. There's still a long way to go today and I don't want to–"

He stopped in mid sentence, eyeing one particular pair of boots that grabbed his attention. He stooped down to closely examine the items in the splashes of sunshine as the clouds sailed steadily eastward and cast uneasy shadows upon the rugged terrain.

"What is it?" Carmella asked.

Caldurian looked up with a stony expression, indicating the wagon with a turn of his head. "I'll tell you when we're moving again. Time to go."

The stars and dual crescent moons blinked and faded behind tattered clouds. Cool breezes stirred the tips of creaking branches in the nearby woods. A fire snapped and sputtered close by, releasing a trail of ghostly smoke into the frosty air. Carmella and Caldurian sat huddled near the flames. A short distance away within the shadowy trees, someone kept watch over them.

An individual leaned protectively behind a gnarled pine, his eyes fixed upon the pair as they engaged in quiet conversation near the blaze. The spy curiously watched, unable to hear Carmella speak as she animatedly moved her hands. The wizard looked on thoughtfully, nodding from time to time, apparently on the receiving end of Carmella's storytelling or a prolonged scolding–the spy couldn't tell which.

What he did know, however, was that he needed to inch closer to gather information and learn the intentions of the two individuals before deciding his next move–whether to continue following them or flee in the opposite direction. He took a deep breath before stepping away from the tree, ready to act. But as he carefully moved one foot away and touched it to the ground, the sharp crack of a brittle twig reverberated through the woods. He froze in place.

With his heart racing, the man took another deep breath and listened closely. Something didn't make sense. He pressed firmly on the foot he had just moved and felt only smooth, hard ground beneath the sole of his boot, suddenly aware that he wasn't the one who had stepped on a twig. The man spun around, ready to bolt, only to face a large black shadow looming before him. The glint of the distant firelight reflected off a metal blade poised in front of him.

"Overheard anything interesting?" Caldurian asked, his voice stern and accusatory as he held a dagger threateningly in front of the man's widening eyes.

The nervous figure involuntarily gulped. "I was just–" But he stopped talking as the wizard's voice fully registered in his ears. "*Caldurian*? How–? How did you–?" The man slowly turned his head and observed the flickering fire just outside the woods, noting that Carmella and the other Caldurian were still sitting there as before with Carmella speaking and the wizard nodding at each sentence with deliberate interest. The spy looked back upon Caldurian's menacing form and deadly weapon, shaking his head in bewilderment. "*Two* of you?" he asked. "How can that be?"

"I'm a wizard, and a good one at that–or have you already forgotten, Mune? I have many intriguing spells up my cloak sleeves." Caldurian sheathed his knife and looked upon Mune with a vague smirk. "Now quit standing there with that silly expression. Follow me to the fire. It's murderously cold out here."

"All right," he replied as if trapped in a confusing dream.

Moments later, Carmella turned her head as she sat by the crackling blaze warming her hands. Her eyebrows slowly arched when she saw Caldurian emerge from the trees and stroll toward her. A short man with a goatee and bundled in a weathered coat walked beside him. When they stepped into the firelight, she immediately recognized Mune as the individual who had run out of the Blue Citadel while she was arguing with her cousin.

"*You!*" she said with contempt.

"Yes, *me*," Mune replied, remembering Carmella from that same moment. But all the while, he couldn't keep his eyes off the second Caldurian who sat by the fire on a small wood crate, nodding occasionally as he looked intently in Carmella's direction while remaining absolutely quiet. "Your twin?" he asked.

"Oh, nothing but a smoke illusion." Caldurian walked over to his three-dimensional double. He rapidly waved a hand several times through the faux wizard until the creation lost its cohesion and disintegrated before their eyes.

"Impressive."

"Carmella and I created it together," he said. "She's becoming quite adept in the magic arts thanks to a bit of training from me."

"Just like her cousin," Mune remarked. "But less edgy I hope. You'll have to tell me how the two of you became fast friends."

"I wouldn't go that far," Carmella said. "But first tell me about Liney. Seeing that you're here, can I assume that her plan to seek an audience with Vellan didn't work out?" she asked hopefully, looking about. "Where is she? Hiding in the trees?"

"Don't assume anything," he replied. "Madeline and I parted company weeks ago when the snow was still flying. She most likely made it to Del Norác, though as to her desire to meet with Vellan, well, I don't dare speculate on that visit."

"What are you saying?" Caldurian asked, clearly worried.

"I'm saying that Madeline got her wish. At least I think so," Mune said, warming his hands by the fire. "We spotted a distant company of Islanders in the middle of winter as we made our way through Kargoth. By that time my desire to be in this dreadful realm had long since disappeared, not that it was strong to begin with. But Madeline was determined to find Vellan and decided she could best achieve that by getting captured on purpose. Companies of Islanders were leaving the southern parts of Kargoth and heading to Vellan's stronghold to regroup after the Enâri were destroyed. Madeline thought it best to abandon our slow and stealthy approach and tag along with Vellan's allies instead."

"Then why are you still here?" Caldurian asked, taking a seat by the fire.

"Because I finally came to my senses, that's why! I was leery about meeting Vellan, especially after failing him at the Citadel. But I tagged along with Madeline out of a begrudging sense of loyalty, hoping that one day before we reached Del Norác that she would come to her senses, too. But when we saw some Islanders while hiding out in the hills, she decided the quickest way to Vellan was through them. At that moment, I knew reaching Del Norác was about to become a terrifying reality, so I did what came naturally to me. I panicked."

"But my cousin went on with her plan?" Carmella inquired.

Mune nodded. "To make a long story short, we debated, then argued, and then decided to go our separate ways. Madeline left our location in the hills and sought out the Islanders, promising not to tell them about me. I assume they took her with them as a prisoner, but they were too far away for me to clearly see anything. Since then, I've been living in empty houses and barns during the winter, slowly making my way back southeast to get out of this place and settle down somewhere. I'm tired and need a long rest. I've decided to be loyal to me for the foreseeable future."

Caldurian grunted. "Apparently you had no loyalty left to spare for *me* after all the lucrative work I've sent you over the years. As soon as plans broke down in Morrenwood, you and Madeline fled south to Vellan, abandoning me as a prisoner in Montavia."

"Things didn't work out there either?" Mune asked. "I had heard rumors."

"No, they didn't." Caldurian explained how Montavia had been liberated and how Tolapari had disabled him with the âvin éska spell. "But things are turning around. I'm nearly my old self again, no thanks to you or Madeline."

Mune sighed. "I'm sorry, but at the time my mind was otherwise occupied. Madeline insisted that we find Vellan as King Justin's soldiers were closing in. I'd have been tossed in prison if they caught me. And as for Madeline, well, she had said that–" He quickly caught himself and went silent, catching Caldurian's probing gaze.

"Had said what?" the wizard asked with an icy calmness. "What did Madeline say as you fled the Citadel?"

Mune glanced at Carmella for advice. But when none was forthcoming, he looked at the wizard, riddled with guilt. "She had said–and it pains me to repeat this, Caldurian, though you're bound to get it out of me sooner or later–but Madeline said that you had *outlived your usefulness.* Her words, not mine!"

Caldurian moved his lips as if about to respond, but then simply stared into the fire, crushed by the comment. Carmella and Mune noted his distress and eyed one another. Mune shrugged, not knowing what to say, so Carmella broke the uneasy silence.

"Caldurian, you know that my cousin has a tendency to speak before thinking," she said in gentle tones. "I'm sure Liney never expected you to hear those sentiments and probably regretted the words the moment they left her lips."

The wizard shook his head as a grim smile crossed his face. "No. Madeline meant every word. And I see her point," he said, briefly looking up. "I was ultimately responsible for the raid on the

Blue Citadel even though I was in Montavia. I must shoulder the brunt of the blame. Still, I don't know if I can ever forgive her."

Mune swallowed hard. "Do you forgive *me*?"

Caldurian flicked his hand back without looking at him. "Fine. You're forgiven. But it feels worse when such devastating words come from Madeline," he admitted, talking to the frenzied flames. "Her betrayal has pierced my heart as I had given her so much over the years." The fire reflected wildly in the wizard's eyes as he sat seemingly paralyzed. "Other than her undivided loyalty to her assignments, Madeline has given me nothing else in return. I had hoped that one day..."

The firewood crackled and a cool breeze played across the brittle grass. Carmella studied Caldurian's face and saw him for a moment more as a man with normal emotions than a conniving wizard, sensing that his heart right now was as empty as the one inside his smoky counterpart.

"Did you have feelings for my cousin?" she asked.

He offered a vague smile. "That's irrelevant now. Whatever dreams this wizard once had when he met that intriguing nursemaid twenty years ago, hoping to take her under his wing and teach her the ways of the world and of magic, well..." He looked up and sighed. "I guess some dreams aren't meant to be realized."

"Did you ever approach Liney with your intentions?"

"Not directly," he replied. "But I could tell early on that Madeline was a focused individual when it came to the magic arts and attaining her place in the world. She hadn't room in her heart for anyone except herself. Deep inside I knew that and should have let my budding sentiments die years ago, but a fool carries on," he sadly admitted. "I took pride in my apprentice, but maybe I should have left Madeline at the Citadel after our failed kidnapping attempt. She may have enjoyed happier years. I might have, too."

A heavy silence fell. Mune looked on uneasily, never having seen Caldurian embroiled in such doubt. He wished he hadn't secretly followed him and Carmella over the last couple days. If the wizard was losing his edge because Madeline had departed, how would he handle meeting her again, only this time possibly at Vellan's side? He wondered if he should go his separate way come morning.

"Getting off topic," he said, "but how did you and Carmella track me down? You had cornered me quite cleverly with the help of that smoke illusion, so I'm guessing you discovered there was only one individual trailing you and not a troop of Islanders."

Caldurian sat up and stretched, happy to talk about something else. He regretted that he had opened up about Madeline, but the deed was done and it was time to move on.

"It was simple, Mune. I had found your boots."

"Excuse me?"

"Carmella and I came across a trail of Enâri boots and garments earlier in the day," he explained. "A sobering sight if ever there was one."

"I'd come across many such displays in my travels," Mune said. "And though I knew the creatures were dead and disintegrated, I always felt that they might arise whole again while I was sleeping nearby. Very disturbing."

"Anyway," Caldurian continued, "something had caught my eye as I walked among them, namely, a pair of boots that you had once owned and discarded. No doubt you had helped yourself to a better pair left behind by a deceased Enâri soldier."

"How could you possibly know that?" Mune sputtered.

"Is it true?"

"Well–yes! But how could…?"

The wizard chuckled. "Because it was the same set of boots that I had created for you with dried leaves and magic when we met inside the Cumberland Forest last autumn. The spell had since lost its potency. I noticed that patches of the leatherwork had begun to turn back into leaves after you had discarded them."

"The soles of my boots were wearing away, and seeing so many Enâri pairs in such good shape, why shouldn't I help myself? Certainly the Enâri had no more use for them."

"Could we change this ghoulish topic?" Carmella interjected.

"Is Jagga still on your mind?" Caldurian asked.

"Or more specifically, what you had done to him?" Mune added. "The poor thing. I learned how you gave that magic medallion to King Justin and set things in motion."

"I did what I had to do," she said defensively. "It wasn't an easy decision."

"But a deadly one."

"Enough, Mune!" Caldurian snapped. "That's all in the past now. Though if you and Madeline had been a tad more competent orchestrating the Citadel raid, then perhaps we wouldn't be having this discussion."

Mune, his arms akimbo, slowly fumed as he took a step closer to the wizard. "I was *this close* to retrieving the key to the Spirit Box!" he said, holding his thumb and index finger close together. "And you have no idea what I went through to get that close." He recalled his fight with Leo in the upper turret, making no mention of the soldier in the King's Guard he had fatally stabbed in the corridor. "Give me some credit for my effort."

"I suppose you're entitled," the wizard coolly replied.

"But I'm glad Leo Marsh got the best of you in the end," Carmella said. "However, Mune, you got off too easily in my opinion. Unlike you, Leo still suffers from the effects of opening that box, so you might want to stop your bellyaching."

Mune scowled. "Just my luck. I leave Madeline only to end up with her equally exasperating cousin. What are the odds?" he muttered. "You women are almost as irksome as Leo Marsh and Nicholas Raven. Those two have been nothing but trouble." He turned to Caldurian, shaking his head in disgust. "Why didn't you hire those locals from Kanesbury to kill Nicholas instead of just getting him out of the village? Would have saved us a whole lot of trouble in the long run."

"Mune!" Caldurian admonished his associate with a caustic glance, but his words had already piqued Carmella's interest.

"*You're* behind Nicholas' troubles?" she said, jumping to her feet and walking over to the wizard, simmering with anger. "*You're* the one who ruined that young man's life?"

"Thank you, Mune," he responded sarcastically before turning to Carmella. "Now before you start lecturing me, too, let me just say that I have no intention of confessing or apologizing for my actions in Kanesbury. I had my reasons for what I did there."

"But what you did there was–!"

He held up a hand to silence her. "I understand you're fond of Nicholas, but what's happened has happened. He unfortunately got caught up in my plans and–"

"What plans?"

"Not important," he replied, suddenly ashamed to reveal what he had done to Otto Nibbs, Maynard Kurtz and an entire village just to satisfy his thirst for vengeance. That Nicholas Raven had become a casualty of his machinations was now beyond his power to reverse. "You are more than free to tell Mister Raven that I was the cause of all his woes the next time you see him, but don't expect me to go into detail about those–*details*!" He looked at Carmella, offering a smile in hopes of salvaging their fragile camaraderie of late. "You may have been harboring vague hopes since we've teamed up that I could change or *may have* changed or might even *want* to change who I was, Carmella. But as I said before, my path is my path, and parts of it are not very pleasant to look upon. You knew who I was before we started this grand adventure, so don't be surprised when new and unpleasant details are accidentally revealed."

Carmella composed herself and took a deep breath. "I suppose you're right. We each know who the other is and probably shouldn't let our recent familiarity cloud our better judgment."

"Agreed," he said. "But still, let's not throw out all that we've accomplished these past few days. There are some genuinely good moments to salvage among all the obvious flaws–most of them mine, I'll freely admit."

"Agreed." Carmella eyed the two gentlemen, wondering what she had gotten herself into but knowing it was too late to turn back. "All right then. So, who wants supper?" she asked, ironing out the wrinkles in her cloak. "It's my turn to cook."

The trio departed early the next morning under hazy blue skies. Mune, though still reluctant to meet Vellan, decided to accompany the others to Del Norác after learning that there was a massive army heading their way from behind. Caldurian assured him that King Justin's scouts would most likely be fanning out through the woods, along the river and among the mountain foothills, making his journey out of Kargoth questionable at best.

"And they will not take kindly to you once your identity is discovered," he warned. "King Justin knows all about your past deeds. You're better off staying with us."

Mune scratched his head. "I suppose this is the safer route, but somehow I feel doomed no matter which way I go."

"Then what have you got to lose?" Carmella said.

CHAPTER 99

The Drusala River

King Justin rode his horse alongside Tolapari beneath a hazy, midmorning sky. It was the day after Caldurian had engineered his smoky disappearance. The long line of troops and supply wagons had been on the road for several hours, trudging determinedly through the lower region of Kargoth. The towering mountains to the north gazed ominously upon them. The King cast an inquisitive eye upon the wizard when he chuckled to himself, apparently in a good mood despite Caldurian's clever escape.

"Will you share with this tired monarch what has put you in such high spirits?" he inquired. "I could use a good laugh to counter my lack of sleep these past nights."

"I was thinking about Caldurian."

"With amusement?"

Tolapari nodded with a relaxed smile. "I've got to hand it to that scoundrel. A smoke apparition of all things! The moment I stepped inside his tent and detected the whiff of stale smoke and noticed a dusting of ash on the floor, I knew what he had done. No doubt with help from Carmella as I'm guessing his powers haven't fully returned. Still, a simple plan elegantly implemented. No wonder Vellan has kept him around for so long."

"You had exploded in anger this morning," the King reminded him. "And nearly a second time when I refused to send out a party to pursue them."

"I apologize again for having been so abrasive," he replied. "However, you should have tracked them down."

"Understood," the King replied as he gazed across the grassy terrain. The woods to their left were dappled with the morning sun, the budding boughs and sinewy trunks obscuring the view of the Drusala River snaking along on the opposite side. "But now that we're back on the road," he continued, lowering his voice, "I'd like to give you my reason."

"The final decision was yours, Justin. You need not explain."

"Still, I want you to know why I didn't send soldiers to track down Caldurian." He leaned in closer as their horses sauntered across the hard ground, mindful of others within listening distance as he lowered his voice further. "And why I allowed him to escape."

"*Allowed*? Did I just hear you correctly, King Justin?"

"You did, my friend. And as you rarely address me as *King* Justin, I shall assume you are a tad upset with the news."

Tolapari, bubbling with consternation, fixed his eyes forward as some uneven terrain unfolded before them. "I don't know any adjectives that would appropriately describe the level of my upset." He kept his voice at a conversational level so as not to draw any attention, but could not conceal his reddening countenance and the wild look of utter disbelief in his eyes.

"Let me explain."

"Please do!" he replied in a sharp whisper. "How could you allow our enemy to escape–and right near Vellan's doorstep?"

"Perhaps I phrased things incorrectly. I didn't actually allow Caldurian to escape as I didn't really know that he was *planning* an escape. However, I did purposely let my guard down and relaxed the restrictions upon him, hoping to nudge him into *contemplating* an escape."

"What's the difference?" Tolapari grunted with mild disgust. "The result is the same–Caldurian is gone! I'll wager you a creel of fresh trout that he's on his way to Del Norác." He glanced at the King with fiery hope in his eyes. "It's still not too late to pursue him."

"I have no intention of doing so, especially when it was you who gave me the idea of allowing Caldurian to slip away."

"*Me?*" Tolapari was aghast. "During my many visits to the Citadel, not once did I utter a supportive word about Caldurian and his reprehensible deeds. Where did you get the idea that I wanted him released, especially when we finally had him under lock and key?"

"You said something several days ago which only grabbed my attention when King Rowan referred to your words two days later. That's when I started to think about how we might use Caldurian to our advantage," he said. "I had no guarantee if anything positive would result, so I kept silent. But I knew I had to try."

"Tell me, Justin, those words I uttered that prompted you to release one of our vilest enemies into the night."

"You spoke them after Caldurian explained how Vellan had deceived Arileez with that magic potion."

"The one that freed him from his island prison?"

"Yes," the King said. "It was then when you had commented that evil tends to collapse upon itself."

"I had said so after learning of the treacherous second spell in that elixir."

"King Rowan later referenced your words, Tolapari. He said that we must give our all in the fight against Vellan since we couldn't manipulate the turmoil within his stronghold. I agreed at first, then began to wonder if we actually *could* secretly manipulate the goings-on inside Vellan's mountain, or at least muddy the waters a little bit."

"What are you saying, Justin?"

"I'm saying that Caldurian was not wholly confident of Vellan's leadership abilities after his defeats in Rhiál and Montavia. Coupled with the destruction of the Enâri, it's no wonder Caldurian was having visions of himself sitting in the seat of power in Del Norác. He told me as much during our conversations this past winter," King Justin said. "I've spoken to Carmella several times, too, who offered similar stories of the wizard's disappointment with Vellan's rule. And do you recall what she told us about her recent confrontation with Madeline?"

The wizard nodded. "Madeline wasn't happy with Caldurian's handling of recent affairs."

"Precisely," he replied with a hint of dark amusement. "The members of Vellan's inner circle are simmering in a stew of deceit and distrust."

"So you think that by allowing Caldurian to escape and run back to Vellan–presumably to where Madeline has also fled–that a power struggle might ensue? And then what? The realm of Kargoth will fall under its own instability?"

"It's possible," the King replied in a less than enthusiastic tone, wondering if he had done the right thing now that he was hearing his plan spoken aloud. "Isn't it?"

Tolapari sighed, digesting the information. "Or have we possibly strengthened their fragile alliance on the eve of war?"

"We?"

Tolapari glanced at his riding companion, his sour mood having lightened. "Well, I did put the idea in your head, Justin. Still, the more I analyze your approach, the more intrigued I become with the possibilities."

"That's how I became entranced with the idea. There is going to be a war when we reach Del Norác. I can't imagine coming to terms with Vellan, though he may want to put on a show of sorts before he launches his troops."

"Agreed."

"So if a battle is inevitable, which would give us the greater advantage? Keeping Caldurian at our side, chancing that he may strike against us if his powers fully return? Or setting him loose upon Del Norác where he might make a play against his master when Vellan's grasp on power grows precarious?" The King shrugged. "So I decided to take a chance. I let Caldurian go."

"With Carmella at his side."

King Justin chuckled. "Oh, I guessed long ago that Carmella would make a run for it sooner or later, eager as she was to locate her cousin. And I suspected that *she* suspected that I knew her intentions all along."

"So why did you do nothing to stop her?"

The King gazed at the melancholy sky as a soft breeze brushed across his face, worrying about Carmella's whereabouts. "After what that woman did to help us in our fight against Vellan, she deserves to determine her fate. I didn't feel I had the right to keep her here against her will despite my better judgment. If

Carmella hadn't brought that medallion to the Citadel, the prospects for this war ending in our favor would have been grim indeed. With the Enâri removed, we now have a fighting chance for victory."

"We do," the wizard said. "And I now see why you allowed her to pursue Madeline all the way to Vellan's abode."

"I just hope it's not to her demise," he replied, visibly worried as their horses ambled contentedly across the grassy terrain. "When Vellan finds out about Carmella's role in the downfall of his Enâri servants…" King Justin shook his head in the dim morning light. "I can't bear to think about it, yet it will haunt my waking hours."

The army advanced the following two days under brighter skies but cooler temperatures. Swiftly moving clouds cast sweeping shadows across wide, grassy swaths and the greening treetops of intermittent woodlands. The air harbored an autumnal chill. The troops slowly rose in elevation, heading northwest along the line of the Drusala River which was often in sight to their left. The next day, the weather changed drastically. Heavy rains again pelted the soldiers as they traversed a narrow tract of land between the river and some woods to their right. Travel conditions were quickly compromised as during the previous storms, so the army halted for the remainder of that day and all the next as the rains let loose down the river valley.

"We still have a little leeway to reach Del Norác by the appointed time," King Cedric reminded King Justin later on the second day of their standstill as they stood beneath the eaves of some towering pines. His breath rose white in the chilly air as the first hints of twilight settled over the land. "Nicholas, Leo and their guides have a much longer journey than ours, so no need to worry that we'll be late with the signal."

"I know you're right, Cedric, but it feels as if we've been on the road for ages since departing Morrenwood. And we're heading directly into the dragon's lair, as it were, while Nicholas and his companions are going around it. I hate being at a standstill now that we're so close." Drops of rainwater found their way through the sweet boughs and tumbled off the hood draped loosely over the King's head. "But I suppose this extra rest is good for the men. Goodness knows that I could use a full night's sleep."

"Then go to your tent while we enjoy this lull. The weather could change in an instant and we'll be on our way," King Cedric told him. "Besides, there's nothing for you to do at the moment except brood. With luck, we shall be on the road tomorrow."

"Regardless of this fickle weather," he replied. "Now if you'll excuse me, I will comply with your wish and seek out a pillow for my tired head. Goodnight."

As hoped for, the weather pattern shifted by morning. The rain ceased before dawn and the clouds broke and dispersed on a warming breeze. By midmorning, the army moved on as the treetops swayed and the swollen waters of the Drusala River rushed by. But the captains in charge kept their lines at a safe distance from the water's edge, not so much out of fear of the Drusala's swift current, but of Vellan's enchantment upon the river. Most suspected that even though the river was transformed into a raging, muddy flow speckled with tiny whitecaps, it probably wasn't enough to dilute Vellan's terrible spell lingering in its watery depths.

After an hour's march, the woods on the right thinned out and the distant mountains were again visible. A short time later, King Justin ordered the lines closer to the river when a garrison was spotted ahead on the water's edge. The King, after consulting with his counterparts, was eager to take a look at the abandoned complex.

The main stone structure stood three stories high and was surrounded by several other buildings of wood or clay. Captain Silas, riding alongside the trio of Kings, guessed that the main building had probably housed over two hundred soldiers. "Possibly more if manned by Enâri alone. The other buildings look like storage facilities and secondary living quarters for additional troops."

King Rowan gazed at the dreary sight, recalling the Enâri horde that had occupied Red Lodge. "Based on estimates of the Enâri population, I imagine there are many more abandoned garrisons like this scattered throughout Kargoth."

"Unless the Islanders occupy them, though they don't come close to the number of Enâri that once defiled these lands," King Justin said, eyeing the structure. "This one looks utterly desolate."

On his order, two dozen soldiers on horseback galloped up to the garrison to inspect the area before the others drew near. The Enâri remains of at least one hundred pairs of boots, tattered clothing and discarded weapons were strewn about the grounds. When Kings Justin, Cedric and Rowan sauntered up, they were transfixed by the sight. King Rowan, having witnessed a similar display at Red Lodge, was intrigued by the fragility of the Enâri despite their brutal demeanor and destructive ways.

"I stood in shock when I returned home with my daughter-in-law after our abduction," he said. "Scattered around the courtyard were countless boots, cloaks and swords, and lingering above it all was a gritty veil of fine sand stirred up by the breezes." A grim smile crossed his face. "I can only imagine the extent of the Enâri annihilation in other locales where they numbered in the thousands."

"Vellan's mountain mining facilities must look like a sorry sight," King Justin remarked.

"Not to mention his stronghold," King Cedric added. "I've heard he relied more on the Enâri creatures than his Island allies to man the corridors in Mount Minakaris. Who knows who he allows close to him now since the Enâri are no more?"

King Justin shrugged as his men started returning from the garrison. "Vellan, I'd wager, prefers his own counsel. Still, it must be a lonely and dreary place to reside."

After the soldiers reported that the garrison and surrounding buildings were abandoned, King Justin and several others examined the swift death that Leo's simple turn of a key had wreaked upon the unsuspecting Enâri troops. The interiors of the buildings were also filled with bodiless boots and uniforms, abandoned weapons and piles of dry soil still intact after having escaped winter's wrath. Brendan and William were among those who toured the morbid sight.

"To be honest," William whispered to his brother as they moved among a handful of soldiers, "when we took our oath, I wondered if Nicholas and Leo would ever return with a reforged key. Being overwhelmed by our escape from Red Lodge, leaving Mother and Grandfather behind, and not knowing if the wizard Frist was even alive, well, I guess my heart was empty of any hope for success. But I kept those thoughts to myself."

"That was wise," his brother replied. He rested a hand upon the younger prince's shoulder as he guided him through a narrow corridor and around a half dozen pairs of scattered Enâri boots. "But don't ever give up hope, Will, even with the slimmest of chances. The enemy will win without a fight otherwise."

William nodded as they moved to another room. "I promised myself not to after witnessing your return. If you can come back from the dead, I suppose there's hope that even Vellan can be defeated." He emitted an anxious sigh, looking up at his brother as memories of their encounter with Arileez flashed through his mind. "When we were in that cabin and I..." He stared at the floor for a moment, searching for the right words. "When Arileez attacked you and I had started to climb up that ladder, well I..."

"If you had rushed to my aid, Will, we might both have been killed. And maybe in a more permanent way, too. So don't lose any more sleep over it," he said with a calming smile, seeing the anxiety in his brother's eyes melt away. "And not another word either. There are more important things to worry about."

"Like knocking on Vellan's front door?"

"Exactly."

The army marched several more hours that day, making camp as gray and purple twilight blanketed the landscape. They continued on to Del Norác the following morning through a cool and hazy dawn. The troops veered away from the river at one point when a stretch of trees grew thick along its banks, temporarily hiding the watery ribbon from view. But as the morning wore on and clouds rolled in from the west, the woods thinned out and the river again made its appearance. Now the terrain grew hilly in parts and numerous streams cut across the land before emptying into the Drusala. But the men and horses drank from and washed in these waterways without fear, knowing that Vellan's enchantment wouldn't pollute these tributaries until their waters touched the river.

By late morning the clouds thickened. Low, rumbling thunder reverberated from time to time down the valley. But the rain held off despite an oppressive cloud cover. The men remained silent during this stretch of the journey, mirroring the melancholic gloom that pervaded the countryside. All were exhausted, many having left the Citadel twenty-seven days ago. Most estimated another two or three days of marching before the real work began, hoping to conserve what strength remained to wield a sword or fire an arrow.

At one point the Drusala River veered sharply northwest as if reaching for the very mountains from which it originated. The high, rapid currents of the previous day had since subsided, transforming the Drusala back into a meandering watery ribbon flowing with a smooth and hypnotic silence. As the footsteps and wheel rotations of the troops and wagons added up to mile upon grueling mile, an occasional dilapidated farmhouse or tiny village long since abandoned slowly drifted past and disappeared behind them like a bird in flight. Low rumbles of thunder continued down the valley, doing more to lull the soldiers into a collective stupor than to shake them into a state of wary vigilance.

"I feel that if I close my eyes, I'll fall into a deep sleep right on my horse," Ranen said as he rode alongside Eucádus and Ramsey, the dark red ribbon secured to his hair the only bright spot in the colorless day. "Perhaps Vellan cast a spell upon the air, too."

"I don't know if even he is powerful enough to control the breezes," Eucádus replied. "But if you doze off, fall from your horse and still remain asleep, then maybe you might be right."

"Just don't expect us to stop and pick you up," Ramsey joked. "You can join us in battle at your leisure."

"Duly noted," Ranen said.

"I won't allow my imagination to bestow additional powers onto Vellan," Eucádus continued. "Such an attitude will not aid us in battle. Besides, if we..." Another roll of thunder rumbled, sounding closer than the previous ones. Yet this particular incarnation, starting low and deep like a dragon's growl, grew louder each moment. Eucádus looked up, glancing ahead with a puzzled look. "That's not thunder," he whispered apprehensively, pointing to a swath of trees at the base of a small hill less than a quarter mile to their right. He said nothing more as frantic shouts from within the company of soldiers farther ahead suddenly filled the air.

Sweeping around the trees at that moment were a hundred enemy soldiers on horseback, galloping like crazed men directly at the King's army. With their swords aloft and clouded eyes fixed on the front line, the men of Kargoth and some of their Island recruits stampeded across the grassy terrain, prepared to plow through the approaching forces like a wildly released arrow. Eucádus and many others immediately broke ranks and rode out to meet the surprise assault head on.

"It's the Kincarin Plains all over again!" Ramsey shouted to Ranen as they galloped side by side toward the onslaught.

"Only then it was but a handful of the enemy," he replied, his face tight and his eyes fixed forward. "This time Vellan sends us a greater force to test our readiness, but they shall meet the same fate!"

The two forces collided in a wide expanse of gently rolling land close to the river as clumps of mud and grass burst forth beneath the pounding horse hooves. Distant rolls of thunder still riddled the thick, gray clouds above. The clash of swords sounded faint from a distance as most of the army was still catching up to where the battle had begun. Kings Justin and Cedric, who had been earlier riding up and down the lines, swiftly rode to the front and dispatched additional units to the skirmish. A volley of arrows streaked low across the sky, sent by a group of the King's archers who targeted some of Vellan's men and toppled them from their horses. Other fighters from Kargoth leapt from their charging steeds with reckless abandon and zeroed in on their opponents, knocking some off the saddle and engaging them in sword fights or hand-to-hand brawls on the grass-tangled ground. When King Cedric looked to consult with Captain Silas who had been with them only moments ago, he worriedly noted that the soldier from Rhiál was riding out to join his comrades in the fray.

"Since he is serving as King Victor's representative, Silas should know the appropriate time to join his troops in a fight and when to direct their movements."

"He is still young, Cedric, and that will always trump protocol," King Justin said. "His fighting instincts took over. Besides, I think Captain Silas still feels he has a debt to repay us on behalf of Rhiál. I will not deny him that opportunity if his heart is so moved."

"Nor will I," he replied with a resigned shake of his head. "Still, it would be a severe blow to the people of Rhiál and Maranac to lose such a fine soldier while they regain their footing."

"My sentiments exactly," King Rowan said, riding up between the two Kings with Brendan and William close behind. "*They* were equally prepared to rush out on a whim," he added, indicating his two grandsons. "But I held them back."

"Grandfather, I am more than ready to hold my own against one of Vellan's soldiers," Prince Brendan remarked with subdued frustration.

"I am not questioning your abilities, Brendan, and you will get your chance," he replied as the clash was already winding down. "But have some pity on a grandfather who has just gotten his grandson back from the dead and is prepared to do anything to return him in one piece to his still grieving mother." King Rowan smiled. "At least humor me until we reach Del Norác. I have earned that much."

Brendan and William nodded as they watched the last fights play out. Most of Vellan's men lay dead or dying as they had driven headlong into an overwhelming force. Arrondale and its allies also suffered grievous losses, though far fewer. Army physicians swooped in upon the injured as the remaining conflicts spread to the periphery along the riverbank or near a thicket of trees on the opposite side of the field. Eucádus and Captain Tiber, having met and drawn swords together, galloped back to the waiting monarchs.

"Your report?" King Justin asked, his voice on edge.

"We dispatched Vellan's men with swift precision," Eucádus replied. "Or nearly so," he added as he stroked Chestnut's mane to calm him. "A few enemy soldiers have taken their fight to the fringes." He indicated the small battles along the water to his left and near the trees off to the right.

"And our men?" King Cedric asked, eyeing his captain.

"We lost three," Captain Tiber sadly informed him, the young soldier's brow damp with sweat. "The enemy charged at us without concern for their own lives, as if they had expected to be killed. Twelve more of our troops at last count have sustained injuries, a few of them serious. But I fear that by the suddenness of this attack, some of our advance scouts may have already met an untimely demise before they could send us word."

"I'll dispatch a few men to search beyond the trees near that hill," King Rowan said, pointing right. "That is where the scoundrels revealed their presence." He turned to his grandsons, eyeing them grimly yet with a reassuring tone of confidence. "Brendan, you will lead the search with your brother. Recruit a number of soldiers from the lines you deem sufficient and make haste."

"At once," Brendan replied. "I'll send a man to report back as soon as I find the others." As he gently turned his horse to ride off, he indicated for his brother to follow. William, equally surprised yet sporting a stony expression, simply nodded as he gently snapped the reins of his horse and rode away.

"This short mission will bolster their spirits," King Rowan remarked, "though what they find may deflate them just as quickly."

"Still, it's good that you let them spread their wings a bit after all they've been through," King Justin said as he watched the two brothers head down the line to assemble their team. "They need to face a challenge to regain their footing, particularly Brendan. He–" Suddenly, a visceral cry of anger from along the river's edge rent the air. All turned and gazed in the distance. "*Now* what's going on?" the King wondered aloud as he and the others headed that way.

As they drew near, they saw two men fighting close to the banks of the Drusala, weaponless, their arms locked around each other in a desperate struggle. The combatants staggered back and forth along the grassy edge as other soldiers rushed toward them. As Eucádus approached the river, a flash of red caught his eye. His heart went cold.

"*Ranen!*" he whispered in horror, though others heard the fear in his voice.

"What's happening?" Ramsey asked.

Eucádus snapped the reins of his horse and bolted toward the water's edge with Ramsey in close pursuit. When he approached a crowd of men rushing on foot to Ranen's defense, he slowed his steed and dismounted, scrambling toward the others with fiery speed to reach his friend. When he finally sped past them, the Drusala River was revealed, reflecting the tired gray sky. Eucádus froze an instant later when Ranen and a soldier from Kargoth, still battling each other with deadly ferocity, slipped on a muddy patch of grass and tumbled sideways into the cold water. They sank beneath the surface just as Eucádus and the others reached the riverbank. Ranen and the enemy soldier quickly rose to the surface, sputtering and catching their breaths before swimming ashore and climbing out of the water like a pair of bedraggled rats.

"Ranen, are you hurt?" Eucádus asked, leaning forward to give him a hand as several other soldiers drew their swords and apprehended the soldier from Del Norác.

"I am quite well," he replied, very much out of breath. Ranen firmly took hold of Eucádus' wrist and pulled himself up. In the same instant, he grabbed the hilt of his friend's sword with his free hand and pulled it from its scabbard. Ranen leapt back and held the others at bay with the weapon. "To be honest, I've never felt better in my life!" he remarked as a wide smile spread across his whiskered face.

"Ranen, what are you–"

Eucádus suddenly understood everything with chilling clarity as he looked into Ranen's eyes, now as cloudy and gray as the skies above. He knew that his dear friend, the leader of the Oak Clearing, was now under Vellan's enchantment.

"Tell them to release my friend at once," Ranen demanded, "or someone else in your ranks will die before you can take my life."

"He is not your friend!" Ramsey shouted as he edged up to Eucádus' side. "Drop your sword, Ranen. You're one of us! You are a proud citizen of Harlow, not of Kargoth."

"You are mistaken. I do the bidding of Vellan. And if you and your comrades have any sense, you will lay down your weapons, march to Del Norác and beg to serve him."

"Oh, we will march to Del Norác," Eucádus replied in a steady voice, knowing it was useless to try to reason with his friend who now stood outside the realm of logic. He wondered if Ranen was doomed to be a slave to Vellan's vicious spell for the remainder of his days. "We will march, but it will not be to join Vellan's ranks. It will be to defeat him."

"Impossible!" Ranen scoffed. "Now release my friend or I will strike and then gladly die here taking at least one of you with me."

"Do as he says!" a voice called out from behind. King Justin emerged from the crowd with Kings Cedric and Rowan behind him. The soldiers guarding the man from Kargoth looked upon King Justin with disbelief. "Release him. Let him go to Ranen," he said in calmer tones. "I want both of those men to return to Vellan with a message from me." Slowly the soldiers lowered their swords and the dripping man hurried to Ranen's side. "Now find them a pair of horses."

"King Justin!" Eucádus gazed at the leader of Arrondale as if he had gone mad. "You cannot be serious."

The King raised a hand, asking Eucádus to indulge him.

Ranen, still holding up his sword, relished the slight discord between the two men. "Why would you want us to return to Del Norác rather than kill us where we stand?"

"There has been enough killing these past few months," the King replied, stepping forward. "And whether there will be more is yet to be determined. That's why I want you to find Vellan and tell him we wish to arrange a parley when we reach the capital city in a few days. Some words before drawn swords might be the wiser path. Unless, of course, you both would rather die right now because you feel unworthy to stand in Vellan's presence and deliver my request."

The soldier from Kargoth sneered with contempt. "If you knew anything, it would be that Vellan values and rewards those who are loyal to him. And though we would happily forfeit our lives in his service, we will gladly deliver your message. If your eventual surrender will spare the lives of the citizens of Kargoth, then we will humble ourselves and inform Vellan of your intentions."

King Justin grimaced. "Agreed. You will be provided two horses and allowed to leave unharmed and unfollowed. Inform Vellan that we request a meeting on the twentieth day of New Spring, four days from today. That will give us time to rest, bury our dead and recover from injuries before we finish our march. Expect us at dawn."

Ranen and the other soldier whispered to one another before turning to the King. "We'll do as you ask," Ranen coolly said, "but Vellan's demands will be harsh after the injustices you have shown his people. Be prepared to pay heavily."

"We'll take our chances." King Justin indicated for one of his troops to find two horses so Ranen and the other soldier could leave at once. He wondered if both men were already dead despite having been spared the point of a sword.

A short time later, Eucádus confronted King Justin with a look of incredulity. "Why would you allow them to run back to the enemy?" They stood near a thicket of trees while the camps were assembled around them in the melancholy light of early afternoon. "And why would you want to arrange a parley with Vellan?"

"No one here has any intention of negotiating with Vellan as he has no intention of negotiating with us. I simply requested a parley to defuse a delicate situation."

"But you allowed Ranen to leave with that villainous soldier."

King Justin sighed, understanding Eucádus' roiling emotions. "If we had forced a resolution, Ranen would most likely be dead now. You could see in his eyes the disregard for his own life. His free will was washed away in the waters of the Drusala." He rested a reassuring hand upon Eucádus' shoulder. "I don't know if Ranen can ever be saved now that he walks among Vellan's horde, but at least he is still alive if that means anything. Perhaps Tolapari can create a counter spell to Vellan's noxious enchantment," he said, though deep in his heart he had serious doubts which Eucádus clearly sensed.

"Maybe it would have been better if Ranen had died," he whispered. "Death released those men from Vellan's grip on the Kincarin Plains and on the battlefields of Rhiál." Eucádus looked wearily at the King. "Maybe only death can save him now."

CHAPTER 100

Like the Breath of a Fiery Serpent

The dead on both sides were buried as the evening shadows deepened. Physicians attended to the wounded. The rumbling thunder had long since ceased like the roars of distant dragons silenced into deep sleep. Brendan had returned earlier that afternoon with William and his team. All looked forlorn as they approached the encampment bearing two dead scouts who had been ambushed and slain by Vellan's troops shortly before the attack. King Rowan thanked them all for performing their duty despite the tragic outcome.

"They are at peace now," Brendan later glumly remarked as he sat by a fire with the King and his brother, quietly studying the snapping flames. "But their families will have to live with the turmoil for the rest of their lives."

"That is one of the sad but inevitable outcomes of war," his grandfather replied. "I hope you never get used to it."

"I assure you that I won't," he replied, glancing at William. He began to fathom the horror that his brother had experienced during the many adventures in his absence.

King Justin let his men rest the next day. But the following dawn, the army again took to the road like a lumbering beast, the winding line of troops and supply wagons moving steadily against a backdrop of trees, mountains and slate gray skies. At midmorning, a light but steady rain fell which lasted until twilight. Overnight, the air chilled as a breeze picked up and moved down the river. The mountains on the right encroached upon them as the land between the water and the towering hills of stone narrowed with every mile they drew closer to Del Norác.

A small sign of hope presented itself to those on guard duty shortly after midnight. The thick mass of clouds began to thin in spots, allowing splashes of light from the Fox and Bear moons above, each near its full phase and partially veiled by the ghostly gray tendrils. Shrouded daylight greeted the army the following morning as the sun rose, providing a subdued yet pleasing luminescence across the river valley. Yet in spite of the increased light, the soldiers remained quiet and contemplative, realizing that by this time tomorrow they would probably be engaged in the defining battle of their lives. Most wondered if they would live to see the days beyond.

Mount Minakaris, their ultimate destination, now loomed in the distance to the northwest, its rocky, snow-covered peak visible like a point of sickly light against the hazy clouds. Below its southern slope lay the city of Del Norác, a collection of barracks and farmsteads occupied by Vellan's Island allies and those native followers under his watery enchantment. Vellan resided in the upper chambers inside his mountain abode far above the stronghold built at the base of Minakaris. Other than his Enâri lieutenants, only those deemed most trustworthy had been allowed inside his personal quarters. But since the destruction of the Enâri, the halls were eerily quiet. Only a skeleton crew served him in the highest levels. The lower levels were well guarded though, and soldiers manning the nearby garrison were always at his call.

About a half mile farther west was Deshla prison, located beyond a tract of woodland and within the base of the mountain. Vellan would visit when the mood struck him, though mostly he had messengers report on the fates of its latest occupants. The wizard kept to himself lately, reflecting on the war and its toll while visualizing the endgame after he completed his long and weary conquest of Laparia.

Later that afternoon, King Justin and Prince Gregory rode up and down the lines to gage the readiness and mood of the troops.

Tolapari caught up with them and asked for a word in private near a scattering of trees on the right flank. They spoke atop their steeds in the growing shadows while the horses snorted and bobbed their heads.

"I did as you asked during our last stop, Justin, and am here to report," the wizard said, his vague expression offering no clues.

"*And?*"

Tolapari shot a frustrated glance at the Drusala River lying beyond a swath of dried grass and weeds. "I carefully scooped up a bucket of river water to perform my tests, but I couldn't craft a counter spell to Vellan's magic. That itself didn't surprise me, though something else that I found *did*."

"What?" Prince Gregory asked.

"Vellan's spell loses its integrity in a water sample shortly after it is separated from the river proper. When I reached camp with the water bucket, I sensed that the magic had dissipated," he said. "I performed further tests, but they all proved the same thing–the spell is confined to the river itself and is constantly regenerated along its course. The magic takes effect only at the source."

"You're sure?" the King asked with hope in his eyes.

"Quite sure," the wizard said. "I consumed some myself."

"Are you mad?" Prince Gregory piped up.

"More confident than mad," Tolapari replied. "However, do not take this as a hopeful sign, but instead merely a curiosity. The results will not help us bring back Ranen to the world of free men should we ever see him again."

"Then there is nothing you can do?" the prince pleaded.

"Perhaps if we had a wizard here comparable in talent to Frist. But recall that it took twenty years for Frist's counter spell against the Enâri to incubate in the Spirit Box. It would require an equivalent effort to defeat the magic now polluting the Drusala."

King Justin sighed. "Eucádus will be devastated to learn of this. His words regarding Ranen will most likely come true."

"And what words were those?" Tolapari inquired.

"He had said, 'Perhaps only death can save him now,'" he somberly replied, gazing ahead while the army weaved its way steadfastly to Del Norác. "And perhaps he is right."

The patchwork of clouds thickened again as daylight waned. The setting sun illuminated their ghostly edges until they coalesced into a single mass that blotted out the remaining light. The men set up tents and lit bonfires under a pall of gray shadows until darkness descended. They were less than two miles from Mount Minakaris, and this would be their last encampment before battling Vellan's forces the following day.

Minutes before sunset, King Justin stood near a thicket of pine trees and gazed at the tip of Minakaris, its snowcapped summit reverently awash in subtle shades of orange and scarlet. King Cedric walked up to him with a faint smile upon his face.

"It's a beautiful mountain," he remarked.

"But we can only see the summit from here," King Justin said, pointing out a distant tree-lined rise that blocked out the lower portion. Del Norác was situated on the other side of the trees. "I'm sure we'd be less enthralled by its grandeur if we were in full view of Vellan's front door."

"Perhaps you're right, but let's enjoy the view while we still have the chance," he said. "It might be the last wondrous sight some of us ever see if things transpire tomorrow as both you and I expect."

Shortly afterward, when King Justin was again by himself beneath the trees, the clouds swiftly mended together, burying the sunlight behind a bank of gray until the mountaintop was drained of all its color and liveliness. For a moment, the hope in his heart nearly faded like the light itself until a chorus of shouts among the troops roused his attention. Heading into the encampment from the northwest were a dozen of his soldiers on horseback led by Captain Grayling. They surrounded a delegation of three men from Del Norác, each one carrying a flickering torch as they sauntered into an open area among the bonfires until ordered to stop. King Justin and many others hurried toward them. He looked up at Captain Grayling for an explanation.

"We spotted them heading this way while on our patrol," the captain said. "They were unarmed and requested to deliver a message from Vellan."

King Justin studied the three men in the firelight, his brow furrowed with distrust. "Deliver your message. What do you want?"

"We'll be brief," replied the trio's spokesman. "Vellan invites you tomorrow morning, as requested, to a parley outside the borders of the capital. A tent has been set up to hold the proceedings. You and any representatives from these gathered armies may attend. Vellan looks forward to substantive talks."

"I doubt that Vellan looks forward to talking after his recent defeats. And the less mentioned about his Enâri debacle, the better," he replied, realizing that this messenger was under the influence of the Drusala. "But my fellow leaders and I will meet with him for what good it will do. Tell Vellan that I look forward to our conversation, such as it will be, at the break of dawn."

"We will relay your message," the soldier replied, signaling the others to turn and follow him back.

"And no need to provide breakfast," the King lightly added. "We'll eat first."

The spokesman ignored the comment, though others broke out in amused smiles. Moments later, Captain Grayling and his men escorted the trio far beyond the perimeter of the encampment and watched them gallop back to Del Norác. Their torch flames disappeared into the darkness like tiny stars behind a veil of clouds.

The air was cool and sweet as the first hint of dawn bled over the eastern horizon the next day. A palpable sense of nervous foreboding hung over the encampment. After a hasty meal, the soldiers on horse and on foot moved out, marching for nearly a mile until they went around and passed the tree-lined rise to the right. In the distance, in all its imagined mystery, lay the city of Del Norác. It was situated along the banks of the Drusala River now flowing closer to the army's left flank. A collection of low stone and brick buildings sprouted up on either side of the water beneath a smoky haze. One building towered modestly above all the others–a former Enâri garrison constructed of large granite blocks which now housed troops from Kargoth and the Northern Isles. Swaths of farmland, orchards and empty fields surrounded the city. Looming silently above Del Norác to the north stood Mount Minakaris. Nestled among patches of green woods, its rocky slopes and snow-frozen tip glimmered in the faint light of morning.

From this vantage point, the small city, mountain and snaking river appeared inviting, but the troops knew their perceptions would change the nearer they drew. But before the first sword was raised or an arrow shot from its bow, King Justin and his royal counterparts planned to ride out to parley with Vellan as promised. Captain Silas, Eucádus and five other soldiers would accompany them. When the army was less than a quarter mile from Del Norác, the order to halt was sounded.

"Vellan isn't to be trusted," William warned his grandfather as the King retrieved a few small items from his saddlebag.

"I know that only too well," King Rowan said as his grandson tugged at his sleeve.

"Will, they know what they're doing, so let them do it," Brendan told him.

The King turned around and looked kindly upon his two grandsons. "This last show with Vellan is simply for that–*show*. We expect nothing from the parley yet are willing to go this one extra step because that is the kind of people we are. Vellan, on the other hand, is a conniver and a liar. But," he added with a glint in his eyes, "we are not naïve and will watch him like a hawk."

"I'd feel much better if I could ride out with you," William said. "I've become handy with a sword lately as I trained to pass the time during our long journey."

"Swords won't be necessary at this stage of the game," remarked Tolapari as he strolled by on his way to see King Justin. He smiled knowingly as his dark blue robes swept across the dewy grass. "Hurry now. The others are waiting."

"Right behind you," William replied. He glanced at his brother and grandfather, wondering if they could decipher the wizard's curious comment.

"You heard the man," King Rowan said, urging them on. "The others are waiting."

Fifteen minutes later, the rumbling of ten galloping horses reverberated across the landscape. William watched as King Justin proudly rode out to a parley tent with Kings Rowan and Cedric accompanying him on either side. Eucádus and Captain Silas rode outside on the left and right flanks. Five other soldiers bearing flags, three in front and two in back, rounded out the party. They advanced upon a large tent in a field on the southeast edge of the city not far from the river. Several tall torches burned in a wide circle surrounding the tent. Two guards stood at the entrance awaiting their adversaries' arrival.

William stood with several others in the shadow of a tall tree. He was about to tap Tolapari on the shoulder to ask him a question when Ramsey, standing nearby, stopped the young prince with a sharp glance.

"Better leave him alone," he whispered as the wizard gazed out upon the ten horsemen with a focused eye, seemingly unaware of those around him. Tolapari's lips moved from time to time as if he were talking to himself.

William pulled back his hand, watching the proceedings in silence as did most of the troops. Several paces to his right, three groups of soldiers waited restlessly near a crackling bonfire as King Justin and his men approached the parley tent.

Moments later, the center guard riding in front of the line raised an arm high in the air, signaling the others to slow down until they were about ten yards away from the tent. The two guards from Kargoth bowed slightly, begrudgingly signaling the arrival of the enemy. One stepped forward as the ten horsemen approached.

"Welcome, King Justin and company, to Del Norác!" he called out in a cold, clear voice. "Our great leader, Vellan, eagerly awaits your visit."

His words had barely left his lips when a torrent of armed soldiers burst out of the tent like a fierce wave, charging at King Justin and his men with raised swords and bows at the ready. Two other groups simultaneously rushed out from behind the tent on either side and joined in the attack. A stream of arrows directed at the King and his companions sailed through the air with brutal swiftness, piercing their marks with bold accuracy. A riot of sharp swords quickly followed. But Vellan's soldiers, ecstatic over the success of their surprise offensive as they rushed upon their enemy, slowly realized what was really happening as they neared the ten horses.

Prince William and the others watched with fascination from their safe positions. They were especially amazed when King Justin and the others, moments after enduring a barrage of arrows and the cruel thrusts of swords, suddenly dissipated into wisps of gray and white smoke. The attacking soldiers from Kargoth stood aghast, many with swords still raised or with new arrows ready to fly, as the ten now-empty horses fled across the field back to their keepers.

At the same moment, Prince William noted that Tolapari grew visibly relaxed. The tension in his facial muscles disappeared in a flash. The wizard turned to him as if casually speaking to a friend. "You had wanted to ask me something?"

"Just wondering how long you could manipulate those smoke apparitions from this distance," he replied with a grin. "But I can now see that it was just long enough."

"Indeed!" a voice piped up from behind. Suddenly King Justin emerged from the crowd where he and the other parley delegates had been keeping a low profile until the wizard's smoke ruse had played out. "I'll give Caldurian this much—it's a simple yet effective trick. But now that we've exposed Vellan's trap, it's time to get on to the real business at hand." He walked over to the bonfire where three groups of a dozen soldiers each had been waiting, all armed with bows and arrows whose tips were each wrapped with a small piece of specially treated cloth. "Let the serpent fly," King Justin instructed the soldiers, nodding to them with steely confidence.

The first group of archers, after readying an arrow in their bows, dipped the wadded points into the fire until a steady flame took hold. The dozen men raised their weapons to the gray sky, aiming northwest as they pulled back on the bowstrings. In unison, they released the burning arrows in a high, spectacular arc that streaked across the sky like a burst of dragon's breath. In quick succession, the second and third groups launched their weapons along the same line, blazing a swift, fiery trail across the morning sky to signal their fellow warriors stationed over a mile away behind a woodland tract, all patiently waiting to liberate Deshla prison. After months of preparation, the war with Vellan had begun.

CHAPTER 101

The Secret of Deshla

Nicholas opened his eyes to darkness. As remnants of sleep dissipated inside his head, the scent of pine and cedar, the crackling of bonfires and the whisperings of men on patrol reminded him that he was encamped several miles south of the Champeko Forest on the southwestern slope of Mount Minakaris.

As he sat up and yawned, several blankets fell from his shoulders. He wrapped them back around himself to ward off the night chill that penetrated his coat underneath. A nearby fire snapped liked forked snake tongues. He couldn't tell how many hours past midnight had drifted by since he first lay down his head. Shimmering moonlight cast an eerie glow through the gauzy clouds drifting above the treetops.

Nicholas noted several sleeping soldiers in the glow of firelight, including Leo who had accompanied him, Max and Hobin to these parts after a nearly uneventful journey. They had said goodbye to King Justin almost two weeks ago, after which Maximilian guided them across the border into Linden. They followed the Bellunboro River for a few days and then traveled west into the mountains, making for the resistance camp on the northern tip of the Champeko Forest. Malek happily greeted their return, upon which they informed him about the King's plan to attack Vellan and of the fiery signal that would be launched at dawn on the twentieth day of New Spring. The next day, Malek and his counterparts led the final march to beyond the southern reaches of the Champeko. Here, nearly eight hundred rebel troops would await King Justin's signal while hiding out in the shadow of Mount Minakaris.

During his trek along the Bellunboro, Nicholas had found few things to lighten his mood as Ivy had been on his mind most of the time. The friendly debates between Hobin and Max contrasting the grandeur and beauty of the Dunn Hills to the Northern Mountains occasionally offered a welcomed distraction. But in the end, neither convinced the other of his position and called it an amicable draw.

As the four had made their way along the river, they avoided larger villages hugging the waterway, uncertain if Vellan's soldiers or his Island allies might have been patrolling there. They did, however, pass through a few hamlets along the way to buy supplies and ask about the latest news. One farmer recounted how a large company of Enâri soldiers had arrived last autumn during the harvest, demanding a share of each farmer's crops as tribute to Vellan.

"As they were armed and outnumbered the fighting-age men in our community, we agreed," the farmer explained. "We had heard horror stories about other villages being burned and its citizens killed when they hadn't cooperated. We didn't want that, so each farmstead set aside what was requested, packing up the crops in crates and barrels until the troops returned in a line of wagons on the first day of New Winter. After we loaded them up, the Enâri spent the night in the area, planning to leave the following morning."

"What happened?" Nicholas asked, anticipating what the farmer was about to say since Leo had opened the Spirit Box on the second day of New Winter.

"Many of us awoke at dawn to see Vellan's creatures off, happy to be rid of the nuisances without any injury or loss of life," he continued. "But then the strangest thing happened as a sudden rush of wind cut across the land." The man moved his hand through the air to mimic the breeze, lowering his voice as if divulging a secret. "Suddenly, every Enâri creature stopped moving and breathing. Even stopped talking, those that were. But that surprise lasted only a moment compared to what happened next."

"What?" Hobin asked, feigning ignorance.

"All the Enâri turned into statues of sand, if you can believe it, and immediately collapsed upon themselves," the farmer excitedly replied. "Our enemy, in the bat of a moth's wing, had been taken down by some inexplicable force, leaving our tribute of food and the enemy's horses and carts unharmed for us to reclaim."

The farmer looked at them as if to say that they would never hear a more amazing story. He told them as much when he led them to his barn and opened a large, cloth bundle pulled from underneath a work bench. Inside were two pairs of Enâri boots, two uniforms and several daggers, as well as a small wooden box filled with a handful of sand.

Max darkly grinned. "You kept some of the remains?"

"Each of us did to serve as proof of our story. Most of the items we later burned. And as for their sandy remains, the autumn rain and winter snow took care of them."

"Quite a story," Leo said. He examined the items, his mind drifting back to that cold dawn in the upper turret in the Citadel. Evidence of the handiwork wrought by the deadly fury released from the Spirit Box was laid out before him. And though he was satisfied to see the results with his own eyes, he was far happier to hear from the farmer how liberty and normalcy had returned to his life and to those of his loved ones. The journey through the Dunn Hills had been well worth the effort.

Nicholas' thoughts drifted back to the present as he sat in darkness among the sleeping soldiers, hours before the dawn attack on Deshla. He had waited for the brutal mountain winter to pass for this chance to find Ivy, a slim chance perhaps, but one he knew he must take. As the fire crackled, he eased his body to the ground and tightened the blankets around him. But as sleep beckoned, he knew that he would first have to survive tomorrow if any of the rest was to matter. Stone-heavy weariness finally overwhelmed him, scattering his thoughts as he surrendered to a deep and restful sleep.

"And some of the best ale and most succulent lamb chops can be had at the Crescent Fox, a small inn located outside my village of Pelico in Surna," a familiar voice whispered. "That's where I first met Malek. He was passing through while recruiting for the resistance movement. And *your* favorite?"

"The Plum Orchard Inn," a second voice responded. "It's ten miles north of Minago, but worth the trip. Always good food and ale, with my favorite meal being the roasted pork dinner I had last autumn with Megan and Nicholas. But then again, when I visited the summer before last—"

"Really? At this hour?" Nicholas groggily looked up at Leo and Sala who sat close by, their voices having invaded his dreams. He sat up as a faint, gray light touched the sky through the treetops. "Discussing favorite places for a meal when we're barely awake?"

"*We're* awake. And can you think of a better conversation to have on the eve of battle?" Sala smiled cheerfully as Nicholas rubbed his eyes. "Leo and I wondered if you were ever going to join us for breakfast."

"Not Plum Orchard Inn fare, but filling nonetheless," Leo said, holding up an herb biscuit and a mug of hot tea. "There are also dried bacon strips and a sack of black walnuts to pick through. You'd better eat up soon. The scouting teams are back."

Leo indicated a small clearing in the camp. There, some of the resistance leaders gathered around a bonfire to speak with several scouts who had returned during the night. Malek and Tradell were present along with a handful of others, including Maximilian and Hobin, who all listened to the latest reports. Everyone anticipated an early raid on Deshla.

"So we're finally going through with it," Nicholas remarked. "Any news?"

"We're waiting for instructions just like you," Sala replied, stretching his arms. "But I don't expect it should be long now."

"That's why you should eat something," Leo said, tossing Nicholas a biscuit.

"Or you'll be forced to eat along the way." Sala glanced at the clearing. He observed Malek and the others filtering away from their meeting with a sense of urgency. "Looks like we're about to get our instructions," he said anxiously. "The years adrift in these mountains fighting for our freedom is about to come to an end." He took a slow sip of tea, the glow from a nearby blaze highlighting the apprehension in his eyes. "But to *what* end?" he ominously added, setting his mug upon a cold, flat rock beside him.

The troops broke camp twenty minutes later, armed with swords, bows and daggers. Dim morning light vaguely illuminated the nearly eight hundred men scattered beneath the creaking boughs like a horde of walking shadows. Soon they stepped out of the tree line into grassy, weed-choked terrain wet with morning dew. No torches were allowed on the march to Deshla prison located a mile away within the stony bowels of Mount Minakaris. The rocky peak loomed left amid a scattering of trees and streams. The Drusala River lay a short distance away on their right, barely visible in the murky light as it swept along in gentle undulations like a snake on a silent hunt.

"This grassy tract narrows between the mountain and the river the closer we get to Deshla," Malek informed the company under his command. "We'll encounter an old Enâri garrison along the water about a quarter mile before the prison. Scouting reports indicate no activity there. I doubt Vellan ever restaffed it after the Enâri were destroyed, unable to spare the troops. But I'm sure the other garrison in Del Norác is bursting with soldiers. Our task, however, is Deshla. I can only imagine how many troops are housed within."

As they marched southeast, another stretch of woodland was visible less than a mile away beyond the garrison and the entrance to Deshla. But that swath of trees extending the narrow width between the river and the mountain was not very deep. It thinned out halfway between Deshla prison and the entrance to Vellan's stronghold in Minakaris on its other side, offering a broad vista of Del Norác from its southern eaves.

Nicholas was on edge with every step, recalling how Ivy was forcibly removed from Brin Mota's raft and taken away as Cale's prisoner. Cold fear overwhelmed him as he imagined the possible harm inflicted upon her and the terror she must be feeling. Now, after a long winter, he was at last marching into the enemy's lair. He forced himself to believe that Ivy was nearby and still alive. He hoped that he could rescue her so they could begin a new life together. If not, he wasn't sure if life would be worth living.

Leo, walking next to him in the shadows, sensed the turmoil in Nicholas' mind and searched for some encouraging words. But a slap on their backs from behind quickly changed the somber mood.

"There you are!" Hobin quietly said, their former guide and dear friend stepping in between the pair to catch up on the latest. "As I've been hobnobbing with Max and some of the others since last evening, I haven't had time to see how you two were holding up."

"On a steady course," Leo said, his mood lifting. "Isn't that right, Nicholas?"

"And finally getting somewhere," he added as his brooding thoughts scattered.

"It's been some rough going since we parted in the Dunn Hills," Hobin said. "For you especially, Nicholas. Compared to you, Leo and I have had it easy lounging around the Blue Citadel while the snow fell."

Nicholas smirked in the gloom. "I think that little incident with Leo and the Spirit Box might count for something comparable."

Hobin nodded, scratching his head. "Yeah, there was that," he said matter-of-factly. "Just make sure to watch each other's back. I'd like to take you both on another hike one day when all this craziness is over. After I meet with Emma, of course."

"Look forward to it," Nicholas said, "if we survive the day."

Hobin grunted with amusement. "That's the spirit."

But before they could comment further, exclamations of awe reverberated across the marching lines. Everyone craned their heads back and raised anxious eyes to the slate gray skies beyond the woods before them. High above the treetops to the southeast flew a brilliant arc of flame, streaming in their direction like a fiery serpent from myths of old. Moments later a second blazing spectacle followed along the same path, and then a third, each briefly igniting the dawn sky like thin, brilliant flashes of lightning. The signal from King Justin had been sent in spectacular fashion, indicating that the battle against Vellan's forces in Del Norác had commenced. Now, with equal fire and fury, the raid on Deshla was ready to launch, too.

Straight to the prison! The battle is on!

Word spread among the troops in brusque whispers. The race to Deshla had been infused with new urgency after viewing the aerial display of fire and light. Malek and the other leaders had planned to march the troops to the abandoned Enâri garrison where they would await King Justin's signal. But as Vellan's forces had been engaged, there would be no last, brief respite for the mountain resistance. The moment to strike was now when the prison would most likely be the least protected while battle raged in the nearby city. Like birds in flight, the soldiers hurriedly veered to the left away from the river, making for the base of Mount Minakaris.

They quickened their pace through weedy grass and around thickets of small trees and scrub brush in the faintly growing light. An outcropping of granite blocks was visible in the distance against the mountain itself. This marked the entrance to Deshla prison, built by Vellan's Enâri laborers years ago. Its gates were guarded by both Island soldiers and men native to the region who had succumbed to Vellan's will. The exterior walls were dotted with burning torches. Their flickering shadows grew pale in the strengthening dawn, and along with it, any hopes for surprise by the raiding forces. Distant shouts and the harsh blast of a horn gave warning to the troops inside Deshla that danger was afoot.

"Here comes the welcoming party," Nicholas said with an uneasy grin, patting the hilt of his short sword as tender thoughts of Ivy raced through his mind. He ran at a moderate pace next to Leo and Hobin, guessing that they both harbored similar notions regarding Megan and Emma.

The three men were positioned in the middle of the pack. A sea of heads and shoulders in front of them rose and fell as the entrance to the prison grew nearer. Suddenly a group of one hundred surprised soldiers burst out through the front metal doors and stormed across the grass to meet the advancing resistance army. The enemy in Kargoth, especially after the demise of the Enâri, had long expected Arrondale and others to attack. What they never anticipated was a military unit rolling out of the neighboring mountains from the west. Vellan had assured his followers that the rebels from Harlow, Linden and Surna were gadflies at best, capable of launching an occasional raid on an Island raft, but not much more. Kargoth had worried little about the resistance, deeming its members ineffective and demoralized after suffering crushing defeats at Vellan's hand.

As the enemy poured out of Deshla, an order was shouted out among the resistance fighters. Fifty soldiers at the front of the line, the best archers among the group, sprinted a short distance toward the charging onslaught and took their positions as the men rushing behind them split in two groups and veered off to either side. With swift and precise motions, the archers loaded their bows and let loose a stinging volley of arrows into the advancing line, the feathered projectiles singing brief notes in the damp morning air before finding their targets with deadly accuracy. About a third of the Deshla guards fell. Malek and his fellow leaders then set loose fighters from both sides of the split formation upon the remaining enemy forces. The rebels converged with raised swords and voices, vastly outnumbering their combatants.

For a few minutes, the clanging of metal blades rent the air as blood was spilled and last breaths were taken. The clouded eyes and disillusioned thoughts of several men from Kargoth cleared and became whole again as they lingered briefly upon the edge of death, many grateful that they had been released from Vellan's spell before a final darkness took hold. Most from the Northern Isles who fell, however, were under no spell except their own burning desire to reap imagined rewards upon Vellan's victory. A few though, dropped their weapons and surrendered as soon as they saw the vast numbers crashing down upon them.

"This must only be the first wave," Leo said to Nicholas and Hobin with a trace of surprise. The fighting had suddenly stopped ahead of them and Leo's sword still rested unused in its sheath.

"I'm guessing you're right," Hobin replied with equal wonder and a hint of uncertainty as an ominous sense of quiet settled upon the land. Nicholas stared at the mountain during the sudden lull, lost in thought.

None of the three men, including many of those around them, had been afforded the chance to raise their swords since the battle had concluded before they reached the fighting front lines. All were sickened and saddened at the loss of life when they viewed the dead bodies sprawled out upon the ground. And despite some minor injuries, all the soldiers from the Northern Mountains had escaped death in this first round against Vellan.

The rebel troops walked about with mystified expressions. They gazed at the now unguarded entrance to Deshla prison forty yards away, its large iron doors flung open. Apparently no second wave of soldiers was going to charge at them by the look of things, and the first wave proved to be merely token resistance. After a few hasty orders were barked out, the army hurriedly advanced to the entrance and took up positions along the mountainside while a smaller force was assembled to take the initial plunge inside. Malek, volunteering to lead that group, chose fifty men eager to step into the shadows beyond the gaping entryway. Nicholas ran over to him.

"I already know what you're going to ask," Malek said with a smile, wiping a sleeve across his sweaty brow.

"*And?*" Nicholas replied.

"And of course you'll be a part of my team," he said. "Leo and Hobin, too. You all deserve more than anyone else to have a first look inside after what you did for us. I had expected a second, larger force to storm out after the initial onslaught, but it appears that that will not be the case. So, my friends, the mystery of Deshla deepens."

"Had the Enâri been here, this wouldn't have been so easy a fight," Tradell chimed in as he walked up to Malek's side. He had participated in the first battle, but other than a torn coat sleeve, he looked none the worse for it. "But I'll accept a bit of mystery in exchange for this first victory and take my chances inside."

"So let's get on with it," Hobin said as he and Leo strolled up.

Malek indicated for his troops to advance, including Max who eagerly desired to see the inner workings of Deshla. With arms at the ready and a scattering of torches in hand, he and his men took their first steps past the thick metal doors, all having pictured this moment occurring amid brutal armed combat instead of with leisurely but cautious steps. Malek, with Tradell and Max shadowing him on either side, entered the prison first, gripping his sword with one hand while holding a torch in the other. Tradell and Max were similarly armed as were Nicholas, Leo and Hobin who followed close behind. They passed through a low, wide passageway built of granite blocks. It extended for a short distance, the end of which was secured by a barred iron gate with a blazing, metal oil lamp affixed to the wall on either side. The gate, though, was unlocked and stood ajar.

"I guess they're expecting us," Malek said.

"Or perhaps nobody else is home," Max suggested.

"Let's hope not," whispered Nicholas, his words eaten up in the darkness.

Tradell swung open the wide gate so everyone could pass down the remaining yards of the entry tunnel which was now carved out of the mountain itself. Two more oil lamps marked the end of the passageway that opened up into a large stone chamber of Enâri construction. But before Malek would allow anyone to enter, he turned and faced the group, lifting his sword and offering a nod of confidence. The others returned an unspoken faith in his leadership, their swords and daggers poised in the flickering glow to face whatever the enemy might throw their way.

Malek, Max and Tradell stepped into the chamber, each scoping out a separate direction for a quick overview of the layout. Tradell, who had spun to his right facing eastward, looked down at a long tunnel with a series of wooden doors on either side, each with a metal barred opening near the top. The series of prison cells were grimly illuminated by oil lamps hanging from the low ceiling at regular intervals, but how far beyond the light the tunnel extended, he could not guess.

Max, looking straight ahead, viewed a sight identical to what Tradell was witnessing–a string of eerily lit prison cells bathed with troubling stillness and a sickly light. Malek, however, was slightly taken aback when he turned left in a defensive stance, his sword held high as if anticipating a skirmish. But all that greeted him was a thin and disdainful laugh.

"What is this?" he whispered, lowering his sword slightly. Nicholas hurried to his side, his weapon at the ready. Leo and Hobin edged up behind them. Max and Tradell turned around when hearing the eerie noise.

"Not what you expected, was it?" said a tall, thin man, darkly dressed. He stood in front of a stone archway framed with burning oil lamps. An armed Island guard waited nearby. Despite knowing that he was defeated, a condescending smile spread across the man's face. The glow of firelight in the chamber behind him illuminated vague outlines of other people passing to and fro within.

"No, it was not," Malek admitted, cautiously taking a step closer. Studying the man's features, he guessed that the individual was under the influence of the Drusala River. The Island guard next to him seemed to possess his own mental faculties unpolluted by Vellan's magic. "Who are you?"

"My name is Istillig. I run this facility," he coolly replied. "What do you want?"

"We're here for our comrades," Malek said, peering across Istillig's shoulder into the room beyond. "By the look of things, you don't have much of a force to back you up. I, on the other hand, have fifty brave men with me and hundreds more outside. So advantage to us, wouldn't you say?"

"I'll give you that," he said, pointing to the darkness beyond them. "But out there is where it counts. In the city of Del Norác, your advantage is falling apart. Vellan's servants are laying waste to King Justin's allied army. It's only a matter of hours before that paltry force is swept away. Your victory here is only temporary."

"*Victory?*" Leo silently mouthed the word to Hobin with much astonishment as Istillig continued to speak. He wondered why the enemy inside was already admitting defeat after the briefest of battles. Where were the backup forces everyone had expected? Leo glanced around when it suddenly struck him just how quiet and motionless Deshla prison seemed. Where were the prisoners?

Nicholas wondered the same thing, having remained quiet despite wanting to know so much about the workings of this facility. All he ever desired since early winter was to make his way to this spot and find Ivy, hoping against all odds to the contrary that she was here. Now he could stand the suspense no longer. His impatience rose with every word the enemy spoke. As he anxiously fingered the hilt of his sword, Malek noted his agitated state and decided to slice through the enemy's bluster.

"I am beyond weary of your words, Istillig," he said. "We will search the prison now, including the room behind you." He motioned to Tradell who hurried out to gather reinforcements.

"Search away," Istillig replied with a shrug of indifference, stepping aside and indicating for his guard to stand down. "There are only nine more of us in the administrative quarters behind me. And as for the prison cells, well, you will see shortly. You'll soon learn the real secret of Deshla which will sting you far more than a cut from the sharpest sword."

"What are you talking about?" Nicholas burst out, unable to contain himself any longer. He suddenly lunged at Istillig, but Leo and Malek both grabbed him from behind before he could do any harm. He struggled for a moment and finally calmed down, promising to control himself. When his friends released him, he calmly addressed Istillig. "Where are the prisoners? Where is Ivy?"

Istillig furrowed his brow. "I don't know anyone by that name. But as I said before, search away. All you will find here is the bitter truth."

"We'll search anyway," Malek replied.

Moments later, Tradell returned with more men bearing torches to help with the search. He directed teams down the two main prison tunnels and the various offshoots soon discovered in the mazelike system. Malek, in the meantime, entered the administrative chamber through the archway with Nicholas and a few others to learn the fate of his missing countrymen. Istillig and his guard surrendered their arms willingly and accompanied them inside where the nine other men awaited.

The chamber was warmed by several round fire pits vented through openings in the low ceiling. A few wooden tables and shelves were cluttered with ledgers, ink wells and quill pens. A larger table off to one side was used for meals and games of dice for the men on duty. Sleeping quarters were located in a connecting chamber.

Scattered among the shadows in back of the room were Istillig's men, their swords raised. Six were from Kargoth and the remaining three stood dressed in garb of the Northern Isles. Before any of them could think about defending themselves, Istillig raised a hand and signaled them to lay down their arms.

"There is no need to fight," he calmly said, "since this minor victory by the mountain rebels will be temporary at best. They'll be dead before the setting of the sun."

Malek barely raised an eyebrow at the comment as he indicated for his men to confiscate the weapons. But before they could conduct a thorough search of the chamber's records, Tradell hurried back into the room and whispered something to Malek.

"In *none* of them?" Malek replied with surprise.

"Not a one," he said. "And most of the adjoining tunnels are dark and empty."

Malek shook his head. "Did I hear correctly? *No prisoners?*"

Tradell nodded. "And hardly any prison cells either."

Istillig laughed tauntingly, guessing that Malek was finally understanding the deceptive workings of Deshla.

Under Tradell's questioning, Istillig revealed the mystery of Deshla prison. Malek and the others listened with great interest as crackling fires filled the chamber with wavering shadows upon the roughly hewn stone walls. Nicholas, leaning against a table, remained silent as the interrogation proceeded. Leo and Hobin noted the growing dark mood of their friend.

"My men searched the two main tunnels," Tradell said. "Yet among those passageways, there are barely forty completed cells, all of them empty. Hardly enough to accommodate the thousand or so citizens of the Northern Mountains who had been ripped from their families and homes over the years. And other cell construction was started but never completed." Istillig, with a knowing gleam in his eyes, remained silent. "As for the connecting tunnels that we've so far checked, not a single cell exists in any of them. It's as if the Enâri dropped their tools before the work of Deshla had barely begun."

Istillig smiled snakishly. "You are not far off the mark, sir. Vellan cancelled his grand design for Deshla many years ago shortly after the Enâri had begun construction."

"But why?"

"It's quite simple." He paused to see if anyone could guess the reason, but only blank stares greeted him. "At that point in the prison's construction, Vellan completed another monumental task, one he had labored upon for months. It was a brilliant design which had sapped much of his strength for a time. When completed, it had rendered this prison complex utterly useless."

"Don't play games with us!" Max sputtered. "Tell us where the prisoners are."

"It should be obvious by now. The answer lies only a short distance outside the gates of this prison, serenely winding its way through Del Norác and for miles beyond." As if sharing the same sickening thought, Nicholas and Malek locked their troubled eyes upon Istillig. "By those horrified looks, I assume you've unraveled the fates of your friends," he said. "Though *friends* might not be an apt description at this point."

"You've led them all to the river!" Malek spoke in a hardened whisper as waves of contempt coursed through him.

"Some went more willingly than others," Istillig replied amid the quiet laughter of his comrades. "But can you envision a more ingenious solution to housing and feeding so many prisoners? Other than killing them all, of course."

"So you forced them to drink of the enchanted river water?" Tradell asked.

"Usually at the point of a sword or an arrow, though some were pushed in depending on the mood of the Enâri guards who handled those messy affairs," he said. "And those who didn't cooperate met a swift end, their bodies left to the whims of the river currents and any predators along the banks. But most of those you seek are now dedicated members of Vellan's army or workers in his mines or on his farms. Many are probably fighting against King Justin's army as we speak."

"Vellan's malice has no bounds," Malek said, trying to comprehend the treachery perpetrated upon the men of Harlow, Linden and Surna. He felt as if a generation of fathers, brothers and sons had been wiped out in a single, dark moment.

"So all our planning and sacrifice has been for nothing!" Max sputtered. "We've been duped for years by the horrible rumors of Deshla that floated among the mountains."

"You have," Istillig replied. "Once Vellan cast his spell upon the river, he realized he no longer needed to waste any time and expense housing his prisoners. After new captives were questioned here and deemed of no further use, they were marched to the Drusala and converted to our side–the majority of them anyway. But Vellan was wise enough to keep the legend of Deshla prison alive, its imagined horrors slowly eroding the hearts and souls of his enemy. He kept this place fully staffed, adding the striking granite façade and metal gates to intimidate any stray passersby. And to completely sell the illusion, Vellan had another Enâri garrison built nearby on the river as an added layer of security against the nonexistent prisoners. The ruse worked beyond his wildest dreams."

"But your secret is out now," Leo said, wondering if Ivy had been taken to the river. Nicholas was thinking the same thing, momentarily paralyzed by the dreaded notion.

"It doesn't matter now. The nations of Laparia are about to fall," Istillig replied. "And fall hard. And you will all witness that glorious spectacle up close."

"Closer than you think!" Malek defiantly stepped back and drew his sword. "My friends and I will join King Justin's army on the battlefield to defeat Vellan once and for all." Swirls of firelight reflected off his burnished blade and in the terrified eyes of Vellan's men standing in the shadows. Istillig, though, appeared unfazed by Malek's bravado.

"So you plan to kill me before you leave?" he asked matter-of-factly. "Not what I expected from the noble souls of the mountain nations, such were the stories I'd heard."

Malek calmly eyed his opponent before glancing at Nicholas who seemed lost in a world of his own, appearing already defeated. "I wouldn't waste a swipe of this weapon on such a worthless being, though you much deserve it." He slipped his sword back into its sheath. "But since you appeared almost too willing to die for Vellan had I attacked you, maybe it's an indication that a part of you is still alive beneath the layers of Vellan's spell, still conscious of what your life once was before the Drusala's hypnotic death imprisoned you. Perhaps a part of you craves death to free you from such misery."

"Nonsense!" Istillig jumped up with a pained look of disgust. Several of Malek's men stepped forward to defend their leader if the situation went awry. "I live to serve Vellan! Your twisted words won't change that fact or my mind." He breathed erratically, his face reddened, flustered for the first time since encountering Malek and his soldiers. He again sat down, gradually regaining his composure.

"Well, Istillig, if you care nothing about your past life, perhaps you can marshal a trace of empathy and try to imagine how other people still treasure their own," Malek said. "Unless, of course, Vellan has wrung that ability out of you as well."

Istillig emitted an impatient sigh. "What is your point? I tire of your words and would rather be locked up in one of the prison cells than sitting here."

"You'll get your chance soon enough," Tradell chimed in.

"My friend is correct," Malek went on. "But if you have any sense of decency left, you can prove it by providing us information on a woman named Ivy who may have been brought to Deshla sometime this past winter."

Upon hearing Ivy's name, a trace of hope stirred inside Nicholas' heart. He glanced up at Malek with a grateful smile, firming his resolve not to give up so easily despite the bleak situation.

"Ivy? Who is this Ivy woman you continue to speak of? There has never been a female prisoner inside these walls. My thorough recordkeeping will attest to that." Istillig noted the looks of consternation between Nicholas and Malek, curious to know the story behind this mysterious woman. "Why do you think this individual would have even been brought here? Is she some famed warrior of the mountains?"

"She may also have been referred to as Princess Megan of Arrondale," Nicholas jumped in, his words uttered as if they were the last possible hope of finding the woman he loved. Istillig looked surprised upon hearing the royal title.

"A princess of Arrondale in my prison? What an honor," he said with amused pride. "Your story grabs my attention. But again, no. I've never seen nor heard of any such individual by either name."

"Are you sure?" Nicholas desperately asked, his pleading eyes locked upon Istillig's narrow face now awash with indifference. But deep inside, he already knew the answer to his vain inquiry.

"Quite sure," he replied, glaring at Nicholas with growing annoyance. "Trust me when I say that there is no one named Ivy or Megan inside Deshla, nor royalty of any kind." He looked up at Malek. "Are we through?"

Malek offered Nicholas a heartfelt gaze, awaiting his response. But Nicholas, his chest aching and his throat tightening, merely shook his head in dismay.

"And none of *you* know of this Ivy?" Hobin shouted to the other men behind Istillig as he stepped forward. "Speak up!"

Most of the men shook their heads, not concerned with the fate of one woman as war waged nearby. One man, however, his face unshaven and hair growing down to his coat collar, stood passively behind the others as he observed the proceedings with interest.

"Then that is that," Max muttered to himself as he walked over to Nicholas, laying a comforting hand upon his shoulder. "He did as you asked," he softly said, referring to Malek. "He led you to Deshla, but I'm sorry things didn't turn out as you'd hoped."

Nicholas, as pale as a winter morning, barely heard Max's words. He felt numb and lifeless just as he had for stretches of time while a prisoner on Brin's raft. His anger, depression and rage momentarily drained out of his body, much like his will to fight on.

"Maybe she was taken elsewhere," Malek said, his words sounding hollow despite his sincerity. "We'll search the local garrisons and Vellan's stronghold when we're able."

"But we should leave now," Tradell said with renewed urgency. "War awaits us. We must give King Justin and the others every advantage while the fight is still young. A narrow road between the mountain and the trees ahead will lead us to Del Norác."

Malek nodded, knowing his duty. He assigned a group of forty men to secure the prison and patrol the area while the rest of the troops marched to the capital city.

"Lock these prisoners and any others still outside in their own cells. Let them experience the same conditions they doled out to so many others over the years," Malek said. "But feed them from the food stores within and treat them kindly. Mercy will be demonstrated in this morbid place, no doubt for the first time."

Malek walked to the archway and signaled for his soldiers to escort the prisoners to the cells, two of his men to every one. Tradell, spotting a set of keys hanging on the wall near where Nicholas was standing, reached for them. He was troubled by Nicholas' plight especially after all he had done to free the Northern Mountains of the Enâri scourge.

"Will you accompany us?" Tradell asked him as Istillig and the other prisoners were being led past. "We may not have found Ivy, but you can help us incarcerate those who have brought much pain to so many others."

Nicholas shook his head, emotionally drained. "I don't care what you do with them," he whispered, gazing at the vacant stares of the men as they trudged by, most of them under Vellan's spell. "They're already dead anyway, looking much like I feel. So it's time that I accepted—"

Nicholas suddenly went silent as a man near the end of the line drifted past. His whiskered face looked oddly familiar as the two briefly locked gazes. The prisoner turned his head away as Nicholas studied his features. For a moment, he was convinced that he had seen this man before yet was unable to place him. Tradell, Leo and Hobin all noticed Nicholas' odd behavior, wondering what had shaken him from his growing stupor.

"Are you all right?" Leo asked as Tradell looked on, the keys locked in his grasp.

"That man, the third from the last. I've seen him before," he said as the prisoner neared the archway. "I know I have. I—"
Nicholas' eyes immediately grew wide with bitter recognition, his

face again flush with color and steely determination. "Don't let him leave!" he cried, excitedly pointing to the last of the prisoners passing into the corridor.

"Halt the line!" Tradell shouted, hurrying out to the archway where Malek was speaking with Max as the prisoners filed past. "Stay your positions!" he called to his men who brought the line to a standstill. Malek and Max looked up.

"Trouble?" Malek asked mischievously. "Prisoners not marching in unison?"

"Not sure yet," he replied, handing Malek the key ring. He grabbed the third prisoner from the end by the upper arm and ushered him back along with the two soldiers who were guarding him. Malek and Max followed. "Is he the one?" Tradell asked Nicholas, holding the prisoner firmly by the arm as the unshaven man kept his head low.

Nicholas breathed deeply, his heart pounding as old memories and familiar faces resurfaced. "That's him," he said with hardened disgust, his spirit reignited as the possibility of finding Ivy again took hold. Nicholas grabbed the prisoner's jaw and turned his face toward him, glaring into the man's clouded eyes. He imagined the individual cleaner cut beneath the now scruffy beard and the disheveled hair.

"Who is he?" Leo asked.

"This is Brin's cousin," Nicholas replied, releasing his grip but still staring down an enemy that at the moment he ranked worse than Vellan. "He and four other Islanders took Ivy away from the raft."

"I assumed you'd be dead by now," the prisoner scoffed, suddenly full of life since his secret was out. "Or at least I had hoped. A pity."

"Nice to see you again too, Cale," Nicholas calmly replied with a grim smile. "Now why don't the two of us have a little talk?"

CHAPTER 102

A Battle of Words

Nicholas and Malek stood outside Deshla prison as daylight grew in the east under a thin veil of clouds. The bulk of the resistance army lined up nearby, preparing to march to Del Norác as Tradell and other group leaders barked out last minute instructions.

"I wish I could have done more to help you find Ivy," Malek said apologetically.

"You brought me this far," Nicholas replied. "If I can get Cale to talk, he'll lead me to her." He swallowed hard, nearly choking up. "I have to believe she's still alive."

"Then get to it," he said, indicating Leo and Hobin who were waiting impatiently in the distance. "Your friends are getting antsy."

"As are yours," he replied as Max and Sala approached to say goodbye, their faces etched with worry.

"Tradell is about to burst from impatience!" Sala remarked. "You'd better step it up, Malek, before he comes over and drags you back to the lines."

"Very well." He shook hands with Nicholas. "All the best, my friend."

"With luck, we may yet all see each other again," Nicholas said, though a hint of uncertainty clouded his words.

After a heartfelt farewell, Nicholas' friends joined the lines of troops bracing for war. Moments later, the small army marched off, following the road between the mountain and the woods until they disappeared into the distant shadows.

"Now we head to our own battle. Are you ready?" Leo asked.

Nicholas turned around, lost in thought as Leo and Hobin approached from behind. He smiled, glad that his friends were with him in these uncertain hours.

"Ready as I'll ever be," he replied with an uneasy sigh. "Let's pay Cale a visit and see if he's in the mood to talk."

Istillig and the other prisoners were locked in cells along the central tunnel, still proclaiming their allegiance to Vellan. Malek, however, had thought it wise to keep Cale isolated in the eastern corridor so Nicholas could question him without disruption. Though Leo and Hobin wanted to accompany him, Nicholas insisted on going alone to start.

"Despite his distrust, Cale is familiar with me," he said in the administrative chamber as the blazing fires drove the chill from the tunnels. A few of Malek's soldiers pored over dusty ledgers and other documents in the background. "Cale might be more likely to open up about Ivy's fate without all three of us breathing down his neck."

"Be careful," Leo said, wearing his knit hat in the coolness of the tunnels."

"And do not go into the cell with him!" Hobin warned. "He'll try to worm his way into your good graces before attacking you."

"I won't do something that foolish—not right away anyway," he joked.

Moments later, Nicholas walked down the eastern passage bathed in sickly light from the hanging oil lamps, passing five empty cells on his left until he reached the sixth wooden door. He paused before cautiously peering through the square barred opening at eye level. Another oil lamp burned inside, lending an eerie glow to the disheveled figure sitting hunched in the corner on a small bench and picking at some food on a tin plate. Nicholas studied Cale's rumpled body. His time in the wild, coupled with Vellan's hypnotic hold on his mind, made him appear far older than his natural years.

"Something you want to say?" Cale asked in a low, strident voice, looking up and tossing his plate aside. "Or are you going to rudely stare at me all day?"

Nicholas felt as if he were viewing a caged animal that would strike if given the chance. He gazed upon Cale with a mix of pity and disgust, knowing the man could not be fully trusted should he offer any information. He would have to evaluate the prisoner's words and mannerisms if he were to have any chance of saving Ivy.

"Where did you and the others take Ivy, the woman on the raft?" The cold, gray days of early winter now seemed an age ago.

"How did you escape from Brin?" Cale replied, stretching his legs and leaning against the stone wall, waiting for a response. But when none was forthcoming, he broke out in a taunting grin. "So here we are–two men with questions, but apparently neither one is willing to answer the other's."

"I'll tell you everything about your cousin if you respond to my questions first."

Cale grunted in amusement. "What a good deal for you. After which, I'm still trapped in here while you're as free as a sparrow."

Nicholas leaned against the door, offering a friendlier tone. "Istillig thinks we'll be defeated before the day is over, so perhaps you'll be free sooner than you think."

"Then why should I give you any information at all about this Ivy, whether she's a princess or otherwise?"

"Because it's the right thing to do, Cale."

"The right thing to do is what benefits Vellan!" He sprang to the door, placing his face against the metal bars, his voice taking on a threatening dimension. "If you have any sense at all, you'll release me at once. You don't know who you're dealing with, sir."

Nicholas stepped back, disturbed by Cale's words though knowing that his speech and demeanor were taking on darker shades because he had drunk from the Drusala. He knew exactly who he was dealing with–a simple thug like Brin who was trying to move up in the world at others' expense. Cale would say anything, whether promises or threats, to keep his plan on track. Nicholas knew he must remain cautious but appear confident and in charge if he were to get good information.

"Where are the four others? Did they make it to Deshla? Did Ivy?"

"This conversation will only go in circles while I'm at a disadvantage," Cale said, turning his head slightly so that one eye gazed ominously at Nicholas through the opening. "Release me so we can talk face to face. Perhaps I'll be more cooperative."

Nicholas, not wanting to give Cale the upper hand by revealing the anxiety eating him up inside, mustered every bit of restraint. He offered a casual shrug and stepped away from the door. "Perhaps you'll be cooperative when you're more familiar with your lovely accommodations. In the meantime, I've earned a proper breakfast. Don't go anywhere."

Nicholas shuffled down the corridor, shoving his hands in his pockets and whistling as he disappeared into the shadows. Cale followed him with a searing gaze, muttering to himself. He trudged back to his seat, kicking his metal plate aside before slumping back down upon the wooden bench, his arms crossed and his breathing heavy as he pondered a way out of his unbearable cage of stone.

Nicholas joined Leo, Hobin and a few other soldiers for a meal in the administrative chamber, though no one seemed to enjoy the food very much. All they talked about were their friends who had marched into battle. On top of that, Nicholas thought only of Ivy, wondering if she had been sent to the garrison in the city that was now most likely engulfed in the flames and ill fortunes of war.

After breakfast, he walked outside with Leo and Hobin to clear his mind before questioning Cale again. The cool morning air was sweet with spring as the clouds began to break and reveal patches of blue sky. Soldiers vigilantly kept watch near the entrance of Deshla and along the base of the mountain. Nicholas and his friends wandered toward the woods, noting the Drusala River eerily flowing past less than a quarter mile to their right.

"I'm going with you when you talk to Cale," Leo said. "That's not a suggestion."

"If you insist," Nicholas replied, happy for the company. With Leo present, he thought Cale might show less bravado and be more inclined to bargain.

"If you want, maybe I could talk to him," Hobin offered, grinding a fist into the palm of his hand. "Perhaps a little less delicate line of questioning might do the trick."

Nicholas chuckled. "I'll keep that in mind if all else fails."

"You do that. And if I…"

Hobin's words trailed off as they neared the tree line, the narrow road to Del Norác to their left. In the quiet of morning, beyond the rustling trees and the songs of birds in flight, the din of distant warfare was barely audible through the woody maze of elm, maple and pine spread out before them. Whether a sharp clanking of metal or the frantic shouts of a warrior, the faraway yet all too near and familiar sounds of bloody battle were carried on the intermittent breezes. Nicholas, Leo and Hobin glanced at one another with a new sense of desperation.

"Time to go back," Nicholas said in urgent tones. "Time to get what I came here for."

Nicholas and Leo stood in front of Cale's prison cell a few minutes later, staring at the man who was again slouched on his low bench in the corner. He glanced up in the dim light and grunted at his interrogators.

"Missed me?" he asked with a crooked smile. Cale rose and ambled to the door, peering at Leo through the opening with a scowl. "What's *he* here for?"

"I asked him–"

"I'm Vellan's representative," Leo said with all seriousness before Nicholas could finish. "He wishes for you to cooperate with us and answer all our questions."

"Do not mock the Wise One!" Cale cried out with unexpected ferocity, wrapping his fingers around the window bars. "Nor those who truly speak for him."

Nicholas and Leo stepped back, glancing at one another. "You hit a nerve," Nicholas whispered. Leo nodded, indicating that he wanted to try a different line of questioning now that Cale was angered and perhaps liable to let some information slip.

He eased up to the door again and locked onto Cale's clouded gaze. "You claim to speak for Vellan?" he asked. "You can't expect us to believe such a farfetched claim. You're merely an underling who has been stuck in these dreary caves for far too long."

"I know more than you think!" Cale snapped, pounding a fist against the door.

"That's not what Istillig told me when I talked to him privately," Leo continued, looking pleased with himself which only infuriated Cale even more.

"You lie! For if you really had talked to Istillig, you'd know that I'm allowed free rein down here according to Vellan's wishes, a fact that Istillig would never deny. Your attempt to fool me to extract information–" Cale suddenly quieted, realizing that the damage had already been done.

"Too late," Leo said. "You've just convinced me that you *do* have a connection to Vellan despite the doubts we harbored earlier."

"Perhaps that's what I want you to think," he replied in a calmer voice.

"No, I also believe you work for Vellan in some capacity," Nicholas said, "though whether that detail gets me closer to finding Ivy remains to be seen."

"It won't," Cale replied. "Unless you're prepared to offer me something valuable in exchange for the information you seek. Otherwise, this conversation is over," he said with a sickening finality before returning to his bench.

"Get back here!" Nicholas ordered, his words strident and bitter, yet they had no effect on Cale. He shook his head, regretting losing his temper. "I'm sounding as pleasant as Brin," he softly remarked to Leo. "Or that insane Captain Lok."

"Maybe just a little," Leo joked. "But after all you've been through…"

Nicholas studied Cale through the door and sighed, knowing that his prisoner would not be responsive any time soon after such an outburst. He signaled for Leo to follow him back up the corridor, hoping to return within the hour and try again.

But their next attempt proved just as futile. Cale refused to speak, barely acknowledging their presence. Even the offer of extra food rations or the promise of a walk outdoors under heavy guard did little to get his attention. And though Nicholas tried to be pleasant and caring, Leo grew increasingly worried as noontime approached.

"This isn't working," he said. He and Nicholas wandered beyond Cale's cell to a spot where the tunnel branched left farther into the mountain. No cells had been constructed in this section or beyond where the last oil lamp hung from the ceiling. "We need a new strategy. Perhaps we should let Hobin have a stab at it."

Though tempted, Nicholas shook his head. "Not yet. I just need a little more time." He scratched his head, gazing into the passage ahead thick with shadows, his mind and heart feeling as lifeless as the dark void before him. "Let's get some lunch and see if any scouts have returned from Del Norác. We'll come back in an hour. That'll give Cale time to think. I could tell him about Brin as a show of good faith."

"But his cousin is dead," Leo said. "That might anger him even more."

Nicholas shrugged. "We have to do something that will grab his interest, Leo! Something he'll feel compelled to bargain for."

"Like what?"

"I don't know," he replied. He walked back up the corridor, his shoulders slouched in expected defeat as he silently passed Cale's cell. "But we better think fast."

A pair of scouts had returned in the meantime, reporting their findings in the administrative chamber. The fighting in Del Norác, now several hours old, raged within the city which straddled the Drusala River about a half mile from Vellan's stronghold in Mount Minakaris. Other battles had broken out in the adjacent field to the east and among the farmland and orchards to the north. Smoke rose like writhing gray snakes in sections of the capital as the deathly sound of clanking swords filled the air.

"Our mountain forces have filtered into all areas in and around Del Norác, but as to their fate, we can only guess," one of the scouts said. "Other teams have gone deeper into the fray and will return later with a more detailed assessment."

"Still, I think we're safe for now," said the second scout. "But if things go ill by mid afternoon, there will be no reason for us to remain here. We should either join the fight or flee back into the mountains." He looked up with a grim smile. "But as my sword is itching for a fight, I know where my place will be if things come to such an end."

"Your opinion is shared by us all," another man replied as nods of agreement rippled among those present.

Hobin, listening in the background, grew disturbed by the news. He led Nicholas and Leo to a corner table near the fire.

"Time's running out for you to reason with Cale," he said, the glow of the flames highlighting his worried expression. "That is if he *can* be reasoned with."

"What else can I do?" Nicholas anxiously asked. "Even if I threaten to kill him, I don't know if that would turn Cale to my side. He might see his death as a necessary sacrifice to Vellan, one he would gladly accept."

Leo agreed. "All that man cares about is pleasing Vellan, so what better way to do that in Cale's twisted mind than to die for the cause."

"Then what have we to bargain with if even death won't motivate him?" Nicholas asked. The soldiers and scouts began to disperse moments later after their meeting had concluded, causing Nicholas to feel as if events were moving out of his control. "Maybe my only recourse is to knock on Vellan's door or go to the garrison in the city and beg for admittance. That's assuming Ivy is even in one of those locations."

Leo and Hobin sensed that Nicholas was beginning to realize the futility of the situation. Both wondered if he may have already accepted the possibility of never seeing Ivy again. Neither though, had the heart to put such a dreadful thought into words.

"Come on now!" Hobin piped up, dispersing their clouds of despair. "It's too soon to give up. You two hiked all the way to Wolf Lake to reforge that key. So why should getting some information from one delusional man be so difficult?"

"When you put it that way…" Leo said before turning to Nicholas. "What do you say? Shall we give it one last try?" But Nicholas hadn't heard Leo's question, lost in thought as he pondered Hobin's simple words. "So, are you with me?" he asked, nudging Nicholas on the shoulder.

"*Hmmm?*" he replied, his tone suddenly calm and carefree as if awakened from a pleasant daydream. "Yes. We'll try again. We definitely will."

Hobin noticed a sudden shift in Nicholas' demeanor. "What notion is rambling through that mind of yours? I've seen that same expression before on Frank and Gus after they've broken into my venison stores and enjoyed a feast."

Nicholas smiled. "Something you just said gave me an idea, Hobin. Something that may get Cale to talk. "

"Oh? So what bit of genius could you possibly take from my words?" he asked.

When they walked back to Cale's cell, he was standing at the door to greet them. Nicholas raised an eyebrow in surprise.

"Eagerly awaiting our return?" he pleasantly asked.

"Not likely. Just inhaling a draft of spring air that swept down the corridor."

"We'll happily take you for a walk in the sunshine," Leo said, "providing you earn it with some information, of course."

"As I said, you must make it worth my while if information is to be forthcoming. Offer me something," he replied, turning away.

"And we will," Nicholas said. "We have information about the people who destroyed Vellan's beloved Enâri. We know where they are at this very moment. I can only guess what Vellan would give to apprehend those culprits." Cale froze in his steps, his back to Nicholas as he listened intently to such startling words. "I'd imagine that whoever provided such information to Vellan would be hugely rewarded."

Nicholas and Leo glanced nervously at one another in the ensuing silence, each wondering if they had hit another stone wall. Cale's face then reappeared at the barred window, a look of curious distrust plastered across his countenance.

"That is a mighty tall tale," he said. "How could you know such a thing when even Vellan wouldn't reveal such information to me, one of his most trusted servants?"

"We know," Nicholas said with a sly smile, "because we're the ones who perpetrated the deed. Leo and I hiked far into the Dunn Hills last autumn to seek out the wizard Frist, the very wizard who twenty years ago created a deadly spirit to annihilate the Enâri. We asked him to reforge the key to the Spirit Box that finally released his lethal handiwork on the second day of New Winter at dawn. Certainly you must have heard at least portions of what I just said if you are in Vellan's inner circle as you claim."

Cale was clearly intrigued, but not entirely sure what to think. "Lies! All lies!" he stated with forced emotion, buying time as he analyzed this new twist. "You're manipulating me with bits of information you might have accidentally overheard."

"We speak the truth," Leo said, describing the trek from Morrenwood to Wolf Lake. He also told Cale about his fight with Mune in the Citadel. Leo and Nicholas both noticed that Cale flinched slightly upon mention of Mune's name.

"You've heard of Mune?" Nicholas asked, giving Cale little time to think. "He and many others, especially the wizard Caldurian, had a hand in the tumultuous affairs of late."

"Many have heard of Caldurian," he replied dismissively. "It is this other wizard you spoke of who intrigues me. Frist, did you say?" Nicholas nodded. "Why did you need to meet with this man to reforge the key? What was wrong with its condition?"

Nicholas, sensing that Cale was trying to test him, believed he was finally making progress. "The original key had been melted down and shaped into a medallion, though it still contained the essence of Frist's magic spell. A woman named Carmella received the medallion by chance from Jagga, one of the Enâri. And though Carmella was fond of him, she did the right thing by taking the medallion to King Justin. From what we had told you previously, you know of the devastating event that happened as a result."

"But whether I believe you is another story," he replied, his mind a swirl of conflicting thoughts as he considered his next move.

At the mention of Carmella's name, just as with Mune's, Cale displayed a hint of recognition. He had recently heard both of those names uttered in Vellan's presence, confirming in his mind that perhaps Nicholas was telling the truth. If he and Leo were responsible for the death of Vellan's prized Enâri race, Cale could think of no greater honor than to hand the two criminals over to receive their much deserved judgment.

Nicholas and Leo realized that Cale probably believed them more than not. They hoped their story was convincing enough to allow him to break through his wall of doubt and open up about Ivy. Cale abruptly cleared his throat as he rubbed a hand over his whiskered face, desiring to get word to Vellan about the two scoundrels standing before him. And if that meant cooperating with them, then he would do what needed to be done.

"Those four men and I took your woman to Del Norác," he said matter-of-factly. Nicholas and Leo stepped closer to the door. "After we left the raft, we followed the Lorren and Gray Rivers for many days. It was an arduous trek even on horseback. With those rivers behind us, we eventually reached the Drusala and followed it to Del Norác, surprised not to encounter any Enâri troops along the way. Now I know why."

"Go on," Nicholas gently encouraged.

"The garrison near Deshla prison was abandoned, so we continued along the river in the black of night until we reached the larger garrison in Del Norác. There we were questioned by Vellan's troops," he explained. "When I informed them that we had Princess Megan with us to present to Vellan, showing the captain in charge the royal medallion around her neck, word was sent to Vellan's stronghold in Mount Minakaris. Soon after, a messenger returned with orders on how to proceed."

"Which were?" Nicholas asked.

Cale taunted them with a hard smile, knowing they hung on to his every word. "We, along with your friend, were to be sent to Mount Minakaris at once."

"How was Ivy when you arrived?" Nicholas inquired, his heart pounding.

"She was fine. A hardy soul. Haven't seen her since."

Leo noted a shadow of dread crossing Nicholas' face. "Where is she now?"

"As I said, the five of us and your woman were escorted to Mount Minakaris. After further questioning, I and the others were allowed to meet with Vellan. At the time I didn't realize that simply meeting with the wizard would mark the pinnacle of my existence, though now I clearly see it."

"What happened to Ivy?" Leo asked impatiently.

"I explained to Vellan how his devoted Island allies came upon the princess, for I, too, at the time, assumed that Ivy was really Princess Megan. I showed Vellan the royal medallion and said that Brin had one of King Justin's spies as prisoner and was on his way to Mount Minakaris to turn him over."

"And Vellan believed you?" Nicholas asked.

Cale grimaced. "He was skeptical, having recently obtained conflicting information. He was convinced we were trying to deceive him and ordered our immediate executions." Nicholas' heart pounded. The color drained from his cheeks. "But not your woman. She was led away, though I didn't know to where. But before the steel blades of his guardsmen were plunged into us, I pleaded with

Vellan to allow us to serve him and told him about the unquestioning devotion of my cousin. Something in my words must have convinced him I may have been telling the truth. He temporarily lifted his order of death. The guards marched us to the snowy banks of the Drusala River just outside the eastern edge of Del Norác. Vellan accompanied us there in the darkness."

"What happened?" Leo whispered, enthralled with the story.

"Under a pale, moonlit sky, the five of us were lined up on the edge of the Drusala. I vaguely saw my reflection in the thin film of icy pieces drifting by. It was then that the mighty wizard spoke, giving us the choice to kneel down, drink the water and become his lifelong servants, or suffer an immediate death. But before Vellan uttered his next word, I shouted out that I would serve him forever and plunged into the Drusala. I arose from its freezing waters with my mind ablaze with a new perspective on life. For the first time in my existence, my thoughts were utterly clear and my vision of the future–*perfect*."

"And your fellow Islanders?" Nicholas asked.

"They hesitated making their decision," he replied with little emotion. "I saw their bodies fall into the river one by one as I was helped out of the water. An arrow was embedded in each of their backs as they floated downstream, disappearing forever into the wintry night. But such is Vellan's high threshold for loyalty."

"And after that incident you became his servant?" Nicholas asked, concealing his horror of the grisly details.

"One of several. Vellan relied heavily upon the Enâri to serve as his aides and messengers. After their terrible fate, he carefully chose their replacements, using only those who had willingly offered themselves to him through the wondrous waters of the Drusala."

"You must have learned much at Vellan's side," Leo said.

"Many of my tasks took me away from him, but even the most menial of them I performed with honor," he replied. "In fact, I had just made my way from Vellan's quarters to Deshla prison shortly before your attack. I had orders to bring some of the guards to Vellan's main gate as reinforcements, but most of them were slaughtered by your comrades."

"Bad timing," Leo deadpanned. "Tell us where Ivy is."

"I haven't seen her since the night we arrived, but I'm certain she is still Vellan's prisoner inside the stronghold," he said. "He doesn't speak to me of her."

"Could you take us to her?" Nicholas asked.

Cale thought for a moment. He wanted to lead them directly to Vellan to face punishment for their horrific crimes, but was vastly outnumbered. He needed to get word to Vellan first, and then have the wizard send an overwhelming force to Deshla and capture his prize. He smiled as a plan formed in his mind. He reached in his pocket and pulled out an iron key, holding it up to the opening.

"I might not be able to take you to Ivy," he said, "but I can get you inside Vellan's stronghold easily enough. His messengers, and those who accompany them, are allowed unrestricted access to certain areas of his fortress without question from the guards. After which, you would have to search for Ivy on your own."

Nicholas stepped closer to the door, his gaze slowly shifting between Cale and the key. "And how do we know that you won't hand us over to Vellan's guards?"

"You don't," he replied. "But that's the chance you must take if you want to see Ivy again. After all, you might have me killed and steal my key once you release me from this cell." Cale shrugged, dropping the key back into his pocket. "It's a chance we'll both have to take."

CHAPTER 103

Through a Dark and Winding Passage

Nicholas explained his plan to Malek's soldiers. He and Leo would escort Cale back to Vellan's stronghold where they would enter through one of the minor gates. A small group of armed men would accompany them along the road between the mountain and the woods, keeping hidden once they neared the entrance.

"Make sure Cale knows that one of my best archers will have him in his sight until you're inside," replied the captain who had approved the mission.

"Also mention that I'm handy with a blade," Hobin added, insisting that he would go along. "I led you to Frist, so I might as well take you to his evil opposite," he added with a chuckle.

A short time later, Nicholas and Leo returned to Cale's cell with the key to unlock his door. They wore daggers at their sides, hoping they wouldn't have to unsheathe them when they led him up the corridor and out of Deshla prison. They assumed the threat posed by the waiting troops would be enough to keep him in line.

"Are you ready?" Nicholas asked, displaying the key.

"As ready as I'll ever be," Cale replied. He briefly held up his key to what Nicholas and Leo hoped unlocked a lightly guarded minor door to Vellan's compound.

"Fine," Leo said, taking charge. "Step back while I unlock the door and open it. And remember, we're both armed and several guards are waiting at the end of the corridor. So no trouble on your part or it's back inside the cell." He took the key from Nicholas, preferring to give the orders to Cale in an attempt to keep the fragile bond of trust strongest between Nicholas and the prisoner.

Cale stepped back as Leo unlocked the door and slowly opened it as if a wild beast were inside. But a moment later, Cale emerged passively into the dimly lit corridor, his head slightly bowed as if his spirit had been broken. Nicholas and Leo stood on either side of him, each with a hand poised above their daggers.

"You won't need those," Cale remarked.

"I hope not," Leo said. "Now let's go. Both the day and the war aren't getting any younger."

Cale smiled pleasantly as the trio proceeded up the corridor. "By the way, you may have my key," he said, fishing through one of his pockets as he walked. "Since you kept your word and released me, I'll entrust it to you as a show of good faith."

"And we'll happily accept it," Nicholas said.

"I suppose," Leo added, being purposefully indifferent.

"Here," Cale said, pulling a hand out of his pocket. Suddenly, he shoved Nicholas and Leo aside in opposite directions, throwing them momentarily off balance as he spun around and bolted back down the corridor past his cell. He faded into the darkness beyond the last oil lamp and passed through another tunnel to his left that burrowed deeper into the mountain.

"Cale!" Nicholas shouted, sprinting after him in anger.

"Wait!" Leo cried, catching up and grabbing him by the shoulder. "Nicholas, he wants us to go after him. But he won't get far. The tunnels don't exit outside according to the earlier searches. Let's do this the smart way."

"And what way would that be?"

"Wait here." Leo hurried up the corridor and informed Hobin about what had occurred. He asked him and another soldier to stand guard inside the main entrance in view of the east and central tunnels in case Cale tried to circle back through either one.

"Watch yourself," Hobin said.

"Cale won't get far in the darkness with all the dead ends."

"Maybe I should go with you."

Leo unsheathed his dagger which glinted in the dull light. "We'll be fine."

Moments later, Nicholas stood similarly armed by Cale's cell when Leo returned. They each unhooked one of the oil lamps suspended from the low ceiling and continued down the gloomy corridor before turning left and plunging into the connecting dark passage. It was low and narrow like the other, with only a few prison cells carved into either side. None of them, however, had any doors attached.

"This must be where Vellan ordered the Enâri to halt construction," Leo said. "The waters of the Drusala would be more than sufficient to lock up the minds and freewill of his captives."

"A brilliant plan," Nicholas remarked. "Deviously creepy, but brilliant."

"With an army of Cales running around, I wonder if Vellan *can* be defeated," he said as they walked farther into the mountain. "The enemy can easily replenish its numbers by pushing captives into a river. How can we compete against that?"

Nicholas sighed, wondering if Leo could be right. "I suppose you need unflinching faith in your cause to carry on," he said, his eyes fixed on the fluttering light guiding them along the narrow passage. "That's what I admire about King Justin, Malek and Eucádus. They never give up no matter how hard the enemy strikes."

"Their perseverance must have rubbed off on you. But since you've never given up in your search for Ivy even before you had met them, I can only conclude that you already possessed the same strength of spirit. What else would explain it?"

Nicholas recalled the recent frenetic months, wondering how he had survived them. "I had great teachers in life, especially my mother, Maynard and Tessa." He thought about his father, Jack Raven, remembering the kind words Frist had said about him. "And some wonderful teachers I had *never* met." He glanced at Leo. "And since you've been at my side through much of this adventure, you must have that same strength of spirit, too." Nicholas laughed. "How else to explain your endless devotion to Princess Megan?"

"Good point," he replied. "But on the other hand, she and I–"

Leo cut short his words. He and Nicholas stared into the dark void ahead, both having heard a noise in the distance. Footsteps? A loose stone hitting the ground? Neither could tell with certainty, but no other sound was forthcoming. Leo signaled to advance with caution as a weighty silence overwhelmed them.

"Perhaps we imagined it," he whispered.

"Both of us?" Nicholas shook his head. "That has to be Cale skulking around, waiting to attack us. But I think he'll find– Hey, what's this?"

Nicholas held out his hand, detecting a cool draft playing across his fingers. Leo felt it, too. When they raised the oil lamps for a better look, the increased illumination highlighted two additional tunnel openings, one to the left and another to the right.

"Wonderful," Leo whispered with exasperation. "Which way did he go?"

"He might have continued straight ahead to fool us."

Leo raised his dagger, the firelight reflecting along its edge. "Stay here and stand guard while I scout ahead and see what kind of maze we're in."

"All right. But watch yourself." Nicholas though, had little time to worry about his friend as the glow from Leo's oil lamp soon reappeared.

"It's a dead end after fifty paces, so that's good news. Cale either took off to the left or right. Choose a direction."

"I'll head right," Nicholas said. "Holler if you find anything."

"You too. And keep that dagger handy."

They split up, their footsteps quickly dying out in each other's ears. Nicholas turned right into the new passageway, finding nothing but crudely chiseled stone walls on either side, imagining with horror Vellan's original plan to imprison the population living among the Northern Mountains. He noticed that the splash of light on the wall to his left had suddenly lessened after he had taken several more steps. He stopped and held up the lamp, shaking his head in dismay. He had found another opening that needed to be investigated and wondered if he would ever see daylight, or Ivy, again.

Ten minutes passed. Nicholas vigilantly stood guard near the entrance to the newest tunnel, though it seemed like an hour. He couldn't risk exploring the next passageway and leave the current one unattended, so he waited patiently for Leo to come back, feeling his chances of finding Ivy slipping away. To his relief, Leo returned a couple minutes later, the glow of his lamp swaying gently as he ambled down the corridor.

"I was about to go searching for you," Nicholas said.

"I had an errand to run," he joked, noticing the new entrance.

"I didn't dare search it and leave the rest of this one unguarded. What'd you find?"

"My tunnel opened up into the main central corridor where Istillig and his friends are relaxing," Leo said. "I recruited a few of Malek's men to keep watch at that intersection in case Cale shows up. A couple others volunteered to check things out farther down in the main section. I'm guessing there are offshoots deeper inside. In the meantime, we can split up and see what you've found here."

Nicholas agreed and continued down the tunnel he had been exploring. Leo stepped into the newly discovered passage to the left. But Nicholas hadn't walked much farther when he came to a dead end. He sighed dejectedly, knowing he mustn't give up, yet found it difficult to retain a positive outlook. He turned around and returned to the spot where Leo had left him and followed him down that passageway. When seeing a lamp coming toward him soon after, he assumed Leo had found a dead end as well.

"Any luck?" he asked perfunctorily, anticipating the answer.

Leo shook his head, noting the anguish in Nicholas' eyes. "None." He held up his lamp and circled around the narrow passage for a final look as if hoping they had missed another tunnel opening somewhere. But both men felt only defeat and frustration as the stale air seemed to slowly suffocate them.

"Cale must have fled to the other side," Nicholas reasoned. "There's nothing left here to explore. Let's go back. Maybe the others tracked him down."

"All right," Leo said as Nicholas turned and trudged back up the tunnel, his head bowed in defeat. "But don't feel that this chase was a waste of time. Now that we know Cale is definitely in the other section of Deshla, we'll find him. And then Ivy, too. I promise."

"If you say so," he muttered, his eyes fixed to the ground.

Leo, watching his friend from behind, couldn't help but feel sorry for him and searched desperately for additional words of support. He was about to speak, knowing that Nicholas was slipping into a state of despair, when he observed a brief but lively fluttering of the flame in Nicholas' oil lamp. But as there were no openings in the rock on either side of the wall, he wondered if his eyes were playing tricks on him.

"Nicholas, wait up a moment."

"*Hmmm?*" He turned around, his thoughts elsewhere. "What'd you want?"

Leo locked his gaze upon Nicholas' lamp, the fluttering of the flame having stopped. "Take a couple of slow steps toward me, holding your lamp aloft."

"*Huh?*"

"Do it please," he said with restrained urgency. "Humor me."

Nicholas shrugged, a puzzled look upon his face. "Fine. But what's your point?"

"I'll tell you shortly." As Leo watched Nicholas draw closer, his concentration focused upon the gentle flame. Then he saw it again when Nicholas passed a particular point along the passageway, a sudden and restless fluttering of the fire as if it had been carried past an open window on a blustery day. "Stop!" he shouted, startling Nicholas who took an additional step before halting.

"Leo, what's going on?" he asked with mild annoyance.

"Take one step back and then don't move. And hold your lamp a little higher and closer to the wall on your right."

"If you insist," he replied, bringing the light toward the rock. "But we're wasting valuable time when we should be–"

Nicholas went silent, his heart beating faster upon seeing and hearing the flame in his lamp suddenly sputter and writhe as he held it near the wall. Yet neither he nor Leo could see an opening in the unevenly chiseled rock that would explain the current of air. He moved the lamp a few inches to the right along the wall and the flame returned to normal.

"Move it back," Leo whispered, watching closely. The flame once again danced when it returned to the same spot.

"What are we seeing?" Nicholas asked with growing interest.

"Not quite sure. Let me take a closer look."

Leo ran the palm of his hand across the stone until he felt a thin stream of air brushing against his skin. As he followed the upward path of the tiny breeze, Nicholas observed with amazement that Leo was tracing an outline of a narrow archway. When he finished, they looked at each other with drunken grins.

"I'm guessing we're thinking the same thing," Leo said.

"Is it possible?"

"Let's find out."

Leo handed Nicholas his oil lamp and then pressed both hands against the rock between the two thin vertical areas where he felt the stream of air, but nothing happened. Slowly, he moved his hands inch by inch to the right until the rock gradually gave way under the pressure as a gust of air washed over his face.

"Leo! There's a–" Nicholas, choking up, couldn't finish his sentence.

"–a doorway," he replied, smiling.

Leo grabbed his lamp and they both took a step back, raising their lights higher as a steady but gentle breeze rustled the hair on their heads. Before them was a low archway and a partially opened stone door expertly cut from the wall. Inside, it looked as black as the night itself. Neither uttered a word, believing that Cale had disappeared into the hidden passageway. Without hesitation, they slipped inside.

The passage was much narrower than the tunnels of Deshla, only the width of three men abreast. Nicholas closed the stone door after they entered to stop the flow of air from extinguishing their lamps. He admired the craftsmanship that had created the smoothly turning door despite the fact that it was the work of the Enâri. Leo, meanwhile, eyeing their way forward, reached up and touched the cold rock ceiling with his fingertips.

"Words of advice–don't jump," he joked as he and Nicholas moved on.

"Where do you think we are?"

Leo furrowed his brow as their footsteps subtly echoed along the tunnel. "I'll bet people used this secret passageway to escort prisoners of particular interest to and from Vellan or his commanders, those few prisoners who were actually kept here. Or maybe it's some sort of escape route. But where it leads to, who knows?"

"I wonder," Nicholas muttered as they trudged on. "Still, wherever it goes, Cale will have to take his time getting there without a light to guide him. But if he reaches the end before we do, we might never find him. Can we pick up the pace?"

They moved faster, gradually rising in elevation. Minutes later, Leo spotted a thin beam of light shooting through the ceiling at a sharp angle and hitting the wall to their left. "What have we here?" he asked, looking up through a narrow hole a few inches wide that had been bored into the stone to reach the fresh air outdoors. The touch of warm sunlight brought a smile to his face.

"An air source," Nicholas said, imagining there were several more scattered along the stone trail. "You've got to hand it to the Enâri–both deadly and resourceful."

"I prefer them in their present state," Leo said. "Let's go."

They continued through the claustrophobic surroundings, aware of the gradual rise and slight turns in their path, though generally heading in an easterly direction. As the cool air brushed against their sweaty brows, both were reminded of their climb up Gray Hawk Mountain with Hobin. They paused a few times to rest, their leg muscles burning, wishing they had brought their water skins. At several points in the trek, Leo set his lamp down and listened for signs of Cale. Except for the fluttering flames, all was silent.

"Maybe he gave us the slip after all and went to the other side of Deshla," Leo said.

"Regardless, we're going to the end wherever this leads," Nicholas replied, signaling for him to move on. "For good or for ill."

A few minutes later they stopped again, tired from the continual rise in elevation and gradually warming air. Nicholas sat against the wall to rest, wondering if they would ever find Cale. Leo plopped down on the opposite side, guessing his friend's thoughts.

"It can't be much farther, Nicholas. We'll move on shortly. We'll find her."

Nicholas nodded, appreciating the comment whether believing it or not. "I wonder how much longer our light will last. The lamp isn't as heavy as when we started. Most of the oil has burned off."

"And unlike our delightful jaunt in the Cashua, we have no wood to start a fire," Leo joked, noting a smile upon Nicholas' face.

"At least we're not lost," he replied, briefly closing his eyes. "We have a well-defined path to somewhere, but I don't know if–"

Suddenly a vague and distant call, cut off immediately after it sounded, startled them both. Nicholas' eyelids popped open. He and Leo scrambled to their feet, staring at one another in confusion.

"You heard that, too?" Leo asked.

Nicholas nodded. "Was it a scream?" He grabbed his oil lamp. "Or a call for help?"

Leo hurried forward. "It has to be Cale, but I can't judge how far ahead."

"Be vigilant. We may not be the only ones here."

As they picked up the pace, sometimes going at a slow run, Nicholas lost sense of how long they had been inside the tunnel, having no clue as to the hour of the day. He assumed that Hobin and the others had probably begun to search for him and Leo within the corridors of Deshla, guessing that the odds were slim that they would stumble upon the secret opening in the wall. As the wavering light and slippery shadows drifted across the floor before his feet, Nicholas looked up to clear his mind. Leo, a few paces ahead, seemed more eager than ever to end this portion of their journey.

"It can't be much farther," he said between breaths, glancing back at Nicholas with a confident smile. "I have a feeling that—"

"Leo! Wait!" Nicholas' blood ran cold as he dropped his lamp and lunged forward, grabbing Leo by the shoulders and pulling him to the ground where they both hit the stone with groan-inducing pain.

"What are you doing?" Leo cried as he rolled on his back, staring up at the pale light flickering upon the ceiling as a momentary spasm of pain shot up his spine. His oil lamp had been extinguished during the fall, but Nicholas' still burned a few feet away.

"Saving your life is what I'm doing," he replied, sitting up. "You all right?"

"I will be," Leo moaned, rubbing the back of his neck.

"Good. Now don't move."

Nicholas stood and retrieved his lamp and then hurried back to Leo's side, letting the light fall on the floor ahead of them. As Leo groggily sat up and stretched his limbs, his eyes focused forward and widened in shock. Just a few steps ahead was a deep pit that extended the width of the tunnel and stretched forward a dozen feet.

Leo walked cautiously to the edge. He glanced at Nicholas with a pale but grateful smile.

"I'm guessing we'll find Cale at the bottom," Nicholas quietly remarked. Leo nodded, trembling at how frighteningly close he had come to joining him there.

After relighting the second lamp, they saw Cale's dead body sprawled out upon the bottom of the pit. Without hesitation, Nicholas began easing himself over the edge.

"What are you doing?" Leo frantically grabbed him before he was halfway over.

"I'll be fine," he said, securing his footing on the unevenly chiseled sides. "Help lower me down. It's not much deeper than my height. I need to get that key."

"All right. I'll follow."

"No," Nicholas replied. "I wouldn't hear the end of it from Megan if you were injured."

A moment later he dropped to his feet and Leo lowered one of the oil lamps. The shadows dispersed and Nicholas saw Cale's body, his eyes gazing lifelessly at the ceiling, a small pool of blood beneath his head. He turned away, sickened. He assumed that this pit had been constructed as a security measure should someone unauthorized find the secret tunnel and wander inside. As swiftly as possible, he rifled through Cale's coat pockets and found the key, relieved that his mission to rescue Ivy might not be in vain after all. He shoved the key in his pocket and handed up the oil lamp to Leo.

"We need to get across," Nicholas said, searching for footholds to hoist himself up high enough to grab hold of Leo's outstretched hand. "Unfortunately, there's no ladder down here to get up the other side."

"Didn't think there would be," Leo said as he felt Nicholas' hand lock around his wrist. After pulling him up, they both sat and rested, breathing heavily as they contemplated their next step.

"How exactly was Cale going to get across that pit?" Nicholas wondered aloud. "He obviously misjudged where he was before he tumbled inside. But unless he was an excellent jumper, how could he possibly scale the distance?"

Leo looked around, seeing nothing but stone. "No wooden planks to set across it. No ladders." He scratched his mop of hair, having earlier removed his knit hat as his body warmed from the hike. "I'm guessing Cale arrived at Deshla through this passageway."

"So am I." Nicholas stood up as an idea suddenly struck him. "Say, if the Enâri could make *one* secret door..."

He walked over to the left wall and pressed his hands against the rock. Leo held up a lamp, watching his friend with interest. Moments later, Nicholas felt a slight movement in the stone and turned to Leo, smiling.

"Find something?"

"Just what I hoped for," he replied, pushing his full weight against the wall as part of it gave way. "Another door. The tunnel within must run to the other end of the pit."

"Nice work." Leo handed him the other lamp.

They stepped inside the narrow corridor, walking in single file until they came to a dead end. Nicholas again pushed against the wall until another stone door opened outward on the opposite side of the pit just as he had predicted.

"One step closer," he said.

"I just want out of this tomb," Leo replied. "Let's move."

They continued on, following the main tunnel and saying little. The path leveled out as they moved beyond the pit, which they took as a good sign. Their anticipation grew with every step, both wondering if they would ever reach the end just as a sudden change of scenery greeted them.

"Look. A *real* door," Leo whispered, not knowing who might be waiting behind it.

Built into the stone wall directly ahead was an iron door, its trio of enormous metal hinges on the right secured with large, round rivets. The door handle and locking mechanism was attached to the left side. Nicholas looked at Leo for some reassurance and then removed Cale's key from his pocket, examining it in the light.

"It's not the Spirit Box," he whispered, inserting the key into the door, "but let's see what trouble is released when I open it." He carefully turned the key, hearing the low, smooth movement of the locking bolt inside. When finished, he glanced at Leo standing protectively nearby, his hand upon the hilt of his dagger. "Shall we?"

Leo nodded, eager to leave the gloomy confines. After setting the oil lamps on the floor to one side, Nicholas grabbed the handle and slowly pushed the door open.

END OF PART TEN

PART ELEVEN
THE LAST STAND

CHAPTER 104

The Battle of Del Norác

Gray smoke rose from a burning structure in the western district of Del Norác, reaching high into the sky as King Justin's soldiers and their allies clashed with Vellan's army. The billowing fumes climbed and then drifted southeast over the Drusala River like a slowly moving snake. The ascending sun burned off thin cloud layers in the late-morning sky, revealing patches of blue above the many skirmishes blazing throughout the city and on its periphery.

Hours earlier, after the launch of fiery arrows against dawn's pale backdrop, King Justin and his counterparts led the army across the final quarter mile of grassy scrubland toward the city's eastern border to confront the enemy. But before they had arrived, Vellan's captains let loose a first strike of their own.

Del Norác was divided into two nearly equal regions by the Drusala River which cut a gently undulating path through the city. Three stone bridges spanned the river, one just inside the western border, one in the center of the city near the garrison, and the third lying outside the eastern edge of Del Norác. The wide, graceful structures were composed of a series of low arches that stretched across the ribbon of water. The easternmost bridge was visible to the left of King Justin's army as it advanced on the capital. But before the frontlines of horsemen and the companies marching behind them had reached the city, a swarm of Vellan's troops on horse and on foot poured out of the barracks located on the river's southern banks. They made for the eastern bridge, preparing to cross and storm the approaching army on the other side before it could reach Del Norác.

At that same moment to the north, another large company in Vellan's army issued forth through the front gates of his stronghold in Mount Minakaris. Those troops marched around the northeastern border of the city and made directly for King Justin's soldiers. Though they would arrive a few minutes after their comrades now crossing the eastern bridge, King Justin feared that a combined strike from both north and south outside the city might result in significant losses right from the start from which they might never recover.

"Divide and conquer?" King Cedric asked his fellow monarch as they trotted across the grassy, tree-dotted expanse. Accompanying them was the wizard Tolapari.

King Justin nodded, signaling his nearby captains to approach. "We need to breach the city and dilute the impact of Vellan's first shot. I'll lead a charge and punch through the eastern border, making for the garrison. Cedric, you and Tolapari must take a force and head off the raid coming from the mountain."

"Captain Tiber, Uland and Torr shall accompany us," King Cedric replied.

The wizard combed a hand through his hair. "My only wish is that Vellan will step outside his front gate when I get there," he said with a mischievous gleam in his eyes. "I have not seen that menace since I was his apprentice decades ago. I'd like to show him a few things I've learned since then from wizards of higher repute."

"Planning a raid without me?" a voice called from behind. King Rowan rode up alongside the others, smiling with fierce resolve as he greeted everyone.

"We have saved the eastern bridge for you," King Justin said.

"I accept," he replied, eager to charge toward the river since those now crossing the bridge included many from the Northern Isles. With him were Captain Grayling and Princes Brendan and William. "We expelled the Islanders once from Montavia. I am eager to do so here as well."

"You shall have your chance," King Justin promised. "But we have only moments to act before our path is blocked. Rowan, have Captain Silas and his forces engage the enemy with you. Gregory and Eucádus shall ride with me. Now onward!"

With that, the trio of Kings separated and transmitted their instructions with eagle-like swiftness. Moments later, the combined armies broke into three units. One headed south to the easternmost bridge under King Rowan's command. A second veered around the northeast corner of the city with King Cedric at the lead to confront the storm from Mount Minakaris. The third, headed by King Justin, raced directly for the eastern border of Del Norác to push into the city and take the garrison on the river's edge.

The clashes at the three battlegrounds were ferocious and swift. Swords were raised and arrows flew through the brisk morning air as both sides directed their men where needed during the intense initial moments of fighting. When at the city's edge, King Justin's forces stampeded across hard, dirt roads to the interior streets. With Prince Gregory, Eucádus and Ramsey at his side, the King was surprised that the waiting troops were less prepared for an offensive than those crossing the eastern bridge or storming out of Minakaris. He guessed that the enemy had probably assumed their dual strikes from the north and south would have blocked any incursion into Del Norác in time.

The initial resistance proved minimal along the various roads lined with low buildings of wood and stone. After engaging in a few halfhearted charges and perfunctory swordfights, Vellan's troops retreated farther into the city and took up new positions while awaiting reinforcements. King Justin briefly took leave of his son and trotted down a side street toward the river with a small company of soldiers.

"That was too easy," Prince Gregory remarked after his father had left, though with caution in his voice. "Vellan was overconfident that our way into the city would be blocked. But I will not savor this minor victory."

"More enemy soldiers will arrive," Eucádus replied. He warily guided Chestnut through a narrow lane of dirty stone buildings that funneled the troops into a common area overgrown with grass and weeds. With an open view on the left, he saw directly across the river to the southern side where some of Vellan's troops were rushing back from the lines that had not yet crossed the eastern bridge. "And here they come now."

"So much for enjoying our minor victory," Ramsey said.

"We shall soon have our hands full!" King Justin's voice boomed as he galloped back toward the common. He pointed in the direction from which he had just traveled. "From there I could see that a third of the troops at the eastern bridge had been redirected back into the city, no doubt making for the central bridge. This fight is not over."

"Father, I'll take a contingent and drive away those on the run on this side of the river before they can return," Prince Gregory said. "We'll thin the herd before rejoining you." He rode off to gather his troops amid the rising volume of clanking swords nearby.

King Justin indicated for Eucádus to accompany him to the garrison. "Time to unleash that same spirited fire as you did in the Citadel," he said, recalling Eucádus' verbal battle at the war council with the emissary from Harlow. "Ramsey, you missed quite a show."

"That spirit served me well in Rhiál," Eucádus replied. "I'm ready to fight."

"Count me in, too," Ramsey said.

"Then let us ride together!" King Justin cried, his words rising on a cool breeze as he signaled for all to press on and follow him.

King Rowan, in the meantime, along with Captains Silas and Grayling, led their troops to the eastern bridge as the enemy crossed the Drusala to attack the northern bank. On the King's command, Silas and Grayling each led a contingent of soldiers, both horsed and on foot, in different directions. They swept wide arcs across the grassy scrubland to points on the riverbank opposite each other from where the bridge touched land. Vellan's troops advanced in frenzied fashion as they streamed off the bridge. Heavily armed Islanders and cloudy-eyed natives of Kargoth and elsewhere attacked as whistling arrows and the pungent smell of blood mingled in the air.

Any organized offensive on either side, however, quickly broke down as several heated battles took on lives of their own along the riverbank and on the bridge. Other skirmishes broke out across the grassy swath, among the scattering of trees and shrubs or upon hillocks and low outcroppings of rock. Prince William gazed upon the raucous confrontations as he and Brendan sat upon their horses on a small rise north of the bridge in the company of their grandfather. King Rowan, assessing the initial clash, consulted with other captains about repositioning the troops as a dozen soldiers on horseback vigilantly kept guard over him and his grandsons.

"This reminds me of the battle below King Basil's estate," William told his brother amidst the echo of ringing metal blades and the shouts of men. "I didn't know if I would survive that day."

"How about today?" Brendan gazed upon him with newfound respect. Though William was two years his junior, he felt that his younger brother appeared the wiser and more self-assured of the pair.

"I feel more or less the same," he replied with a faraway look as mental images of Lake LaShear were superimposed over the Drusala River. He turned to his brother. "But I'll know for sure once Grandfather gives us permission to join in the fray."

Brendan was surprised by the casualness William displayed regarding the unfolding battle. Though he realized his brother had matured much in the last few months, he hoped that William wasn't eager to fight to prove himself an adult, or worse yet, to make, in his mind, amends for his actions in the cabin when Arileez had attacked.

"After Grandfather conveys his final orders, he'll take to the fight and we shall accompany him," Brendan said. "But not a moment sooner, just as we'd promised." William sighed with impatience and Brendan couldn't help but grin, seeing hints of his more recognizable younger brother again. "Grandfather lost me once, Will. He had to watch Mother endure the grief of my death which must have broken his heart to no end."

"That's why we should have sent word to Mother that you're alive. Imagine the depth of her pain still to this day."

"Grandfather and I agreed that until this fight is over and our fates are determined, we'll withhold the news of my current state," Brendan insisted. "It would be beyond cruel to tell Mother that I'm alive while war wages on, only to have me struck down again and make her grieve all over. It would be the death of her."

"I suppose you're right," he muttered.

"I am right, including respecting Grandfather's request that we keep out of battle until the last possible instant. But I assure you, we shall have our moment." The two princes saw King Rowan nod to his captains and send them on their way with new orders. "Perhaps sooner than you think. Here he comes."

The King guided his steed toward his grandsons as the men keeping watch moved in closer. "I've provided all the insight I can," he said, indicating his troops spread out across the field. "It is in their hands now, so let us join our fellow warriors with haste." King Rowan noted a hint of a smile upon William's face which the young prince quickly suppressed. "But not reckless haste," he cautioned.

"We'll follow wherever you lead," Brendan replied as William nodded in agreement.

"Your orders, sir?" one of the soldiers inquired.

King Rowan surveyed the battlefield one last time, noting the fierce fighting close to the bridge. "Captain Grayling's men have taken the upper hand by converging on the bridge, preventing half of Vellan's troops from crossing. That situation looks under control." He pointed to an area along the riverbank east of the bridge where Captain Silas and his soldiers were making a determined stand among a scattering of trees and high grass. "Let us make our charge there and give Silas some assistance." King Rowan unsheathed his sword and raised it high in the morning light. Brendan and William mirrored their grandfather's action. The King pointed his weapon toward the Drusala. "Onward, for Montavia and all the free lands of Laparia!"

His steed bolted toward the riverbank with Brendan, William and the other dozen soldiers following. The rumbling of their horses rose in volume like a swift and growing thunderstorm ready to unleash its fury.

Minutes earlier, King Cedric peeled away several companies from the right flank of the coalition army. They charged around the northeast corner of Del Norác and then directly toward Vellan's soldiers pouring out of the main gates of Mount Minakaris. With Captain Tiber and Tolapari at his side, the King thrust his sword into the air and called out a charge for victory. The army defiantly advanced, some on horseback but most on foot, entering the farmland and grassy fields lying between the mountain and the northern edge of the city. Morning sunshine streamed down through a thin layer of clouds, highlighting an array of swords, short spears and tightly strung bows at the ready. But as the men prepared to collide with the seemingly endless line of soldiers still marching out of Vellan's stronghold, a flash of doubt flickered in King Cedric's mind. He briefly wondered if this might be a symbolic charge only, a last swift stand to the death.

The inevitable clash materialized like a strong wave pounding a stone breakwall. The equine lines, stretching across the width of the field, ripped through Vellan's front forces with explosive fury. King Cedric, Captain Tiber and Tolapari guided the center lines into the eye of the storm while Uland and Torr led the remaining troops to opposite ends. Sharp blades quickly met flesh and the maelstrom turned bloody. The wails and groans of the wounded on both sides soon blanketed the battlefield.

"They pour out of the mountain like a colony of spike ants!" Tolapari shouted to King Cedric. His sword quickly cut down an enemy soldier in his path. "And just as annoying, too!"

The wizard wiped a sleeve across his sweaty brow before plunging his sword into the throat of a cloudy-eyed native of Kargoth who charged at him with an axe. As death quickly took hold, the soldier's eyes cleared to their natural, light brown color that matched the long strands of hair framing his narrow and confused face. The man's body collapsed to the ground in a senseless pile when Tolapari removed his sword in a single, swift motion, deriving no satisfaction from his brief victory.

As the morning wore on, bodies on both sides of the conflict fell to the ground at the point of a blade or stumbled backward upon an arrow's impact. The bright daylight of a warm spring day faded to black in the eyes of many. As the deadly minutes accumulated, King Cedric saw that his forces were still outnumbered and that achieving victory upon this particular battlefield was nearly impossible.

"We've done all we can here!" he shouted to Captain Tiber while racing to his aid. Tiber and another soldier, both on horseback, were fighting off five Islanders who attacked them on foot. King Cedric's steed clipped one of the Island troops as he sped by and knocked him hard to the ground. Tiber's sword pierced the shoulder of another and rendered him incapacitated. Moments later, the remaining three foes were killed in the brief skirmish.

"What are you saying?" Tiber replied at last, his brow dotted with sweat as he guided his horse alongside the King. "Retreat?"

King Cedric nodded. "We cannot weather the numbers Vellan has thrown our way for much longer. We should make for the city and regroup. Besides, we've achieved what we came here for, breaking up the enemy's initial attack. Call the retreat before our forces erode to naught."

Captain Tiber singled for the other soldier to ride out with him toward the central and western portions of the battlefield and sound the new orders. The King snapped his reins, preparing to ride and spread the word along the eastern lines. But he suddenly held back when, out of the corners of his eyes, he caught the distant gates of Vellan's stronghold slowly reopen.

"Nothing good can come of that," he whispered to himself. Suddenly, another slew of enemy soldiers emerged from behind the iron gates to aid their comrades and push them on to victory. King Cedric scowled and raced to sound the retreat before his forces faced complete annihilation.

The word to withdraw spread fast as several clashes still raged. Most soldiers, as ordered, fled south toward the northern border of Del Norác, moving with added haste when seeing the new wave of enemy troops flowing out of Minakaris. All sense of order broke down as King Cedric's men dashed across the field away from Vellan's troops whose fiery zeal was bolstered with additional lines marching their way. As King Cedric urged his men to the city, he glanced back one last time at Mount Minakaris, gazing indignantly upon the stronghold's impenetrable walls built outward from the base of the mountain. He knew that Vellan was probably watching from one of his lofty perches and smiling with smug delight.

A nearby voice then cried out in surprise, indicating the patch of woodland to the northwest alongside the mountain far beyond the gates of Vellan's abode. "Where'd *they* come from?" he asked.

King Cedric heard the comment but continued ushering his men toward the city, the words not registering in his mind. Only when he noticed some of his men turning around to glance back at the mountain did his scattered thoughts crystallize. He reined his horse to a slow trot and circled back so that Mount Minakaris lay once again in view. With mouth agape, he saw a second army appear in the north, but this time the advancing troops were charging directly at the fresh lines pouring out of Vellan's gates.

"Who are they?" another soldier uttered with incredulity.

King Cedric, overwhelmed with amazement, couldn't believe his eyes. Members of the mountain resistance from Surna, Linden and Harlow were barreling down the road between the woods and the mountain, fully armed and heading their way. He wiped a hand across his balding head, smiling with disbelief.

"Surely the raid on Deshla cannot be over this soon," he whispered, wondering if Nicholas and Leo were among those now charging full bore into Vellan's astonished troops who were still filing out of Minakaris.

Nearly the same question was posed by Torr who rode up alongside the King. "How is it possible they are here so quickly? Did they forgo the prison raid?"

"I don't know," he replied with a broad smile. "But they will not battle alone. There will be no retreat today. Onward!"

King Cedric snapped the reins of his horse and drew his sword, urging his men to return to the fray. But most, upon seeing the new arrivals, had already halted their flight to the city as a new spirit of hope infused the air. A sense of impending doom, however, infected the hearts of Vellan's troops as they watched their welcomed reinforcements scatter in disarray from the surprise attack behind them. The discordant clanking of swords and whistling of arrows again filled the air. But it wasn't until about an hour later amidst the ebb and flow of the fighting that King Cedric crossed paths with Malek and Max. The two were wiping fresh blood off their swords after defeating a trio of Islanders among a low mound of half buried rock. The King, now upon his feet with sword in hand, had been thrown from his steed nearly half an hour ago.

"Those three Islanders looked as wild-eyed as their allies who had drunk from the Drusala," Max joked as he greeted the King and a few other soldiers standing with him. He then introduced Malek before explaining the surprising turn of events at Deshla Prison.

"I look forward to hearing all the details later," the King said. "But your arrival couldn't have been better timed. We were about to retreat to Del Norác."

"We may yet do that," Malek said, gazing across the field and soaking in a panoramic view of the bloody proceedings. "I'm seeing pockets of retreat by Vellan's troops near the east and west edges of the field. But his men are escaping to the city, not back to Vellan's stronghold along the mountain."

"So we'll pursue them there!" Maxed chimed in.

"At once," the King agreed. "King Justin and his men made for the garrison earlier. I don't know how they're faring, but more enemy troops can't bode well for them."

"Then let us mop up the remaining mess here," Malek said.

"I'll get word out to reconstitute the lines for a march into the city, though I'll leave a small force here to deal with the aftermath," King Cedric told him. "But with luck, King Justin may already have the situation at the garrison under control."

He hurried west with a handful of men to gather his troops while Malek and Max sprinted toward a rocky stream to the north to aid some fellow fighters. Deep in their hearts though, neither of the two parties expected King Justin to be facing anything but an excruciating battle in the center of Vellan's capital. All, nonetheless, were eager to join in the conflict as soon as possible.

The garrison in Del Norác was constructed of granite blocks, its long southern wall abutting the Drusala River. It rose four stories high with a square watchtower in the center. Lines of small, deep windows punctured the walls, appearing like deadened eyes that gazed tirelessly upon the city. A set of metal doors within an archway marked the main entrance. Several minor doorways were scattered about, all securely locked from the inside. A few smaller buildings of similar design were located nearby on both sides of the river, serving as additional barracks, armories, food storehouses and stables. Though the garrison was not filled to capacity as when housing its former Enâri occupants, Vellan had worked tirelessly in recent months to approach those previous numbers. He had gathered his remaining forces throughout Kargoth and the other mountain nations, supplementing them with his Island allies.

When King Justin and his men had arrived there earlier that morning, they met only light resistance until Vellan's troops on the other side of the river dashed across the central bridge to help defend the garrison. Soon the fighting scattered among various buildings and adjacent streets, though the garrison stood well defended. Blood was drawn in swift fashion, staining grass, stone and hard ground while glistening in the sun.

"How are your arms holding out?" Ramsey asked Eucádus as they swung swords by the shadowy northeast corner of the building, having abandoned their horses in an earlier scuffle. They stood with a handful of their compatriots holding off a sudden attack from a dozen men who had charged at them, their eyes clouded with a cold, fierce devotion to Vellan.

"My arms still have life," Eucádus replied between breaths as droplets of sweat trickled down his forehead. "But the throat is nearly parched. Perhaps we should take a drink from the river!" he joked, eliciting grins from Ramsey and others in earshot.

"Vellan would like that," he said, shifting sideways to avoid a well-aimed blade that nearly impaled him. Ramsey spun around as his attacker sailed past and shoved the man from behind with his foot, sending him face first into the garrison wall. Without missing a beat, he lunged forward and buried his sword into the man's back. When he swiftly removed his weapon, the man collapsed to the ground, freed from Vellan's hold. Ramsey had no time to contemplate the man's tragic fate as he was instantly swept up again in the fight against the remaining troops from Kargoth.

But moments later, the arrival of King Justin and a small group of men on horseback helped Eucádus, Ramsey and the others make swift work of their opponents. The dozen men from Kargoth soon lay dead around them while Eucádus' troops, despite a few minor bruises and cuts, were none the worse for wear.

"Well timed!" Eucádus called out to the King before eyeing the surrounding conflicts unfolding before him.

The sharp clash of swords up and down several streets opposite the garrison grew louder and deadlier with each passing moment. When Eucádus glanced above to the west, he noticed a line of gray smoke snaking its way across the sky and over the river to the southeast. The acrid smell of a fire somewhere in the western district wafted upon the breeze. He eyed King Justin, both their thoughts turning to Prince Gregory.

"Apparently my son has stirred up a hornet's nest," the King remarked without a trace of worry. The men around him, looking at their leader in a leather battle jerkin over a gray woolen shirt while sitting comfortably upon his steed, took much solace in his steady demeanor. But that reassuring moment was short lived.

"Above you!" one of King Justin's men shouted from across the road, pointing animatedly at the top of the garrison. "They're coming from above!"

Looking like a brood of dangling snakes, a series of long, thick ropes were suddenly dropped off the garrison roof from one end to the other. Scrambling down the lines hand over hand were Vellan's troops, all armed with swords and sliding along the granite wall like a colony of rats scurrying from their nest. As nearly two dozen men simultaneously dropped to the ground and drew their weapons, an equal number above then climbed over the edge of the roof in unison and let themselves down. A third and fourth wave followed until a swarm of enemy soldiers infested the street, overwhelming King Justin's forces as the din of clattering swords tainted the air.

"Follow me!" Eucádus cried to Ramsey and his men as he plunged into the sea of enemy combatants.

At the same time, King Justin and those of his troops still on horseback waded through the expanding, deadly crowd, their swords swinging from side to side as they confronted their newest foes. Other soldiers in the streets, upon seeing the spectacle, rushed to help. Several of them though, fell in the first few bloody moments as the magnitude of the shock attack rushed over them like a raging fire.

Then something strange and unforeseen happened, though unnoticed at first by most as the chaos up and down the street intensified. As the thrust of cold blades through air and flesh continued unabated, two additional teams of Vellan's troops dropped down from the rooftop along the suspended ropes. Working in concert, they slowly waded through the tumultuous crowd toward the King's horse, furtively channeling the animal and its rider through the bedlam and closer to the garrison wall. King Justin fought off other attackers clamoring around him, unaware that he was being gradually separated from his riders and foot soldiers.

As the King neared the shadowy north side of the wall, another pair of men on the rooftop peered over the edge directly above him. They climbed over the side close to one another, each holding onto a rope. Going hand over hand, they slid down swiftly and silently above the mayhem while the King's horse was backed against the garrison wall. As King Justin fought off a few soldiers to his right, he didn't see the two men on ropes above, lowering themselves the last few feet. Suddenly, they grabbed hold of the

King from opposite sides, each placing an arm underneath one of his shoulders while tightly holding onto their ropes with the other hand.

"King Justin!" Ramsey bellowed out just as the King craned his neck backward in stunned surprise, eyeing the two assailants who had him in their grips.

But before he could utter a word, King Justin was lifted off his horse by the two men as several of their comrades on the roof furiously pulled on the ropes. The King and his captors rose up the garrison wall with mesmerizing speed that left onlookers below shocked and senseless. Upon hearing Ramsey's frantic call, Eucádus spun around and gazed up with dread as King Justin ascended while futilely hacking at one of the ropes with the restricted use of his sword. Eucádus' blood ran cold as he desperately calculated a way to rescue the King of Arrondale. But a moment later King Justin was gone, pulled onto the roof by a bevy of outreached hands and arms that engulfed the monarch like tentacles and carried him away. Seconds later, the ropes were pulled up and disappeared, and with them, any chance for a rescue.

CHAPTER 105

Blood on the Eastern Field

The battle near the eastern bridge on the city's edge was as brutal and bloody as the fighting inside Del Norác. The hostilities had separated into smaller conflicts along the river and among the trees and knolls across the field. Brendan and William inhaled the bitter stench of combat as they guided their steeds through the fires of warfare. King Rowan remained close to them after they were swept into the initial battle, brandishing their swords with expertise thanks to much training during weeks of traveling. But as the confidence of the sibling princes increased, they followed the natural flow of the fighting.

As the day wore on, they were seamlessly integrated into the conflict much like their fellow soldiers. Many unfortunate others though, lay scattered about in lifeless poses, dirt-grimed and bloodstained. A few had expelled their last breaths while face down in the Drusala River, their bodies drifting eastward with the current and leaving behind a diffuse trail of pinkish water.

"I never imagined it so," Brendan said to his brother as they briefly rested in the shade of a tree after an exhausting bout with one of Captain Silas' companies. They had both long ago lost their horses after a punishing clash. Brendan's face was stained with sweat and dust, and his mop of blond hair was matted down like wet straw.

"Imagined what?" William asked, appearing similarly disheveled.

Brendan looked at his brother, his eyes filled with an unspoken horror. "I never imagined that I'd get used to the death and misery around me–and so quickly."

William wiped the perspiration from his brow, recalling his experiences in Rhiál. "You'll never get used to this, Brendan. Right now our minds are tolerating it, even ignoring parts while we go about this unpleasant business. But the day will always haunt us," he said with grim certainty. "Some day if we're fishing on the Gestina River again or eating breakfast in our rooms, this day will find us, and there's nothing we can do to stop it."

Brendan placed a consoling hand upon his shoulder. "Nor would I want to, Will. The path we walk today is a part of who we are, for good or ill, and we'll have to accommodate it into our lives." He offered a heartfelt smile as he tousled his brother's hair. "And now I'm better understanding your thoughts regarding my demise. But as I'm back at your side alive and well, I hope you'll not visit them so often, though I suspect they'll knock on your mind's door from time to time."

Will offered a playful grin. "I'll try to keep that door locked."

"Good," he replied, eyeing the nearby soldiers who were surveying an area along the river. To the left of the bridge, a company of Islanders were making a charge at Captain Silas' men who had just fended off several troops from Kargoth. "I believe this respite is over," he added. Brendan took a deep breath, straightened his shoulders and patted the hilt of his sword before following the troops who started racing toward the Drusala River. William joined in the chase, wondering if this day would ever end.

When they reached the river, over fifty men were tearing up the grass and wielding swords along the water's edge. Captain Silas, embroiled in a deadly swordfight with a brawny soldier from the Isles, briefly looked up upon seeing the two princes of Montavia and their allies, his spirits lifting. An instant later, the tip of Silas' blood-stained sword tore across the chest of the Islander, sending the man flailing backward and tumbling to the ground just before he was finished off with a single thrust of the blade. When Silas turned to seek out the new arrivals, he eyed another determined Islander racing toward him amid the chaos. The captain sighed and gripped his sword tightly, ready to do it all over again.

Prince Brendan rushed over to give Silas a hand, much to William's wide-eyed consternation. As the Islander bolted headlong toward Silas while running parallel to the river, Brendan charged at him from the north. As he drew his blade, he shouted out to get the man's attention. The Islander slowed down upon hearing the frantic cry. When seeing the young prince barreling toward him, he repositioned his weapon just in time as Brendan's well-aimed blade met his with a swift and sharp strike.

Their swords clattered as each fended off strike after deadly strike, but Brendan never relented and edged forward with each swing of his blade. The Islander grudgingly retreated toward the riverbank, his back to the water while his eyes remained fixed upon the prince's steely gaze and his unfathomable burst of fury. As their swords rose to repel the other's strike, Brendan advanced another step and the Islander found himself poised precariously on the river's edge as the prince's fearless blade again came at him. He shifted to his right to avoid the expected hit, but misjudged his step and slipped, tumbling into the Drusala with a terrific splash. Brendan leaped back to avoid the spray of water as William ran up to his side.

"That's one way to fight," he said as the man surfaced in the water, coughing and sputtering between gasps for breath.

Suddenly the Islander was overcome with an eerie sense of calm as he waded to shore, his sword missing. The stark contrast to his fiery temper moments ago unnerved Brendan. He grabbed William's arm and pulled him back as Captain Silas joined them.

"Well played!" Silas said, observing the Islander as he crawled up the bank and fell flat on his chest in utter exhaustion. "And well timed, too. I'm not ashamed to say that I was on my last legs, though I'm feeling better now."

"Glad to be of service," Brendan replied as the fighting raged around them. He pointed to the beached Islander. "What about him?"

"Let him lie there and dream about the greatness of his new master," he remarked as the Islander breathed heavily while face down on the ground, apparently asleep. "He is now a prisoner of the enchanted water, and if he awakens and rejoins the fight, then he shall take his chances. But I will not slay him while in a defenseless state."

"Though he probably deserves it," William muttered.

"Agreed. But there is more work to be done." Silas pointed to a thicket of scraggly trees farther to their right where Captain Grayling and others were engaged in a skirmish with men from Kargoth. "Let's give our friends a hand."

Drawing their weapons, Captain Silas, Brendan and William headed toward the fighting as the clattering of swords and shouting of men blanketed the area. But beneath the din, the subtle sound of heavy boots moving through the grass caught William's ear. A fleeting shadow behind him grazed the corners of his eyes. The young prince glanced instinctively over his shoulder but hardly had time to shout out to Brendan and Captain Silas who were a few steps away to his right. The Island soldier they had left upon the riverbank had stealthily raced up from behind, stooping low and moving quickly, a dagger clutched in his muddy, wet hand. He zeroed in on Silas, his eyes ablaze with a newly heightened devotion to Vellan.

"Behind you!" William cried, but an instant too late. The Islander lunged at Silas' legs and drove the dagger into his right calf.

Captain Silas fell with an agonizing cry. Spasms of pain coursed through his body, though he managed to roll on his back and face his assailant after the Islander removed his knife and jumped to his feet. He was ready to attack again, this time his eyes focused upon Brendan who had spun around and raised his sword. But before they clashed, William flew past his brother with an outstretched blade and charged at the enemy with one purpose in mind. The world went silent, seemingly frozen in time as the tip of his sword met its mark and effortlessly tore through layers of the enemy's protective gear, clothing and soft flesh. While clutching the hilt of his sword, William noted a glimmer of life flickering in the dying eyes of the Islander, unaware of the dagger still in the man's grip. But before the man let loose a last deadly swipe, his body was thrust backward by a sudden force. He stumbled and fell dead to the ground with William's sword still buried inside him.

William, nearly toppling over upon the corpse, turned swiftly aside and scrambled back on his feet. When his eyes focused, he saw an arrow protruding out of the Islander's chest as he lay gazing at the sky with a vacant stare. When he glanced left, he saw a soldier from Arrondale standing there clutching a bow in his outstretched arm with another arrow at the ready. Beside him upon a horse, wearing a vague smile, sat King Rowan. William smiled back as if all the fighting around them had faded away.

"Were things so dull near the bridge that you moseyed on back to this part of the war?" he asked his grandfather.

"It's a good thing I spotted you from afar and decided to have a look." King Rowan dismounted and raced to Captain Silas' side where Brendan was already tending to his wound. William joined him while the archer unsheathed his sword and kept watch.

"I don't think you'll be leaving us just yet," Brendan said to Silas with a comforting smile. He carefully cut off a portion of the soldier's ripped pant leg with a dagger and used it to temporarily bind the bleeding wound. "It's not life threatening as far as I can tell, but you'll need the immediate attention of a physician."

"Agreed," King Rowan said. He pointed to some distant trees. "There is an area to the northeast less than half a mile beyond that thicket of pine. People from our supply lines have congregated there with some of the food stores. Physicians are also present to tend to those who can be brought to them. You must get on my horse, Silas, and go there."

Captain Silas shook his head, wincing in pain. "King Rowan, I can't leave while–"

"You'll serve no good in your condition," he bluntly told him, examining the bandage. "Blood continues to seep through your wrap. You'll not be much use to us unconscious." He looked at his grandsons. "Help me get him on the horse. King Victor and Queen Melinda will never forgive me if I let their most respected representative expire upon the field of battle."

After a bit more prodding, Captain Silas relented. He wrapped an arm around Brendan and William's shoulders so they could help him stand and get him to the horse. The archer keeping watch urged them to hurry.

"The fighting upon the low rise over there seems to be intensifying, and not in our favor," he ominously remarked. "Hostilities may spread this way."

"Then we had better move now," King Rowan said as Silas was gingerly helped upon the horse.

When he was secure in the saddle, Silas grabbed onto the reins and took several deep breaths until the throbbing pain in his leg subsided for a moment. His face was as pale as snow and his shoulders slumped forward, causing all to wonder if he might pass out before he made it to his destination.

"I'll be fine," he said with a faint smile. "It is all of you I'm worried about."

"Worry no more as our fates are out of your hands." King Rowan pointed to the northeast, indicating a relatively clear path for him to follow. "Go now."

"I shall give you a bit of maneuvering room," the archer said, again raising his bow and firing two arrows in rapid succession. He struck dead a pair of Vellan's troops who were headed their way along the path Silas intended to take.

King Rowan slapped the back of his steed whereupon it galloped away at breakneck speed. As Silas disappeared beyond the last area of fighting and toward the thicket of pine, the King was satisfied that he'd soon be in competent and caring hands.

"Now it's time for the men of Montavia to make our move," he said, looking proudly at his grandsons. He indicated a skirmish raging near a clump of scraggly trees in the distance where Brendan, William and Silas were earlier heading. "We'll go and give Captain Grayling a hand. Keep close to me and Marello," he calmly remarked, referring to the archer who now had his bow slung across his back and a sword in hand. "Let's go!"

The King, with his grandsons to the right and Marello on his left, raced to the tree-dotted area where the fighting had flared up. They passed the two dead bodies pierced by Marello's arrows. But before the quartet reached their destination, the fighting upon the low rise to the left appeared to be spreading toward their position. A new influx of Vellan's troops temporarily gave the enemy the upper hand. Suddenly, an arrow flew by from that direction, nearly striking Brendan as it blasted past his left side before dying in the grass several yards behind him.

"They have an archer in their ranks," Marello said as they hurried along, having heard the arrow streak by like an angry wasp.

"And he's apparently taken an interest in us," Brendan replied with dark humor.

"We're almost there," King Rowan said, glancing ahead at Grayling and his men near the trees. "I think we've dodged the chaos to our left."

But just as those words left his mouth, five soldiers near the low rise broke away from their battle and raced toward the King and his companions. William spotted them first, observing a burning rage in their eyes that only death itself could extinguish.

"We've got company!" he cried, wondering if the advancing soldiers were close friends of the two men Marello had slain.

As they drew closer, William noted by their garb that three of the men were native to Kargoth and the other two were from the Isles. By their speed across the trampled grass, they would arrive in mere moments before he and the others could reach Grayling. William clenched his teeth and reached for his sword, only to recoil with icy terror when his fingers clutched an empty sheath. In all the excitement, he had neglected to retrieve his weapon still imbedded in the body of the dead Islander who had stabbed Silas. He quickly procured a small dagger attached to his belt and hoped for the best.

"Our next fight will be here," King Rowan said with gritty determination as he slowed down to take a defensive stance as the five enemy soldiers zeroed in.

"I have a few arrows left," Marello replied, sheathing his sword and grabbing the bow off his back in the same breath. He pulled one of the arrows from his quiver and fitted it to the bowstring while reducing his stride to get a better aim. A second later he released the arrow and hit one of the Islanders in the right shoulder, knocking him to the ground. Marello skidded to a halt and dropped on one knee, firing another arrow which found its intended target, striking dead one of the men from Kargoth as the remaining three soldiers readied their attack. Marello swiftly abandoned bow for sword as King Rowan and his grandsons ran into his line of sight and headed toward the trio. He quickly joined them, rushing at the remaining Islander to his left.

The clattering of swords rose above their heads as King Rowan, Brendan and Marello battled their opponents, swinging their blades as weariness, hunger and thirst were pushed aside in the lengthening, late afternoon shadows. William, unwilling to be left out of the fray, maneuvered toward the right side of the towering soldier from Kargoth who was battling his brother and prepared to lob his dagger at him. But he held back as the tip of Brendan's blade sliced across his opponent's right wrist, causing the soldier to bellow in agony as the weapon flew out of his hand. The man fell to his knees as Brendan scrambled backward to avoid being hit by the falling sword. But in his rush, his foot caught a protruding rock, causing Brendan to twist and topple hard upon his back, hitting his head as the wind was temporarily knocked out of him.

"Brendan!" William shouted in warning. For at that same moment, the injured soldier rose slowly to his feet. Though shaken and in pain, he seethed with vengeance as he displayed a sharp dagger and hobbled toward Brendan, determined to finish him off.

King Rowan and Marello, engaged in their own ferocious battles, each heard William's frantic shout and saw the deadly events unfolding a short distance away. But before either could safely evade their own attackers to lend any assistance, their eyes widened in horror as William raced toward the wounded soldier who was now just steps away from his brother. Brendan, at the same time, tried to sit up and shake off the swirling haze in his mind, his fingers blindly groping through the grass for his sword.

"Your life belongs to Vellan now!" the soldier from Kargoth muttered as he loomed over Brendan, his knife rising to strike.

"And your worthless life is *mine!*" William shouted. He jumped onto the man's back, wrapping one arm tightly around his thick neck and plunging his dagger into the soldier's chest with a single, powerful thrust. The man's head snapped backward as a bolt of pained coursed through him, paralyzing him for an instant. William gazed briefly into his eyes and witnessed a cloud of delusion and bewilderment dissipating like morning mist before death quickly took hold. His body collapsed to the ground with Prince William stuck between it and the cool, green grass.

Using his remaining strength, William rolled the body off and sat up, his eyes watering, his breathing labored and his head swimming with sounds of discordant voices and clattering metal blades. When his vision and hearing refocused, his gaze was immediately drawn to his grandfather who was still fighting yards away with the soldier from Kargoth, their blades expertly repelling one another's furious strikes. Beyond them, Marello and the Islander were in a struggle of daggers and fists, both having lost their swords. As William frantically looked for his brother's weapon to assist his grandfather, the King's blade ripped a gash across his opponent's chest, sending him stumbling backward to the ground. King Rowan swiftly finished off the soldier with a single thrust to the midsection, releasing him from Vellan's spell.

With sweat streaming down his face, he raced to his grandsons who sat on the ground beside each other, both somewhat disoriented. King Rowan dropped his sword in the grass, the blood of his enemy clinging to the blade. He knelt down and placed a hand on William and Brendan's shoulders to reassure himself that they were really alive and spared of serious injury.

"You two are aging me fast," he said. The sun, dipping in the west, reflected off their blond locks, dirt-smudged faces and crooked smiles. King Rowan saw in their lively eyes a glimpse of his son, Kendrick, and was reminded of better days in their youth. "Can you both stand?"

"I think so," William said as he slowly got to his feet. "But Brendan might need a hand up as he got the worst of it."

"I'll be fine," he insisted, putting on a brave face. Brendan grabbed his brother's arm and got to one knee, resting for a moment as a bout of lightheadedness swept over him. His eyes widened in dread when he glanced over his grandfather's shoulder. "Look behind you!" he shouted, jumping up and searching for his sword with unsteady steps, nearly stumbling as he did so.

King Rowan spun around and rose to his feet, only to see that the Islander who had been fighting Marello was now barreling toward them with a bloody dagger in his hand. Just moments before, he had knocked Marello to his chest after a prolonged hand-to-hand struggle, causing him to twist his ankle. But before Marello righted himself, the Islander leapt upon his back and sank his blade deep into Marello's side, leaving him slumped upon the ground in a motionless mass. Now, the Islander charged at King Rowan and his grandsons with vengeance in his eyes, his blade catching the setting sun.

With no time to reach his sword, King Rowan unsheathed a dagger and sped forward, pushing William aside. He ran straight toward the Islander, knowing that the fanatical soldier would stop at nothing to slaughter the three of them. Gripping his dagger until his fingers ached, the King locked his gaze upon his enemy's clouded eyes, knowing he had only one chance to save his grandsons as the distance between them disappeared. Seconds later, their bodies collided like a pair of crashing boulders.

They eyed each other with contempt while still upon their feet. Brendan and William looked on with shock. King Rowan, his hand gripping the hilt of his dagger, bared his teeth with defiance as he watched the clouded eyes of his enemy turn crystal clear before they turned up into his skull. With a quick jerk of his arm, the King pulled his blade from the Islander's body which fell to the ground in a deadened pile. He took an awkward step backward and turned slowly toward his grandsons. Brendan and William sighed with relief and looked up smiling at their grandfather, ready to race to him with much deserved accolades. But when they noted his pallid complexion and saw the dagger slip out of his hand, their smiles faded. They spotted the Islander's knife handle protruding from the King's abdomen and noted the fine trail of crimson streaking down his vest.

"Watch over one another," King Rowan said to them, his lips barely moving, his voice a hoarse, weak whisper. Suddenly his body collapsed to the ground, warmly awash in the thin rays of the sun that slowly descended in the western sky.

CHAPTER 106

Mountain Rumblings

Nicholas stepped cautiously through the doorway into silent darkness. Suddenly he stopped. The tips of his right fingers touched a barrier in front of him, though not one of hard stone like the tunnel walls. To his puzzlement, the substance felt somewhat soft as he carefully moved his hand over the surface. It yielded to the slight force of his palm as if he were pressing against heavy drapery or a large rug hanging from a line on cleaning day.

"What is it?" Leo whispered from behind, his hand on the hilt of his dagger. A suffocating stillness permeated the air.

"Something's blocking the way. A wall, but not really."

Leo furrowed his brow. "Then *what*?"

Nicholas glanced left and right, his eyes growing accustomed to the murkiness. He noted a faint glow several yards away on each end, though it was more pronounced toward the right side. He stepped that way to allow Leo room to pass through the doorway. A moment later, Leo admitted that he saw a vague light in both directions, too. Nicholas suggested that they walk to their respective ends to explore.

"All right," Leo whispered, gently pushing the door closed.

They slowly walked in opposite directions down a shoulder-width corridor, the cold stone mountain to one side and the slightly undulating wall of heavy material on the other. After each had gone several paces, both sensed a dryer, fresher change in the air, convinced they were about to finally escape the stuffiness of the main tunnel. As Nicholas drew closer to his end, the subtle glow intensified and he noted the outline of some stonework. He soon recognized the profile of a large fireplace directly ahead where the soft wall to his left had come to an end. He smiled, realizing what was suspended in front of the tunnel door.

He moved out from behind his shadowy location and craned his head toward the other end of the room. There stood Leo, staring back at him after he had also stepped out from behind the mysterious piece of textile. Both glanced up at the barrier, a huge, thick tapestry suspended from the ceiling and nearly touching the floor, running almost the length of the entire wall. A fireplace to its left emitted a steady glow from the wispy flames and lustrous embers of a dying fire. They stood inside a shadowy, vacant room lined with wooden shelves crammed full of leather-bound books and numerous scrolls. A table was cluttered with parchment sheets and ink bottles, and a single wooden chair kept a lonely vigil near the fireplace. A stone archway across the room led out to a corridor.

As Nicholas and Leo walked toward one another, their eyes couldn't help but gaze with appreciative wonder at the colorful wall hanging. It depicted portions of the snowcapped Northern Mountains and the surrounding trees and valleys of Kargoth. Both guessed that it was Mount Minakaris looming in the foreground, hardly believing they were deep inside the mountain itself, most likely in one of Vellan's private studies.

"Nice place," Leo said. "I suspect Vellan sits here to concoct his vile plans."

"Or unwinds by the fire after a hard day of inflicting misery," Nicholas replied. "I suppose even a tyrant needs a place to relax."

"No doubt. Now let's find Ivy and get out of here."

Before stepping into the corridor, Leo peeked through the archway and glanced up and down the silent passageway. After signaling that all was clear, they exited the room and turned left. The stone walls had been expertly cut, smoothed and tinted a light reddish brown shade by the Enâri. All were decorated with intricate engravings, some depicting scenes similar to those on the tapestry. Lit candles affixed to the walls cast a calming glow along the gently curving passage. Soon they reached a dead end, but on their right was an oak door with a curved brass lever handle. Nicholas glanced at Leo who offered a reassuring nod, so he slowly opened the door.

Inside was a darkened set of stone stairs that curved right and rose parallel to the corridor. Leo grabbed a candle from the wall and he and Nicholas climbed the nearly twenty steps to the top. Awaiting them was a metal door locked with a sliding bolt. Leo carefully moved the bolt and pulled the door open just a crack. A stab of late afternoon sunlight and a cool blast of air greeted them. When he pulled it open all the way, both realized with delight that they had reached the outdoors, though quickly ruled out the exit as a future means of escape.

"What is this?" Nicholas whispered in amazement. They stepped onto a small, semi-circular balcony with a waist-high railing that had been carved out of the mountain.

A cool, steady breeze brushed across the face of Mount Minakaris. Its stony sides were splashed with soft shades of reddish orange light as the sun dipped in a brilliant blue sky above the snowy peaks to the northwest. Nicholas and Leo stood nearly halfway up the southern slope of the mountain with an unobstructed view of Del Norác and the Drusala River below. A snaking line of gray smoke lingered over the city. Distant cries of men and the clattering of swords were barely perceptible from such a dizzying height.

As they leaned against the thick stone railing to take in the panoramic view, they noted a sheer sheet of rock cascading below them until the tree line gradually developed along the lower, wider portion of the mountain. Far down to their left they spotted a few dirt roads presumably leading from some minor gates toward distant fields and stables on the lower elevations of the mountain's southeast slope. Another road led directly to Del Norác. A wide stream rushing down the mountain wended its way among the trees and fields until it finally emptied into the Drusala River farther to the east. Glancing right, they noticed that the trees lower on the mountain slope in that direction grew thicker and wilder in spots. A swath of woodland at the base of Mount Minakaris gently hugged the southwest edge.

Directly below them lay an impressive example of Enâri stonework. At the southern foot of the mountain, Vellan's creatures had constructed an elaborate stone bastion connecting to Mount Minakaris that rose nearly five hundred feet and stretched about three times the length. It seamlessly conformed to the side of the mountain as if it had been a natural extension. Several square towers and a few spires dotted the upper portions of the stronghold. The iron gates below ominously observed the nearby city like a sleepless eye. Nicholas and Leo looked down upon the top of Vellan's fortress, their breaths taken away as they imagined falling from such a height to its various levels of rooftops and surrounding parapets. Nicholas didn't want to guess how many thousands of Vellan's soldiers occupied the chambers below, hoping that Ivy wasn't imprisoned in a lonely cell in one of them. Without a word to one another, they turned around and stared up in awe at the rocky slope above them, their gazes rising to the snowy and icy peak of Mount Minakaris shimmering in the late sunshine of an early spring evening.

"I imagine we're barely a visible speck to anyone down below who happens to look up," Leo said as he turned to stare once more across the sweeping vista.

Nicholas agreed as a cold gust of wind rushed past. "I suspect all of them are otherwise occupied." He could only wonder what life-and-death circumstances King Justin and his troops were embroiled in at the moment and hoped for their safety.

"No doubt Vellan climbs up here to look upon his realm," Leo said with a bitter edge. "Such a spectacular view probably fed his warped sense of imagined greatness. I wonder if that wizard ever really appreciated all this beauty surrounding him."

"I doubt it," Nicholas replied, indicating that they should head inside and continue their search for Ivy.

A short time later they were back in the main corridor. They entered another unoccupied room at the opposite end, but finding nothing of interest, they left and exited through an archway in the center of the passage. They descended a stone staircase to the level below which brought them to another candle-lined corridor. Nicholas led the way west along the passage until they came upon another archway in the wall to their right. The room within swirled with shadows. He peered inside as Leo glanced up and down the hallway with mounting apprehension, wondering how long their luck would last at not being spotted.

"See anything?" he whispered.

"Too dark," Nicholas replied. "But there's a faint line of light on the left wall. I think there's a door slightly ajar."

When they entered the chamber, a thin stream of cool air drifted past them, apparently coming from the vertical slit of light across the room. As their eyes adjusted, Nicholas spotted a small round fire pit rising two feet off the ground and filled with a bed of glowing orange and red embers that continually brightened and dimmed like hundreds of opening and closing eyes watching their every move. But that added little light to the room as they moved gingerly across the floor. Just as Nicholas had guessed, a metal door stood slightly open against the side wall, allowing a splash of light to slip through. When he opened the door wider, a blast of cool air brushed their faces.

But instead of a small balcony as before, they walked out onto a larger, rounded stone terrace extending over the mountainside and supported beneath with meticulously carved blocks of granite. Several oak benches were scattered about. A stone railing encircled the structure which offered a tree-filled view of the southwest slope. Along the terrace's left side, the uppermost tips of a few tall pine trees shot up for several feet behind the railing, their sweet scent perfuming the air. The view was mostly unobstructed on the center and right sides where Nicholas and Leo took in another stunning vista. There, the drop was less severe than on the balcony, though still as deadly. And instead of sheer rock, small trees and patches of vegetation blanketed areas of the slope below.

"Incredible," Nicholas muttered, shaking his head.

"The view is every bit that and more," Leo replied. "Hobin would be impressed."

"I agree, but I wasn't referring to the scenery. I just meant it's incredible that Vellan produced a race that could create so many wondrous things, yet he trained them to bring damage and death throughout the region. What would possess him to do so?" He shrugged with bewilderment and headed back inside.

"Isn't that usually the case with tyrants?" Leo asked, his whispered words laced with dark mirth as he followed Nicholas into the room. He closed the door, concealing them once again in a tomb of suffocating shadows. "I'm not even sure if Vellan knows for certain what's kept him going all these years. Probably bitterness and spite. But if we ever run into the wizard, I'll make it a point to ask."

"You might as well ask me *now*," a low, raspy voice replied from somewhere in the darkness. "Whoever it is you are."

Nicholas and Leo froze. Their hearts pounded as the soft words shot pangs of dread through them. As they tried to pinpoint the location of the voice, a fresh blaze rose from the circle of embers and increased the light within. Nicholas noticed an aged hand ascending above the fluttering flames as if it were magically drawing out fire from the stone pit. Slowly, the hand pulled away and rested upon the lap of its equally wizened owner. An old man sat upon a cushioned wooden chair close to the fire pit as ghostly threads of bluish smoke rose up and disappeared through an opening in the stone ceiling.

The elderly figure stooped slightly sideways as if he had been napping or deep in thought, clad in layers of brown robes with a dark gray cloth cap wrapped loosely about his head. Tufts of white hair bulged out from beneath the covering around his ears, and a set of tired eyes above a slightly furrowed face keenly observed his visitors. A long oak staff leaned against the side of his chair, its misshapen top splintered and brittle like the fingers of an arthritic hand. The man breathed heavily as he gazed upon Nicholas and Leo, unsurprised by their sudden appearance, his lips barely moving as he whispered to himself. Nicholas and Leo glanced at one another, knowing they were in Vellan's presence.

"Nothing to say?" the wizard calmly asked, straightening up in his chair. He leaned back and caressed his chin while studying the two strangers with curiosity rather than fear or surprise. "You enter my abode uninvited, yet look at me as if I owe *you* an explanation."

"You do," Nicholas said, finding it an effort to utter those simple words as the shock of seeing Vellan constricted his breathing. But as he slowly absorbed the image of the old man, an image quite unlike what he had envisioned through the years, he grew calm and less afraid. Looking squarely into his eyes, he posed the one question foremost on his mind. "Where is Ivy, the young woman Cale brought to you many weeks ago? What have you done with her, Vellan?"

A thin smile spread across the wizard's lips. "So you know my name, young man," he replied. "And you've apparently met

Cale, a most devoted Islander to me and my cause if ever there was one."

"You should have met his cousin," Nicholas said. "Cale was a pale imitation."

"And now he's a corpse at the bottom of a pit," Leo added, his courage growing.

Vellan twitched with a flash of anger as he met Leo's gaze. "You've killed him?"

"Cale accidentally killed himself," Nicholas said, not wishing to rile Vellan. Despite a grandfatherly appearance, he knew the man was a powerful wizard who could strike them dead if the mood took him. He wondered why Vellan had already *not* killed them, but Leo spoke again, chasing the thought from his mind.

"We followed Cale through your secret tunnel connecting to Deshla prison after he escaped from us," he explained. "Cale had no light with him and took a fatal fall."

"I see." Vellan nodded, touching his fingers to his dry lips as he assessed the situation. "So you two were clever enough to discover the private entrance to my mountain home. I suppose I'll have to post a guard behind the tapestry until I can change the locks," he added with a dry smirk.

"Speaking of which," Nicholas said as he looked around, "your corridors here are barren. I would have expected more security from such a renowned wizard."

Vellan scowled. "This renowned wizard doesn't appreciate your patronizing tone. But rest assured, I have more than enough loyal troops to keep me safe. The lower levels are flooded with men who would give their lives to protect me. And though I usually keep a few of my most loyal servants roaming these upper levels where I make my home, I dismissed them an hour ago so as not to scare you away." Vellan delighted in the flummoxed expressions upon Nicholas and Leo's faces, neither having the slightest clue as to what he meant. "You see, I was expecting you just now and didn't want to risk an unnecessary confrontation before I had a chance to speak with you."

"Expecting us?" Nicholas asked. "How can that be?"

"Perhaps it's more accurate to say that I was expecting *someone*, not you two in particular," he elaborated. "A short while ago I sensed a growing presence as you made your way up the tunnel, specifically, Frist's presence." Vellan nodded, seeing a splash of uneasy surprise in Nicholas' eyes. "I'm guessing that you have seen the wizard recently. I detect his strong presence surrounding you." He stared sharply at Leo. "Not so much on you. Unfortunately for both your sakes, I can easily surmise the reason why you had met with him. But before you disclose those fascinating details, tell me your names, though I'm convinced I already know those, too."

"How could you know?" Nicholas asked. "Cale may have revealed mine, but he never met my friend here. So unless you–" A sickening feeling suddenly overwhelmed him as he imagined Ivy's cruel interrogation and treatment at the hands of her captors. "What have you done to her? Where is Ivy?"

Vellan chuckled, delighting in his visitor's distress. But as Nicholas prepared to lunge at him despite any consequences to his own life, the wizard raised a hand and slowly shook his head. "There's no reason to worry about her safety, Nicholas Raven. Your pretend princess has been well looked after since arriving in Mount Minakaris. She is in no danger. No immediate danger anyway, so you had better not push your luck."

"Nor *you*," Leo coolly challenged, wanting to draw Vellan's attention away from Nicholas for Ivy's sake. "I suppose you know my name, too."

Vellan grunted. "Am I forced to endure a petty apple grower gracing the corridors of my beloved residence? Consider yourself fortunate, Leo Marsh, to behold what most people of Laparia will never have the chance to see." He noted Leo's surprise when he uttered his name. "My informant long ago provided me with both your identities and other particulars."

"And if he didn't, I surely would have," a woman's voice curtly chimed in near the doorway behind them.

Nicholas and Leo spun around. A diminutive woman stood just inside the archway, her lips in a thin, straight line as she stared at them with icy disdain. The firelight gently reflected off the wayward locks of flaming red hair protruding beneath a black silk kerchief wrapped around her head. A fur-lined shawl was draped over her shoulders. Nicholas immediately recognized the face he saw six months ago along the Trillium Sea.

"Madeline," he whispered in disbelief.

"I'm flattered you recognize me after all this time," she said, stepping into the room and standing at Vellan's side. She studied Nicholas and Leo with much interest. "These are the two individuals who implemented the deception with Princess Megan," she reminded the wizard. "It's nice to finally have two faces to go along with the names I had learned of a while back. Shall I summon guards to take them away?"

Vellan gently patted her wrist. "Not yet, Madeline. I wish to speak with these gentlemen and find out more about their dealings with Frist, a vile collaboration that led to the destruction of my cherished Enâri." He slowly cast a hardened gaze upon Nicholas and Leo as his fingers tightened around the armrests of his chair. "The three of you helped to destroy my greatest achievement–and nearly myself in the process."

"That achievement brought misery and death to the people of Laparia," Nicholas said. "Frist clearly saw that, as I'm sure did the other wizards of your order."

"Don't speak of things you know nothing about! Frist and the rest of them mocked my ideas to expand our race and to make it flourish–to save it from time's eventual decay. They had a narrow vision." Vellan paused, breathing heavily as Madeline placed a soothing hand upon his shoulder and advised him to remain calm. The wizard nodded appreciatively at her and slowly relaxed. "And when I saw my beloved Enâri disintegrate before my eyes, Frist had managed to kill *my* vision, draining from me much of my power and energy that had been invested in their creation and maintenance." A morbid smile spread across his lips. "Part of me wishes that I had also been extinguished as the Enâri were when that loathsome spirit was released, yet still I breathe."

"And you'll get better until you're fully recovered," Madeline assured him. "You must. That is why you should have your supper now which is ready in the next room. Or do you wish for me to bring a tray to you instead?"

"Madeline takes care of me, overly so at times," he remarked as Nicholas and Leo looked on. "My indispensable nursemaid. And if I recover, I shall owe it all to her. You see, I have not long been in this feeble condition. Three and a half months ago I would have been fit enough to join the battle now raging in Del Norác despite the nearly eighty years I carry upon my shoulders. Now I'm not sure if I have many years left."

"The wizards from the Gable Mountain Range are a long-lived race," Madeline stated. "But look at what you've done to one of their greatest by cooperating with King Justin. Shameful!"

"And look at what you've both done to Laparia," Nicholas replied with equal contempt. "Along with Caldurian, you've created nothing but havoc in your wake, including in my home village of Kanesbury. I will not feel sorry for either of you."

"Nor would I expect it," Vellan returned defiantly. "But don't think that I am without power, young man. I'm still a potent force to be reckoned with. You and your friend will pay for your deeds."

"Shall I send them below with my cousin?" Madeline asked. "It will do your heart and mind good to have them out of your sight."

"Carmella is *here*?" Nicholas asked with foreboding. "She was under the King's protection. How did this happen?"

"I have had several uninvited guests over the past few days," Vellan said, "including your co-conspirator. That Carmella willingly brought the medallion to the Blue Citadel makes her as much of an accomplice in the annihilation of the Enâri as the two of you. I also include King Justin in your little group and his underling who turned the key. And if there is a modicum of justice in the world then they, too, shall get what's coming to them," he remarked in an almost snarling manner as Nicholas and Leo exchanged troubled glances. "Yet in deference to Madeline, I have postponed any decision on Carmella's fate for the time being, allowing that woman to work as her cousin's servant in the quarters below."

"But humility is slow to come to my cousin," Madeline said. "Perhaps other methods should be employed, though I wonder if she is even worth the trouble."

"Time will tell," Vellan told her, turning to Nicholas and Leo. "Now suddenly you two drop in, giving me more to ponder regarding the meting out of punishments. And though I expected you to arrive here someday, Nicholas Raven, as Cale had informed me that his cousin was bringing you to me, I never expected your friend to show up, too." He shot a glance at Leo. "Don't even think about reaching for your weapon," he said as Leo's fingers inched toward his dagger. "Madeline and I can take you both down with a well chosen spell before either one of you draws your blade. Such a rash attempt would not bode well for Ivy either, so keep that in mind."

"Fine," Leo grudgingly replied, his hand dropping to his side. He knew they were already at a severe disadvantage, wondering how much worse it could get if Vellan ever found out that he was the person who opened the Spirit Box.

"I feel like a bit of supper," Vellan said in an upbeat tone, much to Madeline's delight. "I've been thinking far too long and have worked up an appetite. Let us move to the dining chamber where we can continue our conversation. There is much yet that I want to learn from Misters Raven and Marsh before I decide their fates." He stood up with a helping hand from Madeline and appeared much taller than his previously hunched position had indicated. After he straightened out his robes, Madeline handed Vellan his gnarled staff. "Perhaps before the stew gets cold, the latest report from the fighting will have arrived if my messenger is on time for once. The many steps up to this level bother his knees though he is far younger than I."

"He'll manage," Madeline replied, extending her hands toward Nicholas and Leo. "I'll have your weapons."

"And should we refuse?" Nicholas gently challenged.

"Don't test my patience," she said in granite-hard tones, prompting Nicholas and Leo to reluctantly remove their daggers and surrender them to her with icy silence. "Now follow me," she added, heading toward the archway.

"Wait a moment," Vellan said, pointing to Leo. "Open the door to the terrace just a little as it had been earlier. You closed it all the way when you came back inside."

"All right," he replied, somewhat perplexed as he carried out Vellan's request. "I'm sorry I disturbed it."

"I'm waiting for my informant to return. He'll need a way inside," he explained while leaning on his staff. "Now let us eat. I'm starving for both food and information." Vellan indicated for them to follow Madeline into the adjoining corridor. "I'll provide the former, and if the two of you value the lives of you and your friends, then you shall supply the latter," he remarked matter-of-factly. "Have I made myself clear?"

They walked into the gently curving hallway and turned left. The pervading stillness and fluttering candle flames created a hypnotic atmosphere that seemed far removed from the violence raging outside. Nicholas was about to inquire about Ivy's welfare when someone was heard ascending the staircase through the archway just ahead to the right. A moment later, Caldurian stepped through the opening, slightly out of breath and holding three pieces of folded parchment, each sealed with a blot of black wax.

"Ah, my messenger has arrived," Vellan said. "And on time, too. Your knees must be getting accustomed to all that climbing."

"My portion of the relay is only three levels, but as it is in service to you, Vellan, I ignore the inconvenience," he replied with feigned respect. He looked up at Nicholas and Leo, immediately recognizing the two men from their encounter near Lake Mara. "The latest military reports," he said as he handed the letters to Vellan, all the while keeping an uneasy gaze upon the new arrivals. "Now if you please, tell me what is going on? What are *they* doing here?"

"They are my supper guests," Vellan replied as he placed the letters into a large pocket of his garments. "I'm glad you're on time to join us while I question them. I hope to learn much before I pronounce their judgments. They might learn a thing or two about what you've been up to as well." He turned to Nicholas. "Caldurian has been my loyal apprentice for years, though his decision-making of late has been less than exemplary."

"I already know about him," Nicholas said. "He disrupted life in my village twenty years ago. And as I recently learned from Prince Gregory, he did so again for nine days late last autumn."

Caldurian returned a sheepish grin. "So you've heard of recent events?"

Nicholas scowled with contempt. "Yes, and among other things, I was informed that my dear friend, Maynard Kurtz, is missing and that Otto Nibbs is in jail. Now you wouldn't have anything to do with those two incidents, would you?"

Caldurian nodded. "And a good many others, too. But let's not quibble about the details. I suppose it wasn't my finest hour for one striving to be a great wizard, but I was pleased with myself for engineering such a grand deception upon your little village."

"And not caring who you hurt in the process."

"Vengeance does carry a price," he stated.

"Were Maynard and Otto both targets of your vengeance?" Nicholas asked as Caldurian stared back with little emotion. "And where is Maynard? Tell me that much."

Caldurian sighed, feeling some sympathy for Nicholas after all he had endured. The wizard held no personal grudges against him, knowing that the young man had been swept away by events out of his control and knowledge. But it was far too late to make amends.

"That is a conversation for another time," he said. "I hope to move beyond talk of misguided deeds and offer you my deepest apology for what it's worth."

"Not much," Nicholas replied, knowing he wouldn't get any answers.

"He apologized to me, too," Vellan chimed in, "after having used my servant, Arileez, for his own purposes in your village. I wasn't pleased, but I have a forgiving nature–to a point. So as part of his punishment, Caldurian now serves as one of my messengers rather than apprentice. Perhaps he can yet be saved."

"I only wish to be in your good graces again and learn whatever more I can," Caldurian coolly replied. "After all, now that I'm aware of the âvin éska, I can only guess that there are numerous other magic spells you can yet teach to this willing student. Though why it has taken this long, I'll never understand." He offered Vellan a halfhearted smile which prompted a look of sour disgust from Madeline.

"See, he is still hurt that I have chastened him so," Vellan remarked to Nicholas and Leo, "but he'll get over it if he expects to remain in my service. I can just as easily take on another apprentice," he added, favorably eyeing Madeline with little heed for Caldurian's wounded pride. "I need someone who thinks as I do and understands the goals I have for this part of the world."

"Then maybe Caldurian isn't your man," Leo said, hoping to fan the underlying dissension between the two wizards.

"Oh?"

"While Nicholas and I were with the King's army a short while ago, Caldurian theorized about Prince Brendan's astonishing return from the grave." He turned to Caldurian, detecting a hint of uncertainty in his dark eyes. "And it was during that conversation when King Justin referenced *another* conversation he had had with you last winter while you were his prisoner in the Citadel."

"You talk too much!" Caldurian snapped.

"I, on the other hand, am very interested in what the young man has to say," Madeline said with a provocative smile.

"As am I," Vellan added, indicating for Leo to proceed.

"If I remember correctly, and I believe I do," he continued, "the King said that Caldurian had told him that Vellan's plans had become–*misguided*?" He placed a finger to his chin, feigning deep thought. "Yes, that was the word–misguided."

Caldurian was about to lash out at Leo but intercepted Vellan's caustic gaze, momentarily holding his temper.

"Misguided?" Vellan remarked, though without a hint of fury. "I suppose, Caldurian, I should be hurt by that comment. But since you neither delivered the kingdom of Montavia to me nor secured the Spirit Box, I really can't put much stock in your disparaging opinion of my endeavors."

"I agree," Madeline replied. "Such behavior is the height of disloyalty."

A flash of disgust ignited in Caldurian's eyes. "*Disloyalty?* You wish to discuss that subject, Madeline? Don't get me started!" He raised a finger to her, his words laced with the hurt and disbelief welling inside him. "In the days before I arrived here, I had many long conversations with Carmella. And let me tell you, your cousin taught me a thing or two about your lack of loyalty to *me*."

Madeline's eyes widened with disbelief. "How could you say such a thing? Any poison my cousin uttered was said simply to drive a wedge between us."

"You've managed to do that brilliantly without her help!" he replied. "After your argument with Carmella behind the Citadel, she informed me that you had said that I had outlived my usefulness. Do you wish to refute that statement?" he asked, his words as prickly as a burdock bush. "And to top things off, you ran to Kargoth like a scared rabbit with that spineless Mune to worm your way into Vellan's confidence instead of seeking me out in Montavia." Caldurian grunted. "Disloyalty? You use that word so freely, ma'am, because you're only too familiar with it!"

Before Madeline could respond, Vellan pricked the bubble of rising tension with a thin laugh, bringing them both to an uneasy silence. "What a quarrelsome family we must seem to our guests," he said, leaning upon his staff. "This is an unbecoming atmosphere inside the corridors of Mount Minakaris, though I suppose it is partly my fault for placing my trust in so few people. But alas, what's done is done. Now can we abandoned these quibbles and attend to matters of war while we enjoy our supper?"

"Please," Madeline said, weary of the verbal strife as Caldurian silently fumed.

As she led the way down the passage to the last room on their left, she wished that neither Caldurian nor her cousin had found their way to Vellan's abode, desiring a fresh start away from her tumultuous past. Madeline felt confident that an apprenticeship with Vellan, despite his recent weakening, would serve her far better than a continued and shaky alliance with Caldurian. Perhaps one day, she speculated, the realm of Kargoth might fall into her own capable hands. As they reached the end of the corridor, a small, swift shape passed over them and sailed down the passageway. It quickly circled back, its fluttering shadow magnified upon the walls by the wavering candle flames.

"What was that?" Leo asked. He and Nicholas ducked briefly as the flying object zeroed in on them when it first zoomed past.

"A bat?" Nicholas guessed, cautiously looking up.

"Not quite. This is my faithful informant," Vellan said with a pleased smile as a large black bird settled upon his left shoulder to everyone's surprise. The messenger crow, Gavin, who regularly met in private with Vellan in the chamber next to the terrace, was accustomed to seeing the place well guarded. The crow was leery of the present situation and whispered into the wizard's ear. Vellan nodded as he listened, his eyes widening with interest as Gavin spilled out a string of astounding details.

"Even the bird has abandoned me," Caldurian muttered.

"Gavin has served you well," Vellan said after the crow had finished talking, "which is why I sent him north to assist you after instilling in him the ability to communicate in our language. He returned to me weeks ago after notifying Vice-Commander Ovek that Princess Megan's kidnapping had been a ruse. Gavin reported his observations about the debacles at both Red Lodge and the Blue Citadel. My feathered informant also provided information about

Mr. Raven and Mr. Marsh's activities. But today he brings good news from the battlefront," he added with delight.

"Are we to learn of this information?" Madeline asked.

"Momentarily," he replied, after which he whispered a few words to Gavin. The crow flew away, disappearing into the far chamber and then slipping back out of the mountain's side. Vellan then eyed Nicholas and Leo with a smile that troubled them both. "The two of you will be especially interested in what I have to say."

"Don't keep us in suspense," Nicholas replied with a brave face, though deep down he felt troubled by the wizard's look of smug satisfaction.

"It seems that King Justin has found himself in an awkward situation. He is a prisoner in the Del Norác garrison." Nicholas and Leo grew pale, fearing the worst. "But don't worry. He is unharmed—for now. And if things play out as I hope, the good King will soon be my guest here in Minakaris where he will face the appropriate judgment for his part in the destruction of my dear departed Enâri."

Caldurian looked at his fellow wizard, hoping to mask his deep concern with an air of practicality. "Aren't you taking a risk by having him transported here, Vellan? Your troops will have to guide King Justin through a horde of enemy soldiers amassing outside the garrison, through the city itself, and then finally to the front gates of this mountain. It's possible he may be rescued during that process. Better to keep the King safely inside the garrison until we achieve victory. Dole out a proper punishment afterward."

Vellan shook his head as he clutched both hands on his oak staff. "There is also a possibility, however slim, that we may not win this battle. I must be bold. I won't postpone the chance to confront King Justin while I can. I've dispatched Gavin back to the garrison with orders to send the monarch here as soon as possible."

"As you wish," Caldurian calmly replied, though his thoughts spun chaotically. He knew he must act swiftly before Vellan complicated matters by bringing King Justin to the stronghold where the monarch's life would be subject to the wizard's volatile mood. A dead or dying King would not serve his purposes at all. With a casual air, Caldurian pointed toward the far end of the corridor. "Shall we proceed? Supper will be cold if we dawdle any further," he said, continuing along the passage at Madeline's side. As they neared the kitchen, Caldurian inhaled deeply and glanced over his shoulder, smiling pleasantly at Vellan. "*Mmmm*, lamb stew with apples and onions. One of your favorites," he added as their shadows wavered erratically upon the walls.

The last chamber on the left housed Vellan's private kitchen and dining quarters. As they passed through an archway, Nicholas and Leo found the atmosphere warm and pleasant. The room had a blazing fireplace built into the walls on either side, the one to the left used to drive away the chills inside Minakaris while the larger one on the right was equipped for cooking. Small open semicircular ovens were built into the sides for baking bread and the like, and piles of dry firewood had been neatly stacked on either side. Several elegantly crafted counters and shelves were built around the room, and in the middle stood a polished oak table with chairs, its burnished surface reflecting an array of flickering candles arranged in the center. A door on the right wall led to a large, well-stocked pantry where several rope-and-pulley operated dumbwaiters were used to haul up food and supplies from the lower levels.

After they entered the room, a short man with thinning black hair and a goatee bounded out of the pantry. He carried a wedge of cheese and a small stone vessel filled with dried tea leaves which he set on one of the counters. A white towel was tucked behind his leather belt as an apron of sorts. He stirred a pot of bubbling stew hanging over the fire as a nearby kettle of water steamed ghostly tendrils out of its spout. Finally, he turned around and glanced at the new arrivals with a flash of annoyed impatience.

"If the lamb is overdone, don't blame me!" Mune said crossly. "If I'm forced to be everyone's cook and plate washer, at least you can show up on time for meals." He ripped the towel out of his belt and patted his brow, noticing with an exasperated sigh the pair of new faces standing with Madeline and the two wizards. "And you've brought guests, so I suppose I'll have to put out extra settings. Luckily I've made a large pot." He trudged over to the others as they lingered near the archway. "So who have we here?"

"Two individuals whose names you are probably familiar with," Vellan said.

"Though in a disapproving sort of way," Madeline added as she placed the daggers she had confiscated upon the fireplace mantel. "Meet Nicholas Raven and Leo Marsh, two prickly nettles who've fouled up some of our fine plans."

"*Nicholas Raven? Leo Marsh?* So at last we meet," Mune said as he studied their faces. But before he could inquire how they ended up in Mount Minakaris, his mouth went agape. He cast a second, longer glance at Leo and took an unsteady step backward.

"*You?*" he shouted with stunned amazement. "You're Leo Marsh? The one who–" He threw his hands up as his companions curiously looked on. "How'd you get here?"

"I'll question them soon," Vellan said. "No need to get so worked up."

"But you don't understand," Mune replied. "You don't know who this man is!" He stepped closer to Leo and locked gazes with him for several tense moments.

"Then why don't you tell him?" Leo challenged.

"Oh, I plan to, sir! I plan to."

"Mune, I know all about their journey to find Frist," Vellan said. "I detected that wizard's arrogant stench all over them before they even stepped foot inside."

Mune edged closer to Vellan. "But you don't understand my meaning, with all due respect. *That man,*" he said, shakily pointing a finger at Leo, "is the individual who opened the Spirit Box. He's the one I had fought with in the Citadel, though at the time I didn't know his name. I just assumed he was a member of the King's Guard."

Vellan stared at Mune, not fully comprehending what he had just heard. But as the realization sank in, he was taken aback and slowly shifted his icy gaze toward Leo. "Is this true?" he asked, his voice barely above a whisper.

Leo's heart beat wildly as Vellan awaited a response. "Yes, I opened the Spirit Box," he admitted, "and happily did so for the sake of Laparia. And particularly for one of King Justin's guardsmen, a loyal soldier whom *he* killed with a knife to the back." He pointed at Mune with contempt. "And I'd do it again without hesitation."

"Oh, would you?" Vellan sputtered, shaking for a moment before he walked to the fireplace to warm himself, clutching his staff. "Valiant words from a simple apple grower!"

"Unlike the poisonous words from a misguided wizard," Nicholas jumped in.

"Watch your tongue!" Madeline snapped, hurrying to Vellan's side and pulling out a chair for him to sit upon.

"I'm fine!" he told her with a brush of his hand before turning to Nicholas. "You know nothing of the power or intentions of either me or my race, Mr. Raven. That is beyond your comprehension."

"I know that all of you in this room have disgraced yourselves by the things you've done to the people of Laparia," he replied. "And you're unaware of the names and faces of most of those you've hurt, nor even care since others do your bidding." Nicholas looked around the room as the flames crackled and the pot of lamb stew bubbled, its sweet aroma wafting through the chamber. "Everything is pleasant inside this mountain while war rages below and others pay the price. But win or lose, I'm guessing you'll do just fine in the end unlike those who wield a sword in your name."

Vellan scowled. "Moralize all you want, but I'm in control. And in matters of war, that is *all* that matters. Yet if I lose the final battle, remember this–I will have a victory regardless because my soldiers will fight until the very last one of them is dead. There'll be no surrender on my side, so even if King Justin manages to declare victory, there'll be so few of his men left alive that it will be a hollow triumph. The nations of Laparia will be stunted for generations because the King of Arrondale was too stubborn to create an alliance with me years ago." He smiled, satisfied that Nicholas and Leo appeared to grudgingly accept the truth of his prediction.

"King Justin will not relent in this battle, nor will the citizens of Laparia during its aftermath," Nicholas said.

"Your King may be on his way over here as we speak, so your words might be a bit premature," Vellan replied. "And when he arrives, Mr. Raven, you can have the honor of watching him receive a just punishment right before I hand down yours."

Nicholas shrugged. "You and others have kept me away from Ivy for more days than I can count. You can't do anything worse to me than what you've already done."

"Really?" Vellan stepped away from the fire and walked toward him. "As punishment for helping to destroy the Enâri, I'm not sure if I should force you to drink from the Drusala River or push you in it myself. But after you've pledged your eternal devotion to me, I'll have you slay the beautiful Ivy to prove your loyalty."

Nicholas shuddered. "You're sick!" he said with defiance, though a growing horror enveloped his heart as he imagined being helplessly subjected to Vellan's will.

"Or instead, maybe I could have you watch as Ivy consumes the nourishing river water and becomes my eternal servant," he continued, goading Nicholas. "And when you realize that the love of your life no longer has feelings for you, and you are grief stricken by the knowledge that that will be the final state of her existence, only then will I have you killed as your last fleeting thought will be of her demise. A fitting end, don't you think?"

"He doesn't know what to think," Madeline remarked.

"Then I will make the decision and spare him further suspense," the wizard replied, tightening his grip upon the oak staff. "And though both options have a delectable twist, I will choose the latter for this simple reason." Nicholas remained silent, teetering between paralyzed revulsion and the urge to lunge at Vellan despite the deadly consequences. "If I make you kill Ivy while you're under my enchantment, it will mean nothing to your heart as your feelings for the girl will have been wiped away. Since I'll derive no satisfaction from that, Mr. Raven, you will instead be condemned to watch helplessly as the woman you love falls completely under my sway–and *then* you can die. Her submission to me will be the last thing on your mind as you draw your final breath, though it will hardly make up for your heinous crime."

As Vellan and Madeline exchanged smiles of vindication, Caldurian and Mune looked on with mixed emotions. Nicholas and Leo glanced at one another with concern, realizing that they must act soon before Vellan's crazed words turned into actual deeds.

"And as for you," Vellan continued, turning to Leo, "I have saved the best for last." His stony expression matched the hard edge to his voice. "I had never expected to avenge the individual who opened the Spirit Box, assuming that King Justin randomly assigned one of his guards to do the deed. I thought I'd have to be content only punishing others from your conspiracy who had found their way here, such as Carmella, Mr. Raven and yourself, and perhaps in time, King Justin. But even with that, I still thought long about what

I'd do if I ever confronted the loathsome being who murdered my Enâri servants, who ended their lives with the turn of a key."

"Did you come up with an answer?" Leo asked unflinchingly.

"Oh, I did," he replied, unaffected by Leo's bravado. "It took me some time to devise the perfect solution, but it was well worth the many hours I pondered over the matter and the subsequent days I utilized to craft the perfect spell for my purpose."

"Can't wait to hear about it sometime," Leo lightly remarked.

"Or maybe I can show you *now!*" Vellan pointed the gnarled tip of his staff at Leo as if he had drawn a sword. "*Thálos weda nón!*" he cried out, sending Leo reeling backward through the air and crashing against a wooden shelf by the archway where he dropped to the floor in a motionless heap.

"*Leo!*" Nicholas ran to his friend and knelt at his side. When he saw Leo's eyes were closed and placed a hand upon his cold, pale face, he feared the worst. He immediately imagined Princess Megan anxiously wandering the corridors of the Blue Citadel while awaiting Leo's return that would never be. He turned and glared at Vellan, his chest tightening, his mind boiling with hate. "What have you done to him?" he shouted. "Tell me!"

"I have given your friend what he truly deserves," Vellan replied. "A fitting conclusion to his wretched life."

CHAPTER 107

Strategic Maneuvers

Fighting continued near the garrison, but the battle gradually spread out into the adjacent lanes and along the banks of the Drusala River. The enemy troops who had earlier descended from the rooftop now filtered out into Del Norác. Eucádus, blaming himself for King Justin's abduction, wielded his sword with an unnatural ferocity by the garrison's northeast corner. Ramsey and several other soldiers alongside him, held onto the slim hope that they could rescue the King of Arrondale. And though their hearts were heavy with the near impossibility of the task, a fresh sense of optimism soon arrived. Horses rumbled up the main road from the west as the sun dipped closer to the golden, snow-tipped peaks looming in the background.

Eucádus spun around and noted a familiar face leading the horsemen who struck down and scattered the enemy troops in their path. Framed in the setting sunlight, Prince Gregory and his men joined in the fray as cheers broke out to welcome them. Eucádus and Ramsey greeted the prince after wading through the chaos, delighted at his return yet dreading the news they had to report.

"Welcome back," Eucádus said as a clash of swords raged around them, only now the enemy was at a disadvantage. "Was your assault on the western district a success?"

"Indeed, but with much effort," the prince replied, his face coated with dust and sweat. He briefly told how he and his men had

335

driven a large contingent of Vellan's forces west after the initial charge into Del Norác. "We battled near one of the armories, and when it was over, the building lay in a smoking heap. Unopened crates of swords and bows were destroyed in a fire and will never get a chance to be used against us."

"For that we are thankful," Eucádus said, ready to inform him of the King's abduction. Prince Gregory, however, beat him to the punch.

"Tell me, where is my father? I wish to speak with him." But when he saw Eucádus and Ramsey's joyful smiles quickly melt away, he knew that something terrible had occurred. He dismounted and locked upon their troubled gazes. "I see there is bad news you are at pains to reveal. Is my father dead?"

"Perhaps worse," Eucádus replied apprehensively.

As he was about to explain, a loud, discordant horn blasted several times from above which caused a stir among the combatants on both sides. Men hurriedly flocked toward the southeast corner of the garrison alongside the river as wild rumors regarding King Justin and his captors spread through the crowd.

"I think we're about to find out," the prince remarked. He mounted his steed and urged his friends to follow him around the corner of the building to the river. There, a crowd had gathered west of the central bridge, their eyes raised to the garrison rooftop.

Four stories up, several men in Vellan's army looked down on the growing throng. All had ceased fighting for the moment, gazing hypnotically above as a soldier on the roof sounded the horn one last time. Two others proudly held up the flags of Kargoth flapping wildly in the wind. The commander in charge stepped forward, his smug smile accented by a pair of dark eyes clouded with Vellan's watery spell. A handful of others stood behind him, and among them, a struggling individual whose face remained hidden.

"Now that I have everyone's attention, I will make a brief announcement," the commander shouted down loudly enough to be heard over the breeze and the distant fighting. "I am Luboc, commander of the Del Norác garrison. To all the brave men of Kargoth, our Island allies and those from the surrounding mountain nations who have joined our cause, I thank you for your spirited defense of this great realm!" He proudly smiled as his troops below cheered. "But I wish to end this war. So to the men of Arrondale, Drumaya and all the kingdoms of the north who have disrupted our peaceful way of life, I say to you this–for the sake of your families back home, lay down your arms and retreat from this land and bother us no more."

"Just like you have never bothered us?" a soldier from Rhiál shouted up. "How many widows and orphans have you already created among our people?"

Luboc raised a hand. "I'll attribute such scurrilous comments to your ignorance about the cause of recent, deadly events throughout Laparia. As you know, King Justin instigated the conflicts in the region, attributing *his* troublemaking to Vellan. He goaded good people like you into believing such nonsense and joining his fight. But perhaps we can end this violence once and for all."

"I don't like the sound of this," Ramsey whispered to Eucádus as they stood among a crowd near the river.

"Nor do I. His words remind me of Irabesh." Eucádus spotted Prince Gregory several yards ahead upon his horse, surrounded by some of his men. "And I suspect that the prince will not be pleased by his speech either."

"If you desire peace, draw back your lines," Luboc continued, scanning the crowd until he spotted Prince Gregory, noting the royal markings of Arrondale on his vestments. "Prince Gregory, will you accept my offer and spare your troops more injury and death? Or will you erode their dwindling numbers just to make a hollow point?"

"Do not expect us to make a hasty exit for your convenience, Luboc. My men know and follow the orders of King Justin," he replied with confidence. "Now enough stalling. What have you done with my father?"

Luboc looked closely at the prince, clearly noting the resolve upon his face even from four stories up. "So, I take it that you will not accept my generous terms."

"No," he replied, leaning back in his saddle. "We'll accept only your defeat."

"Duly noted. And as to your inquiry, your father is well. In fact, he was kind enough to join our little gathering up here."

Luboc pointed to the man who had been struggling among the other soldiers. And though his face was not visible, most who were near enough below could distinguish the individual's shortly cropped silvery hair and see flashes of Arrondale's royal markings upon his outer garment, giving them no doubt that King Justin was still alive.

"Release him at once," Prince Gregory demanded with calm authority, "or even Vellan will not be able to save your wretched life when I get through with you."

"You are hardly in a position to make threats as I am quite safe inside this garrison while you and your men are not." Vellan's troops erupted in laughter, prompting a modest bow of self-congratulations from Luboc. "But since you insist that I release your father, I will do the gentlemanly thing and accede to your wish."

Luboc signaled to his men. They ushered their prisoner to the edge of the rooftop facing the Drusala River. Prince Gregory's heart froze when he realized what was happening, and though he couldn't see his father's face with the other men surrounding him, he imagined with great pain what King Justin must be thinking as the dark waters of the Drusala flowed past him far below.

"Let him go!" the prince pleaded.

"Oh, I will," Luboc replied. "And then your men can follow the good King's orders just as you said they would. But I suspect that the orders King Justin will issue will be far different from what you're used to after he tastes the Drusala's refreshing waters."

"Do not do this!" Prince Gregory cried out. "It is depravity of the lowest order."

"Then you had better catch him," he said with a snakelike smile before turning to his guards. "Throw him in!"

Without hesitation, the soldiers pushed their captive off the roof. He flailed his arms while plummeting four stories to the water below. As Eucádus and the others rushed to the riverbank, Prince Gregory felt as if he had just seen his father felled by an arrow. Yet a part of him also believed that that would have been a better fate than the horror now consuming the King's mind and free will.

"To the river, sir?" one of Prince Gregory's captains asked with a sense of urgency, fearing that the King's son was in a state of shock. "We must rescue your father regardless of his condition."

"Of course," he replied, forcing himself to focus. "Find a path through the crowd!"

Eucádus and Ramsey, in the meantime, had pushed through the onlookers and raced to the water's edge, its glossy surface highlighted by the setting sun. As the Drusala flowed past beneath the arches of the nearby bridge, they spotted a silvery-haired man swimming east until he neared a low spot on the riverbank. There he climbed out and collapsed upon the grassy slope, exhausted. Eucádus bolted toward him with several other soldiers. As he approached the man lying face down on the ground, he unsheathed his sword and called to him with apprehension as more troops gathered around.

"King Justin? Can you hear me?" he asked. "Can you speak?"

"Of course I can," he muttered into the soaking arm that pillowed his head. "And you should listen carefully to what I'm about to say." Slowly, he looked up with clouded eyes as a crazed smile gradually spread across his face. "Long live Vellan!" he cried, breaking into a fit of delighted, almost maniacal laughter as he lay there in a wet pile.

Eucádus' eyes widened with surprise, though not because of the man's words but because of the haggard face staring back at him. This devoted follower of Vellan slowly getting to his knees was not King Justin of Arrondale, though he possessed similar features and wore the monarch's outer vestment. A glance at Ramsey's equally astonished face proved to him that he was not imagining things.

"Who are you?" Eucádus demanded. "Where is the King?" But before the man could answer, a soldier by the northeast corner of the garrison shouted down to the river.

"The garrison gates have opened!" he cried, urging his fellow soldiers to return to the main street in front of the building. "The gates are open! Men are leaving!"

"What's going on?" Ramsey asked, looking to Eucádus for guidance as his mind swirled with confusion. A similar question was upon the lips of many.

Eucádus suddenly realized the horrifying truth and turned to locate Prince Gregory in the bustling crowd. But there was no need as the prince and his men were already racing back toward the north side along with a company of others he urged onward to the front gates, having pieced together what had just happened.

"This was a distraction!" Eucádus said as the crowd dispersed along the side of the garrison and made for the main gate as sporadic fighting again broke out along the way. "Luboc put on a show to clear a path from the front gate to the north part of the city."

"But why?" Ramsey asked.

"To transport the real King Justin out of this building!" he replied, returning his sword to its sheath. "And bring him safely to Mount Minakaris. To Vellan."

"Then let us join in his rescue!" Ramsey eagerly said.

As he headed up the small slope on the riverbank, Eucádus followed his friend into the lengthening shadow of the garrison, wondering how far King Justin and his captors had ventured into the hostile city streets. But as he turned his head to survey the movement of soldiers around him, he caught a familiar flash of red color in the softening rays of sunlight to his right. As Ramsey continued forward with the others, Eucádus slowed his pace. He spotted a tall man farther down the river near the bridge heading his way. A growing light below the eastern horizon tinted the skyline. Eucádus stopped, his eyes drawn to the vaguely familiar figure with long black hair tied up in back with a blood red piece of cloth. The man suddenly recognized Eucádus and stopped. Both stood silently as the crowd scattered and the sounds of distant warfare faded in their minds.

"So, Eucádus, I see you still prefer to wage your battle on the losing side," Ranen called out, smiling confidently as he took a few slow steps toward his former friend. "You should have killed me days ago when you had the chance."

"This battle is far from over," Eucádus sternly replied. His heart ached upon seeing the shell of a man that Ranen had been reduced to by Vellan's cruel hand.

"Perhaps you're right. The battle between Kargoth and your feeble army may be far from over," he said, slowly unsheathing his sword and raising it to catch the golden light of the setting sun. "But our fight, Eucádus, is about to begin."

Inside Mount Minakaris, Leo lay sprawled upon his back near the archway wall, his face cold and pale. Nicholas, kneeling by his side, feared that Vellan had driven all life out of his friend. But when he noticed a slight rise and fall of Leo's chest, a flicker of hope ignited in his weary heart.

"Don't worry," Vellan said, lowering his oak staff to support himself. "Your friend isn't dead–yet. The spell I cast is an inspired one, not intended to deliver an instant death."

"What are you talking about?" Nicholas glared at the wizard who appeared much frailer than he had only moments ago.

But before he could reply, Vellan grew suddenly pale, appearing ready to pass out. Madeline raced to his aid in horror, grabbing him by one arm in case he might fall.

"Mune!" she cried, trying to hold him steady. Mune bolted to her side and helped her lead the wizard to a chair at the table. Vellan slowly took a few deep breaths, appearing more comfortable as the color gradually returned to his face.

"Thank you," he said, sounding exhausted as he leaned back. He handed his staff to Madeline, indicating for her to place it against the mantelpiece. "Casting that spell took more out of me than I had anticipated, but it was well worth it." Vellan sprouted a vindictive smile while gazing upon Leo's seemingly lifeless body with malicious delight.

"It won't be worth it if you die," Madeline told him. "Your strength has weakened since the demise of the Enâri. Let me take care of you as I suggested until you're back to your old self again." She turned to Caldurian who waited quietly near the opposite end of the table, snapping her fingers at him. "Don't stand there like a courtyard statue. Fetch some stew and tea for Vellan! He needs nourishment."

"At once," he replied, grudgingly tolerating another of Madeline's many orders she had spouted ever since worming her way into Vellan's good graces. But as long as Vellan fancied her companionship, Caldurian thought it best to play along. "Do you want stew as well, Madeline?" he inquired while leaning over the steaming pot and stirring it carefully with a large wooden spoon.

"Tea only," she replied, taking a seat at the table. She frowned when Mune looked her way expectantly. "You can eat later. Stand guard over our guests. The one is stirring."

"Fine."

As Mune trudged toward them, he noticed Leo moving as if awakening from a deep sleep. Nicholas anxiously looked on. Mune kept a respectful distance, standing near the archway and wondering how different things would be if he had only stopped Leo from turning that key. Such a simple action had altered the landscape of the war and of his life. King Justin's army would have already been defeated had the Enâri still lived, and Mune realized his own situation would have been vastly improved over the uncertainty that now plagued him. He wished he could relive that moment and set things right. His alliance with Caldurian, Madeline and Vellan had lost its allure, and he regretted not leaving Kargoth days ago. He sadly shook his head and sighed. Then Leo opened his eyes.

"Are you all right?" Nicholas asked, helping him sit up against the shelf.

"What happened?" he asked groggily, for a moment not sure of his location or the hour. He rubbed the back of his head and winced. "I remember waking up miserably on Hobin's floor that one morning after drinking too much ale the night before. That felt good compared to this."

Nicholas couldn't help but smile, glad to see Leo's sense of humor still intact. But he wondered how long Leo could fight off the effects of Vellan's spell. "Rest for a while. I don't think we're going anywhere just yet."

Leo stubbornly shook his head, placing a hand on Nicholas' shoulder. "Help me stand," he said. "I won't give him the satisfaction of remaining on the floor."

Nicholas helped Leo to his feet, noting the faint hint of an encouraging smile from Mune, though not sure how to interpret it. Leo placed a hand upon the shelf to steady himself, pausing to catch his breath before turning to Vellan.

"You need to practice your spells," he said, gazing defiantly at him and Madeline. "You get a failing grade for that attempt."

"Ah, but you're wrong," Vellan replied as Caldurian walked over with a tray laden with a bowl of lamb stew and two cups of steaming tea. "Things are not always as they appear. The spell I cast was more successful than you know," he said as Caldurian placed the bowl before him along with a hand cloth and a spoon. He also set down a cup of tea each for Vellan and Madeline, smiling humbly before returning to the serving counter. "You see, Mr. Marsh," Vellan continued, "this particular spell will slowly drain the life out of you, but not too slowly. You'll have time to think about the heinous act you perpetrated upon the Enâri by aligning yourself with Frist. And if you have any sense of decency, you'll come to regret what you did before death finally takes you." He ate a spoonful of stew and drank from his cup. "That should happen sometime around dawn. I suggest you use your remaining time wisely."

"Well said," Madeline whispered with an ingratiating smile. She sipped from her tea while Vellan ate his meal as if it were just an ordinary day.

"Frist is a better wizard in death than you'll ever be in your lifetime," Nicholas said, overwhelmed by a sense of helplessness. "He gave his life to remake that key. You've only sacrificed others to achieve your aims."

"If Frist is such a great wizard, then see if he can help you now!" Vellan felt his strength returning to both mind and limb. "Unlike me, Frist squandered his power on trivialities. And when he took his last breath, he wound up just like the race of wizards will some day end, dead and forgotten. It's as simple as that."

Leo took a deep breath and managed a few steps toward the table, looking at Vellan with a mix of pity and contempt. "Frist did much good for people, but in small ways, never seeking praise for it. His accomplishments will far outlast anything you've done. He helped people instead of using them." While Vellan remained stone silent, staring fixedly at his bowl, Madeline turned a shade of crimson as she slowly fumed. Leo dismissed them with a shake of his head. "Believe it if you want that Frist squandered his powers, but you two have squandered your lives," he said. "Simple as that."

Vellan eyed him with scorn. "Oh, is it?" He slowly rose from his chair, grabbing his staff for support as he stepped away from the table. "Believe what you like, Mr. Marsh, but in the end it only matters who has accumulated power and isn't afraid to use it. I have succeeded on both counts! So in what little time you have left, enjoy your moral victory. I, on the other hand, have a realm to oversee, and that gives me a vast sense of accomplishment." He turned to Nicholas. "And don't think I've forgotten about you, Mr. Raven. I no longer have any interest in speaking to you or your friend, so it's time to rid my home of you both. Caldurian! I have a task for you."

"Yes?" he said, stepping forward.

"Inform some guards below to escort Ivy to the river. She may be thirsty," he said with a grim smile. "Then have her brought back here so Mr. Raven can speak to her one last time before he receives his just reward at the point of a sword."

"You can't do this!" Nicholas shouted. "Ivy has done nothing to you. Let her go!"

Vellan pointed his staff at him, prompting Nicholas to hold his ground. "Care to receive the same punishment as your friend?" he asked. "I'll be happy to oblige."

Madeline grabbed one of the daggers on the mantelpiece and shoved it into Mune's hand. "Guard them properly!"

"All right!" He waved the dagger until Nicholas and Leo stepped back toward the wall. Vellan sighed heavily as he lowered his staff and clutched it for support, again appearing as tired as he was after casting his spell upon Leo.

"Are you all right?" Caldurian asked with concern.

"I'm fine!" he snapped, attempting to shake off his weariness as he trudged back to the table. "Now carry out my instructions while I finish eating supper. Be gone!"

"Yes, please do as you're told!" Madeline shouted, indicating for Caldurian to leave as she hurried to Vellan's side.

"Very well. I shall go now," he calmly replied. He stepped through the archway and turned right down the corridor, looking askance at Vellan and Madeline as he brushed past the opening and continued along the candlelit passageway.

But Caldurian had no intention of carrying out Vellan's order. Instead, he stopped and stood with his back to the wall, listening for any sounds from the dining chamber. If things had gone according to plan, he expected to hear something at any moment other than the faint murmur of voices above the flickering candlelight. This was his one chance to strike before events got completely out of hand, but as he listened, he worried that he might have made a mistake and had already been found out. Then a harrowing shriek blasted through the corridor. Caldurian's heart pounded as a smile formed upon his lips.

He waited a few moments as the commotion grew in the other room and then raced back up the corridor. He barreled through the archway, feigning surprise at the scene before him. "Madeline, what happened? I heard your scream from the stairwell." She looked up in a frazzled panic, kneeling on the floor beside Vellan. He had collapsed face down in an unconscious pile upon his oak staff.

"Help me!" she cried, desperately trying to turn him over. Caldurian ran to her aid as Mune guarded Nicholas and Leo who looked on in stunned silence.

Caldurian helped Madeline roll the wizard onto his back. Vellan, his eyes closed and face pale, breathed steadily which calmed Madeline as she tried to shake him awake, calling to him in desperate tones.

"Vellan, please come to," she whispered. "Open your eyes! Speak to me!"

"Apparently the stress from casting that last spell has taken a toll upon his already weakened state," Caldurian said, standing up. He folded his arms and massaged his chin, stepping back to observe the fallen wizard.

"What should we do?" she asked, annoyed by his seeming lack of concern.

"I would suggest you let him rest, Madeline."

"Rest? We need to revive him!"

"And I think that you should take a long rest as well," he added. "After all, you've been operating on little food and sleep these past few days as war has encroached upon us. Perhaps some lamb stew might do you a bit of good as well."

"Forget about my health, you fool! What about Vellan?" she screamed, unable to comprehend Caldurian's indifference as he stood there wearing a vague smile. "Tell me what to do! Tell me how to–" A fearful chill shot through Madeline as it suddenly hit her. She suspiciously eyed the bowl of stew upon the table, her face ashen as a growing sense of betrayal became apparent. "What have you done?" she whispered.

In the field near the eastern bridge, the sickly smell of blood and death saturated the air. William and Brendan rushed to their grandfather after he had collapsed, the Islander's knife lodged in his abdomen. The man who had assaulted King Rowan and killed Marello now lay dead a few feet away. Marello's body hugged the ground several yards to the west. A clash of swords intensified in the distance as twilight neared.

When the sibling princes reached King Rowan, they saw him gazing at the eastern horizon, grateful that he was still alive. William took his hand and caressed it as Brendan examined the bloody wound. He hesitantly touched the handle of the deadly dagger.

"Don't," King Rowan told him, his voice tired yet firm. He placed his free hand upon Brendan's fingers and gently moved them aside. "There is nothing you can do," he said, smiling faintly as he looked upon his cherished grandsons.

"I must try!" Brendan pleaded.

King Rowan took a shallow, painful breath as he squeezed William's hand for support. "You must both save yourselves for the sake of Montavia. You need to watch over our dear homeland in my absence," he said. "You must be there for your mother, too. My death will be but a passing bad dream when Vilna and the citizens of Montavia look upon Prince Brendan once again, alive and prepared to rule in my stead."

"Grandfather, don't talk like that," Brendan replied. His eyes misted as he removed and folded his vest, placing it under the King's head as a pillow.

"You will return with us to Red Lodge," William added encouragingly, though deep in his heart, seeds of doubt and despair took root as he accepted the inevitable.

"If today we are victorious," the King continued as the color drained from his cheeks, "then the two of you will escort my body back to Triana. And when you become king, Brendan, keep your brother close by for counsel and companionship." He glanced at William and grinned. "And *you* keep him on his toes."

"But we still need you, Grandfather," Brendan replied as he choked up, wishing his heartfelt words would enable the King to stave off death itself.

"And I you," he said, his eyes drawn to the eastern horizon looming behind his grandsons' shoulders. "But now I must leave you both for a time until we meet again in the afterworld. This is to be our fate. But I think that–"

"Think *what?*" Brendan asked, grasping desperately at their remaining time together.

King Rowan took several shallow breaths as his hold on the moment weakened, the images before him fading slowly in his mind. But at that same time, William and Brendan noted a lively light growing in his eyes as their grandfather gazed upon them, each feeling a flicker of warmth and hope igniting inside them. "I think that… Nay, I *know* that you will both succeed and make me proud when all is done." The King smiled as he gazed eastward, whispering his final words. "I can see it in the heavens."

He closed his eyes for the last time, his face and body relaxing as he lay upon the cool grass. The Drusala River flowed silently by to the south. William bowed his head and kissed his grandfather's hand while Brendan brushed his fingers across the dead monarch's face as tears fell from his eyes.

"He is at peace now, and safe," Brendan said, his voice hoarse as he stared up at the sky and wondered how he and his brother would ever endure the dreary days ahead. "But we are *not*," he added ominously when looking westward again.

"What?" William asked, his thoughts elsewhere as he laid the King's hand upon his chest. But when he noted the stern expression on Brendan's face, he looked in the same direction, immediately understanding his brother's point.

While they had been tending to their grandfather, a small contingent of enemy soldiers fighting near the low rise to the west had broken away and made for the patch of land where King Rowan lay. They moved swiftly, some in front leading the way on horseback. Before they arrived, Brendan jumped up and retrieved his sword lying close by. William grabbed the dagger he had used to kill the soldier from Kargoth. With quiet courage, they stood in front of their grandfather's body and held their weapons aloft, silently challenging the approaching soldiers who were led by a cloudy-eyed native of Kargoth named Meegs.

"How touching," he said mockingly to the amusement of his followers. "The King's loyal pages guard his corpse in one last act of bravery before they are slaughtered." His men raised their swords. "I watched with interest from over there as your King fought, which is why I didn't interfere. I wanted to see what he was made of. But he was no match for one of Vellan's determined soldiers. And you two are no match for us."

"We do not fear you!" Brendan said, his eyes locked onto Meegs' smug face. "And whether we live or not, your hours are numbered. King Justin and his allies will soak this field with your blood."

"Strong words from a young man," he coolly remarked before addressing William. "And have you no last words to add?"

Prince William smiled to the man's dismay. "I agree with everything my brother said," he replied, tilting his head toward Brendan. "We are of like minds, usually."

"Soon you will be of like conditions–dead." Meegs signaled to a nearby captain. "We have work to do. Kill them now."

"With pleasure," he replied, stepping forward with a few other troops. William and Brendan stood their ground and raised their weapons higher, bracing themselves for what they realized would be their final moments.

Just then, a soldier from the Northern Isles sitting atop a horse alongside Meegs leaned over and whispered a few hurried words to his leader, pointing at William and Brendan. Meegs slowly raised his eyebrows as he absorbed the information.

"Wait!" he shouted. "Do not touch them."

The soldier leading the charge quickly turned around. "Sir?"

"You heard me," he replied as he climbed off his horse and waded through the group of men circling William and Brendan like vultures. Meegs, his sword still resting in its sheath, stood in front of the two brothers and glanced at their right hands as they each gripped their weapons. "Now is your chance to finish me off," he said with a chuckle, indicating his defenseless posture. "But I suppose that wouldn't be an honorable act by two princes of Montavia even against someone you find as abhorrent as me." Meegs pointed at their matching silver rings. "My associate from the Isles just informed me that we have something more valuable here than two royal pages."

"What of it?" William asked. "Dead is dead regardless of our identities."

"Oh, I must allow you to live for a while longer, at least until I get orders from Vellan." He glanced at Brendan. "Same goes for the next king of Montavia who might come in handy for Vellan after he controls all of Laparia. With the proper guidance, I think you'd be much more amenable to Vellan's ideas than King Rowan."

"My brother and I will never serve Vellan," Brendan replied, sheathing his weapon. "Even upon the threat of death."

"Even upon the threat of your brother's death?" Meegs noted a glimmer of fear in Brendan's eyes. "I think you'll be more inclined to return to Montavia and serve as its King according to Vellan's wishes if your brother remains in Kargoth as our guest."

"Guest?" William grunted in amusement. "Brendan, ignore his silly threats," he said before addressing the mildly irritated Meegs. "My brother would never undermine Montavia even if you vowed to toss me off the top of Mount Minakaris. Our home is more valuable than either of our lives." He copied his brother's action and disarmed himself, placing his dagger underneath his belt. "As I said, we are usually of like minds."

"Admirable stances by the both of you. But in the end, Vellan doesn't need to force your loyalty through grandiose threats or at the point of a sword. That's too much work," Meegs said. He glanced at the gently flowing river to his right before casting a hardened stare upon the two princes. "*Hmmm,* but I believe a simple drink from the Drusala will produce far better results in less time, don't you?"

"What have you *done?*" Madeline repeated. She jumped to her feet and stood toe-to-toe with Caldurian as Vellan lay asleep upon the floor. The dual fireplaces crackled wildly, casting subtle shadows upon the walls. "Did you cast a spell on him? Is he dying?"

Caldurian shook his head. "Nothing that dramatic. I merely added a little something to his lamb stew while nobody was paying attention. Vellan will recover in a day."

Madeline gasped. "A day? There is war outside! The enemy has infiltrated these chambers," she cried, indicating Nicholas and Leo who stood under Mune's watch.

"Those two are the least of my concerns," he said. "And unless this war comes to a halt soon, there might be nothing left of Kargoth or the rest of Laparia worth living for even if we are victorious. Vellan has made a fine mess of things because of his desire to exact vengeance on his kindred wizards."

"And *you* haven't made a mess of things?" Nicholas piped up.

"Who told you to speak? Hold your tongue!"

"Not a chance," he replied, tired of silently standing by while they bickered and Ivy remained a prisoner. "Before I parted ways with the King's army, his son told me about your visit to Kanesbury last autumn. For nine days you and your troops terrorized my village. Now Otto Nibbs sits in jail and Maynard Kurtz is missing."

"Don't believe everything you hear," Caldurian said.

"I can only guess that it was your need for vengeance against Otto that has gnawed at you all this time. You finally seized your chance to pay him back for the humiliation you suffered twenty years ago." Nicholas sadly shook his head. "You've made your own fine mess, though I don't know how or why you involved Maynard Kurtz and me in your twisted plans."

Caldurian scowled. "You give me too much credit. But I haven't time for explanations. There are more pressing matters now," he said, indicating Vellan's body.

"Then revive him!" Madeline demanded in strident tones.

"I have neither the proper ingredients on hand nor the desire to restore him to consciousness," he replied, no longer intimidated by Madeline. "I used a potent dose of rasaweed combined with other items I had pilfered from your cousin's rolling pharmacopeia. Vellan will wake on his own long after I have implemented my plans."

"Plans?" she asked, though already having an inclination as to what he had in mind. "You want Kargoth for yourself. Admit it!"

"I'll admit nothing," he replied as he turned aside, but only for a moment before flinging a sharp glance her way. "And you don't want Kargoth for *yourself*?" he asked, his arms akimbo as he towered over Madeline. "Can you honestly tell me that all of your fawning and fussing over Vellan was done out of compassion for his health rather than as a ploy to grasp the reins of power in Minakaris?"

Madeline's face tightened. She glared at the wizard, unable to speak as her ire rose. "Yes it was!" she finally shouted. "Whether you believe it or not, I cared only about his wellbeing and nothing more."

Caldurian looked deeply into her eyes, detecting that blend of innocence and toughness he noticed upon their first meeting in the Citadel courtyard when he was immediately taken with her. But now he also perceived glimmers of betrayal and fierce self-reliance which pained the wizard, yet it also freed him from her hold.

"I don't believe you," he whispered, turning away. "So stop denying it."

"Only if you do the same," she calmly replied, realizing they recognized each other's designs on Kargoth only too well. "It seems we both desire Vellan's seat inside this mountain above all else, only that…" Madeline's words trailed off as she grabbed onto the edge of the table to steady herself as if she were about to faint.

"Are you all right?" Mune asked, still standing guard at the archway with the dagger in hand.

"I feel lightheaded," she replied, quickly coming to. "Perhaps all the excitement has–" She suddenly stood upright as if paralyzed, gripping the table's edge as a jolt of pain shot up her spine. She remained immobile for several seconds until the unsettling episode passed, leaving her pale and breathless. "What's happening to me?" she asked, touching her forehead as Caldurian watched with growing curiosity. "I feel as if I were–" Her eye caught Vellan's bowl of stew upon the table and she turned to Caldurian. "Did you drug me with the rasaweed as well? Did you put some in my tea?"

"Of course not," he replied as if wounded by her words. "If I had, you'd be sleeping right now, much like Vellan."

"If you didn't drug her, Caldurian, why does she look as pale as a stickle slug?" Mune inquired as Nicholas and Leo looked on.

"You must have done something to me!" Madeline insisted as she sat down near the fireplace to rest. She looked up at Caldurian, about to say something more, but then was unable to remember the point she wanted to make. "Are you sure you didn't put rasaweed into my drink? I don't feel at all myself."

"I'm absolutely sure," he replied, taking a seat next to her. "However, I must admit that I'm not entirely sure how the substance that I *did* pour into your tea will affect you. Actually, I'm not quite sure at all."

Madeline's eyes widened with a mix of fear and horror. "What are you saying?"

"I'm saying–and perhaps now with the tiniest bit of regret– that you have consumed some of the potion Vellan entrusted to me over three years ago. It was the same potion that Arileez drank to free himself from his island prison." Caldurian nodded to indicate that he was quite serious as she gazed upon him with disbelief. "That potion would have slowly drained him of his powers were he not killed in the Citadel," he added.

"I don't understand," Madeline replied. "You already gave Arileez the potion. So how could you give it to me? And why?"

"I never intended it to come to this, Madeline. I really didn't." Caldurian spoke with genuine compassion as he looked upon his once loyal associate in her dazed state. "Before I entrusted the vial of potion to Commander Jarrin who delivered it to Arileez, I secretly kept some of the potent liquid for myself, intending someday to use it on Vellan."

Madeline couldn't believe what she was hearing. "You were plotting Vellan's demise over three years ago?"

Caldurian nodded sheepishly. "I suppose so, though I wasn't sure if it would work upon him to slowly and imperceptibly eliminate his powers. I hoped to secretly introduce it into one of Vellan's meals when I returned here for more training, but recent events have prevented me from doing so. Now that war is upon us and other conflicts have spun out of control, I knew I had to act fast, knowing there wouldn't be time to wait for the effects of the potion to kick in. Now seemed like the perfect time for the rasaweed."

"So you drugged him into a sleep state instead," she muttered with disgust.

"Carmella had an abundance of items, though she knew nothing of my intentions. And Vellan's weakened state made the rasaweed mixture that much more efficient."

"What do you intend to do with Vellan?" she asked as Caldurian's image and words faded in and out as if he were speaking to her in a dream.

"I can't reveal everything," he replied with a scheming smile.

"Then tell me what you intend to do with *me!*" Madeline shouted, refocusing her attention with much effort. "I won't give up without a fight."

"You are in no condition to fight."

"Don't try me!" She stood and slapped her hands upon the table, seething with anger. "I'm still handy with a spell, Caldurian, and am not afraid to use one against you. Remember, you taught me the…" Madeline furrowed her brow as she tried to recall the name of a spell. "You taught me the…"

"What's wrong?" Mune asked.

"I can't remember the spell," Madeline whispered, sitting back down and staring at her hands in bewilderment. "Caldurian, what have you done to me?"

"Madeline, I–"

"Arileez was of the race of true wizards," she said. "We are not. How could you give that potion to me without knowing its effects? It might kill me for all you know."

"I don't think it will come to that," he replied, though not completely sure.

"Not that you even care at this point."

Caldurian stood and looked kindly upon her. "Madeline, I will always care about you despite our recent differences. I've been fond of you since we first met."

"Then why would you do this?" she asked on the verge of tears. "Why would you take away the most important part of me?"

Caldurian stroked his beard as he stared at the tabletop, searching for the most comforting answer considering Madeline's current state. But as he raised his eyes and saw the desperation in her face, he knew she deserved only the truth.

"There are many reasons, Madeline, though betraying me for Vellan is the one that hurt me most," he told her. "When I learned that you had fled to Kargoth to be at his side while I was imprisoned, well, that cut me to my heart. I thought I deserved more."

"I didn't think that I could save you."

Caldurian shook his head. "You didn't even try! According to Carmella, you fled to Kargoth immediately after the debacle in the Citadel, spouting some not so kind words about me having outlived my usefulness."

"I apologize," she said, wiping away some tears.

"I suppose your emotions got swept away in the chaos, so I'll forgive you," he replied. "But that wasn't the only reason. You see, Madeline, you've grown much as a wizard over the years, and the more you perfected your powers, the less you needed me. As I said, I was always fond of you and imagined us one day ruling Kargoth together and expanding our realm into other regions of Laparia. We would have done a far better job than Vellan, using a forceful but wise hand. But you've always been far too independent to need me at your side." He sat down, staring into Madeline's troubled eyes. "I suppose I always realized that but was loath to admit it."

"So you're punishing me now for what you helped to create?"

"No, don't think that! I'm not punishing you. I'm *freeing* you. Freeing you to start a brand new life that suits you."

"*This* life suited me, Caldurian!"

"But it was a life unfairly influenced by me," he explained. "I may have led you down a path that you weren't ready for at the time, denying you the opportunity to make a life for yourself. Your situation would have been far different if I had never coaxed you into helping me try to kidnap Princess Megan twenty years ago."

Madeline scowled. "Yes, I could still be a nursemaid in the Citadel. Or maybe I'd have graduated to kitchen help. Some life!"

"Don't be bitter. You might have gone further on your own– and Carmella, too. Because of me, she pursued a life in the magic arts, all in an attempt to draw you back from the ruinous path I had led you down," he said. "I created the enmity between the two of you. Who knows where your lives might be had I not interfered?"

Madeline looked at him with disbelief. "Who *are* you? And why do you speak this way? You've never harbored such feelings before. You've grown soft, Caldurian."

"I never lost my powers before either, if only temporarily," he replied. "That caused me to reexamine my priorities. But you can thank your cousin for some of my change of heart. Carmella and I had long and profound talks after she helped me escape."

"Leave my cousin out of this!"

"I can't, for it was she who helped me realize that maybe you would have fared better in life without my interference. Though your cousin is a bit eccentric, she has spoken wise and heartfelt words because she truly cares about your wellbeing."

Madeline breathed deeply, her shoulders rising and falling as her face tightened. "My cousin is responsible for this? Carmella convinced you to eradicate my powers?"

"Of course not!" he replied. "She knows nothing of this. All I'm saying is that Carmella enlightened me about my own life and how things might have been different had I trained in the magic arts with someone other than Vellan. It got me to thinking about our relationship, Madeline, and how I may have led you astray while you were too young and naïve to understand the consequences."

"It's up to me to decide my fate, not you, Caldurian. *Or* my cousin!"

"Carmella spoke those words about me. But I applied them to our relationship because I care about you. I was trying to help, trying to perform one genuine good deed in my life, though it may not seem so right now," he said. "Please don't be bitter."

"Bitter?" She rose to her feet, feeling lightheaded as Vellan's potion worked its way through her system. "Both you and my cousin conspire against me, and now–" Madeline held a hand to her heart, feeling the love and knowledge of the magic arts draining from both mind and body, rendering her cold and empty inside and realizing that she could do nothing to stop it. "And now you expect me to accept my new fate with merely a shrug? Why don't you just thrust a dagger in my side and ask me to live with that trifling inconvenience as well?" she added, choking up.

"Madeline, be reasonable. You have much yet to live for."

"I have nothing to live for!" she shouted, pointing an accusing finger at the wizard. "Thanks to you and Carmella, my life has been ruined. And that goes for all of you, too!" she added, glaring at Nicholas, Leo and Mune.

"What did I do?" Mune asked.

"None of you are worthy to stand in Vellan's presence, deserving only his wrath!"

"Madeline, I think that is the potion talking," Caldurian said, standing and offering her his hand. "Let me take you outdoors for a breath of fresh air where we can speak in private. Your world is not as bleak as you imagine it."

Madeline slapped his hand away. "My world is ruined, and it's your fault! Talking won't change a thing."

"Please, Madeline, I–"

"Aren't you listening?" she cried, her face reddening and her body shaking as she clenched her fists. "You've killed me, Caldurian. And nothing you can say will ever fix it!"

Madeline lunged at him and nearly knocked him over, but he held her tightly as she struggled like a fish pulled out of water. They spun about the floor awkwardly as Madeline tried to free herself, nearly stumbling over Vellan's body at one point. Mune watched in horror along with Nicholas and Leo, but he decided not to interfere lest he let his guard down. He motioned for his prisoners to move toward the fireplace along the right wall to get out of the way.

"Let me go!" Madeline shouted, pounding Caldurian's chest.

"Not until you calm down!" he said, grabbing her by the shoulders as they neared the archway.

"I am calm!" she shrieked, shoving Caldurian against the side of the archway and slipping out of his grasp. She bolted to the right down the candlelit corridor. Caldurian pursued her, his mind whirling with confusion. "Stay back!" she cried, spinning around and stopping halfway down the passage. "I have much yet to do while I still can. I will remain loyal to Vellan if no one else will!"

"You're in no condition to do anything," he said in a gentler tone, holding out his hand. "Please, come back and let us talk."

"I can't do that," she replied, her voice suddenly calm as her body began to quiver. Her eyes darted rapidly back and forth as she gazed aimlessly at the flickering candles and the smoothly carved ceiling. "I know I can't do that. And I don't know if I... Caldurian, do you...?" Madeline slowly began to sway like a slender reed in a steady wind. "Do you...?"

A look of dread spread across the wizard's face. "Madeline, are you all right?"

"I really...don't know," she softly said before collapsing to the floor. Caldurian rushed to her aid in fearful silence.

CHAPTER 108

Apples and Arrows

Gripping the reins of his steed, Prince Gregory led his men north in pursuit of King Justin and his captors. Moments earlier, upon rounding the corner of the garrison, he was horrified to see about thirty horses bolting from the open main gates, making a beeline into the heart of the city. Among the fleeing soldiers, the prince saw his father being ushered away atop one of the steeds in the fierce stampede. The garrison's main gates were quickly closed and barred from the inside after the soldiers had departed. Prince Gregory directed his men both on horse and on foot to save the King.

"Stop them from reaching Minakaris!" he shouted, knowing it would be impossible to breach Vellan's stronghold. He also realized that because intense fighting still raged throughout Del Norác, the enemy troops would not be able to push through the streets in one attempt. They would have to slog their way forward, giving slim hope to the prince that he might yet save his father. "Split up and flood the city!"

He signaled for two captains to veer off left and right with some troops and filter through several side streets to cover more ground. Ramsey, following on foot, trailed the prince into the center of the city along a narrow road. Corpses were strewn among several low buildings pocked with smashed windows and broken doors. Here the fighting had been particularly harsh in the past hour, though now the area was serenely painted with golden rays of the setting sun that gently touched the faces of the dead. But as the lane opened up onto a grassy common, a new skirmish erupted when enemy troops swooped in through a thicket of trees and from behind a row of crumbling brick shops.

"Well, Eucádus, it's time we earned our pay!" Ramsey grimly joked as he unsheathed his sword, glancing over his shoulder. "Maybe this time we'll–" But when he saw no sign of his friend, he worriedly looked about, assuming that Eucádus had been a few steps behind him all along.

But Ramsey's concern was driven from his thoughts as he charged headlong into the fray with several fellow soldiers. Their swords clattered sharply as blade met blade in the latest round of the war. The attack was brutal as their foes swarmed at them like angry hornets, but as the enemy's numbers were limited, the onslaught was short-lived. Prince Gregory and his men swiftly gained the upper hand and defeated their opponents, though a few on the periphery escaped to regroup elsewhere.

"This was a hastily arranged ambush to delay us," the prince remarked as he brought his horse to a halt and sheathed his blood-stained sword. Though the air had cooled appreciably in the approaching twilight, he wiped a forearm over his sweaty brow and took a much needed gulp from a nearly empty water skin.

"Then let us move on," Ramsey said as he cleaned his sword in a tuft of grass. "The mountain looms eerily close in the north."

"It does," he replied, gazing upon Mount Minakaris before calculating the number and strength of his remaining troops. He noted the weariness in their eyes yet also a fiery determination to press forward. With an encouraging smile he urged them onward. They followed Prince Gregory across the trampled common and through another maze of streets, needing little motivation other than securing the safety of their King.

Soon they approached the northern part of the city, overwhelming a scattering of the enemy along the way. Prince Gregory, not wanting to appear overconfident, saw that his father's army had secured at least this section of the city, though the chaotic sounds of battle reverberated from afar, especially to the east beyond the city's border. But his brief illusion of partial victory was shattered when they emerged from several narrow streets into a large area of farmland, grazing pastures and budding orchards. The cultivated parcel encompassed the northernmost strip of Del Norác before it gradually transformed into a large swath of grassy scrubland that lay in the shadow of Minakaris. The mountain loomed a quarter mile away, its slopes bathed in the glow of the setting sun.

Spread out before them, running east to west, were several battles raging at once across multiple terrains. Over the course of the day, the fighting inside the city had moved northward into these more open areas. The clashes here had been joined by troops led by King Cedric and Tolapari who then gradually moved southward after their earlier encounter with Vellan's troops from the mountain stronghold. This sudden re-eruption of the war darkened any hope in the prince's heart for victory. But when he glanced westward at a field parallel to a sprawling apple orchard just beyond it, his mood changed.

"Over there!" he cried, pointing to a large group of enemy troops on horseback trying to break through a line of soldiers pushing back from the north. "That has to be them!" Prince Gregory charged forward while others followed as best they could. Some of his soldiers though, were diverted along the way when pulled into other fights spread out upon the vast canopy of grass, trees and soil. The setting sun dipped slowly into the blazing western peaks. In the east, a string of snow-tipped mountains stood proudly against a crisp blue sky as a silvery-white glow steadily rose from just below the horizon.

Prince Gregory led three dozen men north across the field, the fragrant orchard of budding apple trees forming a natural border to their left. Suddenly, one of his captains who had broken away earlier, burst forth with a contingent of soldiers from the southern streets. Though weary and bruised, the men, most of them on foot, charged forth to catch up with their fellow soldiers in the rescue attempt.

"*Now* let's see the enemy reach the mountain with the King," Ramsey said with renewed hope to a soldier running beside him. "We'll block them from the south while our allies act as a wall to the north. And if we each stream out to the east and meet, we can pen in Vellan's troops with the orchard as a barrier to their west."

As Ramsey drew nearer, he guessed that Prince Gregory was thinking along those same lines since a portion of his men began to circle about to the northeast. Whoever was in charge of the northern company had given a similar order as a line of men veered southeast and linked up with their fellow soldiers to loosely lock in the enemy.

As the allied forces moved in, several of Vellan's troops on horseback saw the futility of their cause and bolted, galloping through the circle at its weaker points. A few succeeded, though others were struck down by well aimed arrows or expertly wielded swords. Ramsey, having joined the fray inside the circle, was drawn into a fight with a soldier from the Isles. But having a bit more energy in reserve, he outmaneuvered the Islander and finished him off with a lethal stroke. It was then that Ramsey locked onto King Justin as he was being pulled off his horse near the apple orchard. The monarch, his hands tied in front, was grabbed by two men from Kargoth and steered into the orchard of low trees as he struggled to get away. Ramsey, knowing that the captors would take the King to Mount Minakaris by any path possible, raced to the orchard.

"King Justin has been taken into the trees!" he shouted to anyone who could hear him as the battle raged on like wildfire.

Moments later, he located Prince Gregory who was fighting a short distance away atop his horse. The prince sparred against a soldier from Kargoth on horseback, their blades harshly clanging. As Ramsey raced to his aid, he grabbed a dagger clutched in a dead Islander's hand that he passed by. With hardly a pause in his stride, he flung the knife at Prince Gregory's foe, striking him in the lower back. The Islander lurched upward in his saddle as a spasm of pain shot through him, rendering him paralyzed for a brief moment. Prince Gregory lunged forward in that instant and plunged his sword through him, toppling the man from his steed. In the approaching twilight, Ramsey noticed the fallen soldier's eyes slowly clear up and his features soften as Vellan's spell dissipated.

"This son of the King thanks you for your assistance," the prince said, very much out of breath as he looked down upon Ramsey, noting a shadow of dread upon his face.

"And *this* son of Linden would like to assist you one more time," he replied, informing Prince Gregory about his father's predicament. He pointed out where along the orchard's border the King had been taken. "Ride to him now, sir! I'll follow with others to help," Ramsey urged, pausing to catch his breath after the prince had sped away. But moments later, he was once again racing toward the apple trees, encouraged to see that other soldiers had caught up and were heading that way as well.

Prince Gregory reached the orchard in breakneck speed, striking down an Island soldier who tried to block his way. He abandoned his steed before entering the grove as the apple trees were too low for the horse to maneuver through. He observed at various points north along the tree line that several allied soldiers had plunged into the orchard as well in pursuit of the King, grateful for their undying loyalty. He slowed down from time to time, dodging branches as he continually scanned through rows of trees dappled with the rays of the setting sun. Soon he spotted three men heading northwest several rows beyond, their movements halting and awkward as if one of the three were impeding their progress. Prince Gregory grinned, knowing his father was putting up a good struggle.

The apple trees were planted in long rows north to south. The prince sped north along a strip of ground between two of the lines, keeping a constant eye on his father and his captors until they were almost directly to his left. As the trio moved northwest, hoping to clear the orchard and make for Mount Minakaris, Prince Gregory shifted west, cutting swiftly across row by row while dodging the hanging branches that scratched at his face like angry wasps. He spotted several other men at various distances and directions, all racing toward the King. He assumed all were from his father's army, though he couldn't make out their faces or garb through the budding branches in the dimming light.

He heard a fluttering noise through the leafy branches just ahead, followed by a single, dull thud as if someone had thrown a stone against the trunk of a tree. He stopped dead in his tracks, the origin of the mysterious noise revealed. Lodged into a tree in front of him was an arrow with orange, brown and black feather fletching, indicative of a weapon from Kargoth. Prince Gregory's heart pounded. Someone behind and to his right was targeting him. He changed directions several times to confuse his assailant, erratically weaving through the shadowy trees. But when he thought he was finally making progress reaching his father, he noticed two more things that sent his heart racing even faster.

One of the two men dragging King Justin through the orchard was suddenly pulled to the left and stumbled to his knees. The King had used the force of his entire body and lunged leftward in mid-run, throwing the enemy soldier off balance. The man lost his hold as he slipped, and with the shift in momentum, King Justin and the second man toppled over between two trees. But the King had anticipated such an outcome. And though his hands were tied in front of him, he scrambled to his feet and raced southward before the others could stop him. Prince Gregory silently cheered on his father.

At the same moment, a group of allied soldiers rushed at the trio from the direction the captors were heading, having earlier cut across the northern border of the orchard to head them off. The man who had stumbled when King Justin escaped, a native of Kargoth, jumped to his feet when he saw the advancing rescue party. He spun around and chased after the King. His counterpart was slain moments later as he charged at the soldiers with a sword. One man from the rescue team then broke away and pursued the soldier from Kargoth before he could reach the King. A second man impulsively followed to help, his pace slower and steps less agile, yet his heart as resolute.

"I'm right behind you, Malek!" shouted Sala, his face dirt-smudged and dewy with perspiration after a day of running and fighting in and north of Del Norác.

Prince Gregory watched the rapid events unfold. He altered his direction once more, hoping to reach his father before the enemy soldier closed in on the King from behind. "Father!" he called out, ducking under a low branch. He finally entered a space between two lines of trees directly south of King Justin who now sped toward his son. With a clear view of his father's determined face, Prince Gregory drew his sword and bolted toward him. The soldier from Kargoth, with Malek and Sala behind him, all madly pursued the monarch from the opposite side.

At once, several enemy arrows shot through the trees with lightning speed, stripping bursts of leaves from the branches as they searched out their marks. King Justin and Sala both fell to the ground in the dusky confusion.

"*Father!*" Prince Gregory cried as he ran, fearing the worst.

But when the King rose to his feet, having apparently only tripped on a tree root, the prince was heartened, but only for a moment. The soldier from Kargoth, now just steps away from King Justin, zeroed in on him with a dagger. Prince Gregory could almost feel the stab of cold metal himself as the soldier rushed at his father with burning hatred. But as the King turned to avoid the brunt of the attack, Malek leaped upon the enemy from behind and tackled him to the ground, taking King Justin down with them in a pile of bodies.

As Malek pulled the soldier off of him, King Justin exhaled a muffled cry of pain that quickly died in the shadows. The haunting sound tore at Prince Gregory's heart. When he finally reached his father, he fell to his knees, his hands trembling, fearing he may have been too late. Malek, without hesitation, finished off the soldier from Kargoth with a single thrust of his sword. He turned away from the corpse in disgust, breathing in the cool twilight air to steady himself.

"Father, speak to me!" Prince Gregory pleaded with quiet urgency as he looked upon the King's pale face staring up at him from beneath an apple tree. Malek watched over them with concern, noting a growing bloodstain below the King's right shoulder.

King Justin, his eyes shifting in a state of confusion, offered his son a faint smile. "It's good to see your face, Gregory, as for a while I thought I would never look upon my son again. But–" He took a slow, deep breath, trying to gather his strength. A flicker of fear shot through the prince as he protectively held his father's hand.

"But what, Father? What do you wish to say?" he whispered, wondering if their time together was nearing its end.

King Justin gazed lovingly upon his son and squeezed his hand as a look of befuddlement slowly crossed his face. "But–who is *he*?" the King inquired, indicating Malek with raised eyes. His voice had grown stronger now, giving hope to his son that maybe his injury was not as severe as it looked.

"My name is Malek, sir. I'm with the mountain resistance," he replied. "Though for the past several hours I've been fighting alongside your troops under the capable direction of King Cedric and the wizard Tolapari."

"Ah, Malek," he replied, recognizing the name. "Nicholas Raven and your friend, Maximilian, had both talked about you when we had met by Lake Mara. In nothing but glowing terms, I should add," he said, trying to sit up.

"I'm flattered," Malek replied. He knelt down and helped Prince Gregory to gently position his father against the tree.

"So you do not intend to die in this apple orchard?" the prince quipped.

"I feel battered and pierced, but with salve and bandaging, I should pull through. That dagger missed any vital organs," he said as his son examined the wound. "Besides, think what a pall I would cast upon Megan and Leo's relationship if I died under an apple tree, of all things." He softly chuckled. "The boy would be devastated!"

"Agreed," Prince Gregory said as he removed his thin, cloth vest and pressed it upon the wound before glancing at Malek. "Can you run for assistance?"

"At once," he replied, racing north up the narrow strip to where most of the soldiers from his group were still gathered.

But he had taken only a few steps when he noticed Sala's body sprawled facedown upon the ground several yards ahead, an arrow buried in his back. He ran to his friend, his chest tightening with every breath. Suddenly a cry of rage erupted from somewhere in the trees far to his right, momentarily drawing away his attention before all went silent. But Malek ignored whatever danger might be lurking and knelt down beside Sala's body, feeling sick to his stomach when gently laying a hand upon the back of the young man's head. But when he did so, Sala flinched as if having been asleep. He slowly turned on his side, the ridge of his nose bloody and bruised as he gazed groggily at Malek.

"My face hurts," he muttered, lightly pressing a finger against his nose. "I lost my footing and tripped. I think someone pushed me."

Malek, on the verge of tears, couldn't help smiling. "And you hurt nowhere else?" he asked in disbelief.

"I scraped my hands, too," Sala said, sitting up. "I guess I passed out."

"If that's the worst of it, you are lucky indeed. But you weren't pushed, my friend." Malek reached around Sala and grabbed hold of the arrow he now realized was only lodged in a small pack around the man's back. "You don't feel this?" he asked, gently wiggling the arrow a few times.

"Feel what?"

"Good." He circled around Sala and examined the arrow which was stuck in the small pack but not firmly so.

"What are you doing? What'd you find?"

"One moment," Malek replied, easing the arrow out of the pack and holding it in front of Sala's stunned eyes. Attached to the point were two of the hardened biscuits he had retrieved from Brin's raft last autumn. "I didn't think these were still edible."

"They're good in a fix, sort of," he sheepishly replied. "I forgot I had any left."

"Well, don't get rid of those," he said, handing Sala the arrow and slapping him on the back before racing northward. "Now attend to the King while I get help."

King Justin walked into the field east of the orchard several minutes later. Prince Gregory and Sala assisted him on either arm, his wound temporarily bandaged. Malek and a few other soldiers accompanied them. The growing white light of an approaching moonrise filled the eastern sky where a string of mountaintops stood silhouetted against the crisp horizon. The battle in the immediate area had since concluded. Most of the enemy lay dead and their horses grazed among the grass as the King's soldiers patrolled the area. But the fighting continued unabated in other parts of Del Norác, especially in the eastern field outside the city's border.

King Justin sat against a tree to rest as allies within the orchard and on the field of battle drew near. Soon King Cedric and Tolapari greeted their old friend. Both men looked exhausted yet were prepared to do whatever needed to be done against Vellan's unrelenting assault. The wizard examined King Justin's wound and provided him with a half-filled water skin. Prince Gregory stood by like a worried parent.

"This bandaging will do for now, but I'll examine it more thoroughly later," he said. "Despite your fine mood, you took a serious hit, Justin. And unlike the cut you received from Arileez, this injury will not magically heal in a day or two."

"I'll be fine," he replied. "I'm one of the fortunate ones today." He gazed somberly across the field littered with corpses. "But there is still more work to do."

"What's our next step?" King Cedric asked. "Though whatever it is, you will most certainly be sitting it out."

"That is yet to be seen. But first I think we should gather what forces we can spare and ride out to the eastern field and assist King Rowan and his men. From this vantage point, I can see the area is thick with fighting. We now have extra horses at our disposal which will greatly help. The remaining troops can head back into the city proper."

"Include me in the former group," a voice spoke from just inside the apple orchard. Seconds later, a disheveled Ramsey caked with dirt, emerged clutching a bow that had been crafted in Kargoth. "I owe my life to Prince William who saved me on the battlefield in Rhiál. I would like to assist him in his fight if even in a small way."

"Then you shall ride with me," King Cedric replied, "for I shall lead the charge." He glanced sharply at King Justin. "And I will tolerate no argument from you," he added with mock indignation, receiving an approving nod from Prince Gregory.

"As you wish," the King said with a tired smile, noticing the bow in Ramsey's hand. "A wartime souvenir?"

Ramsey shook his head. "I ripped it from the hands of the enemy assassin hidden in the trees before I killed him," he said, tossing the bow to the ground. "I don't want it. I'll have enough bad memories of this day if I survive."

"Assuming that the day ever ends," Tolapari remarked as he gazed upon Mount Minakaris looming ominously to the north. "For I can't stop wondering if Vellan has more surprises awaiting us in the dark corridors of his lair."

CHAPTER 109

Views from On High

Candles flickered against the corridor walls, casting somber shadows in the silence. Caldurian gazed wistfully at Madeline as he knelt by her side. She lay fast asleep on the floor, her breathing steady and her face relaxed, giving the wizard a sense of relief that she would survive the effects of the potion he had slipped into her tea.

"I'm sorry, Madeline, but it was for the best," he whispered, gently touching her cheek. "Return to your old life. In time you'll see that I was right to push you away."

Caldurian studied her face, noting with fond amusement a wisp of fiery red hair sticking out from beneath the black silk kerchief wrapped about her head. He knew that it was really she who had pushed *him* away despite all he had taught her about the magic arts. But the wizard forgave her, realizing he had led her down a twisting road of mayhem and magic when she was too young to grasp the ramifications of such a life. And though he never expected to see her again after today, she would always have a place in his heart.

Caldurian then heard a commotion back in the dining area. *Was that shouting? Was that–Mune's voice?* He jumped to his feet and dashed down the corridor, chiding Mune under his breath while assuming the prisoners had gotten the best of him.

When he stormed through the archway, his instincts were proven correct. Nicholas had tackled Mune to the floor and was trying to wrest the dagger from his hand. Leo, in his weakened state, picked up Vellan's staff to use as a weapon. But before he could render any assistance, Caldurian stealthily ran up from behind and grabbed it.

"I'll take that!" he said, ripping the staff from Leo's hand and pushing him to the floor. He raised the gnarled piece of wood above Leo's body and shouted, getting Nicholas and Mune's attention. "Enough! We don't have time for this nonsense! Now on your feet, both of you," he ordered, eyeing Nicholas in particular, "or I shall put your friend here out of his misery."

Nicholas released his hold on Mune and reluctantly rose to his feet. Mune, red-faced and panting, retrieved the knife and pointed it directly at Nicholas.

"One step closer and I swear I'll use it!" he sputtered.

Caldurian sighed in frustration. "Put the knife down!" he said as if disciplining a child. Mune, with a sour grimace, reluctantly obeyed and slipped the blade behind his belt. Caldurian lowered the staff, indicating to Nicholas to attend to his friend.

"Are you all right, Leo?" he asked as he helped him off the floor. He could plainly see that Leo appeared weaker and paler than even a few minutes ago, wondering if the stress of the situation was hastening the effects of Vellan's spell. He guided Leo to a chair at the table and insisted he sit down and rest.

"Let me catch my breath and I'll be fine," he said without a hint of levity or sarcasm, causing Nicholas to think that maybe Leo was in worse shape than he was letting on.

Doing all he could to keep his temper in check, Nicholas glared at Caldurian. A part of him desired to attack the wizard regardless of the consequences, but he knew that both Ivy and Leo needed him now more than ever.

"Tell me what you want, Caldurian," he said. "Tell me now or we'll both regret it before the day is out."

Caldurian appeared more amused than intimidated. "That sounds like a threat, Mr. Raven, but rash words are hardly necessary," he calmly replied. "Because what I intend to do for you and your friend is to, well, let you go."

Nicholas and Leo stared dumbfoundedly at the wizard, not sure if they had heard him correctly. Even Mune looked on with his mouth agape, wondering if Caldurian had accidentally consumed some of the disorienting potion he had given to Madeline.

"Come again?" Nicholas asked, his senses fully on alert as if expecting Caldurian to initiate some sleight-of-hand. "You're letting us go?"

"Yes. But don't look so surprised. It will benefit me, too."

"That I don't doubt," he replied with growing suspicion. "But that doesn't offset my initial surprise. Why would you let us go?"

"Yes, why?" Mune added, equally puzzled.

"Because I have plans for them," the wizard replied matter-of-factly, noting the lingering skepticism upon all their faces. "You'll just have to trust me."

"Trust you?" Leo said, exhaling deeply as he leaned back wearily in his chair. "After watching what you just did to Vellan and Madeline–your so-called friends–how can Nicholas and I expect anything but deceit from you?" He glanced at Mune. "If I were you, I'd watch myself. By my calculations, you're next."

Caldurian noted the startled look upon Mune's face. "You're speaking nonsense, Mr. Marsh. Mune has nothing to worry about. He will remain loyal to me and do my bidding because he knows he's on the winning side and will be justly rewarded. Who in his right mind would scoff at a deal like that?"

Mune, after a moment of contemplation, nodded at the wizard yet remained silent.

"I really don't care what deals you two make," Nicholas said. "Just tell us about the plans you have for Leo and me."

Caldurian removed a sealed piece of parchment from one of his cloak pockets and handed it to Nicholas. "I'm letting you go as a sign of good faith to King Justin. I want you to deliver this message to him. I wrote it earlier today, planning to have Mune deliver it. But the two of you showing up here only strengthened my plan."

Mune winced. "Me?"

"Yes, you. But don't worry, Mune. Your new assignment won't take you outside the walls of Minakaris. You'll be far away from the swords and bloodshed."

"What does it say?" Nicholas asked, still not trusting the wizard. "I won't deliver anything to the King until I know what you're planning. And I'm definitely not leaving here without Ivy and Carmella at my side."

"Fine!" he sputtered. "Mune will take you to the women before you leave. You can slip out one of the lower exits on the southeast slope. It's less steep on that side and there are roads from the upper stables leading into Del Norác. And considering all the troops Vellan has unleashed today, some of those exits are probably lightly guarded by now, if at all." He looked wide-eyed at Nicholas. "Satisfied?"

"I will be once you tell me about the contents of the letter," he replied, not yet fully convinced. Deep inside though, his thoughts whirled and his heart beat wildly, hoping that he would soon see Ivy.

Caldurian let out a deep sigh, irritated that he had to explain his every move. But to give himself the best chance for success, he needed Nicholas' cooperation.

"As you wish," he said. "My message, which I need you to get to either King Justin or Prince Gregory, outlines a deal I want to make in order to end this war before every last man in both armies is slaughtered."

"Go on," Nicholas said, intrigued but cautious.

"And the key to my deal," he continued, pointing to Vellan who was still sprawled upon the floor in a deep sleep, "is to hand over *him*."

"You're serious?" Nicholas asked in stunned disbelief.

"Yes. I'll hand over Vellan, the bane of Laparia and the scourge of the mountain nations for these past fifty years. I will offer him to King Justin and his allies for their cooperation." The wizard smiled gleefully. "Quite a bargaining piece, don't you think?"

"A good first step," Leo admitted.

"It's a tremendous first step! In addition, if King Justin and his counterparts agree to leave Kargoth, I will also halt the flow of troops from the Northern Isles into this region. But to be truthful, that benefits me as well. I have no desire to ally myself with that thuggish lot. Vellan trusted them, but I certainly don't," he said. "Everything is explained in the letter. King Justin will be pleased with my offer and my trustworthiness."

"Don't be so sure," Nicholas said.

"That is why you must deliver the letter to the King, Mr. Raven. He needs to see that you and your friends are in fine health thanks to my efforts. You must tell him what I did on your behalf. Convince King Justin that I have changed–at least enough in the right direction for him to deal with me now."

"Anything you did today was for your own benefit," Leo tiredly remarked. "The change you talk about is only on the surface."

"Let's not quibble over details."

"I'll quibble over one of them," Nicholas said. "Leo is not in fine health after what Vellan did to him. Can you help?"

Caldurian looked down for a moment, genuinely troubled about Leo's condition and not taking any delight in what he was about to say. "Even if I had weeks to spare, it wouldn't be enough time for me to figure out the complexities of Vellan's spell to reverse it. Remember, I am not a true wizard, but was only an apprentice to one. I am truly sorry."

"Can't you at least slow the effects?" Nicholas pleaded. "Or what if you consulted with Tolapari? He is out there on the field of battle. Perhaps between the two of you…"

"Tolapari is no more a true wizard than I. Neither of us would be very much help in the end." He glanced at Leo with regret. "I hate to be blunt, Mr. Marsh, but my best advice is to use wisely what little time you have left. Save your friends and help stop this war. That would be an honorable deed in your final hours."

"But you have to do something!" Nicholas implored.

Leo stood up, his strength returning for the moment. "He's right, Nicholas. What's done is done, and time is running out. Let's find Ivy and Carmella and get out of this place. If I'm to permanently depart this world by dawn," he added with a familiar trace of humor in his voice, "I don't want to be stuck in here when it happens."

Nicholas managed to smile through the anger churning inside him if only to make Leo feel better. He held up the parchment letter, eyeing the wizard. "What if I can't locate King Justin or his son? What should I do with this? According to Gavin's report, the King had been kidnapped and might already be on his way over here."

"I cringed when I heard those words, fearing that I wouldn't be able to present my offer to him," Caldurian said. "Yet in light of recent developments, it would be a good thing if King Justin were now brought here, saving me a lot of uncertainty. But the point is to get word to him or his associates as soon as possible. King Cedric,

King Rowan and Tolapari are all in the vicinity. Deliver the message to whoever is in charge and tell him about what has happened here. I need to gain the trust of someone on your side–and fast! I, in the meantime, will seek out Gavin. He among all of us may be able to locate the King and deliver word to him expeditiously. One of us must succeed."

"How will you find Gavin?" Mune inquired doubtfully.

Caldurian flashed a knowing smile. "Oh, where I am going, Gavin will most certainly find *me*," he said before removing another sealed letter from his cloak pocket. He handed it to Mune. "This is your assignment."

"It is?" he said distrustfully, gazing at the letter as if it were a poisonous object.

"Deliver it below to the captains in charge in the stronghold. It is an order from Vellan to draw down our troops so we can parley with King Justin."

"When did Vellan compose this letter? And why?"

"I wrote the letter, you fool, earlier today when I was preparing to enact my plan." A shadow of doubt crossed Mune's face. "Don't worry. The handwriting is identical to Vellan's and all the official markings are in place. You won't be arrested as a suspected traitor when you deliver it. As I was obliged to act as Vellan's courier these past few days, I closely studied his messages and devised a spell to transform my own script to match his. Clever actually, but no time to go into details. Now we must be off."

"One more thing," Nicholas said.

Caldurian put his hands to his face, shaking his head. "Now what?"

"What makes you think King Justin will agree to any of this? Why would he want you ruling Kargoth instead of Vellan?"

"What other choice does he have? It's either total defeat or strike a deal with me. Compared to the chaos that Vellan has released upon Laparia, I'm a fine alternative."

"You helped to bring about that chaos," Leo pointed out, "including in Nicholas' village. You're no different from Vellan."

"But I'm willing to end this war!" he snapped. "And I will rule Kargoth more wisely than Vellan ever did, promising to keep my nose out of the rest of Laparia."

"But for how long?" Nicholas asked. "In the end, you'll be grasping for more power and riches at others' expense just like Vellan. It's all a matter of time."

"Think what you like, but that's the chance King Justin will have to take. It's either that or certain death to what remains of his army. *You* must make the first move."

Nicholas looked at Leo, and sensing that he had come to the same conclusion, realized they had no other choice. "Fine," he muttered. "We'll do as you ask."

"You won't regret it. Now I must be off if we're to make this plan work. And Mune, as soon as you show them the way out, get those orders to the stronghold below. I'll be heading in the opposite direction."

"All right. But what about Madeline?"

"I'll have a long talk with her when she awakens. She should be in a better state by then and more amenable to my suggestion that she start a new life far away from here. But let me worry about that. Now go."

"Very well," he said. "But first I'll throw together a bag of provisions in the pantry for our guests. Even along a dirt road, it'll still be quite a hike for them down the remainder of the mountain into Del Norác."

"Just don't dawdle!" The wizard hurried to the exit, nodding goodbye as he swept through the archway and sped down the corridor. When he reached Madeline, who still slept soundly on the floor, he paused and gazed kindly upon her. "Don't worry, love. In time, life will be worth living for you again. And for me, too," he said, flashing a tender smile. "But first things first." He moved on, slipping through the exit and rushing up a staircase to the level above, unaware that Madeline had slowly raised her head after he departed, her mind racing with wild and vindictive thoughts.

After reaching the next level, Caldurian hastened down the corridor. Soon he neared the door with the curved brass handle that Nicholas and Leo had earlier discovered. The wizard grabbed a lit candle from the wall, opened the door and bounded up the shadowy staircase until he reached the locked door at the top. He drew the bolt back and opened the door a crack, feeling a sense of exhilaration about the new life that awaited him. A blast of cool evening air rushed inside when he opened the door all the way, extinguishing the candle. Caldurian tossed it aside as he stepped out onto the stone balcony carved out of the mountain. He gasped in awe as he placed his hands on the railing and gazed upon his realm. The sky to the east was filled with a growing icy white glow along the horizon. In the west, the sun descended into the red and gold tinged mountain peaks. He had stood here only once before at Vellan's side many years ago as a reward for designing a particularly well-crafted spell.

"Now I can look upon my dominion at my leisure," he whispered, pleased with himself as he scanned the sky for any sign of Gavin. He hoped that Vellan's faithful crow would spot him against the side of the mountain, so he patiently waited for his arrival, happy to enjoy the scenery. He savored the moment and his impending victories over both Vellan and King Justin's army, envisioning the extraordinary life nearly within his grasp.

In time. All in good time.

Eucádus placed a hand upon the hilt of his sword but did not draw the weapon. He looked at Ranen with deep sadness in his heart. Ranen, his raised sword catching rays of the setting sun, smiled arrogantly as the two men stood alone on the grassy banks of the Drusala River. The other soldiers near the garrison had fled north in pursuit of King Justin. Eucádus did not want to fight Ranen, but he knew that his mind, warped by Vellan's magic, was focused on nothing else except a contest to the death.

"You threaten to kill me after all we've shared together as friends?" Eucádus asked, displaying neither fear nor intimidation. "Do you not recall your successes as leader of the Oak Clearing? For years, along with Jeremias, Uland and Torr, we fought against Vellan's incursion into our homelands."

"We were mistaken in our thinking," Ranen replied. "And as you can see and hear from the distant fighting, those past efforts were in vain. Today Vellan will demonstrate his supremacy when your side is finally defeated."

"That will not be the case." Eucádus took a few steps closer until he could see the cloudy deadness in Ranen's eyes. "I have not traveled this far just to let Vellan step on us like ants. If anyone is to taste defeat today, it will be his troops, though you, Ranen, need not be one of the casualties." He took another step forward and held out his empty hands. "Lay down your arms. Leave this place. I will not pursue you."

"I would never desert my leader!"

"Then come back to our side. Search deep in your thoughts. Remember your old life. You are not one of the people of Kargoth who are still breathing yet dead. We are both men of Harlow."

Ranen smirked, amused by what he thought were the naïve utterances of a man without purpose and hope. "I no longer give my allegiance to Harlow, and if you had any sense, neither would you." He stepped closer, his eyes fixed on Eucádus who stood in the shadow of the garrison wall. "But to be fair, I will extend a similar offer. Come to my side, Eucádus. Drink the waters of the Drusala to free your mind, to refocus your mind. See the world clearly for the first time in your pitiful existence."

Eucádus sighed and shook his head, not hearing the slightest change in Ranen's frame of mind. But deep down, he never expected that he would. "It appears my efforts here have been in vain."

"Apparently so."

"But if you will not listen to me, Ranen, at least think of your wife who waits for you back at the Clearing. She tore off the red piece of material that binds your hair from one of her favorite dresses. How can you forget such a loving gesture? Does not even that tender act stir up fond memories and make you want to reclaim your life?"

Ranen set the tip of his sword upon the grass and gazed curiously at Eucádus. "Despite a losing argument, you do tend to go on. But flailing words, or a piece of red material, can never compete with Vellan's crystalline vision. Now let us do what we must." He raised his weapon. "The time for talk is over."

"I have no desire to do battle with you."

"Good," he replied. "Then it should take but a moment for me to finish you off!"

Ranen sprang forward. In that same instant, Eucádus drew his weapon, having expected nothing less than a fierce attack. Their blades clashed along the water's edge, the sharp metallic strikes echoing off the garrison wall. Agile footwork carried them eastward over the trampled grass closer to the stone bridge spanning the Drusala. Their view of the river opened up to the west, its mirrory surface shimmering red and gold from the setting sun. A bluish white glow rising just below the eastern horizon painted the water east of the bridge in cool shades of daylight, as if morning and night were in defiant competition on either side of the low, stone arches.

"You may as well give up, friend," Eucádus taunted as the two men stepped back from one another to catch their breaths. "I've fought against you many times in practice and know your style of swordsmanship. You will not defeat me."

"Ah, but I have since trained with Vellan's finest," Ranen confidently replied. "So prepare for some unexpected moves, *friend*."

Eucádus signaled for him to advance. "And I'll show you all I've learned from the brave warriors of Arrondale and elsewhere."

Ranen rushed forward, his sword slicing through the air as each forceful strike met Eucádus' blade with a ringing clash. The fight stretched out for long moments at a time with the combatants periodically stepping back to gather their strength. Yet neither seemed fully aware of their surroundings or the passage of time. But with stealthy finesse, Ranen carefully choreographed his steps so that the two men moved closer to the bridge with every few swipes of their swords. Eucádus, whose back was now to the river, appeared unmindful of the changing path of their fight even as he took his few first steps backward onto the stone bridge. Ranen kept his gaze fixed upon him as if not noticing the change of venue either. Eucádus offered a knowing grin, indicating that he had indeed been aware of his intention all along.

"Are you plotting to push me into the Drusala instead of killing me, Ranen?" he asked. "For that is the only way I would ever join your side in this ugly affair."

"You'd make a worthy addition to Vellan's army once your philosophy was properly adjusted. Something to consider in the few moments you have left to live," he said with another forceful strike.

Eucádus fought back with equal vigor as they moved slowly across the bridge, circling one another at times or inching closer to the low stone rails on either side. As they neared the western edge, the last rays of the setting sun splashed upon their faces and up and down the deadly edges of their swords. Eucádus suddenly shifted to one side to avoid Ranen's blade and swiftly countered, slicing deeply into his right wrist. Ranen's arm involuntarily snapped backward, causing him to drop his sword and grab at the wound with his left hand. When he looked up, Eucádus was charging at him full bore to deliver a second, fatal strike. But just before he plunged his sword into Ranen's chest, Eucádus tossed the weapon aside and dove upon his enemy, tackling him to the ground.

"I will not kill you, Ranen," he said as he struggled on the stone with his former friend, "though you may deserve it!"

"You are a fool!" Ranen sputtered, ignoring his pain and fighting with renewed ferocity. "Giving up the advantage because of sentiment will be the death of you."

"At least I am not already dead!" he shouted as they scuffled on the ground, trying to regain their footing.

In the commotion, Ranen landed a sharp elbow against Eucádus' chest, disabling him long enough while he scrambled to his feet. Eucádus, though in pain, rolled to one side just as Ranen lunged at him. He quickly stood up and grabbed Ranen from behind who fought back like a wild animal, spinning swiftly around and freeing himself before shoving Eucádus backward against the west railing. He locked his hands around Eucádus' neck, staring into his eyes with bitter contempt as he slowly choked him.

"Now you will learn what death is!" he cried as he pushed Eucádus' head backward against the railing. "Unless you take this last chance to open your mind and join Vellan's army."

Eucádus, gasping for breath as Ranen's fingers tightened around his neck, could see the flowing waters of the Drusala below, knowing that a plunge into the poisonous river would result in a fate worse than death. But as he locked gazes with Ranen, a faint smile formed upon his lips, causing Ranen to snarl with rage.

"So that is your answer? You would rather die?" he asked, maintaining his hold with mounting anger. "Well then, *friend*, I will abide by your wishes." Ranen tightened his grip. "And the world will be a better place because of it!"

Nicholas looked at Mune with growing anxiety, eager to leave the mountain. "Forget about gathering any provisions. Take me to Ivy and Carmella." He also wanted to find Tolapari to see if he could help Leo, though after hearing Caldurian's grim words, he wondered if it might simply be an effort in futility. "We have to go now!"

"We will," Mune replied as an inscrutable smile grew beneath his sea gray eyes. "And I had no intention of rummaging though the pantry for your benefit. I just said that to Caldurian as an excuse to stay behind. I need to speak with you privately."

"What?" Leo asked, eyeing the dagger at Mune's side. "We don't want trouble."

"And you won't get any if you hear me out," he promised. "I just want to talk. Like Caldurian, I'm now ready to lay out *my* deal."

"What are you talking about?" Nicholas asked. "We don't have time for this!"

"If you want me to lead you safely out of Minakaris with your friends, then you'll make time," he replied, jabbing a finger in the air. "Now button up your mouths so I can explain myself, then we'll be on our way."

"Fine," he said with a sigh. "Tell us what you want."

"I need you to deliver a message to King Justin."

"Are you serious?" Leo asked. "What could you possibly have to say to the King of Arrondale?"

"I'm hurt by that comment," he replied, feigning indignation. He walked over to Vellan's sleeping body and stared at it, his back to Nicholas and Leo. "Though I'm not a great wizard like him, I have made valuable contributions to recent events."

"Deadly contributions," Nicholas said. "What's your point?"

Mune turned around. "My point is that I won't be remaining here to act as some lackey for Caldurian. I'm fed up with this job which I've done for too many years at a wage far below my worth," he crossly replied. "To tell you the truth, I'm fed up with Caldurian. And Vellan and Madeline, too! All of them are far too eager to dispense orders to me as if I were one of the Enâri, bred to do their bidding without question."

"What's that got to do with King Justin?" Nicholas asked.

"Plenty! I plan to start a new life far from here. I'm not sure where, but after all I've been through, I just want to be left alone." He rubbed his temples, looking tired as he paced about the room. "I want to sleep late in a proper bed and eat meals at my leisure. For too many years I've followed others' schedules, and frankly, I don't have much to show for it, though I was promised plenty."

Leo smirked. "Are we supposed to feel sorry for you, Mune? You've had a difficult life, poor soul, ruining other people's lives."

Mune bristled. "Think what you like, but I want a life free of complications–and that includes King Justin!" Nicholas looked at him, not quite sure of his point, but Leo immediately noted the man's guilt-ridden expression and grasped his meaning.

"Fearful that you may have to pay for your ill deeds some day?" he asked. "King Justin probably has a list of your offenses as long as his arm."

"I'm sure," he uncomfortably replied, "including a particularly unsavory one."

"Yes. Killing a member of the royal guard will probably land you in one of the King's prison cells for the rest of your life," Leo said. "Or maybe you'll feel a noose around your neck instead."

Mune paled as he contemplated the scenario, wishing he had never followed Leo to that upper chamber in the Citadel. "Though I know I deserve it, I'm afraid I might be hunted down after the war ends. The possibility will hang over me regardless where I go."

"You could turn yourself in," Nicholas suggested.

"And you could jump in the Drusala River!" he snapped. "But neither of those things is going to happen. That's why I need you to deliver my message."

"Which is…?"

"First, do you promise?" he asked, glaring at Nicholas. "If you want to see Ivy and escape this miserable mountain, promise you'll deliver my message to the King himself."

"I promise!" he shouted, more annoyed than angered. "How many times do I have to say it? Now get on with it so we can leave."

Mune, suddenly calm and composed, walked over to Vellan's body again and stared down upon it with a mix of fear and curiosity. "The message I need you to relay should forever absolve me of my crimes against Arrondale and all of Laparia. The King must realize that this message is being delivered at my behest." He turned and faced them. "And, Nicholas–and I can't emphasize this enough–but you must make him swear that he will pardon all my offenses and leave me alone until the end of my days."

"I'll try my best," he said. "Now tell me the message already."

"I'll do better than that," Mune replied. He slowly removed the dagger tucked behind his belt and knelt down at Vellan's side. "I'll *show* you."

"What are you doing?" Nicholas asked in alarm as Mune placed the tip of his dagger a few inches above Vellan's heart.

He looked up at Nicholas and Leo who appeared frozen in disbelief. "I am about to rid Laparia of a poison that has affected these lands for the last fifty years," he calmly stated. "Caldurian was close to the right idea regarding Vellan's fate, but he was either too timid or lacked the foresight to take it all the way to its logical conclusion. I, on the other hand, will get to the heart of the matter."

"Mune, think about what you're proposing," Nicholas said, stepping forward. But when Mune raised the dagger higher, threatening to plunge it into Vellan that instant, Nicholas stopped, indicating that he would keep his distance. "Leave Vellan's fate in the hands of King Justin and his fellow monarchs. It is not your place to decide."

"Isn't it?" he asked. "I have done some dreadful things at Vellan's bidding. Is it not right that I should put an end to his terrible reign?" He chuckled nervously. "Who knows, but perhaps I'll be praised for this deed. And when you tell King Justin what I did here today, how could that kindly old man not pardon me for my transgressions?"

"Nicholas is right," Leo jumped in. "This decision is not yours. Besides, Vellan is a true wizard. None of us knows what will happen if you kill him. You're playing with fire."

Nicholas held out his hand. "Listen to Leo, Mune. Give me the knife," he kindly requested. "When I deliver Caldurian's letter to the King, I'll tell him that you're an equal part of the wizard's proposal to hand over Vellan and are deserving of his pardon."

Mune stared at the dagger as their words swirled in his mind. He looked at them askance. "You'd really do that? Or are you simply humoring me to get to your friends?"

"You have my word," Nicholas said. "I'll secure a promise from King Justin to leave you alone as a reward for your part in ending this war." He immediately regretted the distasteful words he had uttered, but silently vowed to hold himself to that pledge. "I'll even beg him to sign a royal decree to that effect. But you mustn't do this deed. None of us know what will result. Please reconsider, Mune, and show us the way out."

Mune gazed at them for several moments, contemplating their argument. He glanced at Vellan's aged face, recalling the unsavory orders he had carried out in his name over the blur of passing years. But after countless miles of travel and unpleasant accommodations, all that he really wanted was to rest and be left alone. His desire to be in the thick of things and make a living from it had since gone cold.

"Mune, do you hear us?" Leo asked, slowly drawing back his attention.

"I'm listening," he replied, sounding more at ease. His face and shoulders relaxed as if he had come to a final decision. "You two have given me a lot to think about," he softly added as his hands slightly loosened their grip upon the dagger. "A *lot*."

"Glad to hear it," Nicholas said with a sense of relief. "Our idea is a good one."

"It is," Mune replied with a cordial smile. "It really is. But after some careful consideration, well, I still think mine is better." With lightning swiftness, he raised the dagger high above the wizard's body.

"Mune, *don't!*" Nicholas shouted as a rush of cold blood raced to his heart.

His warning went unheeded. Mune plunged the dagger into Vellan's chest with all his might as a burst of searing pain shot up his arms. The wizard's eyelids popped open. His eyes darted back and forth as if seeking out the perpetrator of such a ghastly and traitorous act. Mune thought he was going to die when Vellan's gaze finally locked onto him while he still clutched the dagger. He stared back in paralyzed terror, trembling and mumbling a silent apology during what he expected to be his final seconds alive. Suddenly, the brief flash of light and liveliness in Vellan's eyes faded. His eyelids closed again for the last time. The remaining dab of color leached out from his cheeks as a final breath was unceremoniously expelled from his lungs. The wizard of Mount Minakaris was dead.

"*Leave at once!*"

Nicholas, mesmerized by what had just happened, turned to Leo. "What'd you say?"

"*Hmmm?*" Leo replied as if in a daze himself, unable to take his eyes off Vellan's corpse. "I didn't say anything."

"*Flee to safety!*"

Nicholas heard the voice again, a commanding whisper that sounded vaguely familiar. "Did you hear it?" he asked, realizing that Leo had not spoken those words.

"Hear *what*?" he asked. But Nicholas' question was forgotten when Leo cringed and pointed at Mune who had just removed the bloodstained dagger from Vellan's body. "What are you doing?"

"Preparing my message," Mune said, his voice chillingly calm. He meticulously wiped off most of the blood from the sharp blade using the folds of Vellan's robes. He then reached over and pulled off the dark gray cloth cap from the wizard's head. With almost a sense of reverence, Mune wrapped the knife in the soft material and looked up at Nicholas. "I left a little blood for show." He slowly got to his feet, trembling. He walked over to Nicholas and handed him the head covering.

"What's this for?" he said, recoiling at the gesture.

"As I said, this is my message. Deliver it to King Justin as you promised." Mune noted Nicholas' bewilderment as he placed the object in his hands. "This is proof that I killed Vellan and saved Laparia from that terrible wizard. This will secure my pardon." Still sensing reluctance on his behalf, Mune gently shook him by the shoulders. "Nicholas, if you want me to take you to Ivy and lead you out of this mountain, you must do as you promised!"

"I will," he softly replied as the surrealism of the moment began to fade. Yet something about the situation still troubled him.

"We both promise," Leo added, observing a faraway look in Nicholas' eyes. "Now take us to Ivy and Carmella."

"This way," Mune said as he headed toward the archway.

As Leo turned to follow, Nicholas grabbed him by the arm. "His body is still here," he whispered.

"What?" Leo asked.

Nicholas indicated Vellan's dead body lying upon the floor. "His corpse is still *here*. He didn't fade into white mist after death like Frist."

Leo noted the discrepancy but could plainly see that Vellan was dead. To make sure, he walked over to the body and felt the wizard's hand which was cold to the touch.

"What's going on?" Mune asked, waiting by the archway.

"Nothing." Leo went to Nicholas and whispered. "He's as dead as stone, but I don't know why he hasn't transformed. But let's leave while we have the chance."

"All right," he replied, making for the archway.

A second mystery soon captured their attention as they hurried down the corridor. Mune stood silently in the middle of the passageway near the exit, glancing up and down the hall. He looked at Nicholas and Leo, his brow furrowed in curiosity.

"Mune, what's wrong?" Leo asked.

"Where's Madeline?" he replied with unease. "Caldurian said she was sound asleep on the floor."

"Maybe she woke up and went after him."

"Or went after Carmella," he replied, rubbing his goatee.

"Where is *she*?" Nicholas asked, sensing that nothing good could come from a confrontation between the two women.

"Carmella is locked in a room two levels below," he said. "Next to Ivy's."

"Take us there!" Nicholas said with growing fear.

"*I can't hold off the inevitable. Leave this place now!*"

Nicholas stood as if paralyzed, again hearing whisperings in his mind. Only this time he recognized the voice of Frist who spoke in urgent tones. Though not knowing how such communication was possible, he trusted the wizard's message without question.

"Mune, take us below at once!"

Minutes earlier, after Caldurian had ascended to the upper level, Madeline groggily raised her head. She lay on the floor, her heart filled with despair and anguish. After glancing up and down the empty corridor, she struggled to her feet and made for the stairwell exit. She suspected that Caldurian had raced to one of Vellan's favorite spots on the mountainside to take in the stunning view of Kargoth at sunset. But Madeline had no interest in confronting him. She instead trudged down the staircase for two levels, guiding her hand along the wall to steady her weakened body as the potion drained away her remaining powers. She wanted to see Carmella, the sole individual she blamed for her downfall. She was certain that her cousin had poisoned Caldurian's mind and set the wizard against her, vowing that Carmella would pay dearly for such treachery.

After entering the corridor, she turned left along a candlelit passage. This section, unlike the others, curved deeper into the mountain. As she neared the midpoint of the long passageway, she noted a pair of guards keeping watch in front of two adjacent doors on her left. The men of Kargoth stood at attention as Madeline approached, knowing she was a favorite of Vellan's and possessed the authority to implement his orders.

"Anything to report?" she bluntly asked the first man.

"No, ma'am," he replied, surprised by her disheveled looks. "The prisoners are secure. Supper was delivered a short while ago."

"Good. I have an assignment from Vellan. I need it carried out with haste."

"Of course," the second man replied. Each guard looked on obediently, both under the influence of Vellan's enchantment and eager to please his representative.

"You are to escort Ivy to the Drusala River," she explained. "It is Vellan's wish that she consume its refreshing waters. I'll keep watch over Carmella's room." Madeline extended her hand and the second guard removed a key from his belt clip and handed it to her. "Take the girl out the southeast entrance two levels down. She'll put up a struggle but will be more than gratified on the return trip. But be sure not to injure her as she holds a special place in Vellan's heart."

"As you wish."

As the guards prepared to enter Ivy's room, Madeline unlocked the adjacent door, eager to talk to her cousin. She knew that Leo would soon be on his deathbed, and it made her feel better that Nicholas would not escape the wizard's punishment either. Seeing Ivy offer her allegiance to Vellan would be a fate worse than death for him.

She stepped into the shadowy room lit by a glowing fireplace and a few candles. Her cousin sat near the blaze at a small table enjoying a supper of soup, bread and tea. She closed the door and walked over just as Carmella set down a steaming cup with her gloved hand and turned her head.

"Hello, cousin," she said, leaning back in the chair. "To what do I owe this visit? Have you and Vellan finally decided what to do with me?"

"That is yet to be determined." Madeline moved into the firelight, her lips pressed in a tight line.

"Well, I wish you'd decide soon since Ivy and I are..." Carmella's words trailed off as she got a better look at her cousin. She stood up, startled by Madeline's disheveled appearance. "What's happened to you, Liney? You look awful."

"Not one to mince words," she remarked, tucking strands of hair underneath her kerchief. "And I won't either." Madeline took another step forward, her watery green eyes smoldering with disdain. "Tell me what words you spoke to Caldurian on your journey here, words that turned him against me."

"What are you talking about?"

"Don't pretend that you don't know, cousin. Speak the truth! What insidious thoughts did you plant into that wizard's mind which caused him to kill me?"

Carmella shrugged. "Kill you? I don't understand. What has Caldurian done to put you in such a crazed state?"

Madeline sighed with disgust. "You wish to claim ignorance? Fine, we'll play it your way. But a short while ago, Caldurian revealed to me a series of conversations he had had with you on your journey to this place."

"We talked about a lot of things. Be specific."

Madeline pointed a shaking finger at Carmella, her voice rising. "You told him that my life would have been better had he never met me and trained me in the magic arts. Now Caldurian believes it and has acted upon it!"

Carmella looked kindly upon her cousin, not wishing to upset her further. "Liney, please sit with me by the fire. We'll talk and have some tea."

"I prefer to stand."

"Suit yourself," she said, taking a seat. "But in all honesty, I think there has been a misunderstanding. My chats with Caldurian were strictly about him. I suggested that *his* life would have followed a much different path–and a far better one–had he not thrown in his lot with the likes of Vellan, though I suppose that applies to you, too. Following Vellan and Caldurian has brought you only grief, though you may not have realized it as you savored the wealth and power resulting from the grief you brought upon others."

"Don't lecture me! Whatever you said to Caldurian has twisted his mind. And because of that, he has turned against me. In fact, he has killed me, though I yet breathe."

"You're speaking nonsense," Carmella replied with a growing sense of unease. "What has been going on upstairs?"

Madeline briefly explained what had happened. "You have fouled matters up by dabbling in the magic arts. Because Caldurian had swiped a vile of rasaweed from your dilapidated home on wheels, Vellan now lies unconscious awaiting who-knows-what fate. You've damaged a lot of lives with your witless meddling, including mine!"

Carmella stood, incensed by the comment. "I've damaged a lot of lives? If that isn't the trout calling the duck wet, Liney, then I don't know what is. What Caldurian did to you was devious, but don't dare compare the swath of destruction you've cut through Laparia to anything I've done. My only intention was to find and help you. Whatever misfortune you're experiencing now is strictly your fault, a result of associating with the worst kind of people." She scoffed at her cousin. "Besides, what kind of damage could I have caused you? I am your prisoner, in case you've forgotten."

Madeline, on the verge of an outburst, kept her composure. "Do you want to see what you've done to me? What you've cost me?" She motioned for Carmella to follow her out of the room. "This way. And you might want to bundle up."

"Gladly. Anything to get out of this room." She grabbed her cloak and draped it over her shoulders. But as soon as they stepped into the corridor, she noticed that both guards were gone and that Ivy's door was ajar, raising her suspicions. After calling out Ivy's name and getting no response, Carmella cast a distrustful glance at her cousin.

"Where's the girl?"

"That is none of your concern."

"It's very much my concern, Liney, and unless you tell me–"

"She is being moved to a new location. Perhaps after our business here is done, I will tell you more."

"Fine. Let's get on with it."

Madeline led the way down the corridor to their left, stopping at a metal door built into the right side of the wall near the end of the candle-lit passage. She produced a key and unlocked the door, turning to her cousin before she opened it.

"Vellan allows only his closest friends inside. Consider yourself privileged."

They stepped into a cool, cavernous room carved out of the mountain on the lower southeastern slope. The chamber was devoid of any furnishings, fireplaces and other light sources. A few stone pillars were scattered about, their smooth sides ornamented with finely chiseled designs. The only illumination came from the glow of white light rising above the eastern horizon that washed into the room through a series of twelve tall, narrow arches cut into the mountain which offered a stunning view of Del Norác and the Drusala River in the distance. Far down and directly below the arches, a wide, frothy stream meandered along the mountain through a canopy of budding trees as it made its way to the Drusala. A narrow dirt road was visible to the east. Faint splashes of red and gold light from the west also spilled into the room through the windowless openings along with a soft, steady breeze. Carmella was fascinated by the room and wondered its purpose.

"The Enâri did some wonderful work," Madeline said as she walked over to one of the arches and placed her hands upon the stone sill that rose to her waist. She enjoyed the view, inhaling the cool evening air.

"What is this place?" Carmella asked. She peered out of an adjacent archway, her breath taken away by the stunning vista as the fresh air brushed across her face.

"Vellan had many areas for his private use constructed into the side of the mountain at various elevations and vantage points," she explained. "A balcony here, a terrace there. This chamber was one of several favorites–sunny or shadowy depending on the time of day, as well as quiet and uncluttered." She smiled wistfully, recalling fond memories. "Vellan would come here to think or enjoy a meal when the weather was accommodating. Even in the middle of winter he would occasionally venture out here to reinvigorate his mind when the snow was flying through the openings." She stepped back and turned to her cousin, her mood momentarily joyful. "On one of my previous visits, Vellan had a table and two chairs placed near one of these arches where we enjoyed a leisurely lunch and a wide-ranging conversation. The hours passed like minutes that delightful afternoon. It was a glorious time."

Carmella stepped back and faced Madeline, not wholly impressed. "I can only imagine what that conversation entailed. His fomenting of war between Rhiál and Maranac perhaps? Or maybe the details of your raid on the Blue Citadel? But I'm sure the discussion nicely complemented your choice of food that day."

Madeline scowled. "Watch you words! You are a guest here."

"I am a prisoner."

"And I am without a future, all thanks to you!" she cried. "I could have held the seat of power in Kargoth one day." Madeline swept an arm across the curving span of arches, on the verge of tears, her chin quivering. "The people and land out there could have been mine to shape into something more magnificent than Vellan had ever imagined. But because of you, it is not to be. Because of you, my dreams have been killed!"

Carmella appeared unfazed. "Your dreams are other people's nightmares."

Madeline's face reddened as she stood toe-to-toe with her cousin. "You had no right to delve into the magic arts and step into my circle. You've ruined everything!"

"Caldurian thought otherwise," she replied, icily staring down her cousin. "And unlike you, he wasn't afraid of a little competition."

"Competition? The only competition that you're on equal footing with me, cousin, is breathing and aging."

"Liney, you'd be surprised by what Caldurian has taught me over these past several days. Not only am I now proficient with smoke manipulation–"

"Child's play!"

"–but he instructed me in the basics of fire manipulation as well." Carmella noted a flash of jealously in Madeline's eyes. "If I'm not mistaken, that is one of your areas of expertise. Or should I say *was* one of your areas of expertise? By the look of you, you're clearly not the same Liney I met behind the Citadel a few months ago."

"Take that back!" she cried, pushing Carmella against one of the arches as a strengthening breeze swept inside. "Or I'll make you regret it for the rest of your life!"

Carmella, fearing that Madeline was losing her hold on reality, forcefully pushed her away and broke free. "Liney, are you mad?"

"I'm angry!"

She rushed at Carmella and nearly tackled her, but Carmella broke free a second time and ran to one of the pillars. She leaned against the stone column to catch her breath, keeping an eye on Madeline who glared at her from across the chamber. Carmella guessed that Caldurian's potion was tearing her apart physically and emotionally.

"Stay where you are, Liney! I don't want to hurt you," she warned. "You are not in your right mind."

"Hurt me?" Madeline scoffed as she stepped closer. "What are you going to do, cousin? Fan some smoke my way?"

"Don't try me!" Carmella peeled off the long beige glove from her right hand and wadded it into a ball. She held it tightly in the same pumpkin-colored hand whose hue extended beyond her wrist.

Madeline stopped, looking upon Carmella with amusement. "Do you plan to throw that glove at me, cousin? *Ouch.*"

Carmella offered a knowing smile. "As a matter of fact, yes."

Loosening her grip on the glove, Carmella whispered a string of inaudible words as she focused her concentration on the item, her voice growing softer with each repetition. Slowly, the wadded material began to glow with a reddish-orange luster until it burst into a controlled flame. She lifted her hand and whispered a few more words, causing the flaming sphere to fly from her palm and speed directly past her cousin. It slammed against one of the arches where it disintegrated in a flash, leaving a black mark upon the stonework. She noted a look of utter disbelief upon Madeline's face, knowing she had tamed her cousin for the moment.

Madeline looked up, her expression uncertain and faraway, her voice languid and without hope. "Apparently Caldurian wasn't wasting his time on you."

"He taught me only a few things," she replied, trying not to sound boastful. "I still need many more lessons before I'll be as proficient as you were."

"Yes," Madeline said with a sigh, shaking her head as she stepped back to the arches and leaned up against the sill. "As I *was*. Now you have taken the prize in the family, cousin. You have won."

"I don't feel like I've won anything, Liney. Not as long as you suffer like this." Carmella took a few tentative steps toward her, sensing her overwhelming pain. "Return with me to Red Fern where we can start mending your life. Maybe I can re-teach you some of the lessons you once knew so well—only this time with the provision that you use them for doing good. Nicholas told me stories of how Frist tended to the sick and injured with his gift. I can't think of a better way for you to make amends."

Madeline smiled halfheartedly as she hoisted herself up and sat on the sill, knowing her cousin meant well. "I doubt King Justin would allow me to wander freely through Arrondale after what I've done. I see a prison cell in my future—or worse."

"Perhaps, but maybe you must pay for your crimes first before you can redeem yourself." A hopeful smile spread across Carmella's face. "Yet seeing that I returned the medallion to the Citadel, I hold a little sway with the King. He might allow me to help rehabilitate you while you serve your time. Years from now you could be roaming through the villages of Arrondale to mend the sick and infirm. That might be your true calling."

"You dream large, cousin," she replied with a sad smile. "Perhaps Caldurian was right. Maybe I would have been better off had I never met him."

"Meeting that wizard was not the best thing for you."

Madeline nodded, calm and agreeable. "I guess it wasn't. My life without him would have been safer and quieter—though I suppose a bit duller compared to all I've experienced over the years."

"Dull is nice every now and then. But would that have been so bad considering all the harm that wouldn't have resulted from your activities?" Carmella felt that Madeline was slowly seeing things her way, certain that if she could get her out of Kargoth, there might be hope for her down the road. It would take years of hard work to help her unravel a lifetime of misdeeds, but Carmella was willing to try with King Justin's permission.

"I suppose that a case could be made for someone to live a dull life after having walked along a path similar to mine," Madeline said with a faint smile. "And it certainly would be a different life after all these years, a different challenge."

"Agreed, but one I'm more than willing to help you adjust to and maybe even enjoy one day," Carmella promised, believing that she had nearly reached through to her.

"Yes, dull certainly would be different for me," she replied, eyeing Carmella with a look of utter surrender. "Different, but not better, mind you–and definitely *not* worth living." Madeline smiled as she sat upon the sill. "Goodbye, cousin," she said, allowing her body to fall backward out of the archway and drop into the cool evening air.

"*Liney!*" Carmella cried, her heart pounding as she rushed to the breezy opening.

She peered over the side just after Madeline's body had hit the smooth, mossy rocks in the rushing stream below. Carmella hugged the stone sill, trembling as she gazed down in disbelief into the watery green landscape tinted with streaks of the dying sunlight. With an aching heart overwhelmed with grief and emptiness, she slowly buried her head into her arms as a flood of warm tears washed down her face.

"Goodbye, cousin," she whispered through her heavy sobs, unaware that the pumpkin color was slowly fading on the edges of her wrists.

CHAPTER 110

River and Mountain

"Flee the mountain! Time is running out!"

Nicholas heard the voice of Frist inside his mind as he and Leo followed Mune down the first long flight of stairs. He clutched Vellan's head cloth with the dagger that had killed him wrapped inside. His heart beat with anticipation that he was about to see Ivy after their long and grueling separation. But when they reached the bottom landing, Leo suddenly succumbed to a fit of pain and nearly fainted. He collapsed to the floor, gasping for breath.

"Leo!" Nicholas cried, racing to him. With Mune's assistance, he helped Leo sit up against the wall near the exit, noting with concern his glazed eyes and pale complexion.

"I need to rest," Leo said, leaning his head back in exhaustion. "This attack was worse than the others."

"Take all the time you need." Nicholas set Vellan's head cloth down as he knelt by Leo's side, feeling helpless.

"But we must go soon!" Mune quietly urged while fidgeting uncomfortably near the exit. "You said so yourself."

"We'll make it."

Leo, breathing a little easier, looked at Nicholas and shook his head. "Or we might not," he said, "at least not with me weighing you down."

"Stop talking like that. We've faced far worse than this. Rest another minute and then we'll take it slower. There's only one more flight before we reach Ivy's room."

Mune glanced at Leo with concern. "And another two flights after that to the southeast exit–and who knows if it's still guarded."

"I said we'll make it!" Nicholas snapped, glaring at Mune. "Have a little faith."

Leo smiled tiredly, placing a hand on Nicholas' shoulder. "I know that you'll make it, but you have to go on without me. It's the only way this will work." But before Nicholas could respond, he held up a hand. "Do it for Ivy's sake."

Nicholas stood, shaking his head as he moved about the small enclosure like a caged animal. "There has to be another way, Leo. I am not leaving you here."

Leo sighed, feeling as heavy as the stonework. "I appreciate your loyalty, Nicholas, but you have no choice. And not wishing to be blunt, but in all likelihood I'm going to be dead by dawn. Save the others and yourself while you have the chance."

"No!"

"I promise to find my way out if I recover my strength, but whatever happens…" Leo went silent, taking a deep breath as he slowly accepted the gravity of the situation.

"*Leo…*" Nicholas looked at his friend, detecting hopeless resignation in his eyes.

"Tell Megan I love her," he softly said, recalling their autumn walk through the Citadel fruit orchard and his proposal of marriage among the white snows of winter.

"You can tell her yourself," he replied, his words beginning to falter. He looked at Mune, desperate for any advice, but Mune merely shrugged and shook his head in reply.

"Nicholas, it's all right," Leo said, drawing back his friend's troubled gaze. "If we can bring this war to an end, then whatever happens to me is a small price to pay." He indicated Vellan's head cloth. "Take that and Caldurian's letter, find the others and leave."

"But maybe Tolapari can help. I'll wager he's a far better wizard than Caldurian."

"Probably, but Tolapari isn't a *true* wizard. He doesn't have the skill or time to undo what's happened," Leo reminded him. "Frist and Vellan are the only true wizards either of us knew, but both, unfortunately, are dead. So where does that leave us?"

A chill shot through Nicholas as a sudden thought ignited in his mind. "*Both dead*? Maybe not." He reached beneath his shirt and removed the silver amulet that Frist had created before his death. "I've carried this for so long that I forget I have it at times." He hurriedly placed the chain around Leo's neck and set the amulet in the palm of his hand.

"Nicholas, I can't take this from you," he protested.

"I'm giving it to you, Leo, so no argument. Frist told me his gift would lead me to those I seek, preserving life where death and destruction lurk. And whether I realized it or not, it has done both. But this of all places is where we need his help the most."

"But do you think that—"

"*On your feet, and then to the outdoors!*"

Nicholas and Mune both noted a flash of surprise upon Leo's face as color began to return to his cheeks. Strained weariness slowly drained from his features. He looked up, wide-eyed and confused.

"Did you hear that?" he asked. "I think it was Frist's voice."

Nicholas smiled. "I didn't, but I believe you *did*."

"What'd he say?" Mune asked anxiously.

"That we should get out of here. And fast."

"Are you able to go on?" Nicholas asked.

Leo, clutching the amulet, nodded. "I still feel a bit weak, but much better than moments ago. I think I can make it down the next flight. We'll see from there."

"Good!" Nicholas replied with renewed hope as he helped him to his feet. "So let's get going. We've lingered here too long."

"I won't argue with that," muttered Mune, signaling for them to follow him down the next flight of stairs.

When they reached the bottom landing, Mune held up a hand, silently indicating for them to wait in the stairwell. He stepped through the archway into the adjoining corridor to assess the way ahead. Nicholas and Leo stood anxiously by, fearing another delay. But a moment later, Mune stuck his head through the opening.

"All clear," he said. "Even the guards are gone."

"*What?*" He and Leo followed Mune into the candlelit corridor, not sure why this unexpected development worried him.

His heart nearly skipped a beat when Mune led them to Ivy and Carmella's rooms. Both doors were ajar.

"Are you sure this is the right level?" Leo whispered.

"Absolutely." He slowly pushed the first door inward. "Ivy? Are you in here?" When Mune saw no one inside, he repeated the procedure in Carmella's room with the same disappointing result.

"What's going on?" Nicholas asked. "Where are they?"

"I don't know!" he fretfully replied. "This is where they had been staying. This is where I brought them their meals. And when they were allowed to go out under supervision, only one of them went at a time, not both."

"Could Madeline have come down here?" Leo asked. "Maybe she ordered them to a more secure location–or something worse."

Mune's face went pale. "I wouldn't put anything past that woman at this point. The potion Caldurian slipped into her tea has sent her mind reeling."

"Let's start searching," Nicholas said, fearing that all might be lost if they didn't move immediately. "Tell us where we should go."

Mune thought for a moment, his mind spinning. "I really don't know. Vellan's mountain abode is, well–*mountainous*. I wasn't allowed access to all areas. But perhaps we should start by exploring–" He paused, eyeing the others with bewilderment. "Do you feel that?" He spun around and faced eastward, holding out a hand as a cool feathery breeze brushed across his fingertips. Nicholas and Leo also felt it, detecting a scent of fresh springtime in the air.

"It's coming down from the end of the passage," Nicholas said, pointing ahead. He noticed a fluttering of the candle flames farther down the corridor. "Is there an exit on this level? Perhaps an open window?"

"None that I know of," Mune said. He slowly walked down the passageway. "Then again, I've never stepped beyond these two doors. Follow me and we'll find out."

At the same moment in the east field, William and Brendan stood by their grandfather's corpse. They stared defiantly at Meegs who threatened to make them drink from the Drusala River. As

Brendan looked at the enemy soldiers surrounding them, most on foot and some atop horses, he knew there was no way to escape such a fate except by death itself. And as he had already experienced death once, he feared only for his brother, saddened at the rich and wonderful years ahead that William would never experience. But for the sake of Montavia, he could never allow themselves to fall under Vellan's spell. He inched his fingers toward the hilt of his sword. Meegs, though, noted the movement of his hand and smiled.

"So, young prince, are you having second thoughts about surrendering? I can tell by the helpless look in your eyes that you would rather die than drink from the river and become Vellan's servant. But how mistaken you are, sir. And you'll realize your error as you serve our great leader, no doubt thanking me in the end."

"Guess again!" William jumped in. "My brother and I will kill you or die in the attempt before stepping anywhere near the Drusala."

"Really?" Meegs discreetly motioned to one of his captains standing behind the siblings as the sounds of distant warfare filled the air like rolling thunder.

"Count on it!"

But before he and Brendan reached their swords, two soldiers grabbed their arms from behind and held them securely upon silent orders from their captain. Meegs chuckled, pleased with the result.

"Bind them tightly!" he said. The soldiers quickly wrapped lengths of thin rope around their wrists.

"Leave my brother alone!" Brendan cried.

Meegs stood in front of the two princes, studying their pained expressions. "The helplessness in your eyes has been replaced by fear," he said. "But moments from now that fear will be washed away and replaced with a glorious devotion to Vellan so fulfilling that you'll wonder how you ever lived without it."

"I think you're confusing devotion with *delusion*," Brendan replied, eyeing Meegs as a faint smile formed upon his lips.

"Why are you smiling?" he snapped, his jovial mood souring.

"Because I am encouraged by what I see in *your* eyes," Brendan said as a sense of serenity enveloped him. William noted his brother's sudden calm demeanor as he looked at him askance, bewildered by his statement.

"I exhibit neither fear nor helplessness!" Meegs insisted.

"You don't," Brendan agreed. "Instead, I see *hope* reflected in your eyes. Exactly what my grandfather saw just before he died."

Meegs, his face wrinkled with contempt, took a step back at what he perceived was Brendan's insolence. William looked on with continued confusion.

"What *are* you talking about?" he whispered to his brother.

Brendan cracked a smile. "Take a look behind you, Will."

Prince William turned around and glanced to the east, the line of snowcapped mountaintops bathed in a luminous white light rising from beneath the horizon. His eyes widened in delight when he noted the dual rims of the full Fox and Bear moons beginning to inch above the skyline side by side, one larger than the other, but each lunar orb defined with a crisp, sharp edge and bathed in a lustrous glow.

"A sign of good fortune if I've ever seen one!" He stared at the twin moonrises in awe along with Meegs and the other soldiers.

"A sign of good fortune? Hardly!" Meegs said with contempt. "Just an old superstition people cling to when the full moons happen to rise together. Or in your case, prince, merely wishful thinking."

Suddenly, everyone felt a faint rumbling underfoot which grew louder in the northwest. They shifted their eyes toward the distant orchards and fields situated above Del Norác. One of the soldiers upon a horse clearly saw what was transpiring and swallowed hard. "Or *is* it?"

Even Meegs appeared shaken when he turned and saw a large contingent of allied forces on horseback galloping at them with raised swords edged with the last rays of the setting sun and the glow of the rising moons. What unnerved him most were the determined figures of King Cedric and Tolapari leading the thunderous charge with unrestrained fury, striking down any of Vellan's troops in their path. Meegs hurriedly consulted with his captains.

"Form your lines and fend them off!" he ordered. "Except for you, Daxen. Grab twenty men and accompany me to the riverbank with those two." He pointed a bony finger at William and Brendan, bound and under guard. "No one is going to stop me from delivering to Vellan two of the finest prizes from today's fight. Now move!"

As most of the troops fell in line and advanced toward King Cedric's approaching storm, Meegs, Daxen and twenty other soldiers surrounded William and Brendan and ushered them toward the river flowing silently in the near distance. The anxiety upon Meegs' face underscored his uncertainty in the success of his plan.

"You'll be dead before we ever reach the water," William said as he and Brendan struggled to slow their progress across the field. "Don't you realize that?"

"Then you will die alongside me!" Meegs shouted.

"And we'll be happy to do so," Brendan taunted.

Suddenly the clattering of swords and guttural shouts of the opposing forces exploded upon the field in the opposite direction. The agitated neighing of horses punctuated a multitude of scattered battles that broke out both on foot and from the saddle, each one unfolding in the shimmering moonlight. Meegs, having seen enough, desperately pointed to the river and urged his men forward.

"There's no time to lose. Run!" he cried out, bitter that his advantage had quickly dissipated when he was on the verge of demonstrating to Vellan his full worth and ingenuity. "Move your feet!" he shouted to his captives.

"Try and make us," William muttered. He dug his heels into the grass, resisting every step of the way much to his brother's pride.

As Meegs angrily pushed them along from behind while surrounded by a contingent of soldiers, he kept peering over his shoulder to gage the enemy's progress. But his protective circle blocked any good view of the conflict.

"I can't see what's going on!" he complained to no one in particular. "Someone give me a report! Daxen, what's happening?"

"The fighting has escalated behind us!" he shouted after maneuvering to the perimeter of their shadowy, moving mass. "Our men are battling bravely despite the overwhelming numbers against them, but—"

"But what?" Meegs sputtered. "What do you see?"

"Trouble!" Daxen eased his way back into the group toward Meegs. "Over a dozen men on horses have broken off from the main force and are heading our way, sir! They are heavily armed."

With a slight turn of his head, Brendan could see the fear and disappointment on Meegs' face at the coming onslaught. And even though the prince knew that he and his brother might be killed in the ensuing clash, he couldn't help but smile that Meegs' plan was about to be disrupted in a most spectacular fashion.

"So much for getting any accolades from Vellan," he said. "Then again, the wizard had no idea that you were planning this abysmal failure. It, like you, will die unnoticed."

"Shut up!" Meegs shouted, resisting the effort to slay Prince Brendan right there.

"Your time is over," William piped up. "That's the cold, hard truth."

"You know nothing!" Meegs snapped. "Keep your mouth closed before I stuff a wad of grass inside and seal it." He leaned in closely between the brothers and dug his fingers into their shoulders as they drew nearer to the river. "Before things end here, and even if I die in the process, I promise that both of you will become servants of Vellan even if I have to pick you up and fling you into the Drusala myself. You will have your eyes opened before the day is done, and that, my friends, is the cold, hard truth!"

But seconds after he uttered those words, the protective ring of soldiers surrounding him began to lose its cohesiveness like a collapsing soap bubble, breaking away in several directions as the deafening sound of thundering steeds drew nearer on either side. Meegs' troops suddenly found themselves engaged in several skirmishes with the swift horsemen weaving about them like a swarm of hornets, their stinging swords finding their foes with ease and making quick work of each one.

"Guess again," Brendan said as Meegs was suddenly exposed in the growing moonlight to the battle raging around him. But he refused to give up.

"It's not over!" he sputtered, grabbing William and Brendan by the arms and trying to pull them toward the river flowing only a few yards away.

But the sibling princes resisted and held their ground despite their bonds. Working together, they dropped to the ground as Meegs had a tight hold on them, causing him to topple over and land hard upon his shoulder. He grunted in pain but quickly shrugged off his injury and jumped to his feet. He unsheathed his sword as William and Brendan struggled to sit up in the grass. When they saw Meegs standing over them with a weapon in hand, their blood ran cold, realizing that he had abandoned his plan to take them to the river. Meegs was about to kill them here, oblivious of the fighting swirling about him.

"You've forced my hand!" he said, his face contorted with rage as he loomed over his prisoners. "Rather than be Vellan's servants in your own land, you will instead be reduced to corpses, rendering Montavia a desolate, kingless realm. You and King Rowan will be forgotten in time, so savor that hollow legacy!" he said while raising his sword to slay them on the spot. "It's all you'll have left after you're–"

Meegs suddenly went silent as he turned, his mouth agape and eyes wide as an armed horseman barreled down upon him, the tip of his sword blazing with moonlight. Meegs barely had time to step backward and fend off the oncoming strike, stunned to near paralysis when the dark haired, unshaven soldier leaped off the charging horse and tackled him to the ground. In one fluid motion, the horsemen unsheathed a dagger and brought it down upon Meegs, killing him instantly before he could utter a word. The cloudiness within his open, lifeless eyes slowly faded beneath the strengthening glow of the Fox and Bear moons. The soldier rushed to William and Brendan who sat staring in awe.

"Did you plan that grand entrance?" William asked with a grin. "Or did it just happen to work out that way?"

"Definitely the latter," Ramsey replied as he knelt down and cut their binding ropes. "And lucky for you it did."

"We can't thank you enough," Brendan said as Ramsey extended them each a helping hand to get back on their feet.

"No need," he replied. "In Rhiál, your brother dramatically saved my life while crouched in the branches of a tree. I thought I'd return the favor. We'll call it even now."

"I'll call it amazing," William said, watching in wonderment as King Cedric and his troops swiftly put an end to Meegs' men. Soon the King and Tolapari trotted over on their horses and looked down upon the two princes.

"I'm delighted beyond words to see both of you breathing and uninjured," King Cedric remarked with a sigh of relief. "But where is your grandfather? I wish to speak with him. There are still war fires blazing all around us."

Any traces of buoyant enthusiasm quickly faded from William and Brendan's faces, replaced with pained and stony expressions. Everyone knew at once that the news would not be good. Brendan pointed farther up the field to the spot where King Rowan had made his last stand, unable to speak the dreadful truth.

"He has passed," William softly spoke, looking up at King Cedric with glassy eyes. "In his last moments, he saved my brother and me, a debt we can never repay."

King Cedric bowed his head, moved by the terrible news. "Your brother can govern Montavia wisely and with boldness in his stead," he responded after gathering himself. "And you, Prince William, can stand by his side in the coming days. That is how you will both repay your grandfather's debt."

"And we shall," Brendan replied, nodding with pride as his heart ached.

King Cedric briefly gazed upon the eastern horizon as the full Fox and Bear moons continued to inch above the mountaintops like two bright, watchful eyes in the heavens. "An augur of good fortune, especially when rising in such a crisp, clear sky. But after the news we just heard, I am not so sure."

"Yet I feel this war is slowly turning in our favor," Tolapari said, gazing upon the dual moons as well. "Perhaps it is a sign of good fortune after all."

"Perhaps," King Cedric replied. He and the wizard followed William, Brendan and Ramsey up the field to King Rowan's body and away from the river as other fighting continued to rage around them in the distance.

Suddenly a tremor shook the ground, agitating the horses that nervously came to a stop. Everyone looked up at Mount Minakaris, instinctively knowing that it was the focal point of the brief vibration.

"What was that?" Ramsey asked.

"I'm not sure," Tolapari replied, combing a hand through his mop of dark hair, visibly distressed.

"Another sign of good fortune?" Brendan said skeptically.

"Nothing about that felt *or* sounded good," William replied as he cast a suspicious eye upon the looming mountain.

Nicholas, Leo and Mune walked to the end of the corridor where they spotted a metal door on the right. It stood ajar, a cool current of air drifting through. Mune carefully pushed it open and stepped into the shadowy chamber. Nicholas and Leo followed, fanning out among the stone pillars to explore. But Nicholas had only taken a few steps when he saw a solitary figure silhouetted against one of the tall arches in the faint glow of the rising moons and the setting sun. When he noted the colorful cloak draped around the person's shoulders, he knew immediately whom he had found.

"Carmella!" he said, hurrying to her.

Upon hearing his voice, she turned around. Her face, wet with teardrops, registered both surprise and joy when she saw him and Leo standing there. Mune kept a cautious distance behind them. She threw her arms around Nicholas and sobbed.

"What happened?" he asked after giving her a moment to compose herself.

"A terrible thing," she said, shaking, her voice hoarse from crying. "Oh, a most terrible thing, Nicholas! And I fear I'm partly to blame."

She explained what had transpired between her and Madeline. Leo leaned over one of the sills and peered down to the coursing stream below, realizing that no one could have survived such a fall. He and Nicholas expressed their deepest sorrow, after which, Carmella insisted on hearing their story. Nicholas explained everything, including their last-minute alliance with Mune. Though knowing Carmella harbored mixed feelings toward him, Mune said he was sorry that Madeline was driven to such a bitter end.

"Though many times she had pushed me to the brink of madness, she certainly didn't deserve this," he said, wiping away a tear. "Caldurian did a horrible thing," he added, catching Carmella's steely gaze. "Well, I shouldn't talk, right?"

"Let's just find Ivy and get out of here," Nicholas said.

"You know where she is?" Carmella asked, taking his hand.

His heart froze as the last bit of hope drifted through the open archways into the dying day. "No," he whispered, crestfallen. "Don't *you*?"

Carmella shook her head. "When Liney released me from my room, Ivy and the guards were already gone. My cousin refused to tell me where they were going."

"So we're back where we started." Nicholas looked at Mune for direction. "Where do we go now? And we haven't much time according to Frist." He glanced at Leo who leaned against one of the arches, visibly tired. "Are you all right? Is the amulet helping?"

"I'm no worse," he said with a faint smile. "But even with Frist's help, I expect my recovery won't be swift. But I'll still be able to leave when you're ready," he promised, gazing out the archway again. He breathed in the fresh air which revived his spirits.

"Mune, tell me where to search," Nicholas pleaded. "Where would Madeline have ordered the guards to take Ivy?"

"The stronghold?" he suggested, not certain of Madeline's intentions. "Ivy would be well protected from rescue down below. Then again, after all the trouble and inconvenience Ivy caused after we kidnapped her, Madeline might have even considered–" He caught himself, not willing to utter the words on his mind. But by their horrified looks, he knew that Nicholas and Carmella had surmised his ghastly thought.

"She wouldn't have!" Nicholas cried. "Not even Madeline would order Ivy's death on a whim. I know she's done some terrible things, but *that*?"

"I can't see her doing that either," Carmella agreed before slowly reconsidering her words. "Then again, Liney was under the influence of that awful potion. I can't begin to imagine how it might have twisted her faculties."

"I won't allow myself to think it!" Nicholas insisted, his patience near a breaking point. "Mune, just make your best guess and tell us where to go."

"Nicholas!" Leo shouted. He turned away from the arch and looked up with nervous excitement. "You may not have to go far," he said, indicating for them to draw near. "Take a look at that dirt road along the stream."

Nicholas hurried over and peered down at the rushing waters not yet fully hidden beneath a stretch of budding trees. He vaguely distinguished the outlines of three people walking down a narrow dirt road east of the stream in the dusky shadows. Two, by the looks of their garments, were soldiers of Kargoth. The third individual between them, shorter in height and wearing a long cloak, was a woman with light brown hair flowing down her shoulders. Nicholas immediately identified the figure in the dimming light.

"*Ivy,*" he whispered, his heart pounding, his mind on fire. But to his horror, Ivy wasn't walking freely with the two men but was being pulled along against her will. To where, he didn't know, but Nicholas vowed not to let her disappear into the wilderness. "Ivy!"

he shouted, his words carried away on a breeze. "*Ivy!*" While struggling to free herself, the woman seemed to have heard something and briefly turned her head. "She can't see me way up here!" Nicholas said frantically, running to Mune. "Tell me how to get down there!"

"What are you going to do?" Leo asked.

"Save her!" he replied, glancing at Mune for instructions.

"Go down two more levels and head east along the corridor," he said. "When you reach the last door on your right, it will lead to another short passageway and then to the outdoors. But I can't promise if any guards will be about."

"All I want are directions."

Leo stepped forward. "I'm going with you."

Nicholas, with an appreciative smile, held his friend back. "No offense, Leo, but you won't be able to keep up with me in your condition. Your job right now is to hold onto that amulet and let Frist bring you back to health."

"A weapon!" Carmella said. "You don't have a weapon!"

Nicholas held up Vellan's head cloth with the dagger still wrapped inside. "I have this for starters. I'll figure out the rest along the way!" he shouted, hurrying to the door. "Now all of you get out of here fast!" He then slipped out of the chamber into the candlelit corridor, rushing for the exit.

Moments later, Nicholas was barreling down a steep set of stairs with his hand against the wall to steady himself, glad that no one else was around. He hurried down a second flight, stopping at an archway on the bottom landing that led into the corridor he sought. He peered into the passageway which was much wider than the ones above and lit with a series of oil lamps similar to those in Deshla prison. He presumed that this area had much more foot traffic than Vellan's personal quarters above, but at the moment, everything was eerily still. Knowing that time was against him, Nicholas darted into the corridor and turned left, hoping for the best as he moved swiftly down the passageway.

Though the corridors had been cut progressively longer both east and west around the mountain on each descending level, Nicholas noted very few chambers on the interior wall to his left to make use of the extra space. To his relief, the doors to each of the rooms were closed. With a rapidly beating heart, he plowed onward, spotting the last two oil lamps just ahead. Each was attached on either side of a metal door to the right with a thin eye slot in its center. With large riveted hinges and an imposing look, the door reminded him of the one he and Leo had stepped through behind the tapestry upon first entering Vellan's abode. This door, however, needed no key and was instead locked with a large sliding bolt that had been slid to one side in the unlocked position. Guessing that Ivy and the two guards had recently passed through, Nicholas cautiously pushed open the door.

He was greeted by the gloom of a short tunnel. Suspended from the center of the low ceiling was an oil lamp producing a sickly light that guided him to the other end and another metal door. It was also unlocked, and through the eye slit, Nicholas saw the faint light of the day's end and a way out of the mountain. He paused before pushing the door open, detecting an odor of smoke. He sniffed the air and realized what he was smelling–pipe smoke. After peering through the slot, his worst suspicion was confirmed. A soldier from Kargoth, grim and unshaven, stood several yards away near a thicket of saplings, smoking a pipe while on guard duty. But knowing that Ivy needed him now more than ever, Nicholas pulled open the door and raced outside, not caring how many soldiers were waiting in the dusky light. But there was only the one guard who tossed aside his pipe, unsheathed a sword and jumped in front of Nicholas to block his way.

"In the name of Vellan, who are you?" His gruff voice rose above the sound of rushing stream water in the near distance. The guard suspiciously eyed Nicholas and the bundle clutched in his hand. "And where'd you come from?"

With his senses reeling, Nicholas uttered the first thing that came to his mind. "I've come with terrible news about Vellan!" he said, staring down the soldier. "I was told by Madeline to deliver it to all the guards."

"I don't believe you," he muttered, taking a step forward. "I think you're a spy."

"I have proof!" Nicholas said, holding up the wizard's head wrap. "Proof to verify my claim that Vellan is dead."

"*Dead?*" The soldier, under the river's influence, clenched his jaw with anger that anyone would say such a thing about his glorious leader. "I should kill you for uttering such traitorous words, but that would deny Vellan the pleasure of witnessing your death."

"It's not a lie!" Nicholas insisted, fearing that Ivy was slipping away. "This material that I hold is the very head covering from Vellan himself." He held up the bundled cloth. "Madeline asked me to deliver it to the garrison in Del Norác."

The soldier noted the familiar dark gray color of the material and wondered if Nicholas might be telling the truth. "Where are your written orders? And why would you go into the city with this information instead of directly to the stronghold below?"

"Another messenger was already sent there," he said, his patience wearing thin. "You must not delay me or you'll have to deal with Madeline's wrath."

The soldier furrowed his brow, still not convinced. "Give me the head wrap!" he ordered, signaling for Nicholas to step forward. He extended his left hand while keeping the weapon raised in his right. "I'll be the judge of where you'll go."

"And I'll be in violation of my orders," he replied with feigned apprehension. "I could get into serious trouble if I give this to you."

"I'll give you serious trouble if you *don't!*" he snapped. "Let me have it!"

"If you insist," Nicholas said with a defeated sigh. He stepped forward as the soldier gazed at him for any sign of deception, the palm of his outstretched hand eagerly waiting to receive the bundle of cloth. "Here you are," he whispered, slowly raising the head wrap as if reluctant to place it into the soldier's hand.

In a swift, single motion, Nicholas slammed the rolled end of the material onto the man's palm. The guard burst out in a bloodcurdling cry as the point of the concealed dagger pierced his hand, sending a bolt of excruciating pain through his body. He dropped his sword and collapsed to the ground, writhing in agony as he yanked the knife from his bloodied skin and bone with an anguished howl. Nicholas, at the same time, swooped down, grabbed the sword and leaped over the soldier. He fled to the nearby dirt road that wound among a swath of budding trees, scattered pines and vibrant green undergrowth.

Nicholas raced down the road which ran parallel to a wide stream on his right, its frothy waters cascading over mossy covered rocks. But he had run only a short distance when the stream curved sharply to the left for a stretch directly in front of him before gradually straightening out again and coursing down the mountainside. A small stone bridge spanned the stream at that point. Nicholas scrambled over it, clutching the sword as he shouted out Ivy's name. When he reached the dirt road on the opposite side, the stream now flowed to his left. On the right side of the road where a portion of the land sloped steeply downward, a low wall of rounded, weather-beaten stones had been constructed following the path of the road for nearly a quarter mile down the mountain.

As Nicholas picked up speed, the trio of figures finally came into view. All moved away from him less than fifty yards ahead. He charged on with silent fury, his heart racing, his lungs burning and his eyes desperately fixed upon Ivy as she grew closer in his sight. To the west beyond the trees, the last red and orange rays of the setting sun filtered through the branches, highlighting their fleshy tips like soft, burning flames. In the east, the diamond white radiance from the rising full moons peeked over the distant mountaintops, stringing the budding leaves and creaking limbs with webs of gauzy light.

"Ivy!" he called out as he drew near, capturing their attention.

"*Nicholas?*" she cried in disbelief, struggling to look back. But the two soldiers pulled her forward, determined to fulfill Vellan's last request. "Nicholas!"

"I'm here, Ivy!" he shouted, gripping his sword as the distance between them melted away.

The soldiers from Kargoth finally took serious notice of their pursuer, throwing worried glances over their shoulders before coming to a halt. They turned around and faced Nicholas while tightly holding Ivy's arms on each side. Nicholas, at last seeing the woman he so dearly loved, came to a sudden stop just a few feet away, his weapon poised and ready to strike.

"Let her go!" he said, his calm, steady words floating upon a sea of rage as the soldiers looked on with uncertainty in their clouded eyes. "I said let her go!"

"Nicholas, how did you find me?" Ivy breathlessly asked, her weary face glowing with hope and amazement at his presence.

"Be silent, girl!" one of the soldiers ordered as he grabbed hold of her with both his arms and pulled her back. The second man unsheathed a sword and stepped forward, staring smugly at Nicholas.

"You don't look like a soldier," he remarked with a grunt.

"But I've been trained by some of the best," Nicholas said, advancing another step.

"Prove it!" The man rushed at him with a sharp blade slicing through the air.

"Look out!" Ivy cried as she fought to break away from the other soldier. But her struggle was to no avail as his strength far outmatched her own.

Nicholas met his attacker with a hardened gaze. They battled along the dirt road, their clattering swords echoing sharply through the trees and off the stone wall as Ivy watched with helpless horror. As Nicholas countered each swipe of the enemy's blade, he recalled his intensive training outside the Blue Citadel and with Malek's men during their long winter in the woods, grateful he had taken the time to properly absorb the lessons.

"Not bad," the soldier begrudgingly remarked as he stepped back for a moment, breathing heavily. "Perhaps you did learn a thing or two from those others."

"I was a quick study," Nicholas said as his foe again rushed at him, each repelling the other's strokes. But when their blades touched on a particularly forceful collision, Nicholas turned slightly to one side upon impact and left his opponent a brief opening. Suddenly he felt the tip of cold steel rip through the clothing on his upper left arm and graze his skin with a stinging bite. He flinched and backed away, gripping his arm.

"You may be a quick study, but humility wasn't one of the lessons!" The soldier leaped up on the stone wall and displayed a triumphant smile.

Nicholas, breathing heavily as he wiped a sleeve across his brow, looked up and shook his head. "Nor was overconfidence, which you seem to be swimming in."

"Are you all right, Nicholas?" Ivy called out.

"I'm fine," he said, glancing her way. "Just give me a moment to finish him off," he added with an uncertain smile before climbing onto the wall and raising his sword, eyeing his foe with disdain. "My blade is just as sharp up here."

"And mine is just as swift," the soldier replied, advancing along the low barrier about the width of his shoulders. The clash of metal swords again rang through the trees.

Nicholas, though, found himself at a disadvantage as he carefully maneuvered each step backward along the wall, glancing at his feet to prevent a fall down the slope to his right. But as the soldier pressed forward, Nicholas noticed in the fading light that one of the surface rocks a few yards behind the man appeared to be loose, the mortar around it having cracked during the frost upheavals of many harsh winters. But every swing of the enemy's weapon pushed Nicholas a step in the opposite direction of the loose rock as the length of wall behind him rapidly disappeared. The hilts of their swords finally crossed with a clang and they glared at each other nose to nose.

"Surrendering in the face of defeat is an honorable option," the soldier remarked.

"Then surrender," Nicholas replied before they pulled back their weapons and again took to the fight.

"Never!" he replied, expertly swinging his sword in an upward arc and grazing Nicholas' left arm in the same spot as before. He leapt backward a few feet atop the wall and gazed at Nicholas' astonished expression. "I've only been playing with you up until now. Rest assured that my third hit will be the last one you'll ever feel."

Nicholas grimaced while clutching his arm, his face sweaty and pale. He wondered if the soldier from Kargoth was speaking the inevitable truth. Yet by leaping back, the man had left more space between them which Nicholas knew he had only a moment to use to his advantage. After glancing at Ivy for support, he charged forward with his weapon raised, catching his opponent momentarily off guard. But the soldier easily repelled each one of Nicholas' sword strikes as he nimbly stepped farther backward along the wall, not intimidated by the change in momentum.

"It would be unsporting of me not to give you at least one moment to shine in this duel," he said as they moved like shadows across the wall, their metal blades clattering in the twilight. "So enjoy it, as it will be a brief one only."

"You now speak without the humility you claim to value," Nicholas said.

"Ah, but a victor doesn't need humility when he is about to stand over the bloodied corpse of his enemy," the soldier replied, once again repelling Nicholas' blade and raising his sword high for what he knew would be a final and fatal strike.

But just as he was about to bring his blade crashing down upon Nicholas, the stone beneath the heel of his left boot suddenly gave way, causing him to lose balance and teeter on the edge of the wall as his bodyweight shifted. The soldier, swinging his arms wildly in the air as he tried to steady himself, saw the point of Nicholas' sword zeroing in on him with deadly precision. He instinctively leaned back to avoid the hit, sending him further off balance until he tumbled over the wall with a harrowing cry and rolled down the steep embankment into the deepening gloom.

Nicholas, breathing heavily as he gripped his weapon, watched the man disappear before turning his attention to Ivy. He jumped off the wall and raced toward her and the second soldier.

"Let her go!" Nicholas cried as he neared them standing alongside the rushing stream, ready to fight the other man on the spot. Then he froze in his tracks.

"You might want to rethink that request," the soldier replied as he held a dagger to Ivy's throat. "Otherwise someone might get hurt."

Nicholas looked worriedly at Ivy as he gripped his sword, unsure how to save her.

"*Nicholas*," she whispered helplessly.

"*Ivy*," he replied, the word barely leaving his lips.

"Are you going to let us continue down the mountain in peace?" the soldier asked. "Or will more blood be spilled?" Nicholas gazed upon the woman he loved as fiery anger burned inside him, yet he was no nearer to a solution as the seconds slipped by. "Answer me!" the man shouted. "What are you going to do?"

As Nicholas was about to reply, a light tremor rumbled through the ground, jarring the pristine landscape for several unsettling seconds. Soon an eerie silence engulfed them. Everyone looked at one another with puzzled concern, feeling as if the mountain had sprung to life and fearing the worst. For a few moments, all stood frozen in uncertainty.

CHAPTER 111

Moonlight and Mist

Caldurian stood on the balcony built into the southern slope of Mount Minakaris, already feeling like the ruler of Kargoth. He was mesmerized by the stunning view while awaiting Gavin's hoped for return. To his left, the brilliant rims of the full Fox and Bear moons ascended above the eastern snowcapped mountains. To his right, the sun had just set between gaps in the stately western peaks. Directly ahead, Del Norác appeared silent, though battles still raged among its streets and fields and along the Drusala River. Far below lay the maze of rooftops and spires of Vellan's stronghold constructed at the foot of the mountain. Caldurian was eager to control the forces stationed inside once he secured a deal with King Justin to end the war, hoping he had acted quickly enough.

He noted a black speck moving through the air far away above the city, but it swiftly closed in on him. Moments later, Gavin landed like a dark shadow on the balcony railing and cawed sharply.

"What are *you* doing here?" the crow asked suspiciously.

"Awaiting your arrival," Caldurian replied.

"Where is the true wizard of Mount Minakaris?" Gavin made no effort to hide his shock that Caldurian was standing on one of Vellan's favorite spots. "I've never talked to anybody at this location except Vellan himself. What mischief is afoot?"

"Mischief? You read too much into this encounter. I am only here to learn if King Justin is being brought to the stronghold."

Gavin bobbed along the railing, eyeing Caldurian with mild distrust. "So Vellan has made you privy to his plan?"

"Of course he did! Though we've had our differences of late, I'm still a valued member of his inner circle," he said, resentful for having to justify his actions to a crow. "Vellan wants to know when the King will arrive, and the sooner, the better."

"Unfortunately, it will be a long wait. I saw an injured King Justin being rescued a short while ago in the apple orchard. Many of Vellan's soldiers were killed in the adjoining field. Soon afterward, King Cedric and the wizard Tolapari led a contingent on horseback to the east field, though I do not know the result of that foray."

Caldurian shook his head, visibly disappointed. "That is not the news I wished to hear, Gavin, but I may yet salvage a victory now that you've arrived. You must take a message to King Justin for me at once. It is of the utmost importance."

"For *you*?" the crow asked, his suspicion again rising.

"For Vellan!" he clarified with growing frustration. "I am implementing his orders, of course, and wish you would follow them without question."

"I do!" Gavin said, snapping his beak. "But I have always taken my direct orders from Vellan *from* Vellan. Where is he?"

"Busy! Now just listen to the message I want you to deliver."

The crow glared loathingly at Caldurian and flapped its wings, causing the wizard to flinch. "Before I take flight again, I demand to know where Vellan is and why you seem to have taken charge."

Caldurian breathed deeply to control his temper. "I am giving orders as Vellan has temporarily transferred rule of Kargoth to me."

"What nonsensical rubbish is this, wizard? Where is Vellan?"

"All you need to know is that—"

"Where is he, Caldurian? Tell me or I will find him myself!"

"I forbid you to do any such thing!" he ordered, shaking his fist. If Gavin ever found Vellan unconscious upon the floor, the wizard feared that his plan would disintegrate. He was certain that the bird would accuse him of the villainous act.

Sensing that Caldurian was lying, Gavin squawked with derision and flew off, skirting the mountain to the west while ignoring Caldurian's angry shouts to return. Soon the crow reached the stone terrace on the southwest slope, its door still ajar. He passed through into Vellan's private room, dismayed to find it empty, and then flew down the adjoining corridor, wondering if the wizard was still eating his supper. But when the crow entered the kitchen chamber bathed in the glow of the fireplaces, he immediately spotted Vellan's lifeless body sprawled upon the floor. Gavin perched on the nearby table and looked down at the cold corpse, shaken with horror when eyeing the large blood stain soaking through the garments over his chest.

"What has he done to you?" the crow sputtered, assuming that Caldurian had killed the wizard of Mount Minakaris. "How could he betray you like this?"

But having been well versed by Vellan in some wizarding lore, Gavin quickly realized that he couldn't possibly be dead as his body still retained its corporeal form. Retaining a flicker of hope that he might yet be alive, the crow alighted upon Vellan's shoulder and gazed upon his pale face. But unable to detect the slightest rise or fall of the wizard's chest, he bobbed his head anxiously, at a loss as to why Vellan's body still remained whole even in death. He let loose a series of loud, desperate caws, trying to revive the corpse though knowing that it was a vain effort.

"Vellan!" he called, gingerly stepping along the body. "Wake up!" Gavin suddenly stopped, frozen in place for several astonished moments as faint mist slowly began to rise from the wizard's body. It enveloped the bird's ebony feathers like ghostly tendrils of fog drifting off the surface of a lake on a cold, autumn morning.

At that same moment four levels below, Carmella and Mune guided a weakened Leo through the short tunnel leading to the southeast exit. The spirit of Frist, working through the amulet around Leo's neck, could no longer hold back Vellan's inevitable fate and relinquished its hold, at last allowing the wizard's imprisoned spirit to escape like a caged, angry beast breaking through its confines. As the trio passed through the door and stepped outside the mountain, the white mist rising from Vellan's corpse intensified. The wizard's body grew more tenuous, weakening and withering away like a fragile bubble of soap. Gavin, his talons sinking into the collapsing garments, flapped its wings and ascended to the tabletop. He looked down upon the body, realizing with horror what was happening and knowing that the mountain interior would not be a safe place to remain.

"My condolences, wise one. But a dangerous mist rises, so I must be off!" Gavin punctuated his words with a powerful squawk before flying through the archway and into the curving corridor.

As Vellan's corpse disintegrated into a voluminous and roiling mist, Gavin sped down the passageway, his fleeting shadow painting the wall in a wild blur. He passed through the west chamber and then burst through the mountainside doorway into the cool evening air. He tore back around the mountain to the balcony on the southern face. There he again perched upon the stone railing, much to Caldurian's surprise.

"I didn't expect you back," the wizard said, noting the crow's agitated state.

"You killed him!" he cried, flapping his wings as he jumped at Caldurian. "How could you, traitor?"

"What are you talking about?" Caldurian slapped the air to keep Gavin at bay. "Vellan is not dead, you fool, but only asleep. I drugged his stew with rasaweed!"

Gavin settled down on the railing, glaring at the wizard. "He's dead, I tell you. I stood next to the bloody stab wound in his chest!"

"Stab wound?" Caldurian's hands began to shake as the color drained from his face. "What dreadful news is this?"

Gavin, realizing that Caldurian was unaware of the wizard's death, tightly folded his wings and dug his claws into the stone. "What I saw only moments ago was white mist rising from Vellan's body—and we both know what that means!"

"*White mist?*" Caldurian's mouth was agape. He placed a hand to his chin as he slowly shook his head. "But how?"

A slight tremor then coursed through the mountainside, forcing Caldurian to grab onto the railing to steady himself. Gavin flapped his wings and rose into the air before settling back down when the quaking stopped.

"What was that?" he asked, though suspecting the answer.

"I'm afraid that Vellan is no more," Caldurian whispered in grave tones. Moments later, a second, stronger tremor rattled the mountainside, throwing him onto the balcony floor where he lay immobilized until the shaking finally stopped. He slowly rose to his hands and knees, wincing in pain as he looked up at Gavin, his eyes filled with fear. "What happened, my friend? Where have I gone wrong in my calculations?"

"I care about neither of those questions," Gavin replied with a skittish flap of his wings. "All I know is that my place is no longer upon this mountainside. And if you had any sense, you would take your leave as well. Goodbye, Caldurian!" He flew off, sailing into the silvery twilight like a leaf caught in a breeze.

"Gavin, wait!" he shouted, slapping his hands upon the railing while still on his knees. He brushed aside the iron gray locks dangling in front of his eyes.

The wizard gazed into the silent void before him, his thoughts twisting. He then noted a subtle sound that caught his ear like a sharp, distant call in a restless dream. He turned his head to the right, noting a blot of slushy snow that had fallen to the floor with a dull splat. The wizard furrowed his brow, confused as to where the snow had come from until a second, larger globule hit the railing close by, the resulting spray of water splattering his face and causing him to jump to his feet.

"What's going on?" he muttered, not grasping the full extent of the situation as a sharp crack rippled through the face of the mountainside far above like a thunderclap. Caldurian spun around with his back to the railing, spooked by the intimidating sound. He cast his eyes up the side of Mount Minakaris, his heart beating wildly. "What *is* that?" he asked as if both expecting and fearing the answer from above. And then he received it.

All at once near the summit, layers of weighty snow, ice and rock separated from the weakened face and began sliding down the steep, southern slope in a single roaring mass, grinding out a vast pathway down the center of the mountain with breathtaking force and speed. Caldurian heard the ear-shattering sound before he saw what was happening. Ice chips and tiny pebbles rolled off the mountainside and rained onto the balcony at his feet, oddly amusing him when he glanced at the bits of debris clattering musically upon the stone surface. Then the truth struck him like an arrow as he looked up. The roar of the descending ice and rock echoed so loudly in his ears that he couldn't hear himself contemplating his final seconds of life while watching the mist-and-dust enveloped avalanche roar at him head-on like a hard wave and erase him instantly as it continued on its wild descent, gouging through rock, trees and streams while gathering strength, until finally crushing, collapsing and burying Vellan's stronghold at the mountain's base and leaving behind a vast pile of muddy, dusty debris towering higher than the surrounding pines that hadn't snapped or toppled in the deadly strike. When the dust cloud eventually settled, a deep, wide scar ran all the way down the southern slope of Mount Minakaris, highlighted in the lustrous glow of the rising dual moons and visible to all for miles around like a fatal gash that had at last taken down a fabled and deadly beast.

Moments earlier, Eucádus struggled to breathe as Ranen tightened his grasp around his neck as they fought on the central bridge. He had Eucádus pinned against the western railing, ready to kill his former friend without regret since he would not join Vellan's side. But as Eucádus grew lightheaded, a slight tremor rolled through the region and shook the bridge as if it had been built upon sand, catching both men by surprise. Ranen loosened his grip just enough in the commotion, allowing Eucádus an energizing breath of air. With his back still pressed over the railing, he grabbed Ranen's injured wrist and dug his thumb into the sword wound until he howled in pain and leapt backward. Eucádus jumped up, ready to retaliate as a flood of rage and betrayal coursed through him. But as he glanced over Ranen's shoulder, a tranquil smile slowly crossed his face when seeing the brilliant edges of the full Fox and Bear moons inching above the eastern mountaintops.

"You think you have won, taunting me with that smug grin?" Ranen asked, rubbing his bloody wrist.

Eucádus shook his head. "This is not smugness, but *wonder*. Look behind you!" He pointed at the dual moons. "They're even more beautiful rising in a clear sky."

Ranen glanced over his shoulder, seemingly unimpressed. "If the full Fox and Bear supposedly herald good fortune, then it is all flowing Vellan's way," he said with confidence. "So that's a strike against you. Now shall we finish this fight with blades?" he asked, indicating their swords lying upon the bridge a short distance away. "Or continue as we were?" he added, holding up his hands.

"You decide the method of your downfall," Eucádus quipped, eliciting a sneer from Ranen. But before he spoke another word, a second, more forceful tremor rocked the bridge and roiled the water below it, throwing them both to the ground.

They met the stone with audible groans and lay there until the shaking stopped. As they slowly stood, a deep and powerful rumbling drifted from the north and filled the air as if an angry herd of cattle were stampeding beneath a thunderous sky. The two men instinctively glanced at the mountain and noted a narrow, cloudy strip of dust and snow racing down the southern slope, seemingly in destructive slow motion.

"That can't be good fortune for Vellan," Eucádus remarked, his astonished eyes glued fixedly to Mount Minakaris. "Don't you agree?" He turned to Ranen who suddenly charged at him like a crazed bull.

"I'll decide the method of *your* downfall!" he cried, lunging at Eucádus and shoving him against the western side of the bridge so that his upper body lay suspended backward above the now swiftly moving river.

Eucádus absorbed the full impact of Ranen's hit which drove the breath out of him and sent a spasm of pain through his body. Both men fought, crazed and wildly off balance, and after teetering upon the top of the railing for a few seconds, they tumbled over the side and dropped like stones with a terrific splash into the choppy waters below.

They plummeted beneath the surface which boiled like a kettle over fire, yet the water remained cold. Eucádus held his breath as his descent slowed, a swirl of strange emotions overwhelming him. He felt as if two faceless voices were competing for his loyalty and devotion, the first promising a life of boundless joy and ease while the other offered only a trail of intermittent struggles and sadness. Yet as he rose to the surface, he detected a dreary emptiness and soullessness in that first voice which repelled him, making him long for the invigorating and strengthening force of the second. But both voices dissipated from his mind when he burst through the surface and gulped down the sweet, cool air of the evening as the Drusala bubbled riotously around him.

When he glanced toward the north bank, he saw Ranen emerging from underwater as well. But before he could shout or swim over to him, the current grew more powerful and carried the two men down the river. With only seconds to spare before being swept under one of the bridge arches, they each swam a few quick strokes toward the other, positioning themselves to be pushed against the nearest bridge support. Moments later, their bodies were slapped against a wide, stone support as they struggled to hold onto the crevices in the masonry. And though they were only a few feet away from each other, neither could communicate over the noisy rush of water that battered them relentlessly. They held on and waited for the river to calm, wondering what had caused the strange and powerful turmoil along the Drusala. Soon their eyes widened in disbelief as they gazed westward, sensing that things were about to get worse.

Just beyond the western border of Del Norác, the Drusala River curved northward into the surrounding mountains and woods. It was here at a point on the river near the southern reaches of the Champeko Forest where Vellan had years ago cast his enchantment upon the water, causing his spell to flow down through Kargoth and beyond. Now, at that same spot, after the second tremor had sent shockwaves through the ground and roiled the waters of the Drusala, a burst of cold stream erupted from below the river like a geyser, sending a thick blanket of mist rolling over the surface and upon the banks on either side. Following the path of the Drusala, a dense, rolling wave of white mist continued to shoot out of the water, moving like a swift snake. Eucádus and Ranen saw the approaching wall of fog racing above the distant treetops like a giant, ghostly apparition until it curved around the western river bend and made straight for them. The men gripped the stonework and tucked their heads into their arms as the wall of mist continued to burst up from the water and swept past them, swooping over and beneath the arches like a wild wind that sped beyond the city until it disappeared down the river valley to the eastern reaches of Kargoth.

The water continued to shove Eucádus against the bridge support, but each successive wave grew weaker until the surface of the river was once again calm. The relentless noise that battered his eardrums had quieted as he slowly lifted his head and looked around. But he could see very little as the river, the bridge and the area along the banks on either side were bathed in a soupy, white mist. He called out Ranen's name, but getting no reply, he feared the worst and swam to the north bank near the garrison.

He reached shore and crawled out dripping wet through the thinning mist and collapsed in exhaustion, not caring if the enemy might be around. After resting a few moments, he raised his head. *The enemy!* Eucádus realized that he still considered Vellan and his army as the enemy. Though lured by the river's magic, he had not succumbed to the enchantment of the Drusala and wondered why, having been awash in its turbulent waters for so long. But before he figured out the answer, a gentle breeze dispersed some of the moonlit mist along the bank. Another body lay facedown close by, apparently asleep as he noted the steady rise and fall of the individual's back. Streaming down the person's shoulders was a rope of long, black hair tied with a familiar blood red ribbon.

Eucádus sat up, tired and sore, yet wary of the danger posed by his former friend. "Ranen?" he softly called. "Can you hear me?"

Ranen's body shifted as he deeply exhaled. Moments later, his eyes opened. He turned his head and faced Eucádus, looking at him with confusion and weariness. Eucádus, however, detected a drastic change in Ranen's expression that he had not seen a quite a while, a familiar air that recalled to mind better times and unbroken bonds of friendship.

"*Eucádus*? Is that you?" Ranen asked, wondering how he had come to be in this place.

"Yes, my friend. Are you hurt?"

"My wrist hurts," he muttered, slowly sitting up and wincing. "And where–" He looked around bleary-eyed, scratching his head. "Where are we?"

"That is a long story," he replied, grinning with joy. "But one I'll be more than happy to tell you after we properly fix your injury."

He observed a vibrant clarity in Ranen's eyes that dispelled the anguish in his heart. Gone was the cloudy veneer of hopelessness and despair that had lately defined Ranen. Vellan's spell had somehow been broken, and because of that, the leader of the Oak Clearing, and Eucádus' dear friend, had at last returned to the land of the living.

William and Brendan somberly led King Cedric and Tolapari to their grandfather's body. As they recounted the story of his valiant death, the second, stronger tremor coursed through the ground. The violent shaking made the land rise and fall in spots as if a giant serpent was burrowing just beneath the surface, toppling several people in their group to the ground. King Cedric and Tolapari, who had just dismounted their steeds, grabbed onto the horses to steady themselves during the powerful upheaval until it subsided.

"I'm beginning to think the good fortune of the rising full moons is but a childish myth," Ramsey said as he stood up and brushed himself off.

"As am I," Brendan agreed, getting to his feet and extending a helping hand to his brother. "Strange things are happening here."

"I even hear a roll of thunder though the sky is clear for miles," William said.

"That isn't thunder," Tolapari said ominously, pointing north at Mount Minakaris. "*Look!*"

Everyone turned and stared in awe at a distant avalanche of snow, ice and rock coursing down the southern slope of the mountain and flattening Vellan's stronghold as if it were crushing a hut of sticks and clay. Left behind was a narrow scar running down the center of Minakaris and an enormous cloud of dust that swirled and somersaulted in the shimmering moonlight.

"A childish myth?" King Cedric remarked to Ramsey with a glint in his eyes.

William shook his head, momentarily speechless. "Can you explain what just happened?" he finally asked the wizard, tugging at Tolapari's sleeve.

"I cannot," he replied, his eyes still fixated on the incredible sight before turning to the prince. "The particulars elude me. But if those tremors and the mountain's fall is any proof, I think I can safely say that Vellan's power no longer holds sway in Kargoth."

"Would that it were so," King Cedric remarked with cautious optimism. "But I should like more proof."

"You may soon have it," Brendan replied with astonishment as he glanced west up the river. He indicated for the others to look as a wall of thick mist shot wildly out of the water among the distant trees. It swiftly emerged around a bend in the river and sailed eastward along the watery course, unhindered by the bridges as it swept past them with lightning fury and disappeared far down the valley, leaving behind in its wake a listless fog drifting lazily over the Drusala and lapping upon its dewy banks.

"Proof enough?" Tolapari asked with a mirthful chuckle.

"It will do for now," the King replied, shaking his head in wonderment as everyone else looked on with similar expressions. Each speculated how badly the interior of the mountain must now look compared to the destruction outside.

Their bewilderment only multiplied moments later when a deafening silence blanketed the field, punctuated with the brief, persistent clattering of discarded swords about the landscape. Everyone was astounded to see that nearly all of the fighting had stopped. Troops from Vellan's army wandered about in a daze, their swords dropping from their hands or tossed aside in horror upon realizing what they had been doing. Soldiers from King Justin's allied armies, who only moments ago were battling Vellan's men to the death, now walked up to them and spoke comforting words, explaining to the confused men where they were and how they had arrived here. Even men from the Northern Isles who had not drunk from the river relinquished their weapons, some surrendering on the spot while others, sensing defeat, fled into the woods and hills, all weary of the long and brutal war.

King Justin witnessed similar scenes along the streets of Del Norác, having walked with Prince Gregory and Malek from the apple orchard to the city's northern border. Despite his injured shoulder that throbbed with pain and greatly tired him, the King listened to many stories by men now freed from Vellan's enchantment as he made his rounds. Soldiers in his army, at first shocked by the enemy's sudden surrender, explained to their former foes where they were and how they had succumbed to Vellan's will.

"I had been captured with several others during an Enâri raid on our village in Linden," a young man told a group of soldiers while King Justin, Prince Gregory and Malek looked on. The man's eyes were now as clear as crystalline water. "We were forced to march for many grueling days to Kargoth. The last thing I remember was stooping down by a river for a drink that the Enâri captain happily allowed us to take. And now I just woke up *here*," he added, looking around in dismay at the injured and dead. "But that was late *last* spring since you say we are now in the year seven forty-three." He sat down on the stone steps of a burnt and battered shop and sighed. "I can't imagine my wife's state of mind right now." He looked up at King Justin, pale with worry. "I wonder if I'll ever see her again. She's the love of my life."

Nicholas looked at Ivy with growing fear after the first tremor had ceased. The soldier from Kargoth, holding her at knifepoint near the rushing stream, awaited his decision to either fight or allow them to proceed down the mountain. Nicholas knew that a sudden attack on his part might alarm the man and end Ivy's life. Letting him leave with her as a prisoner seemed the only viable option, though Nicholas was already planning a silent pursuit through the woods afterward.

"Decide now!" the man shouted, his whiskered face contorted beneath a pair of clouded eyes that looked on in a deadened stare. "Or I will decide for you." He pressed the flat end of the blade against Ivy's neck as her hands and lips trembled.

"Wait!" Nicholas called out, gazing upon Ivy as tears welled in his eyes. He knew he must let her go one more time in order to have any chance of saving her, and the decision shattered his already broken heart. But as he was about to concede to the enemy, Ivy offered a wisp of a smile, indicating that she understood his dilemma.

"It's all right, Nicholas," she softly said as a tear rolled down her cheek. "The day is not yet over."

He tried to offer a comforting smile as he gripped the hilt of his sword, understanding that he couldn't win this particular battle by fighting. "I love you, Ivy, and I'll never stop searching for you," he said. "*Never.*" He wiped a tear from his face and let the sword fall to the ground.

"I love you too, Nicholas. And we *will* be together one day. I know it."

"But not today," the soldier remarked, knowing he had bested Nicholas and could get on his way. "Kick that sword over here."

With grudging obedience, Nicholas struck the sword hilt with the tip of his boot and sent it sliding over the dirt road until it lay within the soldier's reach. The man bent down and grabbed the weapon, his eyes and dagger upon Ivy all the while. He cast it into the stream where it disappeared into the frothy, moonlit waters.

"Now what?" Nicholas said with contempt.

"Turn around and walk away," he said. "And if I glance over my shoulder and see you following, she'll pay the price." He gripped Ivy by the arm until she nearly cried out.

"Stop hurting her!" Nicholas shouted, using all his willpower to keep from lunging at the soldier.

"She'll be fine," he replied with a smirk, "once she drinks from the river."

"I'll never do such a thing!" Ivy said as she put up a struggle.

"You'll die if you don't!" he told her before glancing sharply at Nicholas. "Now leave!" he ordered, placing the knife close to Ivy's throat. "This is my last warning."

Nicholas, reluctantly preparing to do as instructed, gazed lovingly upon Ivy, still not fully convinced that leaving was the right thing to do. Seeing the hesitation in his eyes, she gently nodded to ease his overwhelming guilt.

"Go on," she whispered. "Do as he says."

"Listen to your woman and leave!" the soldier angrily replied. "It is time to end this madness."

"*Very much so.*"

Nicholas was about to walk away when he thought he heard a familiar voice whispering in a breeze. He hesitated, not sure if he had imagined it as a heavy silence settled among the trees and mossy rocks. Ivy noted the puzzled look upon his face while her captor clenched his jaw in frustration, ready to explode. Then the second tremor mercilessly rocked the mountain.

All at once, Nicholas, Ivy and the enemy soldier were knocked to the ground. The trees around them swayed and creaked in the sudden upheaval and the stream water sloshed over the sides of its stony banks. The shaking lasted for a few seconds and then stopped. Nicholas, easing himself up on one knee, saw that Ivy and the soldier had been separated in the fall and jumped to his feet, ready to leap between her and her captor. But the soldier, anticipating such a move, scrambled to his feet with the dagger in hand and planted himself between Nicholas and Ivy, ready to strike.

He and Nicholas glared at one another, silently daring the other to make a move, when a deep, distant rumbling reverberated through the air. Around the mountainside to their west, at a higher elevation and out of their sightline, an avalanche let loose and roared down the rocky slope in a thunderous din. And though the trio couldn't see a thing, they heard the cracking of stone, the shattering of ice, and soon thereafter, what sounded like the snapping of trees as the growing roar gained speed in its descent. Moments later, clouds of dust and fine snow billowed high into the sky to the west in a line that began near the summit of Mount Minakaris and extended down the center of the southern slope. Soon a steady gust of wind blasted past them, swaying the tree branches and raining specks of sand and ice. Finally, a horrific crash sounded below near the mountain base before all went eerily quiet.

The soldier from Kargoth, still poised between Nicholas and Ivy, looked around in a daze. He wondered where he was and why he was holding a knife as the shimmering moonlight filtered through the trees. Nicholas noted that the glazed, cloudy appearance of the man's eyes had cleared up and the tension in his face had vanished, making him appear younger and unthreatening compared to seconds ago.

"Where am I?" he asked, stepping aside so that Nicholas and Ivy now faced one another with similarly perplexed expressions. The man dropped his dagger with a look of disgust and remorse, fearing he may have threatened the two strangers. "Forgive me if I tried to hurt you," he softly told them, rubbing his hands across the sides of his head as if trying to jog his memory. "But I am at a loss."

"It's all right," Ivy whispered with a gentle smile, walking toward him without fear. "You have not been yourself lately."

"Nor have many others," Nicholas said. "But I think that's about to change."

The man, whose name was Lacarus, explained that he was a farmer miles outside the southeastern border of Kargoth near the Drusala River. "It seems like years since I was plowing my land, but I'm not entirely sure. The last thing I remember was watering my horses along the river while transporting a load of hay. I bent down to cup some water for myself, and then..." He stared at Nicholas and Ivy. "I don't remember anything more until just now as I stand here between the two of you. What has happened?"

"More than we can say," Nicholas said, briefly telling him about Vellan's spell upon the river and of the recent war. "And since the spell has apparently been broken, something tells me that this conflict might be over, too." He glanced south toward Del Norác and his eyes widened. "Look!" he said, pointing at a distant white line snaking its way through the city. "A thick fog covers the river."

"It's both ghostly and beautiful," Ivy whispered in awe.

"Indeed," Lacarus said, turning to them in a daze. "I am far from my family and home. May I now leave and seek them out?"

"Of course!" Ivy said. "You needn't ask our permission. You belong with them."

"Go at once," Nicholas insisted, "though you may first want to stop in Del Norác for provisions and information. We shall do the same. I suspect lots of people will soon be traveling in all directions to reunite with their loved ones."

"Then I'll be off," he said, thanking them for their kindness. Nicholas picked up his knife and handed it back to him with a smile. Moments later, the man hurried down the dirt road until he disappeared into the distant trees.

Nicholas and Ivy looked at one another with joyful amazement, their minds and bodies on the verge of exhaustion, yet their hearts and souls as warm and light as a summer morning. With uncontainable smiles, they walked the last few steps between them and collapsed into each other's arms. They sobbed and whispered loving words long held in their hearts during a separation that seemed to have gone on for a lifetime since first meeting in the evening shadows in Castella's backyard in Boros.

Nicholas gazed into Ivy's eyes and touched her soft hair as she stood with the moonlight behind her, knowing that her presence wasn't a dream but at last a glorious reality. When she smiled with his same blissful wonder, he couldn't help but smile in return, knowing they had walked through fire and darkness to reach this moment in time. Holding each other tenderly, they kissed in the cool mountain air. The rushing stream flowed past, its waters imbued with the glow of the Fox and Bear moons rising above the snowcapped mountains in the east on their long trek together across the starry sky in search of the far horizon.

CHAPTER 112

A City of Tents

"I feel as if I'm dreaming," Ivy whispered. She held tightly to Nicholas in the moonlit woods, listening to his calming heartbeat and never wanting to let go as her spirit soared to joyous heights.

"You are not dreaming," he assured her, looking deeply into her eyes. "And I promise this will never happen to you again."

"*Never?*"

He kissed her and smiled. "I'll always be at your side, Ivy, to protect you and share your life." He chuckled. "You'll probably grow tired of seeing my face."

"That will never happen," she replied, suddenly shifting her gaze beyond his shoulder. "Though *his* face I wouldn't regret never seeing again."

"*Hmmm?*" Nicholas turned around as three figures strolled down the dirt road toward them. He grinned with relief upon seeing Leo and Carmella walking alongside the stone wall with Mune a few paces behind. He took Ivy's hand and hurried over to greet them, guessing that she would be less than pleased that he and Leo had made an alliance with Mune to rescue her.

"You're both safe!" Carmella exclaimed, rushing forward and wrapping her arms around Nicholas and Ivy at the same time. She and Ivy had become fast friends during their imprisonment in the mountain.

Leo gave her a hug as well. "It's good to see you again, Ivy, and under better circumstances than last time," he said, recalling their adventure along the grasslands. He started to remove the amulet from around his neck, planning to return it to Nicholas. "I think it's time this went back to its rightful owner."

"Not so fast," Nicholas said, preventing him from taking it off. "Though the color has returned to your face, you are far from cured. Keep that amulet close to you until we're fully certain. At the very least you shall wear it until after dawn tomorrow. If not for your sake, then for Megan's."

Leo nodded appreciatively and placed the amulet beneath his shirt. "Understood. I'll wait to see what tomorrow brings. But in the meantime, where shall we go?"

"Straight down the mountain," Carmella said, pointing along the road. "When I arrived here with Caldurian and Mune, we entered the mountain through a lower doorway perhaps another mile below. There's a patch of flat land nearby with stables and a row of smithies. Hopefully, my wagon is still there in one piece."

Mune, meanwhile, stood uncomfortably in the background, averting his eyes whenever Ivy looked at him. Nicholas intervened to defuse the awkward situation.

"We all have questions we can answer on our way down, but I think Ivy needs to know now why Mune is walking freely with us," he said.

"Instead of being bound and gagged?" Leo joked.

"Very amusing," Mune dryly remarked. "Especially after I guided you out of Minakaris before it crashed in on itself."

"That is a point in your favor," he admitted.

Nicholas told Ivy how Mune had set off the chain of recent events by killing Vellan and explained how he had led them to her. Ivy was more than understanding, though her distrust of Mune remained unchanged. When she learned of Madeline's fate, she expressed sincere condolences to Carmella despite the hardships that the woman had caused her.

"Liney proceeded down a dark and twisted path many years ago," Carmella said with deep sadness, "though unfortunately I wasn't able to reach her in time and turn her back. But she is at rest now, though I shall miss her despite her deeds." She wiped away a tear. "But we should move on, luckily with the moonlight to guide us. So follow me. It's quite a hike to the bottom of the mountain."

When they reached the stables in a large clearing, Carmella found her wagon alongside one of the smithies just as she had left it several days ago. A few horses grazed freely among the grass, but not a soul was around. After Vellan's spell had been broken, Nicholas guessed that everyone had probably left to return to their homes after releasing the animals. Leo chose two sturdy and cooperative horses to hitch to Carmella's wagon, and after Ivy insisted on bandaging Nicholas' wound, they were soon back on the road following the course of the stream. Mune served as Carmella's driver, saying it was the least he could do after all he had put her through. But after only a few minutes, he reined the horses to a stop, having caught sight of something along the stream bank to their left. Mune jumped off the seat and ran to the water.

"What's he doing?" Ivy asked.

"I'm not sure," Nicholas replied.

They stood with Carmella near the horses, waiting for Mune to return. Leo was resting in back of the wagon. Nicholas eyed Mune through the shadows and saw him drop to one knee near the water's edge, frantically signaling everyone to join him. They did so, shocked at his discovery.

Mune, with head buried in hand, knelt somberly next to Madeline's body which had washed up onto the bank along a stony section of the stream. Nicholas, after giving him a moment to compose himself, helped him carry her body away from the water and set it on a tuft of tall grass and weeds. Ivy wrapped a comforting arm around Carmella as they stood over her cousin's body a short time later to pay their respects. After letting Carmella grieve for a time in private, Nicholas and Mune buried the body beneath a white birch tree and marked the gravesite with a ring of stones gathered from the edge of the stream.

"May she find rest and peace here," Carmella said while standing near the burial site. She dabbed away a few tears with the remaining beige glove that she used to wear. When she was ready to leave, she noticed Mune leaning against the birch tree with one arm. "Are you all right?" she softly asked, walking over to him.

Mune looked up, his eyes red and his face damp from crying. "I'm going to stay here a while longer," he said. "And after that, I..." He sighed, shaking his head in sorrow. "I shall leave in the morning, I suppose, and go where the road takes me. But right now I just want to sit here beside Madeline's resting spot and spend some time with her, if you have no objections. To be honest, I need to have a long think with myself."

"I have no objection," Carmella said, patting him lightly on the shoulder. She and Ivy returned to the wagon, leaving Nicholas alone with him.

"I'll tell King Justin what you did inside the mountain," Nicholas told him. "I no longer have Vellan's head wrap or the knife that killed him, but with all the resulting signs of destruction, I don't think the King will need much additional proof."

Mune offered a vague smile. "I suppose I can't ask for more than that," he said, nodding with thanks. "Have a safe journey now."

"We will," he replied, then turned and walked away.

As they started down the road with Nicholas at the reins, Carmella cast a final look at her cousin's gravesite. She took comfort that Mune was holding a silent vigil by the circle of stones among the thick shadows, his shoulders trembling, his head bowed to his chest, and a hand, wet with teardrops, pressed to his face.

They traveled at a leisurely pace. Nicholas, guiding the horses with Ivy at his side, was happy not rushing someplace or fleeing someone as he had done for the last six months. Life had been a whirlwind, but now he savored this tranquil moment with her, their arms interlocked as they shared quiet and heartfelt words. He glanced at her from time to time as the wagon rattled on, reassuring himself that she was not merely part of a restless dream like the many he had had over the past several weeks.

"Don't worry, Nicholas. I'm not going anywhere," she said when catching him gazing at her. "Unless, of course, it's with you."

"Glad to hear it," he replied playfully. "I'm tired of chasing you all around Laparia."

Moments later, she rested her head upon his shoulder. "I missed you," she whispered before closing her eyes to sleep. Nicholas focused on the road ahead, a contented smile upon his face.

When he glanced at Carmella on the opposite end of the seat, he noticed that she had closed her eyes as well, exhausted from her many adventures and overwhelming grief. Nicholas guessed that Leo, too, was still sound asleep in back of the wagon, hoping that Frist's magic would heal him.

He guided the wagon through the silvery light of the dual moons, happy to watch over his friends. He would gladly forego some much needed sleep to get them safely down Minakaris. Despite all the hardships he had endured in recent months, Nicholas believed that his three traveling companions had suffered the most lately and deserved this brief respite before their journey home.

He thought of Kanesbury and all the complications he had left behind after fleeing during the Harvest Festival. But he harbored none of the fears that had plagued him earlier. He was now armed with new information, and more importantly, the support of new friends, and looked forward to returning and clearing his name. Nicholas sighed as he gazed at the Fox and Bear moons through the branches, hoping that his friends and acquaintances back home looked forward to seeing him return as well.

After reaching the bottom of the mountain early that evening, Nicholas stopped along a stream near some trees and built a fire. He, Ivy and Carmella shared a meager dinner from the provisions inside the wagon. As Leo hadn't yet stirred, they decided to let him be, knowing that a recuperative slumber would serve him well. Soon afterward, they drifted off to sleep themselves.

Nicholas awoke at sunrise and sat up yawning by the cold embers while wrapped in a blanket. A faint mist hung over the distant river, though it was much diminished from the night before. In the gaps between the western peaks, he watched as the Fox and Bear moons dipped below the horizon. After breakfast with Ivy and Carmella, he decided that it was time to wake Leo and then drive into Del Norác to see how their friends had fared.

"He should be rested for the next three days," he joked to Ivy. Nicholas opened the wagon door and let in the morning light. He gently prodded Leo's shoulder as he lay on his side bundled in several blankets, his breathing steady and his complexion fair. "Time to rise and roll," he said. "Better hurry before the kitchen closes."

Leo forced his eyes open and greeted them with a perplexed stare. "Is Hobin waiting for us?" he asked. He slowly sat up and dangled his feet over the edge of the wagon as the blankets dropped off his shoulders. "I can't climb another mountain today."

"There'll be no hiking, Leo. You're in Kargoth," Ivy said with a warm smile as she brushed back his tousled hair. "And you look quite healthy after all you've been through." Leo appeared confused as remnants of sleep still overwhelmed him.

"She means that you're not dead," Nicholas said, pointing at his chest to indicate the amulet beneath his shirt. "Vellan's spell, remember? I guess Frist showed him a thing or two. But now Megan will have to live with the consequences of you surviving."

"Good one," he replied with a smirk that quickly transformed into a yawn. "Now where can a guy get a hot meal around here? I'm starving."

They ate breakfast and then moved southwest toward the fields and farmland on the northern border of Del Norác. As they pulled away from the trees along Mount Minakaris and headed into open land between the mountain and the city, they were shocked to see a massive pile of stone and melting ice that had been deposited at the southern base where Vellan's stronghold once existed. The debris rose higher than the nearby pines. Even from a half mile away, Nicholas thought it was a surreal sight.

"That explains all the noise from last evening," he said as they stopped to stretch their legs and absorb the astounding view.

Carmella put her hands to her face in disbelief, the pumpkin color on them completely gone. "Imagine, Leo, if we had still been inside the mountain when it let loose," she said. "We wouldn't be having this conversation right now."

"I think Frist was watching out for the two of you," Nicholas remarked.

"I think he was watching out for all of us," Ivy said, gently taking his hand.

Soon they neared the northern fields. Scores of gray and white tents had sprouted up there overnight and also in the eastern field after the supply wagons had arrived, having kept their distance during the fighting. The war dead and injured had been brought to the tents and tended to by hundreds of soldiers who had traded in swords for bandages and balms. Nicholas thought about the friends he and Leo had left behind seventeen days ago when they bid King Justin farewell, wondering who among them might still be alive. They were the grimmest of thoughts beneath a clear blue sky and a brilliant rising sun.

They stopped at one of the nearest tents, now a beehive of activity as men scurried about the bonfires where water was being boiled, meals prepared and bloodstained clothing laundered. After climbing off the wagon and waving down a young soldier from Harlow, Nicholas learned that this particular station housed some of the men with only minor injuries who were expected to make full recoveries.

"But there are so many of them," the man said. He rubbed his shirt sleeve across a sweaty brow. "Even in victory, there is much hardship."

"Your efforts will not go unnoticed," Nicholas told him with heartfelt gratitude, amazed at the organization among the smoke-filled and ember-crackling chaos. "But if you have knowledge of King Justin's whereabouts, we'd be more than grateful for your assistance. We have information for him."

"The King's quarters are set up along the eastern border of the city," the soldier replied, pointing southeast beyond the field. "But I must inform you that the King–"

"–doesn't have time to be your guide!" a familiar voice called out. "But I *do!*"

Nicholas spun around, seeing a man walking briskly toward them through the drifting white smoke, his whiskered face, aqua-colored eyes and easy smile as pleasant and familiar as a crisp autumn morning. "Hobin!" he cried out with relief, greeting him with a hug. "It feels like ages since Leo and I left you behind at Deshla."

"Maybe one of these days I'll forgive you for disappearing," he joked.

"It wasn't on purpose," Leo said, hurrying down from the wagon to say hello to his former guide.

Carmella and Ivy walked up and Nicholas took Ivy's hand. After Carmella greeted Hobin, Nicholas, with a beaming smile upon his face, at last introduced him to Ivy.

Hobin looked upon the young woman with fatherly affection. "So this is the beautiful lady who Nicholas told me so much about during our travels," he said, giving her a hug. "I'm glad he found you safe and sound, dear," he whispered into her ear.

"Thank you," she replied.

As Hobin stepped back, he smiled at Nicholas. "She's worth every day of your search, so don't lose her again."

"I don't plan to," he said, again taking her hand. After the soldier departed to continue his duties, Nicholas and Leo gave Hobin a brief account about what had happened after they left him in Deshla. "But we could stand here for hours talking about that. Tell us what you're doing here, Hobin."

"I was seeking out you two, of course!" he replied. "When you never returned from your search for Cale, several of us tried to track you down through the tunnels, but with no luck. We assumed there was a secret exit, but we never found it."

"There was," Leo said. "But it's tricky to find."

"Anyway, we searched outdoors, hoping you were still in the vicinity," he continued. "But you were chatting with Vellan and his friends. Then around sunset, there was a small tremor inside the mountain which rattled us in more ways than one. We bound our prisoners and hustled them outside, fearing the worst. Soon after, a second, more powerful quake shook the land. Deshla collapsed in on itself. We were far enough away but witnessed a dragon-like breath of dust and debris pour out of the entrance when the ceilings fell in. There'll be no more going inside that place ever again."

"So how did you end up here?" Carmella asked.

"Strange story," he replied. "Suddenly, a wall of white mist tore down the river and then all the prisoners woke up from whatever trance Vellan had them under. It was the most amazing thing. We released them and headed into Del Norác. When we saw Vellan's stronghold was a pile of rubbish, we assumed he was in no better condition. But to make a long story short, I've been searching tent to tent and along the edge of the mountain for the past several hours hoping to locate you two. I didn't know what else to do, thinking you might've made your way back here and got swept up in the fighting. But I see you had your own adventure instead. I can't wait to hear the particulars."

"Right now I'd just like to find King Justin and the others," Nicholas said. "We can inform you all at once about Vellan's fate and Ivy and Carmella's rescue."

"Both intriguing stories, I'm sure," he replied, uncomfortably scratching his whiskers as a cloud of worry enveloped him.

"What's the matter?" Carmella asked. "You look absolutely glum."

Hobin nodded uneasily. "I am. And it concerns King Justin."

When they neared Del Norác, rows of tents stretched across the field along the eastern border from the northern pastures and farms down to the grassy banks of the Drusala River. Two large tents were in the middle of the first row adjacent to the city. A pair of soldiers stood guard outside each one. King Justin lay upon a cot inside the tent on the left, trapped in a restless sleep with a burning fever after a severe infection from his shoulder wound took hold during the night. In the tent on the right, the body of King Rowan lay in state as Brendan and William kept a melancholy vigil inside.

Nicholas and Leo approached King Justin's tent, devastated when they had learned the news about the two monarchs' conditions. Swirls of white smoke from scattered bonfires moved gracefully with the breezes as they neared the entrance, both doubtful that they would be allowed to visit. Carmella, Ivy and Hobin stayed near the wagon, believing that too many visitors would be inappropriate at such a delicate time.

"He may not be conscious," Nicholas speculated. "Perhaps we should meet with King Cedric."

Before Leo could respond, the front flap was pulled aside and out stepped King Cedric and Tolapari. When they saw Nicholas and Leo, both smiled with astonishment.

"If you two aren't a breath of spring air around here, then I don't know what is!" the wizard said, greeting each with a hearty handshake. "I ran into Hobin late last night and he told me of your disappearance in the tunnels. I wasn't sure if we'd see you again."

"Welcome back," King Cedric added, delighted to see them unscathed.

"I wish our visit was under better circumstances," Nicholas said glumly. "Hobin informed us about what had happened to King Justin and King Rowan."

"Such sorrowful news after the mostly good tidings we bring from inside Minakaris," Leo said.

"We will welcome any good news," the King replied. "We've won the war, but at a terrible cost."

"Still, I'll take the victory," Tolapari said, eyeing Leo with concern. "Forgive me for changing the subject, but I sense the strong presence of the wizard Frist about you–and a hint of something else which greatly disturbs me as I cannot explain it."

"Your instincts are accurate," Nicholas said, informing him that Leo was now wearing Frist's amulet and giving the reason why.

"But I believe I am nearly recovered from Vellan's spell," Leo told him, "the proof being that I am not dead."

"Compelling evidence," King Cedric said with a worrisome smile. "Still, perhaps Tolapari can administer an additional remedy of his own as a precaution."

"I'm greatly relieved that Vellan's spell has been neutralized through Frist's intervention," Tolapari said. "I think a good long sleep would aid in a full recovery, too. In the meantime, tell us what happened inside the mountain."

"Happy to," Nicholas said. "But first tell us of King Justin's condition."

They walked to the side of the tent for some privacy. There, Tolapari said that King Justin had grown ill around midnight, having succumbed to chills and a fever from his injury. "Other physicians and I have tended to him as best we could. But a virulent infection has gotten hold of him. He now lies on a cot drifting in and out of consciousness. I cannot say if he will survive the next few days."

Leo's heart ached upon hearing the news, knowing how hurt Megan would be if her grandfather should die. "Where is Prince Gregory? I'd like to speak with him."

"He sat with his father in the early morning hours and recently returned to the city," King Cedric said. "Gregory is overseeing the repairs to many of the structures in Del Norác. Some of our soldiers will remain here for a time to tend to the injured and help revitalize the city after the bulk of our army leaves."

"Gregory will visit later," Tolapari said. "But it would be good if you sat with King Justin, Leo. He has called out to Megan and you a few times in his fevered state."

"*Me?*" Leo felt both puzzled and moved.

"During our journey here, Justin had told me and Tolapari of your and Princess Megan's affection for one another," King Cedric replied. "He is quite fond of you, Leo, and proud of your service to Arrondale. It would be more than appropriate for you to sit at his side and comfort him. He may or may not hear your words, but other than his son, you are almost like family to him."

"I would be honored to do so."

"Excellent," Tolapari said. "I'll escort you to the King now as I think it best not to leave him alone. Then Cedric, Nicholas and I can find a quiet little corner to hear of your adventures inside Mount Minakaris."

"Just make sure that little corner is large enough for six people," Nicholas said, indicating where Ivy, Carmella and Hobin patiently waited. "I brought guests."

Moments later, awash with apprehension, Leo entered King Justin's tent with Tolapari. The flickering light inside was dim from the few burning oil lamps scattered about on small wooden tables and vented through openings in the ceiling.

King Justin lay upon a cot in one corner and Leo walked over to him. The monarch, pale and fast asleep, was covered with several blankets. A cool, wet cloth was set upon his forehead. Several bowls of steaming water infused with curative herbs had been placed about the tent, enveloping the air with a sweet aroma that both refreshed and soothed. Tolapari pointed to a cushioned chair next to the cot facing the King and indicated for Leo to sit down.

"If there is any change in his condition, send for me at once. In the meantime, keep him company. Call one of the guards if you need anything."

"I will," Leo said, sitting down. He immediately noticed the slow rise and fall of the King's chest beneath his blankets. King Justin appeared frail, nothing like the vigorous man who had led his army from Morrenwood to Del Norác with nary a complaint. Leo thought it a shame that he had been reduced to such a sickly state, glad that Megan couldn't see him this way. "Perhaps Carmella could examine him. She has an assortment of dried herbs and such in her wagon," he suggested to the wizard, glancing behind his chair. But Tolapari had already left.

"I guess he *was* eager to hear Nicholas' story," he softly joked to break the tension even though he assumed that King Justin couldn't hear him. The man's eyes were closed, his face pale and haggard in the fluttering shadows. Yet Leo still felt intimidated while in his presence, much like the time when he and Nicholas had first met him.

He sighed and reached over, taking King Justin's hand while contemplating what Megan's reaction would be if she were here. It tore him apart when he considered the possibility that the King might die. Though Prince Gregory would make a fine monarch, the citizens of Arrondale would have a void in their hearts upon King Justin's absence. And Megan, he knew, would be devastated at a time when she should be joyous at life's possibilities instead. Leo thought the situation most unfair.

"If there is anything I could do, sir, I would have you ask it of me," he whispered, gazing forlornly upon the King. "But under the circumstances, I will instead ask your son the next time I see him and let his words guide my actions. Yet I hope..." Leo's words trailed off with unease. He took a deep breath to compose himself. "Yet I hope that any favor either of you might ask would involve me being at your granddaughter's side to protect her and keep her company. For what you don't know—and I wanted Princess Megan to be the first to tell you, but again, under the circumstances..." Leo cleared his throat, nervous to utter his next words. "You see, sir, I have already asked your granddaughter to be my wife. With your permission, of course! And your son's, too."

Leo froze, holding his breath as if he had just confessed to a traitorous crime against Arrondale. But King Justin's eyes remained closed, his breathing as slow and steady as before. There would be no words or sign of either assent or disapproval. Leo exhaled and leaned back in his chair, releasing the King's hand. Yet a part of him felt emboldened that he had at least voiced those words foremost in his mind, believing that the next time he and Megan approached King Justin or Prince Gregory with the same request, his heart wouldn't be pounding and his lungs wouldn't feel like crystallized rock.

He imagined what Megan might be doing at that moment, whether wandering the Citadel corridors or walking about the grounds on a beautiful spring morning. Yet the weather north might be far different than in Kargoth, with steady spring rains a possibility. Leo rested his head against the chair, closing his eyes for a moment as he inhaled the soothing and intoxicating aroma from the medicinal water wafting from the bowls, hoping that Megan wasn't enduring a stretch of bleak days. As his heavy eyelids closed again, he wondered if she missed him as much as he missed her, convincing himself that she did as a tranquil smile crossed his lips while he drifted off into a deep and restful sleep.

Nicholas, in the meantime, had strolled off with Ivy, Hobin and Carmella behind the line of tents along the city's edge. They gathered around a small fire with King Cedric and Tolapari in back of a stone building warmed by the climbing sun. The wizard and King were delighted to meet Ivy, fascinated by the details of her rescue. As they listened, both were amazed to learn how Caldurian had betrayed Vellan and Madeline, and stunned that Mune had slayed the wizard of Minakaris in the end.

"Many of Vellan's spells were finally broken upon his death," Tolapari said. "Complex spells must be continually maintained by the one who cast them which forges a connection between the wizard and his target. A most taxing proposition that explains why Vellan was weakened after the Enâri were destroyed. His thoughts and will were constantly focused on them to do his bidding. Frist, no doubt, would have lived many more years had he not put so much of himself into incubating the spirit that destroyed the Enâri."

"Fortunately for us he did," King Cedric replied. "Otherwise, this war would have taken a far different turn, and not in our favor."

"Frist was there in the end," Nicholas said. "He guided us safely out of the mountain, and more importantly, he led me to Ivy."

"Frist's presence from beyond the grave might also explain the destruction that followed Vellan's demise," Tolapari continued. "With Frist preventing Vellan's transformation from life to death for as long as he could, I believe that the reversals of Vellan's spells were multiplied in their intensity when his spirit finally escaped from his body with a vengeance. Caldurian, no doubt, was buried among the dust and rubble."

"No great loss," Hobin muttered.

Tolapari expressed his condolences to Carmella on the death of her cousin. "Despite what she had done, I know you still cared for her a great deal."

"I thought I could lead her back to who she once was," she said with a melancholy air while gazing into the flames. "But too many years had passed since we last met. I didn't really understand how much Liney had changed. May she now have some peace."

"If only she had had your sensibility," King Cedric remarked. "Her life might have turned out much differently, Carmella."

"Perhaps. But I think Liney's encounter with Caldurian was her downfall," she replied, glancing at Tolapari. "Had she met you instead, and learned under your guidance, she might have used well the gifts she had buried deep inside her. But that is the way of the world." She looked back into the flames, feeling empty and lost.

"Not always," Tolapari said, drawing back her gaze. "Maybe you can develop and use your gifts properly to make up for the errors of her way."

"What are you saying?" she asked.

"From the stories you just told me, you've apparently learned much from Caldurian, and in such a short time, too. I'd like a demonstration of your smoke apparitions when you have some time," he said. "I've been thinking of taking on an apprentice. It's been far too long since I've done so, what with all the turmoil throughout Laparia that has consumed my time these last few years." The wizard looked at Carmella with an encouraging smile. "Might you consider yourself in such a role?"

"*Me*? An apprentice?" She placed a hand to her heart, deeply touched by the offer. "I am at a loss for words."

"The only word I need is *yes*. Of course, I'll understand if you want time to think about it or wish to–"

"*Yes!*" Carmella exclaimed. "But may I keep my wagon for our journeys? After some repairs and a new coat of paint, of course."

"I wouldn't have it any other way," he insisted. "But only if I take the reins."

"That'd be delightful," she replied. "When do we start?"

Later that morning, Nicholas and Ivy visited Brendan and William in the tent where King Rowan's body lay upon a wooden bier draped with black cloth. Carmella and Hobin accompanied them. Boughs of fragrant pine surrounded the bier, and candles flickered on small stands on either side. Nicholas noted how much the two brothers had matured in the six months since he first met them, but it was a maturity tempered with heartache and strife that would forever shape their futures.

"My brother and I have traveled many miles since taking our oath in the Citadel," Brendan said. "The events that happened along the way have scaled both dizzying heights and depths unimaginable. My grandfather's death is one of the latter."

"But with his death, he has saved your life, Prince Brendan, and your brother's," Carmella softly said as she placed a comforting arm around him. "Value that second chance, that gift he has given you when you return to Montavia and begin your reign."

"Brendan more than anyone can appreciate such a second chance," William replied, his eyes reddened with grief. "But I, too, will never forget how Grandfather gave his life for us. It is a wound my heart will always carry."

After leaving them a short time later, Nicholas checked in on Leo in the adjoining tent. But seeing him sound asleep in the chair at King Rowan's side, he let him be and informed Tolapari. The wizard, tending to some injured soldiers in another tent farther up the line, was glad to hear the news.

"After you told me about Vellan's spell, I suspected Leo could use hours more sleep in addition to the healing powers from Frist's amulet," he said while examining a soldier's broken wrist. "That is why I urged him to spend time at King Justin's side. I knew the aromas from the medicinal waters would lull him into a deep sleep. Though Leo appeared in good health when you arrived, neither of you fully understand the trauma he suffered. I'll have another cot brought in there and let him sleep until he awakens naturally."

"Thanks for helping, Tolapari. If there's anything I can do–"

"As a matter of fact there is," he jumped in, reaching for an empty wooden bucket. "I need boiling water to refresh the bowls in here. Send Carmella and Hobin this way, too. I'd like to scour through her inventory of herbs. She can assist me here and begin her apprenticeship. And if Hobin is agreeable, I'll send him out to gather various leaves, roots and tree bark that I need. There will be much to do in the days ahead."

"I'll find them at once," Nicholas said, offering additional help on behalf of himself and Ivy. "Just tell us where to go and what to do. Despite all I've been through, I feel as if I contributed nothing to this fight. Those lying in these tents have taken the brunt of the storm."

"Oh, you have done more than your share, Nicholas Raven, but I understand your point. When you return, I shall find plenty for you both to do."

Nicholas and Ivy delivered food and water as instructed, happy to lend a hand even at small tasks as they made their way through the city of tents and around smoky bonfires. As they worked together, Nicholas grew closer to Ivy. He was impressed at how well and with such ease she could comfort a wounded soldier and offer an encouraging smile, knowing she would make a wonderful mother some day.

But he departed shortly after noontime, called away to help transport additional firewood to the multitude of camps throughout the north and east fields. He missed Ivy so much during their separation, yet kept his mind focused to while away the hours. As twilight approached, he cheered up when hearing someone call out to him while he and a few others unloaded a pile of split wood for a camp near the river's edge.

"I guess hauling firewood on a horse-drawn wagon is a lot easier than pushing crates on a sled," a familiar voice said. Malek walked up to Nicholas through the shadows and slapped him on the back. "I'm glad to see you're still breathing and unhurt."

"I would say the same about you," Nicholas replied as he shook Malek's hand, noting a few scratches upon his face and a bandage around his left forearm. "But I see you must have stumbled into a tight spot or two since you marched away from Deshla."

"Nothing I couldn't handle," he said with his familiar and easy smile. "But we can compare notes later. First I need to know—did you find Ivy?"

Nicholas burst out in a smile. "She's delivering food among the tents, but I'll introduce you later. She and I are both in your debt for saving me so I could save *her*."

"I'm happy for you," he replied. "And after you unload that cart, you and your friends can join us for a meal around the fires. I'm guessing you haven't eaten in hours."

"I haven't," he said, noting a deep weariness in Malek's eyes despite his jovial manner. "I doubt you have either. What have you been doing all day?"

"As I said, we can compare notes later," he replied with a slightly somber demeanor, indicating for Nicholas to follow him to the bonfire when his work was done.

Shortly afterward, Nicholas and his crew were sharing a meal of stew and biscuits near the river's edge around a blazing fire, its yellow, red and orange glow splashing across the water's surface in warm, oily strokes. Max and Sala were present among the large group, both in good health and high spirits. Nicholas was glad to hear about their adventures over the past two days. When he learned that these men had been burying the dead in a swath of land to the northeast, he guessed that their emotions must have run the gamut between restlessness and melancholy all day while performing such a grim task. He realized that they now needed time to unwind as they would be at it again in the morning.

"Tradell, no doubt, is off sitting by one of the other fires and preparing for tomorrow's task," Max later commented to Nicholas and Sala as they enjoyed hot tea by the snapping flames. "He is one of several men helping to organize the burying, and if possible, the identifying of the corpses."

"His military training in Linden made him a perfect candidate for such a difficult job," Sala remarked. "Still, it is a sobering ordeal all around."

"Maybe after Kargoth is resettled, people might travel here to pay their respects to those who died to save Laparia," Max said. "It will be a solemn sight in the shadow of the mountain."

"It will indeed," Nicholas softly replied, gazing up at Mount Minakaris to the north, the scar running down its southern slope barely visible in the dimming light.

As everyone enjoyed a second helping of stew, Nicholas leaned back against a pile of wood near the fire and gazed up at the budding white stars scattered across the clear eastern sky, again thinking of Ivy. He hoped she had taken some rest during the day, having endured a traumatic ordeal of her own. He also wondered if Leo had awakened, knowing the long rest would do his friend good.

He noticed a fiery glow beneath the snowy mountaintops along the eastern horizon, watching for several minutes as the intensity of the light increased. A few minutes later, the rim of the Fox Moon, just past full phase, peeked over the horizon to reveal its luminous presence. Slowly it climbed above the mountains as Nicholas watched in lazy fascination, unaware of the passage of time as voices drifted in and out on the periphery of his consciousness until his eyes closed and sleep found him.

His eyes opened wide moments later, or so he first thought, when somebody's laughter cut through the darkened landscape. But when Nicholas looked up, he saw that the Fox Moon had risen a bit higher in the eastern sky and that its faithful companion, the Bear Moon, also a day past full, had already climbed above the horizon as well, now following the Fox across the night sky at arm's length. Nicholas guessed that he had dozed off for almost half an hour, knowing he should be on his way. Soon afterward he said goodbye to his friends and walked through the sea of tents toward the eastern border of Del Norác, assuming that Ivy, Carmella and Hobin would be somewhere in the vicinity.

Leo opened his eyes, noting a flicker of light dancing upon the tent ceiling. He stretched his arms, feeling refreshed and alert, when suddenly realizing he was lying on a cot along the side of the tent adjacent to where King Justin lay fast asleep. He sat up and plopped his feet on the ground, vaguely remembering being led from his chair to the cot by two individuals. He couldn't recall what time that had happened, but when he noted the blackened sky through the small vents in the ceiling, he realized he must have slept the day away. He then heard a faraway whisper inside his head.

"You are healed. Save the King."

Leo automatically reached for the amulet beneath his shirt and removed it, forgetting that he had been carrying it around for the past day. He wondered why he hadn't thought about giving it to King Justin until just this moment. Leo felt the best he had in several months, realizing that Frist's healing power had brought him to this point. Even the constant chill he felt since opening the Spirit Box had disappeared. With urgent strides, he walked over to King Justin and placed the amulet in his right hand.

"Get well, sir," he whispered. "If not for your sake, then for Megan's."

He watched the King for a moment, the monarch's face as pale as snow and his breathing slow but steady, knowing there was nothing more he could do. As he turned to leave, he noticed King Justin's fingers slowly tighten around the amulet. A hint of color returned to his face. He stared in amazement as those two subtle changes revitalized the King's appearance. But since he still slept soundly, Leo left him to his rest and slipped through the tent flap into the cool night air.

The stars above were muted by the glow of the Fox and Bear moons, the one ahead of the other as they ascended together in the evening sky. Leo guessed that he had been asleep for half the day as he wandered toward a nearby fire. But just before he reached the outer glow of the firelight, a voice called to him.

"Thank you for keeping my father company," Prince Gregory said, walking over and greeting Leo with a handshake. "I'm glad you and your friends survived that ordeal in the mountains."

"Barely," he replied, happy to see Megan's father.

"I was inside the tent a half hour ago to check on you both as I have recently returned from my duties in the city," the prince explained. "I saw no change in him. But how do you feel now? Tolapari informed me of your encounter with Vellan."

"The effects of the wizard's spell are no longer a concern," Leo said. "It has been some time since my body and spirit felt whole, though my appetite needs looking after."

"Then head to the fire where both food and your friends are waiting," Prince Gregory instructed. "I'll go inside and sit with my father, but I fear his prospects are bleak despite our best efforts."

"You may think otherwise when you see him again," Leo said, offering unlooked for hope. "There has been a remarkable change in him only moments ago."

"A change you say?" Prince Gregory was nervously excited, scanning Leo's shadowy expression for an explanation. "Tell me what you've seen!"

"I think it best that you see for yourself," he replied, walking him back to the tent. With a vague smile, the prince nodded gratefully and disappeared behind the flap as Leo headed back to the bonfire.

Greeting him were Carmella, Ivy and Hobin, all delighted that he appeared to be in fine spirits. They insisted that he sit down on a log while they found him something to eat. Tolapari, in the meantime, hurried over from another fire after learning that Leo had awakened. The wizard observed his demeanor, convinced that Leo had been fully cured.

"And the amulet? Where is it?" he asked.

"Now working its magic on King Justin," Leo replied.

"Ah, well done!" the wizard told him before rushing off to examine the King.

Hobin quickly ladled out some stew into a bowl and handed it to Leo with a spoon and some bread. "This will fix you up nicely," he said, taking his seat near the fire to finish his own meal. "Carmella prepared it herself. Eat up."

"Hobin is on his third helping, but there's still plenty more," she said with a cheerful laugh that lightened the evening. "Don't feel shy about asking for seconds."

"I won't," he replied as Ivy gave him a cup of steaming tea.

"Freshly steeped from the kettle," she said, handing Leo the drink and stepping back into the edge of the light. "Now enjoy your supper and don't let us bother you too much."

"You've all been more than kind," he said, glad to be among friends as he listened to Hobin and Carmella tell him stories of their busy day.

As Ivy looked upon them in the fire's glow, she was happy that some of the people who had aided in her rescue were enjoying a few hours of rest and camaraderie, knowing how much they deserved this special time. But her thoughts were soon drawn to Nicholas, contemplating where he might be among the vast city of tents and sadly wondering if she might not see him again until morning. She then noted the soft sound of footsteps behind her and soon felt a pair of warm arms wrap lovingly around her waist. She smiled and tilted her head back, catching the glimmer of firelight in Nicholas' eyes and noting his boyish grin as he smiled back contentedly and kissed her cheek.

"I missed you," he whispered, holding her closely under the stars and rising moons.

"And I missed you," Ivy softly replied. She gently clasped his hands as the two of them gazed upon their friends around the crackling flames, both simply happy to stand there all night in each other's treasured company until the sun rose in the eastern sky.

CHAPTER 113

The Long Road Home

As the sick and injured recuperated over the next few days, repairs and renovations proceeded in Del Norác at a steady clip. Stonemasons and carpenters worked from first light to dusk each day, attacking short term structural problems on some buildings while others fixed roads and tended to the fields and orchards. A contingent of men from King Justin and King Cedric's armies, and some from Surna, Linden and Harlow, would stay to oversee the necessary work for the long haul and reestablish order in Kargoth.

"There are many good men native to this region who would provide excellent leadership when a population reestablishes itself up and down the Drusala." Prince Gregory spoke to his father three days after Leo had slipped the amulet into his hands, spurring on his recovery. "Sadly, many people who weren't ensnared by Vellan's spell have fled over the years, most probably never to return."

"Give them time. Word will spread of Vellan's demise," he assured his son. "Families will come back."

They sat on a bench beneath a budding maple tree in one of the grassy commons in Del Norác. It was late morning on the twenty-fourth day of New Spring and they had stopped to rest after touring parts of the city to assess the repairs. A light breeze blew in the warm sunshine. Other soldiers with them tended to their horses as the sounds of hammers and shovels echoed through the streets.

The King claimed to be in perfect health now, his ruddy cheeks and vibrant steps attesting to that opinion. With Nicholas' permission, he had given the amulet to Tolapari to help some of his most ill patients.

"The men have made much progress under your direction, Gregory," he continued. "Most of our troops can leave in three days. The individuals you've chosen to leave in charge will manage nicely."

"It was less a matter of choosing than of volunteering," the prince informed his father. "After enduring Vellan's rule, there are concerned people who want to provide guidance and make sure his replacement will be a leader and not a subjugator."

"A wise precaution." King Justin pointed to a nearby street where several men on horseback headed their way. "And speaking of those concerned people, here come a few of them now."

Sauntering across the green on their steeds were Eucádus, Ranen and Ramsey accompanied by Nicholas and Leo, who were invited on a tour of the city. Eucádus wished to hear details of their adventure inside Mount Minakaris, but since he was busy overseeing some of the reconstruction at Prince Gregory's bidding, he suggested that Nicholas and Leo follow him around for the day. Riding behind them was Captain Tiber, and on either side of him were Uland and Torr, the former with his left arm in a sling and the latter with a bandaged forehead. Each had received his injury when battling in the northern field under Tiber's command.

"Everyone seems to be having a fine time today," Prince Gregory said, noting their jovial moods as the group moved into the shade. "You make my father and me look like a couple of old men sitting here discussing our aches and woes."

"Then Uland, Torr and I should join you if you want to speak of aches and pains," Captain Silas replied. He ambled up on his horse from the very back with William and Brendan at his side.

The three of them had toured Del Norác at Tolapari's urging. The wizard believed the fresh air and company would do them good, especially the two princes still mourning their grandfather's death. Silas' right calf, bandaged after his knife injury, was slowly healing. And as he needed a cane to walk, he was excited to climb on a horse and move freely around. William and Brendan accompanied him, discussing the events in the eastern field. And though the horrible memory of that day would never be erased, their pain was momentarily eased with abundant talk and sunshine among friends.

"We're having a fine time," Nicholas said, "though parts of our conversation have been dreary and dark."

"That is to be expected after what we've been through," King Justin said as the men dismounted. Ramsey assisted Captain Silas in stepping down and then handed him his cane which had been tied to the side of the saddle.

"You and King Victor will be able to swap cane stories when you return home," he joked. "That is, if the King is still using his when you return."

"His knee was nearly healed when I left Maranac," Silas replied. "But if not, I suspect we'll both be caneless by the time New Maranac officially comes into existence this autumn. It will be a magnificent day."

"A day as equally magnificent as the end of Vellan's reign," Eucádus remarked. "And now that Nicholas and Leo have provided me details of the wizard's last moments, I'll return to Harlow with numerous tales for my countrymen." He turned to Prince Gregory. "But now I must report to you on matters inside the city."

"But you and Ranen have yet to tell us about your battle on the bridge," Leo said with disappointment. "Nicholas and I have heard only rumors."

"I would also like the firsthand details," Brendan jumped in. But when seeing the two men glance at each other with reluctance and unease, he and the others guessed that the experience was still too painful to discuss.

But Ranen relented slightly and spoke up. "As horrible as it was being under Vellan's sway, it was nothing compared to declaring enmity toward such a dear friend as Eucádus. I will speak of it no further right now."

"And until Vellan's spell was broken, the toxic waters of the Drusala could not be resisted by even the strongest among us," Eucádus added, not willing to fully delve into the incident. "But I will admit that I experienced a hint of what Ranen and many others endured who succumbed to the river's enchantment. I partly understand the horror they lived with, some for years of their lives."

"What are you saying?" Nicholas asked.

"When Ranen and I fell into the water, I instantly felt the force of Vellan's will upon my mind and soul," he continued, glancing at the ground from time to time as he formed his thoughts with difficulty. "I experienced how easy and tempting it was to reach out to him and obey his every command, believing that I would be rewarded beyond my imagination. Yet at the same time, I knew I had the choice to reject his orders and stay on the path I was already treading, difficult as it might be." Eucádus looked up as he rubbed a hand across his whiskered face. "I had spoken to Tolapari in private about the incident. He believed that Vellan's spell was disintegrating just as I hit the water, so while I wasn't forced to surrender to his will, I did experience the essence of the enchantment in a less potent form, able to distinguish between Vellan's call and my own life."

"A choice, sadly, none of the others ever had," King Justin remarked.

"That's exactly what the wizard believed," he continued. "And while in the water, I also perceived that the rewards I was promised in my mind were empty and unfulfilling, merely a sham to entice my allegiance. Again, a perspective that the others were never allowed when the spell was fully potent."

"It was a pernicious device Vellan used to ensnare his people," Ranen said. "But on this beautiful day, I would rather not pursue the subject further. Perhaps another time."

"Understood," Prince Gregory said as a light breeze swept across the common. "Let us talk of something else."

"Preferably over lunch," King Justin quipped. "I'm famished."

Soon the men shuffled off to one of the nearby camps for a brief meal, the conversation turning to less serious matters as their voices and laughter rose high above the sun-splashed roofs and treetops within the slowly healing city.

The weather turned cloudy three days later when the armies from the north prepared to set out for home, yet the air remained warm and pleasant as the journey commenced from the east field. Nicholas and Leo bid a fond farewell to Malek, Max and Sala, wondering if they would ever see them again.

"You and Leo must visit Surna in another year or two," Malek suggested. "My wife and daughters would be delighted to meet you both. Afterward, we can travel to Kargoth and see what kind of nation grows here in Vellan's absence."

"Something sweet and pure I hope," Nicholas said, eager to make the trip. "We can meet up with Sala and Max along the way."

"We'll bring Hobin along," Leo said, "and make it a reunion."

"In that case, you'll have to make a trip to Harlow, too," Eucádus said as he, Ranen and Ramsey joined in the goodbyes. "But first we have much work to do here." Eucádus, Malek and the others would be staying in Del Norác for a few more weeks before returning to their homes, helping with the transition to a newly ordered society.

King Justin, who had been talking with King Cedric, Tolapari and his son, overheard their conversation and offered a farewell before commenting on their desire to reunite. "You may be onto an idea that the realms of Laparia should adopt in the future," he said. "It would be to our advantage if, from time to time, we leaders came together to keep a more vigilant eye on our corner of the world lest another Vellan sprout up. Though we send messages across the miles, we've been lax about cultivating stronger bonds."

"Then allow me to volunteer Grantwick as the location for our first get-together," King Cedric offered. "Perhaps early autumn of next year or the following spring. I'll dispatch messengers to hash out the particulars."

"Though Eucádus and Malek are not official representatives of their respective homelands," King Justin said with a mischievous smile, "I suspect they may be so in one capacity or another by then."

"Your confidence in us is appreciated," Eucádus said. "But first we must make sense of this mess in Del Norác."

"But if I had to guess," Malek said, "I think that swift change will come to all the halls of power in the mountain nations. With word of Vellan's defeat spreading far and wide, those who curried favor with him out of cowardice or for profit might soon find themselves out of a job. The people will clean house of such useless politicians."

King Justin chuckled. "Regardless of your future careers, you two and your associates shall be high on our list of invitees to any future gatherings. After all, we'll need some curt words and blasts of commonsense to air out the puffery that usually billows to the rafters during these assemblies. Agreed?"

"You have my word," Eucádus said.

"And mine," Malek agreed as each shook hands with the two Kings as well as Prince Brendan, the future King of Montavia. "It will be our honor."

After everyone said goodbye, the lines of marchers, horses and wagons began their homeward trek. They halted for a few minutes in the vast field where the dead had been buried, offering heartfelt words and moments of silence for the sacrifices so many had made to keep Laparia free. They continued on in silence, drifting past the sacred site as everyone took a last look amid prayer and quiet contemplation. Prince Brendan took the reins of the wagon that carried his grandfather. The King's prepared and wrapped corpse lay beneath a low, black canopy raised over the rear of the wagon. William sat next to his brother in a melancholy haze as four soldiers from Montavia rode along on horseback, two on either side of the wagon, carrying flags of the realm.

Carmella followed in her wagon with Hobin at the reins. Close behind them on two horses were Nicholas, Ivy and Leo, all lost in thought about the war and the changes wrought because of it. Nicholas, wearing Frist's amulet beneath his shirt and with Ivy sitting behind him, looked at the array of burial mounds, overwhelmed by how many men had been forever separated from their loved ones to safeguard the lives and liberty of those whom they had never met. He couldn't fully comprehend the magnitude of such sacrifice yet thought of nothing else as he guided his steed past the field with Ivy, her arms wrapped around his waist. All absorbed the somber moment as the vast assemblage moved on in respectful silence.

They journeyed over the next several days along the Drusala River under gray skies and light rain, crossing the eastern border out of Kargoth as the brilliant green of the Rhoon Forest slowly came into view. After skirting around its leafy eaves, the army turned northward through the gap between the Rhoon and the Braya

Woods. In time they entered the southern reaches of Drumaya and eventually arrived on the western shore of Lake Mara as the skies cleared and the sun shone brilliantly upon its lapping waters. Though it seemed a lifetime ago, just over one month had passed since they first reached the lake and discovered with astonished joy that Prince Brendan had returned from the grave. As the sibling princes now rode past the water, the joy of that special time had evaporated as they transported the body of their beloved grandfather. Both sensed that fate had been determined to claim one life in their royal line before the war had drawn to a close.

"If that is to be the way of things, I'm sure Grandfather was glad that he had departed this world so that you could breathe and walk again," William told his brother as the wagon rolled on.

"If that truly is the way of things, then I suppose he was," he replied with a tired sigh. "Still, that brings little comfort to me or to those at home awaiting his return."

"I suppose it doesn't." William stared blankly across the lake, eager to reach the Swift River. "It shall be a tearful homecoming."

In time, the travelers reached the north tip of Lake Mara where the Swift River flowed into the water. Lines of men and wagons hugged the riverbank and extended into the adjacent field as they pressed northward and entered the heart of Drumaya. As they passed though small villages, locals lined the way to cheer on the returning troops and beg for information. King Cedric, with Captain Tiber by his side, expressed joy to be back home, yet was filled with melancholy when thinking about those who were left behind.

"In time, after their grief has subsided somewhat and people return to a semblance of normalcy, the full stories of what our brave soldiers did in Kargoth will be told and celebrated," King Cedric told him. "Much like after the battles in Rhiál. And perhaps families and friends will make the journey to Kargoth one day to view the final resting spot of their loved ones and reminisce about such glorious lives."

"It will be a bittersweet journey," the captain replied, "though some may be hesitant to ever step foot in Kargoth even though Vellan is no more."

The King nodded as he wrestled with another thought. "I see your point, which is why we should construct a remembrance of some sort in Grantwick, a memorial citizens can visit to honor those who died in these two wars. I'll put Minister Nuraboc in charge."

"If anyone will put her heart into such an honorable task, it is Judith Nuraboc."

"It is the least we can do for a debt that can never be fully repaid," King Cedric replied as he guided his horse along the grassy banks while the vast army moved about him as a single mass. "And may such a debt never need repaying again," he softly added as a sweet breeze whispered across the field from the west.

As twilight neared on the tenth day of traveling, the coalition army reached the village of Wynhall. Captain Silas and his troops took their leave, crossing the stone bridge on the Swift River to camp below the Bressan Woods. There they would rest for a few days and resupply before the long trip back to Rhiál across the Kincarin Plains.

"After New Maranac comes to be in five months, King Victor and Queen Melinda will send ambassadors to formalize treaties of friendship with our neighbors," Captain Silas told King Justin and the others before he departed. "I guarantee that your next visit will be much more pleasant than the last one."

"If you see Aaron," William said, "give him my best."

"I will," he promised. "And though Aaron continues to work in the kitchens in Melinas, he has accepted an offer to serve on the King and Queen's personal staff when they take up residence in Bellavon. A suitable reward for helping to capture a spy."

After Captain Silas and his men had left, the remainder of the army made camp in the fields outside of Wynhall. They departed early the next day for Grantwick, arriving late that afternoon. King Justin and Prince Brendan's soldiers stayed for five days, pitching tents in the field overlooking the Ebrean Forest to the west. One evening while sitting by a fire, William and Brendan recalled their harrowing adventure in the cabin somewhere deep inside the woods, feeling as if it had been a bad dream long since past. They shared a meal with Nicholas, Ivy, Leo, Carmella and Hobin beside the crackling flames. The canopied wagon holding King Rowan's body stood close by in the thickening shadows surrounded by an honor guard.

"Shortly after I had first looked upon this forest, I lost my brother," William remarked as the fire's gentle glow brushed across his face. "And now that I gaze upon these woods for what may be the last time, my heart again is overwhelmed with sorrow."

"Whenever I look upon the mountains in the days ahead, I'll always think of Liney with sadness for the life that she abandoned," Carmella said, empathizing with the young prince's grief. "We've all been touched cruelly by this war, with reminders all around us."

"But don't get so lost in those dark moments that you abandon the joyful ones," Ivy said, briefly glancing at Nicholas. "You have found your brother again, Prince William, and against the most impossible odds. Hold onto that."

"I'll remind him often," Brendan chimed in to lighten the mood, "though he'll probably tire of me when I am king as I'll no longer be able to attend to his every whim whenever he gets bored."

"You'll be begging me to entertain you when affairs of state interfere with fishing or rambling about the foothills," William shot back with a playful smirk. "Time will tell after we get back home."

"And what are your plans?" Leo asked Hobin who sat silently by, gazing into the flames as he drank from a steaming mug. "Taking any trips north of Woodwater by chance?"

Hobin affected an annoyed scowl. "You mind your business with a certain young lady in the Blue Citadel and I'll mind mine with another one living along the Crescent." He sipped his drink, hiding a vague smile behind the cup. "Yes, I will be traveling north to see Emma, most likely by late spring—not that it's any of your business. And Frank and Gus will come with me this time."

"They'll be a handful on such a long trip," Nicholas said as he leaned back next to Ivy and stretched his legs. "Constantly at your heels, begging for food and attention."

"A lot less trouble than you and Leo," Hobin ribbed, eliciting laughter from the others. "And I won't have to answer their endless questions either."

Nicholas smiled fondly, gazing at their valued guide across the snapping flames. "We'll miss you too, Hobin."

"But don't be surprised if Nicholas and I come knocking at your door one day and take you up on your offer to climb another mountain," Leo added. "If you plan to do some mapmaking for King Justin, you'll need qualified assistants on your long treks."

"I suppose I will," he replied. "But if I'm out when you arrive, tap an ale cask, start a fire and tend to the place until I return–just not in that order."

"I look forward to it," Leo said. "With Megan's permission, of course."

Nicholas glanced at Ivy who stared back at him with feigned displeasure. "And with Ivy's permission, too!" he quickly added, taking her hand as they both smiled. "Something I look forward to asking her for a very long time."

Five days later, with their men rested and resupplied, King Justin and Prince Brendan led the armies north, thanking King Cedric and bidding him goodbye. The ties between Arrondale, Drumaya and Montavia had been strengthened over the course of two long and weary wars. King Justin was confident that such powerful bonds would serve well in uniting the whole of Laparia in the long run.

"When we meet in Grantwick for our initial gathering, we'll see just how strong a connection we've woven," King Cedric had earlier remarked as he and King Justin made their rounds upon horseback as the armies broke camp.

"But don't be surprised if you and your wife are invited to the Citadel long before that," King Justin replied with a knowing smile. "I suspect there may be a wedding in the not-so-distant future, but the information is not yet for public consumption."

"Princess Megan and Leo?"

The King raised a hand. "I am just speculating as nothing has yet been confirmed, Cedric. But let's just say that I was privy to some reliable words during my illness that such is the plan. I believe my hunch is near the mark."

"Beatrice and I look forward to journeying to Morrenwood," he replied. "But until I receive an invitation, no word on this matter shall pass my lips. Far be it from me to spoil the young couple's day. Gregory, though, must be bursting to announce the news."

The King chuckled. "Even he doesn't know yet, though I suspect he will shortly."

"Then I'll double my discretion and treat this matter as a state secret, particularly since a woman's input is involved."

"A wise policy," he agreed as they continued meandering across the field. "A wise policy indeed."

The dwindling army pressed forward at midmorning, keeping west of the Swift River until the Red Mountains loomed into view. Soon they crossed the tributaries of the river's upper region and passed eastward through the lush, green valley between the second and third peaks at the lower end of the chain. In time, the southern portion of Lake Lasko came into view which again stirred up vivid memories for William as he neared the village of Parma farther up the coast. Only this time the young prince didn't fall into a fit of melancholy since his brother now sat at his side, alive and well. But other feelings of emptiness and sorrow blanketed the sibling princes to varying degrees for every mile of road they traversed in the company of their deceased grandfather.

In the middle of a cool, gray morning on their eighth day since leaving Grantwick, King Justin brought his army to a halt. They had crossed into Arrondale a while ago and were assembled on the road and fields skirting the west bank of the Pine River in southern Bridgewater County. Here Prince Brendan separated his troops from King Justin's army so they could continue northeast along River Road. They would ride and march through the heart of Arrondale before passing through the Black Hills and Keppel Mountains farther east, finally reaching the end of their journey in Montavia. King Justin and his men would continue north, leaving the main road to cut across country, making for Morrenwood on their final day's march and planning to arrive at the capital before sundown.

"It has been an honor riding with you," Prince Brendan said to the King as he and his brother shook the monarch's hand.

"Thank you again for saving our kingdom," William added as he said goodbye to Prince Gregory. "As we whiled away the hours to Kargoth, Grandfather told me many stories about how you and your troops liberated Triana."

"I had a little help," he replied, referring to Nicholas and Leo who stood nearby. "Had they not eliminated the Enâri, the war in Montavia might have taken an ugly turn."

"As would have the war in Kargoth," King Justin said, turning to Nicholas and Leo. "The fates of many were tied to your actions."

"Don't give us all the credit," Nicholas said. "Many played a part in that mission, including Carmella and Hobin."

"And others along the way," Leo added. "Without the help of any single one of them, Nicholas and I might have failed."

"Thankfully you did not," Brendan replied, glancing up at King Justin. "And now we must take our leave, sir, and embrace the bittersweet days ahead."

Soon the army of Montavia departed. Prince Brendan and Prince William solemnly led the way with an honor guard of horsed soldiers surrounding King Rowan's wagon. As Nicholas and the others looked on, all wondered how the citizens of Montavia would react upon learning the news of the King's death and of Prince Brendan's miraculous return.

They would learn weeks later how villagers throughout Montavia had greeted the arriving troops as they neared the capital, showering them with praise and hearty greetings along the way until informed that their beloved King Rowan had paid the ultimate price. But before the shock of his death registered among each group of people, they were then told the news that Prince Brendan, still mourned throughout the kingdom, had astonishingly returned to the land of the living. Those who glimpsed him atop the wagon at the head of the line respectfully guiding his grandfather back home could not mistake his familiar blond hair and sea blue eyes. Word spread quickly far and wide, so that when the returning army had finally reached Triana and the main gates of Red Lodge itself, a crowd of tearful onlookers lined the way in respectful silence for their dead King. Yet whispers of amazement were tossed like flowers upon the path at Prince Brendan's return.

The most tears were shed by Lady Vilna when she stepped through the front doors of Red Lodge and hurried down the stairs as the canopied wagon pulled through the front gate. The clip clopping of horses echoed off the cobblestone courtyard. When she saw her two sons upon the wagon, her senses reeled and her heart beat wildly. Brendan and William climbed down and ran to their mother, both hugging her at the same time and not wanting to let go as tears freely flowed. Neither boy had seen her in over seven months since the night they escaped through the west gate to seek help. Neither then had imagined the journey they would take, and both now could hardly believe that they had made it back home as their mother's loving arms and warm words tenderly embraced them.

After Prince Brendan and his troops departed, King Justin ordered the army of Arrondale to make for the open fields to the north. He was eager to gaze upon the bluish-gray speckled stonework of the Citadel before sunset. The King rode at the head of the line with his son, both discussing events of the last few weeks. But foremost on their minds was getting back home to their loved ones. It had been sixty days since they passed through the gates of the Blue Citadel in the waning days of winter to commence their assault against Vellan, though it seemed like a year. Now that the last miles were before them, neither King Justin nor his son could fully fathom that the journey was nearly over.

"Only when we're sitting comfortably by a fire with Megan, getting peppered with one question after another, will the reality of what we went through finally sink in," the prince remarked. "Though I eagerly look forward to every one of my daughter's inquiries."

"And hearing about the administrative woes that Nedry most certainly endured in our absence, too," the King added. "Then I'll feel as if I'm back where I belong and can start to put things in perspective." Neither could help but laugh.

"What has put the two of you in such a good mood?" Tolapari asked as he guided his steed alongside them. Accompanying the wizard on another horse was Carmella who immediately caught the attention of Prince Gregory and his father since both were used to seeing her riding upon her cherished wagon.

"We were discussing family and such," the King said as a freshening breeze rolled across the field from the west.

"And what about you two?" the prince asked curiously. "What did you say, Tolapari, to persuade this woman to abandon her usual mode of transportation?"

"I would never abandon such a valuable piece of property," Carmella insisted. "It holds my most cherished possessions. But since Tolapari has graciously offered to take me on as his apprentice, we were discussing the course of my training over the next year."

"Though I will happily accompany Carmella along the roads and fields of Laparia, there will be some places where horses alone, or study legs, will be the only way to travel," the wizard explained. "Carmella is getting some practice."

"Well best of luck," King Justin said. "But I expect a visit from both of you from time to time whenever you're in the area."

"Count on it," Tolapari promised. "Even though the war is over, I could never deny the King of Arrondale my sage advice and stellar company."

"And I look forward to conversing with Princess Megan now and then over a steaming pot of tea," Carmella added. "Especially if she continues her relationship with Leo. No offense, gentlemen, but she'll need a woman's advice from time to time."

"Duly noted," King Justin said. "By the way, Carmella, where *is* your wagon?"

"A half mile behind us," she replied. "But don't worry. It is in very capable hands."

Farther back among the steadily moving lines, Nicholas sat atop Carmella's wagon with the reins in hand, gazing out upon the familiar landscape unfolding before them. Ivy sat next to him with Leo on her other side. Hobin rode to their right on his steed, keeping a watchful eye on them as if they were his children. All had moved on in tranquil silence for the past several minutes as if mesmerized by the steady sounds of the turning wheels and muffled clip clopping of the horses across the grassy terrain.

"I've never heard you all so quiet before," Hobin said as he looked up at the trio. "None of you are dozing off, are you?"

Leo, nearest to him, turned his head as he leaned back in his seat. "Not dozing, Hobin, though close to it," he said, stretching his arms with a relaxed smile upon his face. "After all that's happened, I'm in a contemplative mood right now. I can't speak for Nicholas or Ivy, but I'm all talked out—even about apples."

"That'd be a first," Nicholas joked as he guided the horses. "And I'm definitely not close to dozing off," he added, glancing at Hobin. "Too much on my mind as I think about returning home."

"I hope you've left some room for me in your thoughts," Ivy playfully remarked.

"Always," he said.

"Well, I guess I'll just talk to my horse then," Hobin answered with a chuckle, "though he was never much of a conversationalist."

"We'll save it for when you get back from visiting Emma," Leo promised as he closed his eyes. "By then, Nicholas and I will have a list of questions longer than my arm."

"I suppose I won't be able to get either of you to clam up then," he muttered, gazing ahead at the iron gray clouds that were thinning far in the west. "So I better enjoy the silence while I can."

His thoughts turned to Emma waiting for him in the north. He wondered what kind of life they could make for themselves after so many years apart. Leo, at the same time, confidently allowed himself to imagine a life together with Megan now that the war had ended, envisioning them collapsing into one another's arms when they reunited at the Citadel as he drifted off to sleep.

Nicholas and Ivy shared similar thoughts about their interweaving paths in life that finally aligned along a parallel course after a tumultuous introduction. It had been a long journey from their first sweet moments in Boros, but they knew deep in their hearts that by surviving the trials of the last few months while apart, surely together they could conquer anything that life might throw their way. Both were eager to find out.

As the day unwound, the last few miles disappeared under foot and hoof and turning wheel. The long, tired lines skirted a patch of woods to their left and made for a familiar stretch of road to the north. Everyone cheered in turns about an hour before twilight when they left the field and moved onto the westernmost section of King's Road a handful of miles outside Morrenwood. The clouds broke and began to scatter by this time, leaving a gauzy patchwork tinted along the edges in soft hues of red, orange and pink. At last, as everyone's minds were saturated with thoughts of home and loved ones, the Blue Citadel came into view. It towered in the distance against the dark Trent Hills and the surrounding deep green pines. Its sturdy granite blocks were gently splashed with the light of the sun descending slowly into the northwest peaks like an eagle alighting gently in its nest. The men and women of Arrondale had finally arrived home.

END OF PART ELEVEN

PART TWELVE
THE JOURNEY HOME

CHAPTER 114

Back to Where it All Began

A day of celebration commenced throughout Arrondale five days after King Justin's army arrived in the capital. Some soldiers had returned to their villages beforehand to be reunited with loved ones. Others remained for a time at the Blue Citadel and the eastern encampment to rest and recover from their injuries. Many families, however, grieved the loss of their fathers, brothers and sons. It was a difficult time for all in the months that followed, particularly for those who had wielded a sword or rode a horse into the fire of battle. But on this special day of celebration, most were in high spirits. For one day, all gave themselves permission to rejoice in their freedom and good fortune that so many had fought and died to secure.

Behind the Blue Citadel, party tents and celebratory bonfires had been set up on that warm spring day, the flames nearest to the Edelin River reflecting upon its swiftly moving waters. Nicholas, sharing drinks with Ivy, Hobin, Carmella and others beneath a large canopy, was reminded of the good times he enjoyed at many Harvest Festivals in Kanesbury over the years despite the dramatics that had occurred at the last one. He also fondly recalled when he and Ivy danced at the winter party in Illingboc.

"They're playing music," Nicholas told her, pointing to a trio of tall pines along the river near which people danced in the sunshine to the lively rhythms of flutes, fiddles and hand drums. "Think our feet can keep up? It's been a while."

"I'm ready if you are," she replied, delighting in the moments she had spent with Nicholas since her rescue on the mountain. She glanced at Carmella and Hobin. "Do you two want to join us?"

"I'll watch," Hobin said. "I'm too tired to compete with you youngsters."

"As am I," Carmella said. "Besides, I have to save my energy. Tolapari and I are giving a demonstration in smoke manipulation later on. It'll be most entertaining."

As Nicholas and his friends left for the dance area through the bustling crowd, they saw Leo and Princess Megan approaching them arm in arm, all smiles and in love.

"Sorry we're late," Leo said. "Megan had some royal duties to attend to."

She glanced knowingly at Leo. Then with a wave of her hand, she indicated for everyone to follow them to a thicket of shrubs on the river for privacy where the waters noisily washed over moss covered rocks. "We have news," she continued excitedly, "though it's still meant to be a secret for just a little while longer."

"Then perhaps you shouldn't tell us," Nicholas said.

"You be quiet, mister," Ivy playfully replied. "If Megan wants to tell us something, kindly let her."

"Of course you're right, dear," he quickly added, amusing both Leo and Hobin.

"Megan, ignore these men folk and tell us what's on your mind," Carmella said. "Ivy and I are eager to hear if they aren't."

"I should hope you will all be," she said, peeking around the shrubbery to make sure no one else was in earshot. She lowered her voice as if divulging a state secret. "Leo and I just had a talk with Father and Grandfather."

"Megan did most of the talking," Leo admitted.

"About what?" Ivy asked.

Megan, holding Leo's arm tightly, couldn't conceal a beaming smile. "Leo, with both poise and confidence–"

"–and *sheer terror*–"

"–just asked them for their blessing to marry me!"

"How wonderful!" Ivy exclaimed as she hugged the princess and then Leo with Carmella mirroring her actions.

"I'm happy for you both," Nicholas said as he wrapped his arms around Megan. "Luckily we met each other in the woods or you might never have met this guy," he added, shaking Leo's hand.

Megan showed them the interlocking silver and copper ring necklace beneath her blouse, telling of Leo's proposal. "I've kept it hidden all this time, but one day soon I shall display it openly." She wore it next to her royal medallion that Ivy had since returned.

"Megan and I decided not to make an official announcement for a few more weeks until after the soldiers have returned home and people can get back to living normal lives," Leo said. "We have plenty of time to share our good news, though we informed Tolapari and Nedry of our intentions so that King Justin doesn't have to tiptoe around everybody."

"I think such good news might boost people's spirits after all that has happened," Hobin said, offering his best wishes. "Still, I'm sure it'll be a fine wedding."

"When is the ceremony?" Ivy asked.

"We're planning an autumn date," Megan said. "I thank you in advance for your discretion, but I had to tell someone before I burst. And I expect you all to be there."

"We wouldn't miss it for the world," Carmella said, wiping a tear from her eye.

"I hope I won't have to call you *Prince* Leo," Nicholas joked.

"I'll make an exception," he replied, "though I do have one favor I'd like to request, seeing as you'll be heading east soon."

"Anything," he said. "Just name it."

Three nights later, King Justin held a private dinner for several close friends who would be leaving over the next few days. Nicholas and Ivy planned to depart the following morning. The King had dispatched a messenger to Laurel Corners days earlier to inform Ivy's parents that she had been rescued and would soon be on her way home, easing her anxiety about lingering at the Citadel for as long as she had.

Prince Gregory, Leo and Megan joined them along with Carmella, Hobin, Tolapari and Nedry. They gathered around a large oak table as servers ladled steaming soup into their bowls and laid out plates of warm bread. Flickering candles lined the center of the table and a roaring fireplace on the far side of the chamber dispelled any chill. Remnants of dusky twilight lingered outside the tall sets of window panes along the west wall.

"For as long as the war and the buildup to it had dragged on," King Justin began, "as I sit here now with you, the preceding days, weeks and months have slipped by like leaves in a passing breeze. I shall miss your companionship."

"But, Grandfather, they shall all be back this autumn for our wedding," Megan told him with a sympathetic smile, gently placing a hand upon his. "Do not let melancholy get the best of you."

"Perhaps it is the wine," Prince Gregory suggested with a smile, drawing light laughter from the others.

"Perhaps," he genially replied. "So I will make the best of our time together." The King glanced across the table at Nicholas. "Since you and Ivy are leaving tomorrow morning, tell me of your plans in the days ahead so it will ease my mind."

"Happy to," he said. "First I will take Ivy home to Laurel Corners, stopping along the way to visit Leo's parents in Minago."

"They'll treat you like royalty," Leo said. "And I'm nearly finished with my letter you promised to deliver to them."

"Better write faster," he said. "Ivy and I are leaving promptly after breakfast."

"But there's a lot to tell," Leo reminded him. "Hiking through the Dunn Hills. Opening the Spirit Box and nearly dying. Facing evil wizards and nearly dying *again*."

Megan smiled, lightly squeezing his hand before turning to her grandfather. "Leo is composing a detailed summary of his adventures, knowing his parents deserve at least that much while he spends a little more time with us at the Citadel."

"But Megan and I will visit Minago in early summer," Leo said. "I have to check on the apple orchards–and my brother."

"I'm sure both have blossomed nicely in your absence," Megan assured him.

"And what about you, Carmella?" the King inquired, glancing at her and Tolapari. "Have you finalized your plans yet?"

She sipped a cup of steaming tea and nibbled on a piece of bread. "After I return to Red Fern to get my house in order, we shall hike through the Trent Hills, following the Edelin River all the way down to the Trillium Sea."

"It's the perfect time of year to head north," the wizard explained. "We shall study the flora and fauna of the region and climb one or two of the lower mountains. Of course, I'll begin teaching Carmella several of the lesser spells from the compendium of the magic arts. We'll return up the west side of the Trent range along the Cashua Forest and be back in time for Megan and Leo's wedding."

"Just don't step *into* the forest," Megan joked, briefly eyeing Leo and Nicholas. "I wouldn't want you to get lost in the woods like a couple of other travelers I know."

"A journey through the Trent Hills sounds like the ideal trip for you, Hobin," Nicholas remarked to his friend at the other end of the table.

"Oh, I shall get my chance," he replied. "King Justin and I have had extensive talks about me mapping regions of Arrondale next year. But first I plan to visit Emma."

"Bring her to the wedding," Leo said. "We want to meet her."

"We'll see," he replied.

"As long as you're traveling that way," Nicholas continued, "could you go a few more miles into Illingboc and deliver a letter to Arch Boland? I want to let him and his family know what transpired in Kargoth and elsewhere. He'll be happy to learn that life along the Crescent will no longer be disrupted by soldiers from the Northern Isles, though I suspect word has already passed that way."

"Of course I will," he said, "as I'm curious to explore that region while I'm there."

"I'm going to tour the area next spring," Prince Gregory announced to the others' surprise. "I'd like to talk with Arch Boland and various leaders up and down the Crescent."

"Why?" Nicholas asked, recalling that Arch wanted him to intercede with King Justin for help in battling the Islanders.

"After speaking with you, Father suggested that it might be wise to establish a treaty of friendship with those along the Crescent," he said. "Since we share a common shoreline, it's time we cast a more serious eye in guarding our coastal borders. I hope to initiate talks with Boland and his ilk to accomplish this goal together."

"As Hobin lives in the southern reaches of the Crescent, he's the ideal man to deliver a letter to Boland from me as well," King Justin said. "We'll see what develops."

"I wish you luck," Nicholas said. "Arch and many others used their own resources to protect that region from the Isles."

"And we must too," Prince Gregory replied. "I'll be visiting Graystone Garrison shortly to initiate plans to build another fort up north near the grasslands. We learned at a terrible cost that Arrondale will not remain secure if its borders are weak."

Nedry, who had been sitting silently at one end of the table, suddenly spoke up. "You see, Nicholas, the brief discussion you had with Arch Boland, and then later with the King, was enough to generate some progress about safeguarding the Crescent. Who knows what might grow because of your words and concern?" he said with a proud smile. "You might have the makings of a royal advisor in you."

"Thanks for the fine compliment," he replied, taking hold of Ivy's hand beneath the table. "And as interesting as your line of work sounds, I believe my path in life leads elsewhere." He felt Ivy's warm fingers gently clasping his own. "But tell me, what are your plans, Nedry? I heard you're retiring from your post."

"I shall finish my duties at the end of this month," he said. "The first day of New Summer will mark my return to private life."

"And to a much deserved rest," Megan told him. "You've worked tirelessly over the years and have been a fine friend to this family. I'll miss seeing you scurrying through the Citadel halls at odd hours on your way to some important meeting or other."

"Your grandfather offered me a choice of two living arrangements upon my retirement," he explained. "One was quarters in the eastern wing of the Citadel with a lovely view of the orchards which I seriously considered, though ultimately declined."

"So where will you go?" Carmella asked.

"I've been provided a cottage in the western district near a thicket of woods with some land for a garden," he said. "Peaceful and idyllic, which I believe is King Justin's way to compensate me for my frazzled state after serving in his employ."

"You will be difficult to replace," Prince Gregory told him.

"Still, don't expect never to see me again. Miss Alb, the head seamstress, and I have been dining together regularly over the winter and have become quite fond of one another. Don't be surprised to bump into me from time to time when I call on her."

"Then don't be surprised if I pull you aside to share some ale," King Justin happily warned him. "I may bend your ear for a while, though in an unofficial capacity, of course."

"I shall be more than happy to listen, sir."

King Justin stood and looked at his family and friends, raising his cup in a toast.

"At this happy moment, let me salute you all for your many contributions to the continued life and freedom of Arrondale and its people," he said, sweeping his gaze across the nine of them with mixed emotions. "But most importantly, let me thank you for your love and friendship, a treasure far beyond what I could ever return in kind, and one I cherish more than these heartfelt words can express. If life repays you by only a tenth of what you have given me, then you shall find yourselves truly blessed indeed."

King Justin drank from his cup, and with a few scattered tears among them, the others did so, too. All felt the poignant weight of an ending chapter in their lives, yet knew in their hearts that more spectacular days and splendid moments were still to come.

Early the following morning after breakfast, Nicholas and Ivy said goodbye to King Justin and his son in a study overlooking the orchards. A short time later they stood outside the main courtyard gates, bidding farewell to their friends. It was a warm and sunny second day of Old Spring. A team of horses and a wagon had been provided for their return journey. Gathered on the grassy edge of the road were Leo, Megan, Hobin and Carmella, all happy to see the young couple together, yet saddened to see them leave.

"We'll be back in autumn for the wedding," Ivy said as she and Nicholas hugged their companions goodbye.

"And if I get my old job back from Ned Adams, I'll be traveling here from time to time making deliveries," Nicholas added. "But first I have to tie up some loose ends."

Megan chuckled. "Those dreadful complications still await you at home. But now that you've solved some of the mystery behind them, I don't expect they'll appear as menacing when you return."

"I hope not," he replied. Though having learned of Mune and Dooley Kramer's connections to that fateful night he had fled home, he still didn't know how it all related to him being framed. Then Carmella spoke up.

"Nicholas, I had meant to tell you this earlier, but the past few days have been so busy that it slipped my mind," she said.

"Tell me what?"

"During one of my conversations with Caldurian, he admitted that he was responsible for the trouble that had befallen you last fall."

"I knew it!" Nicholas said, eager for the details. But he was quickly disappointed.

"However," she continued, "the wizard refused to provide me any specifics regarding how or why. But I hope that gives you some solace in your search for answers."

Nicholas sighed. "A little, but I may have to resign myself to the fact that I might never find out the entire truth."

"Still, it's something," Leo said. "Maybe others back home found out what really happened. At the very least, you can confront Dooley and pry the answers out of him."

"Oh, that I plan to do," he promised.

"But first things first," Hobin said. "You have a young lady to escort home. If you gab with us any longer, it'll be time for Megan and Leo's wedding. So get going already!"

"Now that's the Hobin I remember," he said.

After a last goodbye, Nicholas and Ivy climbed aboard the wagon. With a gentle flick of the reins, they slowly headed down the main road through Morrenwood, leaving the Blue Citadel, many fond memories and their dearest friends behind.

Once out of the capital, they turned onto King's Road and headed east into the warming hours of midmorning. The sun rose against a cobalt blue sky blooming with languid white clouds. The fields on either side of the road and the distant southern hills were alive with vibrant shades of green, dotted here and there in bright blues, pinks and yellows as the wildflowers of late spring burst forth. Ivy smiled and wrapped an arm around Nicholas as they leisurely moved, enjoying their time alone. He smiled back while guiding the horses onward.

"Leaving Morrenwood is by far a better journey than the one getting there."

"And why is that?" she asked.

"Well, there was the raw autumn weather and a string of rainstorms for starters, not to mention all the trouble across Laparia. And, of course, you weren't beside me," he added, kissing her cheek. "That was the worst reason. But now that we're together under a beautiful sky with all the time in the world, well, it's like…"

"Ivy glanced up. "*A dream*?"

Nicholas smiled again. "A dream come true."

They passed through a few villages during the day, enjoying a late lunch in one and wandering about to stretch their legs. Near twilight, Nicholas pulled over by a grove of trees along a stream where they spent the night. The following day was nearly a repeat of the first in both the weather and their itinerary. As dusk settled in, they neared the end of King's Road and passed the night by a blazing fire below Darden Wood where Nicholas had first met Princess Megan. He told Ivy the story of their encounter and how he promised to accompany Megan all the way to Boros.

"Meg, however, said that I was just trying to avoid my problems back home."

"And were you?" Ivy asked as the flames crackled, bathing them in its gentle glow.

"I suppose, but I promise to make it all the way home after I take you to Laurel Corners," he said. "But it's a good thing I went to Boros or I'd never have met you."

"Excellent point," she said, leaning over to kiss him. "I guess we both gained something from your procrastination."

"We did," he returned with a smile, kissing her tenderly as a cool, spring breeze rustled through the grass beneath the starry sky.

After an earlier start the next day, they reached the end of King's Road before midmorning and veered left onto River Road. Though they were still many miles away from his village, Nicholas knew that this road passed directly through Kanesbury, making him yearn for home. He drove with few stops that morning to make up for their leisurely pace the two previous days, but their time together had strengthened the bonds of love and friendship between them. Nicholas wanted to reach Laurel Corners tomorrow, knowing that

Ivy was homesick. He planned to arrive at Minago before sundown where they would spend the night with Leo's family and no doubt enjoy a wonderful meal compliments of Joe and Annabelle Marsh.

Along the way, Nicholas pointed out Graystone Garrison upon a gently rolling field to the left. He recalled the night he had met soldiers from Montavia camping along the road outside the village of Mitchell, some of them on their way to train at this very garrison. Then, he had desired to be in the King's Guard, yearning for a bit of adventure. But after all the adventures that he and Ivy had just shared, Nicholas realized that he had had enough excitement to last half a lifetime and simply looked forward to spending some lazy and contented days with her in the future.

Shortly after noontime, they neared the turnoff to Orchard Road. After traveling north about a half mile along it, Nicholas pulled the wagon over near a large oak beside a grassy field so they could rest and have lunch. The horses drank from a stream as Nicholas built a fire and Ivy prepared a small meal. After eating, they sat under the shade of the tree and whiled away half an hour, holding hands and talking about what to do with the rest of their lives. Nicholas then got up and excused himself.

"I want to check on the horses and give them each an apple," he said. "They've had a long journey, too."

"Hurry back," Ivy said as a warm breeze played through her hair.

She leaned against the tree trunk and relaxed as Nicholas disappeared behind the wagon, watching the dwindling flames of the fire flutter in the gentle swirls of air. She recalled the morning in Castella's kitchen when she and Nicholas knelt on the hearth to build a fire before sharing some bread and cinnamon tea in the gray dawn while the others slept. Ivy imagined sharing many such moments with Nicholas in the years ahead, realizing how fortunate they were to have met despite the chaotic circumstances. Nicholas soon appeared around the corner of the wagon, one hand hidden behind his back.

"Miss me?" he asked playfully.

"As soon as you left," she replied, curiously eyeing him. "What have you there?"

He sat down beside her and revealed a bouquet of wildflowers he had gathered in the field, presenting it to Ivy who smiled with delight. "I thought someone as pretty as you deserved these," he said, his gaze fixed lovingly upon her.

"They're beautiful, Nicholas! Thank you."

"And," he continued with a hint of nervousness, "I'm hoping you think that I deserve someone like you as nothing would make me happier than being your husband. So with all my heart I ask—will you marry me, Ivy?"

Her eyes misted when Nicholas uttered those words she had longed to hear. Yet deep in her heart, Ivy had always known that she and Nicholas would spend their lives together. She couldn't imagine going through the years ahead without him.

"Of course I'll marry you!" she said, wrapping her arms tightly around him before pulling back and looking into his eyes. "And you're more than I deserve," she added, kissing him and feeling as if she were starting a new life.

Nicholas shared similar sentiments. And though the trouble he had yet to face in Kanesbury lingered in back of his mind, this blissful moment with Ivy was all that mattered right now. He couldn't wait to start his new life as well.

They arrived at Leo's parents' house as the setting sun tinted the weeping willow in front, igniting it in a blaze of golden hues. Joe, Annabelle and Henry greeted Nicholas when they saw his wagon pull up. All were excited to finally meet Ivy. When Nicholas handed Leo's letter to Mrs. Marsh, she beamed with relief.

"I'd rather he were here so I could give him a hug," she said while hustling everyone to the house. "Still, hurry inside now. I have a letter to read!"

"Leo plans to visit in early summer with Princess Megan."

"That's wonderful!" Mrs. Marsh replied, clutching the letter to her heart as Joe opened the door. "So he and the lovely princess are still fond of one another?"

Nicholas and Ivy exchanged glances and smiled. "You'd better read the letter first. That'll explain everything."

Moments later, Mrs. Marsh, wanting to be a gracious host, threw on an apron and placed the letter in her pocket. She hurriedly sat everyone down at the table and served them from a kettle of pork stew simmering over the fire.

"There's rhubarb pie on the sill!" Henry said, anticipating the sweet treat.

"Yes, yes," his mother said distractedly as she placed a plate of herb biscuits on the table and urged her guests to dig in to their meals. "Don't wait for me now. Eat! Eat!" After filling everyone's cup with apple cider, Mrs. Marsh finally sat down in her seat in front of an empty bowl and cup, satisfied that her duties were fulfilled. She removed Leo's letter from her apron pocket with trembling hands and began reading it as the others conversed, stopping moments later with a loud exclamation.

"My goodness, Joe! Our son is going to marry the princess!" she said with a stunned smile before rereading the passage. "Can you imagine that?"

"I imagine more work for me in the apple orchards after he moves away," he joked, happy to hear the news.

"Is that going to make my brother a prince?" Henry asked, furrowing his brow. "He bosses me around enough as it is."

"I suppose it will," his mother replied with her eyes glued to the letter, delighted with the prospect. "Just imagine, my son the *prince*. What will I wear to the wedding?"

"I'll buy you a new dress when we drive up north," her husband replied before addressing Nicholas and Ivy. "We're going to get apple orders for the season shortly and enjoy a well-earned, leisurely day at the Plum Orchard Inn."

"I look forward to another visit there myself when I take Ivy back to Laurel Corners," Nicholas said. "Next to your wife, Ron and Mabel Knott are the kindest hosts."

Mrs. Marsh again looked up from the letter. "Leo writes that he's inviting the Knotts to the ceremony. Oh, it will be a lovely time, visiting Morrenwood for such a grand celebration! We haven't been to a fancy wedding in ages."

Ivy looked at Nicholas with a raised eyebrow, silently questioning him. He smiled knowingly and nodded, sensing her desire to tell the Marshes about their engagement.

"Then perhaps you might like to attend *two* weddings," she suggested, happily recounting Nicholas' proposal earlier that day and their plans to marry next spring. Annabelle, tearing up, hugged them both upon hearing the good news.

"This calls for dessert!" she said, hurrying to the counter.

"Let me give you a hand," Ivy said, joining her as the men talked at the table. She leaned in and whispered to Annabelle as she sliced up the rhubarb pie. "I need to ask you something, Mrs. Marsh, though I hardly know you and don't wish to impose."

"Nonsense. You and Nicholas are like family. What do you need, dear?"

"A favor."

The next morning dawned cool and overcast as if autumn had returned and spring was a fading memory. But Nicholas felt the change in weather appropriate as it reflected his somber mood. He walked with Ivy about the Marshes' property after breakfast, the colorful flowers and blooming trees muted in the dim light.

"A few more days on the road won't matter to me," he told her as they strolled hand in hand along the side of the barn. "I've put in enough miles already. I'm used to it."

"Just more hours for you to stew about what awaits you at home," Ivy said. She stopped and faced Nicholas, taking his hands in hers. "I want our life together to start as soon as possible, so the quicker you deal with your troubles back home, the sooner that can happen." She kissed him. "I'll go with you for support," she offered.

"No," he insisted. "I want your first visit to Kanesbury to happen only after I have my affairs in order. I don't want you involved with this mess."

"We've faced enough messes already. What's one more?"

Nicholas grinned. "You're probably right, but I'd still prefer that your introduction to my village be on a happier note. Or on second thought, I could never go back and we could spend the rest of our lives along the sea."

Ivy smiled. "Even I know you're not serious. But considering how you cleverly broke into Vellan's abode, straightening things out back home should be easy."

"I hope so," he replied, hugging her. "I miss you already."

"And I miss you." She looked him in the eyes with endless reassurance. "But the faster you get on the road, the happier you'll be when it's over. So not to sound pushy, but I think it's time that you left, Nicholas, before we both lose our resolve."

"Sure you'll be fine without me?"

"I'll accompany Joe and Annabelle on their trip north, enjoy a lovely meal at the Plum Orchard Inn as you suggested, and then return home to Laurel Corners. Mrs. Marsh was more than happy to assist when I asked. She quite agreed with my reasons."

Nicholas took her arm in his and continued their walk as a gentle breeze weaved among the leafy trees and lush green grass. "So who am I to argue with *two* women? But I'm still going to miss you, Ivy, now more than ever."

Nicholas departed later that morning, waving to Ivy and the Marshes as he rattled down the road in the wagon. Ivy's smile was the last thing he saw before turning his head and focusing on the path before him. Soon after leaving Minago, he was back on Orchard Road driving south, realizing that he was finally going home. Despite thickening clouds and a steady breeze, the rain held off for several miles before he reconnected with River Road. When he reached the intersection, he turned left and journeyed eastward, feeling that he might avoid the worst of the weather. But moments later, the skies opened up.

Nicholas flipped the hood of his coat over his head and pressed on. Only when the rainfall grew nearly blinding did he finally pull off the road underneath some trees to wait out the storm. Another hour passed before the rain let up, though the sky still remained dark, the clouds bulging with moisture. He continued miserably onward, plagued by intermittent showers, but eventually reached the village of Foley. The streets were deserted as its residents had taken refuge in their homes glowing with warm firelight in the late afternoon dusk. Nicholas guided the wagon straight through, determined to reach home later that night. When he arrived in Mitchell a couple miles farther east, the rains let loose again and he resigned himself to spending one more night away from Kanesbury.

Nicholas found a small inn just off the main road. After housing his horses and wagon, he ate a light meal in his second floor room, warmed himself by the fireplace until the chills of the day had left, and then crawled into bed and fell promptly asleep. Other than a dream about Ivy, his slumber was undisturbed.

Nicholas rose late the following morning, waking to a pounding rain against the window panes. He hadn't slept for that many hours in quite some time and felt refreshed. But when he separated the curtains and gazed through the window at the gray deluge, he knew he would be staying put indefinitely.

He ate lunch in the common room with other lodgers who accepted the idea that some or all of their day would be wasted because of the intolerable weather. As Nicholas consumed a bowl of hot soup and bread at a table near a crackling fireplace, he realized how much he missed Ivy and his friends. For a moment it seemed as if all of the people he had met and all the adventures he had shared with them over the last eight months were just figments of his imagination. He felt as empty and alone as on the evening he had said goodbye to Katherine Durant in the ice cellar before disappearing into the night. Overcome with melancholy, he quickly finished his meal and returned to his room, flopping upon the bed to take a nap in hopes that this grim mood would soon pass.

He awoke several hours later to the sound of eager voices and the opening and closing of distant doors. Nicholas glanced out his window and noted the waning daylight, realizing he had taken a longer nap than he had wished. Yet the rain had ceased and the clouds had taken on lighter hues of gray, giving him hope that he could reach Kanesbury by nightfall. After paying his bill and retrieving his wagon from the stables, he was back on the road in the cool dampness, leaving the village of Mitchell behind. He headed home, eager to navigate the final ten miles between him and the uncertain days ahead.

When darkness finally engulfed the landscape, Nicholas realized that he was traveling the last mile of roadway before the western border of Kanesbury. His heart pounded and he took a slow, deep breath, contemplating all he had experienced since leaving. He had fled the village last year on the tenth day of New Autumn and was now returning on the sixth day of Old Spring. Yet all the problems he had once escaped still hung over him like the dreary clouds above.

Soon the lights of Kanesbury beckoned to him in the near distance north and south of River Road, the gentle glow of warm, yellow windows scattered among the thickets of pine and maple trees like curious, unblinking eyes. When reaching the western border, he reined his horses to a stop and gazed out upon the narrow streets through the leafy trees. No one was around in the immediate vicinity, though a few distant voices were vaguely audible from somewhere within the middle of the village. All in all, it was a typically quiet evening in Kanesbury. And despite the many trials still ahead, Nicholas was glad to be back.

CHAPTER 115

A Familiar Face

Nicholas entered Kanesbury awash in the murky shadows of early evening. He stayed on River Road, guessing that anyone who might pass by would not recognize him in the gloom. To his relief, the road remained deserted. He decided to scout about first before confronting Dooley Kramer. He intended for that meeting to take place in the presence of Constable Brindle and Ned Adams, the two men to whom Nicholas most wanted to prove his innocence. He knew that Maynard, wherever he was, already believed him innocent.

As he guided the wagon east, Nicholas was comforted by the warm display of houselights peeking through the trees. It conjured up memories of pleasant walks to the Water Barrel Inn and to and from the gristmill. Most residents lived north of River Road where the houselights were numerous among the leafy trees. To the south, the lights were fewer and scattered. He detected the glow from the Iron Kettle Tavern, a popular haunt for Dooley Kramer and the late Arthur Weeks. But it only made him angry to think about what those two had done to him.

Soon he neared a street branching off River Road to his left. Katherine and her mother lived in the corner house at the far end, so Nicholas decided to pay them a secret visit and hear the latest about life in the village. He guided the wagon off the north side of River

Road among a thicket of trees and climbed down, deciding to walk up the street to see if any light was coming from the house.

He strolled north along the narrow lane, passing Matilda Grute's house on his right. Shortly thereafter, he approached a thicket of trees beyond it. From here he had a direct view of the Durant household across the street on the corner, its windows as dark as coal. He guessed that Katherine and her mother were out for the evening or had retired early, so he prepared to leave. But as he was about to turn around, he detected movement among the tall, shadowy pines in back of their house.

Nicholas, though concealed among the trees in darkness, bent down as a precaution and took a second look. A man moved among the trees on the Durant property, his face periodically aglow as he drew on a pipe. Nicholas couldn't identify the figure and was warily curious as to why he was secretly watching Katherine's house.

He stealthily made his way back down the street and returned to his wagon just around the corner. Moments later, Nicholas headed farther into the village along River Road, anticipating his next stop and hoping to find some answers.

A short time later, he neared Adelaide Cooper's house at the other end of the village. Here the trees were sparser, offering a magnificent view of the stars in the moonless sky. Nicholas recalled talking to Adelaide on her porch two days before the Harvest Festival. Now the house stood dark and deserted. He noted the outlines of Maynard's home and his own cottage across the road, both equally dead. Hoping to find a familiar face, he decided to check one other place before calling it a night.

First he hid the wagon behind Adelaide's house and unhitched the horses, allowing them to graze along a nearby stream. He then walked along River Road back into the village. Moments later, he weaved his way among the shadowy shrubs and trees behind Oscar and Amanda Stewart's house, the light from the windows splashing upon the lawn. Nicholas recalled leaving their ice cellar eight months ago, fleeing to an uncertain future. Now here he was again, nearly as uncertain about his fate as he was back then.

He cautiously approached the house and peered into a kitchen window but saw no one inside. He considered knocking on the back door, yet feared that if the Stewarts had company, his presence would be advertised throughout the village in no time. To make certain, he decided to peek through a window on the south side to gauge his next move. But as soon as he turned the corner of the house, he quickly retreated and pressed his back to the building, his heart beating rapidly. As on the Durant property, Nicholas spotted someone lingering in the shadows here as well.

He carefully peered around the corner and saw a figure leaning against a tree and gazing west toward the front of the property. As the person wasn't looking in his direction, Nicholas observed the individual for a moment, knowing it wasn't the same person he had seen earlier as he appeared taller. Nicholas slipped back around the corner and wondered why someone was skulking about. When he saw a shadow pass across the light on the lawn, he realized that someone had entered the kitchen. He ducked and scurried back to where he had first looked into the house and again spied through the window. This time he saw someone he recognized, a soft and familiar, yet troubled face.

There in the kitchen hanging a kettle of water over a fire in the hearth was Katherine Durant, her long, brown hair cascading over a beige knitted sweater. A veneer of worry clouded her face. Nicholas wanted to speak with her at once and made his way to the ice cellar. He hurried down the stone stairs and opened the door into the familiar cool and dark confines.

After feeling his way to the staircase, he quietly ascended in utter darkness until a faint outline of a door appeared at top. He pressed his ear to it, and hearing no voices, he slowly opened the door just enough to peek through. Seeing no one, he stepped into the pantry, keeping to one side of the doorway leading into the kitchen. He heard a clattering of tea cups and saucers, but detecting no voices, he assumed that Katherine was still alone.

With mounting apprehension, Nicholas slowly craned his head around the doorway. At that same moment, Katherine looked up as she was preparing the tea. Their surprised gazes met, their breaths nearly taken away. Katherine, her mouth agape and her heart racing, was confused and elated at once. Before she could utter a word, Nicholas raised a finger to his lips and beckoned her to the pantry. She hurried to him, throwing her arms around his shoulders.

"Is it really you?" she whispered.

"It's me, Katherine," he whispered back, delighted to hear her voice again.

He indicated that they should go downstairs to speak more freely. Understanding his concern, Katherine found a spare candle and lit it from a burning oil lamp affixed to the wall and led Nicholas down to the ice cellar. They sat on wooden crates in the same corner like eight months ago. The candle was wedged between blocks of straw-covered ice cut from Neeley's Pond last winter.

"When did you get back?" she whispered.

"Within the hour," he replied, telling her of his previous stops. "I'm so glad to see you again, but did I arrive at a bad time?"

Katherine shook her head. "The Stewarts invited my mother and me over for dinner tonight. No one else is around. Morris has the night off and is holed away in his room. I was making tea."

"I saw you through the kitchen window. And I saw something else." He told her about the two figures watching this house and her home. When he noted her cheerful expression melt away, he guessed that she was in trouble. "What's going on?"

"More than you could imagine. But I know you've had your share of adventures, too, so anything I say will pale in comparison."

"We can talk about me later. First tell me everything that happened since I left," he said with growing concern.

"First let me serve tea. I'll return, excusing myself to replenish the firewood," she said. "Though Oscar, Amanda and my mother would be delighted to see you, I don't want anyone I associate with to know that you're back just yet. And I suspect you want to keep your arrival secret as well."

"Hiding out in this ice cellar was a dead giveaway, right?"

Katherine smiled. "I'm so glad you're home, Nicholas."

She returned a few minutes later with a cup of steaming tea and a plate of biscuits for Nicholas which he gratefully devoured as they talked. But before he could pry any information from her, she eagerly requested details about his time away.

"That could take hours," he explained, tiding her over with a few highlights.

While Katherine was fascinated by the sparse account, she detected an unspoken reluctance on Nicholas' part to delve further into detail. She suspected where his story might lead because of something that Dooley had told her. She folded her arms, feigning a chill to change the subject. Nicholas removed his coat and draped it over her shoulders.

"We need to schedule these meetings down here in the middle of summer," he joked. "Now tell me what happened since I left. I've heard a few rumors on the road, the most disturbing one being that Maynard has been missing since late last autumn."

"Let me assure you that Maynard is alive. I know where he is. And Adelaide Cooper, too."

Nicholas was relieved to hear the news. "You know quite a bit of the comings and goings here. What have you been up to?"

Katherine smiled. "I'd ask you the same, but I'm already privy to some details."

"How?"

"I have my source."

Nicholas furrowed his brow, taking a sip of tea. "Who?"

Her expression turned somber. "Let me say that I *had* my source."

He was intrigued when she informed him that the bulk of her information was obtained from Dooley Kramer. And though Nicholas harbored ill feelings toward him, he exhibited genuine remorse when he learned of his accidental death.

"Dooley, along with Zachary Farnsworth, framed you for the gristmill robbery and Arthur Weeks' murder," she said.

Nicholas shook his head in disbelief. "I knew Arthur was involved since he lied to my face. And while away, I came to the realization that Dooley ripped the missing button off my jacket," he said. "But why would Farnsworth have anything against me? He was always personable whenever I met with him while on business for Ned Adams."

Katherine smirked with disdain. "Behind his amiable façade is a scheming manipulator. Zachary's connections went beyond people in and around the village. He had dealings with Caldurian himself."

"Now *his* involvement doesn't surprise me. He confided to a woman named Carmella that he was behind my troubles. I even heard he overran our village again."

"It's true. For nine days we lived under Caldurian's rule, backed up by an army of horrid soldiers from the Isles. Well, except for one," she cryptically added. But her focus suddenly shifted. "*Carmella*? Isn't she the woman who brought the medallion to King Justin? The one you and Leo Marsh took to the wizard Frist?" She noted the look of stunned incredulity upon Nicholas' face, certain he was wondering how she could know such facts. "I suppose you enjoyed playing hero," she added lightly, though deep down she was very proud of Nicholas.

"Are you a mind reader?" he inquired, flabbergasted by her knowledge of his exploits and the names of the people with whom he had associated.

"Remember, I had a good source—Dooley Kramer."

"But how could he have possibly known all that information?"

"Because Dooley was spying from the rafters during your meeting with King Justin," she explained. "The meeting where you had volunteered to find the wizard Frist."

"Dooley was *there*?" he said in amazement, recalling that King Justin had learned of a spy's existence from Caldurian. "But the King was never told the name of the spy. He certainly would have informed me had he known it was Dooley Kramer, of all people."

"Well, Dooley admitted it to me, and a good many other things, too. It allowed me to piece together some of the strange goings-on during the Harvest Festival."

Nicholas was impressed with her ingenuity. *And a good many other things, too*? Suddenly he wondered if Dooley had told her about Ivy and his request to King Justin to help rescue her. Even though he and Katherine were only friends, he felt a tiny bit guilty for not revealing that part of his adventure and his relationship with Ivy to her. But whether she knew or not, there were more pressing matters to discuss first.

"Since you've apparently solved this mystery, I'd logically assume that Constable Brindle was informed of the facts," he said. "Yet earlier you mentioned you didn't want others associated with you to know that I was back. If that's the case, I'm guessing that you also didn't want others to know about any information linked to me that you had, including Dooley's confession." He noted Katherine's troubled gaze, and with a nod, she confirmed his suspicions. "So Brindle knows nothing of this?"

"Not a thing."

He raked a hand through his hair and sighed. "This makes no sense, Katherine."

"It will once you know all the particulars."

"Then please tell me."

"All right," she said, explaining how Caldurian had seized the village, her association with Paraquin, Otto Nibbs' reappearance and her journey with Lewis to the swamp. Nicholas listened with subdued anger, heartbroken at the misery and chaos his friends had endured. "The wizard, at the urging of the crowd, arrested my uncle. And for six months he has been languishing in the lockup awaiting trial."

"When will that be?"

"Your guess is as good as mine. Farnsworth insisted that it would only be proper to hold a trial when Maynard returns. And though most agreed at first, the months have dragged on. There are misgivings about Uncle Otto still being locked up and about how he ended up in prison in the first place. Though few speak it aloud, many now see how they unfairly condemned my uncle, realizing the wizard manipulated their emotions to get his revenge for events of twenty years ago." She looked at Nicholas as if reaching out for help. "And I can prove it, though I fear for the safety of others if I go after Farnsworth with the truth."

Nicholas took her hands, seeing the aguish in her eyes. "If I had stayed, this might not have happened. But tell me more about Farnsworth. Has he threatened you, knowing you're aware of his role in recent events? And does he know that Maynard isn't missing?"

"Yes to both," she said with a defeated sigh, "though he hadn't directly admitted his involvement. He made veiled threats to people close to me to force my silence."

"How'd you learn of Dooley and Farnsworth's involvement? It was a gutsy move for you and Lewis to follow Dooley to the swamp where a killer awaited him."

"We didn't know that at the time," she said. "But after spying on them for nearly two weeks, I discovered they were making late-night journeys there every six days. I was determined to follow them the next time they left. And since Lewis suspected I was up to something, I let him accompany me," she said. "Dooley finally confessed to everything that he, Farnsworth and Caldurian did, particularly to you and Uncle Otto."

"But how did Farnsworth discover that you were on to him?"

"I'm not quite sure," she said. "But something clued him in. He made subtle yet chilling threats against those closest to me on the day following my journey to the swamp. It was the same morning that Constable Brindle was attacked."

"*Attacked?*" Nicholas raised his voice upon hearing such disturbing information. "What happened? Is Clay all right?"

"He's back on the job and uses a cane to get around," she said, explaining how the constable was assaulted before she could divulge what she had discovered at the swamp. "I can't prove it, but I know Zachary Farnsworth was behind that incident. He probably hired some unsavory individual to attack the constable just like he paid someone to kill Dooley. That's why I've kept silent, fearing for the lives of others around me."

"I understand."

"And to make matters worse, Zachary told me he would hire several men out of his own pocket to keep an eye on the village and prevent trouble in the future. But I know that was just a threat to keep me in line," she said with disgust.

"That explains who I saw tonight spying in the shadows," Nicholas said. "But surely others in the village must have seen these strangers."

"They have, but there are different faces from time to time," Katherine continued. "When inquiries were first made, Zachary said that the scouts were hired to search for Maynard and were reporting in from time to time. He also said that some would patrol the village to prevent trouble from returning. Most people found that admirable and accepted his story, happy to have extra eyes around after all of our recent trouble." She looked wearily at Nicholas in the glow of the candlelight. "People have been spooked and distrustful even though months have since passed."

"I can see that you are, too, Katherine, despite the brave fight you've waged."

"My resolve has waned while I was constantly monitoring my movements," she admitted. "I dare not visit Maynard and Adelaide as I would surely be followed, putting their lives and those who harbor them at risk. But I don't know how long Farnsworth will tolerate this uneasy truce between us. His patience and wealth must be growing thin having to finance those men. Maybe it's time to publicly confront him regardless of the consequences."

"Have you kept in contact with Maynard and Adelaide?"

Katherine nodded, reluctant to reveal their location. "The morning after I left them was the same day Farnsworth had made his veiled threats, promising to hire the watchers. Guessing that that would take some time even for him, I immediately rode out to where Maynard and Adelaide were staying. I arranged to communicate with their guardians from then on without me ever having to leave the village."

"How?"

"Every ten days or so, I cross paths with one of them at a prearranged spot in the village, such as the bakery or the butcher shop, never speaking to nor acknowledging the other," she said. "Instead, we slip a note unobtrusively to one another about the latest news. In the note I receive, the next meeting place and time is provided. I can't take the chance and speak to these individuals in case one of Zachary's men is watching."

"How are Maynard and Adelaide faring?"

"Adelaide is fully recovered and is helping to nurse Maynard back to health, though it has been a slow ordeal," she said. "Maynard had finally awakened sometime in New Winter, but is still very weak, needing assistance to walk. He sleeps several times throughout the day as if Arileez' spell still has a lingering effect upon him."

"Arileez?" Nicholas was shocked to learn that the wizard had caused some of the problems in Kanesbury. "I heard stories about his plan to replace King Justin in the Citadel, though he was killed in the attempt. Apparently Arileez had the ability to transform his appearance to resemble anyone or anything he desired."

"That's what Dooley told me. After Arileez cast a sleeping spell on Maynard, he assumed his likeness and position in Kanesbury to implement Caldurian's plan against my uncle."

A sickening feeling washed over Nicholas. "He impersonated Maynard?"

Katherine nodded. "That is why Caldurian needed you out of the way, Nicholas, so you wouldn't stumble upon his elaborate plan."

"But Dooley knew that I was going to leave Kanesbury and join up with the King's Guard. Why bother framing me?"

Katherine told him how Dooley had stolen the key to the Spirit Box when he was a boy, and of Farnsworth's attempt years later to return the key to Caldurian in exchange for control of the village. "With you gone, Dooley had a chance to demonstrate his worth to Ned Adams by easing his way into your job at the gristmill. It was all Zachary's idea to curry favor with the wizard. Since Dooley would be required to make deliveries to the Citadel, Zachary thought that Caldurian might be able to use him as a spy of sorts and reward him further for his ingenuity."

"The idea sounds preposterous," Nicholas said, "yet Dooley did act as a spy as you mentioned earlier, so..." He shook his head, his emotions in a whirl.

"And we may never know all the harm that resulted from it."

Nicholas agreed, yet knew that Dooley Kramer had paid for his transgressions with an untimely death. "What's done is done, I suppose. And between you, me, Maynard and Adelaide, we have more than enough evidence to clear my name. But that's the least of my worries. We need to expose Farnsworth without endangering you or anyone else."

"There is nothing I'd like more, but I fear that once we make a move against him, he'll unleash his private forces upon everyone I care about. I couldn't bear to see what happened to Constable Brindle–or something even worse–happen to others."

"Or happen to you, Katherine."

"That is the least of *my* worries, Nicholas. Whether Zachary is arrested or flees, I can't risk having his men attack others in a final act of crazed vengeance." She shuddered. "I've seen the heartless acts he has committed. He's a vicious animal."

"Then we'll defang him and eliminate the others in his pack."

"But how? The two of us are outnumbered."

Nicholas smiled encouragingly. "We'll just have to trust in a few more people."

Katherine nodded, letting go of her fear and accepting the reality that more help was required. "You're right, Nicholas. But with Zachary's men all over the village, I'm worried that someone will get hurt no matter what we do."

He thought for a moment, the candle glow highlighting a sly smile inching across his face. "First we need to get Zachary and his men in one place before making our move."

Katherine was skeptical. "How are we ever to do that? You don't realize what kind of people I've been dealing with, Nicholas."

"Oh, I have a good idea considering some of the people I've had to endure," he replied. "But it may not be as difficult as you think. We just have to lure those wild animals of sorts to us with a tempting piece of bait."

"And what exactly would that be?"

"*Me.*" Nicholas was about to say something more, but held back. "Let me mull over the details for a few days. I need to come up with a solid plan first," he said. "But I know the perfect place to do my thinking, providing you'll help me, of course."

Katherine returned to the ice cellar twenty minutes later, having gone upstairs to talk with Oscar, Amanda and her mother so as not to arouse suspicion. She gave Nicholas a small sack of food to take on his visit to Maynard and Adelaide, whose whereabouts she finally revealed.

"It's a small thank you for Emmett and Lorna for all their help over the past few months, though I'm still in their debt," she said. "The Stewarts won't miss the leftovers."

"Thanks for trusting me with their location," Nicholas said.

"I suppose I have to start trusting someone."

"Since no one but you knows that I'm back in Kanesbury, I'll simply be a shadow in the night. Maynard and Adelaide will be safe."

Katherine nodded, realizing that the next few steps in their plan were out of her hands. "But you mustn't go until after Mother and I leave and Oscar and Amanda retire for the night. Whoever is watching this house will most likely depart after we head home. When all the lights are off, you can slip away."

"And all you have to do is wait for your next secret meeting where I'll get word to you about my plan."

"That will be in four days at the poulterer's shop."

"I'll have all the details worked out by then, or at least I hope so," he teased, standing up. He smiled at Katherine with a mix of pride and affection. "Though I often wondered how Kanesbury was faring during my absence, I never suspected how much misery and chaos you all had to deal with. Some of my adventures pale in comparison."

"From what little you already told me, I doubt that. And when this is all over, I expect a more detailed account from your first day on the road to the last, including all of your dealings with wizards, mountain guides and secret tunnels."

"You have my word." They hugged goodbye before she made her way to the staircase. Nicholas eyed her as she ascended the first few steps, debating whether he should tell her about his relationship with Ivy. "Katherine, wait," he called out.

"Yes?" she asked, moving down the steps and walking back into the candlelight.

Nicholas looked uneasily at the ground for a moment, glad they were immersed in shadows. He took a deep breath and slowly exhaled, his stomach knotting up. "Katherine, there's something I need to tell you about."

Sensing his apprehension, Katherine sat down and invited him to do so, too. "Nicholas, you're my friend and can tell me anything. What's on your mind?"

He looked briefly away before raising his eyes to meet hers. "While I was on the road, I met a woman and..." His voice faltered and he looked down.

Katherine touched his trembling hands and smiled kindly. "And fell in love?"

He lifted his eyes, sensing nothing but her support and good wishes. "Yes. I guess *fell in love* is the proper description."

"Then I'm happy for you!" she said excitedly, wrapping her arms around him. "So very happy."

As she pulled away, Nicholas wondered if she had heard him properly. "That wasn't the reaction I expected," he replied, a wave of relief washing over him. "I *did* say that I was in love, so I thought that maybe you'd be..."

"A bit more upset?"

Nicholas smiled awkwardly. "Well, when I had invited you to the dance, I was thinking that maybe our friendship might develop into something more, though I never said so directly. And when you accepted, I sensed–or maybe I hoped at the time–that you might have thought so, too." He shrugged. "But I guess running away quashed any chance for us to ever find out. Even still, I was a bit hesitant talking about this just now in case you *had* felt something more for me back then."

Katherine sighed despondently, her eyes downcast. "I must confess that the notion had crossed my mind, Nicholas." She slowly looked up and caressed his cheek with the back of her fingers, her mesmerizing gaze momentarily clouding his thoughts.

"*Oh?*" he replied, his voice quavering, wondering if he had hurt her feelings.

"And now after hearing this news..." Katherine slowly leaned back, apparently upset, until she broke out in a broad smile, once again his old friend. "Oh, don't think too highly of your charms, Nicholas Raven," she teased. "After all, you weren't the only man on my mind in your absence. I've found someone else, too."

Nicholas swallowed hard and grinned. "You had me going there for a moment. I–" He raised an eyebrow in surprise. "Uh, what are you talking about?" he asked, noting a faint blush upon her cheeks. "Or should I say–*who* are you talking about?"

"Well, since I assume the new love you're referring to is that woman named Ivy–"

"You know her name?" he asked in amazement.

"Dooley overheard a lot while up in the rafters."

"He apparently did," he responded with a chuckle.

"Anyway, from what little information he gleaned about Ivy– her being kidnapped and your search for her–Dooley guessed that you cared deeply for this woman. I thought as much, too. Because of that, I didn't want to mention her name until I better understood where you stood with her, lest you thought I was prying."

"I would never think that about you," he said.

"So can I assume you found Ivy safe and sound?"

"Very much so, and on two occasions, but both after long and wearisome searches." Nicholas felt as if those adventures were part of another life. "After I fled this ice cellar, my road took me all the way to the Trillium Sea–twice–and then to Kargoth and inside the heart of Vellan's mountain before sending me right back here. Quite a journey for one man," he admitted.

"And to think that I didn't have to leave the borders of Litchfield County to experience my adventure," she replied. "Seems we've both had quite a time."

"We sure did," he said, delighted that Katherine had a newfound love. "By the way, you never mentioned who you've taken a fancy to. Someone I know?"

She nodded with a mischievous smile. "But you may not recognize him since you last saw the man in Amanda's kitchen up to his elbows in soapy water. He's since gotten a proper haircut and now works for Oscar harvesting and hauling firewood."

Nicholas thought for a moment. "Lewis?"

"He's turned into a charming man, if you must know, and we get along swimmingly," she said. She recounted how Lewis had protected her and immobilized the man who had tried to kill Dooley near the swamp.

"One of these nights, you, Lewis and I will have to meet at the Water Barrel Inn and compare notes of our adventures over a few mugs of ale."

"Not until our current mess is settled," Katherine reminded him. "Your work tonight isn't over."

"And neither is yours. You'd better go before Amanda comes looking for you."

Katherine gave him a final hug and hurried upstairs, already anticipating the note he would send to the poulterer's shop in four days. Nicholas, in the meantime, bided his time in the ice cellar until Katherine and her mother left for the night. Shortly afterward, Oscar and Amanda extinguished the houselights before retiring to bed. Nicholas, noting that the faint glow outlining the door at the top of the stairs had disappeared, guessed that it was safe to depart. He grabbed the sack of food Katherine had provided, blew out the candle and, just as he had done eight months ago, slipped through the doorway behind the house and disappeared into the shadowy night.

CHAPTER 116

A Plan Takes Shape

Nicholas returned to Adelaide's house to retrieve his wagon, then traveled east along River Road, contemplating how to wrest the village of Kanesbury from Zachary Farnsworth's grasp. About a mile outside the village, he turned left onto Willow Road. Emmett and Lorna Trout lived a few minutes north on a farm with their three children. When Nicholas arrived, he found it dark and still, guessing that the family had long since gone to bed. Then a swift shadow sped from the barn and made directly for him, shattering the silence with loud, piercing barks. A light appeared in an upper window of the small house nearby. Nicholas placed his head in his hands, sorry he had abruptly awakened the household.

"Horace! Quiet!" growled a deep voice in the night. A tall man emerged through the front door, holding an oil lamp in one hand and a stick of firewood as a weapon in the other. He hurried to the wagon with the dog now silently at his side, both suspiciously eyeing the new arrival. "Who's there?" Emmett asked, raising the lamp high.

"Katherine Durant sent me," Nicholas said as he introduced himself. "I'm here to see Maynard and Adelaide."

"About what?" he asked, his doubts quickly allayed since he had heard Adelaide fondly mention Nicholas' name several times in conversation.

"About taking them home," he said. "But it'll require some hard work."

"Well, I'm all for that!" Emmett spouted with delight as he tossed aside the piece of wood and scratched his whiskered face. "Let's go inside and hash out the details. I'll have Lorna put on a hot kettle." He signaled for Nicholas to step down from the wagon. "It's about time, too. From all the stories we've heard about Farnsworth, his day of reckoning has been a long time coming."

Nicholas followed Emmett Trout and his dog into the house, the cool kitchen scented with the aroma of freshly baked bread that the family had shared at dinnertime. Emmett's wife, Lorna, was soon downstairs, happy to meet Nicholas and delighted that a solution to their problem was perhaps just around the corner.

"Adelaide has been like a doting grandmother to us and the children," she said, hanging a kettle of water for tea over a fire and fixing up a plate of cheese and biscuits, two of the items Katherine had included in the sack of food Nicholas presented to them. "But Maynard needs better care than we can provide."

"And I don't know how long we can keep his presence a secret," Emmett added as they sat around the kitchen table.

"Your help is beyond appreciated," Nicholas said. "But with luck, Maynard and Adelaide may soon be back home where they belong. Can I see him now?"

"Of course," Lorna said, bringing over three mugs of tea on a wooden tray with the cheese and biscuits. "But he's probably fast asleep."

"He does that quite a lot after what he's been through," her husband said.

"But I, on the other hand, am wide awake," someone spoke in soft tones near the doorway to an adjacent room.

Nicholas turned around upon hearing the familiar voice and smiled when seeing his dear friend and neighbor wrapped snugly in a shawl. "Adelaide!" he said, jumping out of his seat and giving her a hug. He was surprised by the vibrant spark of life in her steel blue eyes and her air of strength and resolve after all she had endured.

"It's wonderful to see you, Nicholas!" she replied, hugging him again as a few tears rolled down her cheeks. "You're the last person I expected to see for a while–if indeed ever–after what Katherine said had happened to you."

"She told me a lot about you and Maynard as well, but it appears that you pulled through despite your harsh ordeal."

Adelaide shrugged as she wiped her face dry. "I have my good days and my bad, but thanks to Emmett and Lorna's kindness, those latter ones don't come around as often or as intensely as they used to."

"How is Maynard faring?"

Adelaide sensed his anxiety. "Let me show you to his room. You can see what Misters Farnsworth and Kramer have reduced him to. I'll come back and sit with Emmett and Lorna until you return, eagerly awaiting your story of life on the road."

He fondly wrapped an arm around Adelaide's shoulder, happy to see her up and about. Yet he silently dreaded what might have become of Maynard, fearing that his condition was quite the opposite of hers.

In a small room in back, Maynard lay asleep in bed beneath several blankets and a patchwork quilt. A candle flickered on a nightstand. Though a tall man, his gaunt face and pale complexion made him appear frail and sickly. His long silver and black hair was gathered about the shoulders as his chest rose slowly beneath the coverings.

"Stay with him awhile," Adelaide gently said as Nicholas sat down on a chair next to the bed. "Join us when you're ready." She patted him on the shoulder before exiting the room, closing the door behind her.

Nicholas looked sadly upon Maynard, wondering if his friend would be in this dreadful condition if he hadn't fled Kanesbury. He fearfully contemplated losing the only father he had ever known, wishing he had better thought out his rash decision of eight months ago. Had he stayed and fought the charges against him, he believed that Maynard would be home right now and in good health. Yet had he not gone, he, Megan and Leo would never have met Carmella and delivered the medallion to the wizard Frist, helping to bring about the downfall of the Enâri, and ultimately, Vellan himself.

Nicholas' head swam as he tried to figure out all the resulting twists and turns of fate based on a single decision, finally admitting that it was impossible. He would deal with the consequences as best he could and wished Ivy and the others were here for support. Then inspiration struck him and he smiled, knowing that help was already close at hand. He chided himself for forgetting so soon and started to reach for the amulet hidden beneath his shirt. But Maynard suddenly stirred and opened his eyes.

"*Nicholas?*" he whispered, slightly confused. "Am I waking up from a bad dream? Some horrible things have happened."

"No and yes," he softly replied, taking hold of his hand.

Maynard looked about, slowly recalling his location. "Ah, I remember now. The horrible things were real. But seeing you here is a turn for the good."

"I'll do my best to make sure of that," he replied, briefly explaining where he had been for the past eight months after Maynard insisted on hearing his story. "But I'll give you more details another time. You need your rest. I didn't mean to wake you."

Maynard closed his eyes for a moment and nodded. "Perhaps tomorrow you can walk with me around the house if I'm up to it. I'm getting better, or Adelaide tells me so." He squeezed Nicholas' hand and looked at him gravely. "Yet I feel as tired as ever. My time on the island was not good for my health. I'm not sure if I'll ever fully recover." A shade of fear crossed his face. "Promise you won't tell Adelaide I said that."

"I promise," he said as Maynard closed his eyes again and breathed deeply, slowly drifting off to sleep. "You rest and let me worry about tomorrow."

"*All right…*" he whispered, his head sinking deeper into the pillow.

Nicholas, noting that Maynard was fast asleep, removed the amulet from around his neck and carefully placed it in his hand, gently folding his fingers over the piece of silver. At once, Maynard took another deep breath, and Nicholas, not sure if he was imagining it at first, noted a hint of color returning to his friend's pallid face as he clutched the amulet more tightly. A sense of tranquility slowly filled the room.

"I'll leave your recovery to the wizard Frist," he softly said as Maynard soundly slept. "There's another matter that now needs my attention." With that, he stood and left the room, confident that Maynard would soon be back to his old self again.

"Young man, you can stay here as long as you need to," Lorna said a short time later as she refilled Nicholas' cup with hot tea. "After all that Adelaide has told us about you over the weeks, you seem like part of the family." She took a seat at the table with Emmett and Adelaide, all eager to hear about his idea to remove Farnsworth from power. "Now tell us this plan of yours."

"The details are sketchy," he admitted, "but I believe there's a way to smoke Farnsworth out of his lair and reveal to everyone how he betrayed Kanesbury."

"Tell us what to do," Emmett said, happy to assist in any way.

Nicholas nodded appreciatively. "Katherine mentioned that she keeps in contact with you from time to time by exchanging notes in secret."

"That's right," Lorna said. "Every ten days or so, Emmett or I will cross paths with her at a prearranged location. We don't speak, pretending we're strangers. But when no one is looking, we slip each other a note with updates on the latest happenings. Emmett and I will include a time, date and location for the next meeting in our note."

"But those latest happenings have been few and far between," Adelaide said with discouragement. "After Constable Brindle was attacked last winter, Katherine informed us about how some of Farnsworth's hired hands have infiltrated the village."

"She was afraid to move against him afterward, certain that someone else close to her would be hurt, or even killed," Emmett said. "And not knowing how many men Farnsworth had hired makes it impossible to mount a resistance. We're not sure if we're dealing with five men or perhaps a few dozen."

"And so we bided our time through winter," Adelaide said. "Lorna and Emmett kindly tolerated Maynard and my presence here."

"Now, Adelaide, don't go talking like that," Lorna replied, patting her hand. "The extra days gave you time to recuperate. Besides, everyone is happy to have you here. You've more than paid your way with all the cooking and cleaning you insist on doing."

"Especially when you make us your bacon breakfast!" another voice chimed in. Gilbert Trout, Emmett and Lorna's oldest son, marched into the room, all smiles and eager to join in the conversation. He had turned sixteen at the beginning of the year and helped out his father on the farm, particularly enjoying plowing the fields in springtime and delivering shipments of hay into the city throughout the season.

"I couldn't sleep with all the chatter," he said after Adelaide introduced him to Nicholas.

"Gill is stuck here, as he often says, having to share a room with his younger brother while Maynard uses his," Emmett explained with a chuckle.

"But Father promised me we can start building a small cottage of my own out back later this summer," Gilbert said. He sat down his lanky frame at the table, combing a hand through a mop of tangled hair.

"*If* you earn it with enough hours on the farm," his mother reminded him.

"No sweat!" he said, grabbing a biscuit from the tray. I'll have enough hours to earn a house before summer is done."

"I had a small cottage behind Maynard's house," Nicholas told him, wistfully amused by the boy's spirit. "But it was more than I could take care of with my jobs on the farm and at the gristmill."

Adelaide asked him if he had heard about what happened at the mill before Caldurian and his troops overran the village. Nicholas shook his head, expecting bad news.

"It burned to the ground," she said. "And though I didn't witness the destruction, all that remained were the charred stone walls, though one of them collapsed according to Katherine's graphic description."

"But Ned Adams has since been rebuilding," Emmett said, relaying information from one of Katherine's recent letters. "Should you ever get your old job back, you'll have a fine establishment to return to."

"That's a big *if*," he said. "There are still lots of obstacles in my way before I can start planning such things. First we have to deal with Farnsworth."

"So tell us what you have in mind," Lorna urged him. "You have me intrigued."

"All right. But just keep in mind that nothing will happen for four more days. That's when you'll pass on your next note to Katherine, correct?"

"Yes. We'll meet at the poulterer's shop. Do you have a message for her?"

Nicholas nodded. "I plan to give her the details of *my* plan before we proceed. I don't want there to be any surprises."

"Am I allowed to help?" Gilbert asked as he munched on a biscuit. "We could stand some excitement around here. I'm bored. A little adventure would do me good."

"That's what I used to think," he replied, noting the urge to explore and see different places in the boy's fiery eyes, a desire which mirrored his own from last autumn. Gilbert also reminded him in subtle ways of William and Brendan, who once, like himself, probably thought they could conquer the world and their dreams simply by wishing it. But living through recent events, not imagining them, had given Nicholas a new perspective on life, offering hard lessons that he learned only too well.

"I think the only help Nicholas needs from you, Gilbert, is for you to do your chores and keep out of the way," Lorna told her son with a sharp eye.

"But, Mom!" he said, frowning with disappointment.

"You heard your mother," Emmett told him. "Now let's hear Nicholas out."

"Adelaide?" Gilbert asked, turning to her in desperation. "What do you think?"

"Oh, I don't get a vote," she replied with an affectionate smile. "But thanks for asking. Now as your father said, let's listen to what Nicholas has to say."

But as the details of Nicholas' developing plan swirled in his mind, he glanced at Gilbert, realizing that there was a part he could play after all, and a crucial part at that. And since Gilbert appeared responsible enough to handle the task, he decided there was no point in looking elsewhere for a recruit.

"Your son has a point," he said, eliciting looks of surprise from Emmett and Lorna. "I need someone trustworthy to deliver a letter for me in secret."

Everyone looked up with puzzlement. "A second letter?" Emmett asked, not sure what Nicholas had in mind. "To Katherine?"

"No. This other letter has a different destination," he said with an inscrutable smile. "It will be going far beyond the borders of Kanesbury, but not too far."

"To where?" Lorna whispered curiously.

"It's all part of my plan," he replied, glancing at her son. "Say, how would you like to go on a little adventure, Gilbert?"

"Seriously?" he asked, gushing with enthusiasm. "When can I leave?"

"Tomorrow, though I'm not sure how long you'd be gone," he said, catching worried looks from his parents. "It depends on how events unfold in Kanesbury."

"What do you have in mind?" Adelaide asked, worrying about Gilbert as she had about Nicholas when he announced his intention to join the King's Guard.

"Where will my son and this letter be going?" Lorna anxiously inquired, reaching over and clasping Gilbert's hand.

"And what will the letter say?" Emmett asked.

"Don't worry," Nicholas assured them. "Gilbert will be quite safe. It's the rest of us who'll be throwing stones at a hornets' nest—and I'll be leading the attack."

CHAPTER 117

Baiting the Trap

Nicholas rode into Kanesbury on a chilly evening four nights later. He left his wagon near Maynard's house beneath the sprawling oak. The horses grunted restlessly under a field of stars as the crescent Fox Moon lingered in the west. As he walked about the farmstead, the scent of fresh, fragrant soil generated a stream of fond memories of the many wonderful years he had spent here with Maynard and Tessa.

Earlier, he had said goodbye to Adelaide and the others after Lorna had returned from the village. There she had delivered the latest secret message to Katherine at the poulterer's shop, allowing Nicholas to proceed with his plan. Gilbert had left three days ago to deliver the second letter, and Nicholas felt confident that the young man would reach his destination without a hitch.

Hours before he had departed, Nicholas spent some time with Maynard who was making a swift and steady recovery after wearing Frist's amulet day and night. They walked about the farm and discussed what had happened since last autumn and what the days ahead might bring. Nicholas was delighted that Maynard had regained much of his strength and stamina, confident that he would soon be living life again on his own farm.

"Nicholas, I have faith in your decision to do this your way," he told him as they neared the main house where Adelaide enjoyed a lively spring breeze from the porch.

"I don't see that I have an alternative if we want to expose Farnsworth. Still, it's good to hear that you have confidence in me, or at least in my plan."

"Definitely *you*," Maynard replied with a smile as he gently slapped him on the shoulder.

Now, as Nicholas stood alone in the darkness on Maynard's farm and observed the gentle glow of yellow houselights sprinkled among the village trees, he felt confident that everything just might work out in the end after all. But there was only one way to find out. He proceeded down the road into the heart of town, hoping that this positive feeling would last until he arrived at the Water Barrel Inn.

Nicholas approached his favorite haunt in the deepening dusk, its windows aglow with soft light that splashed upon the boot-trodden ground beyond the sills. Sweet pine smoke wafted through the air as ghostly bluish tendrils rose from the chimney in elegant swirls. Friendly faces passed in front of the window panes, reminding him of happier days. But now was not the time for reminiscing. He had put this moment off long enough. He placed his hand on the doorknob, knowing he was about to stir things up in Kanesbury, or at least more than they had been in recent months. Taking a deep breath, he pushed open the door and stepped inside.

The inn was filled with the hum of competing conversations, some in whispered tones in the corner shadows, others of a more lively nature from tables filled with plates of roasted meats and mugs of frothy ale. A large blaze crackled in the fireplace, casting shadows upon the walls of stone and knotty pine. Nicholas inhaled the warmth and laughter of the treasured surroundings as he closed the door behind him, having missed the place like a long lost friend.

As he walked inside on a wave of cool air that slipped through the doorway, he scanned the faces of the crowd, hoping to spot someone he knew. But with each step across the floor, heads started to turn and conversations began to fade. Within moments, Nicholas noticed that all eyes were focused on him amid the thick and uneasy quiet. And though he had hoped for and expected such a reception, he still felt intimidated by the barrage of curious and icy stares flung his way.

"What are you doing here?" Bob Hawkins shouted out. He stood up at one end of a table with his hands pressed indignantly upon the surface. "Where do you get the nerve to show your face around this place, Nicholas Raven?"

Nicholas locked gazes with the man nearly twice his age, whiskered with unkempt hair and well on the road to inebriation. He recalled Bob Hawkins' grating voice on the night he was arrested by Constable Brindle. Having nothing better to do back then except stick his nose into somebody else's business, Hawkins had egged on the constable when Nicholas was accused of robbery. And though Nicholas could slough off such taunting comments now, they had stirred up anger and doubt in him during the Harvest Festival.

But even worse than that blathering of a slightly drunken man eight months ago was facing the betrayed disappointment of Ned Adams. After Clay Brindle had held aloft the missing jacket button, apparently proving to everyone that he was a thief, Nicholas had been devastated to see Ned's trust and confidence in him disintegrate before his very eyes. And though now he would have proof to the contrary through the testimony of his friends, he still couldn't help feeling ill at ease.

"I'm looking for Maynard Kurtz," he said, his heart racing. "I just went to his place, but no one is there. He wasn't at Adelaide Cooper's house across the road either."

"That's because they're both missing!" Bob Hawkins shouted, glaring at Nicholas. But before he could spout further, a man at another table, who had transacted business with Nicholas at the gristmill, calmly looked up.

"Maynard hasn't been seen since the middle of Old Autumn," he said. "And Adelaide has been missing since the time you left."

Nicholas feigned a worried expression upon hearing the news. "Maynard is missing? What are you talking about, Mr. Canby?" he asked. "I recall him asking me about Adelaide's whereabouts shortly before I departed, but I assumed she was preparing for the festivities. Now you're saying they're *both* missing?"

"And Dooley Kramer, too!" another man jumped in. "He disappeared about two weeks after Maynard left to visit the King about Caldurian's reappearance."

"*Caldurian?*" Nicholas furrowed his brow in feigned surprise. "What has been going on here?"

"You tell *us!*" Bob Hawkins cried. "What with you robbing, murdering and fleeing the law, how do we know that you weren't behind some of those incidents?"

"Oh, sit yourself down and shut up, Bob!" someone else shouted. "Nicholas has been gone for months, so how could he have anything to do with the disappearances? You're just trying to cause trouble as usual."

"This is my village, too. I have a right to know what goes on inside it!" he retorted. "Especially when a suspected criminal traipses back into our midst."

"I'm no criminal!" Nicholas protested. "I never robbed Ned Adams' gristmill nor murdered Arthur Weeks. And though it was wrong of me to flee when first accused, I've come back to turn myself in and stand trial in hopes of clearing my name. I'll accept whatever judgment my fellow citizens decide, but before I do so, I want to find Maynard."

"Fine. But that doesn't prove your innocence!" Bob Hawkins snapped. "At least not to me. I want to know the whole story about where you've been and what kind of mischief you've been up to. Save me a front row seat at the trial."

"And I want to know what's been going on around here." A chorus of voices suddenly erupted, all eagerly taking turns explaining to Nicholas what had happened in recent months, most never having believed that he was really guilty of either thievery or murder. A few, however, did protest, saying that Constable Brindle should be contacted at once as Nicholas was a fugitive from the law, though their voices were quickly drowned out.

As the crowd converged around Nicholas and individuals took turns adding to and embellishing the events from last fall, Bob Hawkins quietly slipped out of the building into the darkness and scurried to the village lockup. The others inside vigorously regaled Nicholas with stories of their lives as prisoners of Caldurian and his soldiers, weaving mostly true tales of bravery and hardship while under the wizard's stern and watchful eye.

As he listened, unable to say a word, Nicholas wondered if he would ever get out of the inn, thinking that maybe he should have gone directly to the lockup instead. But he wanted news of his reappearance and impending trial to spread through Kanesbury like wildfire, and stopping here first would do just that. He needed to make sure a trial was inevitable if his plan was to succeed, hoping to put the unsuspecting Mayor Farnsworth on trail at the same time.

But just as he was feeling overwhelmed by all the attention, the front door opened. Constable Brindle strode into the room, cane in hand, with his deputy, Tyler Harkin, close behind. Lurking in back with muted glee was Bob Hawkins who had raced to fetch the constable, more interested in creating an entertaining spectacle than a desire for justice. Regardless, Nicholas was glad to see Clay Brindle, though he greeted him with a façade of doubt and worry as the crowd went silent.

"So it's really you, Nicholas, and not just a figment of Bob's pickled imagination," the constable said, eliciting chuckles.

"See, I told you he was here!" Bob excitedly pointed out as Deputy Harkin quieted him with a sour expression.

"Clay, I was planning to visit you next," Nicholas replied apologetically, glancing curiously at the constable's cane. "What happened to you?"

"Long story," he replied. "But I want to hear yours first."

"I intend to tell you everything," Nicholas promised, detecting a hint of disappointment beneath Clay's friendly exterior. "But first I wanted to speak with Maynard. I came here looking for him since he wasn't at home. Now I've learned that he's been missing for quite some time. Has anyone been searching for him?"

"We can talk about that later as well," Clay said, noting Bob Hawkins' eyes widen with anticipation. "In private!" Bob frowned along with most of the others as the constable coldly stared them down. "This is a legal matter and will be treated as such. Nicholas, accompany me and Tyler to the lockup where we can talk." He threw an extra sharp glance at Bob Hawkins for good measure.

"All right," Nicholas agreed, "though I hope one day soon to address everyone in public and explain my actions of last autumn. I'm not a thief or a murderer, and if it takes a trial to clear my name, I'll happily comply."

"Good to hear," Clay said. "But let's talk first." He, Nicholas and Tyler stepped outside the inn, but like a shadow, Bob Hawkins and several of the other men trailed behind them.

"Now don't go following us!" Deputy Harkin snarled. "This is an official matter."

"And these are public streets!" Hawkins insisted. "You can't stop us from wandering up the lane in the same direction."

"Oh, let them follow," Clay remarked with an exasperated sigh, wiping a handkerchief across his brow. He glowered at Bob and the others in the light of the doorway. "But get in my way and you'll be guests in one of my cells. Are we clear?"

When they arrived at the lockup, about twenty people had breathlessly followed them up the road. Others were congregating near the front steps and areas closeby, word having spread about Nicholas Raven's sudden return. Nicholas appeared overwhelmed by their presence, but inside was delighted that Kanesbury was waking up to his reappearance. With so many people curious about his past whereabouts, he was confident that they would demand a quick trial if only to get to the bottom of the mystery regardless whether anyone thought him guilty or not.

"Can we speak to him?" someone shouted from beneath the sprawling maple tree rising solemnly between the lockup and the village hall.

"No you cannot!" Clay shouted. He and his deputy hurried Nicholas up the stairs and inside the shadowy entryway of the lockup, closing the door behind them.

"Like a gaggle of nosey geese!" Deputy Harkin sputtered. "Don't they have anything better to do this evening? I'd like to—" Suddenly the front door reopened. A steady chorus of voices from outdoors flowed into the entryway as a tall figure stepped inside before hastily shutting the door.

"Didn't I say no one was to come in here?" Constable Brindle fumed as he angrily turned to greet the intruder. "I'll put a guard outdoors if I—" He quickly caught himself when Zachary Farnsworth stepped through the shadows into the light from the main room. "Oh, it's you," he said apologetically. "Mayor Farnsworth, what brings you here?"

"*He* does," he replied, pointing at Nicholas as he unbuttoned his coat and hung it on a wall peg. "I'd been working late in the banking house when word of his arrival reached my ears. When I saw the crowd, I correctly assumed you were all on your way here."

Nicholas tilted his head slightly, appearing a bit bewildered. "*Mayor* Farnsworth? I don't understand. Otto Nibbs is no longer our mayor?"

"You've been gone far too long," the constable said. He led everyone into the main room where a blaze snapped in the fireplace. "It's a long story, but Otto is sitting in one of the lockups in back. And Maynard, who has been missing as you heard at the inn, served as acting mayor until he departed for Morrenwood months ago."

"Mr. Farnsworth now serves in that capacity," Deputy Harkin said.

"A role I took on reluctantly after some turbulent days in Kanesbury," Farnsworth replied with an air of weariness. "But we can discuss those particulars later. Your reappearance is what the village is buzzing about."

Constable Brindle shot a stern look at his deputy. "Tyler, please leave Zachary and me alone for a few minutes so we can talk to Nicholas in private. Keep an eye on the crowd and make sure we're not disturbed."

"Certainly, sir," he said with a trace of disappointment.

As Tyler left the room, the constable offered Nicholas a chair in front of his desk while he sat down behind it, setting his cane to one side. Farnsworth stood near the fireplace, the flickering light casting a coppery glow upon his face.

"Nicholas, I'll get right to the point. It's been eight months since you left," Clay said matter-of-factly. "Where have you been?"

Nicholas leaned back in his chair. "I wish I could say I had been leading a life of adventure," he replied, his eyes cast downward from time to time, "but I was just going from job to job where I could find one, scratching out an existence. I worked on a few farms here and there, and in late winter I helped collect and boil sap in an old sugarhouse in Bonner County. Nothing exciting, but I survived and had some time to think." He looked up with regret. "A *lot* of time."

"Well, I'm glad it brought you to your senses about coming back and facing the mess you'd left here," Clay said. "Though all of that was nothing compared to the chaos Caldurian rained down upon us in your absence."

"Yes, someone at the inn mentioned that the wizard had been here," he said. "What happened? And why did Maynard travel to Morrenwood?"

"To alert King Justin of the wizard's presence," Farnsworth stated, leaning against the mantelpiece.

Though he wasn't eager to talk about Caldurian since his secret dealings with the wizard weighed heavily upon his mind, Farnsworth thought it best to attack the subject head on, knowing that avoiding the topic might raise subtle suspicions. He also wondered why Nicholas made no mention of having gone to Morrenwood, meeting King Justin and taking part in the quest to reforge the key. Dooley had told him about Nicholas' surprise appearance at the Blue Citadel, but Farnsworth couldn't reveal such information without implicating himself to a long list of crimes against the kingdom. But why wouldn't Nicholas speak of those deeds? Out of modesty? Or did he plan to reveal all at a public trial to build up sympathy for himself? Whatever his reason, Farnsworth felt confident that Nicholas couldn't connect him to Dooley and Arthur's actions against him during the Harvest Festival, nor should he have any reason to suspect him in the first place. He would hear him out further before making any decisions.

"Maynard wanted to speak to the King after Caldurian and his Island soldiers had slipped away in the dead of night," Farnsworth continued. "Sadly, he hasn't been heard from since his departure over five months ago."

"Is anyone searching for him?" Nicholas asked with alarm.

"Yes, but to no avail. I wish I had good news to report."

"As do I," Clay added. At Nicholas' urging, the constable explained all that took place in Kanesbury since the Harvest Festival. He listened with the same fascination and horror as when Katherine first told him those same stories four nights ago in the ice cellar.

"I have to go and find him!" Nicholas said frantically, jumping up. He looked at Zachary and the constable and let his emotions settle as he slowly dropped back into his seat. "But I suppose I must deal with matters here first." He shook his head. "I wish I had never run away that night, Clay. It was a poor decision on my part."

"It was, but I understand how the fear of seeing your world falling apart had prompted you to take off like a jackrabbit into that field. Murder and robbery are heavy charges. And though I have no proof to the contrary, seeing you return to face judgment helps to convince me that you're not guilty."

"Really?" Nicholas asked hopefully.

Clay nodded sympathetically. "You see, Nicholas, after things settled down, I got to thinking about what had happened, as have many people. Those Enâri creatures were released from the caves on the same night Arthur Weeks was killed, the very night you were accused of robbery and murder. In hindsight, people found it difficult to believe those events were coincidental. Weeks later, Caldurian and his Island hooligans invaded our village, riling up folks and pitting one against the other. It was a horrible time."

"No doubt," Nicholas said. "But what are you getting at?"

Clay leaned back and folded his arms. "Though I don't have any proof–especially since Arthur Weeks is dead and Dooley Kramer is missing–I can't shrug off my suspicions that your misfortunes were connected to all the troubles brought about by that awful wizard. I've known you too many years to believe you're capable of such horrific acts."

"Thanks, Clay," he said. "I appreciate you saying so."

"And though I've only known you through your transactions on behalf of Ned Adams, Nicholas, I have to say the same about you as Clay just did." Farnsworth spoke amiably, walking toward the desk and taking a nearby seat. "After listening to comments over the past weeks, many people have regrets about how the wizard had so easily manipulated them to turn against Otto. It was a confusing time, and to this day no one is exactly sure what happened, or why. But the worst was brought out in the citizens of Kanesbury by a great deceiver. And as Constable Brindle stated, perhaps you were swept up in that wizard's devious plan."

Nicholas offered the acting mayor a grateful smile. "You don't know how good it makes me feel to hear you say that, sir. My thoughts have been jumbled lately, not understanding any of what had happened to me nor able to disprove it to the rest of Kanesbury. But I must be allowed to try, which is why I'm requesting a trial to plead my case and perhaps gain the forgiveness of my fellow villagers."

"It would be good to have someone back on Maynard's farm to make it productive again," Clay told him.

"I'd like nothing better. But if I'm set free, it would be my duty to search for Maynard no matter how hopeless the cause. He's family, after all. I owe it to him."

"That's commendable," Farnsworth said, warming up to the idea that a trial clearing Nicholas of all charges might play to his advantage.

As Nicholas spoke, Farnsworth wondered if testifying in the young man's favor might endear himself to the public. Most people seemed to be on Nicholas' side after putting events and emotions in perspective. But that didn't solve the Otto Nibbs debacle that prevented Farnsworth from fully enjoying the fruits of his labors. Until the situation was resolved, there was a chance that Katherine Durant would connect him to the wizard's schemes whether she had proof or not. It irked him not knowing the location of Maynard Kurtz and Adelaide Cooper. He was convinced that Katherine had helped them escape from the swamp. But even with hired hands to keep a close eye on her, Farnsworth knew he could only hold her at bay for so long before she'd grow brave enough to move against him. And now that Nicholas had returned, people would be scrutinizing details from the past. Rumors and accusations, once leveled, could quickly overwhelm and destroy him. He needed to get out in front and manipulate the public's perception to protect himself before the truth unraveled his web of deceit. But how?

"And so, Mr. Mayor, I leave my fate in your hands," Nicholas concluded as Farnsworth nodded sympathetically at his request for a quick trial.

"Don't give me credit for having that much sway over people," Farnsworth replied. "And just because Constable Brindle and I support you, it will be the decision of a jury as to whether or not you are set free," he warned. "Fifteen out of twenty-one of your fellow villagers will have your fate in their hands, not me. You may be eager to put this affair behind you, but think through about how fast you really want to proceed."

"I've done my fair share of thinking. More than was probably good for me. So the sooner I can get this trial behind me, the happier I'll be."

"Unless you're found guilty," Constable Brindle cautioned, his words punctuated by a furrowed brow above his dark eyes and apple red cheeks. "And though I'll be in charge of presenting the case against you, I promise to be fair yet meticulous. I have no evidence to support your claim of innocence other than your own word since no one has come forward in your defense."

"On the other hand," Farnsworth said, "Mr. Raven has neither Arthur Weeks nor Dooley Kramer to testify against him, one being dead and the other missing." He eyed Nicholas with a steely gaze. "It will essentially be a judgment on your character, sir."

"Well," Nicholas replied as he shifted anxiously in his seat, "most people in Kanesbury seem to have found me a decent person—or so I've always thought," he said, sprouting a nervous grin. "But I suppose we'll find out for certain very soon."

"We shall, so tailor your words accordingly," Farnsworth said, confident that Nicholas now viewed him with a heightened sense of respect and admiration for being so cooperative. At the same time, he was privately amused at reaping the praises from this naïve, young man whose downfall he had secretly engineered. He wished Katherine Durant had been as easily fooled, though he still wasn't certain what facts she actually knew about his corrupt ways. It was that lack of knowledge which gnawed at him. "Clay, would a week be enough time for you to ready a trial?"

"More than enough time." He looked sadly at Nicholas. "I don't relish this task and will be glad when it's over."

"Very well," Farnsworth said. "Today is the tenth day of the month. Let's plan for one week from tonight, the nineteenth of Old Spring. That will give us time to select a jury. In the meantime…" He lifted his eyes uncomfortably to the constable who immediately understood his meaning.

"In the meantime," Clay continued, staring at Nicholas with a heavy heart, "you'll have to stay here in the lockup. There's one cell available as Otto has made the other one his home for far too long."

"I understand," Nicholas said without hard feelings. "I had expected to spend my first night back in Kanesbury in this building."

"Deputy Harkin is here until midnight when his relief shows up. I'll send him off to secure any items you want from your cottage while I ink up the parchment and make this case all nice and legal."

"Thanks, Clay." Nicholas stood and shook his hand. "And I apologize again for running off. I should have trusted you." Clay Brindle nodded appreciatively. Nicholas turned and extended his hand to Zachary Farnsworth as he rose from his chair. "And thank you, Mr. Mayor, for your understanding and assistance, though I'm not sure I deserve it."

Farnsworth shook his hand as if they were old friends. "Happy to oblige, Nicholas. I've heard enough good things about you to know that this is the right way to proceed."

"That's more than fair," he said. "And though I'm saddened that Otto and Maynard have succumbed to misfortune, I'm certain the mayor's office is in good hands. You're a credit to the position, Mr. Farnsworth."

"I try," he replied with a modest shrug. "Now I'll leave Clay and his deputy to attend to things here. With patience, the next nine days should pass swiftly, Mr. Raven."

"A visitor or two might help with that," Clay suggested. "As Otto's sister and niece stop by here often enough, maybe they'd like to call on you, too."

Farnsworth, feigning indifference, felt his heart beat rapidly at the prospect of Nicholas and Katherine meeting. Though not certain what specifics Katherine knew of his dark deeds, he knew nothing good could come from those two discussing past events. He feared that innocent details of their conversation could inadvertently be connected and pieces of the puzzle put in place should they start questioning one another.

Nicholas, guessing that Farnsworth might be thinking along such lines, knew he must quickly dispel any fears on his part in order for a trial to proceed unhindered. "Yes, about that, Clay," he replied. "If anyone should show up in the next week to see me, let them politely know that I don't wish to have any visitors as I'm preparing for my defense. *Especially* Katherine Durant. I think it's best I be left alone from any distractions."

"Are you sure?" Clay asked, wrinkling his brow in confusion.

Nicholas nodded. "I'm a bit embarrassed to say, but I had promised to take Katherine to the village dance with me during the Harvest Festival. Then I ran off because of all the commotion, leaving her without an escort or an explanation as to why, just a few days before the dance." He smiled grimly. "To tell you the truth, I don't think that she would want to talk to me after how I behaved. And if she did, I imagine it would only be to scold me. So please, if you don't mind, I'd rather be left alone."

"Understood," Clay replied with a thin smirk, slapping him supportively on the shoulder. "Now wait here and I'll go find Tyler so we can get this thing moving."

"I'll walk you out," Farnsworth said, nodding goodbye to Nicholas before he strolled into the entryway with the constable, his fears happily allayed.

Nicholas watched them depart, hoping his demeanor came across as vulnerable and unthreatening to Farnsworth. But it would be one week from tonight that the real test would take place. He sat down and leaned back in his chair and sighed as he stared at the fire, his thoughts turning to Ivy to give him strength and peace of mind to make it through the next nine grueling days.

Zachary Farnsworth left Constable Brindle shortly afterward. He walked back to the banking house in the inky darkness, happy to leave the crowd still gathered around the lockup. He needed time to think as tonight's events had caught him off guard. He wondered if he should have granted Nicholas a trial so quickly, a trial that would dredge up events from the Harvest Festival, events tightly entwined with his misdeeds. Yet not doing so would have raised suspicions since Nicholas had requested it. More than anything, Farnsworth wanted to appear concerned while at the same time placing himself above the messy conflict.

He entered the empty banking house and locked himself in his office. A single oil lamp provided the only light as he sat hunched behind his desk, his arms folded as his mental gears spun at breakneck speed. Since Nicholas Raven would be recalling events on the night of his arrest, naturally bringing up the names Arthur Weeks and Dooley Kramer, Farnsworth wondered if he could be associated with either of those individuals in any way. But as he racked his brain, knowing that both men were dead, he convinced himself that Nicholas would not be able to make the connection. Nicholas had been more than respectful to him inside the constable's office, even thanking him several times which helped calm his lingering fears. It was Katherine Durant who gave him pause.

What did she know? That question plagued him since winter shortly after he had pulled those prickly burrs from Katherine's cloak and then caught the young woman in a lie. It was then he first began to suspect that she had traveled to the swamp. Had she rescued Maynard and Adelaide and sent them somewhere safe until they were ready to point the finger of blame at him? If so, his veiled threats against her and her loved ones had successfully kept her at bay so far, though he wondered for how long. Sooner or later, she might find her courage and come after him.

On the other hand, even if Katherine had been to the swamp, Farnsworth still clung to the hope that perhaps Maynard and Adelaide had already been killed and disposed of by his hired assassin before she arrived. If so, she would know nothing about either of them ever having been there in the first place. Or was it possible Katherine had arrived when Dooley and his killer were engaged in deadly combat and watched them each die, burying them both later herself? Perhaps she had killed one or both, causing him to wonder if either man had revealed his role in the kidnappings to her before dying.

Farnsworth sighed as he ran his hands through his hair. There were endless scenarios regarding what might have happened at the swamp, and in all of them, Katherine's knowledge of his involvement might range from knowing nothing to knowing everything. Now with Nicholas' return, he feared that with events of the Harvest Festival replaying in people's minds, loose threads of someone's story or random tidbits of information might somehow lead back to him. Was it possible? Had he covered his tracks?

Farnsworth sighed again, unable to think anymore, unable to juggle all the lies he had told. He rested his head on the desk and closed his eyes, knowing that it all boiled down to Katherine Durant. She held the key to his fate.

A dark idea whispered to him from the shadowy corners of his mind. Was it time for another mysterious assault against one of Katherine's loved ones to remind her of his power? Or should he order one of his hired hands to move against Katherine herself? Farnsworth wondered if another unexplained disappearance might sweep aside all his troubles once and for all. A stranger's encounter with Katherine while she was walking alone on a dark street might do the trick. Or perhaps a visit to her home in the dead of night while her mother was out would accomplish the same thing. All of it was possible. And though another disappearance would be the talk of the village, the shock would eventually fade and his problems would at last be solved.

Another possibility struck Farnsworth as his eyelids slowly lifted, an air of resignation hovering above him like rain clouds. Maybe it was time to flee Kanesbury and start a new life elsewhere before his empire crumbled down upon him. Perhaps life here had run its course and it was time to seek out new ventures elsewhere. With the experience gained here, he was certain he could repeat his achievements more cleanly a second time without incompetents like Dooley Kramer and Arthur Weeks holding him back. It was a move to seriously consider.

With his head still buried in his arms, Farnsworth allowed whirls of indecision to overwhelm him. More than anything, he wanted to keep this job and his place in Kanesbury society after all the years of hard work to attain it. Katherine Durant had no right to take it away. It angered him that he had to play this game with her, pretending to be civil while each imagined that the other was preparing to strike a fatal blow. This was not supposed to be the end result of all his secret dealings. It was most unfair.

Farnsworth sat up and scowled, not prepared to give up just yet. He knew he would never be able to trust Katherine, and making a deal with her would be all but impossible. Getting his hands dirty just one more time—or at least the hands of his hired men—might end these nagging doubts once and for all. He would do it as soon as this trial was over. It was the only way.

But just to be safe in case events went awry, he would prepare for a quick departure and have his hired hands armed and at the ready. If Katherine made a move to expose him, feeling secure in the company of her fellow residents, then Farnsworth vowed to let loose his men upon the village hall like the Enâri themselves while he made a getaway, not caring about the resulting bloodbath. After coming this far, he wasn't going to surrender without a fight. He vowed to forge ahead until grasping victory or gasping for his last breath. There would be no compromise. Only one of them could win.

CHAPTER 118

The Trial

The days leading up to Nicholas' trial passed swiftly and with much excitement. Residents of Kanesbury anticipated a show unlike any they had seen, not counting Otto Nibbs' trial of sorts which many now admitted had been a sham. These latest proceedings would be different as Nicholas Raven would face a jury of his fellow citizens without the deadly threats of a devious wizard hanging over them. The benches in the village hall quickly filled as the late afternoon sun drifted westward on the last day of a frenetic week. With the building bulging beyond capacity, others listened near the main entrance or from outdoors by the open windows.

Also lingering outside were six of Zachary Farnsworth's hired hands awaiting his orders should their services be needed. Another individual was stationed within. They blended in with the villagers as if they were residents of Kanesbury, though Katherine spotted them easily as she made her way to the hall with Lewis and her mother. By their ominous presence, she knew that Farnsworth was sending a message that she should hold her tongue at the trial or face severe repercussions. She and her loved ones were still at risk and she had expected nothing less, convinced that Farnsworth would do anything to maintain his position in society.

As she walked up the front steps, Katherine cast a subtle backward glance while adjusting her shawl, noting two additional men in Farnsworth's employ who had discreetly followed her from the house, having kept a vigilant eye upon her all week. They mingled with the outdoor crowd, awaiting Farnsworth's orders.

Fragrant breezes wafted inside through the windows, carrying upon it a scent of sweet roses in bloom throughout the village and a hint of fading lilac that had blossomed weeks ago in explosions of dark purple, lavender and white. Though the sun still shone brightly, the oil lamps had already been lit inside as no one could predict how long the trial would last. And though summer was on the horizon, the fireplace crackled against the west wall as reliably hot weather had not yet arrived. Many wore hats, cloaks or light coats inside the cool interior to keep comfortable, especially some older residents who took their time transitioning from season to season.

In back of the hall, the pine table normally used for village council meetings had been removed. In its place were three rows of seven chairs where twenty-one villagers now sat as Nicholas' jury. A few whispered to one another while waiting for the trial to begin, but most were silent and observed the chattering throng before them, feeling the heavy burden of the decision they would soon make regarding a man's life.

Off to the front left was a single chair. Mayor Farnsworth would sit there after he opened the trial and Constable Brindle and Nicholas Raven made their respective cases. The latter two would sit on a pair of chairs on the opposite side to the right of the jury. At the moment, the three principals were gathered in one of the upstairs offices, waiting for the signal to come down and begin the proceedings. Moments later while the room was still abuzz, three loud peals of the village bell reverberated through the hall and the streets of Kanesbury, signaling the start of the trial. Spectators both inside and out went silent, preparing for the weighty moments ahead.

Footsteps descended the creaky wooden staircase in the front entryway. Those standing in that section raised their eyes in unison as Mayor Farnsworth led the way down, a stern yet thoughtful expression upon his face. Behind him walked Nicholas Raven and Constable Brindle, with his cane in hand, both sporting similar demeanors. The room was silent until Farnsworth reached the last step. The crowd quickly separated to create a pathway into the main hall. Without a word, the trio passed by, each man occasionally acknowledging someone with a brief smile or nod. The path behind them disappeared as quickly as it was formed as onlookers filled in the space to get a better view.

Nicholas, Farnsworth and the constable maneuvered down the center aisle between the rows of benches. People on either side hung off the ends as they were crammed shoulder to shoulder like fence pickets. Nicholas was surprised by the crowd's size, unable to spot Katherine in the blur of faces. He had not spoken to her in nine days and wondered if she was as nervous as he was, guessing that it would be a long night ahead.

They took their places in front, Farnsworth on the left and Nicholas and Constable Brindle on the right. Clay gently placed a hand on Nicholas' back as he escorted him to his chair and whispered that he should sit down. Nicholas did so, taking a deep breath as he gazed out upon the crowd. Clay sat down beside him, holding his cane. Nicholas was reassured by the man's presence even though the constable would be arguing the case against him. Beyond Clay to his right, Nicholas noted the twenty-one jury members, avoiding eye contact with any of them.

He then observed Farnsworth standing beside his chair on the other side of the room. The mayor was dressed in his finest vest and evening coat, his hand resting on the back support as he looked across the crowded hall in silent wonder. The rows of benches from front to back and along the side walls contained the lifeblood of Kanesbury, the young and old alike, its history and its future. As Farnsworth cast his eyes upon his fellow villagers, Nicholas carefully studied the man's face, wondering what he really thought of these people after having used them and ruined them just like Caldurian. He couldn't help recalling when he had first met Vellan alone in his stony chamber, no doubt cultivating dark thoughts similar to those of Zachary Farnsworth right now. And though Vellan's ideas had been on a much grander scale, Nicholas realized that the aims of both men were equally pernicious. All eyes were drawn to Farnsworth as he began to speak.

"It is too lovely a day to be cooped up inside, but events have played out in such a way that that is our fate," he said with a folksy eloquence that appealed to those present. "I won't jabber on long, but as mayor, it is my job to facilitate this trial to ensure a just verdict. Today we will judge the case against Nicholas Raven, accused of robbing Ned Adams' gristmill of money and flour sacks last autumn. He is also charged with fleeing the village after being arrested for that crime. Finally, Mr. Raven is accused of the murder of Arthur Weeks who was stabbed to death that same night in the home of Dooley Kramer.

"According to our laws, Constable Brindle will present the case against the accused. Mr. Raven will then offer words in his defense. Both men can call on any available witnesses to support their side. Afterward, our jurors will decide the innocence or guilt of Mr. Raven after discussing the case among themselves in private." He extended a hand to indicate the three rows of jurors who sat listening in stony contemplation. "If at least fifteen of the twenty-one jurors reach the same finding, then Mr. Raven shall be declared either innocent or guilty in accordance with their pronouncement. And by law, if neither finding is recorded by at least fifteen jurors, a second jury will be seated three days hence to hear the presentations one last time. If no decision of innocence or guilt is reached that second time, the case against Mr. Raven will be dropped and he shall be set free." Farnsworth stepped away from his chair to address the jury. "Do you understand your task and vow to carry it out with honest reflection?"

"We do," they replied in unison.

He nodded appreciatively, and after glancing at Nicholas and Constable Brindle, the mayor returned to his chair and addressed the spectators one last time. "And with that, we will begin," he simply stated, taking his seat with an air of cool confidence. His stomach, however, was riddled with knots, his thoughts in a violent whirlwind.

Clay Brindle planted his cane on the floor and stood up, wiping his forehead with a handkerchief. After eyeing Nicholas and offering a thin smile, he stepped forward to address the mass of anxious faces before him.

"Afternoon, everyone. My job today is to present the case against Nicholas Raven on your behalf," he said, uncomfortably clearing his throat. "And though I don't relish this task as I have known Nicholas to be a fine citizen, I will relate the facts as I honestly know them." Clay Brindle observed the nodding of many heads and heard faint whispers of agreement, taking comfort that all was going well. "So let me start on the tenth day of New Autumn last year, the first day of the Harvest Festival, when Ned Adams told me that his gristmill had been robbed. And so began my investigation."

Constable Brindle recounted his trek to the gristmill with Ned, where Dooley Kramer had been tallying up the number of stolen flour sacks when they arrived. Ned also discovered that a leather pouch of silver half-pieces had been stolen from his office strongbox. Clay told everyone he had spotted a brown button among some spilled flour near one of the crates that had been broken into, guessing that it probably popped off the thief's coat during the robbery. With fumbling fingers, he removed the button from his pocket and held it up for all to see. Murmurs of excitement rippled through the hall. Nicholas remained still in his seat while everyone was mesmerized by the constable's words, their gazes fixed upon Clay as if they had never heard his story before.

With a flicker of surprise, Nicholas caught someone staring back at him from the middle of the crowd with an expression of pained regret. As Clay talked about tracking down Arthur Weeks to question him about the robbery, Nicholas noted that Ned Adams, sitting next to his wife, was looking at him with saddened eyes. He guessed that Ned was conveying a sense of remorse for having believed that he was responsible for the robbery. Nicholas bestowed a tender smile of friendship upon his old boss, silently conveying that there were no hard feelings. He noted a faint smile upon Ned's face just before the man bent his head down and raised a hand to his cheek.

As Clay continued speaking, a movement in the crowd drew Nicholas' attention away from Ned. Several rows behind and to the right, he spotted Emmett and Lorna's son, Gilbert, who was jostling past a few people to reach someone farther down on the bench. When he squeezed between two people and sat down, an older woman on his left appeared miffed that the boy had invaded the already crowded row, turning her head away in silent irritation. The younger woman on his right, however, offered a familiar and comforting smile as Gilbert sat next to her and cupped a hand to her ear to speak.

Nicholas was glad to see that Gilbert had returned from his assignment, presumably having delivered his letter and now telling Katherine Durant all about it in whispered words. Katherine nodded a few times, seemingly pleased at what she was hearing. Sophia, sitting to her daughter's right, curiously looked on. Next to Sophia was another vaguely familiar face, though it took a few moments before Nicholas realized he was looking at Lewis Ames, not used to seeing him with short hair. But his thoughts were abruptly jarred when Katherine raised a hand to her mouth, her eyes widening in surprise at something Gilbert had just uttered. She cast an incredulous gaze upon the boy but said nothing as they both continued watching Constable Brindle speak.

Nicholas' heart pounded. He wondered what devastating news Gilbert had delivered, for that was all he could imagine by the shocked expression upon Katherine's face. He causally drew his eyes away and looked at Clay, but the constable's words didn't reach him as he envisioned his plan having already failed.

"When I questioned Arthur Weeks in the Iron Kettle Tavern," the constable recounted, "he reluctantly told me that Nicholas Raven had visited him late on several nights while he was cleaning the gristmill. Arthur, who had been instructed by Ned Adams to lock up each night, claimed that Nicholas insisted that he leave when his work was done, promising to lock up the mill himself."

"And did Arthur say why Nicholas had visited the mill late at night?" Farnsworth asked while remaining seated in his chair. As it was his job to oversee the trial, he was allowed to ask questions as necessary to help clarify a point or elicit more information. And though the constable was doing a fine job, the mayor nonetheless wanted to exhibit an image of caring and concern to keep the focus on him from time to time.

"Arthur claimed that Nicholas had returned to work on the bookkeeping," Clay replied, "yet Ned told me that the books were already up to date."

Nicholas, hearing Constable Brindle describe Arthur's blatant lie, ignored the episode between Katherine and Gilbert and focused on the trial. He remembered facing Arthur Weeks in the Water Barrel Inn where the man had flung his vile accusation, though he now felt no anger toward him as he had earlier. Knowing that Arthur died at the hands of an Enâri creature, he could only conjure up compassion for his former coworker. For a little money, Arthur had been duped by Dooley and Farnsworth, and in the end paid for it with his life. Nicholas would save his indignation for those who deserved it more.

"We then walked to Nicholas' cottage on Maynard Kurtz' farm," the constable continued. "I wanted to question him about Arthur's accusation, though I didn't find him on the property. I found something else instead."

The misery and confusion that had plagued Nicholas eight months ago again stirred inside him, but this time the emotions didn't overwhelm him since he knew of the intricacies behind the grand deception. As Clay described finding the flour sacks and silver half-pieces in the shed, Nicholas again wondered how individuals and events might have been affected differently if he hadn't fled. Might people have escaped much suffering if he had stayed and faced the charges against him from the start?

He knew he would never satisfactorily answer that riddle, knowing he must accept his path in life as it unwound. As Malek had once told him, he might have been destined to have a role in the troubled events of the day. Maybe leaving Kanesbury was what he was supposed to have done. He would never have met Megan on the road otherwise, launching a chain of events that helped topple the evil growing in Kargoth and spreading across Laparia. He knew he must accept that logic and get on with life.

"I tracked down Nicholas at the Water Barrel Inn," Clay continued. "I told him about the accusations against him which he immediately denied to Arthur Weeks' face. When I displayed the button found near the spilled flour, it matched the buttons on Nicholas' jacket, one of which was missing." A few surprised gasps were audible in the hushed silence. "As Nicholas again denied the charges, I returned with him to the shed and revealed the stolen items. Nicholas once more claimed his innocence, unable to explain how the items had gotten there. But as all the evidence pointed to him, I had no choice but to escort him to the lockup until I could further investigate." Clay Brindle again removed a handkerchief and wiped his brow. "But while stopping by his cottage to get another jacket, as I had to keep the one with the missing button as evidence, Nicholas gave me the slip and ran off into a field.

"To complicate matters, Arthur Weeks was murdered later that night while visiting Dooley Kramer. The poor man had been stabbed to death. I heard Dooley's frantic screams while I was a few streets away, so I rushed to his house with a curious crowd in tow. Looking frazzled and terrified, Dooley told me that Nicholas had been to his house and killed Arthur because he had implicated him in the robbery. I immediately increased the scope of my search for Nicholas, rounding up additional volunteers. But by dawn, I assumed that he was long gone and called everybody back. And though I sent a description of Nicholas and a list of his alleged deeds to other authorities in the region, we never had any success in locating him."

Clay briefly turned to Nicholas, catching his eye. "But the only reason Nicholas Raven stands trial now is because he returned of his own accord to face these charges, placing himself at the mercy of the village. The jury must weigh that action as it sees fit. And so, ladies and gentlemen, that is the extent of my story. As the two key witnesses against him are no longer here–Arthur Weeks being deceased and Dooley Kramer missing–I have no one else to provide testimony since no one has come forth during my investigation to substantiate the charges. Unless anyone steps forward now with pertinent information, I'll sit down and allow Nicholas to present his case."

Clay Brindle looked about the room, making a perfunctory effort to encourage any reluctant witnesses to come forth. But expecting none, he took his seat by Nicholas, again dabbing his forehead with the handkerchief while clutching his cane in the other hand.

"You did a fine job, Clay," Nicholas whispered.

"Thanks," he replied. "Hope I didn't build a wall too high for you to climb over."

"I'll do my best," he said as Farnsworth stood to speak.

"Thank you, Clay, for a fine summation of some complex and grisly details," he said. "I'm sure the jurors have gleaned much from your descriptions. However, they must balance your words against those of Nicholas Raven who will now offer his statement before calling forth any witnesses." Farnsworth extended a hand, indicating for him to proceed. "You may now make your case, sir."

As he sat down, Nicholas rose from his chair, his unease apparent to all. But with the fates of several people in the balance and thoughts of Ivy on his mind, he knew that much rested on his performance. After taking a deep breath, his nerves settled and soon the words poured forth from his heart.

"Thank you for allowing me to speak today," Nicholas said, gazing about the hall and at the jury. "And though I also agree that Constable Brindle gave a fine speech, I hope to prove the accusations leveled against me are false even though my accusers are not around to defend their charges. I say to you in all honesty that I did not steal money or flour from Ned's gristmill. I worked as an accountant for him, a man I deeply respect, for almost two years. I labored in his mill for an additional two years before that, so I couldn't conceive of committing such an act against someone whose trust I've worked to attain and whose friendship I was honored to have earned.

"As for the murder of Arthur Weeks, I didn't commit that horrible deed either, even though Arthur lied and accused me of the robbery. His action was inexcusable, but he didn't deserve to die because of it," he said as the golden glow of sunlight illuminated the western windows. "I didn't kill Arthur, because at the time of his death, I was nowhere near him." He paused and scanned the faces of those nearest to him, sensing their polite skepticism. "And I can prove it, too. You see, I have a witness."

Whispers of disbelief spread across the room. Nicholas knew he had grabbed everyone's attention, including Farnsworth and Clay Brindle's, both of whom he guessed were wondering why he hadn't mentioned this fact to them during the past week.

Farnsworth was thinking exactly that as pangs of uneasiness swept over him, yet he kept his composure and feigned a level of surprise equal to those around him. What worried him most about the stunning revelation was the door it might open to other avenues of discussion. If Nicholas could produce a witness to exonerate him, then people would begin to ask who had really killed Arthur Weeks, and more importantly, why. Everyone would then wonder why Dooley Kramer had lied about Nicholas' involvement in the murder, igniting further speculation about the events of that night. Farnsworth fumed inside, believing that Nicholas had deceived him. He desperately wanted to know why, but more importantly, he wanted the name of the mysterious witness.

"I'm telling the truth!" Nicholas said, raising his voice until the crowd calmed down. "And that witness is here tonight. But before I call on the individual, you must know that this person wanted to speak to Constable Brindle months ago, but at my stubborn insistence, kept silent. Since the witness is a close friend, I feared that until the real murderer was found, her life might be in danger if she stepped forward to defend me."

Upon hearing Nicholas utter the word *her*, many heads in the room turned to Katherine Durant. Farnsworth starred coolly at her, knowing he must keep his composure until he knew all the facts. But a wave of anxiety slowly engulfed him when realizing that a secret alliance existed between Nicholas and Katherine. He knew that Nicholas had deceived him, having told him a week ago that he had never said goodbye to Katherine before he fled the village. It had been a lie, but for what purpose?

A chill shot up his back when he considered that the couple might have talked to each other since his return to Kanesbury despite Nicholas' statement to the contrary. If they had met, what might have been discussed? Farnsworth gripped the edge of the chair, his fingernails digging into the wood as he helplessly listened to Nicholas address the spellbound citizens of Kanesbury.

"So if she is willing," he continued as the crowd held its collective breath, "I would ask Katherine Durant to explain how I secretly met with her that night while hiding in the ice cellar in Oscar and Amanda Stewart's home." He looked at Katherine with an encouraging smile, silently wishing her good luck. She stood, nervously pressing the creases out of her dress as she confronted a barrage of inquisitive stares.

"What Nicholas said is true," she remarked, her soft voice barely filling the hall. Oscar and Amanda were seated a few rows ahead to her left across the center aisle. She gazed at them apologetically, but seeing nothing except kindness and understanding in their eyes, her confidence was bolstered. "I had been working in Amanda's kitchen on the first night of the Harvest Festival to help with their annual party. When I stepped into the adjoining pantry, someone whispered to me from behind the door leading to the ice cellar. To my surprise, it was Nicholas Raven. I followed him downstairs to talk in private.

"I was relieved to see him after hearing rumors of his involvement in the robbery. He said that he had no idea how the items from the gristmill had ended up in his shed, but what disturbed him more was that Arthur Weeks had falsely accused him. Nicholas regretted running away from the constable and wanted to turn himself in, but I urged him to rest on his decision overnight. He agreed, planning to return later to Maynard Kurtz' farm and sleep in the barn, hoping by then that Constable Brindle and his men would be gone." Katherine paused, lowering her eyes. "But that didn't happen as an even more horrible event gripped Kanesbury later that night, with Nicholas again being thrust into the center of the new controversy."

"And that new controversy was the murder of Arthur Weeks?" Farnsworth asked from his chair, his distrust of Katherine escalating though he looked pleasantly upon her.

"That's correct," she replied, not rattled by his interruption. "After Nicholas and I talked, I left him alone to rest. But after learning about the murder a couple of hours later and hearing that Nicholas was being accused of the crime, I rushed back to the ice cellar. I found him fast asleep and woke him with the bad news. He was confused in his exhausted state, feeling that people and events were conspiring against him. So at my urging, he reluctantly fled Kanesbury later that night, not telling me in which direction he would be leaving. I promised not to reveal this information to anyone since he feared for my safety. And I kept my promise—well, for the most part." She looked at Nicholas with a trace of guilt. "I ended up telling one other person."

Murmurs of surprise spread through the hall. Even Nicholas looked upon her with a befuddled expression as she had never mentioned that fact during their encounter thirteen days ago. When the room quieted, he again addressed her.

"I'm curious, Katherine—as I'm sure is everyone—as to whom you shared this information with," he said. "And why?"

"I'll gladly tell you," she replied, glancing ahead a few rows to her right, "though I don't know if this individual had expected to be called upon to speak today."

Ned Adams turned around in his seat and looked at her. "It's all right, dear," he said, standing up. "I'm more than happy to speak in Nicholas' defense. I believe with all my heart that he is innocent of these crimes." He turned to Nicholas. "Shall I begin?"

"Please," he said, signaling for Katherine to take her seat.

"Very well. And I shall not take up much of your time as my story is brief," he began. "The reason Miss Durant confided in me is the result of a chance meeting in front of the village hall one evening six months ago. It was the second day of Old Autumn, a date I remember as I'm sure many here do, since later that same night, Caldurian's hired troops from the Isles stormed our village and raided our homes. And on the night before that, my gristmill had been razed to the ground in a devastating fire."

"Why were you and Katherine talking about me?" Nicholas inquired.

"She and I were discussing Otto's strange reappearance," Ned told him. "Katherine's uncle, having warned some villagers that trouble was afoot, didn't seem like his old self when he had stopped by to see me one night. Even Katherine agreed that Otto had appeared distant and aloof. That he fled the village he loved so dearly before the forewarned attack only added to our confusion. That wasn't the Otto we knew. And though we attributed his strange behavior to his having been kidnapped by the Enâri creatures at Barringer's Landing–or so we believed at the time–Katherine and I also shared those similar feelings about another individual."

"And who would that be?" Nicholas asked.

"Maynard Kurtz. He was exhibiting a distant personality quite opposite his usual affability," he explained. "What I'm trying to say is that the odd behavior of both Otto and Maynard, coupled with the gristmill robbery, Adelaide Cooper's disappearance and Arthur Weeks' murder–all happening just as the Enâri reawakened and escaped from the Spirit Caves–well, it made me regret that I had even for a minute believed Nicholas Raven was responsible for his accused crimes. Though I couldn't prove it, I suspected that that conniving wizard Caldurian had his dirty hands in those goings-on. Nicholas, I believe, had somehow gotten tangled in the web of events for reasons that none of us could explain.

"Sensing my emotional turmoil and wishing to allay my fears, Katherine informed me that Nicholas had been in the ice cellar at the time of Arthur's death." Ned looked about, grateful to see that people were beginning to understand that Nicholas had been falsely accused. "Upon hearing the information, I knew that Dooley Kramer had lied and that he and Arthur must have been involved in the robbery. But why they framed Nicholas, I cannot guess. We even speculated that maybe Dooley had committed the murder." He sadly shook his head and shrugged. "It's a muddled mystery for sure."

"But perhaps a mystery someone else can shed some light upon," Katherine remarked. She again stood to the surprise of her mother who looked on in stunned silence. Lewis and Gilbert, however, remained stone-faced as they listened, knowing that each word she spoke drove the narration of events closer to Zachary Farnsworth's role.

Farnsworth sat stiffly upon hearing this, knowing that Katherine was taunting him, prodding his patience, but he didn't know to what purpose. Was she simply pushing back and testing him? Or did she mean to expose him? The nine men he had hired to watch Katherine and her family and friends had assured him that she had never left the village or made contact with any strangers over the weeks. No one out of the ordinary had visited her home either, not even in the dead of night. That knowledge calmed him a little bit, but just to be safe, he glanced at his paid operative seated along the east wall. After quietly getting his attention, Farnsworth raised an eyebrow and signaled him to be ready to alert his associates outside and take action if necessary. Waiting near the lockup was a horse loaded with money and supplies in case he needed to make a quick getaway, though he hoped it wouldn't come to that.

"You have another witness?" Nicholas asked, feigning surprise.

"Yes," Katherine replied as Ned took his seat. "There is someone here who has firsthand information about the robbery at the gristmill–and more. I think you'll find the story interesting, yet disturbing in its chilling details." As she turned and looked behind her, everyone stared in the same direction, eager to hear from the mysterious individual. "You may come forward now," she gently beckoned.

Slowly emerging from the crowd inside the front entryway was a short woman in a plain, gray dress with a knitted shawl draped over her shoulders and a kerchief tied about her head. The room went silent as she walked up the center aisle, her shoulders slightly stooped while she held a handkerchief to her mouth as if recovering from a cold. She appeared thoroughly nondescript, having seamlessly blended in with the others and drawing no attention to herself until now. When the woman reached the point directly across from Katherine, she stopped, straightened her shoulders and lowered the handkerchief from her face. And though several stunned people close by recognized her instantly, only when she removed her head covering and looked around did the entire room finally realize that it was Adelaide Cooper. All were astonished, none more so than Zachary Farnsworth. He locked a hardened stare upon her, momentarily paralyzed by the sight of the gray haired woman who countered his gaze with steel blue eyes that burned with such fearlessness and vigor that it caused him to momentarily look away. But nobody observed Farnsworth's moment of distress as they were focused upon Adelaide, all eager to hear her story.

"Where've you been?" someone shouted.

"*Shhh!*" chided another. "She'll speak when she's ready."

Upon seeing familiar faces, Adelaide smiled as a sense of relief and serenity enveloped her. She was happy to be home again and unafraid, ready to help put an end to Farnsworth's fraudulent hold upon the village. After signaling Katherine to take her seat and offering a brief acknowledgment to Nicholas, she began her story.

"I'm guessing that I was the last person you expected to see here tonight," she said with good humor. "And as to where I've been, well that is quite a captivating story. But first you must know this, my friends. Everything that happened to me is connected to the troubles that plagued Nicholas Raven." A buzz of speculation swept across the room as everyone wondered what juicy bits of information Adelaide was about to reveal. "There is more of a foul nature behind what has gone on in Kanesbury than meets the eye," she said. "The wizard Caldurian was only the beginning of your problems."

Farnsworth remained seated as his anxiety intensified, the color draining from his face. All he had worked for was about to be taken away by Adelaide's sudden appearance. After all the time, money and effort he had put into tracking Katherine's whereabouts and contacts of late, he couldn't comprehend how he had slipped up, allowing Adelaide to fearlessly saunter up the aisle right under his nose. *Where had she been hiding?*

The question seared itself into his mind as he wondered what the citizens of Kanesbury would do to him once Adelaide revealed the reason for her disappearance. His spirit deflated even further as another horrible notion took hold. If Katherine had managed to bring Adelaide to this public trial, then could *he* be inside the building as well?

Farnsworth eyed a few faces in the crowd, desperately seeking out Maynard Kurtz. Like a hawk, he zeroed in on a tired, dusty farmer with his coat collar pulled up to his neck a few benches back, and then on a tall man standing in the shadowy corner to his left behind cluttered rows of people. Off against the right wall sat an individual in a rumpled coat and a ragged, brown cloth hat shadowing his eyes while his outstretched legs kept warm near the blazing fireplace. Farnsworth's effort to seek out Maynard was in vain, yet he knew the man must be somewhere in the vicinity. He could feel his unsettling presence. It was only a matter of time, he realized, until they buried him with their words. Should he flee now before they had the chance? His palms sweated as the lustrous western light slowly faded behind the windows. He knew he had to act fast.

While Adelaide recounted the night she had first heard voices across the road from her house, Farnsworth again eyed his paid operative on the side. With an imperceptible nod, he signaled the man to casually leave and alert his eight colleagues outside to prepare for the worst, promising himself that he would ride out of the village a free man, putting as much distance between himself and Kanesbury as possible. It would be up to the villagers whether or not blood would be shed in the process if they tried to thwart his escape.

"On the following evening two nights before the Harvest Festival, I heard those voices again in the darkness," she said, explaining that she also noted a flicker of light among the shadows across the road. "Grabbing an oil lamp, I walked to Maynard's property to explore. The windows of his house and Nicholas' cottage were black, so I assumed both were asleep. I saw another flicker of light near the back shed, and despite the unnerving situation, I pushed ahead to investigate." Adelaide's eyes grew wide as she relived the fear of that dreadful night. "Even more shocking was what I discovered inside Nicholas's shed. Or rather I should say *who* I discovered."

"*Who?*" whispered a young girl as if enthralled in the words of a campfire tale, eliciting a few smiles and momentarily breaking the tension.

"When I opened the shed door, I saw two men inside. One held a sack of flour and was setting it down," she continued. "Both were mortified to see me, and I knew on the spot that I was interrupting something criminal. I asked them what they were doing and said I was going to wake Nicholas, but the other man had pulled out a knife." Adelaide fanned herself as the unpleasant memories stormed back. "I was terrified and ran speechless from the shed, their footsteps directly behind me as I raced across the field back to the road, hoping to reach the safety of my house."

"Who were the two men?" Nicholas asked in soothing tones.

"One of them, the one with the flour sack, was none other than Dooley Kramer," she replied. A chorus of stunned whispers flooded the chamber. Many concluded on the spot that Dooley had successfully framed Nicholas to get his job at the gristmill. "And regarding the identity of the other man—"

Farnsworth gripped the edge of his chair, ready to jump to his feet once his name was uttered and disgraced before his fellow citizens. He hoped his men outside were ready to clear a path for escape upon his signal and prevent anyone from pursuing him until he fled to the countryside. Holding his breath, he waited for Adelaide to finish.

"Well, for the moment, Nicholas, I'd like to keep that individual's name private as there is much more of my story to tell that concerns him," she said to the disappointment of many. "But that isn't the only reason," she quickly added, garnering everyone's rapt attention once more and sending their emotions on another upward spiral. "To keep this trial proceeding smoothly, I don't want to reveal the name just yet because…"

"Because why?" Nicholas inquired upon her nervous pause.

Adelaide took a deep breath, laying a hand over her chest. "Because that individual is sitting in this chamber," she told him, sending rumblings of shock, suspicion and fear throughout the hall.

Everyone looked about, wondering who might have committed such an atrocious deed. Many were angered, demanding to know who it was so they could apprehend the culprit, while others considered fleeing with their families, wondering if it was safe to remain in the presence of such a criminal. But curiosity ultimately got the best of them. Everyone remained glued in their seats to hear out the story to its bitter end.

Farnsworth, in a slow exhale, realized that Adelaide had offered him a short reprieve. He wondered if she was toying with him or perhaps wanted to fashion an unspoken deal of some sort on orders from Katherine Durant. In either case, he decided to seize the opportunity and take charge, wanting to deflect any suspicions that might be directed his way. He stood up to calm the crowd.

"Please, everyone, let us hold our comments and allow this kind lady to finish speaking," he said with a veneer of warmth and concern, though still ready to run if it came to that. "This is a trial, after all, and it should be conducted with the utmost restraint." When the gathering finally settled down, he nodded pleasantly to Adelaide, indicating for her to continue.

"Thank you, Mr. Farnsworth," she replied. "As I was saying, I fled Maynard's property, but I wasn't fast enough. I was apprehended by the two men before I could get inside and lock the door. And as the one had me at knifepoint, I dared not scream, fearing for my life.

"You were held captive in your house?" Nicholas asked.

"Yes, for a few hours. Before dawn I was taken to the man's house and locked in the cellar. I was held prisoner for several days, promised that I wouldn't be hurt if I cooperated." She recounted her time of fear and isolation in the dank and dreary room. "I couldn't figure out why these awful things were happening to me and Nicholas, but a partial answer was revealed a few nights later. I was bound and gagged by my captor. He explained that an important meeting was about to take place in his house and he couldn't risk me being discovered. If I knew what was good for me, he said, I would agree to his terms. Fearing the worst, I relented, promising to be quiet while he conducted business."

Adelaide explained that she had fallen asleep, and then hours later a loud voice in the room above abruptly woke her. "I can't be sure if someone was angry or merely expressing himself forcefully, but it sent a chill through me. Realizing that my host was attending to the business he had spoken of, I listened carefully as bits of conversation filtered through the floorboards. I couldn't hear any specifics as many words were muffled, but I heard enough to learn who was meeting with my kidnapper."

"*Who?*" Constable Brindle asked, leaning forward in his chair with owl-like eyes. He glanced at Nicholas, his face flush with embarrassment. "Oh, sorry. Just getting a little carried away by the testimony. This is your witness."

"Nothing to be sorry about," Nicholas replied, taking it as a good sign that Clay was enthralled with Adelaide's account. He looked kindly upon the woman, impressed with the ease and grace with which she was handling herself under such difficult circumstances. "Please tell us the name of that mysterious visitor, Adelaide."

"It was the wizard Caldurian," she calmly stated.

"Caldurian!" a man in back whispered loudly enough for everyone to hear. "One of our own was making deals with that horrible wizard?"

"Yes," Adelaide replied. "I can't tell you precisely what they had discussed, but I heard mention of a key and some talk of the Enâri creatures that terrorized our village. Also, the name Nicholas Raven came up from time to time, and I can't imagine that that boded well for the young man."

"Nor can I," Nicholas joked, momentarily lightening the mood. "Did any additional meetings occur between the wizard and this unnamed individual?"

"I cannot say, because several days later I was taken to a new location. It was to be my home for the next several weeks until my rescue on the last day of autumn."

"You were held prisoner elsewhere?" Nicholas curiously asked. "Where?"

"I was locked in a crude house built on a small island deep in the swamplands east of Kanesbury," she explained. "It was well hidden from view of passersby, and I can only guess what criminal activity was conducted there before it became my temporary home. But luckily, Katherine Durant cleverly discovered my location. With the help of Lewis Ames, they freed me from that desolate prison. Well, not just me," she cryptically added. "Somebody else was held on that island, too, though in another location. Unfortunately, I didn't know who nor was able to get to him as I was securely locked inside my house."

"But you know the name of this person now?" Nicholas asked, noting out of the corners of his eyes how the jurors leaned forward to hear the latest twist in the tale.

"I do," she said. "But I think now would be a good time for Katherine to speak again. She can explain how she rescued me while shedding more light on the nature of the dealings between Caldurian and my captors."

Everyone looked at Katherine as she stood up. "Adelaide is correct. Just before Lewis and I freed her from the island, we learned about the mysterious goings-on in Kanesbury and elsewhere from Dooley Kramer. He confessed to a string of wrongdoings with his accomplice who had helped kidnapped Adelaide."

Nicholas scratched his head, appearing confused. "Why would Dooley Kramer tell you about all the crimes he had committed? That doesn't make sense."

"It will when you learn that Dooley revealed this information only after Lewis and I saved his life from a hired killer." Katherine waited for another spontaneous display of surprise from the crowd to dissipate before continuing. "You see, the individual Dooley had been working with had secretly turned against him and was about to have Dooley murdered along with the other two people on the island. Lewis and I were there to stop it and learned a good deal afterward."

As Katherine spoke, Farnsworth took a slow, deep breath, letting his shoulders slump as he exhaled, realizing that she and her friends had no intention of making any sort of deal with him. They were simply laying out to the residents of Kanesbury the sordid details of how they had been used, robbed and deceived. It was only a matter of time before the name *Zachary Farnsworth* would be uttered as a participant in those crimes, and then all would be over. He glanced around the room, knowing that the false trust he had secured from his fellow villagers would forever be replaced with loathing and disrespect once the truth was revealed. He had little time left to make his getaway, desperately looking to see if the man he sent outside to alert his other hired help had returned. *Where was he?* Farnsworth knew he would have to act fast once the signal to proceed was given. *Should I run for it right now?* He considered the possibility, but knew he would be stopped in his tracks without assistance from outside. He tugged at his collar as Nicholas posed his next question, feeling the heat rising in the room.

"So tell us, Katherine, about how you discovered Adelaide on the island. How did you and Lewis arrive there unseen and just in time to save Dooley's life?"

"It wasn't easy," she replied. "And though Adelaide and the other prisoner were both rescued, not everyone survived the grueling ordeal that night."

A weighty silence overwhelmed the room. Everyone who sat shoulder to shoulder, or stood crowded in the front entryway or outdoors near the open windows listened with undivided attention. The dimming rays of the sinking sun streaked the western windows as Katherine recounted the nine turbulent days when Caldurian and his soldiers had taken over Kanesbury. Some were at first taken aback when she mentioned befriending an Islander named Paraquin, but she assured them that the young man regretted his actions and wanted to escape his situation.

"I distrusted him in the beginning, too," she admitted, "but when he knocked on my door one evening with information, I slowly warmed up to the fact that not everyone I assumed was an enemy really *was* an enemy. Sadly, the opposite proved true as well, namely, that some people I supposed were on our side were really not."

She explained how Paraquin had told her about Dooley and his unnamed associate's late night travels outside the guarded borders of Kanesbury, confirming that they were in league with Caldurian. "After Paraquin overheard Adelaide's name being discussed between Dooley and this other individual, I spied on them, learning that they left the village late at night every six days. It wasn't until about two weeks after Caldurian had disappeared that I managed to accompany Dooley in secret to the swamp to get to the bottom of this mystery."

All were impressed how Katherine had concocted a ruse to draw away Dooley's associate from one of those late-night journeys so she and Lewis could hide in back of the wagon and follow him. She didn't mention that Amanda Stewart had unwittingly assisted her in the endeavor. She painted in chilling detail how the hired assassin had nearly killed Dooley before he met his own demise by falling upon his knife.

"Afterward, Dooley confessed his involvement in Adelaide's abduction and a multitude of other crimes," she said. "He also revealed the name of the second person who had been kidnapped and placed on the island."

"Who?" Nicholas asked, his voice just above a whisper in the deathly silence.

"Maynard Kurtz," she said to everyone's utter bewilderment. "He had been held captive on the island for most of last autumn, though he has since been hiding out with Adelaide just a few miles from here."

"Maynard?" a woman asked, ignoring trial protocol because Katherine's statement sounded so absurd. "How could that possibly be? Maynard was in Kanesbury most of that time!" Rumblings of suspicion spread through the room. "I've spoken to him myself during the time period you've suggested."

"Yes, how could that be, Miss Durant?" Farnsworth asked with skepticism. He stood and stepped forward, sensing a chance to shed doubt upon her testimony. Even if Katherine dared to produce Maynard at this trial, he didn't see how she could prove that he had been kidnapped while everyone in the village saw Arileez walking around as Maynard's double. Surely they would think she was delusional. "Maynard Kurtz was alive and well in Kanesbury for most of last autumn as all of us here are aware, particularly me. He appointed me to the village council after Ned Adams resigned. And he didn't depart for Morrenwood until the thirteenth day of Old Autumn, nearly at the end of the season when I took his place as acting mayor. So with all due respect, why would you present such a fanciful story? I don't understand."

Katherine, guessing that Farnsworth believed she knew nothing about Arileez and finally had her cornered, looked at him with a trace of concern as he sprouted a thin but vindictive smirk. She returned a relaxed and confident smile, causing him to flinch when he caught a steely gleam in her eyes.

"I admit that my story may sound fanciful to anyone who interacted with Maynard last autumn," she continued. "But my claim will make sense when those people realize they were not associating with the real Maynard Kurtz. As Dooley explained to me, the Maynard Kurtz so many of us know and love had been replaced by an impostor, a powerful wizard named Arileez who could transform into anyone or anything he desired." Dead silence greeted her words, followed by whispers of disbelief and nervous laughter. But Katherine took the expected response in stride and smiled pleasantly.

"Now I don't blame you for thinking I may have embellished my testimony with a bit of silliness."

"A *bit*?" someone commented with a snicker.

"I reacted the same way when Dooley said he had witnessed that strange wizard change shape before his very eyes. You see, Dooley and his associate were hired by Caldurian to remove Nicholas from his residence on Maynard's farm. The wizard needed to freely meet with the impostor Maynard to implement his plan without being observed."

"And what plan would that be?" someone else asked.

"To take over our beloved village," she replied, "an event you all witnessed firsthand. But even that wasn't Caldurian's main objective, but only a means to an end. What the shameful wizard truly wanted, and sadly achieved, was to destroy the life of Otto Nibbs for the humiliation my uncle brought upon him twenty years ago. It was an act of revenge," Katherine said, wiping away a tear, "and for a time, it tore our village apart."

Nobody spoke for a few moments as they digested her words. Though the existence of a wizard powerful enough to transform his appearance was difficult for most to accept, nearly everyone quietly admitted that the ill fortunes that had befallen Otto Nibbs were easily traced back to Caldurian now that the confusing haze of those chaotic nine days had dissipated. Nicholas broke the silence.

"Katherine, do you have any proof of your claim?" he asked. "Though I sense your words are sincere, I believe most would take your story to heart if you offered something a bit more substantial."

"I couldn't agree more," she replied, "which is why a few words from Maynard Kurtz himself might help to convince them."

"But Maynard got lost on his way to Morrenwood!" someone called out. "If Constable Brindle's men couldn't find him during all this time, how could you?"

Katherine couldn't help but grin as did many others in the assembly who began to believe her statement. "The real Maynard Kurtz never went to Morrenwood," she explained. "It was the wizard Arileez, in Maynard's form, who had left our village, departing two days after Caldurian and his troops had disappeared. But if you don't believe me, then perhaps Maynard can ease your doubts."

In unison, people looked over their shoulders to the crowded front entrance of the hall, expecting Maynard Kurtz to emerge from the swarm of people and stroll up the center aisle in dramatic fashion, much like Adelaide had done a short while ago. But when nothing happened, they turned back around in their seats and looked at Katherine, wondering if she had misspoken or was playing a trick. A local pumpkin grower, sitting with his wife on one of the front benches and whispering into her ear, stood up and pointed at the jury.

"Hey, look up there!" he called out, indicating one of the jury members on the right end of the back row who had slowly stood up and gazed across the rows of spectators in a strangely familiar manner. "Isn't that...?"

All eyes locked onto the tall, unshaven man standing silently before them, wearing brown, weather-beaten pants and a matching coat over a heavy woolen shirt. A sun-baked hat rested upon his head, covering the long strands of dark brown hair that fell down his neck and disappeared beneath his coat. As everyone carefully studied the individual, including Nicholas, Constable Brindle and Zachary Farnsworth, most saw a vague resemblance to someone they had known long ago but were unable to identify. A moment later, his eyes widening, Clay Brindle finally recognized the man and rose from his chair, standing with both hands upon his cane for support.

"Maynard!" he shouted with a mix of disbelief and delight. "Where've you been?"

"At the swamp, just as Katherine told you," he replied, removing his hat and coat and setting them on the chair, allowing his recognizable long hair to be seen by all, though it was now tinted dark brown to disguise its trademark silvery-black color. He stepped forward in front of the other jury members who appeared equally surprised by his presence, not having recognized him when they convened inside the hall minutes before the public as he had remained quiet and kept to himself. "I apologize for the theatrics, but I, like Adelaide, was cautioned that my presence should be concealed until the last possible moment. But I did have to confide in one person near the end to secure this seat." Maynard glanced at Deputy Tyler Harkin who stood off to the side, his eyes cast down. "Well, two people actually." He signaled to a man hiding among the crowd at the other end of the hall to step forward and take his rightful place on the jury. Chase Kevic, sporting a mop of gray hair and ruddy cheeks, hurried sheepishly down the aisle and took his assigned jury chair, addressing Nicholas and Constable Brindle as he passed by.

"I hope I didn't foul up this trial," he said, "but Maynard insisted that he had a good reason to temporarily assume my place. And him being an old friend..."

"I understand," Nicholas said. "Maynard can be persuasive."

"Apparently so," Clay Brindle agreed. "But if Nicholas has no objections to continuing after this strange twist during his own trial, then I have none either." He glanced at Farnsworth for a ruling.

Farnsworth, seething inside at Maynard's reappearance, hastily put on a façade of objectivity now that the crowd's focus was temporarily upon him. "We shall proceed," he ordered as everyone's attention quickly shifted back to Maynard while Farnsworth silently stewed, envisioning his modest empire crumbling before his eyes. After everyone took their seats, Maynard strolled up closer to address the crowd.

"I suppose you're all wondering if what Katherine told you about the wizard Arileez is true," he began, heartened to look upon the faces of the many friends and acquaintances he hadn't seen in a long time. "Let me assure you that she *is* telling the truth, hard as it is to believe. Despite the fantastical nature of her account, Arileez visited my farm late one evening about a week and a half after Nicholas had left Kanesbury.

"It was a chilly night. I was in the barn at my workbench. I had been restless and unable to sleep much, worried about how Nicholas was faring and fretting about what had happened to Adelaide. Despite Constable Brindle's investigation and the efforts of many local search parties, no progress had been made as to her whereabouts. And so I carried on as best I could, enduring the void that had been visited upon me.

"But on that particular night as I stood hunched over my bench in the light of an oil lamp whiling away the hours, I heard a faint noise behind me as if something had scurried into the barn. I grabbed the lamp and turned around, expecting to see a stray cat taking refuge from the cold. What I saw instead was a small red fox looking hungry and chilled, though to my surprise it didn't appear the least bit afraid of me, its yellowish eyes locked onto mine. It struck me as a most surreal sight for some reason, and feeling sorry for the creature, I decided to go to the house and find it some scraps to eat.

"I had only taken a few steps toward the barn door when I turned around to see if the fox was following me. But when I looked down in the faint light, I saw that the creature was gone. In its place, however, was a set of mud-stained boots identical to the ones I was wearing. Upon seeing such an odd sight, I rubbed my eyes, wondering if I was imagining things. As I slowly raised the oil lamp, I saw a pair of legs in those boots, then a whole body, and finally the face of an individual standing there in absolute silence, his sharp stare cutting through the gloom and burning into my soul. I was flabbergasted by the sight, unable to speak for a few moments as I stood there looking directly at–*me*."

Maynard paused, rubbing a trembling hand over his face as he recalled the strange and shocking images from that night while his mesmerized audience looked on. Though he had already told Adelaide and Nicholas this story in private after he had regained consciousness, revealing these details in public now made the incident sound highly implausible to his ear. But he knew he must continue for Nicholas' sake.

"When I was finally able to utter a few words, I asked the individual–my twin–who he was. He replied in a voice identical to mine, 'I am you,' and then curiously eyed me as if studying my features and subtle mannerisms. After my nerves settled, I asked him what he wanted and where he had come from. 'Where I come from doesn't concern you,' he told me. 'But I want your life,' he added with little emotion, whereupon I saw him raise a hand in the air toward me. And though he possessed no weapon, I heard him utter a series of strange, whispered words in a language I had never heard before. I found myself mesmerized by the sound of his voice, unable to move my limbs or draw my eyes away. As his voice faded in the recesses of my mind, the faint light from my oil lamp also seemed to grow dimmer. Soon I was overwhelmed in darkness and then–"

Maynard paused again as he swept his gaze across the villagers, taking solace in their presence. "And then I remembered no more until I woke up in a stranger's farmhouse with Adelaide looking down upon me. It was the seventh day of New Winter as I was informed, meaning that I had been asleep for about seven and a half weeks under that strange sleeping spell, most of the time spent lying in a small shed on an island in the swamp. Adelaide told me that while locked inside her prison home, she had seen Dooley Kramer and the other gentleman she referred to earlier carrying my body onto the island one night. They took me to a shed where I remained asleep until Katherine and Lewis found me. I recall nothing during that time except for scattered dreams, nor do I remember the manner in which I was removed from my barn after that wizard had cast his spell."

As Maynard elaborated upon a few of the compelling details, Farnsworth looked on in silent dismay, knowing it was only a matter of time until he was publicly exposed for his crimes. He recalled the night he and Dooley were instructed by Arileez to wait in a wagon just down the road from Maynard's property, prepared to implement the next phase in Caldurian's complicated plan. When Arileez silently signaled to them from the barn with a wave of an oil lamp, Farnsworth drove the cart inside the gaping doors and saw Maynard's sleeping body sprawled upon the ground.

"Get rid of him far from here," Arileez had instructed. "*Permanently*," he added in a sinister tone that belied his kindly appearance as Maynard Kurtz. It was then that Farnsworth fully understood Caldurian's reason to remove Nicholas Raven from the property, though he had no idea just what devious intentions either wizard had in store for the other residents of Kanesbury. At the time he only wanted to get away from Arileez as quickly as possible as he felt a looming sense of dread in the wizard's presence. He and Dooley loaded Maynard's body onto the cart and covered it with a blanket, promising the wizard to bury it deep in the woods outside the village.

"No one must ever see him again," Arileez had told him, his words cold. "*Ever*."

"And no one ever will," Farnsworth promised before he and Dooley drove out of the village to the swamp, neither having the nerve to kill Maynard despite him being fast asleep and unable to put up a struggle.

Now, as Zachary Farnsworth watched Maynard in front of the packed hall, he regretted not possessing more hardened nerves back then to finish the job they had promised to do. He bit the inside of his cheek, determined to resort to any ruthless means to extricate himself from his imploding world in the next few minutes, knowing that it was just a matter of time before the finger of blame pointed his way. He again scanned the room for the hired hand he had sent outside to alert his other help, wondering what was delaying the man's return. The time to act was drawing near.

"At this point," Maynard concluded, "I would ask that Katherine fill in the remaining details of the story as I was fast asleep during this most curious affair."

"Thank you for your helpful words," Nicholas said, standing up to shake Maynard's hand before he took a seat among the crowd.

Nicholas signaled to Katherine with a grateful smile, silently indicating that they were nearing the end of their plan. And though he suspected that Farnsworth might attempt something rash before the trial concluded, he also worried that Katherine already knew what that something was after he had earlier witnessed Gilbert Trout whispering into her ear and causing her to register a look of stunned disbelief. He guessed that Gilbert had warned her about a gathering of Farnsworth's men outside, perhaps in numbers greater than they had anticipated. With uncertainty in the air, Nicholas knew they must be extra cautious once they implicated Farnsworth. But one way or another, his ulcerating presence would end here tonight, though in what manner, fate was yet to decide.

"Now, Katherine, after all the astounding information we've heard this afternoon, is there anything you might have left out?" Nicholas asked.

She stood. "There are three matters left that I wish to address," she replied, "the first one regarding the fate of my Uncle Otto. Maynard explained how he had been kidnapped and replaced by the shape-shifting wizard. So, too, was my uncle. As Dooley informed Lewis and me at the swamp, the man you all thought was Otto Nibbs skulking about in the dead of night and warning certain people about the impending danger to our village, and who then fled our borders out of selfish safety for his own concern, was not Otto at all. That man was the wizard Arileez in Otto's form, working on Caldurian's order to stoke up your hatred and disrespect for my uncle until his unexpected return in this very hall. At that fateful moment, the citizens of Kanesbury collectively vented their wrath upon Otto and cheered for his imprisonment, handing Caldurian the victorious revenge he had been seeking for over twenty years."

Silence filled the room saturated with the guilt and remorse that was buried just below the surface of the village for these past few months. Katherine saw in the faces of her friends and neighbors a genuine sense of sorrow and a desire for forgiveness at how horribly they had treated Otto and for succumbing so easily to Caldurian's fraudulent words. She knew they were good people at heart who had been led temporarily astray, certain that even Otto himself would forgive them. And the kind, soothing tone of her next words conveyed that notion to them, at once lightening the mood.

"But as I stand here among you," she continued, "I am wholly convinced that whatever shortcomings we've all committed over the past several months are far outshone by the many good deeds and earnest efforts to right the wrongs that have been visited upon us during that dark and wayward chapter in our lives."

As the crowd soaked in her healing words, Nicholas detected a shift in everyone's mood, as if a shadow of melancholy and lingering guilt had been lifted off their shoulders and scattered to the fair breezes of approaching twilight. And though he would never fully forget the pain and hardship he had suffered on his long journey, he only now began to appreciate how much his fellow villagers had suffered locally at the hands of the same forces who had cast their poison across Laparia. He was proud of Katherine and so many others who had fought tirelessly at home with as much grit and determination as individuals like Eucádus, Malek and Max.

"Secondly, I'd like to discuss the fate of Dooley Kramer," Katherine went on as the afternoon light softened upon the darkening window panes. "As you know, Dooley provided much information to Lewis and me. And though he had much to pay for to redeem himself, I'd like to think that his confession may have partially absolved him. Still, I must regretfully report that Dooley, whether due to destiny or bad luck, paid the ultimate price for his participation." Concerned whispers drifted among the spectators.

"What are you saying?" asked a woman sitting nearby. "You know of Dooley's whereabouts?"

Katherine nodded to the surprise of many. "While all of you are aware that Dooley has been missing for quite some time, I know what happened to him at the swamp after he led Lewis and me to Adelaide and Maynard." She detailed Dooley's encounter with Adelaide, his fatal fall off the staircase and his subsequent burial in the nearby woods. "The following morning I went to inform Clay Brindle of all that had happened on the island, but the constable was attending to other business. Sadly, before I could contact him the next day, Clay had been attacked that very dawn. It was a most tragic coincidence as I later learned from the person who I assumed was behind Clay's assault."

"What are you saying?" Nicholas asked. He and everyone in the room were chilled by Katherine's insinuation even though he had heard her speak those very words thirteen days ago when they talked in the ice cellar.

"Yes, what *are* you saying?" Clay chimed in. He stood up next to Nicholas with the help of his cane, teetering on the verge of anger, his eyes wide with wild speculation. "You know who attacked me and didn't tell me? *Who*?" he angrily demanded. "And why did you keep it secret?"

"Please forgive me, Clay, for not stepping forward sooner," she replied in apologetic tones. "And let me stress that while I do not know the name of the specific individual who attacked you, I am more than convinced I know who hired that person. And that is the third and final matter I wish to address." She paused as everyone looked at her, all yearning to hear the name of the person behind such an awful attack. "It was the same man who worked with Dooley Kramer to frame Nicholas. I have no definitive proof, but I can say that I was subtly threatened by this man shortly after Clay's attack."

"But why would he threaten you?" Clay asked, his brow furrowed in confusion.

"He wanted me to keep silent about what had happened at the swamp," she said. "At the time, this man correctly suspected that I had been there and knew of his involvement in Maynard and Adelaide's abductions. How he discovered this, I do not know, but he made it eerily clear that what had happened to Clay Brindle–or perhaps even something worse–could just as easily happen to my loved ones and friends unless I held my tongue. Until this trial today, I have kept silent on these matters out of fear of violent reprisals. But for the sake of this village, I can no longer hide the truth. This individual and his criminal deeds must be exposed so all can see who has been lurking among them in plain sight, slowly poisoning their very lives."

Everyone sat silent, letting Katherine's sobering words sink in. Clay finally stepped forward, still unable to logically connect all the pieces of her riveting account.

"Pardon me, Nicholas, but I must ask Katherine one more question if that's all right with you," he said amidst a swirl of muddled thoughts.

"Take as much time as you need," Nicholas replied, stepping back. Everyone directed their attention to the constable who stood leaning upon his cane.

"Katherine, while I appreciate the thoroughness of your testimony which has answered quite a few lingering questions–"

"And poses more," someone softly called out, followed by a sprinkling of mirthful laughter across the benches.

"Yes, yes!" Clay replied with mild annoyance, holding up a hand to keep order. "But what I still don't understand are the motives of this yet unnamed individual who worked with Dooley Kramer and two powerful wizards. You haven't yet told us why he committed these horrible deeds," he stated, scratching his head. "What exactly did he gain from all his troubles–and ours?"

Katherine pondered the question with sadness in her eyes. "I suppose, Constable Brindle, that the accumulation of money and power at other people's expense is what motivates individuals like the man of whom we speak. And just as in the far off corners of Laparia, here, too, in Kanesbury, the same sinister forces have been at work while most of us have gone about our daily business.

"You see, this man has slowly climbed his way up in Kanesbury society while in league with Caldurian and his associates. After Uncle Otto disappeared and Maynard was abducted and replaced by Arileez, it was the impostor Maynard who was appointed by the village council as acting mayor in Otto's absence, just as Caldurian had planned. The wizard knew that one of Maynard's duties as head of the council would be to fill in for the mayor during any absence. And later, after Caldurian and his men had left after terrorizing us and imprisoning my uncle, who did this impostor appoint to replace Ned Adams on the council after he resigned to rebuild his gristmill?"

Without mentioning a name, Katherine had caused all gazes to shift to Zachary Farnsworth who remained quietly seated in his chair, suddenly caught in the wilting glare of suspicion. Though he didn't make eye contact with anyone, Farnsworth felt his skin grow warmer and could hear his heart beating rapidly as he tried to take in a lungful of air to prepare for the coming onslaught. He again glanced about the corners of the room, desperately looking for any of his men to signal that the time to act was now.

"And one day later, our impostor acting mayor announced that he would travel to Morrenwood to consult with King Justin about Caldurian's return to these parts," she continued, pressing forward with a cool, calm demeanor that belied the fiery spirit inside her. "And before the false Maynard had left Kanesbury, who did he recommend as his replacement for what all of us thought would be a temporary absence?" Once more, all eyes shifted to Farnsworth, the man's name whispered bitterly upon a few lips.

"After hearing today's testimony, one might conclude that the appointment of this individual to the office of mayor could be the reward he was promised from Caldurian." Katherine looked directly at Zachary Farnsworth who returned a bitter, smoldering gaze. "But unfortunately for you, Mr. Farnsworth, there were far too many loose ends in such a complicated endeavor. Though it took some time, your plans have finally unraveled."

Katherine kept her hard gaze fixed upon him as he silently challenged her, his reddened face slowly contorting as a burning anger welled inside him.

"Why are you staring at me like that?" he snapped. "Why are any of you looking at me?" he added, addressing the crowd with a dismissive swipe of his hand. "Surely you don't believe this young girl's fanciful stories, do you?" He looked about from face to face, but not a single individual offered a hint of support. All first wanted to hear his explanation after such incriminating testimony.

"Can you give us any reason to disbelieve her?" Constable Brindle asked. He took a few slow steps toward Farnsworth, the tip of his cane tapping the wooden floorboards with sobering finality. "Tell me, Zachary, did you hire the individual who attacked me?"

"I am insulted by such harsh words!" he said with offense, jumping to his feet.

"Insulted or not, I would still like an answer," the constable replied, taking one step closer. "Did you hire the man who attacked me—*yes* or *no*?"

Farnsworth's jaw went slack. "I cannot believe such questions are being hurled at me after this outlandish testimony! You have nothing to say to *her*, constable?" he asked, pointing at Katherine. "She, who makes up stories on behalf of Dooley Kramer, and then conveniently says he is dead and buried. How do we know that she isn't telling lies in a plot against me? Can she produce the body? Or maybe that has conveniently disappeared." He stepped toward the first row of benches, eyeing several of the villagers gazing warily upon him. "And most preposterous of all is a fabrication about a wizard changing his appearance at will, using such a yarn against me without a shred of proof. Have any of you seen that wizard change shape from Maynard Kurtz into another man? Or a dog? Or even a loaf of apple bread? Have you, Miss Durant?"

"No, I have not," she softly replied, "though Dooley claimed to have seen Arileez' transformation. And coupled with Maynard's testimony about seeing his own double, you cannot completely refute what I've said. It would logically explain the unusual behavior of the impostor Otto Nibbs who acted in a manner so unlike my real uncle."

"Again we have these suspect facts, these malleable facts that apparently can be shaped into whatever truth Miss Durant desires as easily as this so-called wizard Arileez could alter his appearance." Farnsworth's words dripped with skepticism. "So I'll ask again–has anyone here ever seen this wizard or witnessed his amazing tricks?"

The room grew quiet. People looked around, hoping that someone might step forward. Others stared at the floor, realizing that Farnsworth had aptly defended himself against one of Katherine's most serious charges. He thought so, too, knowing that not a single person inside the hall had ever seen Arileez in his true form. He hoped that if he could refute Katherine's biggest claim, perhaps he could chip away at her other charges to sow some doubt and buy enough time to flee before everyone came to their senses. Just as Caldurian had done, he wanted to keep everyone off balance with theatrics and bombast so, whether they believed him or not, he would have confused them enough to get what he needed, namely, a means of escape. He dramatically cupped a hand to his ear.

"Well, I hear no support of Miss Durant's outrageous claim," he said, taking a step back. "That makes me wonder what else she said that might not stand up to a bit of rigorous scrutiny." He chuckled amiably before glancing at the jury. "I'm not even the one on trial today. So should I sit down and let Mr. Raven conclude? Or may I proceed with another line of questioning to defend my besmirched honor?"

An uneasy silence took hold. But before anyone in the jury could reply, a man sitting on a crowded bench adjacent to the fireplace cleared his throat. Several people turned their heads toward that shadowy spot on the west side of the room. Farnsworth did so as well, casting an irritated glance at the individual. "Yes?" he asked, his eyebrows arched sharply. "Do you have something to say?"

The man, dressed in a long, rumpled coat with a ragged, brown cloth hat tilted over his eyes, slowly stood and faced the curious onlookers. He stepped into the glow of the crackling flames, slightly pushing back the brim of his hat.

"Yes, I do," he said, his voice pleasant and folksy yet with a streak of authority lingering just beneath the surface. "With your permission, of course."

"*Fine*," Farnsworth muttered, eyeing the man suspiciously. He couldn't make out the entirety of his face in the thin shadows nor identify him by name. "First, who are you? And what bizarre bits of information could you possibly add to this outlandish trial?"

"What I have to say relates directly to the particulars of these proceedings," he replied as he strolled closer to the front of the crowd. "I'm sure you'll be enlightened."

"Oh, really?" Farnsworth's tone was slightly mocking as if not expecting much from the man, though his curiosity was piqued nonetheless. "What have you to say?"

Nicholas also watched with growing curiosity as the man strode forth, not recognizing him yet detecting a familiarity to his voice. The situation at last became apparent when he looked beyond the man's unkempt clothing and weatherworn hat. He immediately cracked a thin smile, unable to believe that such a person had time to concern himself with the trifling matters of a small village.

"I wish to address the matter you have expressed much skepticism about, Mr. Mayor." The man spoke in easy tones, eyeing Farnsworth from beneath the brim of his hat. "Namely, the existence of the wizard Arileez. I believe Miss Durant's account regarding his transformational abilities. You, however, have dismissed it."

"And by the mere act of stating that you take her word over mine is supposed to convince everyone of the veracity of her story?" Farnsworth asked. "I think most would agree with me, sir, that your statement needs a bit more meat on its bones."

The man cast a steely gaze at him before breaking out with an easy smile. "The information I bring here is anything but skeletal." He slowly removed his hat and overcoat. "You see, Mr. Farnsworth, I stand here as an eyewitness. I met Arileez face to face and saw his phenomenal abilities up close. *Too* close in fact, as I received a wound from his very hand. And were it not for some courageous men, I most likely would have died from a second, swift stroke of his blade," he said. "Is that proof enough to start?"

Farnsworth looked at the stranger, intimidated by the man's ice blue eyes that stared him down, and the confidence and certainty of his words that had overwhelmed the hall. Slowly he realized who this person was, having seen images of him depicting the same short cropped, silvery hair and fine vestments now on display, but unable to comprehend how or why he would be here. Yet Farnsworth knew he hadn't succumbed to delusion when others began to murmur the individual's name, all delightfully stunned by his presence.

But before he could welcome the visitor to the village hall, Len Harold rose to his feet with deference and breathlessly called out his name. "King Justin!"

CHAPTER 119

The Verdicts

The men, women and children in the village hall rose to their feet, astounded that the King of Arrondale had graced them with his presence. Len Harold, seated across the chamber among the first few rows, recalled having talked with King Justin several times during the war council and always appreciated his kindness for taking the time to meet with a total stranger. Now his admiration for the man rose to new heights. "What an unexpected honor and surprise," he said with heartfelt gratitude.

"The honor is mine, Mr. Harold. But please sit down," the King replied, signaling for all to do so. "Today's proceedings are not of a royal nature, but instead a trial of local interest. I am here merely as a witness and neither want nor expect special treatment. I wish only to testify on behalf of my friend, Nicholas Raven." He glanced at Nicholas with an encouraging smile. Everyone looked at the young man, astonished that King Justin knew him, yet even more amazed that he had addressed him as *friend*.

"Thank you," Nicholas replied, wondering how the monarch had arrived here at such a crucial time.

Twelve days ago, Nicholas had bid Gilbert Trout farewell on his journey with the second letter addressed to Prince Gregory. The teenager road directly to Graystone Garrison located about thirty miles away. Nicholas knew that Prince Gregory had planned to be there for a time as he was helping to organize the construction of a new garrison up north along the coastline. In his letter, he requested if it would be possible for the prince to spare a few troops and send them to Kanesbury in secret upon the day of the trial, suspecting that Zachary Farnsworth and his men would likely cause trouble of some sort once Farnsworth's connection to Caldurian was exposed. But how King Justin ultimately came to be here, he could not guess.

"I'm honored by your presence and kind words," Nicholas continued, gazing at the King as if still not sure he was really standing there. "And I'm more than happy to have you speak at my trial. I, like everyone else, am eager to hear what you know about Arileez. Please, tell us of your encounter with him, sir."

"It took place in the Blue Citadel last year on the second day of New Winter," the King replied. He stood in front of the crowd, occasionally turning to Nicholas and the jury. "It was a day I learned just how secretive and insidious Vellan's plans were to extend his poisonous grip across Laparia. But fortunately, the reign of Vellan ended in spectacular fashion. I'm sure many of you have heard stories of his demise slowly begin to arrive home with your brave friends and neighbors who fought against him.

"Now for the particulars about Arileez. I had met that wizard in one of the Citadel corridors, though at first I didn't know who he was because he looked exactly like, well–like *me*." The King noted the surprised looks before him as whispered comments made their way from row to row. He smiled, offering his reassurance. "Yes, I see you already recognize the link between my account and the one given by Maynard Kurtz. The strange transformational abilities of Arileez are completely true–or *were* true, I should say–as Arileez was killed in the attack against me." King Justin turned slightly and pointed to his upper right arm, showing everyone a torn section of his shirt sleeve. "This is the garment I wore when Arileez sliced through my skin with a talon-like extension of his own hand. I keep it as proof of that horrible act and to remind myself how fragile our freedom is against those who wish to extinguish it. You see, Arileez, on Vellan's behalf, tried to usurp the rule of Arrondale by replacing me after having assumed my form, speech and mannerisms. Had he succeeded, no one would have been the wiser because Arileez, under Vellan's direction, would have slowly rewoven the fabric of our free lands to suit his purposes, slowly killing us from within.

"But Vellan's foul design was revealed and we defeated that aspect of his horrible plan. And after learning about the events in Kanesbury, we now realize that Caldurian had also used Arileez for a similar purpose here. Before sending that shape-shifting wizard to Morrenwood, Caldurian had borrowed Arileez to seek his revenge on your mayor and my dear second cousin, Otto Nibbs, who I've learned sits in a cell in the lockup next door." He paused a moment, aware of a deep sense of regret that filled the room.

"And so, ladies and gentlemen, if you value my word, then you should also accept the word of Maynard Kurtz. He was telling the truth about how Arileez had infiltrated your village in the guise of both Maynard and Otto." King Justin turned to Farnsworth, eyeing him with cool contempt. "And if today's testimony is to be believed, then you, Mr. Farnsworth, had clearly conspired with Caldurian to help him seek vengeance upon this village, and also involved yourself in kidnapping, hiring of an assassin and other assorted thugs, and additional crimes as well. And for what? Financial gain? A position of power? A bit of public adulation?" The King sadly shook his head. "Is that what you sold out your village for, Mr. Farnsworth? Is that all that really mattered to you in life?"

The room succumbed to silence. Everyone cast their eyes upon Zachary Farnsworth who remained seated in his chair, frozen in the moment. He countered the barrage of accusatory stares with a hardened sneer, his face reddening in the dying golden light upon the windows. He rose defiantly to his feet, pushing back against the growing disdain of the crowd by the sheer force of his will.

"Why are you all looking at me like that?" he asked, his tone sharp yet controlled. He shot a callous glance at King Justin before eyeing Katherine Durant seated among the crowd. "The two of you are in on this together!" he said, waving a finger back and forth between her and the King. "And did *you* know anything about this?" he inquired of Nicholas, stepping away from his chair. "Were you aware of this conspiracy against me?"

"I knew nothing about King Justin being here today," he replied. "I'm as stunned by his arrival as you are, Mr. Farnsworth. But as long as we're posing questions, let me ask you one. Was it your idea to frame me for the gristmill robbery?"

Farnsworth bit his lower lip, trying to remain composed, yet each moment spent looking at Nicholas set his mind ablaze. "Did I frame you? How dare you ask me such a slanderous question!"

"And were you the one who set my gristmill on fire?" Ned Adams shouted out as several villagers quietly urged him on.

"That is a vile accusation indeed, Mr. Adams, and not worthy of a response!" he shouted, stepping past the King to address the onlookers up close. "May I remind you that I am not the one on trial. As the facilitator of this proceeding, I shall suspend it at once if these scathing attacks continue. Do you hear me?"

"These are not attacks," Katherine said as she rose from her seat. "We speak the truth, Mr. Farnsworth, a harsh truth from which you can no longer hide. Your reprehensible deeds have finally caught up with you, and whatever punishment awaits you will never compensate for the damages you've inflicted. But mark my words, this village and its fine citizens will recover from the poison you've spilled here. We will rebuild our lives, hopefully never to be fooled by the likes of you again."

Farnsworth smirked. "What a fine speech. But just because you've paraded Maynard and Adelaide before us, doesn't prove that I kidnapped them. And I want to see the corpses of Dooley Kramer and this alleged assassin before I'll even consider believing that other part of your story."

"But you *did* kidnap me!" Adelaide shouted, standing up and pointing a finger at him. "And I'll testify so in front of your jury."

"And you still didn't answer my question!" Ned Adams shot back as he jumped to his feet, glaring at Farnsworth. "Did you burn down the gristmill before that wizard invaded our village? Did you?"

"*No!*" he hysterically exclaimed, waving a finger in the air. "I knew nothing about that! It was all Caldurian's idea to—"

Farnsworth went silent, his heart pounding and his chest heaving as all looked at him with disgust. At that moment, Constable Brindle signaled to Tyler Harkin to approach. He whispered into his ear and then the young deputy slipped out the door on the west side, unnoticed by Farnsworth who continued to stare down the other villagers.

"So you have had discussions with the wizard," Maynard said, adding his voice to the mix. "Nice of you to finally admit it."

"I'll admit nothing! And as you people have made a farce of this trial, I hereby suspend it until such time as saner arguments can be made."

"I'm afraid you can't do that, Zachary," Constable Brindle told him. He walked toward the acting mayor, his cane in hand and a grim expression upon his face.

Farnsworth spun around and eyed him with distrust. "What are you talking about? Get back to your seat!"

Clay calmly shook his head. "With all due respect, sir, I am in charge of bringing the case against Nicholas Raven, not you. So in light of what has been revealed today, I am hereby withdrawing all charges against him."

"You cannot do that!" Farnsworth cried out. "You have no right!"

"Yes, I do, Zachary. And it's done." He glanced at Nicholas with a contrite smile. Nicholas nodded once and smiled back as if to say that all had been forgiven long ago.

"I will not allow it!" Farnsworth pressed on, stepping toward the constable.

"Furthermore," Clay continued in the same steady tone, "I am hereby leveling charges against you, Mr. Farnsworth, that include kidnapping, attempted murder, conspiring with the enemies of Arrondale, and well, a long list of other things I have yet to sort out. But we'll have time to discuss the particulars while you're sitting in one of the lockup cells."

"Have you lost all sense of reason, constable? You cannot treat me like this!" he fired back. "I am mayor of this village."

"I beg to differ, sir," Len Harold replied as he rose to his feet. "Now that Maynard Kurtz has returned, he automatically resumes the duties of that office which he temporarily transferred to you when he left for Morrenwood." Len snapped his fingers and feigned an absentminded laugh. "Pardon me, but I just realized that it was the *impostor* Maynard Kurtz who appointed you to the village council and then as acting mayor. So in reality, you hold no political office at all and therefore have no say over these proceedings."

Farnsworth, his mouth agape, desperately searched for a reply. When he finally gathered his faculties, the side door reopened as Tyler Harkin returned, only this time he accompanied someone into the hall. Everyone noticed at once and a collective gasp erupted, followed by excited whispers, buoyant smiles and a scattering of applause. Zachary Farnsworth caught sight of the individual walking alongside the deputy, slapped by another stunning turn of events.

"What's he doing here?" he whispered in disgust. "I didn't authorize this!"

"You have to stop saying things like that," the constable said, "as you have no authority around here, Mr. Farnsworth." Clay turned to Otto Nibbs who was walking toward him at Tyler Harkin's side. He placed a hand upon his shoulder. "Welcome back, Otto," he said. Otto looked on in stunned silence as Constable Brindle addressed the crowd. "And let me also announce that I am withdrawing all charges against Otto Nibbs in light of today's testimony, though most of us believe this is an action long overdue."

Otto turned to the constable with a bemused grin on his face. "You're telling me this is over, Clay?" he asked, not quite sure that he wasn't dreaming.

"You're a free man, Otto!" he replied, shaking his hand as everyone broke out in spontaneous cheering.

Katherine and Sophia rushed up to Otto and wrapped their arms around him as tears of joy flowed among the reunited family. Nicholas, watching from close by, basked in the joy that radiated from them, grateful that his village had begun the long, slow process of healing. At the same time, Clay whispered into Farnsworth's ear before indicating to Deputy Harkin to immediately escort him out of the hall to the lockup.

"Please come with me," the deputy quietly told Farnsworth amid the cheers swirling around them in a sea of lively emotions. Tyler gently placed a hand on his upper arm to guide him to the side door before the crowd around Otto grew any larger.

"*Fine!*" he bitterly muttered. "I'm ready to leave."

"Thank you, sir. Now this way please," the deputy instructed, indicating the side door to the right of the fireplace. "And then later I'll have to—"

But those were the last words Tyler spoke as Farnsworth abruptly turned his shoulder to one side and broke free of the deputy's hold. He bolted down the center aisle toward the main entrance, shoving people aside as they made their way up to offer congratulations to Otto and Nicholas.

"Stop him!" Tyler shouted, racing down the aisle in pursuit.

"Don't let him get away!" Clay hollered above the commotion punctuated by scattered screams and wildly flung commands to apprehend the traitorous Farnsworth.

But despite his swift start, Zachary Farnsworth didn't get very far. As soon as he had cleared the aisle and barreled into the entryway, he found the front doors blocked by a wall of irate citizens, their arms interlocked and their feet planted firmly to the floor. He knew at once that he wouldn't escape that way.

"Get out of my way!" he shouted, his face scarlet with rage.

"You're not going anywhere," a man in front told him.

"Your only option is to come peacefully with me," Deputy Harkin called from behind where another wall of people had formed alongside him, penning Farnsworth inside the entryway. "How shall we do this?" he asked. "Do you want to accompany me to the lockup? Or would you rather be carried there by these nice people? Your choice."

Farnsworth, inhaling short, shallow breaths as he looked from side to side, slowly walked backward until he came to a halt near the bottom step of the staircase where the day's proceedings had begun.

"Ingrates, every one of you!" he snarled, his face contorted as if a trapped animal. "I was turning this village into something more than it is, something special. It could have been a place worth living in one of these days, but you've just thrown that chance away!"

"Kanesbury already is a place worth living in," Nicholas said as he and Clay Brindle emerged through the crowd protectively surrounding Deputy Harkin.

"And we're quite happy with it that way, Zachary." Otto's unflappable voice cut through the tension as he also made his way through the wall of people. "Now go quietly with the deputy and put an end to this unbecoming spectacle. It's all over."

Farnsworth glanced at Otto Nibbs, wishing that Caldurian had simply killed him instead of concocting such an elaborate scheme for his revenge. "No, Otto. This isn't over until I say it is!" he lashed out. In a flash, he spun around and bolted up the staircase to the offices above. At once, several people prepared to rush up after him.

"Hold on!" Tyler Harkin called out, ordering them all back.

"You heard my deputy!" Clay shouted from behind as he briskly hobbled through the crowd, clutching his cane for support. "There's no way for Zachary to escape now. He's trapped. Let Tyler and a few of my other men go upstairs in an orderly fashion. I'll have no one else in this village getting hurt again on his account."

"But, Clay, some of us want to…"

"Is that understood?" the constable ordered.

"*Yes…*" another voice disappointingly replied, speaking for the others.

With the crowd momentarily under control, Constable Brindle consulted with Tyler in hushed tones about securing reinforcements as everyone looked on. But just as the deputy nodded, ready to act on the constable's plan, a chorus of shouting could be heard outdoors, steadily rising in volume. When someone in back of the crowd opened the front door, the frantic calls from the street were unmistakable.

"*Now* what's going on?" Clay sputtered, wading through the throng of people blocking the entrance. "Let us through please!"

"Zachary Farnsworth is on the roof!" somebody shouted outside as a wave of cool, early evening air wafted indoors. "He's climbing out through the bell tower!"

At once, the villagers inside the building spilled out into the dusky street as the last rays of the setting sun filtered through scattered pines and leafy trees. A handful of stars emerged against a dark, velvety blue backdrop, keeping company with the quarter Bear Moon hanging above. Lounging above the eastern horizon was the nearly full Fox Moon emitting a shimmering, silvery glow.

The rush of people through the front and side doors subsided as everyone spread out into the street and around the village hall. All were stunned by the sight of Zachary Farnsworth crawling like a frightened rat out of the north exit of the four small arched openings comprising the bell tower. Its lemon-yellow painted sides were dully illuminated by the sun's dying light and the glow of the dual moons. Yet the citizens of Kanesbury who had just emerged from the village hall were more surprised by a second spectacle. Farnsworth, too, was taken aback by the same sight once he wormed his way out of the bell tower and gingerly got to his feet, straddling either side of the sloping roof. But unlike the triumphant sense of joy quietly exhibited by the others, Farnsworth's heart sank as he gazed down upon the gathering below. Any hopes of escape were instantly dashed.

As he craned his head forward, holding onto the eaves of the bell tower to steady himself, he counted twenty of King Justin's soldiers on horseback positioned in a sweeping arc along the front and west sides of the building where the two exits were located. Several other soldiers walked about the area and mingled with the crowd. The large maple tree between the village hall and the lockup next door cast an ominous shadow. Some of the upper branches touched the edges of the roof like groping fingers that brushed against the structure whenever a slight breeze passed by.

Farnsworth sighed with a heavy heart when spotting his nine hired hands, all now reluctant guests of the King. He wiped his brow and grimaced, staring at them sitting on the grass off to one side under the watchful eyes of three guards. Their hands were tied behind their backs after having been easily apprehended by the overwhelming force.

"Zachary, get down here before you fall and break your neck!" Clay Brindle shouted from below. Standing beside him were King Justin, Otto Nibbs, Maynard Kurtz and Len Harold in a united front, all hoping to defuse this last obstacle so the village could begin to heal. Deputy Harkin soon joined them, awaiting orders from the constable.

Nicholas stood nearby with Adelaide, Katherine, Lewis and Sophia, all looking up at Farnsworth's shadowy figure balanced upon the rooftop, each feeling as if they were immersed in a nonsensical dream. Gilbert Trout stood a short distance away with his parents and siblings, all of them equally enthralled.

"And I thought I had seen everything when inside Mount Minakaris," Nicholas said to Katherine with grim humor as they watched the spectacle unfold.

"Apparently the thirst for power affects both the great and the small," she replied. "It's like a horrible fever, I suppose."

"But just as in Kargoth, this fever should break soon," remarked a familiar voice.

Nicholas turned, noting an approaching figure in the dusky light. He smiled with boundless gratitude, surprised again for a second time this evening. "Prince Gregory!" he said, extending a hand to King Justin's son. "I was only hoping that a few of your soldiers would show up, never expecting you or your father."

"And miss this exciting trial that you wrote to me about?" he replied. Nicholas introduced him to everyone, mentioning that Katherine was Otto Nibbs' niece.

"Since your mother and Otto are second cousins to my father," Prince Gregory said, "that makes us third cousins. This gathering has become a family reunion of sorts."

"And we can thank Nicholas for arranging it," Katherine lightly replied.

"But I didn't expect you or King Justin to attend. How'd that happen?" he asked.

"When Gilbert arrived at Graystone with your request for troops, I decided to lead them here myself," the prince said. "And as there were several days to spare before the trial, I sent word to the Citadel and informed my father of your plight, guessing he may have wanted to lend words of support. We arrived a few hours ago. I held my men back just beyond the river until the trial started so as not to cause any commotion."

"Your help is beyond appreciated," Nicholas replied, signaling for Gilbert and his family to join them. He introduced Emmett and Lorna to the prince who thanked them for their son's service.

"With Gilbert's assistance, we located Farnsworth's allies and quietly rounded them up, though most surrendered on the spot."

"If only Zachary would recognize his fate and surrender as well," Katherine said, glancing up at the disgraced man who still pondered his next move while precariously balanced upon the roof.

"I don't think he's the surrendering type," Lewis said, standing at her side.

Constable Brindle's voice boomed through the air again, his patience wearing thin. "Zachary, I'm giving you one last chance to end this before I send a team up there to drag you down!" he hollered. "It's your choice. What do you want to do?" But when Farnsworth didn't respond, Clay glanced uneasily at his companions. "Well, I guess that's that," he quietly told them.

Otto stared at the rooftop, the figure of Zachary Farnsworth transforming into a shadowy silhouette as moonlight filtered through the treetops. "I can't imagine what that man must be thinking right now," he remarked. "Dark thoughts, no doubt."

Farnsworth, at the moment, was paralyzed by his muddled reflections. He gazed down at the crowd, torn between attempting a blatant escape which would most likely end in his capture, or retreating back inside the village hall and turning himself in to Constable Brindle and perhaps retaining a shred of dignity. But either option ended up with him behind a locked door with a small barred window for perhaps the remainder of his life.

As his fingers gripped the edge of the bell tower, he recalled when he had first seen Dooley Kramer fingering that iron key around his neck over five years ago, wishing that he had minded his own business. If he had simply walked down the street then and passed his neighbor with only a brief hello, he might now be enjoying dinner in the Iron Kettle Tavern or perhaps running his own business like he had always wanted. But now it was too late, he realized. A decision had to be made soon or it would be made for him.

As Farnsworth looked down at the shadowy faces, the cold, empty pit of his stomach signaled that all was lost. There would be no more meetings or fancy dinners to attend, nor a title of respect to parade about the village on a warm summer afternoon, nor even the simple turning of heads when visiting a local shop. All that remained was to determine the best method of surrender that would cause the least amount of shame.

As the light faded, he shifted his gaze between the bell tower and the villagers below, knowing it was time to choose. Taking a deep breath, he gathered his remaining courage and made up his mind, hoping his final move would draw back some of the citizens of Kanesbury to his side. When he heard Clay call to him again from the street, he could no longer distinguish the constable's outline in the gloom. He had to act now as he possessed only this one last chance to sway the public.

"Zachary, unless you answer me this instant, my men and I are coming after you!" Clay hollered up to the rooftop, though expecting that Farnsworth would persist in his stubborn silence. When no response was forthcoming, he turned to the others and sighed. "Well, he had his chance, so I guess this will end ugly." The constable signaled to Tyler Harkin who had been standing attentively nearby. "Round up a handful of men and follow me inside. Let's get this over with."

"Yes, sir," he replied, hurrying off to recruit his team.

"Shall we accompany you?" Maynard asked, looking on with Otto, Len and King Justin.

"No, this is something my men and I need to take care of. I think we'll–"

Clay was suddenly interrupted by a single, loud clang of the village bell, its deep, sonorous reverberations wafting through the streets while startling all who were gathered nearby. Everyone simultaneously looked up at the bell tower, its outline vaguely visible against the starry sky. Below, the soft yellow light from inside the first floor poured through the windows and front doorway, splashing gently upon the grassy perimeter.

"*Now* what is that fool up to? Is he trying to annoy me to death?" the constable sputtered, pounding the tip of his cane into the ground. "Tyler, where are you?"

"Here, sir!" The deputy hurried over with three other men in tow and followed the constable to the door.

"Listen up," Clay began, pausing at the front steps to explain his plan. But he had barely opened his mouth when the village bell pealed loudly once again, shocking everyone to attention a second time. A few oil lamps began to ignite one by one among the crowd, bathing pockets of people in a subtle glow.

"What is Zachary doing?" someone commented nearby in disgusted tones.

Nicholas wondered the same thing as he stared up at the bell tower, thinking that Farnsworth had gone mad. "Perhaps the dreadfulness of all he had done is finally sinking in," he remarked to Katherine and the others.

"Or more likely the consequences he is about to face," she replied.

At that moment, Nicholas felt the tiniest bit sorry for the man whose world was crashing down around him, recalling his own brush with a similar fate last autumn. Yet he had serious doubts that Farnsworth could ever redeem himself after what he had done, wondering if the man would ever accept responsibility for his actions.

The village bell sounded one more time, but unlike the first two deafening clangs, this particular ring was swift and deadened, its crippled sound eaten up by the night before it had a chance to drift beyond the bewildered gathering. Everyone stared curiously at the bell tower after hearing the strange metallic clunk. Constable Brindle thought it was a most odd and unsettling sound.

"I don't know what to make of that," he said to Tyler, his words barely above a whisper. "Light the spare oil lamps in the entryway and race upstairs with your team. Farnsworth is up to some sort of mischief or my name isn't Clay Brindle." He tapped his cane on the floorboards after they all went inside, wordlessly indicating that he wouldn't have the strength to make it up the set of stairs wrapped around the inside of the tower. "Hurry and report back. And bring that insufferable Farnsworth with you."

"I plan to," Deputy Harkin said.

He and the other three men each grabbed an oil lamp sitting on a recessed shelf in the entryway and lit them from one of the flickering lamps upon the wall. In funereal silence, the four men proceeded up the stairs to the next floor now fully immersed in darkness, making their way to the bell tower door that stood slightly ajar. After placing a finger to his lips, Tyler carefully pushed open the door and entered the darkened stairwell. And though the light from their lamps helped cast away the gloom as they ascended the angular staircase in single file, a murky oppressiveness closed in upon them with each step despite the cooling breeze that drifted inside through the arched openings at the top.

After Tyler had taken a few right turns up the creaky staircase and heard no sound above, he began to wonder if Farnsworth had escaped onto the roof again or had possibly hurried back down before he and the others had reentered the building, perhaps hiding in a second floor office or in the main room where Nicholas' trial was held. As he ascended another short flight, Tyler considered sending some of his men downstairs to search the rest of the building and inform Constable Brindle of his change in tactics. He raised his oil lamp higher while making the turn up the next flight, glancing to his right as the flickering flame dispersed the gloom.

Tyler suddenly stopped, his heart racing. He locked gazes with Farnsworth who glared back at him from just a few feet away with a cold, horrifying stare. Tyler instinctively lurched backward, pressing against the tower wall as he lifted his lamp even higher as a defensive motion, expecting Farnsworth to lunge at him.

"Are you all right?" asked one of his men on the flight below.

"Stay there!" Tyler replied protectively in case Farnsworth prepared to attack. "I found him," he added, not taking his eyes off the man for even an instant.

But as the deputy gazed at Farnsworth, he grew cautiously calm as his sense of disorientation slowly dissipated and his eyes began to make sense of the spatial peculiarity before him. Tyler leaned forward, grasping the staircase railing with his free hand as he held aloft the oil lamp with the other to better illuminate the area. He could now see Zachary Farnsworth in whole, seemingly floating in the air before him while cloaked with the evening gloom. But Farnsworth said nothing while continuing to stare in Tyler's direction, his head tilted as he slowly turned his entire body to one side as if purposely ignoring the deputy. Tyler carefully leaned over the railing, bringing the lamp closer to Farnsworth until the reality of the situation icily took hold.

The sickly glow fell upon Zachary, highlighting his oddly discolored countenance and slightly distorted features. Tyler cringed upon closer inspection. He noticed a piece of rope wrapped tightly around Zachary's neck. Slowly raising his eyes and the oil lamp, Tyler followed the taut line all the way up the center of the tower to the pulley wheel connected to the side of the bell unit. The large bell was raised upward at a sharp angle, frozen in place because of the weight of Farnsworth's cooling corpse, and as utterly and eerily mute as the dead man dangling silently beneath it.

CHAPTER 120

The Many Roads Ahead

The village awoke to cool air and clear skies the following morning. When its residents took to the streets, a lightness of heart and freedom from worry enveloped them as they went about their business. Talk of Nicholas' trial was rampant, stories of which took on new and more exciting dimensions depending upon who was telling the tale. But in any version, Nicholas and Otto were painted as heroes and treated like royalty for a time wherever they showed their faces, particularly Nicholas when rumors of his adventures abroad made the rounds through Kanesbury.

"I heard that he and King Justin drove Vellan from his very stronghold," remarked Arlo Brewer as he chatted with Zeb Walker outside the bakeshop as the aroma of fresh honey bread wafted out an open window. "Just the two of them–unarmed, mind you."

Zeb shook his head as he leaned on a fencepost. "I don't know where you get your facts, Arlo, but a reliable source at the Water Barrel Inn said that Nicholas was under secret orders to track down the Enâri leader. Said that he cast some wizard's spell on the creature, destroying the entire horde in the process."

"A wizard's spell?" he replied with a derisive grunt. "Who at the Water Barrel told you such nonsense? Someone pickled in ale, no doubt! In case you haven't noticed, Nicholas Raven isn't a wizard."

"He's no soldier either!" Zeb fired back.

"Well, one of us is wrong," he replied with a laugh, slapping Zeb on the shoulder. "We'll have to discuss it later at the inn until we get our facts straight, okay?"

"Excellent idea!" he heartily agreed, promising to meet Arlo there at dusk, both certain they would get to the bottom of the contradictory stories as soon as a few mugs were drained in such a worthy endeavor.

On the day after the trial, Katherine and Lewis accompanied Clay Brindle and his men to the swamp to recover the bodies of Dooley Kramer and the hired assassin. The climbing sun, pasted upon a cobalt blue sky, warmed the line of horse-drawn wagons rattling east down River Road.

"A proper burial will help close this sad chapter in Kanesbury, but it'll take place outside the village," the constable said on the ride over. "Zachary's corpse will join them."

When they arrived at the watery stretch, now overwhelmed by trees in full bloom and the wild, leafy undergrowth of late spring, Katherine was not surprised that the assassin's body was not to be found where Lewis had buried it.

"No doubt Zachary returned after he suspected that I had been here," she guessed. "He must have stumbled upon the body, dug it up and disposed of it elsewhere." A chill ran through her at the thought of it.

"And there's no way to get to the island," Lewis said after having searched for the rowboats. "Both vessels are missing. I'll wager Dooley's body is, too."

Clay leaned on his cane, assessing the situation. "If Farnsworth moved the corpses, we're out of luck. But the two boats are missing. Zachary might have feared he had to work fast and..." His words lazily trailed off as he gazed across the murky water with a shrewd gleam in his eyes. "Maybe King Justin's men can help us." He glanced at his deputy. "Tyler, we need to build a few rafts."

Later the following day, Prince Gregory directed his men to construct two makeshift rafts upon the water's edge to conduct a search. After Clay's men and the garrison soldiers methodically dragged the swamp for a couple hours, the decaying bodies of Dooley Kramer and Dell Hawks–and the boat they had been tethered to—were pulled up from the bottom with several grappling hooks. The other sunken boat had been located earlier in less deep water and raised, a large gash visible on the bottom.

"Nothing can stay hidden forever," the constable remarked as the evidence was hauled onto shore. "Sooner or later, Farnsworth was going to get caught."

"I'm glad it was sooner," Katherine replied as she and Lewis watched the grim proceedings unfold. "Even the short time he was in power proved far too long a stretch. Still, I suppose things could have been so much worse for Kanesbury," she said, feeling Lewis' comforting arm wrap around her, grateful he was at her side through it all and certain he would be there in the days and years to follow.

Three days later, King Justin and Prince Gregory departed Kanesbury to much fanfare. The prince returned to the Graystone Garrison with some of his soldiers, taking into custody the nine men whom Zachary Farnsworth had hired, all with Clay Brindle's blessing. King Justin, however, had other plans as he explained at a farewell dinner the night before at Oscar and Amanda Stewart's home. He would trek to Arrondale's eastern border with his troops as he hadn't visited that region lately. If time allowed, he would visit King Brendan of Montavia, anxious to see how he and Prince William were faring.

Maynard and Adelaide were also settling in, both again comfortable at home now that the trial and all the attendant secrecy were behind them. Nicholas savored his newfound freedom as well, finding a quiet hour that afternoon to sit in his cottage near a sunny, open window and write a long letter to Ivy. It was six days until summer. A balmy breeze and the call of blue jays drifted through the window, soothing his mind.

Later, after Nicholas strolled over to the posting house and paid his fee, the attendant handed him another letter. "This arrived earlier," he said, handing him a piece of folded parchment sealed with blue wax. Nicholas smiled upon seeing the royal embossing upon the wax. "It looks important, but at the rate Edgar is moving these days, you probably wouldn't have gotten it until tomorrow."

"Thanks." Nicholas meandered outdoors into the sunlight, standing across the street opposite the banking house. He ignored Farnsworth's old place of employment and scanned the neatly penned words upon the front of the parchment–*Mister Nicholas Raven, Village of Kanesbury, Litchfield County, Arrondale*. His invitation to Megan and Leo's wedding had arrived. Before he broke the seal, a voice called to him from up the street.

"Nicholas, glad to see you out and about," Ned Adams said. "I had wanted to speak with you sometime after the trial, but it seems we're all too busy lately."

"I wanted to talk to you, too," he replied. "I was hoping to–"

"Oh, may I go first?" Ned asked as the two wandered a short distance to a large maple tree and stopped in its cooling shade.

"Certainly," he said. His former employer appeared tired and careworn as if the events of the past few months still weighed heavily upon his mind.

"I want you to know that the gristmill repairs are progressing nicely," Ned informed him. "If all goes according to plan, we should be operating by late summer, well in time for the final harvest."

"That's great news!"

"And though you probably haven't decided your future plans in light of all that's happened, I want you to know that your old accounting job is still available if you want it." Ned stared at the ground for a moment, raking a hand through his thinning hair. "You must have mixed feelings because of the way I treated you after the robbery, but–"

"The evidence was rather incriminating," Nicholas said, "so I can't blame you for how you reacted. I might have done the same thing in your place."

"I appreciate that," he said with a grateful smile, "but I know you've been a solid citizen for a long time. I shouldn't have let my emotions fight against what I really knew deep in my heart. I should have trusted my instincts," he added in apologetic tones. "I'm sorry for not having stood by you."

"You're doing that now," Nicholas replied, shaking his hand. "As far as I'm concerned, that's all that really matters."

"Thank you." Ned choked up as the stress and anxiety evaporated from his countenance. "So, what did you want to speak to me about?"

Nicholas grinned. "Just about getting my old job back. I'm glad you haven't filled the position yet."

"It's yours for the taking! And with a new, larger desk to boot. I'd love to have you assist in the final stages of the mill's rebuilding as well."

"I accept," Nicholas said before quickly raising a hand and catching Ned off guard. "There is one condition, however. If all goes according to plan, I won't be available for a couple of weeks during Mid Summer."

"Of course, of course! Take off any time you need to attend to Maynard and your duties on his farm. I understand."

"Oh, Maynard is mending nicely," he said. "And he hired extra help for planting and harvesting. I should have been more precise about that short absence, Ned. I might not be available for part of Mid Summer because, hopefully, I won't *be* here."

Nicholas rode through the streets of Boros on the first day of Mid Summer, guiding his wagon to Aunt Castella's house where Ivy, in one of her letters, had promised to meet him. A light breeze blew off Sage Bay, laced with fond and heartwrenching memories from nearly a year ago. That time seemed of another age, yet the depths of horror and the heights of joy he had experienced would always be near to his heart, reminding him of the wild and unexpected journey he had been swept away upon without a lifeline. But when it was all over, he had been happily washed ashore alongside Ivy, which, he realized with a faraway smile, had made it a journey more than worth taking.

He arrived at Castella's house near the end of a winding, cobblestone lane. A wreath of spring berries, daisies and other wildflowers adorned the front door. As he tied up the horses by the water trough, Nicholas noted a stack of chopped wood in back of the property among the tall grass and pines. He recalled first meeting Ivy near that spot last autumn in the fading twilight when his world was falling apart. Now, on a sun-splashed summer day, he was about to meet her again after nearly six weeks of grueling separation, barely able to contain his excitement that life, at last, was back on its proper course.

He walked to the front entrance, his spirit as buoyant as the billowing clouds above. Just as he raised a hand to knock, the door opened inward. Ivy stood there, warming his heart like the rising sun. The two couldn't help but smile knowingly at one another, realizing that their lives could go forward after having together endured many dark and dangerous roads.

"I saw you from the upper window," she said breathlessly. "I was so happy to see you finally arrive that I ran down the stairs."

"And I'm happy to see you," Nicholas replied, calmed and energized by Ivy's smile. "It's been far too long."

They embraced in the doorway with the same longing and depth of concern as when reunited on the slopes of Mount Minakaris. The busy streets and fragrant breezes faded in the background as they held one another, sharing whispered words between tender kisses as the passage of time no longer registered for a few, sweet moments.

"Who's calling at this hour, distracting my housekeeper when there's so much work to be done?" Aunt Castella's voice resonated with feigned annoyance as she walked into the sitting room, spotting Nicholas and Ivy by the open door in each other's arms.

Nicholas grinned upon seeing Megan's great aunt, a light blue checkered shawl draped over her shoulders and a beaming smile upon her face. He greeted Castella with a hug, delighted to see her again.

"You look as healthy as ever," he said, kissing her cheek.

"Not having to fret about Megan and Ivy these past several weeks has done wonders for my wellbeing!" She invited Nicholas and Ivy to sit down so they could all catch up on the latest. "I have a tea kettle on. No doubt you've had a tiring journey."

"But I'm as refreshed as ever now," he said, smiling at Ivy. Nicholas soon gave an account of his travels to Boros, mentioning how he had spent the night with Leo's parents in Minago and stopped for lunch at the Plum Orchard Inn. "Ron and Mabel Knott send their best. They'll ride along with us to Meg and Leo's wedding."

"They're a delightful couple," Ivy said. "When the Marshes took me home, we stopped at the inn for lunch."

"I look forward to meeting them," Castella said.

"You should visit the Plum Orchard," Nicholas suggested. "A day away from Boros now and then would do you good."

"No doubt it would," she agreed, standing up to check on the tea. "But I'm afraid that won't be possible now."

"Why not?" he asked, mildly perplexed.

"Because I won't be living here much longer, Nicholas. I'm selling my house."

As they enjoyed their tea, Nicholas learned that Castella was readying her house for sale, having decided to move to Morrenwood. At the urging of Megan and King Justin, she planned to take up residence in the Blue Citadel that autumn.

"I'd been hemming and hawing about whether to remain in Boros another year or so," she said. "It wasn't an easy decision."

"I didn't write of it as Castella was of two minds for so long," Ivy said.

"But age is creeping up on me whether I care to admit it or not," she continued, "and the winters are becoming more than I can handle alone. Besides, as I'll be attending Megan and Leo's wedding there, it seemed like the perfect time to make the move."

"I'm sure you'll be happy. Morrenwood is a beautiful city," Nicholas said.

"Still, I shall miss our many talks at your kitchen table," Ivy told her.

"As shall I," Castella replied, wiping away a tear. "But whether I sold this house or not, I suspect our separation would come soon regardless." She looked at them with a tender smile. "I see the love between the two of you and imagine you'll soon be joining hands at your own wedding. Am I right?" she asked, eliciting smiles from them both.

"We've decided sometime next spring," Ivy said. "I didn't want to tell anyone that Nicholas had proposed until he was with me and all of his troubles at home were settled."

"Which they are," he happily chimed in. "Though we did let the news slip when we stayed with the Marshes. But now I suppose we can tell everyone."

"I'm honored to be among the first to know," Castella said, raising her steaming cup to toast the couple. "And may you find a lifetime of happiness together."

"Thank you," Ivy replied, her eyes misting.

"And visit me when you can. I shall miss you both terribly!"

Nicholas stayed in Boros for a few days to help Castella get the house ready for market. Later, he and Ivy traveled east to Laurel Corners to spend several days with her family, promising to check in on Castella from time to time. Nicholas had briefly met Ivy's father, Frederick, last fall after returning from the grasslands, and was happy to finally meet her mother, Constance, and two younger sisters, Martha and Jane. All felt as if they already knew him after Ivy had told them so much about Nicholas since her return. Constance thanked him profusely for rescuing her daughter.

"I would have journeyed twice around Laparia to find Ivy," he admitted with all sincerity, assuring her parents that she would forever be safe at his side when they announced their plans to marry to the delight of all.

A few days later, Nicholas and Ivy walked along a deserted stretch of grassy shoreline dotted with trees and colorful, flat pebbles that had been smoothed by the constant string of waves embracing the shoreline. "The days are drifting by too fast," she said with a hint of melancholy. "I'll miss you when you return to Kanesbury."

"And I'll miss you," he said, stopping to reassure her as a balmy breeze drifted across the bay. "But I'll be back in autumn when we go to Meg and Leo's wedding."

"That'll seem forever, but I suppose I'll survive."

"You'll be so busy helping Castella, planning our wedding and dealing with your two excitable sisters that you won't even notice," Nicholas joked, kissing her tenderly. "Trust me–the rest of summer will fly by."

"But even after we visit Morrenwood, next spring will still seem like a hundred years away." She lowered her head upon Nicholas' shoulder with a dejected sigh.

"At least winter won't be as horrendous as the last one we endured," he said, causing Ivy to look up with a halfhearted smile.

"It'll still be unbearable without you."

"Well, if the snowfall isn't too formidable, I'll visit again in Mid Winter," he promised. "In the meantime, I think it's only fair that you visit Kanesbury on our way back from the Citadel. I want you to meet Maynard before our ceremony."

"That would be lovely!" she said, her mood brightening. "Since Kanesbury is to be our home, I think it's my duty to interrogate your friends and find out exactly who it is I intend to marry," she teased. "I expect nothing but glowing reports."

Nicholas was just as eager to introduce her to them, knowing in his heart that they would welcome her into their lives as if she had been an old friend. He wanted Ivy to fall in love with her new home as easily as he had fallen in love with her.

"*Hmmm*," he muttered, keeping a straight face. "If this marriage is to work out, a few well placed bribes among some friends should conceal my shady past from you."

"You can try," she replied, "but I think I'd keep you anyway." Ivy took his hand as they looked down the lazy, grassy shoreline. "If the weather cooperates next spring, why don't we get married right here? This is such a lovely place and not too far from the house for the festivities afterward. Oh, I can't wait, Nicholas! What do you think?"

"It's a fine idea," he agreed, imagining them standing here less than a year from now and promising to share the rest of their lives together, a moment he doubted might ever happen while traipsing through the Dunn Hills, sailing up the Lorren River or wandering through the mountain tunnels in Kargoth. But as he held Ivy's hand, all those dark moments faded as they gazed over the stretch of lovely blue water. "A brilliant idea." He turned and kissed her. "And I can't wait either."

On the third day of New Autumn, Princess Megan and Leo Marsh were married in the main courtyard of the Blue Citadel. Several hundred guests attended, toasting the joyful couple beneath sunny blue skies. A gentle rain of colorful leaves occasionally fell from the surrounding trees, the branches of each one festooned with ribbons and glass enclosed oil lamps that cast droplets of light far into the night. Amid lively music and dancing, free flowing plates of food, and the unending cups of wine, spiced cider and ale, not a note of disappointment was expressed other than that the celebration should have gone on for a second day, or perhaps even a third.

Earlier that evening, after twilight had settled in and the warming flames from a fire pit cast flickering shadows upon the crowd, Nicholas and Ivy spent time with old friends at a table near a thicket of white birch trees. Megan and Leo, along with Carmella, Hobin and Emma, sat with them. Candles in the center of the table added a soft sheen to the smiling faces as they discussed past adventures and future hopes.

"I've had quite an adventure exploring the Trent Hills with Tolapari," Carmella said when asked about her training. "And I still have much to learn, but the *old* Carmella looks like a dilettante compared to the woman before you now, not meaning to boast."

"I never had any doubts," Megan said proudly.

"But where to next?" Ivy asked, detecting a deep sadness in Carmella's eyes which made her believe that the woman still grieved over the loss of her cousin.

"We'll travel to Drumaya and points farther south during winter," she said. "Tolapari and I talked with King Cedric yesterday. He invited us to spend a few days in Grantwick when we pass through. But our path will not take us into Kargoth, at least not this time. I don't have the heart to go there just yet despite Vellan's defeat."

Ivy glanced at Nicholas, silently questioning him with a faint smile. He immediately understood her concern and nodded.

"Wherever your path takes you, Carmella, make sure you're back in the area come springtime for another journey," Ivy said.

"A journey to where?" she asked.

"To Laurel Corners," Nicholas said with a playful grin. "More specifically, on the fourteenth day of Mid Spring. And make sure the rest of you keep that date open, too," he added, waving a finger at the others in mock warning.

Megan beamed with delight, realizing that Nicholas and Ivy were planning to marry that day. She congratulated them with hugs, prompting a barrage of similar sentiments from all around.

"I was wondering when you two would announce," she said, adorned in a silken dress of blue and white with a ringlet of matching colored flowers in her hair.

"We planned to wait until after your wedding before springing the news," Ivy said.

"But since we're all here together..." Nicholas added, happy to let some of his closest friends in on the secret.

"I think I'll be able to slip away from my princely duties to attend," Leo joked.

"Expect us as well," Hobin said as he and Emma expressed their delight with the news. "Since Emma and I were married over the summer, that now leaves Nicholas as the last of our hiking trio to take a wife. It'll be a solemn moment indeed," he said with a feigned sniffle, pretending to wipe away a tear.

"Oh, you are a wit!" Emma said with a laugh as she playfully slapped his arm. A polished, blue stone pendant dangled from her neck, its tiny embedded silver sparkles catching the candlelight. "And whether fate planned for us to find those identical stones along Lake Lily or not, I'm still the best thing that ever happened to you."

"That you are, dear," he affectionately replied, kissing her on the cheek.

"May we please?" Megan quietly asked of Hobin and Emma, looking at them with bottled excitement as she lightly traced a finger along the line of her collar.

Hobin nodded. "Oh, go ahead. You're the bride, after all. Far be it from me to say no to you on your special day."

"Thanks! I've been dying to show it to Ivy though you wanted it kept secret."

"Show me what?" she asked, intrigued by the mystery.

"A present that Hobin and Emma gave us," she replied. Megan removed a fine, metal chain from around her neck with a stone pendant attached to it that had been hidden beneath her dress. The small, rounded stone was awash in vibrant swirls of autumn hues, its polished surface glossy and smooth. She handed it to Ivy as Leo removed a nearly identical stone from his pocket and slid it over to Nicholas.

"It's beautiful," Ivy said, examining the craftwork so elegant in its simplicity.

"Hobin thought that Megan and I should have our own matching set much like he and Emma," Leo said. "He told me he had scoured the shoreline along the Crescent for hours to find them when he was up north visiting her."

"He's a romantic at heart," Emma replied, "no matter how much he hides it."

"*Hmmm…*" Hobin gruffly replied, winking at Emma before turning to Nicholas and Ivy. "So next spring the two of you can expect your own set, though I'll keep the color a secret."

"That's more than kind of you," Ivy said, handing the pendant to Carmella so she could admire it. "I can't wait to see what you've found for us."

"Neither can I," Nicholas said with a grin, slapping Hobin on the back. "A romantic indeed. But don't worry, your secret is safe with us. Wouldn't want to ruin your reputation as a crusty, old guide, after all. Bad for business."

Hobin grunted. "If you and Leo ever follow me up one of the Five Brothers peaks, you'll be wishing I were an old softie by the time we reach the summit."

"Name the day and the mountain," Leo challenged teasingly. "Right, Nicholas?"

"Just no Northern Islanders this time," he insisted. "Though Frank and Gus are more than welcome to tag along."

After the wedding, Ivy stayed in Kanesbury for over two weeks, having arrived four days before the start of the Harvest Festival. Nicholas had nearly forgotten about the celebration as recent events and much traveling had pushed it out of his mind. He and Ivy made an appearance at the Stewarts' party on the festival's first night, but were content spending the bulk of those three days walking about the village or attending quiet dinners with Maynard, Adelaide and a few close friends. Nicholas did, however, take Ivy to the pavilion dance on the final night, holding her close in the moonlight as music played throughout the evening, much like they had done in Illingboc beneath the frosty stars.

About ten weeks later, after autumn's radiant palette had dissolved into somber shades of winter, Nicholas visited Ivy in Laurel Corners. They walked hand-in-hand along a worn snow path on the frozen shores of Sage Bay. Beneath a cloak of ashen gray clouds, the sharp call of seagulls and the salty summer mist had been replaced by a cold, weighty silence pressing upon a vast tract of misshapen ice chunks piled like wreckage up and down the shoreline. The wintry edge of the sea was located a quarter mile across the bay, pushing outward a little farther each day as the biting cold held firm its grip.

Ivy, bundled in a blue hooded cloak, paused near a sturdy willow tree, its sinewy branches flailing in the breeze. She held Nicholas close to keep warm as he wrapped a reassuring arm around her, wearing the long, hooded wool coat he had donned when leaving the Citadel on his quest to Wolf Lake, and ultimately, to Ivy.

"Why'd you stop?" he asked, noting a faraway smile upon her face. "Too cold to keep walking? Do you want to turn back?"

"No," she replied, kissing him in the bracing breeze. "I wanted to show you this spot. I'd like us to get married here this spring. What do you think?"

Nicholas looked around, and despite the mischievous weather, he could envision the scenic possibilities running through Ivy's mind that would bloom here come next spring after a bit of warmth and sunshine reawakened the area. "I like it," he said, noting the delight in her eyes now that their plans were falling into place. "And in a little over three months when everyone is gathered here, I know they'll all be pleased, too."

"I hope so," she said as they gazed upon the wintry landscape, imagining a future together that now seemed as distant as the miles that once separated them.

They clasped hands, gazing into one another's eyes. Nicholas and Ivy visualized the snowy, desolate shoreline slowly melting beneath spring's reviving breath in the weeks ahead. They imagined the cries of seagulls returning to the turquoise waters lapping upon stony shores, along which stood the budding willow tree and a grassy path strewn with wildflowers beneath the warmth of a rising sun. As they leaned forward in a loving kiss, each wished that the cold, lumbering days ahead could fly by like an eagle in swift flight.

And when their lips met again on that spot three months later, the gray chill had dissolved into balmy shades of green, their winter attire replaced with a silken dress and a vested suit, and the lonely landscape now blossomed with applause from a circle of guests who cheered on the wedded couple as they basked in each other's undying love. And for a brief time, two lives were made perfect on the water's edge on that late, sunny morning. The daunting and circuitous path leading to that special moment had been more than worth the heartache and trouble in the end, all of which had now faded like a troubling memory or the ethereal remains of a whispered word.

By Mid Summer, Nicholas and Ivy had adjusted comfortably to their roles as husband and wife, enjoying each other's company over a span of lazy, carefree days. They had moved out of the cottage and into the main house with Maynard as there was plenty of room to spare, allowing Ivy's sisters to spend the nights in the cottage when they were invited to visit. One evening shortly after their arrival, amid much talk and laughter while sitting down to dinner, Nicholas realized how fortunate he had been despite the wild twists and turns in the past. Life in Kanesbury and in the world beyond seemed to have settled down, an observation which greatly eased his mind when imagining himself and Ivy seated around a table someday with their own children.

A post from Leo a couple of weeks later confirmed his view. As he read the letter regarding arrangements for a trek into the Dunn Hills with Hobin, Leo made reference to the recent gathering in Grantwick that he had attended with Megan, King Justin and Prince Gregory. A sense of optimism had been expressed by the leaders of the region after Kargoth and its allies had been defeated, yet all agreed that eternal vigilance was required to prevent the rise of another Vellan. But for the time being, Leo believed, the world was in safe hands which gave him much hope.

"Everyone plans to meet again two years from now in New Maranac," Nicholas said to Ivy as he read the letter while sitting together on the porch steps. In it, Leo described his reunion with Malek, Eucádus and others who had helped bring stability back to Kargoth and their respective homelands. "Perhaps we can attend the next gathering. I hear the communities along Lake LaShear are a sight to behold."

"I look forward to it," Ivy said, remarking admirably on the tone of Leo's letter. "He sounds more *prince* than *apple grower* on parchment. I suppose life at the Blue Citadel has rubbed off on him just a bit."

"I guess so," Nicholas agreed, noting that Leo's sometimes dry sarcasm was absent in his friend's written words. "Perhaps Megan has turned him into a respectable member of the royal family," he added with a chuckle, sensing that a different version of Leo had composed that letter instead of the one he had first met tumbling uncontrollably into a huge mud puddle.

But just over a month later, Nicholas discovered the reason for the change in his friend's demeanor when he and Ivy traveled to Morrenwood with the final flour shipments for the King's stores. They remained at the Blue Citadel, happy again to see Leo, Megan and Castella in such fine spirits. While at lunch in a quiet chamber later that afternoon, Megan and Leo announced that they were expecting their first child late next spring, delighted to share such joyous news.

"Leo has been such a dear, reluctant even to leave my side when we first learned," Megan said. "Still, my husband desperately needs to get out of the Citadel for a spell."

"Or perhaps *you* need him to," Nicholas joked.

"As much as I love him, a few weeks of fresh air will do him good," she replied.

"Though it'll pain me deeply, I will depart for the Dunn Hills in two days as scheduled," Leo said, gazing fondly at his wife. He removed from his pocket the polished stone that Hobin and Emma had given him as a wedding present, matching the one that Megan wore as a pendant around her neck. "But I'll always be thinking about you," he added, holding up the stone with a loving smile. "Both of you."

Two days after, Nicholas and Leo left on horseback for the village of Woodwater to meet up with Hobin. They traveled around the southern edge of the Cashua Forest and crossed the Lorren River over a stone bridge a few miles south of the village. Hobin was delighted to see them while Frank and Gus greeted them as enthusiastically as on their first arrival.

"Emma is staying with her niece in Illingboc for a few weeks," Hobin said, "so it'll be like old times as we trek through the hills."

"Minus the Island assassins," Leo deadpanned as Nicholas glanced at Hobin's latest cartographic creations spread out upon a work table.

"Are these portions of the Trent Hills?" he asked, impressed with the drawings.

"One of the projects King Justin commissioned from me," he replied. "They still need a bit of work that I'll finish up over winter. But now we'll be tramping in the opposite direction to the Five Brothers range. We passed between the two easternmost mountains on our way to Wolf Lake two years ago, but in a few days we'll climb up the central peak in the chain."

"Let me guess–the tallest of the Five Brothers?" Leo asked.

"And toughest," Hobin replied, grinning in anticipation. "We leave in two days."

Hobin led Nicholas and Leo north through the woods for several days until they reached the clearing between Beetle Lake and Gray Hawk Mountain. There the trio veered northwest and made for the third mountain in the Five Brothers range as the orange, red and yellow leaves of autumn blanketed the trails before them. On a cool, misty morning two days later, they began their ascent of the mountain. Its elevation slowly rose as they traversed dirt and stony paths and followed cold stream banks whose waters rushed over mossy rocks that glittered like emeralds in the sunlight. Shortly before mid afternoon, the weary climbers stepped foot on the breezy summit beneath a crystalline blue sky and swiftly passing clouds. And the view from this peak, like on Gray Hawk Mountain, took their breaths away.

"Words can't express it," Nicholas said as he and the others took in the colorful vista stretching out in all directions around them.

Gazing northeast, Nicholas looked upon the first two peaks of the Five Brothers standing proudly nearby, sun-splashed and tinted in contemplative shades of deep blue. The last two Brothers took on a similar appearance when he glanced over his shoulder to the southwest. And for miles about, other distant peaks rose majestically above a vast mantle of deciduous trees ablaze in autumn hues and punctuated with rich, green lines of stately pines and blue lakes glistening like open eyes looking up to the heavens.

Looking northward, he soaked in the view of Wolf Lake embedded in the forest below like a blue sapphire. He noted the dark dot of an island lying off its southern shoreline, recalling the day they had approached Frist's home as a fine veil of snow flurries peppered the air. Nicholas placed a hand to his chest and felt the wizard's silver amulet beneath several layers of clothing, grateful that Frist's sacrifice had helped the nations of Laparia defeat Kargoth and guide him on his search for Ivy. He reached into his pocket and removed a small polished stone the color of lush green clover. He held it close to his heart and imagined with a contented smile that Ivy had just reached for the matching stone hanging from a delicate chain about her neck.

"Ready?" a voice called to him as if from a deep and faraway dream, slowly rousing Nicholas from his hypnotic state. "Are you ready?"

"*Hmmm?*" he replied in a fog, drawn back to the moment as he placed the gift from Hobin and Emma in his pocket and turned to his friends. "*Ready?* Ready for what?"

"For lunch," Hobin said, slipping the pack off his weary shoulders. "Let's find a spot and enjoy a bit of dried beef and biscuits with this nice view."

"Unless you'd rather nap first," Leo joked, stretching his arms after he dropped his pack on the rocky summit. "I'm not too proud to admit that I could use one."

"I'm as wide awake as ever," Nicholas said, breathing in the crisp mountain air as he enjoyed the stunning vista. "And eager for my next climb, wherever it might take me."

Nicholas and Ivy returned to Kanesbury in late Mid Autumn, happy to enjoy some uneventful days for a time. After the first deep snowfall of winter arrived, Ivy took ill for a few days and Nicholas dutifully looked after her as she rested in bed. Though he initially worried that her travails in the wild had finally caught up with her, he was relived when she swiftly recovered late one sunny morning when the snow was piled high outside their bedroom window.

"I'd like to thank Frist for my quick mend," she remarked to Nicholas, "but I never wore his amulet around my neck when you placed it in my hands a few nights ago. I was so tired that it must have slipped between the blankets," she said, handing back his treasured gift. "I found it just now."

"It was near you, if that counts," he replied. "I'm just happy you recovered. Now we can take our winter walks together along the river. They won't be as grand as along Sage Bay–"

"–but lovely nonetheless," she chimed in with a smile. "I can't wait to start."

"Rest for another day," Nicholas suggested. "Just to be sure."

Over the next two weeks they had taken several walks as Ivy showed no signs of relapsing into her brief illness. On one stroll a few days later as they wandered along the snowy, ice-coated Pine River, she took Nicholas' hands and stopped. Ivy turned to him with a faint smile that warmed his heart despite the gray clouds above.

"After you had left this morning to purchase that load of firewood, Maynard drove me to the physician as I was feeling dizzy again like I did just before I'd gotten ill," she told him, causing Nicholas to immediately fear the worse.

"Are you all right?" he asked, holding his breath as he gently squeezed her hands, yet puzzled by the tranquil look upon her face.

"I'm quite healthy," she assured him. "In fact, the physician said that both of us are doing fine, so there's no need to worry."

"*Both* of us?" he asked, his brow furrowed. Nicholas' eyes widened, suddenly understanding what Ivy had meant. He beamed, dumbfounded for a moment before wrapping his arms around her in utter joy. "When?" he whispered, holding Ivy tightly as the cold and snow around them seemed to melt into springtime.

Jack Frederick Raven was born on the first day of Old Summer the following year, having been given the names of both Nicholas and Ivy's fathers as his own. Maynard was delighted to sit and hold his grandson on the front porch while the weather stayed warm, and Adelaide didn't lack for excuses to walk across the road to visit as often as she could, feeling like a grandmother just as she had toward Nicholas while he was growing up on the farm with Maynard and Tessa.

The tenth day of New Autumn the following month marked the start of the Harvest Festival. It was exactly three years ago to the day that Nicholas had found himself embroiled in local troubles beyond his imagining. He and Ivy decided to attend the annual party at the Stewarts' residence for a short while as Maynard and Adelaide were more than happy to watch young Jack while he slept soundly in the next room.

"You both deserve a little time to yourselves," Adelaide said as they finished a light supper at the table. "And a bit of fresh air will do you good."

"You heard the woman," Maynard joked as he leaned back in his chair, shooing the young couple away. "Why, in a few years you'll be begging us to babysit. Enjoy this free time while you can."

"If you insist," Nicholas said with a smile, grateful for their unending support.

"Thank you," Ivy replied. "We won't be long. But first I want to check on Jack."

She and Nicholas strolled quietly into their bedroom and knelt on an oval rug beneath a cradle against the side wall. The room was softly lit by a single oil lamp casting flickering shadows. Beneath a patchwork quilt, their young child lay upon his back sound asleep, his chest rising and falling in peaceful rhythms. The silver amulet from the wizard Frist hung loosely on a corner post at the foot of the cradle. Nicholas and Ivy glanced at one another and smiled in the gauzy light, neither in a hurry to leave their child just yet.

"A few minutes more," she whispered, taking his hand as they watched their son.

"I'm sure the party has barely gotten underway," he assured her, equally content to enjoy this special time. "Knowing Oscar and Amanda, the celebration is sure to go on far into the night."

"So no need to hurry?" Ivy softly asked, gazing at her son.

Nicholas placed an arm around his wife's shoulder and gently kissed her cheek, his other hand resting steadily upon the edge of Jack's cradle. "No hurry at all," he said.

THE END

POSTSCRIPT
A WRITER'S WEB

ABOUT THE BOOK

When spinning the tale of *Nicholas Raven and the Wizards' Web*, I had to utilize more than my right brain creative writings skills to craft such a long story. To help me effectively lay out the various plotlines and to keep track of where and when characters were at a particular moment (including those two moons), I had to use a bit of left brain technical skill, too. And though what follows is unnecessary for the reader to know to enjoy the story, I decided to include it for those who may find it of interest. On the following pages, I will briefly discuss the calendar I developed to keep this sprawling narrative on course and have prepared a story timeline detailing where characters and events are each day relative to one another. Also included are a few words about the Fox and Bear moons that were featured throughout the novel, as well as a brief geneology about King Justin and his family line. And since I was inspired to write this book after reading J. R. R. Tolkien's *The Hobbit* and *The Lord of the Rings* in 1975, I've added one of my website updates detailing my first introduction to his works.

The Calendar

In June 1999, after typing the first few paragraphs in Chapter 1 of this novel, I realized that I needed to draw a map to keep my writing on track because of the book's complex plot and varied geography. I ended up creating four of them. I also realized that having a short prologue would help to better set up the narrative, so I wrote that, too. Likewise, as the linear storytelling branched off into various plot threads, I decided that having a calendar for Laparia, the featured section of this world I had imagined, would help me to keep my characters and plot points in order especially if I ever had to reference a particular point in the book while writing, which I did regularly. I would never have accurately keep track of things if I hadn't done so.

My calendar consists of twelve months, three for each season, with weeks that are nine days long. The first day of the year begins on the first day of spring, and nine of the months consist of twenty-eight days each. The remaining three each have twenty-nine days. Because of that setup, the calendar repeats itself every three years. The months are named for each of the seasons, beginning with New Spring, Mid Spring and Old Spring, similarly continuing through the year with summer and autumn, and ending with New Winter, Mid Winter and Old Winter.

Though the vast majority of the novel takes place in a span just a little over three years long, events are referenced from years past and are chronicled in the timeline. Chapter 1 begins on the fifth day of New Autumn in the year 742. Chapter 120 ends on the tenth day of New Autumn in 745. The calendars of those four years are featured on the next pages with a few key dates in the book indicated below each one.

Year 742

New Spring

1	2	3	4	5	6	7	8	9
10	11	12	13	14	15	16	17	18
19	20	21	22	23	24	25	26	27
28								

Mid Spring

1	2	3	4	5	6	7	8
9	10	11	12	13	14	15	16	17
18	19	20	21	22	23	24	25	26
27	28							

Old Spring

1	2	3	4	5	6	7
8	9	10	11	12	13	14	15	16
17	18	19	20	21	22	23	24	25
26	27	28	29					

New Summer

1	2	3	4	5
6	7	8	9	10	11	12	13	14
15	16	17	18	19	20	21	22	23
24	25	26	27	28				

Mid Summer

1	2	3	4
5	6	7	8	9	10	11	12	13
14	15	16	17	18	19	20	21	22
23	24	25	26	27	28	29		

Old Summer

1	2
3	4	5	6	7	8	9	10	11
12	13	14	15	16	17	18	19	20
21	22	23	24	25	26	27	28	29

New Autumn

1	2	3	4	5	6	7	8	9
10	11	12	13	14	15	16	17	18
19	20	21	22	23	24	25	26	27
28								

Mid Autumn

1	2	3	4	5	6	7	8
9	10	11	12	13	14	15	16	17
18	19	20	21	22	23	24	25	26
27	28							

Old Autumn

1	2	3	4	5	6	7
8	9	10	11	12	13	14	15	16
17	18	19	20	21	22	23	24	25
26	27	28						

New Winter

1	2	3	4	5	6
7	8	9	10	11	12	13	14	15
16	17	18	19	20	21	22	23	24
25	26	27	28					

Mid Winter

1	2	3	4	5
6	7	8	9	10	11	12	13	14
15	16	17	18	19	20	21	22	23
24	25	26	27	28				

Old Winter

1	2	3	4
5	6	7	8	9	10	11	12	13
14	15	16	17	18	19	20	21	22
23	24	25	26	27	28			

The main story begins on the 5th day of New Autumn in 742.
Nicholas flees Kanesbury on the 10th day of New Autumn.

Year 743

New Spring

						1	2	3
4	5	6	7	8	9	10	11	12
13	14	15	16	17	18	19	20	21
22	23	24	25	26	27	28		

Mid Spring

		1	2
3	4	5	6	7	8	9	10	11
12	13	14	15	16	17	18	19	20
21	22	23	24	25	26	27	28	

Old Spring

								1
2	3	4	5	6	7	8	9	10
11	12	13	14	15	16	17	18	19
20 / 29	21	22	23	24	25	26	27	28

New Summer

1	2	3	4	5	6	7	8
9	10	11	12	13	14	15	16	17
18	19	20	21	22	23	24	25	26
27	28							

Mid Summer

	1	2	3	4	5	6	7
8	9	10	11	12	13	14	15	16
17	18	19	20	21	22	23	24	25
26	27	28	29					

Old Summer

			1	2	3	4	5
6	7	8	9	10	11	12	13	14
15	16	17	18	19	20	21	22	23
24	25	26	27	28	29			

New Autumn

				1	2
4	5	6	7	8	9	10	11	12
13	14	15	16	17	18	19	20	21
22	23	24	25	26	27	28		

Mid Autumn

		1	2
3	4	5	6	7	8	9	10	11
12	13	14	15	16	17	18	19	20
21	22	23	24	25	26	27	28	

Old Autumn

								1
2	3	4	5	6	7	8	9	10
11	12	13	14	15	16	17	18	19
20	21	22	23	24	25	26	27	28

New Winter

1	2	3	4	5	6	7	8	9
10	11	12	13	14	15	16	17	18
19	20	21	22	23	24	25	26	27
28								

Mid Winter

1	2	3	4	5	6	7	8
9	10	11	12	13	14	15	16	17
18	19	20	21	22	23	24	25	26
27	28							

Old Winter

	1	2	3	4	5	6	7
8	9	10	11	12	13	14	15	16
17	18	19	20	21	22	23	24	25
26	27	28						

Vellan is defeated on the 20th day of New Spring in 743.

Year 744

New Spring
	1	2	3	4	5	6
7	8	9	10	11	12	13	14	15
16	17	18	19	20	21	22	23	24
25	26	27	28

Mid Spring
		1	2	3	4	5
6	7	8	9	10	11	12	13	14
15	16	17	18	19	20	21	22	23
24	25	26	27	28

Old Spring
			1	2	3	4
5	6	7	8	9	10	11	12	13
14	15	16	17	18	19	20	21	22
23	24	25	26	27	28	29

New Summer
						1	2
3	4	5	6	7	8	9	10	11
12	13	14	15	16	17	18	19	20
21	22	23	24	25	26	27	28

Mid Summer
							1
2	3	4	5	6	7	8	9	10
11	12	13	14	15	16	17	18	19
20/29	21	22	23	24	25	26	27	28

Old Summer
1	2	3	4	5	6	7	8
9	10	11	12	13	14	15	16	17
18	19	20	21	22	23	24	25	26
27	28	29

New Autumn
	1	2	3	4	5	6
7	8	9	10	11	12	13	14	15
16	17	18	19	20	21	22	23	24
25	26	27	28

Mid Autumn
		1	2	3	4	5
6	7	8	9	10	11	12	13	14
15	16	17	18	19	20	21	22	23
24	25	26	27	28

Old Autumn
			1	2	3	4
5	6	7	8	9	10	11	12	13
14	15	16	17	18	19	20	21	22
23	24	25	26	27	28

New Winter
						1	2	3
4	5	6	7	8	9	10	11	12
13	14	15	16	17	18	19	20	21
22	23	24	25	26	27	28

Mid Winter
							1	2
3	4	5	6	7	8	9	10	11
12	13	14	15	16	17	18	19	20
21	22	23	24	25	26	27	28

Old Winter
								1
2	3	4	5	6	7	8	9	10
11	12	13	14	15	16	17	18	19
20	21	22	23	24	25	26	27	28

Nicholas and Ivy marry on the 14th day of Mid Spring in 744.

Year 745

New Spring
1	2	3	4	5	6	7	8	9
10	11	12	13	14	15	16	17	18
19	20	21	22	23	24	25	26	27
28

Mid Spring
1	2	3	4	5	6	7	8
9	10	11	12	13	14	15	16	17
18	19	20	21	22	23	24	25	26
27	28

Old Spring
1	2	3	4	5	6	7
8	9	10	11	12	13	14	15	16
17	18	19	20	21	22	23	24	25
26	27	28	29

New Summer
				1	2	3	4	5
6	7	8	9	10	11	12	13	14
15	16	17	18	19	20	21	22	23
24	25	26	27	28

Mid Summer
					1	2	3	4
5	6	7	8	9	10	11	12	13
14	15	16	17	18	19	20	21	22
23	24	25	26	27	28	29

Old Summer
							1	2
3	4	5	6	7	8	9	10	11
12	13	14	15	16	17	18	19	20
21	22	23	24	25	26	27	28	29

New Autumn
1	2	3	4	5	6	7	8	9
10	11	12	13	14	15	16	17	18
19	20	21	22	23	24	25	26	27
28

Mid Autumn
1	2	3	4	5	6	7	8
9	10	11	12	13	14	15	16	17
18	19	20	21	22	23	24	25	26
27	28

Old Autumn
1	2	3	4	5	6	7
8	9	10	11	12	13	14	15	16
17	18	19	20	21	22	23	24	25
26	27	28

New Winter
			1	2	3	4	5	6
7	8	9	10	11	12	13	14	15
16	17	18	19	20	21	22	23	24
25	26	27	28

Mid Winter
				1	2	3	4	5
6	7	8	9	10	11	12	13	14
15	16	17	18	19	20	21	22	23
24	25	26	27	28

Old Winter
					1	2	3	4
5	6	7	8	9	10	11	12	13
14	15	16	17	18	19	20	21	22
23	24	25	26	27	28

The story concludes on the tenth day of New Autumn in 745.

The Story Timeline

Year 684
Mid Spring

Vellan journeys from the Valley of the Wizards in the Gable Mountains to explore Laparia at age twenty.

Year 686
Mid Autumn

Vellan returns to the Gable Mountains and tells his fellow wizards of his travels.

Year 687
Mid Autumn

Vellan marries Audriana.

Year 689
New Autumn

Vellan leaves on a second journey to Laparia, spending much time in the Northern Mountains.

Year 692
Mid Autumn

Vellan returns to the Gable Mountains, encouraging his fellow wizards to impose their order and wisdom on the outside world, not only for the sake of common men, but to ensure the survival of the race of wizards. After weeks of instigating unrest in his society to achieve his goal, Vellan is banished from his order at age twenty-eight and departs for Laparia. Three days later, he leaves the wizards' realm on its eastern border, crossing the Mang River. The globe on his oak staff is blackened when he steps into the water. He smashes it against a rock on the other side of the river, vowing revenge on his order.

Year 692 - 702

Vellan transforms a region in the Northern Mountains of Laparia into Kargoth. He casts a spell on the Drusala River so that whoever touches or drinks the water will be devoted to him and carry out his orders.

Year 707

Vellan's created Enâri race is revealed to the world.

Year 707 - 710

The Enâri build Vellan's stronghold at the base of Mount Minakaris north of the city of Del Norác and carve out his residence inside the mountain.

Year 710 - 715

Vellan wields economic influence over the mountain nations of Surna, Linden, Harlow and the nearby kingdom of Drumaya. He also cements a relationship with the Northern Isles.

Year 715 - 720

Vellan meets Caldurian in the Red Mountains and trains him as his apprentice.

Year 720 - 722

Caldurian, at Vellan's behest, tries to forge an alliance with other kingdoms in Laparia but is turned down.

Year 722

Caldurian, with help from Madeline, a nursemaid in the Blue Citadel in Arrondale, fails in his attempt to kidnap the infant Princess Megan to use as leverage to gain King Justin's support for an alliance with Vellan. Caldurian and Madeline flee with the eagle Xavier and their Enâri force of five hundred to the village of Red Fern where they stay temporarily with Madeline's cousin, Carmella. When Carmella learns about their activities and threatens to turn them in to the authorities, she has a fight with Madeline who casts a spell and turns her hands a pumpkin orange color. Caldurian later casts a spelling spell upon Carmella. Then he, Madeline, Xavier and the Enâri escape to the east, hiding in the northern reaches of the Cumberland Forest near the village of Kanesbury.

After learning by chance that Mayor Otto Nibbs of Kanesbury was a second cousin to King Justin, Caldurian promises Otto riches and power to persuade the King into an alliance with Vellan. Otto, however, secretly sends word to the King about Caldurian's whereabouts. The wizard grows suspicious of Otto and unleashes his Enâri horde on Kanesbury. Jack Raven dies after being wounded in the attack. His son, Nicholas, is born to Alice Raven a week later. King Justin's troops arrive and arrest Caldurian, Madeline and Xavier. The Enâri flee to some caves outside the village and are placed under a sleeping spell by the wizard Frist who had accompanied the King to Kanesbury. Frist creates the Spirit Box which the King gives to Otto Nibbs. Xavier escapes, stealing the key to the Spirit Box from Otto. King Justin releases Caldurian and Madeline, expelling them from Arrondale with a warning for Vellan not to interfere in the kingdom ever again. Ten-year-old Dooley Kramer steals the key from Xavier after wounding the eagle with a rock. Xavier later dies. Caldurian vows revenge upon both Kanesbury and Otto Nibbs.

Year 742
New Autumn

5th day of month Nicholas Raven announces his plan to join the King's Guard in Morrenwood.

8 Nicholas invites Katherine Durant to the Harvest Festival dance. Dooley Kramer steals Nicholas' jacket button. Adelaide Cooper is kidnapped by Zachary Farnsworth and Dooley Kramer.

10 On the first night of the Harvest Festival, Nicholas is framed and arrested for robbing the gristmill and flees custody. Mune bribes a drunken George Bane to enter the Spirit Caves and unwittingly release the Enâri from their twenty year sleeping spell. Jagga breaks away from the other Enâri to search for the key to the Spirit Box. Nicholas hides in the ice cellar at the home of Oscar and Amanda Stewart where a party is being held for the Harvest Festival. Jagga kills Arthur Weeks, who is waiting in Dooley's house, and steals the key to the Spirit Box. Nicholas flees Kanesbury in secret after being accused of Arthur's murder.

11 Before dawn, Mune meets with the messenger crow, Gavin, and then later with Caldurian for his next orders. Nicholas has breakfast with the Nellis family while on the road but runs away before they learn of his troubles in Kanesbury. Caldurian meets with Farnsworth that night to retrieve the key, telling him to expect a visit from the wizard Arileez. Nicholas encounters soldiers from Montavia later that night who are traveling to train with King Justin's men.

12 At dawn, Caldurian meets with the Enâri at Barringer's Landing, planning to invade Montavia. They leave that evening. Nicholas passes through the villages of Mitchell and Foley.

13 Jagga asks a farmer to melt down the key in his forge, turning it into a medallion.

14   Nicholas reaches King's Road. Later that night, he meets Princess Megan in the Darden Wood.

15   Nicholas joins Megan on the road to Boros so she can stay with her Great Aunt Castella.

16   Nicholas and Megan spend the night with Leo Marsh and his family in the village of Minago.

17   On the road, Nicholas reveals to Megan and Leo what had happened to him in Kanesbury. They arrive at the Plum Orchard Inn. Megan is nearly kidnapped and later reveals that she is Princess Megan of Arrondale.

18   Nicholas, Megan and Leo leave the Plum Orchard Inn as Madeline spies on them through a window. They arrive in Boros. Aunt Castella says they are being followed. Nicholas meets Ivy Brooks.

Caldurian and the Enâri meet Commander Jarrin on shore above the Black Hills. Caldurian meets with Arileez on shore and gives him instructions for his assignments in Kanesbury and Morrenwood.

Madeline meets Mune at the Plum Orchard Inn. He tells her of the planned assault on the Blue Citadel. They will go north to the grasslands and meet with Commander Uta. Madeline informs him that Dell Hawks is tracking Princess Megan to kidnap her and that there will be a war council in Morrenwood. Mune later tells Gavin of the war council so he can send the message to Caldurian.

19   Ivy goes alone to her aunt and uncle's candle shop in Boros that morning. Later, Megan arrives there with Nicholas and Leo. Megan and Ivy switch places. On the way home, Ivy is kidnapped in Boros and brought to a root cellar in Cavara Beach. Sims, who was hired to help kidnap Ivy, tells Nicholas and Leo where she was taken in exchange for money.

Gavin informs Caldurian of the planned war council in nineteen days.

20 Nicholas and Leo leave for Cavara Beach shortly after midnight. Madeline and Mune take Ivy from the root cellar before dawn and travel to the grasslands.

Jagga meets Carmella on the road, strikes up a friendship and gives her the medallion as a gift.

22 Madeline, Mune and Ivy meet with Uta and discuss the proposed raid on the Blue Citadel. Captain Lok is ordered to take Ivy, who all believe is Princess Megan, to Karg Island near the mouth of the Lorren River for safekeeping. Nicholas and Leo sneak up on the tents along the shoreline. Nicholas frees Ivy who is later recaptured. Nicholas and Leo are both rendered unconscious as Ivy is taken away by boat.

23 Caldurian, the Enâri and troops from the Northern Isles attack and take over Montavia, taking King Rowan prisoner in Red Lodge. Prince William and Prince Brendan escape from Triana that evening to get help in Morrenwood.

Otto is visited by an Enâri creature that night who is really the wizard Arileez in Enâri form.

Nicholas and Leo leave the grasslands.

24 Otto leaves for Barringer's Landing in the morning, expecting to meet with the Enâri creatures to prevent them from attacking Kanesbury again. He never returns. Maynard is placed under a sleeping spell by Arileez who has taken his shape. Farnsworth and Dooley bring Maynard's sleeping body to a shed in the swamp that evening. They also bring supplies to Adelaide who is their prisoner in a small locked house nearby. A public meeting is held in the Kanesbury village hall about Otto's disappearance. Maynard (Arileez) is appointed as acting mayor and Ned Adams replaces him on the village council. Len Harold volunteers to go to Morrenwood to seek help from King Justin about the possible Enâri threat.

27 Nicholas and Leo return to Boros from the grasslands. They decide to accompany Megan back to Morrenwood and ask King Justin to help rescue Ivy.

Mid Autumn

3rd day of month Nicholas, Leo and Megan leave Boros and arrive back at Leo's parents' house in Minago.

4 Dooley leaves for Morrenwood with flour shipments for the King's stores, hoping to be able to spy on the war council.

7 Nicholas, Leo and Megan leave for Morrenwood from Leo's parents' house in Minago.

8 Dooley arrives in Morrenwood and by chance meets Len Harold who promises to give him a tour of the Blue Citadel. Len had already met King Justin and is invited to speak at the war council.

9 Nicholas, Leo and Megan meet Carmella and Jagga on the road.

10 Dooley hides in the rafters in the war council chamber and spies on the meeting, falling asleep during most of it. William and Brendan arrive during the council and tell of the invasion of Montavia. Len wonders why Otto Nibbs had said he was to meet with the Enâri creatures when at the time the Enâri were already in Montavia. Eucádus speaks at the council, explaining how citizens of Harlow, Linden and Surna had left their nations and banded together, preparing to attack Vellan. King Justin persuades him to join in on an attack of Rhiál, getting everyone to agree to send forces there as well as to Montavia. Nicholas, Leo, Megan, Carmella and Jagga arrive at the Citadel after the war council. Nicholas and Leo volunteer to take the medallion to the wizard Frist to have it reforged. Dooley overhears this information after waking up and later passes it on to Gavin who will stay around to spy and follow the travelers before informing Caldurian where they are heading.

11 Nicholas and Leo plan their route to Wolf Lake with the wizard Tolapari, King Justin and Nedry, the King's top advisor. Nedry spots a crow (Gavin) on the windowsill. Nedry has extra travel clothes made for Brendan and William who want to travel in their spare time before the army moves out to Montavia.

13 Nicholas and Leo depart before midnight from the Citadel on their journey.

14 William and Brendan leave the Citadel at dawn. Brendan tells Will that he is going to Grantwick to ask King Cedric to join in the fight against Vellan in Rhiál. Gavin, spying on them, hears they are going to the Drumayan capital and flies off to tell Caldurian.

Nicholas promises himself to abandon Leo and search for Ivy after completing his mission with Leo to find the wizard Frist and reforge the key to the Spirit Box.

15 Nicholas and Leo journey through the Gliwice Gap in the Trent Hills.

16 Nicholas and Leo enter the Cashua Forest.

19 Brendan and William spot a deer (Arileez) on their travels. That night in the village of Parma, they meet Sorli (Arileez) who buys them dinner. Brendan, suspicious of the man but not knowing why, leaves with William in secret.

21 Nicholas and Leo walk along a ravine in the Cashua Forest.

23 Nicholas and Leo rest for a day in the Cashua Forest as Nicholas takes ill.

25 William and Brendan arrive in Grantwick at night. The gates around King Cedric's quarters are barred until sunrise. They go to the Ebrean Forest to sleep under the eaves.

Nicholas and Leo emerge from the western eaves of the Cashua Forest.

26 Brendan and William confront Arileez in a cabin in the Ebrean Forest. Brendan is killed. William awakens later that day and meets Ramsey and his friends, refugees from Surna, Linden and Harlow, who tell him that Brendan had died. They leave for the Star Clearing where William again meets Eucádus, its leader.

Nicholas and Leo spot three rafts from the Northern Isles poling up the Lorren River at night.

27 Just after midnight, Farnsworth and Dooley host a secret meeting in Ned Adams' gristmill with Caldurian, Arileez, Madeline, Mune and Gavin. Dooley and Farnsworth learn that Caldurian wanted Nicholas Raven removed from his home so he could meet with Arileez in secret while Arileez was assuming the form of Maynard Kurtz. Caldurian tells everyone that Arileez will later replace King Justin as part of Vellan's plan to conquer Arrondale.

Nicholas and Leo meet Will Fish and his family across the river from Woodwater.

28 William, Eucádus and others from the Star Clearing march through the Ebrean Forest to Grantwick and camp outside the city borders.

Nicholas and Leo meet Lane Fish who agrees to help them find a mountain guide in Woodwater.

Old Autumn

1st day of month Arileez, in Otto Nibbs' form, visits several people in Kanesbury in the predawn hours, warning them that trouble is heading to the village.

William, Eucádus, Ranen and the other Clearing leaders meet with King Cedric of Drumaya who tells them he will march with them to Rhiál to free that kingdom from Vellan's grip.

2   Before dawn, Ned Adams' gristmill is burned to the ground. Constable Brindle arranges for village patrols to begin that evening to protect Kanesbury. Katherine tells Ned Adams that Nicholas was hiding in the ice cellar when Arthur Weeks was murdered. Later in the evening, men from the Northern Isles invade Kanesbury and take control of the village. The impostor Maynard, Clay Brindle and the five members of the village council are taken as prisoners to the village hall.

Nicholas and Leo arrive in Woodwater with Lane Fish and eat at the Mossy Boulder. Two spies from the Northern Isles overhear them talking and plan to track them, believing they are the people Caldurian is seeking. Nicholas and Leo meet Hobin who agrees to guide them to Wolf Lake.

3   The impostor Maynard, Clay Brindle and the five members of the village council are taken to see the wizard Caldurian who has taken up residence in Otto Nibbs' house. As they have breakfast with him, he tells him of his plans to take over the property and food supplies in the village. Caldurian later meets with the residents in the village hall, shattering all the windows to quell their growing resentment of him. Katherine meets Paraquin, a soldier from the Northern Isles.

Nicholas, Leo and Hobin begin their trek through the Dunn Hills. During the night, they think they are being followed.

4   The armies of Drumaya and the Five Clearings leave Grantwick and assemble on the east side of the Swift River near Wynhall.

Maynard (Arileez), Oscar, Ned and seven others hold a secret meeting in an empty root cellar to plan an escape from Kanesbury and get help from Morrenwood and some neighboring villages.

5   The armies of Drumaya and the Five Clearings begin traveling east to Rhiál across the Kincarin Plains.

Katherine learns from Paraquin that Farnsworth and Dooley are conspiring with Caldurian and may know something about Adelaide's disappearance.

6 The impostor Maynard feigns a confrontation with Caldurian about the mass arrests in the village, bringing them to a halt. Lewis Ames expresses his fond feelings for Katherine.

Nicholas admits to Leo that he wants to depart and search for Ivy after their mission is completed. Hobin says he will accompany Leo back to Morrenwood in Nicholas' place.

7 King Cedric finds that some of his forward scouts were ambushed and killed on the Kincarin Plains. Soon after, a small band of soldiers from Kargoth attacks the armies of Drumaya and the Five Clearings, but all are quickly killed. One of the soldiers, before dying, expresses his devotion to Vellan. When he dies, a vague cloudiness in his eyes clears up and his facial features relax. Others believe the dead soldiers had drunk from the Drusala River in Kargoth and were under Vellan's spell until death released them.

Nicholas, Leo and Hobin reach Beetle Lake and climb Gray Hawk Mountain.

8 Thirteen members of the resistance movement in Kanesbury set their escape plan in motion but are stopped by the soldiers from the Northern Isles and are arrested.

9 Before dawn, Nicholas, Leo and Hobin are attacked by two men from the Northern Isles who had been tracking them. Nicholas wounds one who flees, but not before he had injured Leo. Hobin kills the other one. They continue hiking later in the day after fashioning a sling for Leo's arm.

Caldurian parades the thirteen members of the resistance before the village, threatening to kill Len Harold and Lewis Ames and send the others to the Northern Isles if the instigator of the rebellion isn't revealed. Otto later returns unexpectedly as Caldurian is about to pass judgment. The crowd clamors for Otto's arrest instead, believing that he had abandoned the village before it was invaded. Caldurian complies with their wishes, arresting Otto and releasing the other prisoners, now satisfied that he has avenged the humiliation

Otto had caused him twenty years ago. Katherine vows to spy on Dooley and Farnsworth, hoping to learn their role behind Nicholas' fate and Adelaide's disappearance. Arileez tells Farnsworth that he will soon appoint him as acting mayor.

10 The armies of Drumaya and the Five Clearings arrive in Melinas, the capital of Rhiál. Captain Silas escorts King Cedric, Eucádus, William, Ranen and Captain Tiber to meet with King Basil. They plan a secret assault of Drogin's troops five days from the following dawn. William befriends Aaron and asks him to give him a tour along the docks on the lake. Later that night, Nyla, a spy for Drogin, informs her husband, Bosh, that William and Aaron plan to walk along the docks the following night and arranges to have them kidnapped to get information from the prince about King Basil's war plans.

11 Caldurian and his Island troops leave Kanesbury in secret before dawn.

Nicholas, Leo and Hobin arrive at Wolf Lake and meet Rustin who takes them to the wizard Frist. The wizard heals Leo's injury with a magic spell. Frist reveals to Nicholas that his father, Jack Raven, had died from wounds during the Enâri invasion of Kanesbury twenty years ago and that he was unable to heal his injuries. Frist retreats to a cave to remake the key.

William and Aaron are kidnapped by Bosh and his men.

12 Ned Adams resigns his seat on the village council. Arileez, in the guise of Maynard Kurtz, appoints Zachary Farnsworth to take Ned's place.

Before dawn, Nicholas, Leo and Rustin go to Frist who awaits them in the cave after reforging the key. Frist presents Nicholas with the key and a silver amulet to protect him in his travels. Frist dies and his body disappears in a white mist. Later, Nicholas, Leo and Hobin leave the island by canoe. Nicholas gives Leo the reforged key to take back to Morrenwood.

William is questioned by Bosh hours before dawn, and to protect Aaron's life, reveals King Basil's war plans. He and Aaron are kept prisoners in a barn outside of Melinas, learning that Nyla was behind their abduction.

13 Nicholas says goodbye to Leo and Hobin and travels east by boat along Wolf Lake.

William and Aaron escape from the barn outside Melinas and flee Bosh's men.

Arileez, in the guise of Maynard Kurtz, leaves Kanesbury, saying he is going to Morrenwood to consult with King Justin about Caldurian's return to the area. Before he leaves, he appoints Zachary Farnsworth as the village's acting mayor.

14 After the morning fog lifts, Drogin's army is revealed on both land and water just outside King Basil's estate in Melinas, prepared to attack. There is a brief parley, with Irabesh, King Drogin's representative, saying that Prince William had been kidnapped and revealed King Basil's secret attack plans. The fighting begins. William and Aaron return and save Ramsey's life. Rafts apparently filled with Drogin's troops sail down Lake LaShear. Jeremias is killed by Irabesh and then Eucádus kills Irabesh. Nyla is arrested for spying. King Justin's men are revealed on rafts along Lake LaShear and others arrive on the field and join in the battle in Melinas. King Basil dies as the battle is won by his men.
Nicholas encounters the man from the Northern Isles whom he had injured five days ago at their campsite after they were attacked. As the man is about to kill Nicholas, he drops dead with an arrow in his back. Nicholas meets Hannah, the woman who saved his life.

15 King Basil of Rhiál is laid to rest.

16 Jeremias is buried in Melinas.

Nicholas and Hannah paddle to Illingboc where they visit Arch and Natalie Boland, Hannah's brother and his wife. Nicholas learns that

Arch and others are secretly conspiring against men from the Northern Isles who have invaded their homeland along the Crescent.

17 King Justin, King Cedric, Captain Silas and their contingent sail across Lake LaShear to Maranac to confront Drogin. Princess Melinda appears and announces that her uncle, King Drogin, was killed in an uprising. She introduces Prince Victor of Rhiál who was held prisoner with her by her uncle. Victor and Melinda confide in Captain Silas that they wish to reunite Rhiál and Maranac as New Maranac with approval of the two populations.

Arch introduces Nicholas to Arteen from the Northern Isles who is planning a raid on the ship *Bretic* and on Karg Island. Nicholas learns that Captain Tarosius Lok is the administrator on Karg Island and assumes that Ivy is being held prisoner on the island under his supervision. Nicholas gets permission from Arteen to join him on the raid so he can rescue Ivy.

20 King Justin, King Cedric, Eucádus and their troops leave Rhiál for their respective homes.

Nicholas, Arteen, Ragus, Brin Mota and other soldiers from the Northern Isles paddle over on rafts and board the *Bretic*. Tarosius Lok is there with Captain Kellig as his prisoner, having been informed of the attack beforehand by Brin Mota who served as his spy. Vice-Commander Ovek arrives and takes possession of the *Bretic* and arrests Lok, privately informing him that the woman he was guarding is not Princess Megan. Lok escapes off the stern, setting the ship afire before he leaves. Nicholas and Ragus follow Lok to Karg Island. Lok is killed and Nicholas is reunited with Ivy. Arteen and his men arrive on the island and Ovek and his crew flee on the *Hara Nor*.

21 Nicholas and Ivy leave Karg Island with a letter from Arteen to deliver to Arch Boland. Brin Mota watches them leave, planning to follow them to Illingboc.

22 On the Kincarin Plains, King Justin's army heads northwest to Morrenwood while King Cedric and Eucádus depart with their troops southwest back to Grantwick.

Katherine spies on Dooley and Farnsworth as they depart secretly at night, confirming that they have been leaving the village every six nights.

23 Katherine asks Amanda Stewart to host a small dinner party with Zachary Farnsworth as guest of honor. Zachary tells Dooley he will have to make the next trip to the swamp alone and pick up a hired assassin on the way to eliminate Maynard and Adelaide from their lives.

24 Prince Gregory and his army leave for Montavia.

26 Prince Gregory's army passes through Kanesbury and he speaks with Len Harold along the roadside, learning about Caldurian's recent takeover of the village and Otto Nibbs' surprise return and imprisonment.

27 Leo and Hobin return to the Blue Citadel with the reforged key.

28 Prince Gregory's troops enter the Keppel Mountains from the west.

Amanda Stewart hosts a dinner for Zachary Farnsworth. Katherine feigns sickness at the party and leaves to meet Lewis. They go to Dooley Kramer's house and secretly follow him to the swamp, saving his life when Dell Hawks tries to murder him. Dooley confesses to all the crimes that he and Farnsworth had done on Caldurian's behalf and takes them to the island to rescue Adelaide and Maynard. Dooley is killed after accidentally falling off the top step of the staircase of the house where Adelaide was kept imprisoned. Lewis and Katherine take Adelaide and the still sleeping Maynard to Emmett and Lorna Trout's farmhouse outside of Kanesbury to hide until they can recover from their ordeals.

New Winter

1ˢᵗ day of month King Justin and his troops return to Morrenwood. Leo presents the reforged key to King Justin who orders that the Spirit Box be opened before dawn the following morning.

Madeline and Commander Uta are concerned that Arileez is having difficulty with his transformational ability on the eve of their attack on the Blue Citadel.

Farnsworth has suspicions about Katherine Durant after learning that she had lied to him about spending the previous night sick at home after leaving the dinner party early. He goes to the swamp and finds that Adelaide and Maynard have escaped, and discovers the dead bodies of Dooley and the hired assassin and dumps them in the swamp.

Brin spies on Nicholas and Ivy at the first day of winter celebration in Ilingboc. Nicholas and Ivy meet Miriam who has a blue stone identical to the one Hobin carries. They promise to visit her Aunt Emma nearby whom Miriam insists never stopped loving Hobin.

Prince Gregory's troops reach the east side of the Keppel Mountains at twilight, preparing to attack Caldurian's troops the following dawn.

2 The Blue Citadel is breached by Commander Uta's troops as Leo takes the key to open the Spirit Box. Carmella and Madeline meet outside the Citadel after twenty years. Arileez is killed after trying to replace King Justin. Leo opens the Spirit Box after Mune attacks him. Jagga's body disintegrates outside the Citadel. Madeline and Mune flee to Kargoth.

Prince Gregory and his troops attack the Enâri and Island forces at Red Lodge. Tolapari casts the âvin éska spell upon Caldurian. Captain Grayling and his troops rescue King Rowan and Lady Vilna from the Enâri riders who are destroyed when the entity from the Spirit Box passes over.

Constable Brindle is attacked before dawn. Farnsworth postpones Otto's trial, offering Katherine veiled threats that harm will come to her family and friends if she exposes his criminal deeds.

3 Nicholas and Ivy visit Emma and show her the blue stone pendant. Brin slips a sleeping potion into Nicholas and Ivy's water skins and kidnaps them when they later fall asleep, planning to take them to Kargoth.

4 Nicholas and Ivy begin their journey up the Lorren River as prisoners on Brin's raft.

5 King Rowan and Vilna receive a letter from Prince William explaining the details of Brendan's death.

6 Prince Gregory and his troops depart Montavia with Caldurian as prisoner.

7 Maynard wakes up from Arileez' sleeping spell at the home of Emmett and Lorna Trout.

11 Prince Gregory and his troops arrive in Morrenwood.

Ivy is removed from the raft and handed over to Cale and a group of Northern Island soldiers who are instructed to take her to Vellan.

12 King Justin talks with Caldurian in the Citadel and learns about Arileez' history. The King later tells Tolapari that he will bring Caldurian along when they march to Kargoth in the spring.

16 Nicholas is rescued from the raft by Malek and his men. A wounded Brin drowns himself in the Gray River. Nicholas accompanies Malek to his camp where he is questioned and learns that the Spirit Box had been opened fourteen days ago and that the Enâri race throughout the Northern Mountains had been destroyed.

20 Max arrives at camp and mentions the planned spring raid on Deshla prison to Nicholas.

23 Max leaves camp for the Thendara Wood to meet his contact from Morrenwood.

25 Nicholas, Malek and the rest of the camp leave south to group with an adjacent camp for the march to Petaras Peak.

26 King Justin holds a second war council at the Blue Citadel.

28 Nicholas, Malek and the combined camps continue south to Petaras Peak.

Mid Winter

3rd day of month Nicholas, Malek and the combined camps are snowbound on their way to Petaras Peak.

5 Nicholas, Malek and the combined camps resume their trek to Petaras Peak in the deep snow.

10 As Nicholas, Malek and the others near Petaras Peak, Dunnic kills Rollin, and when trying to escape, is killed with an arrow by Malek. Max returns with a letter from Prince Gregory explaining that the armies of King Justin and his allies will march to Kargoth in the spring to confront Vellan.

20 Nicholas, Malek and their other camp members leave Petaras Peak and begin their trek to the Champeko Forest to meet up with the other groups in the mountain resistance.

Old Winter

14th day of month King Justin, sensing an early spring, wants to launch an attack on Vellan as soon as possible. Leo asks Princess Megan to marry him.

17 The armies of Arrondale and Montavia depart through the gates of the Blue Citadel for Kargoth. Megan bids farewell to Leo, Carmella and Hobin.

19 Brendan awakens without memory in the Ebrean Forest in the spot where he was buried.

21 The armies of Arrondale and Montavia reach the northern tip of Lake Lasko.

22 The armies of Arrondale and Montavia pass by the village of Parma.

Nicholas and Max leave the Champeko Forest, beginning their journey to Lake Mara.

Brendan leaves the cabin in the Ebrean Forest and begins his trek out of the woods.

23 The armies of Arrondale and Montavia enter the Red Mountains.

Nicholas and Max reach the Bellunboro River on Linden's western border at nightfall.

25 The armies of Arrondale and Montavia enter the kingdom of Drumaya and march to Grantwick. Kings Justin and Rowan are welcomed by King Cedric. Eucádus and Ranen meet Leo and learn of his role in ridding their nations of the Enâri.

26 Nicholas and Max begin traveling along the southwestern border of the Ebrean Forest in Linden.

27 The armies of Arrondale, Montavia, Drumaya and the Five Clearings march south to the village of Wynhall where they meet Captain Silas and his troops from Rhiál and Maranac.

28 The allied armies of Arrondale, Montavia, Drumaya, the Five Clearings, Rhiál and Maranac reach the northern tip of Lake Mara.

Nicholas and Max enter the kingdom of Drumaya.

Year 743
New Spring

1ˢᵗ day of month Prince Brendan appears alive along the shore of Lake Mara.

Nicholas and Max reach Lake Mara farther south of King Justin's army.

2 Nicholas and Max meet up with Prince Gregory and King Justin's army on Lake Mara. Nicholas is reunited with Leo, Hobin and Carmella. Hobin learns of Emma's location and that she still loves him. Caldurian reveals that Vellan had placed a second, secret spell in the potion that freed Arileez from his island prison, guessing that it was responsible for bringing Brendan back to life and quickly healing King Justin's wound. Nicholas meets Caldurian and blames him for the death of his father twenty years ago.

3 King Justin and the allied armies reach the Braya Woods.

4 Prince Gregory informs Nicholas of Caldurian's invasion of his village for nine days last autumn and of Maynard's disappearance. Nicholas, Leo, Hobin and Max take their leave of King Justin and travel back into Linden. King Justin gives Caldurian permission to meet with Carmella.

5 Carmella and Caldurian meet for the first time in twenty years, with the wizard agreeing to teach Carmella some magic and help find her cousin, Madeline, if she will help him escape from King Justin's guards.

7 The allied armies halt on the southwest edge of the Rhoon Forest during a severe rainstorm. Carmella learns to create smoke spheres.

8 The allied armies enter the southern portion of the Northern Mountains, traveling a few miles north of the Drusala River. Carmella and Caldurian create colorful smoke butterflies.

9 Using a magic smoke illusion, Carmella helps Caldurian escape from King Justin's encampment. King Justin and the allied armies enter Kargoth.

Nicholas, Leo, Hobin and Max meet a farmer in Linden who describes witnessing the destruction of the Enâri creatures who had been confiscating food from their community.

10 While traveling through Kargoth, Carmella and Caldurian stop at an abandoned farmhouse near dawn to sleep. There they find the sandy remains of several Enâri creatures. They feel they are being watched.

King Justin tells Tolapari that he purposely let Caldurian escape, hoping his dissatisfaction with Vellan's rule will cause strife between them and aid their fight in the coming war.

11 Carmella and Caldurian come upon a long trail of destroyed Enâri creatures, their boots, weapons and garments being all that remain. The sight of one pair of boots intrigues the wizard. Later that evening, they meet Mune who was leaving Kargoth after parting ways with Madeline weeks ago. He said that Madeline had gotten caught on purpose by some Island soldiers, hoping to be taken to Vellan. Carmella learns that Caldurian was responsible for Nicholas' troubles in Kanesbury.

12 Mune decides to accompany Carmella and Caldurian to Vellan's stronghold in Del Norác.

13 A torrential rainstorm halts the progress of the allied army into Kargoth for two days.

15 King Justin and the allied army continue their journey northwest into Kargoth, exploring an abandoned Enâri garrison along the way.

16 A band of Vellan's troops attacks the allied army along the Drusala River. Ranen falls into the Drusala during a fight and falls under Vellan's spell. To prevent another fight and spare his life, King Justin asks Ranen to go to Vellan to request a parley.

19 Three of Vellan's soldiers inform King Justin that Vellan will await him near Del Norác the following day.

20 Fiery arrows are launched by King Justin's men to signal the start of the war with Vellan.

Nicholas, Leo, Malek and their troops raid Deshla prison, only to find it empty. Nicholas and Leo question Cale about Ivy's whereabouts and later pursue him through the tunnels when he escapes. He later dies in a fall in a pit, after which, Nicholas and Leo find a door at the end of the tunnel.

King Justin's troops enter Del Norác with Prince Gregory, Eucádus and Ramsey. King Rowan, William, Brendan and Captains Silas and Grayling take the fight to the eastern bridge. King Cedric, along with Tolapari, Captain Tiber, Uland and Torr, fight against Vellan's troops pouring out of Mount Minakaris. Soon Malek, Max and their men join the fray from the north and break up Vellan's initial assault near the mountain before heading into the city. King Justin is kidnapped at the garrison. Captain Silas is wounded and King Rowan is stabbed while saving his grandsons.

Nicholas and Leo meet Vellan and Madeline in the upper chambers of Mount Minakaris. Vellan casts a dying spell upon Leo when learning he had opened the Spirit Box.

An impostor King Justin is thrown from the garrison roof as a diversion, enabling Luboc's troops to spirit away the real King to Mount Minakaris. Eucádus meets Ranen, still under Vellan's spell, along the river.

Leo revives from Vellan's spell, learning that he will be dead by dawn. Later, after eating the stew Caldurian had served him, Vellan passes out and Madeline suspects treachery on Caldurian's part.

King Rowan dies and then Meegs, a soldier from Kargoth, apprehends Brendan and William when he learns they are the King's grandsons.

Caldurian admits he drugged Vellan to gain control of Kargoth before the war destroys his only chance. Then Madeline feels faint and Caldurian tells her that he drugged her tea with some of the potion Vellan gave him three years ago to release Arileez from his island prison, having originally planned to use it on Vellan, but never finding the right opportunity. He says that he may have led Madeline down the wrong path in life and wants her to start over again, mentioning that his earlier talks with Carmella helped lead him to this decision. Madeline is angered at him and Carmella for destroying her life and runs off, passing out as Caldurian chases her down the corridor.

Prince Gregory chases his kidnapped father into an apple orchard north of the city and runs to him after he is wounded by an enemy soldier whom Malek pulls off the King and kills. King Cedric and Ramsey plan to ride to the aid of King Rowan's men in the eastern field.

Caldurian frees Nicholas and Leo on the condition that they deliver a letter to King Justin informing him that Caldurian will end the war and hand over Vellan if King Justin's army leaves Kargoth. Nicholas agrees after Caldurian promises that Ivy and Carmella will be released.

Eucádus and Ranen fight on the central bridge in Del Norác. Ranen pins him against the western rail and chokes him as Eucádus will not turn to Vellan's side.

Caldurian awaits Gavin's report from Vellan's balcony overlooking Del Norác.

Mune stabs Vellan to death after making Nicholas promise to deliver a message to King Justin in exchange for helping him find Ivy and Carmella. Mune wraps the bloody dagger in Vellan's head cloth and gives it to Nicholas to deliver to the King as proof he killed Vellan in exchange for a pardon for all his crimes throughout Laparia.

Madeline orders two guards to take Ivy to the Drusala River and then argues with Carmella in one of Vellan's open chambers on the mountainside. Though Carmella vows to help her turn her life around, Madeline realizes that her magic abilities and her dreams have both disappeared and kills herself by falling backward out one of the open arches, falling into the rocky stream below. The pumpkin color on Carmella's hands begins to fade.

Nicholas, Leo and Mune search for Carmella and Ivy. Nicholas gives Leo the amulet from Frist which helps to restore his strength.

King Cedric, Tolapari, Ramsey and their troops rescue William and Brendan from Meegs as the full Fox and Bear moons begin to rise. Moments later, a tremor rumbles across the landscape.

Nicholas, Leo and Mune locate Carmella and then see that Ivy is being taken away outside the mountain. Nicholas follows her, and after battling one of her two captors, demands that Ivy be released. Just then, a tremor rumbles across the landscape.

Gavin locates Caldurian on Vellan's balcony, being suspicious when he will not tell him of Vellan's location. Gavin flies away into the mountain and finds Vellan's dead body. When it starts to fade to mist, he returns to Caldurian who said he drugged Vellan to sleep but didn't kill him. When a large tremor hits, Gavin flies off. Caldurian is killed when an ice and rock slide takes him out, and then afterward, the stronghold below.

Eucádus and Ranen fight on the bridge when the tremor occurs. Ranen pushes him against the bridge rail and they both fall into the water which begins to coldly boil as Vellan's spell on it weakens. After a wall of fog engulfs them, the river calms but a mist remains. Eucádus swims to shore and finds Ranen asleep. When he awakens, Ranen recognizes his friend, no longer under Vellan's spell.

William, Brendan, King Cedric, Tolapari and Ramsey witness the avalanche on Mount Minakaris from the eastern field. Moments later, the enemy soldiers awaken from Vellan's spell and cast aside their weapons.

King Justin, Prince Gregory and Malek wander through Del Norác, hearing stories from the former enemy about the last things they remembered before succumbing to Vellan's will.

When Vellan's spell is broken, the soldier holding Ivy at knifepoint remembers who he is and drops his knife, sorry for what he has done. Nicholas and Ivy tell him to go find his family and he leaves. Then Nicholas and Ivy embrace, at last reunited. Leo, Carmella and Mune show up shortly after and they head down the mountain. When they discover Madeline's body washed up along the stream, Nicholas and Mune bury it. Mune decides to remain at her gravesite for a time, not sure where he will go afterward. Nicholas, Ivy, Leo and Carmella continue down the mountain.

21 Nicholas, Ivy, Leo and Carmella approach the northern border of Del Norác where a tent city had been set up to tend to the injured and dying soldiers. There they meet Hobin who had been searching for them. He tells them King Justin has been injured and is unconscious due to an infection from his wound. They travel to his tent, meeting King Cedric and Tolapari. Leo sits with the injured King and falls asleep in his chair. Tolapari offers Carmella an apprenticeship. Nicholas and Ivy help to assist with the wounded soldiers. Nicholas later meets Malek, Max and Sala along the river while delivering firewood among the tents. Leo awakens refreshed and places the amulet from Frist into King Justin's hand who then immediately begins to recover in his sleep.

24 King Justin and Prince Gregory tour Del Norác as it undergoes repairs.

27 The allied armies depart Kargoth, stopping at the burial field to pay their respects to the war dead.

Mid Spring

8th day of month The allied armies reach the village of Wynhall in Drumaya. Captain Silas and his troops depart across the Swift River and head back home to Rhiál and Maranac.

9 The remaining allied army arrives in Grantwick to rest for a few days.

14 King Justin and Prince Brendan leave Grantwick and lead their armies north.

21 Prince Brendan's army bids farewell to King Justin and continues east through Arrondale to Montavia. King Justin leads his troops northward to Morrenwood, arriving home near sunset.

26 Festivities are held throughout Arrondale to celebrate the end of the war in Kargoth. Megan and Leo announce their engagement to their friends.

Old Spring

1st day of month King Justin holds a farewell dinner for his family and close friends.

2 Nicholas and Ivy leave the Blue Citadel and head for home.

4 Nicholas and Ivy leave King's Road and turn onto River Road, passing Graystone Garrison along the way. After stopping on their way up Orchard Road, Nicholas asks Ivy to marry him. Nicholas and Ivy visit Leo's parents in Minago.

5 Nicholas leaves Minago and heads home to Kanesbury, spending the night in the village of Mitchell during a severe rainstorm.

6 Nicholas arrives in Kanesbury as darkness falls. He secretly meets with Katherine in the Stewarts' ice cellar and discusses how to expose Zachary Farnsworth's crimes to the village. He later goes to Emmett and Lorna Trout's farmhouse to see Maynard and Adelaide and explain his plan to defeat Farnsworth, recruiting their son, Gilbert, to deliver a secret letter.

7 Gilbert Trout leaves to deliver Nicholas' letter to Prince Gregory at the Graystone Garrison.

10   Nicholas returns to the Water Barrel Inn to the surprise of everyone there. Constable Brindle arrives and escorts him to the lockup to hear his story. With Zachary Farnsworth's permission, Nicholas accepts a trial date in one week.

19   Nicholas' trial takes place in the Kanesbury village hall. Adelaide Cooper and Maynard Kurtz reappear in public and testify on Nicholas' behalf. King Justin appears and makes a statement verifying the existence and capabilities of the wizard Arileez. Zachary Farnsworth is implicated in the crimes against Kanesbury and for conspiring with Caldurian. He is arrested, all charges are dropped against Nicholas, and Otto Nibbs is set free. Farnsworth breaks free and escapes to the bell tower roof where he sees Prince Gregory with King Justin's troops surrounding the village hall, having already captured Farnsworth's men. Farnsworth then slips back inside the bell tower and hangs himself.

21   The bodies of Dooley Kramer and Dell Hawks are located and removed from the swamp.

24   Nicholas receives an invitation to Megan and Leo's wedding. Ned Adams offers Nicholas his old job back at the gristmill that is still being rebuilt.

Mid Summer

1st day of month   Nicholas travels to Boros and visits Ivy at Aunt Castella's house. Castella announces that she will move to Morrenwood in the autumn after Megan and Leo's wedding. Nicholas and Ivy tell her they plan to marry next spring.

5   Nicholas and Ivy travel to Laurel Corners to spend some time with Ivy's family, announcing their engagement.

New Autumn

3rd day of month   Princess Megan and Leo Marsh are married in the Blue Citadel in Morrenwood.

6 Nicholas and Ivy leave Morrenwood and head for home after the wedding festivities.

9 Nicholas arrives in Kanesbury with Ivy who visits for a couple of weeks.

Mid Winter

2nd day of month Nicholas and Ivy walk along frozen Sage Bay when he visits her in Laurel Corners during winter. Ivy shows him a spot near a willow tree along shore where she wants to get married.

Year 744
Mid Spring

14th day of month Nicholas and Ivy are married along Sage Bay in Laurel Corners.

Old Spring

22nd day of month King Cedric of Drumaya hosts a gathering of public officials in Grantwick to discuss the state of affairs in the region.

Mid Summer

1st day of month Ivy's sisters, Martha and Jane, arrive in Kanesbury to visit.

22 Nicholas receives a letter from Leo detailing their plans to accompany Hobin into the Dunn Hills in autumn.

New Autumn

6th day of month Nicholas and Ivy depart for Morrenwood.

9 Megan and Leo tell Nicholas and Ivy that they are expecting a child late in the spring.

11 Nicholas and Leo depart the Blue Citadel for Woodwater.

16 Nicholas and Leo arrive at Hobin's home in Woodwater.

26 Nicholas, Leo and Hobin climb the middle peak of the Five Brothers mountain range.

Mid Autumn

19th day of month Nicholas and Ivy return to Kanesbury.

New Winter

10th day of month Ivy tells Nicholas she is expecting their first child.

Year 745
Old Summer

1st day of month Jack Frederick Raven, Nicholas and Ivy's first child, is born.

Fox Moon and Bear Moon

To help give my story a more otherworldly feel, I decided to have two moons grace the skies above it, namely, the Fox Moon and the Bear Moon, the latter being the larger of the two lunar orbs. And as two rising full moons are supposed to be a sign of good fortune in this world, a concept first introduced with an engraving of the full moons on Princess Megan's royal medallion, the full Fox and Bear rise above the mountains at the end of the story upon Vellan's defeat.

In order to keep track of which phase of which moon was visible on a particular day if I made mention of it, I ended up devising a numbered shorthand for each moon phase in their respective cycles and jotted them down on one side of the yearly calendars I drew up to keep track of my characters and plotlines. After committing to this concept, I wanted the presentation to be as accurate as possible.

And to make things mathematically simple for me, I gave the Fox Moon a twenty-eight day orbit and the Bear Moon a thirty-two day orbit, which means that the two full moons would rise together every 224 days, or just about every eight months by this calendar. Though most people who read the book won't give any of this a second thought, I strived for accurate calculations nonetheless, usually being a stickler for details. Any mistakes about this or anything else in the book are strictly mine.

What follows is an image of one of my calendars (Year 742) that I used to keep track of my storyline. The numbers in parentheses represent the chronological days of the story beginning in the first chapter, again, for my writing benefit. The second image is the moon chart I drew to follow the Fox and Bear in their orbits.

One of four calendars I constructed to help me keep track of the timeline of events in the novel. The numbers on the right margin indicate the weekly moon phases for the Fox and Bear.

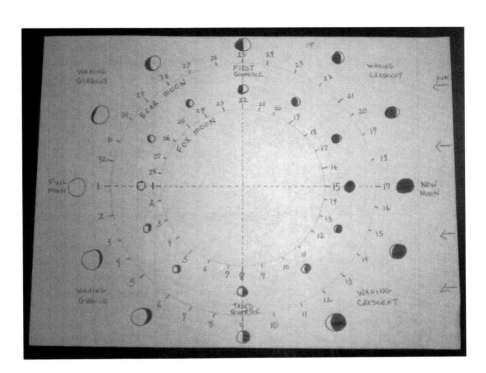

A sketch I drew charting the Fox and Bear moons so I could track their phases when I made mention of them in the book.

A Brief Geneology

As the family members of King Justin of Arrondale are related to the Nibbs/Durant residents of Kanesbury, I constructed a partial family tree to illustrate those connections. I extended the family line as far back as needed to show this, though several people listed in earlier generations do not appear nor are mentioned in the book. The line begins with King Vincent and his sister, Elizabeth, who would be King Justin's grandfather and great aunt, respectively.

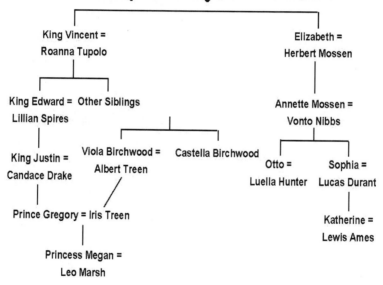

Partial Family Tree of King Justin and Relations

Inspiring Words

While working on this book, I began to post monthly updates on my website starting in April 2011 that presented various aspects of writing this novel, some delving into the background of the story while others were more nuts and bolts in nature about my page progress. One, printed below, details how I was inspired to begin this project a few years after reading J. R. R. Tolkien's *The Hobbit* and *The Lord of the Rings* in 1975 when I was twelve years old.

Update #17 - August 24, 2012

I'm particularly happy to be writing this update today for two reasons. One, it's not the last day of the month, which too many times I found myself nearly breaking my rule to post one update per month. Two, and more importantly, I'm delighted to report that I completed Chapter 96 a few days ago and finished editing it on Wednesday. This chapter, along with Chapters 92 - 95, are what the storyline has been building to and where many plot points are finally resolved. These five chapters together run 215 pages, more than I first anticipated, but it was well worth the effort to reshape my original ideas over the last few months and produce a better story than I once imagined in my teens and twenties. The total page number right now stands at just a bit over 2300, not including what I've already completed for Chapter 97 which I started writing three days ago. Now just six chapters to go!

I feel as if I have climbed over a high wall to get to this point in my book, with only a few minor hurdles left to complete. So I thought I'd write about how and why I decided to take on this enormous literary effort. In my first post (April 17, 2011), I mentioned how in the spring of 1975 when I was twelve years old I had read J. R. R. Tolkien's *The Lord of the Rings*, and then later *The Hobbit*, which inspired me to write my own epic fantasy novel.

In that post I had written: *Besides the interesting characters and events in Tolkien's story, I was greatly impressed by the grand narrative sweep of the work, so much so that I reread it several times in my youth (along with The Hobbit) and a few more times since. After reading the three volumes the first time, I felt as if I had taken the journey myself, often thinking back to particular sections of the book and consulting his maps as if they represented a real place. It wasn't long after my first couple of readings* [in the fall of 1978] *that I began to imagine snippets of my own narrative, some more developed than others, and many not even connected to one another in a proper storyline. But I knew then that I wanted to write my own grand narrative someday. And nearly thirty-three years later, I'm almost there.*

Let's now make that thirty-four years later. And when I think about how I first stumbled upon Tolkien's works in 1975, it was, like Bilbo Baggins finding the One Ring of power, just a matter of chance.

While in sixth grade, the textbook series that I was using in my reading class contained some stories that were chapters from various novels, though no mention of the novels themselves was provided as I recall. One of the stories was titled *Riddles in the Dark*, which Tolkien fans know is Chapter Five from *The Hobbit*, a key chapter where Bilbo Baggins finds the One Ring. I remember reading that story in April of 1975, not realizing it was an excerpt from a novel, and then plowing through the rest of the volume since I liked to read ahead even before the stories were assigned as homework.

One afternoon shortly afterward, during a free period where students were allowed to work on their own and talk quietly, I was seated at my desk doing some homework when a classmate in the next row to my right began telling another student about a book he had read. I couldn't help but overhear the conversation about someone named Frodo who inherited a magic ring and had to drop it in the Cracks of Doom to destroy it. I didn't know who this Frodo character was or where exactly the Cracks of Doom were located, but I had heard something about a magic ring and quickly realized that my classmate was referring to the One Ring mentioned in *Riddles in the Dark*.

As my interest was piqued, I later asked him about what book he had been discussing. He told me that the story we had read was a chapter lifted from a novel called *The Hobbit*. I was further intrigued when he mentioned there was a three-part sequel called *The Lord of the Rings* which recounted the journey to destroy the One Ring. I was immediately hooked by his description, and so after school that day, we went to the public library just down the block to find the book. Unfortunately, when we got there, the book had already been checked out. And worse, there was a waiting list.

It seems around that time, *The Hobbit* and *The Lord of the Rings* were quite popular, being the *Harry Potter* of its time. And that was before the Internet and 24-hour news. So I put my name on the waiting list, disappointed that I couldn't take the book home. But my classmate suggested that I check out the first volume of *The Lord of the Rings* instead since I had already read the key chapter about the ring in *The Hobbit*. So I did, eager to get on with this literary adventure. But after reading the first few pages of Chapter One of *The Fellowship of the Ring*, I set the book aside and remember it sitting on the second shelf of the small desk my brother and I shared in our bedroom.

As I recall the stretch of weather at the time being warm and sunny, I can only guess that I was more drawn to play outdoors than flip through the pages of a book, though I was a voracious reader during those years. But each time I walked past my desk, I always noticed the book and felt a tinge of guilt for not reading it because of all the help offered from my classmate. So as the book's May due date drew closer and closer, I again picked it up and started from the beginning, only this time I never put the book down and flew through the pages. Soon I was back in the library to check out *The Two Towers*, and later, *The Return of the King*. I was enthralled with the story, feeling as if I had gone on that journey myself.

Then one sunny day in August, I received a telephone call from the library informing me that *The Hobbit* had been returned and that I was next on the list to check it out. In a flash, I walked down to the library (or possibly ran, I can't remember), signed out the book and hurried home. I do remember how excited I was to finally be able to read this novel and recall pouring myself a tall glass of iced tea, grabbing a lawn chair and unfolding it in the backyard and then plopping down and losing myself in its pages. And though I can't remember the book cover illustration for the volumes of *The Lord of the Rings* that I first read (even an online search didn't jog my memory), I clearly recall the tan cloth hardcover edition of *The Hobbit* that I read containing a small, red, bowing hobbit impression on the upper right hand side.

I guess why I remember these minor details with such clarity is because they are important to me and helped formed who I am in part as a writer. I think it's important that everyone have a passion of one sort or another. Mine is writing, and more specifically, writing this current book. And whether one's passion is grand or simple, or provides you with a living or not, hopefully it will give you joy and sustain you through life's ups and downs, inspire you and possibly others, and ultimately make you a better person.

As you can see, this has been one of my longest posts, so why stop now? I'll leave you with one more interesting nugget (to me, anyway) about my first encounter with *The Hobbit*. When first thinking about writing this post several months ago, I suddenly remembered that reading the *Riddles in the Dark* chapter was not the first time I had heard about *The Hobbit*. I had actually seen the book many times before but never knew anything about it.

In the grade school I attended, the fifth through eighth grades were located on the second floor and shared a small, one-room library at the end of the hallway. I remember often scanning the wall on the left side of the room after entering the library to find a book to read, and while doing so, one book spine always caught my attention. Perhaps it was the bold blue, green, black and white colors that jumped out at me, since being colorblind, the stark color contrasts probably appealed to me more than subtler shades. Or maybe the unusual title *The Hobbit* intrigued me as well. What was a hobbit, I probably asked myself.

But what surprises me most in retrospect is that, one, I don't specifically recall noting the titles of any of the other books on that shelf, only *The Hobbit*, and two, not once did I ever pull the book down to take a look at it. Go figure! I guess the creative writer part of me would like to think that whenever my eye caught sight of that book and for some reason never took it off the shelf, it was a sign of some sort, as if the book were quietly telling me that it would be an important part of my writing life, but not just yet. I'd still have to wait a while longer before I should read it.

But the funny thing I only realized a short time ago when thinking about writing this post was that it never occurred to me to check out this edition of *The Hobbit* when my classmate and I went to the public library to find the book. Events in life though, whether large or small, happen as they do. And if I had read *The Hobbit* earlier, I would have missed out waiting for that telephone call all summer, racing to the library to see the return date stamped inside as I checked out the book, and then enjoying a cold, iced tea in my backyard on a warm August afternoon while I savored each page.

So I guess it was worth the wait. And for those of you waiting for me to finish this book as well, I hope it's worth it for you too. Back in September.

To those of you who have read
all three volumes and made it this far,
my sincere thanks and appreciation.

~ Books by Thomas J. Prestopnik ~

Nicholas Raven and the Wizards' Web
an epic fantasy in three volumes

A Christmas Castle
a novella

The Endora Trilogy
a fantasy-adventure series for pre-teens & adults

The Timedoor - Book I
The Sword and the Crown - Book II
The Saving Light - Book III

Gabriel's Journey
an adventure novel for pre-teens & adults

Visit Thomas J. Prestopnik's official website
www.TomPresto.com